VLADIMIR NABOKOV

VLADIMIR NABOKOV

NOVELS 1955–1962

Lolita

Pnin

Pale Fire

Lolita: A Screenplay

THE LIBRARY OF AMERICA

The paper used in this publication meets the
minimum requirements of the American National Standard for
Information Sciences—Permanence of Paper for Printed
Library Materials, ANSI Z39.48—1984.

Distributed to the trade in the United States
by Penguin Books USA Inc
and in Canada by Penguin Books Canada Ltd.

Library of Congress Catalog Number: 96–15256
For cataloging information, see end of Notes.
ISBN: 1–883011–19–1
———
First Printing
The Library of America—88

Manufactured in the United States of America

BRIAN BOYD

ADVISED ON TEXTUAL MATTERS AND
WROTE THE NOTES FOR THIS VOLUME

Contents

Lolita 1

Pnin 299

Pale Fire 437

Appendix
   Lolita: A Screenplay 669

Chronology 837

Note on the Texts 869

Notes 873

LOLITA

To Véra

Foreword

*"Lolita, or the Confession of a White Widowed Male," such were
the two titles under which the writer of the present note received
the strange pages it preambulates. "Humbert Humbert," their
author, had died in legal captivity, of coronary thrombosis, on
November 16, 1952, a few days before his trial was scheduled to
start. His lawyer, my good friend and relation, Clarence Choate
Clark, Esq., now of the District of Columbia bar, in asking me
to edit the manuscript, based his request on a clause in his
client's will which empowered my eminent cousin to use his discretion in all matters pertaining to the preparation of "Lolita"
for print. Mr. Clark's decision may have been influenced by the
fact that the editor of his choice had just been awarded the Pol-
ing Prize for a modest work ("Do the Senses make Sense?")
wherein certain morbid states and perversions had been discussed.*

*My task proved simpler than either of us had anticipated. Save
for the correction of obvious solecisms and a careful suppression
of a few tenacious details that despite "H.H.'''s own efforts still
subsisted in his text as signposts and tombstones (indicative of
places or persons that taste would conceal and compassion spare),
this remarkable memoir is presented intact. Its author's bizarre
cognomen is his own invention; and, of course, this mask—
through which two hypnotic eyes seem to glow—had to remain
unlifted in accordance with its wearer's wish. While "Haze"
only rhymes with the heroine's real surname, her first name is
too closely interwound with the inmost fiber of the book to allow
one to alter it; nor (as the reader will perceive for himself) is
there any practical necessity to do so. References to "H.H.'''s
crime may be looked up by the inquisitive in the daily papers for
September–October 1952; its cause and purpose would have continued to remain a complete mystery, had not this memoir been
permitted to come under my reading lamp.*

*For the benefit of old-fashioned readers who wish to follow the
destinies of the "real" people beyond the "true" story, a few details may be given as received from Mr. "Windmuller," of*

"Ramsdale," who desires his identity suppressed so that "the long shadow of this sorry and sordid business" should not reach the community to which he is proud to belong. His daughter, "Louise," is by now a college sophomore. "Mona Dahl" is a student in Paris. "Rita" has recently married the proprietor of a hotel in Florida. Mrs. "Richard F. Schiller" died in childbed, giving birth to a stillborn girl, on Christmas Day 1952, in Gray Star, a settlement in the remotest Northwest. "Vivian Darkbloom" has written a biography, "My Cue," to be published shortly, and critics who have perused the manuscript call it her best book. The caretakers of the various cemeteries involved report that no ghosts walk.

Viewed simply as a novel, "Lolita" deals with situations and emotions that would remain exasperatingly vague to the reader had their expression been etiolated by means of platitudinous evasions. True, not a single obscene term is to be found in the whole work; indeed, the robust philistine who is conditioned by modern conventions into accepting without qualms a lavish array of four-letter words in a banal novel, will be quite shocked by their absence here. If, however, for this paradoxical prude's comfort, an editor attempted to dilute or omit scenes that a certain type of mind might call "aphrodisiac" (see in this respect the monumental decision rendered December 6, 1933, by Hon. John M. Woolsey in regard to another, considerably more outspoken, book), one would have to forego the publication of "Lolita" altogether, since those very scenes that one might ineptly accuse of a sensuous existence of their own, are the most strictly functional ones in the development of a tragic tale tending unswervingly to nothing less than a moral apotheosis. The cynic may say that commercial pornography makes the same claim; the learned may counter by asserting that "H.H."'s impassioned confession is a tempest in a test tube; that at least 12% of American adult males—a "conservative" estimate according to Dr. Blanche Schwarzmann (verbal communication)—enjoy yearly, in one way or another, the special experience "H.H." describes with such despair; that had our demented diarist gone, in the fatal summer of 1947, to a competent psychopathologist, there would have been no disaster; but then, neither would there have been this book.

This commentator may be excused for repeating what he has

stressed in his own books and lectures, namely that "offensive" is frequently but a synonym for "unusual"; and a great work of art is of course always original, and thus by its very nature should come as a more or less shocking surprise. I have no intention to glorify "H.H." No doubt, he is horrible, he is abject, he is a shining example of moral leprosy, a mixture of ferocity and jocularity that betrays supreme misery perhaps, but is not conducive to attractiveness. He is ponderously capricious. Many of his casual opinions on the people and scenery of this country are ludicrous. A desperate honesty that throbs through his confession does not absolve him from sins of diabolical cunning. He is abnormal. He is not a gentleman. But how magically his singing violin can conjure up a tendresse, a compassion for Lolita that makes us entranced with the book while abhorring its author!

As a case history, "Lolita" will become, no doubt, a classic in psychiatric circles. As a work of art, it transcends its expiatory aspects; and still more important to us than scientific significance and literary worth, is the ethical impact the book should have on the serious reader; for in this poignant personal study there lurks a general lesson; the wayward child, the egotistic mother, the panting maniac—these are not only vivid characters in a unique story: they warn us of dangerous trends; they point out potent evils. "Lolita" should make all of us—parents, social workers, educators—apply ourselves with still greater vigilance and vision to the task of bringing up a better generation in a safer world.

Widworth, Mass.   John Ray, Jr., Ph.D.

August 5, 1955

Part One

LOLITA, light of my life, fire of my loins. My sin, my soul. Lo-lee-ta: the tip of the tongue taking a trip of three steps down the palate to tap, at three, on the teeth. Lo. Lee. Ta.

She was Lo, plain Lo, in the morning, standing four feet ten in one sock. She was Lola in slacks. She was Dolly at school. She was Dolores on the dotted line. But in my arms she was always Lolita.

Did she have a precursor? She did, indeed she did. In point of fact, there might have been no Lolita at all had I not loved, one summer, a certain initial girl-child. In a princedom by the sea. Oh when? About as many years before Lolita was born as my age was that summer. You can always count on a murderer for a fancy prose style.

Ladies and gentlemen of the jury, exhibit number one is what the seraphs, the misinformed, simple, noble-winged seraphs, envied. Look at this tangle of thorns.

I was born in 1910, in Paris. My father was a gentle, easy-going person, a salad of racial genes: a Swiss citizen, of mixed French and Austrian descent, with a dash of the Danube in his veins. I am going to pass around in a minute some lovely, glossy-blue picture-postcards. He owned a luxurious hotel on the Riviera. His father and two grandfathers had sold wine, jewels and silk, respectively. At thirty he married an English girl, daughter of Jerome Dunn, the alpinist, and granddaughter of two Dorset parsons, experts in obscure subjects—paleopedology and Aeolian harps, respectively. My very photogenic mother died in a freak accident (picnic, lightning) when I was three, and, save for a pocket of warmth in the darkest past, nothing of her subsists within the hollows and dells of memory, over which, if you can still stand my style (I am writing under observation), the sun of my infancy had set: surely, you all know those redolent remnants of day suspended, with the midges, about some hedge in bloom or suddenly entered and traversed by the rambler, at the bottom of a hill, in the summer dusk; a furry warmth, golden midges.

My mother's elder sister, Sybil, whom a cousin of my father's had married and then neglected, served in my immediate family as a kind of unpaid governess and housekeeper. Somebody told me later that she had been in love with my father, and that he had lightheartedly taken advantage of it one rainy day and forgotten it by the time the weather cleared. I was extremely fond of her, despite the rigidity—the fatal rigidity—of some of her rules. Perhaps she wanted to make of me, in the fullness of time, a better widower than my father. Aunt Sybil had pink-rimmed azure eyes and a waxen complexion. She wrote poetry. She was poetically superstitious. She said she knew she would die soon after my sixteenth birthday, and did. Her husband, a great traveler in perfumes, spent most of his time in America, where eventually he founded a firm and acquired a bit of real estate.

I grew, a happy, healthy child in a bright world of illustrated books, clean sand, orange trees, friendly dogs, sea vistas and smiling faces. Around me the splendid Hotel Mirana revolved as a kind of private universe, a whitewashed cosmos within the blue greater one that blazed outside. From the aproned pot-scrubber to the flanneled potentate, everybody liked me, everybody petted me. Elderly American ladies leaning on their canes listed toward me like towers of Pisa. Ruined Russian princesses who could not pay my father, bought me expensive bonbons. He, *mon cher petit papa*, took me out boating and biking, taught me to swim and dive and water-ski, read to me *Don Quixote* and *Les Misérables*, and I adored and respected him and felt glad for him whenever I overheard the servants discuss his various lady-friends, beautiful and kind beings who made much of me and cooed and shed precious tears over my cheerful motherlessness.

I attended an English day school a few miles from home, and there I played rackets and fives, and got excellent marks, and was on perfect terms with schoolmates and teachers alike. The only definite sexual events that I can remember as having occurred before my thirteenth birthday (that is, before I first

saw my little Annabel) were: a solemn, decorous and purely
theoretical talk about pubertal surprises in the rose garden of
the school with an American kid, the son of a then celebrated
motion-picture actress whom he seldom saw in the three-
dimensional world; and some interesting reactions on the part
of my organism to certain photographs, pearl and umbra, with
infinitely soft partings, in Pichon's sumptuous *La Beauté Hu-
maine* that I had filched from under a mountain of marble-
bound *Graphics* in the hotel library. Later, in his delightful
debonair manner, my father gave me all the information he
thought I needed about sex; this was just before sending me,
in the autumn of 1923, to a *lycée* in Lyon (where we were to
spend three winters); but alas, in the summer of that year, he
was touring Italy with Mme de R. and her daughter, and I
had nobody to complain to, nobody to consult.

3

Annabel was, like the writer, of mixed parentage: half-
English, half-Dutch, in her case. I remember her features far
less distinctly today than I did a few years ago, before I knew
Lolita. There are two kinds of visual memory: one when you
skillfully recreate an image in the laboratory of your mind,
with your eyes open (and then I see Annabel in such general
terms as: "honey-colored skin," "thin arms," "brown bobbed
hair," "long lashes," "big bright mouth"); and the other
when you instantly evoke, with shut eyes, on the dark inner-
side of your eyelids, the objective, absolutely optical replica of
a beloved face, a little ghost in natural colors (and this is how
I see Lolita).

Let me therefore primly limit myself, in describing Annabel,
to saying she was a lovely child a few months my junior. Her
parents were old friends of my aunt's, and as stuffy as she.
They had rented a villa not far from Hotel Mirana. Bald
brown Mr. Leigh and fat, powdered Mrs. Leigh (born Vanessa
van Ness). How I loathed them! At first, Annabel and I talked
of peripheral affairs. She kept lifting handfuls of fine sand and
letting it pour through her fingers. Our brains were turned
the way those of intelligent European preadolescents were in
our day and set, and I doubt if much individual genius should

be assigned to our interest in the plurality of inhabited worlds, competitive tennis, infinity, solipsism and so on. The softness and fragility of baby animals caused us the same intense pain. She wanted to be a nurse in some famished Asiatic country; I wanted to be a famous spy.

All at once we were madly, clumsily, shamelessly, agonizingly in love with each other; hopelessly, I should add, because that frenzy of mutual possession might have been assuaged only by our actually imbibing and assimilating every particle of each other's soul and flesh; but there we were, unable even to mate as slum children would have so easily found an opportunity to do. After one wild attempt we made to meet at night in her garden (of which more later), the only privacy we were allowed was to be out of earshot but not out of sight on the populous part of the *plage*. There, on the soft sand, a few feet away from our elders, we would sprawl all morning, in a petrified paroxysm of desire, and take advantage of every blessed quirk in space and time to touch each other: her hand, half-hidden in the sand, would creep toward me, its slender brown fingers sleepwalking nearer and nearer; then, her opalescent knee would start on a long cautious journey; sometimes a chance rampart built by younger children granted us sufficient concealment to graze each other's salty lips; these incomplete contacts drove our healthy and inexperienced young bodies to such a state of exasperation that not even the cool blue water, under which we still clawed at each other, could bring relief.

Among some treasures I lost during the wanderings of my adult years, there was a snapshot taken by my aunt which showed Annabel, her parents and the staid, elderly, lame gentleman, a Dr. Cooper, who that same summer courted my aunt, grouped around a table in a sidewalk café. Annabel did not come out well, caught as she was in the act of bending over her *chocolat glacé*, and her thin bare shoulders and the parting in her hair were about all that could be identified (as I remember that picture) amid the sunny blur into which her lost loveliness graded; but I, sitting somewhat apart from the rest, came out with a kind of dramatic conspicuousness: a moody, beetle-browed boy in a dark sport shirt and well-tailored white shorts, his legs crossed, sitting in profile, looking away. That photograph was taken on the last day of our fatal summer and just a few minutes before we made our second and final attempt to thwart fate. Under the flimsiest of pretexts (this was our very last chance, and nothing really mattered) we escaped from the café to the beach, and found a desolate stretch of sand, and there, in the violet shadow of some red rocks forming a kind of cave, had a brief session of avid caresses, with somebody's lost pair of sunglasses for only witness. I was on my knees, and on the point of possessing my darling, when two bearded bathers, the old man of the sea and his brother, came out of the sea with exclamations of ribald encouragement, and four months later she died of typhus in Corfu.

4

I leaf again and again through these miserable memories, and keep asking myself, was it then, in the glitter of that remote summer, that the rift in my life began; or was my excessive desire for that child only the first evidence of an inherent singularity? When I try to analyze my own cravings, motives, actions and so forth, I surrender to a sort of retrospective imagination which feeds the analytic faculty with boundless alternatives and which causes each visualized route to fork and re-fork without end in the maddeningly complex prospect of my past. I am convinced, however, that in a certain magic and fateful way Lolita began with Annabel.

I also know that the shock of Annabel's death consolidated the frustration of that nightmare summer, made of it a permanent obstacle to any further romance throughout the cold years of my youth. The spiritual and the physical had been blended in us with a perfection that must remain incomprehensible to the matter-of-fact, crude, standard-brained youngsters of today. Long after her death I felt her thoughts floating through mine. Long before we met we had had the same dreams. We compared notes. We found strange affinities. The same June of the same year (1919) a stray canary had fluttered into her house and mine, in two widely separated countries. Oh, Lolita, had *you* loved me thus!

I have reserved for the conclusion of my "Annabel" phase

the account of our unsuccessful first tryst. One night, she managed to deceive the vicious vigilance of her family. In a nervous and slender-leaved mimosa grove at the back of their villa we found a perch on the ruins of a low stone wall. Through the darkness and the tender trees we could see the arabesques of lighted windows which, touched up by the colored inks of sensitive memory, appear to me now like playing cards—presumably because a bridge game was keeping the enemy busy. She trembled and twitched as I kissed the corner of her parted lips and the hot lobe of her ear. A cluster of stars palely glowed above us, between the silhouettes of long thin leaves; that vibrant sky seemed as naked as she was under her light frock. I saw her face in the sky, strangely distinct, as if it emitted a faint radiance of its own. Her legs, her lovely live legs, were not too close together, and when my hand located what it sought, a dreamy and eerie expression, half-pleasure, half-pain, came over those childish features. She sat a little higher than I, and whenever in her solitary ecstasy she was led to kiss me, her head would bend with a sleepy, soft, drooping movement that was almost woeful, and her bare knees caught and compressed my wrist, and slackened again; and her quivering mouth, distorted by the acridity of some mysterious potion, with a sibilant intake of breath came near to my face. She would try to relieve the pain of love by first roughly rubbing her dry lips against mine; then my darling would draw away with a nervous toss of her hair, and then again come darkly near and let me feed on her open mouth, while with a generosity that was ready to offer her everything, my heart, my throat, my entrails, I gave her to hold in her awkward fist the scepter of my passion.

I recall the scent of some kind of toilet powder—I believe she stole it from her mother's Spanish maid—a sweetish, lowly, musky perfume. It mingled with her own biscuity odor, and my senses were suddenly filled to the brim; a sudden commotion in a nearby bush prevented them from overflowing—and as we drew away from each other, and with aching veins attended to what was probably a prowling cat, there came from the house her mother's voice calling her, with a rising frantic note—and Dr. Cooper ponderously limped out into the garden. But that mimosa grove—the haze of stars, the tingle, the flame, the honeydew, and the ache remained with me, and that little girl with her seaside limbs and ardent tongue haunted me ever since—until at last, twenty-four years later, I broke her spell by incarnating her in another.

5

The days of my youth, as I look back on them, seem to fly away from me in a flurry of pale repetitive scraps like those morning snow storms of used tissue paper that a train passenger sees whirling in the wake of the observation car. In my sanitary relations with women I was practical, ironical and brisk. While a college student, in London and Paris, paid ladies sufficed me. My studies were meticulous and intense, although not particularly fruitful. At first, I planned to take a degree in psychiatry as many *manqué* talents do; but I was even more *manqué* than that; a peculiar exhaustion, I am so oppressed, doctor, set in; and I switched to English literature, where so many frustrated poets end as pipe-smoking teachers in tweeds. Paris suited me. I discussed Soviet movies with expatriates. I sat with uranists in the Deux Magots. I published tortuous essays in obscure journals. I composed pastiches:

> . . . Fräulein von Kulp
> may turn, her hand upon the door;
> I will not follow her. Nor Fresca. Nor
> that Gull.

A paper of mine entitled "The Proustian theme in a letter from Keats to Benjamin Bailey" was chuckled over by the six or seven scholars who read it. I launched upon an *"Histoire abrégée de la poésie anglaise"* for a prominent publishing firm, and then started to compile that manual of French literature for English-speaking students (with comparisons drawn from English writers) which was to occupy me throughout the forties—and the last volume of which was almost ready for press by the time of my arrest.

I found a job—teaching English to a group of adults in Auteuil. Then a school for boys employed me for a couple of winters. Now and then I took advantage of the acquaintances I had formed among social workers and psychotherapists to visit in their company various institutions, such as orphanages and reform schools, where pale pubescent girls with matted eyelashes could be stared at in perfect impunity remindful of that granted one in dreams.

Now I wish to introduce the following idea. Between the age limits of nine and fourteen there occur maidens who, to certain bewitched travelers, twice or many times older than they, reveal their true nature which is not human, but nymphic (that is, demoniac); and these chosen creatures I propose to designate as "nymphets."

It will be marked that I substitute time terms for spatial ones. In fact, I would have the reader see "nine" and "fourteen" as the boundaries—the mirrory beaches and rosy rocks—of an enchanted island haunted by those nymphets of mine and surrounded by a vast, misty sea. Between those age limits, are all girl-children nymphets? Of course not. Otherwise, we who are in the know, we lone voyagers, we nympholepts, would have long gone insane. Neither are good looks any criterion; and vulgarity, or at least what a given community terms so, does not necessarily impair certain mysterious characteristics, the fey grace, the elusive, shifty, soul-shattering, insidious charm that separates the nymphet from such coevals of hers as are incomparably more dependent on the spatial world of synchronous phenomena than on that intangible island of entranced time where Lolita plays with her likes. Within the same age limits the number of true nymphets is strikingly inferior to that of provisionally plain, or just nice, or "cute," or even "sweet" and "attractive," ordinary, plumpish, formless, cold-skinned, essentially human little girls, with tummies and pigtails, who may or may not turn into adults of great beauty (look at the ugly dumplings in black stockings and white hats that are metamorphosed into stunning stars of the screen). A normal man given a group photograph of school girls or Girl Scouts and asked to point out the comeliest one will not necessarily choose the nymphet among them. You have to be an artist and a madman, a creature of infinite melancholy, with a bubble of hot poison in your loins and a super-voluptuous flame permanently aglow in your subtle spine (oh, how you have to cringe and hide!), in order to discern at once, by ineffable signs—the slightly feline outline of a cheekbone, the slenderness of a downy limb, and other indices which despair and shame and tears of tenderness forbid me to tabulate—the little deadly demon among the wholesome children; *she* stands unrecognized by them and unconscious herself of her fantastic power.

Furthermore, since the idea of time plays such a magic part in the matter, the student should not be surprised to learn that there must be a gap of several years, never less than ten I should say, generally thirty or forty, and as many as ninety in a few known cases, between maiden and man to enable the latter to come under a nymphet's spell. It is a question of focal adjustment, of a certain distance that the inner eye thrills to surmount, and a certain contrast that the mind perceives with a gasp of perverse delight. When I was a child and she was a child, my little Annabel was no nymphet to me; I was her equal, a faunlet in my own right, on that same enchanted island of time; but today, in September 1952, after twenty-nine years have elapsed, I think I can distinguish in her the initial fateful elf in my life. We loved each other with a premature love, marked by a fierceness that so often destroys adult lives. I was a strong lad and survived; but the poison was in the wound, and the wound remained ever open, and soon I found myself maturing amid a civilization which allows a man of twenty-five to court a girl of sixteen but not a girl of twelve.

No wonder, then, that my adult life during the European period of my existence proved monstrously twofold. Overtly, I had so-called normal relationships with a number of terrestrial women having pumpkins or pears for breasts; inly, I was consumed by a hell furnace of localized lust for every passing nymphet whom as a law-abiding poltroon I never dared approach. The human females I was allowed to wield were but palliative agents. I am ready to believe that the sensations I derived from natural fornication were much the same as those known to normal big males consorting with their normal big mates in that routine rhythm which shakes the world. The trouble was that those gentlemen had not, and I *had*, caught glimpses of an incomparably more poignant bliss. The dimmest of my pollutive dreams was a thousand times more dazzling than all the adultery the most virile writer of genius or the most talented impotent might imagine. My world was split. I was aware of not one but two sexes, neither of which was mine; both would be termed female by the anatomist. But to me, through the prism of my senses, "they were as different as mist and mast." All this I rationalize now. In my twenties and early thirties, I did not understand my throes quite so clearly. While my body knew what it craved for, my mind rejected my body's every plea. One moment I was ashamed and frightened, another recklessly optimistic. Taboos strangulated me. Psychoanalysts wooed me with pseudoliberations of pseudolibidoes. The fact that to me the only objects of amorous tremor were sisters of Annabel's, her handmaids and girl-pages, appeared to me at times as a forerunner of insanity. At other times I would tell myself that it was all a question of attitude, that there was really nothing wrong in being moved to distraction by girl-children. Let me remind my reader that in England, with the passage of the Children and Young Person Act in 1933, the term "girl-child" is defined as "a girl who is over eight but under fourteen years" (after that, from fourteen to seventeen, the statutory definition is "young person"). In Massachusetts, U.S., on the other hand, a "wayward child" is, technically, one "between seven and seventeen years of age" (who, moreover, habitually associates with vicious or immoral persons). Hugh Broughton, a writer of controversy in the reign of James the First, has proved that Rahab was a harlot at ten years of age. This is all very interesting, and I daresay you see me already frothing at the mouth in a fit; but no, I am not; I am just winking happy thoughts into a little tiddle cup. Here are some more pictures. Here is Virgil who could the nymphet sing in single tone, but probably preferred a lad's perineum. Here are two of King Akhnaten's and Queen Nefertiti's pre-nubile Nile daughters (that royal couple had a litter of six), wearing nothing but many necklaces of bright beads, relaxed on cushions, intact after three thousand years, with their soft brown puppybodies, cropped hair and long ebony eyes. Here are some brides of ten compelled to seat themselves on the fascinum, the virile ivory in the temples of classical scholarship. Marriage and cohabitation before the age of puberty are still not uncommon in certain East Indian provinces. Lepcha old men of eighty copulate with girls of eight, and nobody minds. After all,

Dante fell madly in love with his Beatrice when she was nine, a sparkling girleen, painted and lovely, and bejeweled, in a crimson frock, and this was in 1274, in Florence, at a private feast in the merry month of May. And when Petrarch fell madly in love with his Laureen, she was a fair-haired nymphet of twelve running in the wind, in the pollen and dust, a flower in flight, in the beautiful plain as descried from the hills of Vaucluse.

But let us be prim and civilized. Humbert Humbert tried hard to be good. Really and truly, he did. He had the utmost respect for ordinary children, with their purity and vulnerability, and under no circumstances would he have interfered with the innocence of a child, if there was the least risk of a row. But how his heart beat when, among the innocent throng, he espied a demon child, *"enfant charmante et fourbe,"* dim eyes, bright lips, ten years in jail if you only show her you are looking at her. So life went. Humbert was perfectly capable of intercourse with Eve, but it was Lilith he longed for. The bud-stage of breast development appears early (10.7 years) in the sequence of somatic changes accompanying pubescence. And the next maturational item available is the first appearance of pigmented pubic hair (11.2 years). My little cup brims with tiddles.

A shipwreck. An atoll. Alone with a drowned passenger's shivering child. Darling, this is only a game! How marvelous were my fancied adventures as I sat on a hard park bench pretending to be immersed in a trembling book. Around the quiet scholar, nymphets played freely, as if he were a familiar statue or part of an old tree's shadow and sheen. Once a perfect little beauty in a tartan frock, with a clatter put her heavily armed foot near me upon the bench to dip her slim bare arms into me and tighten the strap of her roller skate, and I dissolved in the sun, with my book for fig leaf, as her auburn ringlets fell all over her skinned knee, and the shadow of leaves I shared pulsated and melted on her radiant limb next to my chameleonic cheek. Another time a red-haired school girl hung over me in the *métro*, and a revelation of axillary russet I obtained remained in my blood for weeks. I could list a great number of these one-sided diminutive romances. Some of them ended in a rich flavor of hell. It happened for instance that from my balcony I would notice a lighted window across the street and what looked like a nymphet in the act of undressing before a co-operative mirror. Thus isolated, thus removed, the vision acquired an especially keen charm that made me race with all speed toward my lone gratification. But abruptly, fiendishly, the tender pattern of nudity I had adored would be transformed into the disgusting lamp-lit bare arm of a man in his underclothes reading his paper by the open window in the hot, damp, hopeless summer night.

Rope-skipping, hopscotch. That old woman in black who sat down next to me on my bench, on my rack of joy (a nymphet was groping under me for a lost marble), and asked if I had stomachache, the insolent hag. Ah, leave me alone in my pubescent park, in my mossy garden. Let them play around me forever. Never grow up.

6

A propos: I have often wondered what became of those nymphets later? In this wrought-iron world of criss-cross cause and effect, could it be that the hidden throb I stole from them did not affect *their* future? I had possessed her—and she never knew it. All right. But would it not tell sometime later? Had I not somehow tampered with her fate by involving her image in my voluptas? Oh, it was, and remains, a source of great and terrible wonder.

I learned, however, what they looked like, those lovely, maddening, thin-armed nymphets, when they grew up. I remember walking along an animated street on a gray spring afternoon somewhere near the Madeleine. A short slim girl passed me at a rapid, high-heeled, tripping step, we glanced back at the same moment, she stopped and I accosted her. She came hardly up to my chest hair and had the kind of dimpled round little face French girls so often have, and I liked her long lashes and tight-fitting tailored dress sheathing in pearl-gray her young body which still retained—and that was the nymphic echo, the chill of delight, the leap in my loins—a childish something mingling with the professional *frétillement* of her small agile rump. I asked her price, and she promptly replied with melodious silvery precision (a bird, a

very bird!) *"Cent."* I tried to haggle but she saw the awful
lone longing in my lowered eyes, directed so far down at her
round forehead and rudimentary hat (a band, a posy); and
with one beat of her lashes: *"Tant pis,"* she said, and made
as if to move away. Perhaps only three years earlier I might
have seen her coming home from school! That evocation settled the matter. She led me up the usual steep stairs, with the
usual bell clearing the way for the *monsieur* who might not
care to meet another *monsieur*, on the mournful climb to the
abject room, all bed and *bidet*. As usual, she asked at once for
her *petit cadeau*, and as usual I asked her name (Monique)
and her age (eighteen). I was pretty well acquainted with the
banal way of streetwalkers. They all answer *"dix-huit"*—a trim
twitter, a note of finality and wistful deceit which they emit
up to ten times per day, the poor little creatures. But in Monique's case there could be no doubt she was, if anything,
adding one or two years to her age. This I deduced from many
details of her compact, neat, curiously immature body. Having
shed her clothes with fascinating rapidity, she stood for a moment partly wrapped in the dingy gauze of the window curtain
listening with infantile pleasure, as pat as pat could be, to an
organ-grinder in the dust-brimming courtyard below. When
I examined her small hands and drew her attention to their
grubby fingernails, she said with a naïve frown *"Oui, ce n'est
pas bien,"* and went to the wash-basin, but I said it did not
matter, did not matter at all. With her brown bobbed hair,
luminous gray eyes and pale skin, she looked perfectly charming. Her hips were no bigger than those of a squatting lad; in
fact, I do not hesitate to say (and indeed this is the reason
why I linger gratefully in that gauze-gray room of memory
with little Monique) that among the eighty or so *grues* I had
had operate upon me, she was the only one that gave me a
pang of genuine pleasure. *"Il était malin, celui qui a inventé
ce truc-là,"* she commented amiably, and got back into her
clothes with the same high-style speed.

I asked for another, more elaborate, assignment later the
same evening, and she said she would meet me at the corner
café at nine, and swore she had never *posé un lapin* in all her
young life. We returned to the same room, and I could not
help saying how very pretty she was to which she answered

demurely: *"Tu es bien gentil de dire ça,"* and then, noticing what I noticed too in the mirror reflecting our small Eden— the dreadful grimace of clenched-teeth tenderness that distorted my mouth—dutiful little Monique (oh, she had been a nymphet all right!) wanted to know if she should remove the layer of red from her lips *avant qu'on se couche* in case I planned to kiss her. Of course, I planned it. I let myself go with her more completely than I had with any young lady before, and my last vision that night of long-lashed Monique is touched up with a gaiety that I find seldom associated with any event in my humiliating, sordid, taciturn love life. She looked tremendously pleased with the bonus of fifty I gave her as she trotted out into the April night drizzle with Humbert Humbert lumbering in her narrow wake. Stopping before a window display she said with great gusto: *"Je vais m'acheter des bas!"* and never may I forget the way her Parisian childish lips exploded on *"bas,"* pronouncing it with an appetite that all but changed the "a" into a brief buoyant bursting "o" as in *"bot."*

I had a date with her next day at 2.15 P.M. in my own rooms, but it was less successful, she seemed to have grown less juvenile, more of a woman overnight. A cold I caught from her led me to cancel a fourth assignment, nor was I sorry to break an emotional series that threatened to burden me with heart-rending fantasies and peter out in dull disappointment. So let her remain, sleek, slender Monique, as she was for a minute or two: a delinquent nymphet shining through the matter-of-fact young whore.

My brief acquaintance with her started a train of thought that may seem pretty obvious to the reader who knows the ropes. An advertisement in a lewd magazine landed me, one brave day, in the office of a Mlle Edith who began by offering me to choose a kindred soul from a collection of rather formal photographs in a rather soiled album (*"Regardez-moi cette belle brune!"*). When I pushed the album away and somehow managed to blurt out my criminal craving, she looked as if about to show me the door; however, after asking me what price I was prepared to disburse, she condescended to put me in touch with a person *qui pourrait arranger la chose.* Next day, an asthmatic woman, coarsely painted, garrulous, garlicky, with an almost farcical Provençal accent and a black mustache above a purple lip, took me to what was apparently her own domicile, and there, after explosively kissing the bunched tips of her fat fingers to signify the delectable rose-bud quality of her merchandise, she theatrically drew aside a curtain to reveal what I judged was that part of the room where a large and unfastidious family usually slept. It was now empty save for a monstrously plump, sallow, repulsively plain girl of at least fifteen with red-ribboned thick black braids who sat on a chair perfunctorily nursing a bald doll. When I shook my head and tried to shuffle out of the trap, the woman, talking fast, began removing the dingy woolen jersey from the young giantess' torso; then, seeing my determination to leave, she demanded *son argent*. A door at the end of the room was opened, and two men who had been dining in the kitchen joined in the squabble. They were misshapen, bare-necked, very swarthy and one of them wore dark glasses. A small boy and a begrimed, bowlegged toddler lurked behind them. With the insolent logic of a nightmare, the enraged procuress, indicating the man in glasses, said he had served in the police, *lui*, so that I had better do as I was told. I went up to Marie—for that was her stellar name—who by then had quietly transferred her heavy haunches to a stool at the kitchen table and resumed her interrupted soup while the toddler picked up the doll. With a surge of pity dramatizing my idiotic gesture, I thrust a banknote into her indifferent hand. She surrendered my gift to the ex-detective, whereupon I was suffered to leave.

7

I do not know if the pimp's album may not have been another link in the daisy-chain; but soon after, for my own safety, I decided to marry. It occurred to me that regular hours, home-cooked meals, all the conventions of marriage, the prophylactic routine of its bedroom activities and, who knows, the eventual flowering of certain moral values, of certain spiritual substitutes, might help me, if not to purge myself of my degrading and dangerous desires, at least to keep them under pacific control. A little money that had come my way after my father's death (nothing very grand—the Mirana had been sold long before), in addition to my striking if somewhat brutal good looks, allowed me to enter upon my quest with equanimity. After considerable deliberation, my choice fell on the daughter of a Polish doctor: the good man happened to be treating me for spells of dizziness and tachycardia. We played chess; his daughter watched me from behind her easel, and inserted eyes or knuckles borrowed from me into the cubistic trash that accomplished misses then painted instead of lilacs and lambs. Let me repeat with quiet force: I was, and still am, despite *mes malheurs*, an exceptionally handsome male; slow-moving, tall, with soft dark hair and a gloomy but all the more seductive cast of demeanor. Exceptional virility often reflects in the subject's displayable features a sullen and congested something that pertains to what he has to conceal. And this was my case. Well did I know, alas, that I could obtain at the snap of my fingers any adult female I chose; in fact, it had become quite a habit with me of not being too attentive to women lest they come toppling, bloodripe, into my cold lap. Had I been a *français moyen* with a taste for flashy ladies, I might have easily found, among the many crazed beauties that lashed my grim rock, creatures far more fascinating than Valeria. My choice, however, was prompted by considerations whose essence was, as I realized too late, a piteous compromise. All of which goes to show how dreadfully stupid poor Humbert always was in matters of sex.

8

Although I told myself I was looking merely for a soothing presence, a glorified *pot-au-feu*, an animated merkin, what really attracted me to Valeria was the imitation she gave of a little girl. She gave it not because she had divined something about me; it was just her style—and I fell for it. Actually, she was at least in her late twenties (I never established her exact age for even her passport lied) and had mislaid her virginity under circumstances that changed with her reminiscent moods. I, on my part, was as naïve as only a pervert can be. She looked fluffy and frolicsome, dressed *à la gamine*, showed a generous amount of smooth leg, knew how to stress the white of a bare instep by the black of a velvet slipper, and pouted, and dimpled, and romped, and dirndled, and shook her short curly blond hair in the cutest and tritest fashion imaginable.

After a brief ceremony at the *mairie*, I took her to the new apartment I had rented and, somewhat to her surprise, had her wear, before I touched her, a girl's plain nightshirt that I had managed to filch from the linen closet of an orphanage. I derived some fun from that nuptial night and had the idiot in hysterics by sunrise. But reality soon asserted itself. The bleached curl revealed its melanic root; the down turned to prickles on a shaved shin; the mobile moist mouth, no matter how I stuffed it with love, disclosed ignominiously its resemblance to the corresponding part in a treasured portrait of her toadlike dead mama; and presently, instead of a pale little gutter girl, Humbert Humbert had on his hands a large, puffy, short-legged, big-breasted and practically brainless *baba*.

This state of affairs lasted from 1935 to 1939. Her only asset was a muted nature which did help to produce an odd sense of comfort in our small squalid flat: two rooms, a hazy view in one window, a brick wall in the other, a tiny kitchen, a shoe-shaped bath tub, within which I felt like Marat but with no white-necked maiden to stab me. We had quite a few cozy evenings together, she deep in her *Paris-Soir*, I working at a rickety table. We went to movies, bicycle races and boxing matches. I appealed to her stale flesh very seldom, only in cases of great urgency and despair. The grocer opposite had a little daughter whose shadow drove me mad; but with Valeria's help I did find after all some legal outlets to my fantastic predicament. As to cooking, we tacitly dismissed the *pot-au-feu* and had most of our meals at a crowded place in rue Bonaparte where there were wine stains on the table cloth and a good deal of foreign babble. And next door, an art dealer displayed in his cluttered window a splendid, flamboyant, green, red, golden and inky blue, ancient American estampe— a locomotive with a gigantic smokestack, great baroque lamps and a tremendous cowcatcher, hauling its mauve coaches through the stormy prairie night and mixing a lot of spark-studded black smoke with the furry thunder clouds.

These burst. In the summer of 1939 *mon oncle d'Amérique* died bequeathing me an annual income of a few thousand dollars on condition I came to live in the States and showed some interest in his business. This prospect was most welcome to me. I felt my life needed a shake-up. There was another thing, too: moth holes had appeared in the plush of matrimonial comfort. During the last weeks I had kept noticing that my fat Valeria was not her usual self; had acquired a queer restlessness; even showed something like irritation at times, which was quite out of keeping with the stock character she was supposed to impersonate. When I informed her we were shortly to sail for New York, she looked distressed and bewildered. There were some tedious difficulties with her papers. She had a Nansen, or better say Nonsense, passport which for some reason a share in her husband's solid Swiss citizenship could not easily transcend; and I decided it was the necessity of queuing in the *préfecture*, and other formalities, that had made her so listless, despite my patiently describing to her America, the country of rosy children and great trees, where life would be such an improvement on dull dingy Paris.

We were coming out of some office building one morning, with her papers almost in order, when Valeria, as she waddled by my side, began to shake her poodle head vigorously without saying a word. I let her go on for a while and then asked if she thought she had something inside. She answered (I translate from her French which was, I imagine, a translation in its turn of some Slavic platitude): "There is another man in my life."

Now, these are ugly words for a husband to hear. They dazed me, I confess. To beat her up in the street, there and then, as an honest vulgarian might have done, was not feasible. Years of secret sufferings had taught me superhuman self-control. So I ushered her into a taxi which had been invitingly creeping along the curb for some time, and in this comparative privacy I quietly suggested she comment her wild talk. A mounting fury was suffocating me—not because I had any particular fondness for that figure of fun, *Mme Humbert*, but because matters of legal and illegal conjunction were for me alone to decide, and here she was, Valeria, the comedy wife, brazenly preparing to dispose in her own way of my comfort and fate. I demanded her lover's name. I repeated my question; but she kept up a burlesque babble, discoursing on her unhappiness with me and announcing plans for an immediate divorce. *"Mais qui est-ce?"* I shouted at last, striking her on the knee with my fist; and she, without even wincing, stared at me as if the answer were too simple for words, then gave a quick shrug and pointed at the thick neck of the taxi driver. He pulled up at a small café and introduced himself. I do not remember his ridiculous name but after all those years I still see him quite clearly—a stocky White Russian ex-colonel with a bushy mustache and a crew cut; there were thousands of them plying that fool's trade in Paris. We sat down at a table; the Tsarist ordered wine; and Valeria, after applying a wet napkin to her knee, went on talking—*into* me rather than to me; she poured words into this dignified receptacle with a volubility I had never suspected she had in her. And every now and then she would volley a burst of Slavic at her stolid lover. The situation was preposterous and became even more so when the taxi-colonel, stopping Valeria with a possessive smile, began to unfold *his* views and plans. With an atrocious accent to his careful French, he delineated the world of love and work into which he proposed to enter hand in hand with his child-wife Valeria. She by now was preening herself, between him and me, rouging her pursed lips, tripling her chin to pick at her blouse-bosom and so forth, and he spoke of her as if she were absent, and also as if she were a kind of little ward that was in the act of being transferred, for her own good, from one wise guardian to another even wiser one; and although my helpless wrath may have exaggerated and disfigured certain impressions, I can swear that he actually consulted me on such things as her diet, her periods, her wardrobe and the books she had read or should read. "I think," he said, "she will like *Jean Christophe*?" Oh, he was quite a scholar, Mr. Taxovich.

I put an end to this gibberish by suggesting Valeria pack up her few belongings immediately, upon which the platitudinous colonel gallantly offered to carry them into the car. Reverting to his professional state, he drove the Humberts to their residence and all the way Valeria talked, and Humbert the Terrible deliberated with Humbert the Small whether Humbert Humbert should kill her or her lover, or both, or neither. I remember once handling an automatic belonging to a fellow student, in the days (I have not spoken of them, I think, but never mind) when I toyed with the idea of enjoying his little sister, a most diaphanous nymphet with a black hair bow, and then shooting myself. I now wondered if Valechka (as the colonel called her) was really worth shooting, or strangling, or drowning. She had very vulnerable legs, and I decided I would limit myself to hurting her very horribly as soon as we were alone.

But we never were. Valechka—by now shedding torrents of tears tinged with the mess of her rainbow make-up,—started to fill anyhow a trunk, and two suitcases, and a bursting carton, and visions of putting on my mountain boots and taking a running kick at her rump were of course impossible to put into execution with the cursed colonel hovering around all the time. I cannot say he behaved insolently or anything like that; on the contrary, he displayed, as a small sideshow in the theatricals I had been inveigled in, a discreet old-world civility, punctuating his movements with all sorts of mispronounced apologies (*j'ai demannde pardonne*—excuse me—*est-ce que j'ai puis*—may I—and so forth), and turning away tactfully when Valechka took down with a flourish her pink panties from the clothesline above the tub; but he seemed to be all over the place at once, *le gredin*, agreeing his frame with the anatomy of the flat, reading in my chair my newspaper, untying a knotted string, rolling a cigarette, counting the teaspoons, visiting the bathroom, helping his moll to wrap up the electric fan her father had given her, and carrying streetward her luggage. I sat with arms folded, one hip on the window sill, dying of hate and boredom. At last both were out of the quivering apartment—the vibration of the door I had slammed after them still rang in my every nerve, a poor substitute for the backhand slap with which I ought to have hit her across the cheekbone according to the rules of the movies. Clumsily playing my part, I stomped to the bathroom to check if they had taken my English toilet water; they had not; but I noticed with a spasm of fierce disgust that the former Counselor of the Tsar, after thoroughly easing his bladder, had not flushed the toilet. That solemn pool of alien urine with a soggy, tawny cigarette butt disintegrating in it struck me as a crowning insult, and I wildly looked around for a weapon.

Actually I daresay it was nothing but middle-class Russian
courtesy (with an oriental tang, perhaps) that had prompted
the good colonel (Maximovich! his name suddenly taxies back
to me), a very formal person as they all are, to muffle his
private need in decorous silence so as not to underscore the
small size of his host's domicile with the rush of a gross cas-
cade on top of his own hushed trickle. But this did not enter
my mind at the moment, as groaning with rage I ransacked
the kitchen for something better than a broom. Then, canceling my search, I dashed out of the house with the heroic
decision of attacking him barefisted; despite my natural vigor,
I am no pugilist, while the short but broad-shouldered Maximovich seemed made of pig iron. The void of the street, revealing nothing of my wife's departure except a rhinestone
button that she had dropped in the mud after preserving it
for three unnecessary years in a broken box, may have spared
me a bloody nose. But no matter. I had my little revenge in
due time. A man from Pasadena told me one day that Mrs.
Maximovich née Zborovski had died in childbirth around
1945; the couple had somehow got over to California and had
been used there, for an excellent salary, in a year-long experiment conducted by a distinguished American ethnologist.
The experiment dealt with human and racial reactions to a
diet of bananas and dates in a constant position on all fours.
My informant, a doctor, swore he had seen with his own eyes
obese Valechka and her colonel, by then gray-haired and also
quite corpulent, diligently crawling about the well-swept
floors of a brightly lit set of rooms (fruit in one, water in
another, mats in a third and so on) in the company of several
other hired quadrupeds, selected from indigent and helpless
groups. I tried to find the results of these tests in the *Review
of Anthropology*, but they appear not to have been published
yet. These scientific products take of course some time to fruc-
tuate. I hope they will be illustrated with good photographs
when they do get printed, although it is not very likely that a
prison library will harbor such erudite works. The one to
which I am restricted these days, despite my lawyer's favors,
is a good example of the inane eclecticism governing the selection of books in prison libraries. They have the Bible, of
course, and Dickens (an ancient set, N.Y., G. W. Dillingham,

Publisher, MDCCCLXXXVII); and the *Children's Encyclope-dia* (with some nice photographs of sunshine-haired Girl Scouts in shorts), and *A Murder Is Announced* by Agatha Christie; but they also have such coruscating trifles as *A Vagabond in Italy* by Percy Elphinstone, author of *Venice Re-visited*, Boston, 1868, and a comparatively recent (1946) *Who's Who in the Limelight*—actors, producers, playwrights, and shots of static scenes. In looking through the latter volume, I was treated last night to one of those dazzling coincidences that logicians loathe and poets love. I transcribe most of the page:

Pym, Roland. Born in Lundy, Mass., 1922. Received stage training at Elsinore Playhouse, Derby, N.Y. Made debut in *Sunburst.* Among his many appearances are *Two Blocks from Here, The Girl in Green, Scrambled Husbands, The Strange Mushroom, Touch and Go, John Lovely, I Was Dreaming of You.*

Quilty, Clare, American dramatist. Born in Ocean City, N.J., 1911. Educated at Columbia University. Started on a commercial career but turned to playwriting. Author of *The Little Nymph, The Lady Who Loved Lightning* (in collaboration with Vivian Darkbloom), *Dark Age, The Strange Mushroom, Fatherly Love,* and others. His many plays for children are notable. *Little Nymph* (1940) traveled 14,000 miles and played 280 performances on the road during the winter before ending in New York. Hobbies: fast cars, photography, pets.

Quine, Dolores. Born in 1882, in Dayton, Ohio. Studied for stage at American Academy. First played in Ottawa in 1900. Made New York debut in 1904 in *Never Talk to Strangers.* Has disappeared since in [a list of some thirty plays follows].

How the look of my dear love's name, even affixed to some old hag of an actress, still makes me rock with helpless pain! Perhaps, she might have been an actress too. Born 1935. Ap-peared (I notice the slip of my pen in the preceding paragraph, but please do not correct it, Clarence) in *The Murdered Play-wright.* Quine the Swine. Guilty of killing Quilty. Oh, my Lolita, I have only words to play with!

9

Divorce proceedings delayed my voyage, and the gloom of yet another World War had settled upon the globe when, after a winter of ennui and pneumonia in Portugal, I at last reached the States. In New York I eagerly accepted the soft job fate offered me: it consisted mainly of thinking up and editing perfume ads. I welcomed its desultory character and pseudo-literary aspects, attending to it whenever I had nothing better to do. On the other hand, I was urged by a war-time university in New York to complete my comparative history of French literature for English-speaking students. The first volume took me a couple of years during which I put in seldom less than fifteen hours of work daily. As I look back on those days, I see them divided tidily into ample light and narrow shade: the light pertaining to the solace of research in palatial libraries, the shade to my excruciating desires and insomnias of which enough has been said. Knowing me by now, the reader can easily imagine how dusty and hot I got, trying to catch a glimpse of nymphets (alas, always remote) playing in Central Park, and how repulsed I was by the glitter of deodorized career girls that a gay dog in one of the offices kept unloading upon me. Let us skip all that. A dreadful breakdown sent me to a sanatorium for more than a year; I went back to my work—only to be hospitalized again.

Robust outdoor life seemed to promise me some relief. One of my favorite doctors, a charming cynical chap with a little brown beard, had a brother, and this brother was about to lead an expedition into arctic Canada. I was attached to it as a "recorder of psychic reactions." With two young botanists and an old carpenter I shared now and then (never very successfully) the favors of one of our nutritionists, a Dr. Anita Johnson—who was soon flown back, I am glad to say. I had little notion of what object the expedition was pursuing. Judging by the number of meteorologists upon it, we may have been tracking to its lair (somewhere on Prince of Wales' Island, I understand) the wandering and wobbly north magnetic pole. One group, jointly with the Canadians, established a weather station on Pierre Point in Melville Sound. Another group, equally misguided, collected plankton. A third studied tuberculosis in the tundra. Bert, a film photographer—an insecure fellow with whom at one time I was made to partake in a good deal of menial work (he, too, had some psychic troubles)—maintained that the big men on our team, the real leaders we never saw, were mainly engaged in checking the influence of climatic amelioration on the coats of the arctic fox.

We lived in prefabricated timber cabins amid a Pre-Cambrian world of granite. We had heaps of supplies—the *Reader's Digest*, an ice cream mixer, chemical toilets, paper caps for Christmas. My health improved wonderfully in spite or because of all the fantastic blankness and boredom. Surrounded by such dejected vegetation as willow scrub and lichens; permeated, and, I suppose, cleansed by a whistling gale; seated on a boulder under a completely translucent sky (through which, however, nothing of importance showed), I felt curiously aloof from my own self. No temptations maddened me. The plump, glossy little Eskimo girls with their fish smell, hideous raven hair and guinea pig faces, evoked even less desire in me than Dr. Johnson had. Nymphets do not occur in polar regions.

I left my betters the task of analyzing glacial drifts, drumlins, and gremlins, and kremlins, and for a time tried to jot down what I fondly thought were "reactions" (I noticed, for instance, that dreams under the midnight sun tended to be highly colored, and this my friend the photographer confirmed). I was also supposed to quiz my various companions on a number of important matters, such as nostalgia, fear of unknown animals, food-fantasies, nocturnal emissions, hobbies, choice of radio programs, changes in outlook and so forth. Everybody got so fed up with this that I soon dropped the project completely, and only toward the end of my twenty months of cold labor (as one of the botanists jocosely put it) concocted a perfectly spurious and very racy report that the reader will find published in the *Annals of Adult Psychophysics* for 1945 or 1946, as well as in the issue of *Arctic Explorations* devoted to that particular expedition; which, in conclusion, was not really concerned with Victoria Island copper or anything like that, as I learned later from my genial doctor; for the nature of its real purpose was what is termed "hush-hush," and so let me add merely that whatever it was, that purpose was admirably achieved.

The reader will regret to learn that soon after my return to civilization I had another bout with insanity (if to melancholia and a sense of insufferable oppression that cruel term must be applied). I owe my complete restoration to a discovery I made while being treated at that particular very expensive sanatorium. I discovered there was an endless source of robust enjoyment in trifling with psychiatrists: cunningly leading them on; never letting them see that you know all the tricks of the trade; inventing for them elaborate dreams, pure classics in style (which make *them*, the dream-extortionists, dream and wake up shrieking); teasing them with fake "primal scenes"; and never allowing them the slightest glimpse of one's real sexual predicament. By bribing a nurse I won access to some files and discovered, with glee, cards calling me "potentially homosexual" and "totally impotent." The sport was so excellent, its results—in *my* case—so ruddy that I stayed on for a whole month after I was quite well (sleeping admirably and eating like a schoolgirl). And then I added another week just for the pleasure of taking on a powerful newcomer, a displaced (and, surely, deranged) celebrity, known for his knack of making patients believe they had witnessed their own conception.

10

Upon signing out, I cast around for some place in the New England countryside or sleepy small town (elms, white church) where I could spend a studious summer subsisting on a compact boxful of notes I had accumulated and bathing in some nearby lake. My work had begun to interest me again— I mean my scholarly exertions; the other thing, my active participation in my uncle's posthumous perfumes, had by then been cut down to a minimum.

One of his former employees, the scion of a distinguished family, suggested I spend a few months in the residence of his impoverished cousins, a Mr. McCoo, retired, and his wife, who wanted to let their upper story where a late aunt had delicately dwelt. He said they had two little daughters, one a baby, the other a girl of twelve, and a beautiful garden, not far from a beautiful lake, and I said it sounded perfectly perfect.

I exchanged letters with these people, satisfying them I was housebroken, and spent a fantastic night on the train, imag-

ining in all possible detail the enigmatic nymphet I would
coach in French and fondle in Humbertish. Nobody met me
at the toy station where I alighted with my new expensive
bag, and nobody answered the telephone; eventually, however, a distraught McCoo in wet clothes turned up at the only
hotel of green-and-pink Ramsdale with the news that his
house had just burned down—possibly, owing to the synchronous conflagration that had been raging all night in my
veins. His family, he said, had fled to a farm he owned, and
had taken the car, but a friend of his wife's, a grand person,
Mrs. Haze of 342 Lawn Street, offered to accommodate me.
A lady who lived opposite Mrs. Haze's had lent McCoo her
limousine, a marvelously old-fashioned, square-topped affair,
manned by a cheerful Negro. Now, since the only reason for
my coming at all had vanished, the aforesaid arrangement
seemed preposterous. All right, his house would have to be
completely rebuilt, so what? Had he not insured it sufficiently?
I was angry, disappointed and bored, but being a polite European, could not refuse to be sent off to Lawn Street in that
funereal car, feeling that otherwise McCoo would devise an
even more elaborate means of getting rid of me. I saw him
scamper away, and my chauffeur shook his head with a soft
chuckle. En route, I swore to myself I would not dream of
staying in Ramsdale under any circumstance but would fly that
very day to the Bermudas or the Bahamas or the Blazes. Possibilities of sweetness on technicolor beaches had been trickling through my spine for some time before, and McCoo's
cousin had, in fact, sharply diverted that train of thought with
his well-meaning but as it transpired now absolutely inane
suggestion.

Speaking of sharp turns: we almost ran over a meddlesome
suburban dog (one of those who lie in wait for cars) as we
swerved into Lawn Street. A little further, the Haze house, a
white-frame horror, appeared, looking dingy and old, more
gray than white—the kind of place you know will have a
rubber tube affixable to the tub faucet in lieu of shower. I
tipped the chauffeur and hoped he would immediately drive
away so that I might double back unnoticed to my hotel and
bag; but the man merely crossed to the other side of the street

where an old lady was calling to him from her porch. What could I do? I pressed the bell button.

A colored maid let me in—and left me standing on the mat while she rushed back to the kitchen where something was burning that ought not to burn.

The front hall was graced with door chimes, a white-eyed wooden thingamabob of commercial Mexican origin, and that banal darling of the arty middle class, van Gogh's "Arlésienne." A door ajar to the right afforded a glimpse of a living room, with some more Mexican trash in a corner cabinet and a striped sofa along the wall. There was a staircase at the end of the hallway, and as I stood mopping my brow (only now did I realize how hot it had been out-of-doors) and staring, to stare at something, at an old gray tennis ball that lay on an oak chest, there came from the upper landing the contralto voice of Mrs. Haze, who leaning over the banisters inquired melodiously, "Is that Monsieur Humbert?" A bit of cigarette ash dropped from there in addition. Presently, the lady herself—sandals, maroon slacks, yellow silk blouse, squarish face, in that order—came down the steps, her index finger still tapping upon her cigarette.

I think I had better describe her right away, to get it over with. The poor lady was in her middle thirties, she had a shiny forehead, plucked eyebrows and quite simple but not unattractive features of a type that may be defined as a weak solution of Marlene Dietrich. Patting her bronze-brown bun, she led me into the parlor and we talked for a minute about the McCoo fire and the privilege of living in Ramsdale. Her very wide-set sea-green eyes had a funny way of traveling all over you, carefully avoiding your own eyes. Her smile was but a quizzical jerk of one eyebrow; and uncoiling herself from the sofa as she talked, she kept making spasmodic dashes at three ashtrays and the near fender (where lay the brown core of an apple); whereupon she would sink back again, one leg folded under her. She was, obviously, one of those women whose polished words may reflect a book club or bridge club, or any other deadly conventionality, but never her soul; women who are completely devoid of humor; women utterly indifferent at heart to the dozen or so possible subjects of a parlor conversation, but very particular about the rules of such conversations, through the sunny cellophane of which not very appetizing frustrations can be readily distinguished. I was perfectly aware that if by any wild chance I became her lodger, she would methodically proceed to do in regard to me what taking a lodger probably meant to her all along, and I would again be enmeshed in one of those tedious affairs I knew so well.

But there was no question of my settling there. I could not be happy in that type of household with bedraggled magazines on every chair and a kind of horrible hybridization between the comedy of so-called "functional modern furniture" and the tragedy of decrepit rockers and rickety lamp tables with dead lamps. I was led upstairs, and to the left—into "my" room. I inspected it through the mist of my utter rejection of it; but I did discern above "my" bed René Prinet's "Kreutzer Sonata." And she called that servant maid's room a "semi-studio"! Let's get out of here at once, I firmly said to myself as I pretended to deliberate over the absurdly, and ominously, low price that my wistful hostess was asking for board and bed.

Old-world politeness, however, obliged me to go on with the ordeal. We crossed the landing to the right side of the house (where "I and Lo have our rooms"—Lo being presumably the maid), and the lodger-lover could hardly conceal a shudder when he, a very fastidious male, was granted a preview of the only bathroom, a tiny oblong between the landing and "Lo's" room, with limp wet things overhanging the dubious tub (the question mark of a hair inside); and there were the expected coils of the rubber snake, and its complement—a pinkish cozy, coyly covering the toilet lid.

"I see you are not too favorably impressed," said the lady letting her hand rest for a moment upon my sleeve: she combined a cool forwardness—the overflow of what I think is called "poise"—with a shyness and sadness that caused her detached way of selecting her words to seem as unnatural as the intonation of a professor of "speech." "This is not a neat household, I confess," the doomed dear continued, "but I assure you [she looked at my lips], you will be very comfortable, very comfortable, indeed. Let me show you the garden" (the last more brightly, with a kind of winsome toss of the voice).

Reluctantly I followed her downstairs again; then through the kitchen at the end of the hall, on the right side of the house—the side where also the dining room and the parlor were (under "my" room, on the left, there was nothing but a garage). In the kitchen, the Negro maid, a plump youngish woman, said, as she took her large glossy black purse from the knob of the door leading to the back porch: "I'll go now, Mrs. Haze." "Yes, Louise," answered Mrs. Haze with a sigh. "I'll settle with you Friday." We passed on to a small pantry and entered the dining room, parallel to the parlor we had already admired. I noticed a white sock on the floor. With a deprecatory grunt, Mrs. Haze stooped without stopping and threw it into a closet next to the pantry. We cursorily inspected a mahogany table with a fruit vase in the middle, containing nothing but the still glistening stone of one plum. I groped for the timetable I had in my pocket and surreptitiously fished it out to look as soon as possible for a train. I was still walking behind Mrs. Haze through the dining room when, beyond it, there came a sudden burst of greenery— "the piazza," sang out my leader, and then, without the least warning, a blue sea-wave swelled under my heart and, from a mat in a pool of sun, half-naked, kneeling, turning about on her knees, there was my Riviera love peering at me over dark glasses.

It was the same child—the same frail, honey-hued shoulders, the same silky supple bare back, the same chestnut head of hair. A polka-dotted black kerchief tied around her chest hid from my aging ape eyes, but not from the gaze of young memory, the juvenile breasts I had fondled one immortal day. And, as if I were the fairy-tale nurse of some little princess (lost, kidnaped, discovered in gypsy rags through which her nakedness smiled at the king and his hounds), I recognized the tiny dark-brown mole on her side. With awe and delight (the king crying for joy, the trumpets blaring, the nurse drunk) I saw again her lovely in-drawn abdomen where my southbound mouth had briefly paused; and those puerile hips on which I had kissed the crenulated imprint left by the band of her shorts—that last mad immortal day behind the "Roches

Roses." The twenty-five years I had lived since then, tapered
to a palpitating point, and vanished.

I find it most difficult to express with adequate force that
flash, that shiver, that impact of passionate recognition. In the
course of the sun-shot moment that my glance slithered over
the kneeling child (her eyes blinking over those stern dark
spectacles—the little Herr Doktor who was to cure me of all
my aches) while I passed by her in my adult disguise (a great
big handsome hunk of movieland manhood), the vacuum of
my soul managed to suck in every detail of her bright beauty,
and these I checked against the features of my dead bride. A
little later, of course, she, this *nouvelle*, this Lolita, *my* Lolita,
was to eclipse completely her prototype. All I want to stress
is that my discovery of her was a fatal consequence of that
"princedom by the sea" in my tortured past. Everything between the two events was but a series of gropings and blunders, and false rudiments of joy. Everything they shared made
one of them.

I have no illusions, however. My judges will regard all this
as a piece of mummery on the part of a madman with a gross
liking for the *fruit vert*. *Au fond, ça m'est bien égal.* All I know
is that while the Haze woman and I went down the steps into
the breathless garden, my knees were like reflections of knees
in rippling water, and my lips were like sand, and—

"That was my Lo," she said, "and these are my lilies."

"Yes," I said, "yes. They are beautiful, beautiful, beautiful!"

11

Exhibit number two is a pocket diary bound in black imitation leather, with a golden year, 1947, *en escalier*, in its upper
left-hand corner. I speak of this neat product of the Blank
Blank Co., Blankton, Mass., as if it were really before me.
Actually, it was destroyed five years ago and what we examine
now (by courtesy of a photographic memory) is but its brief
materialization, a puny unfledged phœnix.

I remember the thing so exactly because I wrote it really
twice. First I jotted down each entry in pencil (with many
erasures and corrections) on the leaves of what is commercially

known as a "typewriter tablet"; then, I copied it out with obvious abbreviations in my smallest, most satanic, hand in the little black book just mentioned.

May 30 is a Fast Day by Proclamation in New Hampshire but not in the Carolinas. That day an epidemic of "abdominal flu" (whatever that is) forced Ramsdale to close its schools for the summer. The reader may check the weather data in the Ramsdale *Journal* for 1947. A few days before that I moved into the Haze house, and the little diary which I now propose to reel off (much as a spy delivers by heart the contents of the note he swallowed) covers most of June.

Thursday. Very warm day. From a vantage point (bathroom window) saw Dolores taking things off a clothesline in the apple-green light behind the house. Strolled out. She wore a plaid shirt, blue jeans and sneakers. Every movement she made in the dappled sun plucked at the most secret and sensitive chord of my abject body. After a while she sat down next to me on the lower step of the back porch and began to pick up the pebbles between her feet—pebbles, my God, then a curled bit of milk-bottle glass resembling a snarling lip—and chuck them at a can. *Ping.* You can't a second time—you can't hit it—this is agony—a second time. *Ping.* Marvelous skin—oh, marvelous: tender and tanned, not the least blemish. Sundaes cause acne. The excess of the oily substance called sebum which nourishes the hair follicles of the skin creates, when too profuse, an irritation that opens the way to infection. But nymphets do not have acne although they gorge themselves on rich food. God, what agony, that silky shimmer above her temple grading into bright brown hair. And the little bone twitching at the side of her dust-powdered ankle. "The McCoo girl? Ginny McCoo? Oh, she's a fright. And mean. And lame. Nearly died of polio." *Ping.* The glistening tracery of down on her forearm. When she got up to take in the wash, I had a chance of adoring from afar the faded seat of her rolled-up jeans. Out of the lawn, bland Mrs. Haze, complete with camera, grew up like a fakir's fake tree and after some heliotropic fussing—sad eyes up, glad eyes down—had the cheek of taking my picture as I sat blinking on the steps, Humbert le Bel.

Friday. Saw her going somewhere with a dark girl called

Rose. Why does the way she walks—a child, mind you, a mere child!—excite me so abominably? Analyze it. A faint suggestion of turned in toes. A kind of wiggly looseness below the knee prolonged to the end of each footfall. The ghost of a drag. Very infantile, infinitely meretricious. Humbert Humbert is also infinitely moved by the little one's slangy speech, by her harsh high voice. Later heard her volley crude nonsense at Rose across the fence. Twanging through me in a rising rhythm. Pause. "I must go now, kiddo."

Saturday. (Beginning perhaps amended.) I know it is madness to keep this journal but it gives me a strange thrill to do so; and only a loving wife could decipher my microscopic script. Let me state with a sob that today my L. was sunbathing on the so-called "piazza," but her mother and some other woman were around all the time. Of course, I might have sat there in the rocker and pretended to read. Playing safe, I kept away, for I was afraid that the horrible, insane, ridiculous and pitiful tremor that palsied me might prevent me from making my *entrée* with any semblance of casualness.

Sunday. Heat ripple still with us; a most favonian week. This time I took up a strategic position, with obese newspaper and new pipe, in the piazza rocker *before* L. arrived. To my intense disappointment she came with her mother, both in two-piece bathing suits, black, as new as my pipe. My darling, my sweetheart stood for a moment near me—wanted the funnies—and she smelt almost exactly like the other one, the Riviera one, but more intensely so, with rougher overtones—a torrid odor that at once set my manhood astir—but she had already yanked out of me the coveted section and retreated to her mat near her phocine mamma. There my beauty lay down on her stomach, showing me, showing the thousand eyes wide open in my eyed blood, her slightly raised shoulder blades, and the bloom along the incurvation of her spine, and the swellings of her tense narrow nates clothed in black, and the seaside of her schoolgirl thighs. Silently, the seventh-grader enjoyed her green-red-blue comics. She was the loveliest nymphet green-red-blue Priap himself could think up. As I looked on, through prismatic layers of light, dry-lipped, focusing my lust and rocking slightly under my newspaper, I felt that my perception of her, if properly concentrated upon, might be sufficient to have me attain a beggar's bliss immediately; but, like some predator that prefers a moving prey to a motionless one, I planned to have this pitiful attainment coincide with one of the various girlish movements she made now and then as she read, such as trying to scratch the middle of her back and revealing a stippled armpit—but fat Haze suddenly spoiled everything by turning to me and asking me for a light, and starting a make-believe conversation about a fake book by some popular fraud.

Monday. Delectatio morosa. I spend my doleful days in dumps and dolors. We (mother Haze, Dolores and I) were to go to Our Glass Lake this afternoon, and bathe, and bask; but a nacreous morn degenerated at noon into rain, and Lo made a scene.

The median age of pubescence for girls has been found to be thirteen years and nine months in New York and Chicago. The age varies for individuals from ten, or earlier, to seventeen. Virginia was not quite fourteen when Harry Edgar possessed her. He gave her lessons in algebra. *Je m'imagine cela.* They spent their honeymoon at Petersburg, Fla. "Monsieur Poe-poe," as that boy in one of Monsieur Humbert Humbert's classes in Paris called the poet-poet.

I have all the characteristics which, according to writers on the sex interests of children, start the responses stirring in a little girl: clean-cut jaw, muscular hand, deep sonorous voice, broad shoulder. Moreover, I am said to resemble some crooner or actor chap on whom Lo has a crush.

Tuesday. Rain. Lake of the Rains. Mamma out shopping. L., I knew, was somewhere quite near. In result of some stealthy maneuvering, I came across her in her mother's bedroom. Prying her left eye open to get rid of a speck of something. Checked frock. Although I do love that intoxicating brown fragrance of hers, I really think she should wash her hair once in a while. For a moment, we were both in the same warm green bath of the mirror that reflected the top of a poplar with us in the sky. Held her roughly by the shoulders, then tenderly by the temples, and turned her about. "It's right there," she said, "I can feel it." "Swiss peasant would use the tip of her tongue." "Lick it out?" "Yeth. Shly try?" "Sure," she said. Gently I pressed my quivering sting along her rolling salty eyeball. "Goody-goody," she said nictating. "It *is* gone." "Now the other?" "You dope," she began, "there is noth—" but here she noticed the pucker of my approaching lips. "Okay," she said co-operatively, and bending toward her warm upturned russet face somber Humbert pressed his mouth to her fluttering eyelid. She laughed, and brushed past me out of the room. My heart seemed everywhere at once. Never in my life—not even when fondling my child-love in France—never—

Night. Never have I experienced such agony. I would like to describe her face, her ways—and I cannot, because my own desire for her blinds me when she is near. I am not used to being with nymphets, damn it. If I close my eyes I see but an immobilized fraction of her, a cinematographic still, a sudden smooth nether loveliness, as with one knee up under her tartan skirt she sits tying her shoe. "Dolores Haze, *ne montrez pas vos zhambes*" (this is her mother who thinks she knows French).

A poet *à mes heures*, I composed a madrigal to the soot-black lashes of her pale-gray vacant eyes, to the five asymmetrical freckles of her bobbed nose, to the blond down of her brown limbs; but I tore it up and cannot recall it today. Only in the tritest of terms (diary resumed) can I describe Lo's features: I might say her hair is auburn, and her lips as red as licked red candy, the lower one prettily plump—oh, that I were a lady writer who could have her pose naked in a naked light! But instead I am lanky, big-boned, woolly-chested Humbert Humbert, with thick black eyebrows and a queer accent, and a cesspoolful of rotting monsters behind his slow boyish smile. And neither is she the fragile child of a feminine novel. What drives me insane is the twofold nature of this nymphet—of every nymphet, perhaps; this mixture in my Lolita of tender dreamy childishness and a kind of eerie vulgarity, stemming from the snub-nosed cuteness of ads and magazine pictures, from the blurry pinkness of adolescent maidservants in the Old Country (smelling of crushed daisies and sweat); and from very young harlots disguised as children in provincial brothels; and then again, all this gets mixed up with the exquisite stainless tenderness seeping through the musk and the mud, through the dirt and the death, oh God, oh God. And what is most singular is that she, *this* Lolita, *my* Lolita, has individualized the writer's ancient lust, so that above and over everything there is—Lolita.

Wednesday. "Look, make Mother take you and me to Our Glass Lake tomorrow." These were the textual words said to me by my twelve-year-old flame in a voluptuous whisper, as we happened to bump into one another on the front porch, I out, she in. The reflection of the afternoon sun, a dazzling white diamond with innumerable iridescent spikes quivered on the round back of a parked car. The leafage of a voluminous elm played its mellow shadows upon the clapboard wall of the house. Two poplars shivered and shook. You could make out the formless sounds of remote traffic; a child calling "Nancy, Nan-cy!" In the house, Lolita had put on her favorite "Little Carmen" record which I used to call "Dwarf Conductors," making her snort with mock derision at my mock wit.

Thursday. Last night we sat on the piazza, the Haze woman, Lolita and I. Warm dusk had deepened into amorous darkness. The old girl had finished relating in great detail the plot of a movie she and L. had seen sometime in the winter. The boxer had fallen extremely low when he met the good old priest (who had been a boxer himself in his robust youth and could still slug a sinner). We sat on cushions heaped on the floor, and L. was between the woman and me (she had squeezed herself in, the pet). In my turn, I launched upon a hilarious account of my arctic adventures. The muse of invention handed me a rifle and I shot a white bear who sat down and said: Ah! All the while I was acutely aware of L.'s nearness and as I spoke I gestured in the merciful dark and took advantage of those invisible gestures of mine to touch her hand, her shoulder and a ballerina of wool and gauze which she played with and kept sticking into my lap; and finally, when I had completely enmeshed my glowing darling in this weave of ethereal caresses, I dared stroke her bare leg along the gooseberry fuzz of her shin, and I chuckled at my own jokes, and trembled, and concealed my tremors, and once or twice felt with my rapid lips the warmth of her hair as I treated her to a quick nuzzling, humorous aside and caressed her plaything. She, too, fidgeted a good deal so that finally her mother told her sharply to quit it and sent the doll flying into the dark, and I laughed and addressed myself to Haze across Lo's legs to let my hand creep up my nymphet's thin back and feel her skin through her boy's shirt.

But I knew it was all hopeless, and was sick with longing, and my clothes felt miserably tight, and I was almost glad when her mother's quiet voice announced in the dark: "And now we all think that Lo should go to bed." "I think you stink," said Lo. "Which means there will be no picnic tomorrow," said Haze. "This is a free country," said Lo. When angry Lo with a Bronx cheer had gone, I stayed on from sheer inertia, while Haze smoked her tenth cigarette of the evening and complained of Lo.

She had been spiteful, if you please, at the age of one, when she used to throw her toys out of her crib so that her poor mother should keep picking them up, the villainous infant! Now, at twelve, she was a regular pest, said Haze. All she wanted from life was to be one day a strutting and prancing baton twirler or a jitterbug. Her grades were poor, but she was better adjusted in her new school than in Pisky (Pisky was the Haze home town in the Middle West. The Ramsdale house was her late mother-in-law's. They had moved to Ramsdale less than two years ago). "Why was she unhappy there?" "Oh," said Haze, "poor me should know, I went through that when *I* was a kid: boys twisting one's arm, banging into one with loads of books, pulling one's hair, hurting one's breasts, flipping one's skirt. Of course, moodiness is a common concomitant of growing up, but Lo exaggerates. Sullen and evasive. Rude and defiant. Stuck Viola, an Italian schoolmate, in the seat with a fountain pen. Know what I would like? If you, monsieur, happened to be still here in the fall, I'd ask you to help her with her homework—you seem to know everything, geography, mathematics, French." "Oh, everything," answered monsieur. "That means," said Haze quickly, "you'll *be* here!" I wanted to shout that I would stay on eternally if only I could hope to caress now and then my incipient pupil. But I was wary of Haze. So I just grunted and stretched my limbs nonconcomitantly (*le mot juste*) and presently went up to my room. The woman, however, was evidently not prepared to call it a day. I was already lying upon my cold bed both hands pressing to my face Lolita's fragrant ghost when I heard my indefatigable landlady creeping stealthily up to my door to whisper through it—just to make sure, she said, I was through with the Glance and Gulp magazine I had borrowed the other day. From her room Lo yelled *she* had it. We are quite a lending library in this house, thunder of God.

Friday. I wonder what my academic publishers would say if I were to quote in my textbook Ronsard's *"la vermeillette fente"* or Remy Belleau's *"un petit mont feutré de mousse délicate, tracé sur le milieu d'un fillet escarlatte"* and so forth. I shall probably have another breakdown if I stay any longer in this house, under the strain of this intolerable temptation, by the side of my darling—my darling—my life and my bride. Has she already been initiated by mother nature to the Mystery of the Menarche? Bloated feeling. The Curse of the Irish. Falling from the roof. Grandma is visiting. "Mr. Uterus [I quote from a girls' magazine] starts to build a thick soft wall on the chance a possible baby may have to be bedded down there." The tiny madman in his padded cell.

Incidentally: if I ever commit a serious murder . . . Mark the "if." The urge should be something more than the kind of thing that happened to me with Valeria. Carefully mark that *then* I was rather inept. If and when you wish to sizzle me to death, remember that only a spell of insanity could ever give me the simple energy to be a brute (all this amended, perhaps). Sometimes I attempt to kill in my dreams. But do you know what happens? For instance I hold a gun. For instance I aim at a bland, quietly interested enemy. Oh, I press the trigger all right, but one bullet after another feebly drops on the floor from the sheepish muzzle. In those dreams, my only thought is to conceal the fiasco from my foe, who is slowly growing annoyed.

At dinner tonight the old cat said to me with a sidelong gleam of motherly mockery directed at Lo (I had just been describing, in a flippant vein, the delightful little toothbrush mustache I had not quite decided to grow): "Better don't, if somebody is not to go absolutely dotty." Instantly Lo pushed her plate of boiled fish away, all but knocking her milk over, and bounced out of the dining room. "Would it bore you very much," quoth Haze, "to come with us tomorrow for a swim in Our Glass Lake if Lo apologizes for her manners?"

Later, I heard a great banging of doors and other sounds coming from quaking caverns where the two rivals were having a ripping row.

She has not apologized. The lake is out. It might have been fun.

Saturday. For some days already I had been leaving the door ajar, while I wrote in my room; but only today did the trap work. With a good deal of additional fidgeting, shuffling, scraping—to disguise her embarrassment at visiting me without having been called—Lo came in and after pottering around, became interested in the nightmare curlicues I had penned on a sheet of paper. Oh no: they were not the outcome of a belle-lettrist's inspired pause between two paragraphs; they were the hideous hieroglyphics (which she could not decipher) of my fatal lust. As she bent her brown curls over the desk at which I was sitting, Humbert the Hoarse put his arm around her in a miserable imitation of blood-relationship; and still studying, somewhat shortsightedly, the piece of paper she held, my innocent little visitor slowly sank to a half-sitting position upon my knee. Her adorable profile, parted lips, warm hair were some three inches from my bared eye-tooth; and I felt the heat of her limbs through her rough tomboy clothes. All at once I knew I could kiss her throat or the wick of her mouth with perfect impunity. I knew she would let me do so, and even close her eyes as Hollywood teaches. A double vanilla with hot fudge—hardly more unusual than that. I cannot tell my learned reader (whose eyebrows, I suspect, have by now traveled all the way to the back of his bald head), I cannot tell him how the knowledge came to me; perhaps my ape-ear had unconsciously caught some slight change in the rhythm of her respiration—for now she was not really looking at my scribble, but waiting with curiosity and composure—oh, my limpid nymphet!—for the glamorous lodger to do what he was dying to do. A modern child, an avid reader of movie magazines, an expert in dream-slow close-ups, might not think it too strange, I guessed, if a handsome, intensely virile grown-up friend—too late. The house was suddenly vibrating with voluble Louise's voice

telling Mrs. Haze who had just come home about a dead
something she and Leslie Tomson had found in the basement,
and little Lolita was not one to miss such a tale.

Sunday. Changeful, bad-tempered, cheerful, awkward,
graceful with the tart grace of her coltish subteens, excruci-
atingly desirable from head to foot (all New England for a
lady-writer's pen!), from the black ready-made bow and
bobby pins holding her hair in place to the little scar on the
lower part of her neat calf (where a roller-skater kicked her in
Pisky), a couple of inches above her rough white sock. Gone
with her mother to the Hamiltons—a birthday party or something. Full-skirted gingham frock. Her little doves seem well
formed already. Precocious pet!

Monday. Rainy morning. *"Ces matins gris si doux . . ."* My
white pajamas have a lilac design on the back. I am like one
of those inflated pale spiders you see in old gardens. Sitting
in the middle of a luminous web and giving little jerks to this
or that strand. *My* web is spread all over the house as I listen
from my chair where I sit like a wily wizard. Is Lo in her room?
Gently I tug on the silk. She is not. Just heard the toilet paper
cylinder make its staccato sound as it is turned; and no footfalls has my outflung filament traced from the bathroom back
to her room. Is she still brushing her teeth (the only sanitary
act Lo performs with real zest)? No. The bathroom door has
just slammed, so one has to feel elsewhere about the house
for the beautiful warm-colored prey. Let us have a strand of
silk descend the stairs. I satisfy myself by this means that she
is not in the kitchen—not banging the refrigerator door or
screeching at her detested mamma (who, I suppose, is enjoying her third, cooing and subduedly mirthful, telephone conversation of the morning). Well, let us grope and hope.
Ray-like, I glide in thought to the parlor and find the radio
silent (and mamma still talking to Mrs. Chatfield or Mrs.
Hamilton, very softly, flushed, smiling, cupping the telephone
with her free hand, denying by implication that she denies
those amusing rumors, rumor, roomer, whispering intimately,
as she never does, the clear-cut lady, in face to face talk). So
my nymphet is not in the house at all! Gone! What I thought
was a prismatic weave turns out to be but an old gray cobweb,
the house is empty, is dead. And then comes Lolita's soft

sweet chuckle through my half-open door "Don't tell Mother but I've eaten *all* your bacon." Gone when I scuttle out of my room. Lolita, where are you? My breakfast tray, lovingly prepared by my landlady, leers at me toothlessly, ready to be taken in. Lola, Lolita!

Tuesday. Clouds again interfered with that picnic on that unattainable lake. Is it Fate scheming? Yesterday I tried on before the mirror a new pair of bathing trunks.

Wednesday. In the afternoon, Haze (common-sensical shoes, tailor-made dress), said she was driving downtown to buy a present for a friend of a friend of hers, and would I please come too because I have such a wonderful taste in textures and perfumes. "Choose your favorite seduction," she purred. What could Humbert, being in the perfume business, do? She had me cornered between the front porch and her car. "Hurry up," she said as I laboriously doubled up my large body in order to crawl in (still desperately devising a means of escape). She had started the engine, and was genteelly swearing at a backing and turning truck in front that had just brought old invalid Miss Opposite a brand new wheel chair, when my Lolita's sharp voice came from the parlor window: "You! Where are you going? I'm coming too! Wait!" "Ignore her," yelped Haze (killing the motor); alas for my fair driver; Lo was already pulling at the door on my side. "This is intolerable," began Haze; but Lo had scrambled in, shivering with glee. "Move your bottom, you," said Lo. "Lo!" cried Haze (sideglancing at me, hoping I would throw rude Lo out). "And behold," said Lo (not for the first time), as she jerked back, as I jerked back, as the car leapt forward. "It is intolerable," said Haze, violently getting into second, "that a child should be so ill-mannered. And so very persevering. When she knows she is unwanted. And needs a bath."

My knuckles lay against the child's blue jeans. She was barefooted; her toenails showed remnants of cherry-red polish and there was a bit of adhesive tape across her big toe; and, God, what would I not have given to kiss then and there those delicate-boned, long-toed, monkeyish feet! Suddenly her hand slipped into mine and without our chaperon's seeing, I held, and stroked, and squeezed that little hot paw, all the way to the store. The wings of the driver's Marlenesque nose shone, having shed or burned up their ration of powder, and she kept up an elegant monologue anent the local traffic, and smiled in profile, and pouted in profile, and beat her painted lashes in profile, while I prayed we would never get to that store, but we did.

I have nothing else to report, save, *primo*: that big Haze had little Haze sit behind on our way home, and *secundo*: that the lady decided to keep Humbert's Choice for the backs of her own shapely ears.

Thursday. We are paying with hail and gale for the tropical beginning of the month. In a volume of the *Young People's Encyclopedia*, I found a map of the States that a child's pencil had started copying out on a sheet of lightweight paper, upon the other side of which, counter to the unfinished outline of Florida and the Gulf, there was a mimeographed list of names referring, evidently, to her class at the Ramsdale school. It is a poem I know already by heart.

> Angel, Grace
> Austin, Floyd
> Beale, Jack
> Beale, Mary
> Buck, Daniel
> Byron, Marguerite
> Campbell, Alice
> Carmine, Rose
> Chatfield, Phyllis
> Clarke, Gordon
> Cowan, John
> Cowan, Marion
> Duncan, Walter
> Falter, Ted
> Fantasia, Stella
> Flashman, Irving
> Fox, George
> Glave, Mabel
> Goodale, Donald
> Green, Lucinda
> Hamilton, Mary Rose
> Haze, Dolores

Honeck, Rosaline
Knight, Kenneth
McCoo, Virginia
McCrystal, Vivian
McFate, Aubrey
Miranda, Anthony
Miranda, Viola
Rosato, Emil
Schlenker, Lena
Scott, Donald
Sheridan, Agnes
Sherva, Oleg
Smith, Hazel
Talbot, Edgar
Talbot, Edwin
Wain, Lull
Williams, Ralph
Windmuller, Louise

A poem, a poem, forsooth! So strange and sweet was it to discover this "Haze, Dolores" (she!) in its special bower of names, with its bodyguard of roses—a fairy princess between her two maids of honor. I am trying to analyze the spine-thrill of delight it gives me, this name among all those others. What is it that excites me almost to tears (hot, opalescent, thick tears that poets and lovers shed)? What is it? The tender anonymity of this name with its formal veil ("Dolores") and that abstract transposition of first name and surname, which is like a pair of new pale gloves or a mask? Is "mask" the keyword? Is it because there is always delight in the semitranslucent mystery, the flowing charshaf, through which the flesh and the eye you alone are elected to know smile in passing at you alone? Or is it because I can imagine so well the rest of the colorful classroom around my dolorous and hazy darling: Grace and her ripe pimples; Ginny and her lagging leg; Gordon, the haggard masturbator; Duncan, the foul-smelling clown; nail-biting Agnes; Viola, of the blackheads and the bouncing bust; pretty Rosaline; dark Mary Rose; adorable Stella, who has let strangers touch her; Ralph, who bullies and steals; Irving, for whom I am sorry. And there she is there, lost in the middle,

gnawing a pencil, detested by teachers, all the boys' eyes on
her hair and neck, *my* Lolita.

Friday. I long for some terrific disaster. Earthquake. Spectacular explosion. Her mother is messily but instantly and permanently eliminated, along with everybody else for miles
around. Lolita whimpers in my arms. A free man, I enjoy her
among the ruins. Her surprise, my explanations, demonstra-
tions, ullulations. Idle and idiotic fancies! A brave Humbert
would have played with her most disgustingly (yesterday, for
instance, when she was again in my room to show me her
drawings, school-artware); he might have bribed her—and got
away with it. A simpler and more practical fellow would have
soberly stuck to various commercial substitutes—if you know
where to go, I don't. Despite my manly looks, I am horribly
timid. My romantic soul gets all clammy and shivery at the
thought of running into some awful indecent unpleasantness.
Those ribald sea monsters. *"Mais allez-y, allez-y!"* Annabel
skipping on one foot to get into her shorts, I seasick with
rage, trying to screen her.

Same date, later, quite late. I have turned on the light to
take down a dream. It had an evident antecedent. Haze at
dinner had benevolently proclaimed that since the weather
bureau promised a sunny weekend we would go to the lake
Sunday after church. As I lay in bed, erotically musing before
trying to go to sleep, I thought of a final scheme how to profit
by the picnic to come. I was aware that mother Haze hated
my darling for her being sweet on me. So I planned my lake
day with a view to satisfying the mother. To her alone would
I talk; but at some appropriate moment I would say I had left
my wrist watch or my sunglasses in that glade yonder—and
plunge with my nymphet into the wood. Reality at this junc-
ture withdrew, and the Quest for the Glasses turned into a
quiet little orgy with a singularly knowing, cheerful, corrupt
and compliant Lolita behaving as reason knew she could not
possibly behave. At 3 A.M. I swallowed a sleeping pill, and
presently, a dream that was not a sequel but a parody revealed
to me, with a kind of meaningful clarity, the lake I had never
yet visited: it was glazed over with a sheet of emerald ice, and
a pockmarked Eskimo was trying in vain to break it with a
pickaxe, although imported mimosas and oleanders flowered

on its gravelly banks. I am sure Dr. Blanche Schwarzmann
would have paid me a sack of schillings for adding such a
libidream to her files. Unfortunately, the rest of it was frankly
eclectic. Big Haze and little Haze rode on horseback around
the lake, and I rode too, dutifully bobbing up and down,
bowlegs astraddle although there was no horse between them,
only elastic air—one of those little omissions due to the absent-mindedness of the dream agent.

Saturday. My heart is still thumping. I still squirm and emit
low moans of remembered embarrassment.

Dorsal view. Glimpse of shiny skin between T-shirt and
white gym shorts. Bending, over a window sill, in the act of
tearing off leaves from a poplar outside while engrossed in
torrential talk with a newspaper boy below (Kenneth Knight,
I suspect) who had just propelled the Ramsdale *Journal* with
a very precise thud onto the porch. I began creeping up to
her—"crippling" up to her, as pantomimists say. My arms and
legs were convex surfaces between which—rather than upon
which—I slowly progressed by some neutral means of locomotion: Humbert the Wounded Spider. I must have taken
hours to reach her: I seemed to see her through the wrong
end of a telescope, and toward her taut little rear I moved like
some paralytic, on soft distorted limbs, in terrible concentration. At last I was right behind her when I had the unfortunate
idea of blustering a trifle—shaking her by the scruff of the
neck and that sort of thing to cover my real *manège*, and she
said in a shrill brief whine: "Cut it out!"—most coarsely, the
little wench, and with a ghastly grin Humbert the Humble
beat a gloomy retreat while she went on wisecracking streetward.

But now listen to what happened next. After lunch I was
reclining in a low chair trying to read. Suddenly two deft little
hands were over my eyes: she had crept up from behind as if
re-enacting, in a ballet sequence, my morning maneuver. Her
fingers were a luminous crimson as they tried to blot out the
sun, and she uttered hiccups of laughter and jerked this way
and that as I stretched my arm sideways and backwards without otherwise changing my recumbent position. My hand
swept over her agile giggling legs, and the book like a sleigh
left my lap, and Mrs. Haze strolled up and said indulgently:

"Just slap her hard if she interferes with your scholarly meditations. How I love this garden [no exclamation mark in her
tone]. Isn't it divine in the sun [no question mark either]."
And with a sigh of feigned content, the obnoxious lady sank
down on the grass and looked up at the sky as she leaned back
on her splayed-out hands, and presently an old gray tennis
ball bounced over her, and Lo's voice came from the house
haughtily: "*Pardonnez*, Mother. I was not aiming at *you*." Of
course not, my hot downy darling.

12

This proved to be the last of twenty entries or so. It will be
seen from them that for all the devil's inventiveness, the
scheme remained daily the same. First he would tempt me—
and then thwart me, leaving me with a dull pain in the very
root of my being. I knew exactly what I wanted to do, and
how to do it, without impinging on a child's chastity; after
all, I had had *some* experience in my life of pederosis; had
visually possessed dappled nymphets in parks; had wedged my
wary and bestial way into the hottest, most crowded corner
of a city bus full of strap-hanging school children. But for
almost three weeks I had been interrupted in all my pathetic
machinations. The agent of these interruptions was usually the
Haze woman (who, as the reader will mark, was more afraid
of Lo's deriving some pleasure from me than of my enjoying
Lo). The passion I had developed for that nymphet—for the
first nymphet in my life that could be reached at last by my
awkward, aching, timid claws—would have certainly landed
me again in a sanatorium, had not the devil realized that I
was to be granted some relief if he wanted to have me as a
plaything for some time longer.

The reader has also marked the curious Mirage of the Lake.
It would have been logical on the part of Aubrey McFate (as
I would like to dub that devil of mine) to arrange a small treat
for me on the promised beach, in the presumed forest. Actually, the promise Mrs. Haze had made was a fraudulent one:
she had not told me that Mary Rose Hamilton (a dark little
beauty in her own right) was to come too, and that the two
nymphets would be whispering apart, and playing apart, and

having a good time all by themselves, while Mrs. Haze and her handsome lodger conversed sedately in the seminude, far from prying eyes. Incidentally, eyes did pry and tongues did wag. How queer life is! We hasten to alienate the very fates we intended to woo. Before my actual arrival, my landlady had planned to have an old spinster, a Miss Phalen, whose mother had been cook in Mrs. Haze's family, come to stay in the house with Lolita and me, while Mrs. Haze, a career girl at heart, sought some suitable job in the nearest city. Mrs. Haze had seen the whole situation very clearly: the bespectacled, round-backed Herr Humbert coming with his Central-European trunks to gather dust in his corner behind a heap of old books; the unloved ugly little daughter firmly supervised by Miss Phalen who had already once had my Lo under her buzzard wing (Lo recalled that 1944 summer with an indignant shudder); and Mrs. Haze herself engaged as a receptionist in a great elegant city. But a not too complicated event interfered with that program. Miss Phalen broke her hip in Savannah, Ga., on the very day I arrived in Ramsdale.

13

The Sunday after the Saturday already described proved to be as bright as the weatherman had predicted. When putting the breakfast things back on the chair outside my room for my good landlady to remove at her convenience, I gleaned the following situation by listening from the landing across which I had softly crept to the banisters in my old bedroom slippers—the only old things about me.

There had been another row. Mrs. Hamilton had telephoned that her daughter "was running a temperature." Mrs. Haze informed *her* daughter that the picnic would have to be postponed. Hot little Haze informed big cold Haze that, if so, she would not go with her to church. Mother said very well and left.

I had come out on the landing straight after shaving, soapy-earlobed, still in my white pajamas with the cornflower blue (not the lilac) design on the back; I now wiped off the soap, perfumed my hair and armpits, slipped on a purple silk dressing gown, and, humming nervously, went down the stairs in quest of Lo.

I want my learned readers to participate in the scene I am about to replay; I want them to examine its every detail and see for themselves how careful, how chaste, the whole wine-sweet event is if viewed with what my lawyer has called, in a private talk we have had, "impartial sympathy." So let us get started. I have a difficult job before me.

Main character: Humbert the Hummer. Time: Sunday morning in June. Place: sunlit living room. Props: old, candy-striped davenport, magazines, phonograph, Mexican knick-knacks (the late Mr. Harold E. Haze—God bless the good man—had engendered my darling at the siesta hour in a blue-washed room, on a honeymoon trip to Vera Cruz, and mementoes, among these Dolores, were all over the place). She wore that day a pretty print dress that I had seen on her once before, ample in the skirt, tight in the bodice, short-sleeved, pink, checkered with darker pink, and, to complete the color scheme, she had painted her lips and was holding in her hollowed hands a beautiful, banal, Eden-red apple. She was not shod, however, for church. And her white Sunday purse lay discarded near the phonograph.

My heart beat like a drum as she sat down, cool skirt ballooning, subsiding, on the sofa next to me, and played with her glossy fruit. She tossed it up into the sun-dusted air, and caught it—it made a cupped polished *plop*.

Humbert Humbert intercepted the apple.

"Give it back," she pleaded, showing the marbled flush of her palms. I produced Delicious. She grasped it and bit into it, and my heart was like snow under thin crimson skin, and with the monkeyish nimbleness that was so typical of that American nymphet, she snatched out of my abstract grip the magazine I had opened (pity no film had recorded the curious pattern, the monogrammic linkage of our simultaneous or overlapping moves). Rapidly, hardly hampered by the disfigured apple she held, Lo flipped violently through the pages in search of something she wished Humbert to see. Found it at last. I faked interest by bringing my head so close that her hair touched my temple and her arm brushed my cheek as she wiped her lips with her wrist. Because of the burnished mist through which I peered at the picture, I was slow in reacting to it, and her bare knees rubbed and knocked impatiently against each other. Dimly there came into view: a surrealist painter relaxing, supine, on a beach, and near him, likewise supine, a plaster replica of the Venus di Milo, half-buried in sand. Picture of the Week, said the legend. I whisked the whole obscene thing away. Next moment, in a sham effort to retrieve it, she was all over me. Caught her by her thin knobby wrist. The magazine escaped to the floor like a flustered fowl. She twisted herself free, recoiled, and lay back in the right-hand corner of the davenport. Then, with perfect simplicity, the impudent child extended her legs across my lap.

By this time I was in a state of excitement bordering on insanity; but I also had the cunning of the insane. Sitting there, on the sofa, I managed to attune, by a series of stealthy movements, my masked lust to her guileless limbs. It was no easy matter to divert the little maiden's attention while I performed the obscure adjustments necessary for the success of the trick. Talking fast, lagging behind my own breath, catching up with it, mimicking a sudden toothache to explain the breaks in my patter—and all the while keeping a maniac's inner eye on my distant golden goal, I cautiously increased the magic friction that was doing away, in an illusional, if not factual, sense, with the physically irremovable, but psychologically very friable texture of the material divide (pajamas and robe) between the weight of two sunburnt legs, resting athwart my lap, and the hidden tumor of an unspeakable passion. Having, in the course of my patter, hit upon something nicely mechanical, I recited, garbling them slightly, the words of a foolish song that was then popular—O my Carmen, my little Carmen, something, something, those something nights, and the stars, and the cars, and the bars, and the barmen; I kept repeating this automatic stuff and holding her under its special spell (special because of the garbling), and all the while I was mortally afraid that some act of God might interrupt me, might remove the golden load in the sensation of which all my being seemed concentrated, and this anxiety forced me to work, for the first minute or so, more hastily than was consensual with deliberately modulated enjoyment. The stars that sparkled, and the cars that parkled, and the bars, and the barmen, were presently taken over by her; her voice stole and corrected the tune I had been mutilating. She was musical and apple-sweet. Her legs twitched a little as they lay across my live lap; I stroked them; there she lolled in the right-hand corner, almost asprawl, Lola the bobby-soxer, devouring her immemorial fruit, singing through its juice, losing her slipper, rubbing the heel of her slipperless foot in its sloppy anklet, against the pile of old magazines heaped on my left on the sofa—and every movement she made, every shuffle and ripple, helped me to conceal and to improve the secret system of tactile correspondence between beast and beauty—between my gagged, bursting beast and the beauty of her dimpled body in its innocent cotton frock.

Under my glancing finger tips I felt the minute hairs bristle ever so slightly along her shins. I lost myself in the pungent but healthy heat which like summer haze hung about little Haze. Let her stay, let her stay . . . As she strained to chuck the core of her abolished apple into the fender, her young weight, her shameless innocent shanks and round bottom, shifted in my tense, tortured, surreptitiously laboring lap; and all of a sudden a mysterious change came over my senses. I entered a plane of being where nothing mattered, save the infusion of joy brewed within my body. What had begun as a delicious distension of my innermost roots became a glowing tingle which *now* had reached that state of absolute security, confidence and reliance not found elsewhere in conscious life. With the deep hot sweetness thus established and well on its way to the ultimate convulsion, I felt I could slow down in order to prolong the glow. Lolita had been safely solipsized. The implied sun pulsated in the supplied poplars; we were fantastically and divinely alone; I watched her, rosy, gold-dusted, beyond the veil of my controlled delight, unaware of it, alien to it, and the sun was on her lips, and her lips were apparently still forming the words of the Carmen-barmen ditty that no longer reached my consciousness. Everything was now ready. The nerves of pleasure had been laid bare. The corpuscles of Krause were entering the phase of frenzy. The least pressure would suffice to set all paradise loose. I had ceased to be Humbert the Hound, the sad-eyed degenerate cur clasping the boot that would presently kick him away. I was above the tribulations of ridicule, beyond the possibilities of retribution. In my self-made seraglio, I was a radiant and robust Turk, deliberately, in the full consciousness of his freedom, postponing the moment of actually enjoying the youngest and frailest of his slaves. Suspended on the brink of that voluptuous abyss (a nicety of physiological equipoise comparable to certain techniques in the arts) I kept repeating chance words after her—barmen, alarmin', my charmin', my carmen, ahmen, ahahamen—as one talking and laughing in his sleep while my happy hand crept up her sunny leg as far as the shadow of decency allowed. The day before she had collided with the heavy chest in the hall and—"Look, look!"—I gasped—"look what you've done, what you've done to yourself, ah, look"; for there was, I swear, a yellowish-violet bruise on her lovely nymphet thigh which my huge hairy hand massaged and slowly enveloped—and because of her very perfunctory underthings, there seemed to be nothing to prevent my muscular thumb from reaching the hot hollow of her groin—just as you might tickle and caress a giggling child—just that—and: "Oh it's nothing at all," she cried with a sudden shrill note in her voice, and she wiggled, and squirmed, and threw her head back, and her teeth rested on her glistening underlip as she half-turned away, and my moaning mouth, gentlemen of the jury, almost reached her bare neck, while I crushed out against her left buttock the last throb of the longest ecstasy man or monster had ever known.

Immediately afterward (as if we had been struggling and now my grip had eased) she rolled off the sofa and jumped to her feet—to her foot, rather—in order to attend to the formidably loud telephone that may have been ringing for ages as far as I was concerned. There she stood and blinked, cheeks aflame, hair awry, her eyes passing over me as lightly as they did over the furniture, and as she listened or spoke (to her mother who was telling her to come to lunch with her at the Chatfields—neither Lo nor Hum knew yet what busybody Haze was plotting), she kept tapping the edge of the table with the slipper she held in her hand. Blessed be the Lord, she had noticed nothing!

With a handkerchief of multicolored silk, on which her lis-

tening eyes rested in passing, I wiped the sweat off my forehead, and, immersed in a euphoria of release, rearranged my
royal robes. She was still at the telephone, haggling with her
mother (wanted to be fetched by car, my little Carmen) when,
singing louder and louder, I swept up the stairs and set a
deluge of steaming water roaring into the tub.

At this point I may as well give the words of that song hit
in full—to the best of my recollection at least—I don't think
I ever had it right. Here goes:

> O my Carmen, my little Carmen!
> Something, something those something nights,
> And the stars, and the cars, and the bars, and the
> ` [barmen—
> And, O my charmin', our dreadful fights.
>
> And the something town where so gaily, arm in
> Arm, we went, and our final row,
> And the gun I killed you with, O my Carmen,
> The gun I am holding now.

(Drew his.32 automatic, I guess, and put a bullet through his
moll's eye.)

14

I had lunch in town—had not been so hungry for years.
The house was still Lo-less when I strolled back. I spent the
afternoon musing, scheming, blissfully digesting my experience of the morning.

I felt proud of myself. I had stolen the honey of a spasm
without impairing the morals of a minor. Absolutely no harm
done. The conjurer had poured milk, molasses, foaming
champagne into a young lady's new white purse; and lo, the
purse was intact. Thus had I delicately constructed my ignoble, ardent, sinful dream; and still Lolita was safe—and I
was safe. What I had madly possessed was not she, but my
own creation, another, fanciful Lolita—perhaps, more real
than Lolita; overlapping, encasing her; floating between me
and her, and having no will, no consciousness—indeed, no
life of her own.

The child knew nothing. I had done nothing to her. And

nothing prevented me from repeating a performance that affected her as little as if she were a photographic image rippling upon a screen and I a humble hunchback abusing myself in the dark. The afternoon drifted on and on, in ripe silence, and the sappy tall trees seemed to be in the know; and desire, even stronger than before, began to afflict me again. Let her come soon, I prayed, addressing a loan God, and while mamma is in the kitchen, let a repetition of the davenport scene be staged, please, I adore her so horribly.

No: "horribly" is the wrong word. The elation with which the vision of new delights filled me was not horrible but pathetic. I qualify it as pathetic. Pathetic—because despite the insatiable fire of my venereal appetite, I intended, with the most fervent force and foresight, to protect the purity of that twelve-year-old child.

And now see how I was repaid for my pains. No Lolita came home—she had gone with the Chatfields to a movie. The table was laid with more elegance than usual: candlelight, if you please. In this mawkish aura, Mrs. Haze gently touched the silver on both sides of her plate as if touching piano keys, and smiled down on her empty plate (was on a diet), and said she hoped I liked the salad (recipe lifted from a woman's magazine). She hoped I liked the cold cuts, too. It had been a perfect day. Mrs. Chatfield was a lovely person. Phyllis, her daughter, was going to a summer camp tomorrow. For three weeks. Lolita, it was decided, would go Thursday. Instead of waiting till July, as had been initially planned. And stay there after Phyllis had left. Till school began. A pretty prospect, my heart.

Oh, how I was taken aback—for did it not mean I was losing my darling, just when I had secretly made her mine? To explain my grim mood, I had to use the same toothache I had already simulated in the morning. Must have been an enormous molar, with an abscess as big as a maraschino cherry.

"We have," said Haze, "an excellent dentist. Our neighbor, in fact. Dr. Quilty. Uncle or cousin, I think, of the playwright. Think it will pass? Well, just as you wish. In the fall I shall have him 'brace' her, as my mother used to say. It may curb Lo a little. I am afraid she has been bothering you frightfully all these days. And we are in for a couple of stormy ones before she goes. She has flatly refused to go, and I confess I left her with the Chatfields because I dreaded to face her alone just yet. The movie may mollify her. Phyllis is a very sweet girl, and there is no earthly reason for Lo to dislike her. Really, monsieur, I am very sorry about that tooth of yours. It would be so much more reasonable to let me contact Ivor Quilty first thing tomorrow morning if it still hurts. And, you know, I think a summer camp is so much healthier, and—well, it is all so much more *reasonable* as I say than to mope on a suburban lawn and use mamma's lipstick, and pursue shy studious gentlemen, and go into tantrums at the least provocation."

"Are you sure," I said at last, "that she will be happy there?" (lame, lamentably lame!)

"She'd better," said Haze. "And it won't be all play either. The camp is run by Shirley Holmes—you know, the woman who wrote *Campfire Girl.* Camp will teach Dolores Haze to grow in many things—health, knowledge, temper. And particularly in a sense of responsibility toward other people. Shall we take these candles with us and sit for a while on the piazza, or do you want to go to bed and nurse that tooth?"

Nurse that tooth.

15

Next day they drove downtown to buy things needed for the camp: any wearable purchase worked wonders with Lo. She seemed her usual sarcastic self at dinner. Immediately afterwards, she went up to her room to plunge into the comic books acquired for rainy days at Camp Q (they were so thoroughly sampled by Thursday that she left them behind). I too retired to my lair, and wrote letters. My plan now was to leave for the seaside and then, when school began, resume my existence in the Haze household; for I knew already that I could not live without the child. On Tuesday they went shopping again, and I was asked to answer the phone if the camp mistress rang up during their absence. She did; and a month or so later we had occasion to recall our pleasant chat. That Tuesday, Lo had her dinner in her room. She had been crying after a routine row with her mother and, as had happened on former occasions, had not wished me to see her swollen eyes: she had one of those tender complexions that after a good cry get all blurred and inflamed, and morbidly alluring. I regretted keenly her mistake about my private aesthetics, for I simply love that tinge of Botticellian pink, that raw rose about the lips, those wet, matted eyelashes; and, naturally, her bashful whim deprived me of many opportunities of specious consolation. There was, however, more to it than I thought. As we sat in the darkness of the veranda (a rude wind had put out her red candles), Haze, with a dreary laugh, said she had told Lo that her beloved Humbert thoroughly approved of the whole camp idea "and now," added Haze, "the child throws a fit; pretext: you and I want to get rid of her; actual reason: I told her we would exchange tomorrow for plainer stuff some much too cute night things that she bullied me into buying for her. You see, *she* sees herself as a starlet; *I* see her as a sturdy, healthy, but decidedly homely kid. This, I guess, is at the root of our troubles."

On Wednesday I managed to waylay Lo for a few seconds: she was on the landing, in sweatshirt and green-stained white shorts, rummaging in a trunk. I said something meant to be friendly and funny but she only emitted a snort without looking at me. Desperate, dying Humbert patted her clumsily on her coccyx, and she struck him, quite painfully, with one of the late Mr. Haze's shoetrees. "Doublecrosser," she said as I crawled downstairs rubbing my arm with a great show of rue. She did not condescend to have dinner with Hum and mum: washed her hair and went to bed with her ridiculous books. And on Thursday quiet Mrs. Haze drove her to Camp Q.

As greater authors than I have put it: "Let readers imagine" etc. On second thought, I may as well give those imaginations a kick in the pants. I knew I had fallen in love with Lolita forever; but I also knew she would not be forever Lolita. She would be thirteen on January 1. In two years or so she would cease being a nymphet and would turn into a "young girl," and then, into a "college girl"—that horror of horrors. The word "forever" referred only to my own passion, to the eternal Lolita as reflected in my blood. The Lolita whose iliac crests had not yet flared, the Lolita that today I could touch and smell and hear and see, the Lolita of the strident voice and the rich brown hair—of the bangs and the swirls at the sides and the curls at the back, and the sticky hot neck, and the vulgar vocabulary—"revolting," "super," "luscious," "goon," "drip"—*that* Lolita, *my* Lolita, poor Catullus would lose forever. So how could I afford not to see her for two months of summer insomnias? Two whole months out of the two years of her remaining nymphage! Should I disguise myself as a somber old-fashioned girl, gawky Mlle Humbert, and put up my tent on the outskirts of Camp Q, in the hope that its russet nymphets would clamor: "Let us adopt that deep-voiced D.P.," and drag the sad, shyly smiling Berthe *au Grand Pied* to their rustic hearth. Berthe will sleep with Dolores Haze!

Idle dry dreams. Two months of beauty, two months of tenderness, would be squandered forever, and I could do nothing about it, but nothing, *mais rien.*

One drop of rare honey, however, that Thursday did hold in its acorn cup. Haze was to drive her to the camp in the early morning. Upon sundry sounds of departure reaching me, I rolled out of bed and leaned out of the window. Under the poplars, the car was already athrob. On the sidewalk, Louise stood shading her eyes with her hand, as if the little traveler were already riding into the low morning sun. The gesture proved to be premature. "Hurry up!" shouted Haze. My Lolita, who was half in and about to slam the car door, wind down the glass, wave to Louise and the poplars (whom and which she was never to see again), interrupted the motion of fate: she looked up—and dashed back into the house (Haze furiously calling after her). A moment later I heard my sweetheart running up the stairs. My heart expanded with such force that it almost blotted me out. I hitched up the pants of my pajamas, flung the door open: and simultaneously Lolita arrived, in her Sunday frock, stamping, panting, and then she was in my arms, her innocent mouth melting under the ferocious pressure of dark male jaws, my palpitating darling! The next instant I heard her—alive, un-raped—clatter downstairs. The motion of fate was resumed. The blond leg was pulled in, the car door was slammed—was re-slammed—and driver Haze at the violent wheel, rubber-red lips writhing in angry, inaudible speech, swung my darling away, while unnoticed by them or Louise, old Miss Opposite, an invalid, feebly but rhythmically waved from her vined veranda.

16

The hollow of my hand was still ivory-full of Lolita—full of the feel of her pre-adolescently incurved back, that ivory-smooth, sliding sensation of her skin through the thin frock that I had worked up and down while I held her. I marched into her tumbled room, threw open the door of the closet and plunged into a heap of crumpled things that had touched her. There was particularly one pink texture, sleazy, torn, with a faintly acrid odor in the seam. I wrapped in it Humbert's huge engorged heart. A poignant chaos was welling within me—but I had to drop those things and hurriedly regain my composure, as I became aware of the maid's velvety voice calling me softly from the stairs. She had a message for me, she said; and, topping my automatic thanks with a kindly "you're welcome," good Louise left an unstamped, curiously clean-looking letter in my shaking hand.

This is a confession: I love you [so the letter began; and for a distorted moment I mistook its hysterical scrawl for a schoolgirl's scribble]. Last Sunday in church—bad you, who refused to come to see our beautiful new windows!—only last Sunday, my dear one, when I asked the Lord what to do about it, I was told to act as I am acting now. You see, there is no alternative. I have loved you from the minute I saw you. I am a passionate and lonely woman and you are the love of my life.

Now, my dearest, dearest, *mon cher, cher monsieur*, you have read this; now you know. So, will you please, *at once*, pack and leave. This is a landlady's order. I am dismissing a lodger. I am kicking you out. Go! Scram! *Departez!* I shall be back by dinnertime, if I do eighty both ways and don't have an accident (but what would it matter?), and I do not wish to find you in the house. Please, please, leave at once, *now*, do not even read this absurd note to the end. Go. Adieu.

The situation, *chéri*, is quite simple. Of course, I know with *absolute certainty* that I am nothing to you, nothing at all. Oh yes, you enjoy talking to me (and kidding poor me), you have grown fond of our friendly house, of the books I like, of my lovely garden, even of

Lo's noisy ways—but I am nothing to you. Right? Right. Nothing to you whatever. *But* if, after reading my "confession," you decided, in your dark romantic European way, that I am attractive enough for you to take advantage of my letter and make a pass at me, then you would be a criminal—worse than a kidnapper who rapes a child. You see, *chéri*. If you decided to stay, *if* I found you at home (which I know I won't—and that's why I am able to go on like this), the *fact* of your remaining would only mean one thing: that you want me as much as I do you: as a lifelong mate; and that you are ready to link up your life with mine forever and ever and be a father to my little girl.

Let me rave and ramble on for a teeny while more, my dearest, since I know this letter has been by now torn by you, and its pieces (illegible) in the vortex of the toilet. My dearest, *mon très, très cher*, what a world of love I have built up for you during this miraculous June! I know how reserved you are, how "British." Your old-world reticence, your sense of decorum may be shocked by the boldness of an American girl! You who conceal your strongest feelings must think me a shameless little idiot for throwing open my poor bruised heart like this. In years gone by, many disappointments came my way. Mr. Haze was a splendid person, a sterling soul, but he happened to be twenty years my senior, and—well, let us not gossip about the past. My dearest, your curiosity must be well satisfied if you have ignored my request and read this letter to the bitter end. Never mind. Destroy it and go. Do not forget to leave the key on the desk in your room. And some scrap of address so that I could refund the twelve dollars I owe you till the end of the month. Good-bye, dear one. Pray for me—if you ever pray.

                                                                C.H.

What I present here is what I remember of the letter, and what I remember of the letter I remember verbatim (including that awful French). It was at least twice longer. I have left out a lyrical passage which I more or less skipped at the time, concerning Lolita's brother who died at 2 when she was 4, and how much I would have liked him. Let me see what else can I say? Yes. There is just a chance that "the vortex of the toilet" (where the letter did go) is my own matter-of-fact contribution. She probably begged me to make a special fire to consume it.

My first movement was one of repulsion and retreat. My second was like a friend's calm hand falling upon my shoulder and bidding me take my time. I did. I came out of my daze and found myself still in Lo's room. A full-page ad ripped out of a slick magazine was affixed to the wall above the bed, between a crooner's mug and the lashes of a movie actress. It represented a dark-haired young husband with a kind of drained look in his Irish eyes. He was modeling a robe by So-and-So and holding a bridgelike tray by So-and-So, with breakfast for two. The legend, by the Rev. Thomas Morell, called him a "conquering hero." The thoroughly conquered lady (not shown) was presumably propping herself up to receive her half of the tray. How her bedfellow was to get under the bridge without some messy mishap was not clear. Lo had drawn a jocose arrow to the haggard lover's face and had put, in block letters: H.H. And indeed, despite a difference of a few years, the resemblance was striking. Under this was another picture, also a colored ad. A distinguished playwright was solemnly smoking a Drome. He always smoked Dromes. The resemblance was slight. Under this was Lo's chaste bed, littered with "comics." The enamel had come off the bedstead, leaving black, more or less rounded, marks on the white. Having convinced myself that Louise had left, I got into Lo's bed and reread the letter.

17

Gentlemen of the jury! I cannot swear that certain motions pertaining to the business in hand—if I may coin an expression—had not drifted across my mind before. My mind had not retained them in any logical form or in any relation to definitely recollected occasions; but I cannot swear—let me repeat—that I had not toyed with them (to rig up yet another expression), in my dimness of thought, in my darkness of passion. There may have been times—there must have been times, if I know my Humbert—when I had brought up for detached inspection the idea of marrying a mature widow (say, Charlotte Haze) with not one relative left in the wide gray world, merely in order to have my way with her child (Lo, Lola, Lolita). I am even prepared to tell my tormentors that perhaps once or twice I had cast an appraiser's cold eye at Charlotte's coral lips and bronze hair and

dangerously low neckline, and had vaguely tried to fit her into
a plausible daydream. This I confess under torture. Imaginary
torture, perhaps, but all the more horrible. I wish I might
digress and tell you more of the *pavor nocturnus* that would
rack me at night hideously after a chance term had struck me
in the random readings of my boyhood, such as *peine forte et
dure* (what a Genius of Pain must have invented that!) or the
dreadful, mysterious, insidious words "trauma," "traumatic
event," and "transom." But my tale is sufficiently incondite
already.

After a while I destroyed the letter and went to my room,
and ruminated, and rumpled my hair, and modeled my purple
robe, and moaned through clenched teeth and suddenly—
Suddenly, gentlemen of the jury, I felt a Dostoevskian grin
dawning (through the very grimace that twisted my lips) like
a distant and terrible sun. I imagined (under conditions of
new and perfect visibility) all the casual caresses her mother's
husband would be able to lavish on his Lolita. I would hold
her against me three times a day, every day. All my troubles
would be expelled, I would be a healthy man. "To hold thee
lightly on a gentle knee and print on thy soft cheek a parent's
kiss . . ." Well-read Humbert!

Then, with all possible caution, on mental tiptoe so to
speak, I conjured up Charlotte as a possible mate. By God, I
could make myself bring her that economically halved grapefruit, that sugarless breakfast.

Humbert Humbert sweating in the fierce white light, and
howled at, and trodden upon by sweating policemen, is now
ready to make a further "statement" (*quel mot!*) as he turns
his conscience inside out and rips off its innermost lining. I
did not plan to marry poor Charlotte in order to eliminate
her in some vulgar, gruesome and dangerous manner such as
killing her by placing five bichloride-of-mercury tablets in her
preprandial sherry or anything like that; but a delicately allied,
pharmacopoeial thought did tinkle in my sonorous and
clouded brain. Why limit myself to the modest masked caress
I had tried already? Other visions of venery presented themselves to me swaying and smiling. I saw myself administering
a powerful sleeping potion to both mother and daughter so
as to fondle the latter through the night with perfect im-

punity. The house was full of Charlotte's snore, while Lolita hardly breathed in her sleep, as still as a painted girl-child. "Mother, I swear Kenny never even *touched* me." "You either lie, Dolores Haze, or it was an incubus." No, I would not go that far.

So Humbert the Cubus schemed and dreamed—and the red sun of desire and decision (the two things that create a live world) rose higher and higher, while upon a succession of balconies a succession of libertines, sparkling glass in hand, toasted the bliss of past and future nights. Then, figuratively speaking, I shattered the glass, and boldly imagined (for I was drunk on those visions by then and underrated the gentleness of my nature) how eventually I might blackmail—no, that is too strong a word—mauvemail big Haze into letting me consort with little Haze by gently threatening the poor doting Big Dove with desertion if she tried to bar me from playing with my legal step-daughter. In a word, before such an Amazing Offer, before such a vastness and variety of vistas, I was as helpless as Adam at the preview of early oriental history, miraged in his apple orchard.

And now take down the following important remark: the artist in me has been given the upper hand over the gentleman. It is with a great effort of will that in this memoir I have managed to tune my style to the tone of the journal that I kept when Mrs. Haze was to me but an obstacle. That journal of mine is no more; but I have considered it my artistic duty to preserve its intonations no matter how false and brutal they may seem to me now. Fortunately, my story has reached a point where I can cease insulting poor Charlotte for the sake of retrospective verisimilitude.

Wishing to spare poor Charlotte two or three hours of suspense on a winding road (and avoid, perhaps, a head-on collision that would shatter our different dreams), I made a thoughtful but abortive attempt to reach her at the camp by telephone. She had left half an hour before, and getting Lo instead, I told her—trembling and brimming with my mastery over fate—that I was going to marry her mother. I had to repeat it twice because something was preventing her from giving me her attention. "Gee, that's swell," she said laughing.

"When is the wedding? Hold on a sec, the pup— That pup here has got hold of my sock. Listen—" and she added she guessed she was going to have loads of fun . . . and I realized as I hung up that a couple of hours at that camp had been sufficient to blot out with new impressions the image of handsome Humbert Humbert from little Lolita's mind. But what did it matter now? I would get her back as soon as a decent amount of time after the wedding had elapsed. "The orange blossom would have scarcely withered on the grave," as a poet might have said. But I am no poet. I am only a very conscientious recorder.

After Louise had gone, I inspected the icebox, and finding it much too puritanic, walked to town and bought the richest foods available. I also bought some good liquor and two or three kinds of vitamins. I was pretty sure that with the aid of these stimulants and my natural resources, I would avert any embarrassment that my indifference might incur when called upon to display a strong and impatient flame. Again and again resourceful Humbert evoked Charlotte as seen in the raree-show of a manly imagination. She was well groomed and shapely, this I could say for her, and she was my Lolita's big sister—this notion, perhaps, I could keep up if only I did not visualize too realistically her heavy hips, round knees, ripe bust, the coarse pink skin of her neck ("coarse" by comparison with silk and honey) and all the rest of that sorry and dull thing: a handsome woman.

The sun made its usual round of the house as the afternoon ripened into evening. I had a drink. And another. And yet another. Gin and pineapple juice, my favorite mixture, always double my energy. I decided to busy myself with our unkempt lawn. *Une petite attention.* It was crowded with dandelions, and a cursed dog—I loathe dogs—had defiled the flat stones where a sundial had once stood. Most of the dandelions had changed from suns to moons. The gin and Lolita were dancing in me, and I almost fell over the folding chairs that I attempted to dislodge. Incarnadine zebras! There are some eructations that sound like cheers—at least, mine did. An old fence at the back of the garden separated us from the neighbor's garbage receptacles and lilacs; but there was nothing between the front end of our lawn (where it sloped along one side of the house) and the street. Therefore I was able to watch (with the smirk of one about to perform a good action) for the return of Charlotte: that tooth should be extracted at once. As I lurched and lunged with the hand mower, bits of grass optically twittering in the low sun, I kept an eye on that section of suburban street. It curved in from under an archway of huge shade trees, then sped towards us down, down, quite sharply, past old Miss Opposite's ivied brick house and high-sloping lawn (much trimmer than ours) and disappeared behind our own front porch which I could not see from where I happily belched and labored. The dandelions perished. A reek of sap mingled with the pineapple. Two little girls, Marion and Mabel, whose comings and goings I had mechanically followed of late (but who could replace my Lolita?) went toward the avenue (from which our Lawn Street cascaded), one pushing a bicycle, the other feeding from a paper bag, both talking at the top of their sunny voices. Leslie, old Miss Opposite's gardener and chauffeur, a very amiable and athletic Negro, grinned at me from afar and shouted, re-shouted, commented by gesture, that I was mighty energetic to-day. The fool dog of the prosperous junk dealer next door ran after a blue car—not Charlotte's. The prettier of the two little girls (Mabel, I think), shorts, halter with little to halt, bright hair—a nymphet, by Pan!—ran back down the street crumpling her paper bag and was hidden from this Green Goat by the frontage of Mr. and Mrs. Humbert's residence. A station wagon popped out of the leafy shade of the avenue, dragging some of it on its roof before the shadows snapped, and swung by at an idiotic pace, the sweatshirted driver roof-holding with his left hand and the junkman's dog tearing alongside. There was a smiling pause—and then, with a flutter in my breast, I witnessed the return of the Blue Sedan. I saw it glide downhill and disappear behind the corner of the house. I had a glimpse of her calm pale profile. It occurred to me that until she went upstairs she would not know whether I had gone or not. A minute later, with an expression of great anguish on her face, she looked down at me from the window of Lo's room. By sprinting upstairs, I managed to reach that room before she left it.

18

When the bride is a widow and the groom is a widower; when the former has lived in Our Great Little Town for hardly two years, and the latter for hardly a month; when Monsieur wants to get the whole damned thing over with as quickly as possible, and Madame gives in with a tolerant smile; then, my reader, the wedding is generally a "quiet" affair. The bride may dispense with a tiara of orange blossoms securing her finger-tip veil, nor does she carry a white orchid in a prayer book. The bride's little daughter might have added to the ceremonies uniting H. and H. a touch of vivid vermeil; but I knew I would not dare be too tender with cornered Lolita yet, and therefore agreed it was not worth while tearing the child away from her beloved Camp Q.

My *soi-disant* passionate and lonely Charlotte was in every-day life matter-of-fact and gregarious. Moreover, I discovered that although she could not control her heart or her cries, she was a woman of principle. Immediately after she had become more or less my mistress (despite the stimulants, her "nervous, eager *chéri*"—a heroic *chéri*!—had some initial trouble, for which, however, he amply compensated her by a fantastic display of old-world endearments), good Charlotte interviewed me about my relations with God. I could have answered that on that score my mind was open; I said, instead—paying my tribute to a pious platitude—that I believed in a cosmic spirit. Looking down at her fingernails, she also asked me had I not in my family a certain strange strain. I countered by inquiring whether she would still want to marry me if my father's maternal grandfather had been, say, a Turk. She said it did not matter a bit; but that, if she ever found out I did not believe in Our Christian God, she would commit suicide. She said it so solemnly that it gave me the creeps. It was then I knew she was a woman of principle.

Oh, she was very genteel: she said "excuse me" whenever a slight burp interrupted her flowing speech, called an envelope an ahnvelope, and when talking to her lady-friends referred to me as Mr. Humbert. I thought it would please her if I entered the community trailing some glamor after me. On the day of our wedding a little interview with me appeared in the Society Column of the Ramsdale *Journal*, with a photograph of Charlotte, one eyebrow up and a misprint in her name ("Hazer"). Despite this contretemps, the publicity warmed the porcelain cockles of her heart—and made my rattles shake with awful glee. By engaging in church work as well as by getting to know the better mothers of Lo's schoolmates, Charlotte in the course of twenty months or so had managed to become if not a prominent, at least an acceptable citizen, but never before had she come under that thrilling *rubrique*, and it was I who put her there, Mr. Edgar H. Humbert (I threw in the "Edgar" just for the heck of it), "writer and explorer." McCoo's brother, when taking it down, asked me what I had written. Whatever I told him came out as "several books on Peacock, Rainbow and other poets." It was also noted that Charlotte and I had known each other for several years and that I was a distant relation of her first husband. I hinted I had had an affair with her thirteen years ago but this was not mentioned in print. To Charlotte I said that society columns *should* contain a shimmer of errors.

Let us go on with this curious tale. When called upon to enjoy my promotion from lodger to lover, did I experience only bitterness and distaste? No. Mr. Humbert confesses to a certain titillation of his vanity, to some faint tenderness, even to a pattern of remorse daintily running along the steel of his conspiratorial dagger. Never had I thought that the rather ridiculous, though rather handsome Mrs. Haze, with her blind faith in the wisdom of her church and book club, her mannerisms of elocution, her harsh, cold, contemptuous attitude toward an adorable, downy-armed child of twelve, could turn into such a touching, helpless creature as soon as I laid my hands upon her which happened on the threshold of Lolita's room whither she tremulously backed repeating "no, no, please no."

The transformation improved her looks. Her smile that had been such a contrived thing, thenceforth became the radiance of utter adoration—a radiance having something soft and moist about it, in which, with wonder, I recognized a resemblance to the lovely, inane, lost look that Lo had when gloating over a new kind of concoction at the soda fountain or mutely admiring my expensive, always tailor-fresh clothes.

Deeply fascinated, I would watch Charlotte while she swapped parental woes with some other lady and made that national grimace of feminine resignation (eyes rolling up, mouth drooping sideways) which, in an infantile form, I had seen Lo making herself. We had highballs before turning in, and with their help, I would manage to evoke the child while caressing the mother. This was the white stomach within which my nymphet had been a little curved fish in 1934. This carefully dyed hair, so sterile to my sense of smell and touch, acquired at certain lamplit moments in the poster bed the tinge, if not the texture, of Lolita's curls. I kept telling myself, as I wielded my brand-new large-as-life wife, that biologically this was the nearest I could get to Lolita; that at Lolita's age, Lotte had been as desirable a schoolgirl as her daughter was, and as Lolita's daughter would be some day. I had my wife unearth from under a collection of shoes (Mr. Haze had a passion for them, it appears) a thirty-year-old album, so that I might see how Lotte had looked as a child; and even though the light was wrong and the dresses graceless, I was able to make out a dim first version of Lolita's outline, legs, cheekbones, bobbed nose. Lottelita, Lolitchen.

So I tom-peeped across the hedges of years, into wan little windows. And when, by means of pitifully ardent, naïvely lascivious caresses, she of the noble nipple and massive thigh prepared me for the performance of my nightly duty, it was still a nymphet's scent that in despair I tried to pick up, as I bayed through the undergrowth of dark decaying forests.

I simply can't tell you how gentle, how touching my poor wife was. At breakfast, in the depressingly bright kitchen, with its chrome glitter and Hardware and Co. Calendar and cute breakfast nook (simulating that Coffee Shoppe where in their college days Charlotte and Humbert used to coo together), she would sit, robed in red, her elbow on the plastic-topped table, her cheek propped on her fist, and stare at me with intolerable tenderness as I consumed my ham and eggs. Humbert's face might twitch with neuralgia, but in her eyes it vied in beauty and animation with the sun and shadows of leaves rippling on the white refrigerator. My solemn exasperation was to her the silence of love. My small income added to her even smaller one impressed her as a brilliant fortune; not because the resulting sum now sufficed for most middle-class needs, but because even my money shone in her eyes with the magic of my manliness, and she saw our joint account as one of those southern boulevards at midday that have solid shade on one side and smooth sunshine on the other, all the way to the end of a prospect, where pink mountains loom.

Into the fifty days of our cohabitation Charlotte crammed the activities of as many years. The poor woman busied herself with a number of things she had foregone long before or had never been much interested in, as if (to prolong these Proustian intonations) by my marrying the mother of the child I loved I had enabled my wife to regain an abundance of youth by proxy. With the zest of a banal young bride, she started to "glorify the home." Knowing as I did its every cranny by heart—since those days when from my chair I mentally mapped out Lolita's course through the house—I had long entered into a sort of emotional relationship with it, with its very ugliness and dirt, and now I could almost feel the wretched thing cower in its reluctance to endure the bath of ecru and ocher and putty-buff-and-snuff that Charlotte planned to give it. She never got as far as that, thank God, but she did use up a tremendous amount of energy in washing window shades, waxing the slats of Venetian blinds, purchasing new shades and new blinds, returning them to the store, replacing them by others, and so on, in a constant chiaroscuro of smiles and frowns, doubts and pouts. She dabbled in cretonnes and chintzes; she changed the colors of the sofa—the sacred sofa where a bubble of paradise had once burst in slow motion within me. She rearranged the furniture—and was pleased when she found, in a household treatise, that "it is permissible to separate a pair of sofa commodes and their companion lamps." With the authoress of *Your Home Is You*, she developed a hatred for little lean chairs and spindle tables. She believed that a room having a generous expanse of glass, and lots of rich wood paneling was an example of the masculine type of room, whereas the feminine type was characterized by lighter-looking windows and frailer woodwork. The novels I had found her reading when I moved in were now replaced by illustrated catalogues and homemaking guides. From a firm located at 4640 Roosevelt Blvd., Philadelphia, she ordered for our double bed a "damask covered 312 coil mattress"—although the old one seemed to me resilient and durable enough for whatever it had to support.

A Midwesterner, as her late husband had also been, she had lived in coy Ramsdale, the gem of an eastern state, not long enough to know all the nice people. She knew slightly the jovial dentist who lived in a kind of ramshackle wooden chateau behind our lawn. She had met at a church tea the "snooty" wife of the local junk dealer who owned the "colonial" white horror at the corner of the avenue. Now and then she "visited with" old Miss Opposite; but the more patrician matrons among those she called upon, or met at lawn functions, or had telephone chats with—such dainty ladies as Mrs. Glave, Mrs. Sheridan, Mrs. McCrystal, Mrs. Knight and others, seldom seemed to call on my neglected Charlotte. Indeed, the only couple with whom she had relations of real cordiality, devoid of any *arrière-pensée* or practical foresight, were the Farlows who had just come back from a business trip to Chile in time to attend our wedding, with the Chatfields, McCoos, and a few others (but not Mrs. Junk or the even prouder Mrs. Talbot). John Farlow was a middle-aged, quiet, quietly athletic, quietly successful dealer in sporting goods, who had an office at Parkington, forty miles away: it was he who got me the cartridges for that Colt and showed me how to use it, during a walk in the woods one Sunday; he was also what he called with a smile a part-time lawyer and had handled some of Charlotte's affairs. Jean, his youngish wife (and first cousin), was a long-limbed girl in harlequin glasses with two boxer dogs, two pointed breasts and a big red mouth. She painted—landscapes and portraits—and vividly do I remember praising, over cocktails, the picture she had made of a niece of hers, little Rosaline Honeck, a rosy honey in a Girl Scout uniform, beret of green worsted, belt of green webbing, charming shoulder-long curls—and John removed his pipe and said it was a pity Dolly (my Dolita) and Rosaline were so critical of each other at school, but he hoped they would get on better when they returned from their respective camps. We talked of the school. It had its drawbacks, and it had its virtues. "Of course, too many of the tradespeople here are Italians," said John, "but on the other hand we are still spared—" "I wish," interrupted Jean with a laugh, "Dolly and Rosaline were spending the summer together." Suddenly I imagined Lo returning from camp—brown, warm, drowsy, drugged—and was ready to weep with passion and impatience.

19

A few words more about Mrs. Humbert while the going is good (a bad accident is to happen quite soon). I had been always aware of the possessive streak in her, but I never thought she would be so crazily jealous of anything in my life that had not been she. She showed a fierce insatiable curiosity for my past. She desired me to resuscitate all my loves so that she might make me insult them, and trample upon them, and revoke them apostately and totally, thus destroying my past. She made me tell her about my marriage to Valeria, who was of course a scream; but I also had to invent, or to pad atrociously, a long series of mistresses for Charlotte's morbid delectation. To keep her happy, I had to present her with an illustrated catalogue of them, all nicely differentiated, according to the rules of those American ads where schoolchildren are pictured in a subtle ratio of races, with one—only one, but as cute as they make them—chocolate-colored round-eyed little lad, almost in the very middle of the front row. So I presented my women, and had them smile and sway—the languorous blond, the fiery brunette, the sensual copperhead—as if on parade in a bordello. The more popular and platitudinous I made them, the more Mrs. Humbert was pleased with the show.

Never in my life had I confessed so much or received so many confessions. The sincerity and artlessness with which she discussed what she called her "love-life," from first necking to connubial catch-as-catch-can, were, ethically, in striking contrast with my glib compositions, but technically the two sets were congeneric since both were affected by the same stuff (soap operas, psychoanalysis and cheap novelettes) upon which I drew for my characters and she for her mode of expression. I was considerably amused by certain remarkable sexual habits that the good Harold Haze had had according to Charlotte who thought my mirth improper; but otherwise her autobiography was as devoid of interest as her autopsy would have been. I never saw a healthier woman than she, despite thinning diets.

Of my Lolita she seldom spoke—more seldom, in fact, than she did of the blurred, blond male baby whose photograph to the exclusion of all others adorned our bleak bedroom. In one of her tasteless reveries, she predicted that the dead infant's soul would return to earth in the form of the child she would bear in her present wedlock. And although I felt no special urge to supply the Humbert line with a replica of Harold's production (Lolita, with an incestuous thrill, I had grown to regard as *my* child), it occurred to me that a prolonged confinement, with a nice Caesarean operation and other complications in a safe maternity ward sometime next spring, would give me a chance to be alone with my Lolita for weeks, perhaps—and gorge the limp nymphet with sleeping pills.

Oh, she simply hated her daughter! What I thought especially vicious was that she had gone out of her way to answer with great diligence the questionnaires in a fool's book she had (*A Guide to Your Child's Development*), published in Chicago. The rigmarole went year by year, and Mom was supposed to fill out a kind of inventory at each of her child's birthdays. On Lo's twelfth, January 1, 1947, Charlotte Haze, née Becker, had underlined the following epithets, ten out of forty, under "Your Child's Personality": aggressive, boisterous, critical, distrustful, impatient, irritable, inquisitive, listless, negativistic (underlined twice) and obstinate. She had ignored the thirty remaining adjectives, among which were cheerful, co-operative, energetic, and so forth. It was really maddening. With a brutality that otherwise never appeared in my loving wife's mild nature, she attacked and routed such of Lo's little belongings that had wandered to various parts of the house to freeze there like so many hypnotized bunnies. Little did the good lady dream that one morning when an upset stomach (the result of my trying to improve on her sauces) had prevented me from accompanying her to church, I deceived her with one of Lolita's anklets. And then, her attitude toward my saporous darling's letters!

DEAR MUMMY AND HUMMY,

Hope you are fine. Thank you very much for the candy. I [crossed out and re-written again] I lost my new sweater in the woods. It has been cold here for the last few days. I'm having a time. Love.

DOLLY

"The dumb child," said Mrs. Humbert, "has left out a word before 'time.' That sweater was all-wool, and I wish you would not send her candy without consulting me."

20

There was a woodlake (Hourglass Lake—not as I had thought it was spelled) a few miles from Ramsdale, and there was one week of great heat at the end of July when we drove there daily. I am now obliged to describe in some tedious detail our last swim there together, one tropical Tuesday morning.

We had left the car in a parking area not far from the road and were making our way down a path cut through the pine forest to the lake, when Charlotte remarked that Jean Farlow, in quest of rare light effects (Jean belonged to the old school of painting), had seen Leslie taking a dip "in the ebony" (as John had quipped) at five o'clock in the morning last Sunday.

"The water," I said, "must have been quite cold."

"That is not the point," said the logical doomed dear. "He is subnormal, you see. And," she continued (in that carefully phrased way of hers that was beginning to tell on my health), "I have a very definite feeling our Louise is in love with that moron."

Feeling. "We feel Dolly is not doing as well" etc. (from an old school report).

The Humberts walked on, sandaled and robed.

"Do you know, Hum: I have one most ambitious dream," pronounced Lady Hum, lowering her head—shy of that dream—and communing with the tawny ground. "I would love to get hold of a real trained servant maid like that German girl the Talbots spoke of; and have her live in the house."

"No room," I said.

"Come," she said with her quizzical smile, "surely, *chéri*, you underestimate the possibilities of the Humbert home. We would put her in Lo's room. I intended to make a guestroom of that hole anyway. It's the coldest and meanest in the whole house."

"What are you talking about?" I asked, the skin of my cheekbones tensing up (this I take the trouble to note only because my daughter's skin did the same when she felt that way: disbelief, disgust, irritation).

"Are you bothered by Romantic Associations?" queried my wife—in allusion to her first surrender.

"Hell no," said I. "I just wonder where will you put your daughter when you get your guest or your maid."

"Ah," said Mrs. Humbert, dreaming, smiling, drawing out the "Ah" simultaneously with the raise of one eyebrow and a soft exhalation of breath. "Little Lo, I'm afraid, does not enter the picture at all, at all. Little Lo goes straight from camp to a good boarding school with strict discipline and some sound religious training. And then—Beardsley College. I have it all mapped out, you need not worry."

She went on to say that she, Mrs. Humbert, would have to overcome her habitual sloth and write to Miss Phalen's sister who taught at St. Algebra. The dazzling lake emerged. I said I had forgotten my sunglasses in the car and would catch up with her.

I had always thought that wringing one's hands was a fictional gesture—the obscure outcome, perhaps, of some medieval ritual; but as I took to the woods, for a spell of despair and desperate mediation, this was the gesture ("look, Lord, at these chains!") that would have come nearest to the mute expression of my mood.

Had Charlotte been Valeria, I would have known how to handle the situation; and "handle" is the word I want. In the good old days, by merely twisting fat Valechka's brittle wrist (the one she had fallen upon from a bicycle) I could make her change her mind instantly; but anything of the sort in regard to Charlotte was unthinkable. Bland American Charlotte frightened me. My lighthearted dream of controlling her through her passion for me was all wrong. I dared not do anything to spoil the image of me she had set up to adore. I had toadied to her when she was the awesome duenna of my darling, and a groveling something still persisted in my attitude toward her. The only ace I held was her ignorance of my monstrous love for her Lo. She had been annoyed by Lo's liking me; but *my* feelings she could not divine. To Valeria I might have said: "Look here, you fat fool, *c'est moi qui décide* what is good for Dolores Humbert." To Charlotte, I could not even say (with ingratiating calm): "Excuse me, my dear, I disagree. Let us give the child one more chance. Let me be her private tutor for a year or so. You once told me yourself—" In fact, I could not say anything at all to Charlotte about the child without giving myself away. Oh, you cannot imagine (as I had never imagined) what these women of principle are! Charlotte, who did not notice the falsity of all the everyday conventions and rules of behavior, and foods, and books, and people she doted upon, would distinguish at once a false intonation in anything I might say with a view to keeping Lo near. She was like a musician who may be an odious vulgarian in ordinary life, devoid of tact and taste; but who will hear a false note in music with diabolical accuracy of judgment. To break Charlotte's will, I would have to break her heart. If I broke her heart, her image of me would break too. If I said: "Either I have my way with Lolita, and you help me to keep the matter quiet, or we part at once," she would have turned as pale as a woman of clouded glass and slowly replied: "All right, whatever you add or retract, this is the end." And the end it would be.

Such, then, was the mess. I remember reaching the parking area and pumping a handful of rust-tasting water, and drinking it as avidly as if it could give me magic wisdom, youth, freedom, a tiny concubine. For a while, purple-robed, heel-dangling, I sat on the edge of one of the rude tables, under the wooshing pines. In the middle distance, two little maidens in shorts and halters came out of a sun-dappled privy marked "Women." Gum-chewing Mabel (or Mabel's understudy) laboriously, absent-mindedly, straddled a bicycle, and Marion, shaking her hair because of the flies, settled behind, legs wide apart; and, wobbling, they slowly, absently, merged with the light and shade. Lolita! Father and daughter melting into these woods! The natural solution was to destroy Mrs. Humbert. But how?

No man can bring about the perfect murder; chance, however, can do it. There was the famous dispatch of a Mme Lacour in Arles, southern France, at the close of last century. An unidentified bearded six-footer, who, it was later conjectured, had been the lady's secret lover, walked up to her in a crowded street, soon after her marriage to Colonel Lacour, and mortally stabbed her in the back, three times, while the Colonel, a small bulldog of a man, hung onto the murderer's arm. By a miraculous and beautiful coincidence, right at the moment when the operator was in the act of loosening the angry little husband's jaws (while several onlookers were closing in upon the group), a cranky Italian in the house nearest to the scene set off by sheer accident some kind of explosive he was tinkering with, and immediately the street was turned into a pandemonium of smoke, falling bricks and running people. The explosion hurt no one (except that it knocked out game Colonel Lacour); but the lady's vengeful lover ran when the others ran—and lived happily ever after.

Now look what happens when the operator himself plans a perfect removal.

I walked down to Hourglass Lake. The spot from which we and a few other "nice" couples (the Farlows, the Chatfields) bathed was a kind of small cove; my Charlotte liked it because it was almost "a private beach." The main bathing facilities (or "drowning facilities" as the Ramsdale *Journal* had had occasion to say) were in the left (eastern) part of the hourglass, and could not be seen from our covelet. To our right, the pines soon gave way to a curve of marshland which turned again into forest on the opposite side.

I sat down beside my wife so noiselessly that she started.

"Shall we go in?" she asked.

"We shall in a minute. Let me follow a train of thought."

I thought. More than a minute passed.

"All right. Come on."

"Was I on that train?"

"You certainly were."

"I hope so," said Charlotte entering the water. It soon reached the gooseflesh of her thick thighs; and then, joining her outstretched hands, shutting her mouth tight, very plain-faced in her black rubber headgear, Charlotte flung herself forward with a great splash.

Slowly we swam out into the shimmer of the lake.

On the opposite bank, at least a thousand paces away (if one could walk across water), I could make out the tiny figures of two men working like beavers on their stretch of shore. I knew exactly who they were: a retired policeman of Polish descent and the retired plumber who owned most of the timber on that side of the lake. And I also knew they were engaged in building, just for the dismal fun of the thing, a wharf. The knocks that reached us seemed so much bigger than what could be distinguished of those dwarfs' arms and tools; indeed, one suspected the director of those acrosonic effects to have been at odds with the puppet-master, especially since the hefty crack of each diminutive blow lagged behind its visual version.

The short white-sand strip of "our" beach—from which by now we had gone a little way to reach deep water—was empty on weekday mornings. There was nobody around except those two tiny very busy figures on the opposite side, and a dark-red private plane that droned overhead, and then disappeared in the blue. The setting was really perfect for a brisk bubbling murder, and here was the subtle point: the man of law and the man of water were just near enough to witness an accident and just far enough not to observe a crime. They were near enough to hear a distracted bather thrashing about and bellowing for somebody to come and help him save his drowning wife; and they were too far to distinguish (if they happened to look too soon) that the anything but distracted swimmer was finishing to tread his wife underfoot. I was not yet at that stage; I merely want to convey the ease of the act, the nicety of the setting! So there was Charlotte swimming on with dutiful awkwardness (she was a very mediocre mermaid), but not without a certain solemn pleasure (for was not her merman by her side?); and as I watched, with the stark lucidity of a future recollection (you know—trying to see things as you will remember having seen them), the glossy whiteness of her wet

face so little tanned despite all her endeavors, and her pale
lips, and her naked convex forehead, and the tight black cap,
and the plump wet neck, I knew that all I had to do was to
drop back, take a deep breath, then grab her by the ankle and
rapidly dive with my captive corpse. I say corpse because surprise, panic and inexperience would cause her to inhale at once
a lethal gallon of lake, while I would be able to hold on for
at least a full minute, open-eyed under water. The fatal gesture
passed like the tail of a falling star across the blackness of the
contemplated crime. It was like some dreadful silent ballet,
the male dancer holding the ballerina by her foot and streaking down through watery twilight. I might come up for a
mouthful of air while still holding her down, and then would
dive again as many times as would be necessary, and only
when the curtain came down on her for good, would I permit
myself to yell for help. And when some twenty minutes later
the two puppets steadily growing arrived in a rowboat, one
half newly painted, poor Mrs. Humbert Humbert, the victim
of a cramp or coronary occlusion, or both, would be standing
on her head in the inky ooze, some thirty feet below the smiling surface of Hourglass Lake.

Simple, was it not? But what d'ye know, folks—I just could
not make myself do it!

She swam beside me, a trustful and clumsy seal, and all the
logic of passion screamed in my ear: Now is the time! And,
folks, I just couldn't! In silence I turned shoreward and
gravely, dutifully, she also turned, and still hell screamed its
counsel, and still I could not make myself drown the poor,
slippery, big-bodied creature. The scream grew more and
more remote as I realized the melancholy fact that neither
tomorrow, nor Friday, nor any other day or night, could I
make myself put her to death. Oh, I could visualize myself
slapping Valeria's breasts out of alignment, or otherwise hurting her—and I could see myself, no less clearly, shooting her
lover in the underbelly and making him say "akh!" and sit
down. But I could not kill Charlotte—especially when things
were on the whole not quite as hopeless, perhaps, as they
seemed at first wince on that miserable morning. Were I to
catch her by her strong kicking foot; were I to see her amazed
look, hear her awful voice; were I still to go through with the

ordeal, her ghost would haunt me all my life. Perhaps if the year were 1447 instead of 1947 I might have hoodwinked my gentle nature by administering her some classical poison from a hollow agate, some tender philter of death. But in our middle-class nosy era it would not have come off the way it used to in the brocaded palaces of the past. Nowadays you have to be a scientist if you want to be a killer. No, no, I was neither. Ladies and gentlemen of the jury, the majority of sex offenders that hanker for some throbbing, sweet-moaning, physical but not necessarily coital, relation with a girl-child, are innocuous, inadequate, passive, timid strangers who merely ask the community to allow them to pursue their practically harmless, so-called aberrant behavior, their little hot wet private acts of sexual deviation without the police and society cracking down upon them. We are not sex fiends! We do not rape as good soldiers do. We are unhappy, mild, dog-eyed gentlemen, sufficiently well integrated to control our urge in the presence of adults, but ready to give years and years of life for one chance to touch a nymphet. Emphatically, no killers are we. Poets never kill. Oh, my poor Charlotte, do not hate me in your eternal heaven among an eternal alchemy of asphalt and rubber and metal and stone—but thank God, not water, not water!

Nonetheless it was a very close shave, speaking quite objectively. And now comes the point of my perfect-crime parable.

We sat down on our towels in the thirsty sun. She looked around, loosened her bra, and turned over on her stomach to give her back a chance to be feasted upon. She said she loved me. She sighed deeply. She extended one arm and groped in the pocket of her robe for her cigarettes. She sat up and smoked. She examined her right shoulder. She kissed me heavily with open smoky mouth. Suddenly, down the sand bank behind us, from under the bushes and pines, a stone rolled, then another.

"Those disgusting prying kids," said Charlotte, holding up her big bra to her breast and turning prone again. "I shall have to speak about that to Peter Krestovski."

From the debouchment of the trail came a rustle, a footfall, and Jean Farlow marched down with her easel and things.

"You scared us," said Charlotte.

Jean said she had been up there, in a place of green concealment, spying on nature (spies are generally shot), trying
to finish a lakescape, but it was no good, she had no talent
whatever (which was quite true)—"And have *you* ever tried
painting, Humbert?" Charlotte, who was a little jealous of
Jean, wanted to know if John was coming.

He was. He was coming home for lunch today. He had
dropped her on the way to Parkington and should be picking
her up any time now. It was a grand morning. She always felt
a traitor to Cavall and Melampus for leaving them roped on
such gorgeous days. She sat down on the white sand between
Charlotte and me. She wore shorts. Her long brown legs were
about as attractive to me as those of a chestnut mare. She
showed her gums when she smiled.

"I almost put both of you into my lake," she said. "I even
noticed something you overlooked. You [addressing Hum-
bert] had your wrist watch on in, yes, sir, you had."

"Waterproof," said Charlotte softly, making a fish mouth.

Jean took my wrist upon her knee and examined Charlotte's
gift, then put back Humbert's hand on the sand, palm up.

"You could see anything that way," remarked Charlotte
coquettishly.

Jean sighed. "I once saw," she said, "two children, male
and female, at sunset, right here, making love. Their shadows
were giants. And I told you about Mr. Tomson at daybreak.
Next time I expect to see fat old Ivor in the ivory. He is really
a freak, that man. Last time he told me a completely indecent
story about his nephew. It appears—"

"Hullo there," said John's voice.

21

My habit of being silent when displeased, or, more exactly,
the cold and scaly quality of my displeased silence, used to
frighten Valeria out of her wits. She used to whimper and wail,
saying *"Ce qui me rend folle, c'est que je ne sais à quoi tu penses
quand tu es comme ça."* I tried being silent with Charlotte—
and she just chirped on, or chucked my silence under the chin.
An astonishing woman! I would retire to my former room,
now a regular "studio," mumbling I had after all a learned

opus to write, and cheerfully Charlotte went on beautifying the home, warbling on the telephone and writing letters. From my window, through the lacquered shiver of poplar leaves, I could see her crossing the street and contentedly mailing her letter to Miss Phalen's sister.

The week of scattered showers and shadows which elapsed after our last visit to the motionless sands of Hourglass Lake was one of the gloomiest I can recall. Then came two or three dim rays of hope—before the ultimate sunburst.

It occurred to me that I had a fine brain in beautiful working order and that I might as well use it. If I dared not meddle with my wife's plans for her daughter (getting warmer and browner every day in the fair weather of hopeless distance), I could surely devise some general means to assert myself in a general way that might be later directed toward a particular occasion. One evening, Charlotte herself provided me with an opening.

"I have a surprise for you," she said looking at me with fond eyes over a spoonful of soup. "In the fall we two are going to England."

I swallowed *my* spoonful, wiped my lips with pink paper (Oh, the cool rich linens of Mirana Hotel!) and said:

"I have also a surprise for you, my dear. We two are not going to England."

"Why, what's the matter?" she said, looking—with more surprise than I had counted upon—at my hands (I was involuntarily folding and tearing and crushing and tearing again the innocent pink napkin). My smiling face set her somewhat at ease, however.

"The matter is quite simple," I replied. "Even in the most harmonious of households, as ours is, not all decisions are taken by the female partner. There are certain things that the husband is there to decide. I can well imagine the thrill that you, a healthy American gal, must experience at crossing the Atlantic on the same ocean liner with Lady Bumble—or Sam Bumble, the Frozen Meat King, or a Hollywood harlot. And I doubt not that you and I would make a pretty ad for the Traveling Agency when portrayed looking—you, frankly starry-eyed, I, controlling my envious admiration—at the Palace Sentries, or Scarlet Guards, or Beaver Eaters, or whatever they are called. But I happen to be allergic to Europe, including merry old England. As you well know, I have nothing but very sad associations with the Old and rotting World. No colored ads in your magazines will change the situation."

"My darling," said Charlotte. "I really—"

"No, wait a minute. The present matter is only incidental. I am concerned with a general trend. When you wanted me to spend my afternoons sunbathing on the Lake instead of doing my work, I gladly gave in and became a bronzed glamor boy for your sake, instead of remaining a scholar and, well, an educator. When you lead me to bridge and bourbon with the charming Farlows, I meekly follow. No, please, wait. When you decorate your home, I do not interfere with your schemes. When you decide—when you decide all kinds of matters, I may be in complete, or in partial, let us say, disagreement—but I say nothing. I ignore the particular. I cannot ignore the general. I love being bossed by you, but every game has its rules. I am not cross. I am not cross at all. Don't do that. But I am one half of this household, and have a small but distinct voice."

She had come to my side and had fallen on her knees and was slowly, but very vehemently, shaking her head and clawing at my trousers. She said she had never realized. She said I was her ruler and her god. She said Louise had gone, and let us make love right away. She said I must forgive her or she would die.

This little incident filled me with considerable elation. I told her quietly that it was a matter not of asking forgiveness, but of changing one's ways; and I resolved to press my advantage and spend a good deal of time, aloof and moody, working at my book—or at least pretending to work.

The "studio bed" in my former room had long been converted into the sofa it had always been at heart, and Charlotte had warned me since the very beginning of our cohabitation that gradually the room would be turned into a regular "writer's den." A couple of days after the British Incident, I was sitting in a new and very comfortable easy chair, with a large volume in my lap, when Charlotte rapped with her ring finger and sauntered in. How different were her movements from those of my Lolita, when *she* used to visit me in her dear dirty blue jeans, smelling of orchards in nymphetland; awkward and fey, and dimly depraved, the lower buttons of her shirt unfastened. Let me tell you, however, something. Behind the brashness of little Haze, and the poise of big Haze, a trickle of shy life ran that tasted the same, that murmured the same. A great French doctor once told my father that in near relatives the faintest gastric gurgle has the same "voice."

So Charlotte sauntered in. She felt all was not well between us. I had pretended to fall asleep the night before, and the night before that, as soon as we had gone to bed, and had risen at dawn.

Tenderly, she inquired if she were not "interrupting."

"Not at the moment," I said, turning volume C of the *Girls' Encyclopedia* around to examine a picture printed "bottom-edge" as printers say.

Charlotte went up to a little table of imitation mahogany with a drawer. She put her hand upon it. The little table was ugly, no doubt, but it had done nothing to her.

"I have always wanted to ask you," she said (businesslike, not coquettish), "why is this thing locked up? Do you want it in this room? It's so abominably uncouth."

"Leave it alone," I said. I was Camping in Scandinavia.

"Is there a key?"

"Hidden."

"Oh, Hum . . ."

"Locked up love letters."

She gave me one of those wounded-doe looks that irritated me so much, and then, not quite knowing if I was serious, or how to keep up the conversation, stood for several slow pages (Campus, Canada, Candid Camera, Candy) peering at the windowpane rather than through it, drumming upon it with sharp almond-and-rose fingernails.

Presently (at Canoeing or Canvasback) she strolled up to my chair and sank down, tweedily, weightily, on its arm, inundating me with the perfume my first wife had used. "Would his lordship like to spend the fall *here*?" she asked, pointing with her little finger at an autumn view in a conservative Eastern State. "Why?" (very distinctly and slowly). She shrugged. (Probably Harold used to take a vacation at that time. Open season. Conditional reflex on her part.)

"I think I know where that is," she said, still pointing. "There is a hotel I remember, Enchanted Hunters, quaint, isn't it? And the food is a dream. And nobody bothers anybody."

She rubbed her cheek against my temple. Valeria soon got over that.

"Is there anything special you would like for dinner, dear? John and Jean will drop in later."

I answered with a grunt. She kissed me on my underlip, and, brightly saying she would bake a cake (a tradition subsisted from my lodging days that I adored her cakes), left me to my idleness.

Carefully putting down the open book where she had sat (it attempted to send forth a rotation of waves, but an inserted pencil stopped the pages), I checked the hiding place of the key: rather self-consciously it lay under the old expensive safety razor I had used before she bought me a much better and cheaper one. Was it the perfect hiding place—there, under that razor, in the groove of its velvet-lined case? The case lay in a small trunk where I kept various business papers. Could I improve upon this? Remarkable how difficult it is to conceal things—especially when one's wife keeps monkeying with the furniture.

22

I think it was exactly a week after our last swim that the noon mail brought a reply from the second Miss Phalen. The lady wrote she had just returned to St. Algebra from her sister's funeral. "Euphemia had never been the same after breaking that hip." As to the matter of Mrs. Humbert's daughter, she wished to report that it was too late to enroll her this year; but that she, the surviving Phalen, was practically certain that if Mr. and Mrs. Humbert brought Dolores over in January, her admittance might be arranged.

Next day, after lunch, I went to see "our" doctor, a friendly fellow whose perfect bedside manner and complete reliance on a few patented drugs adequately masked his ignorance of, and indifference to, medical science. The fact that Lo would have to come back to Ramsdale was a treasure of anticipation.

For this event I wanted to be fully prepared. I had in fact begun my campaign earlier, before Charlotte made that cruel decision of hers. I had to be sure when my lovely child arrived, that very night, and then night after night, until St. Algebra took her away from me, I would possess the means of putting two creatures to sleep so thoroughly that neither sound nor touch should rouse them. Throughout most of July I had been experimenting with various sleeping powders, trying them out on Charlotte, a great taker of pills. The last dose I had given her (she thought it was a tablet of mild bromides— to anoint her nerves) had knocked her out for four solid hours. I had put the radio at full blast. I had blazed in her face an olisbos-like flashlight. I had pushed her, pinched her, prodded her—and nothing had disturbed the rhythm of her calm and powerful breathing. However, when I had done such a simple thing as kiss her, she had awakened at once, as fresh and strong as an octopus (I barely escaped). This would not do, I thought; had to get something still safer. At first, Dr. Byron did not seem to believe me when I said his last prescription was no match for my insomnia. He suggested I try again, and for a moment diverted my attention by showing me photographs of his family. He had a fascinating child of Dolly's age; but I saw through his tricks and insisted he prescribe the mightiest pill extant. He suggested I play golf, but finally agreed to give me something that, he said, "would really work"; and going to a cabinet, he produced a vial of violet-blue capsules banded with dark purple at one end, which, he said, had just been placed on the market and were intended not for neurotics whom a draft of water could calm if properly administered, but only for great sleepless artists who had to die for a few hours in order to live for centuries. I love to fool doctors, and though inwardly rejoicing, pocketed the pills with a skeptical shrug. Incidentally, I had had to be careful with him. Once, in another connection, a stupid lapse on my part made me mention my last sanatorium, and I thought I saw the tips of his ears twitch. Being not at all keen for Charlotte or anybody else to know that period of my past, I had hastily explained that I had once done some research among the insane for a novel. But no matter; the old rogue certainly had a sweet girleen.

I left in great spirits. Steering my wife's car with one finger, I contentedly rolled homeward. Ramsdale had, after all, lots of charm. The cicadas whirred; the avenue had been freshly watered. Smoothly, almost silkily, I turned down into our steep little street. Everything was somehow so right that day. So blue and green. I knew the sun shone because my ignition key was reflected in the windshield; and I knew it was exactly half past three because the nurse who came to massage Miss Opposite every afternoon was tripping down the narrow sidewalk in her white stockings and shoes. As usual, Junk's hysterical setter attacked me as I rolled downhill, and as usual, the local paper was lying on the porch where it had just been hurled by Kenny.

The day before I had ended the regime of aloofness I had imposed upon myself, and now uttered a cheerful homecoming call as I opened the door of the living room. With her cream-white nape and bronze bun to me, wearing the yellow blouse and maroon slacks she had on when I first met her, Charlotte sat at the corner bureau writing a letter. My hand still on the doorknob, I repeated my hearty cry. Her writing hand stopped. She sat still for a moment; then she slowly turned in her chair and rested her elbow on its curved back. Her face, disfigured by her emotion, was not a pretty sight as she stared at my legs and said:

"The Haze woman, the big bitch, the old cat, the obnoxious mamma, the—the old stupid Haze is no longer your dupe. She has—she has . . ."

My fair accuser stopped, swallowing her venom and her tears. Whatever Humbert Humbert said—or attempted to say—is inessential. She went on:

"You're a monster. You're a detestable, abominable, criminal fraud. If you come near—I'll scream out the window. Get back!"

Again, whatever H.H. murmured may be omitted, I think.

"I am leaving tonight. This is all yours. Only you'll never, never see that miserable brat again. Get out of this room."

Reader, I did. I went up to the ex-semi-studio. Arms akimbo, I stood for a moment quite still and self-composed, surveying from the threshold the raped little table with its open drawer, a key hanging from the lock, four other household keys on the table top. I walked across the landing into the Humberts' bedroom, and calmly removed my diary from under her pillow into my pocket. Then I started to walk downstairs, but stopped halfway: she was talking on the telephone which happened to be plugged just outside the door of the living room. I wanted to hear what she was saying: she canceled an order for something or other, and returned to the parlor. I rearranged my respiration and went through the hallway to the kitchen. There, I opened a bottle of Scotch. She could never resist Scotch. Then I walked into the dining room and from there, through the half-open door, contemplated Charlotte's broad back.

"You are ruining my life and yours," I said quietly. "Let us be civilized people. It is all your hallucination. You are crazy, Charlotte. The notes you found were fragments of a novel. Your name and hers were put in by mere chance. Just because they came handy. Think it over. I shall bring you a drink."

She neither answered nor turned, but went on writing in a scorching scrawl whatever she was writing. A third letter, presumably (two in stamped envelopes were already laid out on the desk). I went back to the kitchen.

I set out two glasses (to St. Algebra? to Lo?) and opened the refrigerator. It roared at me viciously while I removed the ice from its heart. Rewrite. Let her read it again. She will not recall details. Change, forge. Write a fragment and show it to her or leave it lying around. Why do faucets sometimes whine so horribly? A horrible situation, really. The little pillow-shaped blocks of ice—pillows for polar teddy bear, Lo—emitted rasping, crackling, tortured sounds as the warm water loosened them in their cells. I bumped down the glasses side by side. I poured in the whiskey and a dram of soda. She had tabooed my pin. Bark and bang went the icebox. Carrying the glasses, I walked through the dining room and spoke through the parlor door which was a fraction ajar, not quite space enough for my elbow.

"I have made you a drink," I said.

She did not answer, the mad bitch, and I placed the glasses on the sideboard near the telephone, which had started to ring.

"Leslie speaking. Leslie Tomson," said Leslie Tomson who favored a dip at dawn. "Mrs. Humbert, sir, has been run over and you'd better come quick."

I answered, perhaps a bit testily, that my wife was safe and sound, and still holding the receiver, I pushed open the door and said:

"There's this man saying you've been killed, Charlotte."

But there was no Charlotte in the living room.

23

I rushed out. The far side of our steep little street presented a peculiar sight. A big black glossy Packard had climbed Miss Opposite's sloping lawn at an angle from the sidewalk (where a tartan laprobe had dropped in a heap), and stood there, shining in the sun, its doors open like wings, its front wheels deep in evergreen shrubbery. To the anatomical right of this car, on the trim turf of the lawn-slope, an old gentleman with a white mustache, well-dressed—doublebreasted gray suit, polka-dotted bow-tie—lay supine, his long legs together, like a death-size wax figure. I have to put the impact of an instantaneous vision into a sequence of words; their physical accumulation in the page impairs the actual flash, the sharp unity of impression: Rug-heap, car, old man-doll, Miss O.'s nurse running with a rustle, a half-empty tumbler in her hand, back to the screened porch—where the propped-up, imprisoned, decrepit lady herself may be imagined screeching, but not loud enough to drown the rhythmical yaps of the Junk setter walking from group to group—from a bunch of neighbors already collected on the sidewalk, near the bit of checked stuff, and back to the car which he had finally run to earth, and then to another group on the lawn, consisting of Leslie, two policemen and a sturdy man with tortoise shell glasses. At this point, I should explain that the prompt appearance of the patrolmen, hardly more than a minute after the accident, was due to their having been ticketing the illegally parked cars in a cross lane two blocks down the grade; that the fellow with the glasses was Frederick Beale, Jr., driver of the Packard; that his 79-year-old father, whom the nurse had just watered on the green bank where he lay—a banked banker so to speak—

was not in a dead faint, but was comfortably and methodically recovering from a mild heart attack or its possibility; and, finally, that the laprobe on the sidewalk (where she had so often pointed out to me with disapproval the crooked green cracks) concealed the mangled remains of Charlotte Humbert who had been knocked down and dragged several feet by the Beale car as she was hurrying across the street to drop three letters in the mailbox, at the corner of Miss Opposite's lawn. These were picked up and handed to me by a pretty child in a dirty pink frock, and I got rid of them by clawing them to fragments in my trouser pocket.

Three doctors and the Farlows presently arrived on the scene and took over. The widower, a man of exceptional self-control, neither wept nor raved. He staggered a bit, that he did; but he opened his mouth only to impart such information or issue such directions as were strictly necessary in connection with the identification, examination and disposal of a dead woman, the top of her head a porridge of bone, brains, bronze hair and blood. The sun was still a blinding red when he was put to bed in Dolly's room by his two friends, gentle John and dewy-eyed Jean; who, to be near, retired to the Humberts' bedroom for the night; which, for all I know, they may not have spent as innocently as the solemnity of the occasion required.

I have no reason to dwell, in this very special memoir, on the pre-funeral formalities that had to be attended to, or on the funeral itself, which was as quiet as the marriage had been. But a few incidents pertaining to those four or five days after Charlotte's simple death, have to be noted.

My first night of widowhood I was so drunk that I slept as soundly as the child who had slept in that bed. Next morning I hastened to inspect the fragments of letters in my pocket. They had got too thoroughly mixed up to be sorted into three complete sets. I assumed that ". . . and you had better find it because I cannot buy . . ." came from a letter to Lo; and other fragments seemed to point to Charlotte's intention of fleeing with Lo to Parkington, or even back to Pisky, lest the vulture snatch her precious lamb. Other tatters and shreds (never had I thought I had such strong talons) obviously referred to an application not to St. A. but to another boarding

school which was said to be so harsh and gray and gaunt in
its methods (although supplying croquet under the elms) as
to have earned the nickname of "Reformatory for Young Ladies." Finally, the third epistle was obviously addressed to me.
I made out such items as ". . . after a year of separation we
may . . ." ". . . oh, my dearest, oh my . . ." ". . . worse
than if it had been a woman you kept . . ." ". . . or, maybe,
I shall die . . ." But on the whole my gleanings made little
sense; the various fragments of those three hasty missives were
as jumbled in the palms of my hands as their elements had
been in poor Charlotte's head.

That day John had to see a customer, and Jean had to feed
her dogs, and so I was to be deprived temporarily of my
friends' company. The dear people were afraid I might commit suicide if left alone, and since no other friends were available (Miss Opposite was incommunicado, the McCoos were
busy building a new house miles away, and the Chatfields had
been recently called to Maine by some family trouble of their
own), Leslie and Louise were commissioned to keep me company under the pretense of helping me to sort out and pack
a multitude of orphaned things. In a moment of superb inspiration I showed the kind and credulous Farlows (we were
waiting for Leslie to come for his paid tryst with Louise) a
little photograph of Charlotte I had found among her affairs.
From a boulder she smiled through blown hair. It had been
taken in April 1934, a memorable spring. While on a business
visit to the States, I had had occasion to spend several months
in Pisky. We met—and had a mad love affair. I was married,
alas, and she was engaged to Haze, but after I returned to
Europe, we corresponded through a friend, now dead. Jean
whispered she had heard some rumors and looked at the snapshot, and, still looking, handed it to John, and John removed
his pipe and looked at lovely and fast Charlotte Becker, and
handed it back to me. Then they left for a few hours. Happy
Louise was gurgling and scolding her swain in the basement.

Hardly had the Farlows gone than a blue-chinned cleric
called—and I tried to make the interview as brief as was consistent with neither hurting his feelings nor arousing his
doubts. Yes, I would devote all my life to the child's welfare.
Here, incidentally, was a little cross that Charlotte Becker had

given me when we were both young. I had a female cousin, a respectable spinster in New York. There we would find a good private school for Dolly. Oh, what a crafty Humbert!

For the benefit of Leslie and Louise who might (and did) report it to John and Jean I made a tremendously loud and beautifully enacted long-distance call and simulated a conversation with Shirley Holmes. When John and Jean returned, I completely took them in by telling them, in a deliberately wild and confused mutter, that Lo had gone with the intermediate group on a five-day hike and could not be reached.

"Good Lord," said Jean, "what shall we do?"

John said it was perfectly simple—he would get the Climax police to find the hikers—it would not take them an hour. In fact, he knew the country and—

"Look," he continued, "why don't I drive there right now, and you may sleep with Jean"—(he did not really add that but Jean supported his offer so passionately that it might be implied).

I broke down. I pleaded with John to let things remain the way they were. I said I could not bear to have the child all around me, sobbing, clinging to me, she was so high-strung, the experience might react on her future, psychiatrists have analyzed such cases. There was a sudden pause.

"Well, you are the doctor," said John a little bluntly. "But after all I was Charlotte's friend and adviser. One would like to know what you are going to do about the child anyway."

"John," cried Jean, "she is his child, not Harold Haze's. Don't you understand? Humbert is Dolly's real father."

"I see," said John. "I am sorry. Yes, I see. I did not realize that. It simplifies matters, of course. And whatever you feel is right."

The distraught father went on to say he would go and fetch his delicate daughter immediately after the funeral, and would do his best to give her a good time in totally different surroundings, perhaps a trip to New Mexico or California—granted, of course, he lived.

So artistically did I impersonate the calm of ultimate despair, the hush before some crazy outburst, that the perfect Farlows removed me to their house. They had a good cellar, as cellars go in this country; and that was helpful, for I feared insomnia and a ghost.

Now I must explain *my* reasons for keeping Dolores away. Naturally, at first, when Charlotte had just been eliminated and I re-entered the house a free father, and gulped down the two whiskey-and-sodas I had prepared, and topped them with a pint or two of my "pin," and went to the bathroom to get away from neighbors and friends, there was but one thing in my mind and pulse—namely, the awareness that a few hours hence, warm, brown-haired, and mine, mine, mine, Lolita would be in my arms, shedding tears that I would kiss away faster than they could well. But as I stood wide-eyed and flushed before the mirror, John Farlow tenderly tapped to inquire if I was okay—and I immediately realized it would be madness on my part to have her in the house with all those busybodies milling around and scheming to take her away from me. Indeed, unpredictable Lo herself might—who knows?—show some foolish distrust of me, a sudden repugnance, vague fear and the like—and gone would be the magic prize at the very instant of triumph.

Speaking of busybodies, I had another visitor—friend Beale, the fellow who eliminated my wife. Stodgy and solemn, looking like a kind of assistant executioner, with his bulldog jowls, small black eyes, thickly rimmed glasses and conspicuous nostrils, he was ushered in by John who then left us, closing the door upon us, with the utmost tact. Suavely saying he had twins in my stepdaughter's class, my grotesque visitor unrolled a large diagram he had made of the accident. It was, as my stepdaughter would have put it, "a beaut," with all kinds of impressive arrows and dotted lines in varicolored inks. Mrs. H. H.'s trajectory was illustrated at several points by a series of those little outline figures—doll-like wee career girl or WAC—used in statistics as visual aids. Very clearly and conclusively, this route came into contact with a boldly traced sinuous line representing two consecutive swerves—one which the Beale car made to avoid the Junk dog (dog not shown), and the second, a kind of exaggerated continuation of the first, meant to avert the tragedy. A very black cross indicated the spot where the trim little outline figure had at last come to rest on the sidewalk. I looked for some similar mark to denote the place on the embankment where my visitor's huge wax father had reclined, but there was none. That gentleman, however, had signed the document as a witness underneath the name of Leslie Tomson, Miss Opposite and a few other people.

With his hummingbird pencil deftly and delicately flying from one point to another, Frederick demonstrated his absolute innocence and the recklessness of my wife: while he was in the act of avoiding the dog, *she* had slipped on the freshly watered asphalt and plunged forward whereas she should have flung herself not forward but backward (Fred showed how by a jerk of his padded shoulder). I said it was certainly not his fault, and the inquest upheld my view.

Breathing violently through jet-black tense nostrils, he shook his head and my hand; then, with an air of perfect *savoir vivre* and gentlemanly generosity, he offered to pay the funeral-home expenses. He expected me to refuse his offer. With a drunken sob of gratitude I accepted it. This took him aback. Slowly, incredulously, he repeated what he had said. I thanked him again, even more profusely than before.

In result of that weird interview, the numbness of my soul was for a moment resolved. And no wonder! I had actually seen the agent of fate. I had palpated the very flesh of fate—and its padded shoulder. A brilliant and monstrous mutation had suddenly taken place, and here was the instrument. Within the intricacies of the pattern (hurrying housewife, slippery pavement, a pest of a dog, steep grade, big car, baboon at its wheel), I could dimly distinguish my own vile contribution. Had I not been such a fool—or such an intuitive genius—to preserve that journal, fluids produced by vindictive anger and hot shame would not have blinded Charlotte in her dash to the mailbox. But even had they blinded her, still nothing might have happened, had not precise fate, that synchronizing phantom, mixed within its alembic the car and the dog and the sun and the shade and the wet and the weak and the strong and the stone. Adieu, Marlene! Fat fate's formal handshake (as reproduced by Beale before leaving the room) brought me out of my torpor; and I wept. Ladies and gentlemen of the jury—I wept.

24

The elms and the poplars were turning their ruffled backs to a sudden onslaught of wind, and a black thunderhead loomed above Ramsdale's white church tower when I looked around me for the last time. For unknown adventures I was leaving the livid house where I had rented a room only ten weeks before. The shades—thrifty, practical bamboo shades—were already down. On porches or in the house their rich textures lend modern drama. The house of heaven must seem pretty bare after that. A raindrop fell on my knuckles. I went back into the house for something or other while John was putting my bags into the car, and then a funny thing happened. I do not know if in these tragic notes I have sufficiently stressed the peculiar "sending" effect that the writer's good looks—pseudo-Celtic, attractively simian, boyishly manly—had on women of every age and environment. Of course, such announcements made in the first person may sound ridiculous. But every once in a while I have to remind the reader of my appearance much as a professional novelist, who has given a character of his some mannerism or a dog, has to go on producing that dog or that mannerism every time the character crops up in the course of the book. There may be more to it in the present case. My gloomy good looks should be kept in the mind's eye if my story is to be properly understood. Pubescent Lo swooned to Humbert's charm as she did to hiccuppy music; adult Lotte loved me with a mature, possessive passion that I now deplore and respect more than I care to say. Jean Farlow, who was thirty-one and absolutely neurotic, had also apparently developed a strong liking for me. She was handsome in a carved-Indian sort of way, with a burnt sienna complexion. Her lips were like large crimson polyps, and when she emitted her special barking laugh, she showed large dull teeth and pale gums.

She was very tall, wore either slacks with sandals or billowing skirts with ballet slippers, drank any strong liquor in any amount, had had two miscarriages, wrote stories about animals, painted, as the reader knows, lakescapes, was already nursing the cancer that was to kill her at thirty-three, and was hopelessly unattractive to me. Judge then of my alarm when a few seconds before I left (she and I stood in the hallway) Jean, with her always trembling fingers, took me by the temples, and, tears in her bright blue eyes, attempted, unsuccessfully, to glue herself to my lips.

"Take care of yourself," she said, "kiss your daughter for me."

A clap of thunder reverberated throughout the house, and she added:

"Perhaps, somewhere, some day, at a less miserable time, we may see each other again" (Jean, whatever, wherever you are, in minus time-space or plus soul-time, forgive me all this, parenthesis included).

And presently I was shaking hands with both of them in the street, the sloping street, and everything was whirling and flying before the approaching white deluge, and a truck with a mattress from Philadelphia was confidently rolling down to an empty house, and dust was running and writhing over the exact slab of stone where Charlotte, when they lifted the lap-robe for me, had been revealed, curled up, her eyes intact, their black lashes still wet, matted, like yours, Lolita.

25

One might suppose that with all blocks removed and a prospect of delirious and unlimited delights before me, I would have mentally sunk back, heaving a sigh of delicious relief. *Eh bien, pas du tout!* Instead of basking in the beams of smiling Chance, I was obsessed by all sorts of purely ethical doubts and fears. For instance: might it not surprise people that Lo was so consistently debarred from attending festive and funeral functions in her immediate family? You remember—we had not had her at our wedding. Or another thing: granted it was the long hairy arm of Coincidence that had reached out to remove an innocent woman, might Coincidence not ignore in a heathen moment what its twin limb had done and hand Lo a premature note of commiseration? True, the accident had been reported only by the Ramsdale *Journal*—not by the Parkington *Recorder* or the Climax *Herald*, Camp Q being in another state, and local deaths having no federal news interest; but I could not help fancying that somehow Dolly Haze had been informed already, and that at the very time I was on my way to fetch her, she was being driven to Ramsdale by friends unknown to me. Still more disquieting than all these conjectures and worries, was the fact that Humbert Humbert, a brand-new American citizen of obscure European origin, had taken no steps toward becoming the legal guardian of his dead wife's daughter (twelve years and seven months old). Would I ever dare take those steps? I could not repress a shiver whenever I imagined my nudity hemmed in by mysterious statutes in the merciless glare of the Common Law.

My scheme was a marvel of primitive art: I would whizz over to Camp Q, tell Lolita her mother was about to undergo a major operation at an invented hospital, and then keep moving with my sleepy nymphet from inn to inn while her mother got better and better and finally died. But as I traveled campward my anxiety grew. I could not bear to think I might not find Lolita there—or find, instead, another, scared, Lolita clamoring for some family friend: not the Farlows, thank God—she hardly knew them—but might there not be other people I had not reckoned with? Finally, I decided to make the long-distance call I had simulated so well a few days before. It was raining hard when I pulled up in a muddy suburb of Parkington, just before the Fork, one prong of which bypassed the city and led to the highway which crossed the hills to Lake Climax and Camp Q. I flipped off the ignition and for quite a minute sat in the car bracing myself for that telephone call, and staring at the rain, at the inundated sidewalk, at a hydrant: a hideous thing, really, painted a thick silver and red, extending the red stumps of its arms to be varnished by the rain which like stylized blood dripped upon its argent chains. No wonder that stopping beside those nightmare cripples is taboo. I drove up to a gasoline station. A surprise awaited me when at last the coins had satisfactorily clanked down and a voice was allowed to answer mine.

Holmes, the camp mistress, informed me that Dolly had gone Monday (this was Wednesday) on a hike in the hills with her group and was expected to return rather late today. Would I care to come tomorrow, and what was exactly— Without going into details, I said that her mother was hospitalized, that the situation was grave, that the child should not be told it was grave and that she should be ready to leave with me tomorrow afternoon. The two voices parted in an explosion of warmth and good will, and through some freak mechanical flaw all my coins came tumbling back to me with a hitting-the-jackpot clatter that almost made me laugh despite the disappointment at having to postpone bliss. One wonders if this sudden discharge, this spasmodic refund, was not correlated somehow, in the mind of McFate, with my having invented that little expedition before ever learning of it as I did now.

What next? I proceeded to the business center of Parkington and devoted the whole afternoon (the weather had cleared, the wet town was like silver-and-glass) to buying beautiful things for Lo. Goodness, what crazy purchases were prompted by the poignant predilection Humbert had in those days for check weaves, bright cottons, frills, puffed-out short sleeves, soft pleats, snug-fitting bodices and generously full skirts! Oh Lolita, you are my girl, as Vee was Poe's and Bea Dante's, and what little girl would not like to whirl in a circular skirt and scanties? Did I have something special in mind? coaxing voices asked me. Swimming suits? We have them in all shades. Dream pink, frosted aqua, glans mauve, tulip red, oolala black. What about playsuits? Slips? No slips. Lo and I loathed slips.

One of my guides in these matters was an anthropometric entry made by her mother on Lo's twelfth birthday (the reader remembers that Know-Your-Child book). I had the feeling that Charlotte, moved by obscure motives of envy and dislike, had added an inch here, a pound there; but since the nymphet had no doubt grown somewhat in the last seven months, I thought I could safely accept most of those January measurements: hip girth, twenty-nine inches; thigh girth (just below the gluteal sulcus), seventeen; calf girth and neck circumference, eleven; chest circumference, twenty-seven; upper arm girth, eight; waist, twenty-three; stature, fifty-seven inches; weight, seventy-eight pounds; figure, linear; intelligence quotient, 121; vermiform appendix present, thank God.

Apart from measurements, I could of course visualize Lolita with hallucinational lucidity; and nursing as I did a tingle on my breastbone at the exact spot her silky top had come level once or twice with my heart; and feeling as I did her warm

weight in my lap (so that, in a sense, I was always "with Lolita" as a woman is "with child"), I was not surprised to discover later that my computation had been more or less
correct. Having moreover studied a midsummer sale book, it
was with a very knowing air that I examined various pretty
articles, sport shoes, sneakers, pumps of crushed kid for
crushed kids. The painted girl in black who attended to all
these poignant needs of mine turned parental scholarship and
precise description into commercial euphemisms, such as *"petite."* Another, much older woman, in a white dress, with a
pancake make-up, seemed to be oddly impressed by my
knowledge of junior fashions; perhaps I had a midget for mistress; so, when shown a skirt with two "cute" pockets in front,
I intentionally put a naïve male question and was rewarded by
a smiling demonstration of the way the zipper worked in the
back of the skirt. I had next great fun with all kinds of shorts
and briefs—phantom little Lolitas dancing, falling, daisying all
over the counter. We rounded up the deal with some prim
cotton pajamas in popular butcher-boy style. Humbert, the
popular butcher.

There is a touch of the mythological and the enchanted in
those large stores where according to ads a career girl can get
a complete desk-to-date wardrobe, and where little sister can
dream of the day when her wool jersey will make the boys in
the back row of the classroom drool. Lifesize plastic figures
of snubbed-nosed children with dun-colored, greenish,
brown-dotted, faunish faces floated around me. I realized I
was the only shopper in that rather eerie place where I moved
about fish-like, in a glaucous aquarium. I sensed strange
thoughts form in the minds of the languid ladies that escorted
me from counter to counter, from rock ledge to seaweed, and
the belts and the bracelets I chose seemed to fall from siren
hands into transparent water. I bought an elegant valise, had
my purchases put into it, and repaired to the nearest hotel,
well pleased with my day.

Somehow, in connection with that quiet poetical afternoon
of fastidious shopping, I recalled the hotel or inn with the
seductive name of The Enchanted Hunters which Charlotte
had happened to mention shortly before my liberation. With
the help of a guidebook I located it in the secluded town of

Briceland, a four-hour drive from Lo's camp. I could have telephoned but fearing my voice might go out of control and lapse into coy croaks of broken English, I decided to send a wire ordering a room with twin beds for the next night. What a comic, clumsy, wavering Prince Charming I was! How some of my readers will laugh at me when I tell them the trouble I had with the wording of my telegram! What should I put: Humbert and daughter? Humberg and small daughter? Homberg and immature girl? Homburg and child? The droll mistake—the "g" at the end—which eventually came through may have been a telepathic echo of these hesitations of mine.

And then, in the velvet of a summer night, my broodings over the philter I had with me! Oh miserly Hamburg! Was he not a very Enchanted Hunter as he deliberated with himself over his boxful of magic ammunition? To rout the monster of insomnia should he try himself one of those amethyst capsules? There were forty of them, all told—forty nights with a frail little sleeper at my throbbing side; could I rob myself of one such night in order to sleep? Certainly not: much too precious was each tiny plum, each microscopic planetarium with its live stardust. Oh, let me be mawkish for the nonce! I am so tired of being cynical.

26

This daily headache in the opaque air of this tombal jail is disturbing, but I must persevere. Have written more than a hundred pages and not got anywhere yet. My calendar is getting confused. That must have been around August 15, 1947. Don't think I can go on. Heart, head—everything. Lolita, Lolita, Lolita, Lolita, Lolita, Lolita, Lolita, Lolita, Lolita. Repeat till the page is full, printer.

27

Still in Parkington. Finally, I did achieve an hour's slumber—from which I was aroused by gratuitous and horribly exhausting congress with a small hairy hermaphrodite, a total stranger. By then it was six in the morning, and it suddenly occurred to me it might be a good thing to arrive at the camp earlier than I had said. From Parkington I had still a hundred miles to go, and there would be more than that to the Hazy Hills and Briceland. If I had said I would come for Dolly in the afternoon, it was only because my fancy insisted on merciful night falling as soon as possible upon my impatience. But now I foresaw all kinds of misunderstandings and was all a-jitter lest delay might give her the opportunity of some idle telephone call to Ramsdale. However, when at 9.30 A.M. I attempted to start, I was confronted by a dead battery, and noon was nigh when at last I left Parkington.

I reached my destination around half past two; parked my car in a pine grove where a green-shirted, redheaded impish lad stood throwing horseshoes in sullen solitude; was laconically directed by him to an office in a stucco cottage; in a dying state, had to endure for several minutes the inquisitive commiseration of the camp mistress, a sluttish worn out female with rusty hair. Dolly she said was all packed and ready to go. She knew her mother was sick but not critically. Would Mr. Haze, I mean, Mr. Humbert, care to meet the camp counsellors? Or look at the cabins where the girls live? Each dedicated to a Disney creature? Or visit the Lodge? Or should Charlie be sent over to fetch her? The girls were just finishing fixing the Dining Room for a dance. (And perhaps afterwards she would say to somebody or other: "The poor guy looked like his own ghost.")

Let me retain for a moment that scene in all its trivial and fateful detail: hag Holmes writing out a receipt, scratching her head, pulling a drawer out of her desk, pouring change into my impatient palm, then neatly spreading a banknote over it with a bright ". . . and five!"; photographs of girl-children; some gaudy moth or butterfly, still alive, safely pinned to the wall ("nature study"); the framed diploma of the camp's dietitian; my trembling hands; a card produced by efficient Holmes with a report of Dolly Haze's behavior for July ("fair to good; keen on swimming and boating"); a sound of trees and birds, and my pounding heart . . . I was standing with my back to the open door, and then I felt the blood rush to my head as I heard her respiration and voice behind me. She arrived dragging and bumping her heavy suitcase. "Hi!" she said, and stood still, looking at me with sly, glad eyes, her soft lips parted in a slightly foolish but wonderfully endearing smile.

She was thinner and taller, and for a second it seemed to me her face was less pretty than the mental imprint I had cherished for more than a month: her cheeks looked hollowed and too much lentigo camouflaged her rosy rustic features; and that first impression (a very narrow human interval between two tiger heartbeats) carried the clear implication that all widower Humbert had to do, wanted to do, or would do, was to give this wan-looking though sun-colored little orphan *aux yeux battus* (and even those plumbaceous umbrae under her eyes bore freckles) a sound education, a healthy and happy girlhood, a clean home, nice girl-friends of her age among whom (if the fates deigned to repay me) I might find, perhaps, a pretty little *mägdlein* for Herr Doktor Humbert alone. But "in a wink," as the Germans say, the angelic line of conduct was erased, and I overtook my prey (time moves ahead of our fancies!), and she was my Lolita again—in fact, more of my Lolita than ever. I let my hand rest on her warm auburn head and took up her bag. She was all rose and honey, dressed in her brightest gingham, with a pattern of little red apples, and her arms and legs were of a deep golden brown, with scratches like tiny dotted lines of coagulated rubies, and the ribbed cuffs of her white socks were turned down at the remembered level, and because of her childish gait, or because I had memorized her as always wearing heelless shoes, her saddle oxfords looked somehow too large and too high-heeled for her. Good-bye, Camp Q, merry Camp Q. Good-bye, plain unwholesome food, good-bye Charlie boy. In the hot car she settled down beside me, slapped a prompt fly on her lovely knee; then, her mouth working violently on a piece of chewing gum, she rapidly cranked down the window on her side and settled back again. We sped through the striped and speckled forest.

"How's Mother?" she asked dutifully.

I said the doctors did not quite know yet what the trouble was. Anyway, something abdominal. Abominable? No, abdominal. We would have to hang around for a while. The hospital was in the country, near the gay town of Lepingville, where a great poet had resided in the early nineteenth century and where we would take in all the shows. She thought it a peachy idea and wondered if we could make Lepingville before nine P.M.

"We should be at Briceland by dinner time," I said, "and tomorrow we'll visit Lepingville. How was the hike? Did you have a marvelous time at the camp?"

"Uh-huh."

"Sorry to leave?"

"Un-un."

"Talk, Lo—don't grunt. Tell me something."

"What thing, Dad?" (she let the word expand with ironic deliberation).

"Any old thing."

"Okay, if I call you that?" (eyes slit at the road).

"Quite."

"It's a sketch, you know. When did you fall for my mummy?"

"Some day, Lo, you will understand many emotions and situations, such as for example the harmony, the beauty of spiritual relationship."

"Bah!" said the cynical nymphet.

Shallow lull in the dialogue, filled with some landscape.

"Look, Lo, at all those cows on that hillside."

"I think I'll vomit if I look at a cow again."

"You know, I missed you terribly, Lo."

"*I* did not. Fact I've been revoltingly unfaithful to you, but it does not matter one bit, because you've stopped caring for me, anyway. You drive much faster than my mummy, mister."

I slowed down from a blind seventy to a purblind fifty.

"Why do you think I have ceased caring for you, Lo?"

"Well, you haven't kissed me yet, have you?"

Inly dying, inly moaning, I glimpsed a reasonably wide shoulder of road ahead, and bumped and wobbled into the weeds. Remember she is only a child, remember she is only—

Hardly had the car come to a standstill than Lolita positively flowed into my arms. Not daring, not daring let myself go—not even daring let myself realize that *this* (sweet wetness and trembling fire) was the beginning of the ineffable life which, ably assisted by fate, I had finally willed into being—not daring really kiss her, I touched her hot, opening lips with the utmost piety, tiny sips, nothing salacious; but she, with an impatient wriggle, pressed her mouth to mine so hard that I felt her big front teeth and shared in the peppermint taste of her saliva. I knew, of course, it was but an innocent game on her part, a bit of backfisch foolery in imitation of some sim-ulacrum of fake romance, and since (as the psychotherapist, as well as the rapist, will tell you) the limits and rules of such girlish games are fluid, or at least too childishly subtle for the senior partner to grasp—I was dreadfully afraid I might go too far and cause her to start back in revulsion and terror. And, as above all I was agonizingly anxious to smuggle her into the hermetic seclusion of The Enchanted Hunters, and we had still eighty miles to go, blessed intuition broke our embrace—a split second before a highway patrol car drew up alongside.

Florid and beetlebrowed, its driver stared at me:

"Happen to see a blue sedan, same make as yours, pass you before the junction?"

"Why, no."

"We didn't," said Lo, eagerly leaning across me, her in-nocent hand on my legs, "but are you sure it was blue, be-cause—"

The cop (what shadow of us was he after?) gave the little colleen his best smile and went into a U-turn.

We drove on.

"The fruithead!" remarked Lo. "He should have nabbed *you.*"

"Why me for heaven's sake?"

"Well, the speed in this bum state is fifty, and— No, don't slow down, you, dull bulb. He's gone now."

"We have still quite a stretch," I said, "and I want to get there before dark. So be a good girl."

"Bad, bad girl," said Lo comfortably. "Juvenile delickwent, but frank and fetching. That light was red. I've never seen such driving."

We rolled silently through a silent townlet.

"Say, wouldn't Mother be absolutely mad if she found out we were lovers?"

"Good Lord, Lo, let us not talk that way."

"But we *are* lovers, aren't we?"

"Not that I know of. I think we are going to have some more rain. Don't you want to tell me of those little pranks of yours in camp?"

"You talk like a book, *Dad*."

"What have you been up to? I insist you tell me."

"Are you easily shocked?"

"No. Go on."

"Let us turn into a secluded lane and I'll tell you."

"Lo, I must seriously ask you not to play the fool. Well?"

"Well—I joined in all the activities that were offered."

"Ensuite?"

"Ansooit, I was taught to live happily and richly with others and to develop a wholesome personality. Be a cake, in fact."

"Yes. I saw something of the sort in the booklet."

"We loved the sings around the fire in the big stone fireplace or under the darned stars, where every girl merged her own spirit of happiness with the voice of the group."

"Your memory is excellent, Lo, but I must trouble you to leave out the swear words. Anything else?"

"The Girl Scout's motto," said Lo rhapsodically, "is also mine. I fill my life with worthwhile deeds such as—well, never mind what. My duty is—to be useful. I am a friend to male animals. I obey orders. I am cheerful. That was another police car. I am thrifty and I am absolutely filthy in thought, word and deed."

"Now I do hope that's all, you witty child."

"Yep. That's all. No—wait a sec. We baked in a reflector oven. Isn't that terrific?"

"Well, that's better."

"We washed zillions of dishes. 'Zillions' you know is schoolmarm's slang for many-many-many-many. Oh yes, last but not least, as Mother says— Now let me see—what was it? I know: We made shadowgraphs. Gee, what fun."

"C'est bien tout?"

"*C'est*. Except for one little thing, something I simply can't tell you without blushing all over."

"Will you tell it me later?"

"If we sit in the dark and you let me whisper, I will. Do you sleep in your old room or in a heap with Mother?"

"Old room. Your mother may have to undergo a very serious operation, Lo."

"Stop at that candy bar, will you," said Lo.

Sitting on a high stool, a band of sunlight crossing her bare
brown forearm, Lolita was served an elaborate ice-cream concoction topped with synthetic syrup. It was erected and
brought her by a pimply brute of a boy in a greasy bow-tie
who eyed my fragile child in her thin cotton frock with carnal
deliberation. My impatience to reach Briceland and The Enchanted Hunters was becoming more than I could endure.
Fortunately she dispatched the stuff with her usual alacrity.

"How much cash do you have?" I asked.

"Not a cent," she said sadly, lifting her eyebrows, showing
me the empty inside of her money purse.

"This is a matter that will be mended in due time," I rejoined archly. "Are you coming?"

"Say, I wonder if they have a washroom."

"You are not going there," I said firmly. "It is sure to be
a vile place. Do come on."

She was on the whole an obedient little girl and I kissed
her in the neck when we got back into the car.

"*Don't* do that," she said looking at me with unfeigned
surprise. "Don't drool on me. You dirty man."

She rubbed the spot against her raised shoulder.

"Sorry," I murmured. "I'm rather fond of you, that's all."

We drove under a gloomy sky, up a winding road, then
down again.

"Well, I'm also sort of fond of you," said Lolita in a delayed
soft voice, with a sort of sigh, and sort of settled closer to me.

(Oh, my Lolita, we shall never get there!)

Dusk was beginning to saturate pretty little Briceland, its
phony colonial architecture, curiosity shops and imported
shade trees, when we drove through the weakly lighted streets
in search of the Enchanted Hunters. The air, despite a steady
drizzle beading it, was warm and green, and a queue of people, mainly children and old men, had already formed before
the box office of a movie house, dripping with jewel-fires.

"Oh, I want to see that picture. Let's go right after dinner.
Oh, let's!"

"We might," chanted Humbert—knowing perfectly well,

the sly tumescent devil, that by nine, when *his* show began, she would be dead in his arms.

"Easy!" cried Lo, lurching forward, as an accursed truck in front of us, its backside carbuncles pulsating, stopped at a crossing.

If we did not get to the hotel soon, immediately, miraculously, in the very next block, I felt I would lose all control over the Haze jalopy with its ineffectual wipers and whimsical brakes; but the passers-by I applied to for directions were either strangers themselves or asked with a frown "Enchanted what?" as if I were a madman; or else they went into such complicated explanations, with geometrical gestures, geographical generalities and strictly local clues (. . . then bear south after you hit the courthouse . . .) that I could not help losing my way in the maze of their well-meaning gibberish. Lo, whose lovely prismatic entrails had already digested the sweetmeat, was looking forward to a big meal and had begun to fidget. As to me, although I had long become used to a kind of secondary fate (McFate's inept secretary, so to speak) pettily interfering with the boss's generous magnificent plan— to grind and grope through the avenues of Briceland was perhaps the most exasperating ordeal I had yet faced. In later months I could laugh at my inexperience when recalling the obstinate boyish way in which I had concentrated upon that particular inn with its fancy name; for all along our route countless motor courts proclaimed their vacancy in neon lights, ready to accommodate salesmen, escaped convicts, impotents, family groups, as well as the most corrupt and vigorous couples. Ah, gentle drivers gliding through summer's black nights, what frolics, what twists of lust, you might see from your impeccable highways if Kumfy Kabins were suddenly drained of their pigments and became as transparent as boxes of glass!

The miracle I hankered for did happen after all. A man and a girl, more or less conjoined in a dark car under dripping trees, told us we were in the heart of The Park, but had only to turn left at the next traffic light and there we would be. We did not see any next traffic light—in fact, The Park was as black as the sins it concealed—but soon after falling under the smooth spell of a nicely graded curve, the travelers became aware of a diamond glow through the mist, then a gleam of lakewater appeared—and there it was, marvelously and inexorably, under spectral trees, at the top of a graveled drive—the pale palace of The Enchanted Hunters.

A row of parked cars, like pigs at a trough, seemed at first sight to forbid access; but then, by magic, a formidable convertible, resplendent, rubious in the lighted rain, came into motion—was energetically backed out by a broad-shouldered driver—and we gratefully slipped into the gap it had left. I immediately regretted my haste for I noticed that my predecessor had now taken advantage of a garage-like shelter nearby where there was ample space for another car; but I was too impatient to follow his example.

"Wow! Looks swank," remarked my vulgar darling squinting at the stucco as she crept out into the audible drizzle and with a childish hand tweaked loose the frock-fold that had stuck in the peach-cleft—to quote Robert Browning. Under the arclights enlarged replicas of chestnut leaves plunged and played on white pillars. I unlocked the trunk compartment. A hunchbacked and hoary Negro in a uniform of sorts took our bags and wheeled them slowly into the lobby. It was full of old ladies and clergymen. Lolita sank down on her haunches to caress a pale-faced, blue-freckled, black-eared cocker spaniel swooning on the floral carpet under her hand—as who would not, my heart—while I cleared my throat through the throng to the desk. There a bald porcine old man—everybody was old in that old hotel—examined my features with a polite smile, then leisurely produced my (garbled) telegram, wrestled with some dark doubts, turned his head to look at the clock, and finally said he was very sorry, he had held the room with the twin beds till half past six, and now it was gone. A religious convention, he said, had clashed with a flower show in Briceland, and— "The name," I said coldly, "is not Humberg and not Humbug, but Herbert, I mean Humbert, and any room will do, just put in a cot for my little daughter. She is ten and very tired."

The pink old fellow peered good-naturedly at Lo—still squatting, listening in profile, lips parted, to what the dog's mistress, an ancient lady swathed in violet veils, was telling her from the depths of a cretonne easy chair.

Whatever doubts the obscene fellow had, they were dispelled by that blossom-like vision. He said, he might still have
a room, had one, in fact—with a double bed. As to the cot—

"Mr. Potts, do we have any cots left?" Potts, also pink and
bald, with white hairs growing out of his ears and other holes,
would see what could be done. He came and spoke while I
unscrewed my fountain pen. Impatient Humbert!

"Our double beds are really triple," Potts cozily said tuck-
ing me and my kid in. "One crowded night we had three
ladies and a child like yours sleep together. I believe one of
the ladies was a disguised man [*my* static]. However—would
there be a spare cot in 49, Mr. Swine?"

"I think it went to the Swoons," said Swine, the initial old
clown.

"We'll manage somehow," I said. "My wife may join us
later—but even then, I suppose, we'll manage."

The two pink pigs were now among my best friends. In the
slow clear hand of crime I wrote: Dr. Edgar H. Humbert and
daughter, 342 Lawn Street, Ramsdale. A key (342!) was half-
shown to me (magician showing object he is about to palm)—
and handed over to Uncle Tom. Lo, leaving the dog as she
would leave me some day, rose from her haunches; a raindrop
fell on Charlotte's grave; a handsome young Negress slipped
open the elevator door, and the doomed child went in followed by her throat-clearing father and crayfish Tom with the
bags.

Parody of a hotel corridor. Parody of silence and death.

"Say, it's our house number," said cheerful Lo.

There was a double bed, a mirror, a double bed in the
mirror, a closet door with mirror, a bathroom door ditto, a
blue-dark window, a reflected bed there, the same in the closet
mirror, two chairs, a glass-topped table, two bedtables, a double bed: a big panel bed, to be exact, with a Tuscan rose
chenille spread, and two frilled, pink-shaded nightlamps, left
and right.

I was tempted to place a five-dollar bill in that sepia palm,
but thought the largesse might be misconstrued, so I placed
a quarter. Added another. He withdrew. Click. *Enfin seuls.*

"Are we to sleep in *one* room?" said Lo, her features working in that dynamic way they did—not cross or disgusted

(though plain on the brink of it) but just dynamic—when she wanted to load a question with violent significance.

"I've asked them to put in a cot. Which I'll use if you like."

"You are crazy," said Lo.

"Why, my darling?"

"Because, my dahrling, when dahrling Mother finds out she'll divorce you and strangle me."

Just dynamic. Not really taking the matter too seriously.

"Now look here," I said, sitting down, while she stood, a few feet from me, and stared at herself contentedly, not unpleasantly surprised at her own appearance, filling with her own rosy sunshine the surprised and pleased closet-door mirror.

"Look here, Lo. Let's settle this once for all. For all practical purposes I am your father. I have a feeling of great tenderness for you. In your mother's absence I am responsible for your welfare. We are not rich, and while we travel, we shall be obliged—we shall be thrown a good deal together. Two people sharing one room, inevitably enter into a kind—how shall I say—a kind—"

"The word is incest," said Lo—and walked into the closet, walked out again with a young golden giggle, opened the adjoining door, and after carefully peering inside with her strange smoky eyes lest she make another mistake, retired to the bathroom.

I opened the window, tore off my sweat-drenched shirt, changed, checked the pill vial in my coat pocket, unlocked the—

She drifted out. I tried to embrace her: casually, a bit of controlled tenderness before dinner.

She said: "Look, let's cut out the kissing game and get something to eat."

It was then that I sprang my surprise.

Oh, what a dreamy pet! She walked up to the open suitcase as if stalking it from afar, at a kind of slow-motion walk, peering at that distant treasure box on the luggage support. (Was there something wrong, I wondered, with those great gray eyes of hers, or were we both plunged in the same enchanted mist?) She stepped up to it, lifting her rather high-heeled feet rather high, and bending her beautiful boy-knees while she walked through dilating space with the lentor of one walking under water or in a flight dream. Then she raised by the armlets a copper-colored, charming and quite expensive vest, very slowly stretching it between her silent hands as if she were a bemused bird-hunter holding his breath over the incredible bird he spreads out by the tips of its flaming wings. Then (while I stood waiting for her) she pulled out the slow snake of a brilliant belt and tried it on.

Then she crept into my waiting arms, radiant, relaxed, caressing me with her tender, mysterious, impure, indifferent, twilight eyes—for all the world, like the cheapest of cheap cuties. For that is what nymphets imitate—while we moan and die.

"What's the katter with misses?" I muttered (word-control gone) into her hair.

"If you must know," she said, "you do it the wrong way."

"Show, wight ray."

"All in good time," responded the spoonerette.

Seva ascendes, pulsata, brulans, kitzelans, dementissima. Elevator clatterans, pausa, clatterans, populus in corridoro. Hanc nisi mors mihi adimet nemo! Juncea puellula, jo pensavo fondissime, nobserva nihil quidquam; but, of course, in another moment I might have committed some dreadful blunder; fortunately, she returned to the treasure box.

From the bathroom, where it took me quite a time to shift back into normal gear for a humdrum purpose, I heard, standing, drumming, retaining my breath, my Lolita's "oo's" and "gee's" of girlish delight.

She had used the soap only because it was sample soap.

"Well, come on, my dear, if you are as hungry as I am."

And so to the elevator, daughter swinging her old white purse, father walking in front (nota bene: never behind, she is not a lady). As we stood (now side by side) waiting to be taken down, she threw back her head, yawned without restraint and shook her curls.

"When did they make you get up at that camp?"

"Half-past—" she stifled another yawn—"six"—yawn in full with a shiver of all her frame. "Half-past," she repeated, her throat filling up again.

The dining room met us with a smell of fried fat and a faded smile. It was a spacious and pretentious place with maudlin murals depicting enchanted hunters in various postures and states of enchantment amid a medley of pallid animals, dryads and trees. A few scattered old ladies, two clergymen, and a man in a sports coat were finishing their meals in silence. The dining room closed at nine, and the green-clad, poker-faced serving girls were, happily, in a desperate hurry to get rid of us.

"Does not he look exactly, but exactly, like Quilty?" said Lo in a soft voice, her sharp brown elbow not pointing, but visibly burning to point, at the lone diner in the loud checks, in the far corner of the room.

"Like our fat Ramsdale dentist?"

Lo arrested the mouthful of water she had just taken, and put down her dancing glass.

"Course not," she said with a splutter of mirth. "I meant the writer fellow in the Dromes ad."

Oh, Fame! Oh, Femina!

When the dessert was plunked down—a huge wedge of cherry pie for the young lady and vanilla ice cream for her protector, most of which she expeditiously added to her pie—I produced a small vial containing Papa's Purple Pills. As I look back at those seasick murals, at that strange and monstrous moment, I can only explain my behavior then by the mechanism of that dream vacuum wherein revolves a deranged mind; but at the time, it all seemed quite simple and inevitable to me. I glanced around, satisfied myself that the last diner had left, removed the stopper, and with the utmost deliberation tipped the philter into my palm. I had carefully rehearsed before a mirror the gesture of clapping my empty hand to my open mouth and swallowing a (fictitious) pill. As I expected, she pounced upon the vial with its plump, beautifully colored capsules loaded with Beauty's Sleep.

"Blue!" she exclaimed. "Violet blue. What are they made of?"

"Summer skies," I said, "and plums and figs, and the grape-blood of emperors."

"No, seriously—please."

"Oh, just Purpills. Vitamin X. Makes one strong as an ox or an ax. Want to try one?"

Lolita stretched out her hand, nodding vigorously.

I had hoped the drug would work fast. It certainly did. She had had a long long day, she had gone rowing in the morning with Barbara whose sister was Waterfront Director, as the adorable accessible nymphet now started to tell me in between suppressed palate-humping yawns, growing in volume—oh, how fast the magic potion worked!—and had been active in other ways too. The movie that had vaguely loomed in her mind was, of course, by the time we watertreaded out of the dining room, forgotten. As we stood in the elevator, she leaned against me, faintly smiling—wouldn't you like me to tell you?—half closing her dark-lidded eyes. "Sleepy, huh?" said Uncle Tom who was bringing up the quiet Franco-Irish gentleman and his daughter as well as two withered women, experts in roses. They looked with sympathy at my frail, tanned, tottering, dazed rosedarling. I had almost to carry her into our room. There, she sat down on the edge of the bed, swaying a little, speaking in dove-dull, long-drawn tones.

"If I tell you—if I tell you, will you promise [sleepy, so sleepy—head lolling, eyes going out], promise you won't make complaints?"

"Later, Lo. Now go to bed. I'll leave you here, and you go to bed. Give you ten minutes."

"Oh, I've been such a disgusting girl," she went on, shaking her hair, removing with slow fingers a velvet hair ribbon. "Lemme tell you—"

"Tomorrow, Lo. Go to bed, go to bed—for goodness sake, to bed."

I pocketed the key and walked downstairs.

28

Gentlewomen of the jury! Bear with me! Allow me to take just a tiny bit of your precious time! So this was *le grand moment*. I had left my Lolita still sitting on the edge of the abysmal bed, drowsily raising her foot, fumbling at the shoe-laces and showing as she did so the nether side of her thigh up to the crotch of her panties—she had always been singularly absentminded, or shameless, or both, in matters of leg-show. This, then, was the hermetic vision of her which I had locked in—after satisfying myself that the door carried no inside bolt. The key, with its numbered dangler of carved wood, became forthwith the weighty sesame to a rapturous and formidable future. It was mine, it was part of my hot hairy fist. In a few minutes—say, twenty, say half-an-hour, *sicher ist sicher* as my uncle Gustave used to say—I would let myself into that "342" and find my nymphet, my beauty and bride, emprisoned in her crystal sleep. Jurors! If my happiness could have talked, it would have filled that genteel hotel with a deafening roar. And my only regret today is that I did not quietly deposit key "342" at the office, and leave the town, the country, the continent, the hemisphere,—indeed, the globe—that very same night.

Let me explain. I was not unduly disturbed by her self-accusatory innuendoes. I was still firmly resolved to pursue my policy of sparing her purity by operating only in the stealth of night, only upon a completely anesthetized little nude. Restraint and reverence were still my motto—even if that "purity" (incidentally, thoroughly debunked by modern science) had been slightly damaged through some juvenile erotic experience, no doubt homosexual, at that accursed camp of hers. Of course, in my old-fashioned, old-world way, I, Jean-Jacques Humbert, had taken for granted, when I first met her, that she was as unravished as the stereotypical notion of "normal child" had been since the lamented end of the Ancient World B.C. and its fascinating practices. We are not surrounded in our enlighted era by little slave flowers that can be casually plucked between business and bath as they used to be in the days of the Romans; and we do not, as dignified Orientals did in still more luxurious times, use tiny entertainers fore and aft between the mutton and the rose sherbet. The whole point is that the old link between the adult world and the child world has been completely severed nowadays by new customs and new laws. Despite my having dabbled in psychiatry and social work, I really knew very little about children. After all, Lolita was only twelve, and no matter what concessions I made to time and place—even bearing in mind the crude behavior of American schoolchildren—I still was under the impression that whatever went on among those brash brats, went on at a later age, and in a different environment.

Therefore (to retrieve the thread of this explanation) the moralist in me by-passed the issue by clinging to conventional notions of what twelve-year-old girls should be. The child therapist in me (a fake, as most of them are—but no matter) regurgitated neo-Freudian hash and conjured up a dreaming and exaggerating Dolly in the "latency" period of girlhood. Finally, the sensualist in me (a great and insane monster) had no objection to some depravity in his prey. But somewhere behind the raging bliss, bewildered shadows conferred—and not to have heeded them, this is what I regret! Human beings, attend! I should have understood that Lolita had *already* proved to be something quite different from innocent Annabel, and that the nymphean evil breathing through every pore of the fey child that I had prepared for my secret delectation, would make the secrecy impossible, and the delectation lethal. I should have known (by the signs made to me by something in Lolita—the real child Lolita or some haggard angel behind her back) that nothing but pain and horror would result from the expected rapture. Oh, winged gentlemen of the jury!

And she was mine, she was mine, the key was in my fist, my fist was in my pocket, she was mine. In the course of the evocations and schemes to which I had dedicated so many insomnias, I had gradually eliminated all the superfluous blur, and by stacking level upon level of translucent vision, had evolved a final picture. Naked, except for one sock and her charm bracelet, spread-eagled on the bed where my philter had felled her—so I foreglimpsed her; a velvet hair ribbon was still clutched in her hand; her honey-brown body, with the white negative image of a rudimentary swimsuit patterned against her tan, presented to me its pale breastbuds; in the rosy lamplight, a little pubic floss glistened on its plump hillock. The cold key with its warm wooden addendum was in my pocket.

I wandered through various public rooms, glory below, gloom above: for the look of lust always is gloomy; lust is never quite sure—even when the velvety victim is locked up in one's dungeon—that some rival devil or influential god may still not abolish one's prepared triumph. In common parlance, I needed a drink; but there was no barroom in that venerable place full of perspiring philistines and period objects.

I drifted to the Men's Room. There, a person in clerical black—a "hearty party" *comme on dit*—checking with the assistance of Vienna, if it was still there, inquired of me how I had liked Dr. Boyd's talk, and looked puzzled when I (King Sigmund the Second) said Boyd was quite a boy. Upon which, I neatly chucked the tissue paper I had been wiping my sensitive finger tips with into the receptacle provided for it, and sallied lobbyward. Comfortably resting my elbows on the counter, I asked Mr. Potts was he quite sure my wife had not telephoned, and what about that cot? He answered she had not (she was dead, of course) and the cot would be installed tomorrow if we decided to stay on. From a big crowded place called The Hunters' Hall came a sound of many voices discussing horticulture or eternity. Another room, called The Raspberry Room, all bathed in light, with bright little tables and a large one with "refreshments," was still empty except for a hostess (that type of worn woman with a glassy smile and Charlotte's manner of speaking); she floated up to me to ask if I was Mr. Braddock, because if so, Miss Beard had been looking for me. "What a name for a woman," I said and strolled away.

In and out of my heart flowed my rainbow blood. I would give her till half-past-nine. Going back to the lobby, I found there a change: a number of people in floral dresses or black cloth had formed little groups here and there, and some elfish chance offered me the sight of a delightful child of Lolita's age, in Lolita's type of frock, but pure white, and there was a white ribbon in her black hair. She was not pretty, but she was a nymphet, and her ivory pale legs and lily neck formed for one memorable moment a most pleasurable antiphony (in terms of spinal music) to my desire for Lolita, brown and pink, flushed and fouled. The pale child noticed my gaze (which was really quite casual and debonair), and being ridiculously self-conscious, lost countenance completely, rolling her eyes and putting the back of her hand to her cheek, and pulling at the hem of her skirt, and finally turning her thin mobile shoulder blades to me in specious chat with her cow-like mother.

I left the loud lobby and stood outside, on the white steps, looking at the hundreds of powdered bugs wheeling around the lamps in the soggy black night, full of ripple and stir. All

I would do—all I would dare to do—would amount to such a trifle . . .

Suddenly I was aware that in the darkness next to me there was somebody sitting in a chair on the pillared porch. I could not really see him but what gave him away was the rasp of a screwing off, then a discreet gurgle, then the final note of a placid screwing on. I was about to move away when his voice addressed me:

"Where the devil did you get her?"

"I beg your pardon?"

"I said: the weather is getting better."

"Seems so."

"Who's the lassie?"

"My daughter."

"You lie—she's not."

"I beg your pardon?"

"I said: July was hot. Where's her mother?"

"Dead."

"I see. Sorry. By the way, why don't you two lunch with me tomorrow. That dreadful crowd will be gone by then."

"We'll be gone too. Good night."

"Sorry. I'm pretty drunk. Good night. That child of yours needs a lot of sleep. Sleep is a rose, as the Persians say. Smoke?"

"Not now."

He struck a light, but because he was drunk, or because the wind was, the flame illumined not him but another person, a very old man, one of those permanent guests of old hotels— and his white rocker. Nobody said anything and the darkness returned to its initial place. Then I heard the old-timer cough and deliver himself of some sepulchral mucus.

I left the porch. At least half an hour in all had elapsed. I ought to have asked for a sip. The strain was beginning to tell. If a violin string can ache, then I was that string. But it would have been unseemly to display any hurry. As I made my way through a constellation of fixed people in one corner of the lobby, there came a blinding flash—and beaming Dr. Braddock, two orchid-ornamentalized matrons, the small girl in white, and presumably the bared teeth of Humbert Humbert sidling between the bridelike lassie and the enchanted cleric, were immortalized—insofar as the texture and print of small-town newspapers can be deemed immortal. A twittering group had gathered near the elevator. I again chose the stairs. 342 was near the fire escape. One could still—but the key was already in the lock, and then I was in the room.

29

The door of the lighted bathroom stood ajar; in addition to that, a skeleton glow came through the Venetian blind from the outside arclights; these intercrossed rays penetrated the darkness of the bedroom and revealed the following situation.

Clothed in one of her old nightgowns, my Lolita lay on her side with her back to me, in the middle of the bed. Her lightly veiled body and bare limbs formed a Z. She had put both pillows under her dark tousled head; a band of pale light crossed her top vertebrae.

I seemed to have shed my clothes and slipped into pajamas with the kind of fantastic instantaneousness which is implied when in a cinematographic scene the process of changing is cut; and I had already placed my knee on the edge of the bed when Lolita turned her head and stared at me through the striped shadows.

Now this was something the intruder had not expected. The whole pill-spiel (a rather sordid affair, *entre nous soit dit*) had had for object a fastness of sleep that a whole regiment would not have disturbed, and here she was staring at me, and thickly calling me "Barbara." Barbara, wearing my pajamas which were much too tight for her, remained poised motionless over the little sleep-talker. Softly, with a hopeless sigh, Dolly turned away, resuming her initial position. For at least two minutes I waited and strained on the brink, like that tailor with his homemade parachute forty years ago when about to jump from the Eiffel Tower. Her faint breathing had the rhythm of sleep. Finally I heaved myself onto my narrow margin of bed, stealthily pulled at the odds and ends of sheets piled up to the south of my stone-cold heels—and Lolita lifted her head and gaped at me.

As I learned later from a helpful pharmaceutist, the purple

pill did not even belong to the big and noble family of bar-
biturates, and though it might have induced sleep in a neurotic who believed it to be a potent drug, it was too mild a
sedative to affect for any length of time a wary, albeit weary,
nymphet. Whether the Ramsdale doctor was a charlatan or a
shrewd old rogue, does not, and did not, really matter. What
mattered, was that I had been deceived. When Lolita opened
her eyes again, I realized that whether or not the drug might
work later in the night, the security I had relied upon was a
sham one. Slowly her head turned away and dropped onto her
unfair amount of pillow. I lay quite still on my brink, peering
at her rumpled hair, at the glimmer of nymphet flesh, where
half a haunch and half a shoulder dimly showed, and trying
to gauge the depth of her sleep by the rate of her respiration.
Some time passed, nothing changed, and I decided I might
risk getting a little closer to that lovely and maddening glimmer; but hardly had I moved into its warm purlieus than her
breathing was suspended, and I had the odious feeling that
little Dolores was wide awake and would explode in screams
if I touched her with any part of my wretchedness. Please,
reader: no matter your exasperation with the tenderhearted,
morbidly sensitive, infinitely circumspect hero of my book, do
not skip these essential pages! Imagine me; I shall not exist if
you do not imagine me; try to discern the doe in me, trembling in the forest of my own iniquity; let's even smile a little.
After all, there is no harm in smiling. For instance (I almost
wrote "frinstance"), I had no place to rest my head, and a fit
of heartburn (they call those fries "French," *grand Dieu!*) was
added to my discomfort.

   She was again fast asleep, my nymphet, but still I did not
dare to launch upon my enchanted voyage. *La Petite Dor-
meuse ou l'Amant Ridicule.* Tomorrow I would stuff her with
those earlier pills that had so thoroughly numbed her mummy.
In the glove compartment—or in the Gladstone bag? Should
I wait a solid hour and then creep up again? The science of
nympholepsy is a precise science. Actual contact would do it
in one second flat. An interspace of a millimeter would do it
in ten. Let us wait.

   There is nothing louder than an American hotel; and, mind
you, this was supposed to be a quiet, cozy, old-fashioned,

homey place—"gracious living" and all that stuff. The clatter of the elevator's gate—some twenty yards northeast of my head but as clearly perceived as if it were inside my left temple—alternated with the banging and booming of the machine's various evolutions and lasted well beyond midnight. Every now and then, immediately east of my left ear (always assuming I lay on my back, not daring to direct my viler side toward the nebulous haunch of my bed-mate), the corridor would brim with cheerful, resonant and inept exclamations ending in a volley of good-nights. When *that* stopped, a toilet immediately north of my cerebellum took over. It was a manly, energetic, deep-throated toilet, and it was used many times. Its gurgle and gush and long afterflow shook the wall behind me. Then someone in a southern direction was extravagantly sick, almost coughing out his life with his liquor, and his toilet descended like a veritable Niagara, immediately beyond our bathroom. And when finally all the waterfalls had stopped, and the enchanted hunters were sound asleep, the avenue under the window of my insomnia, to the west of my wake—a staid, eminently residential, dignified alley of huge trees—degenerated into the despicable haunt of gigantic trucks roaring through the wet and windy night.

And less than six inches from me and my burning life, was nebulous Lolita! After a long stirless vigil, my tentacles moved towards her again, and this time the creak of the mattress did not awake her. I managed to bring my ravenous bulk so close to her that I felt the aura of her bare shoulder like a warm breath upon my cheek. And then, she sat up, gasped, muttered with insane rapidity something about boats, tugged at the sheets and lapsed back into her rich, dark, young unconsciousness. As she tossed, within that abundant flow of sleep, recently auburn, at present lunar, her arm struck me across the face. For a second I held her. She freed herself from the shadow of my embrace—doing this not consciously, not violently, not with any personal distaste, but with the neutral plaintive murmur of a child demanding its natural rest. And again the situation remained the same: Lolita with her curved spine to Humbert, Humbert resting his head on his hand and burning with desire and dyspepsia.

The latter necessitated a trip to the bathroom for a draft of water which is the best medicine I know in my case, except perhaps milk with radishes; and when I re-entered the strange pale-striped fastness where Lolita's old and new clothes reclined in various attitudes of enchantment on pieces of furniture that seemed vaguely afloat, my impossible daughter sat up and in clear tones demanded a drink, too. She took the resilient and cold paper cup in her shadowy hand and gulped down its contents gratefully, her long eyelashes pointing cupward, and then, with an infantile gesture that carried more charm than any carnal caress, little Lolita wiped her lips against my shoulder. She fell back on her pillow (I had subtracted mine while she drank) and was instantly asleep again.

I had not dared offer her a second helping of the drug, and had not abandoned hope that the first might still consolidate her sleep. I started to move toward her, ready for any disappointment, knowing I had better wait but incapable of waiting. My pillow smelled of her hair. I moved toward my glimmering darling, stopping or retreating every time I thought she stirred or was about to stir. A breeze from wonderland had begun to affect my thoughts, and now they seemed couched in italics, as if the surface reflecting them were wrinkled by the phantasm of that breeze. Time and again my consciousness folded the wrong way, my shuffling body entered the sphere of sleep, shuffled out again, and once or twice I caught myself drifting into a melancholy snore. Mists of tenderness enfolded mountains of longing. Now and then it seemed to me that the enchanted prey was about to meet halfway the enchanted hunter, that her haunch was working its way toward me under the soft sand of a remote and fabulous beach; and then her dimpled dimness would stir, and I would know she was farther away from me than ever.

If I dwell at some length on the tremors and gropings of that distant night, it is because I insist upon proving that I am not, and never was, and never could have been, a brutal scoundrel. The gentle and dreamy regions through which I crept were the patrimonies of poets—*not* crime's prowling ground. Had I reached my goal, my ecstasy would have been all softness, a case of internal combustion of which she would hardly have felt the heat, even if she were wide awake. But I still hoped she might gradually be engulfed in a completeness of stupor that would allow me to taste more than a glimmer of her. And so, in between tentative approximations, with a confusion of perception metamorphosing her into eyespots of moonlight or a fluffy flowering bush, I would dream I regained consciousness, dream I lay in wait.

In the first antemeridian hours there was a lull in the restless hotel night. Then around four the corridor toilet cascaded and its door banged. A little after five a reverberating monologue began to arrive, in several installments, from some courtyard or parking place. It was not really a monologue, since the speaker stopped every few seconds to listen (presumably) to another fellow, but that other voice did not reach me, and so no real meaning could be derived from the part heard. Its matter-of-fact intonations, however, helped to bring in the dawn, and the room was already suffused with lilac gray, when several industrious toilets went to work, one after the other, and the clattering and whining elevator began to rise and take down early risers and downers, and for some minutes I miserably dozed, and Charlotte was a mermaid in a greenish tank, and somewhere in the passage Dr. Boyd said "Good morning to you" in a fruity voice, and birds were busy in the trees, and then Lolita yawned.

Frigid gentlewomen of the jury! I had thought that months, perhaps years, would elapse before I dared to reveal myself to Dolores Haze; but by six she was wide awake, and by six fifteen we were technically lovers. I am going to tell you something very strange: it was she who seduced me.

Upon hearing her first morning yawn, I feigned handsome profiled sleep. I just did not know what to do. Would she be shocked at finding me by her side, and not in some spare bed? Would she collect her clothes and lock herself up in the bathroom? Would she demand to be taken at once to Ramsdale— to her mother's bedside—back to camp? But my Lo was a sportive lassie. I felt her eyes on me, and when she uttered at last that beloved chortling note of hers, I knew her eyes had been laughing. She rolled over to my side, and her warm brown hair came against my collarbone. I gave a mediocre imitation of waking up. We lay quietly. I gently caressed her hair, and we gently kissed. Her kiss, to my delirious embarrassment, had some rather comical refinements of flutter and probe which made me conclude she had been coached at an early age by a little Lesbian. No Charlie boy could have taught her *that*. As if to see whether I had my fill and learned the lesson, she drew away and surveyed me. Her cheekbones were flushed, her full underlip glistened, my dissolution was near. All at once, with a burst of rough glee (the sign of the nymphet!), she put her mouth to my ear—but for quite a while my mind could not separate into words the hot thunder of her whisper, and she laughed, and brushed the hair off her face, and tried again, and gradually the odd sense of living in a brand new, mad new dream world, where everything was permissible, came over me as I realized what she was suggesting. I answered I did not know what game she and Charlie had played. "You mean you have never—?"—her features twisted into a stare of disgusted incredulity. "You have never—" she started again. I took time out by nuzzling her a little. "Lay off, will you," she said with a twangy whine, hastily removing her brown shoulder from my lips. (It was very curious the way she considered—and kept doing so for a long time—all caresses except kisses on the mouth or the stark act of love either "romantic slosh" or "abnormal".)

"You mean," she persisted, now kneeling above me, "you never did it when you were a kid?"

"Never," I answered quite truthfully.

"Okay," said Lolita, "here is where we start."

However, I shall not bore my learned readers with a detailed account of Lolita's presumption. Suffice it to say that not a trace of modesty did I perceive in this beautiful hardly formed young girl whom modern co-education, juvenile mores, the campfire racket and so forth had utterly and hopelessly depraved. She saw the stark act merely as part of a youngster's furtive world, unknown to adults. What adults did for purposes of procreation was no business of hers. My life was handled by little Lo in an energetic, matter-of-fact manner as if it were an insensate gadget unconnected with me. While eager to impress me with the world of tough kids, she was not quite prepared for certain discrepancies between a kid's life and mine. Pride alone prevented her from giving up; for, in my strange predicament, I feigned supreme stupidity and had her have her way—at least while I could still bear it. But really these are irrelevant matters; I am not concerned with so-called "sex" at all. Anybody can imagine those elements of animality. A greater endeavor lures me on: to fix once for all the perilous magic of nymphets.

30

I have to tread carefully. I have to speak in a whisper. Oh you, veteran crime reporter, you grave old usher, you once popular policeman, now in solitary confinement after gracing that school crossing for years, you wretched emeritus read to by a boy! It would never do, would it, to have you fellows fall madly in love with my Lolita! Had I been a painter, had the management of The Enchanted Hunters lost its mind one summer day and commissioned me to redecorate their dining room with murals of my own making, this is what I might have thought up, let me list some fragments:

There would have been a lake. There would have been an arbor in flame-flower. There would have been nature studies —a tiger pursuing a bird of paradise, a choking snake sheathing whole the flayed trunk of a shoat. There would have been a sultan, his face expressing great agony (belied, as it were, by his molding caress), helping a callypygean slave child to climb a column of onyx. There would have been those luminous globules of gonadal glow that travel up the opalescent sides of juke boxes. There would have been all kinds of camp activities on the part of the intermediate group, Canoeing, Coranting, Combing Curls in the lakeside sun. There would have been poplars, apples, a suburban Sunday. There would have been a fire opal dissolving within a ripple-ringed pool, a last throb, a last dab of color, stinging red, smarting pink, a sigh, a wincing child.

31

I am trying to describe these things not to relive them in my present boundless misery, but to sort out the portion of hell and the portion of heaven in that strange, awful, maddening world—nymphet love. The beastly and beautiful merged at one point, and it is that borderline I would like to fix, and I feel I fail to do so utterly. Why?

The stipulation of the Roman law, according to which a girl may marry at twelve, was adopted by the Church, and is still preserved, rather tacitly, in some of the United States. And fifteen is lawful everywhere. There is nothing wrong, say both hemispheres, when a brute of forty, blessed by the local priest and bloated with drink, sheds his sweat-drenched finery and thrusts himself up to the hilt into his youthful bride. "In such stimulating temperate climates [says an old magazine in this prison library] as St. Louis, Chicago and Cincinnati, girls mature about the end of their twelfth year." Dolores Haze was born less than three hundred miles from stimulating Cincinnati. I have but followed nature. I am nature's faithful hound. Why then this horror that I cannot shake off? Did I deprive her of her flower? Sensitive gentlewomen of the jury, I was not even her first lover.

32

She told me the way she had been debauched. We ate flavorless mealy bananas, bruised peaches and very palatable potato chips, and *die Kleine* told me everything. Her voluble but disjointed account was accompanied by many a droll *moue*. As I think I have already observed, I especially remember one wry face on an "ugh!" basis: jelly-mouth distended sideways and eyes rolled up in a routine blend of comic disgust, resignation and tolerance for young frailty.

Her astounding tale started with an introductory mention of her tent-mate of the previous summer, at another camp, a "very select" one as she put it. That tent-mate ("quite a derelict character," "half-crazy," but a "swell kid") instructed her in various manipulations. At first, loyal Lo refused to tell me her name.

"Was it Grace Angel?" I asked.

She shook her head. No, it wasn't, it was the daughter of a big shot. He—

"Was it perhaps Rose Carmine?"

"No, of course not. Her father—"

"Was it, then, Agnes Sheridan perchance?"

She swallowed and shook her head—and then did a double take.

"Say, how come you know all those kids?"

I explained.

"Well," she said. "They are pretty bad, some of that school bunch, but not that bad. If you have to know, her name was Elizabeth Talbot, she goes now to a swanky private school, her father is an executive."

I recalled with a funny pang the frequency with which poor Charlotte used to introduce into party chat such elegant tidbits as "when my daughter was out hiking last year with the Talbot girl."

I wanted to know if either mother learned of those sapphic diversions?

"Gosh no," exhaled limp Lo mimicking dread and relief, pressing a falsely fluttering hand to her chest.

I was more interested, however, in heterosexual experience. She had entered the sixth grade at eleven, soon after moving to Ramsdale from the Middle West. What did she mean by "pretty bad"?

Well, the Miranda twins had shared the same bed for years, and Donald Scott, who was the dumbest boy in the school, had done it with Hazel Smith in his uncle's garage, and Kenneth Knight—who was the brightest—used to exhibit himself wherever and whenever he had a chance, and—

"Let us switch to Camp Q," I said. And presently I got the whole story.

Barbara Burke, a sturdy blond, two years older than Lo and by far the camp's best swimmer, had a very special canoe which she shared with Lo "because I was the only other girl who could make Willow Island" (some swimming test, I imagine). Through July, every morning—mark, reader, every blessed morning—Barbara and Lo would be helped to carry the boat to Onyx or Eryx (two small lakes in the wood) by Charlie Holmes, the camp mistress' son, aged thirteen—and the only human male for a couple of miles around (excepting an old meek stone-deaf handyman, and a farmer in an old Ford who sometimes sold the campers eggs as farmers will); every morning, oh my reader, the three children would take a short cut through the beautiful innocent forest brimming with all the emblems of youth, dew, birdsongs, and at one point, among the luxuriant undergrowth, Lo would be left as sentinel, while Barbara and the boy copulated behind a bush.

At first, Lo had refused "to try what it was like," but curiosity and camaraderie prevailed, and soon she and Barbara were doing it by turns with the silent, coarse and surly but indefatigable Charlie, who had as much sex appeal as a raw carrot but sported a fascinating collection of contraceptives which he used to fish out of a third nearby lake, a considerably larger and more populous one, called Lake Climax, after the booming young factory town of that name. Although conceding it was "sort of fun" and "fine for the complexion," Lolita, I am glad to say, held Charlie's mind and manners in the greatest contempt. Nor had her temperament been roused by that filthy fiend. In fact, I think he had rather stunned it, despite the "fun."

By that time it was close to ten. With the ebb of lust, an ashen sense of awfulness, abetted by the realistic drabness of a gray neuralgic day, crept over me and hummed within my temples. Brown, naked, frail Lo, her narrow white buttocks to me, her sulky face to a door mirror, stood, arms akimbo, feet (in new slippers with pussy-fur tops) wide apart, and through a forehanging lock tritely mugged at herself in the glass. From the corridor came the cooing voices of colored maids at work, and presently there was a mild attempt to open the door of our room. I had Lo go to the bathroom and take a much-needed soap shower. The bed was a frightful mess with overtones of potato chips. She tried on a two-piece navy wool, then a sleeveless blouse with a swirly clathrate skirt, but the first was too tight and the second too ample, and when I begged her to hurry up (the situation was beginning to frighten me), Lo viciously sent those nice presents of mine hurtling into a corner, and put on yesterday's dress. When she was ready at last, I gave her a lovely new purse of simulated calf (in which I had slipped quite a few pennies and two mint-bright dimes) and told her to buy herself a magazine in the lobby.

"I'll be down in a minute," I said. "And if I were you, my dear, I would not talk to strangers."

Except for my poor little gifts, there was not much to pack;

but I was forced to devote a dangerous amount of time (was she up to something downstairs?) to arranging the bed in such a way as to suggest the abandoned nest of a restless father and his tomboy daughter, instead of an ex-convict's saturnalia with a couple of fat old whores. Then I finished dressing and had the hoary bellboy come up for the bags.

Everything was fine. There, in the lobby, she sat, deep in an overstuffed blood-red armchair, deep in a lurid movie magazine. A fellow of my age in tweeds (the genre of the place had changed overnight to a spurious country-squire atmosphere) was staring at my Lolita over his dead cigar and stale newspaper. She wore her professional white socks and saddle oxfords, and that bright print frock with the square throat; a splash of jaded lamplight brought out the golden down on her warm brown limbs. There she sat, her legs carelessly high-crossed, and her pale eyes skimming along the lines with every now and then a blink. Bill's wife had worshiped him from afar long before they ever met: in fact, she used to secretly admire the famous young actor as he ate sundaes in Schwab's drug-store. Nothing could have been more childish than her snubbed nose, freckled face or the purplish spot on her naked neck where a fairytale vampire had feasted, or the unconscious movement of her tongue exploring a touch of rosy rash around her swollen lips; nothing could be more harmless than to read about Jill, an energetic starlet who made her own clothes and was a student of serious literature; nothing could be more innocent than the part in that glossy brown hair with that silky sheen on the temple; nothing could be more naïve— But what sickening envy the lecherous fellow whoever he was—come to think of it, he resembled a little my Swiss uncle Gustave, also a great admirer of *le découvert*—would have experienced had he known that every nerve in me was still anointed and ringed with the feel of her body—the body of some immortal daemon disguised as a female child.

Was pink pig Mr. Swoon absolutely sure my wife had not telephoned? He was. If she did, would he tell her we had gone on to Aunt Clare's place? He would, indeedie. I settled the bill and roused Lo from her chair. She read to the car. Still reading, she was driven to a so-called coffee shop a few blocks south. Oh, she ate all right. She even laid aside her magazine to eat, but a queer dullness had replaced her usual cheerfulness. I knew little Lo could be very nasty, so I braced myself and grinned, and waited for a squall. I was unbathed, unshaven, and had had no bowel movement. My nerves were a-jangle. I did not like the way my little mistress shrugged her shoulders and distended her nostrils when I attempted casual small talk. Had Phyllis been in the know before she joined her parents in Maine? I asked with a smile. "Look," said Lo making a weeping grimace, "let us get off the subject." I then tried—also unsuccessfully, no matter how I smacked my lips— to interest her in the road map. Our destination was, let me remind my patient reader whose meek temper Lo ought to have copied, the gay town of Lepingville, somewhere near a hypothetical hospital. That destination was in itself a perfectly arbitrary one (as, alas, so many were to be), and I shook in my shoes as I wondered how to keep the whole arrangement plausible, and what other plausible objectives to invent after we had taken in all the movies in Lepingville. More and more uncomfortable did Humbert feel. It was something quite special, that feeling: an oppressive, hideous constraint as if I were sitting with the small ghost of somebody I had just killed.

As she was in the act of getting back into the car, an expression of pain flitted across Lo's face. It flitted again, more meaningfully, as she settled down beside me. No doubt, she reproduced it that second time for my benefit. Foolishly, I asked her what was the matter. "Nothing, you brute," she replied. "You what?" I asked. She was silent. Leaving Briceland. Loquacious Lo was silent. Cold spiders of panic crawled down my back. This was an orphan. This was a lone child, an absolute waif, with whom a heavy-limbed, foul-smelling adult had had strenuous intercourse three times that very morning. Whether or not the realization of a lifelong dream had surpassed all expectation, it had, in a sense, overshot its mark— and plunged into a nightmare. I had been careless, stupid, and ignoble. And let me be quite frank: somewhere at the bottom of that dark turmoil I felt the writhing of desire again, so monstrous was my appetite for that miserable nymphet. Mingled with the pangs of guilt was the agonizing thought that her mood might prevent me from making love to her again as soon as I found a nice country road where to park in peace.

In other words, poor Humbert Humbert was dreadfully unhappy, and while steadily and inanely driving toward Lepingville, he kept racking his brains for some quip, under the
bright wing of which he might dare turn to his seat-mate. It
was she, however, who broke the silence:

"Oh, a squashed squirrel," she said. "What a shame."

"Yes, isn't it?" (eager, hopeful Hum).

"Let us stop at the next gas station," Lo continued. "I want
to go to the washroom."

"We shall stop wherever you want," I said. And then as a
lovely, lonely, supercilious grove (oaks, I thought; American
trees at that stage were beyond me) started to echo greenly
the rush of our car, a red and ferny road on our right turned
its head before slanting into the woodland, and I suggested
we might perhaps—

"Drive on," my Lo cried shrilly.

"Righto. Take it easy." (Down, poor beast, down.)

I glanced at her. Thank God, the child was smiling.

"You chump," she said, sweetly smiling at me. "You revolting creature. I was a daisy-fresh girl, and look what you've
done to me. I ought to call the police and tell them you raped
me. Oh, you dirty, dirty old man."

Was she just joking? An ominous hysterical note rang
through her silly words. Presently, making a sizzling sound
with her lips, she started complaining of pains, said she could
not sit, said I had torn something inside her. The sweat rolled
down my neck, and we almost ran over some little animal or
other that was crossing the road with tail erect, and again my
vile-tempered companion called me an ugly name. When we
stopped at the filling station, she scrambled out without a
word and was a long time away. Slowly, lovingly, an elderly
friend with a broken nose wiped my windshield—they do it
differently at every place, from chamois cloth to soapy brush,
this fellow used a pink sponge.

She appeared at last. "Look," she said in that neutral voice
that hurt me so, "give me some dimes and nickels. I want to
call mother in that hospital. What's the number."

"Get in," I said. "You can't call that number."

"Why?"

"Get in and slam the door."

She got in and slammed the door. The old garage man beamed at her. I swung onto the highway.

"Why can't I call my mother if I want to?"

"Because," I answered, "your mother is dead."

33

In the gay town of Lepingville I bought her four books of comics, a box of candy, a box of sanitary pads, two cokes, a manicure set, a travel clock with a luminous dial, a ring with a real topaz, a tennis racket, roller skates with white high shoes, field glasses, a portable radio set, chewing gum, a transparent raincoat, sunglasses, some more garments—swooners, shorts, all kinds of summer frocks. At the hotel we had separate rooms, but in the middle of the night she came sobbing into mine, and we made it up very gently. You see, she had absolutely nowhere else to go.

Part Two

IT WAS then that began our extensive travels all over the States. To any other type of tourist accommodation I soon grew to prefer the Functional Motel—clean, neat, safe nooks, ideal places for sleep, argument, reconciliation, insatiable illicit love. At first, in my dread of arousing suspicion, I would eagerly pay for both sections of one double unit, each containing a double bed. I wondered what type of foursome this arrangement was ever intended for, since only a pharisaic parody of privacy could be attained by means of the incomplete partition dividing the cabin or room into two communicating love nests. By and by, the very possibilities that such honest promiscuity suggested (two young couples merrily swapping mates or a child shamming sleep to earwitness primal sonorities) made me bolder, and every now and then I would take a bed-and-cot or twin-bed cabin, a prison cell of paradise, with yellow window shades pulled down to create a morning illusion of Venice and sunshine when actually it was Pennsylvania and rain.

We came to know—*nous connûmes*, to use a Flaubertian intonation—the stone cottages under enormous Chateaubriandesque trees, the brick unit, the adobe unit, the stucco court, on what the Tour Book of the Automobile Association describes as "shaded" or "spacious" or "landscaped" grounds. The log kind, finished in knotty pine, reminded Lo, by its golden-brown glaze, of fried-chicken bones. We held in contempt the plain whitewashed clapboard Kabins, with their faint sewerish smell or some other gloomy self-conscious stench and nothing to boast of (except "good beds"), and an unsmiling landlady always prepared to have her gift (". . . well, I could give you . . .") turned down.

Nous connûmes (this is royal fun) the would-be enticements of their repetitious names—all those Sunset Motels, U-Beam Cottages, Hillcrest Courts, Pine View Courts, Mountain View Courts, Skyline Courts, Park Plaza Courts, Green Acres, Mac's Courts. There was sometimes a special line in the write-

up, such as "Children welcome, pets allowed" (*You* are welcome, *you* are allowed). The baths were mostly tiled showers,
with an endless variety of spouting mechanisms, but with one
definitely non-Laodicean characteristic in common, a propen-
sity, while in use, to turn instantly beastly hot or blindingly
cold upon you, depending on whether your neighbor turned
on his cold or his hot to deprive you of a necessary complement in the shower you had so carefully blended. Some motels
had instructions pasted above the toilet (on whose tank the
towels were unhygienically heaped) asking guests not to throw
into its bowl garbage, beer cans, cartons, stillborn babies;
others had special notices under glass, such as Things to Do
(Riding: *You will often see riders coming down Main Street
on their way back from a romantic moonlight ride.* "Often at
3 A.M.," sneered unromantic Lo).

Nous connûmes the various types of motor court operators,
the reformed criminal, the retired teacher and the business
flop, among the males; and the motherly, pseudo-ladylike and
madamic variants among the females. And sometimes trains
would cry in the monstrously hot and humid night with heart-
rending and ominous plangency, mingling power and hysteria
in one desperate scream.

We avoided Tourist Homes, country cousins of Funeral
ones, old-fashioned, genteel and showerless, with elaborate
dressing tables in depressingly white-and-pink little bedrooms,
and photographs of the landlady's children in all their instars.
But I did surrender, now and then, to Lo's predilection for
"real" hotels. She would pick out in the book, while I petted
her in the parked car in the silence of a dusk-mellowed, mysterious side-road, some highly recommended lake lodge which
offered all sorts of things magnified by the flashlight she
moved over them, such as congenial company, between-meals
snacks, outdoor barbecues—but which in my mind conjured
up odious visions of stinking high school boys in sweatshirts
and an ember-red cheek pressing against hers, while poor Dr.
Humbert, embracing nothing but two masculine knees,
would cold-humor his piles on the damp turf. Most tempting
to her, too, were those "Colonial" Inns, which apart from
"gracious atmosphere" and picture windows, promised "unlimited quantities of M-m-m food." Treasured recollections

of my father's palatial hotel sometimes led me to seek for its like in the strange country we traveled through. I was soon discouraged; but Lo kept following the scent of rich food ads, while I derived a not exclusively economic kick from such roadside signs as TIMBER HOTEL, *Children under 14 Free.* On the other hand, I shudder when recalling that *soi-disant* "high-class" resort in a Midwestern state, which advertised "raid-the-icebox" midnight snacks and, intrigued by my accent, wanted to know my dead wife's and dead mother's maiden names. A two-days' stay there cost me a hundred and twenty-four dollars! And do you remember, Miranda, that other "ultrasmart" robbers' den with complimentary morning coffee and circulating ice water, and no children under sixteen (no Lolitas, of course)?

Immediately upon arrival at one of the plainer motor courts which became our habitual haunts, she would set the electric fan a-whirr, or induce me to drop a quarter into the radio, or she would read all the signs and inquire with a whine why she could not go riding up some advertised trail or swimming in that local pool of warm mineral water. Most often, in the slouching, bored way she cultivated, Lo would fall prostrate and abominably desirable into a red springchair or a green chaise longue, or a steamer chair of striped canvas with foot-rest and canopy, or a sling chair, or any other lawn chair under a garden umbrella on the patio, and it would take hours of blandishments, threats and promises to make her lend me for a few seconds her brown limbs in the seclusion of the five-dollar room before undertaking anything she might prefer to my poor joy.

A combination of naïveté and deception, of charm and vulgarity, of blue sulks and rosy mirth, Lolita, when she chose, could be a most exasperating brat. I was not really quite prepared for her fits of disorganized boredom, intense and vehement griping, her sprawling, droopy, dopey-eyed style, and what is called goofing off—a kind of diffused clowning which she thought was tough in a boyish hoodlum way. Mentally, I found her to be a disgustingly conventional little girl. Sweet hot jazz, square dancing, gooey fudge sundaes, musicals, movie magazines and so forth—these were the obvious items in her list of beloved things. The Lord knows how many nickels I fed to the gorgeous music boxes that came with every meal we had! I still hear the nasal voices of those invisibles serenading her, people with names like Sammy and Jo and Eddy and Tony and Peggy and Guy and Patti and Rex, and sentimental song hits, all of them as similar to my ear as her various candies were to my palate. She believed, with a kind of celestial trust, any advertisement or advice that appeared in *Movie Love* or *Screen Land*—Starasil Starves Pimples, or "You better watch out if you're wearing your shirttails outside your jeans, gals, because Jill says you shouldn't." If a roadside sign said: VISIT OUR GIFT SHOP—we *had* to visit it, *had* to buy its Indian curios, dolls, copper jewelry, cactus candy. The words "novelties and souvenirs" simply entranced her by their trochaic lilt. If some café sign proclaimed Icecold Drinks, she was automatically stirred, although all drinks everywhere were ice-cold. She it was to whom ads were dedicated: the ideal consumer, the subject and object of every foul poster. And she attempted—unsuccessfully—to patronize only those restaurants where the holy spirit of Huncan Dines had descended upon the cute paper napkins and cottage-cheese-crested salads.

In those days, neither she nor I had thought up yet the system of monetary bribes which was to work such havoc with my nerves and her morals somewhat later. I relied on three other methods to keep my pubescent concubine in submission and passable temper. A few years before, she had spent a rainy summer under Miss Phalen's bleary eye in a dilapidated Appalachian farmhouse that had belonged to some gnarled Haze or other in the dead past. It still stood among its rank acres of golden rod on the edge of a flowerless forest, at the end of a permanently muddy road, twenty miles from the nearest hamlet. Lo recalled that scarecrow of a house, the solitude, the soggy old pastures, the wind, the bloated wilderness, with an energy of disgust that distorted her mouth and fattened her half-revealed tongue. And it was there that I warned her she would dwell with me in exile for months and years if need be, studying under me French and Latin, unless her "present attitude" changed. Charlotte, I began to understand you!

A simple child, Lo would scream no! and frantically clutch at my driving hand whenever I put a stop to her tornadoes of temper by turning in the middle of a highway with the implication that I was about to take her straight to that dark and dismal abode. The farther, however, we traveled away from it west, the less tangible that menace became, and I had to adopt other methods of persuasion.

Among these, the reformatory threat is the one I recall with the deepest moan of shame. From the very beginning of our concourse, I was clever enough to realize that I must secure her complete co-operation in keeping our relations secret, that it should become a second nature with her, no matter what grudge she might bear me, no matter what other pleasures she might seek.

"Come and kiss your old man," I would say, "and drop that moody nonsense. In former times, when I was still your dream male [the reader will notice what pains I took to speak Lo's tongue], you swooned to records of the number one throb-and-sob idol of your coevals [Lo: "Of my what? Speak English"]. That idol of your pals sounded, you thought, like friend Humbert. But now, I am just your *old man*, a dream dad protecting his dream daughter.

"My *chère Dolorès*! I want to protect you, dear, from all the horrors that happen to little girls in coal sheds and alley ways, and, alas, *comme vous le savez trop bien, ma gentille*, in the blueberry woods during the bluest of summers. Through thick and thin I will still stay your guardian, and if you are good, I hope a court may legalize that guardianship before long. Let us, however, forget, Dolores Haze, so-called legal terminology, terminology that accepts as rational the term 'lewd and lascivious cohabitation.' I am not a criminal sexual psychopath taking indecent liberties with a child. The rapist was Charlie Holmes; I am the therapist—a matter of nice spacing in the way of distinction. I am your daddum, Lo. Look, I've a learned book here about young girls. Look, darling, what it says. I quote: the normal girl—normal, mark you—the normal girl is usually extremely anxious to please her father. She feels in him the forerunner of the desired elusive male ('elusive' is good, by Polonius!). The wise mother (and your poor mother would have been wise, had she lived) will encourage a companionship between father and daughter, realizing—excuse the corny style—that the girl forms her ideals of romance and of men from her association with her father. Now, what association does this cheery book mean—and recommend? I quote again: Among Sicilians sexual relations between a father and his daughter are accepted as a matter of course, and the girl who participates in such relationship is not looked upon with disapproval by the society of which she is part. I'm a great admirer of Sicilians, fine athletes, fine musicians, fine upright people, Lo, and great lovers. But let's not digress. Only the other day we read in the newspapers some bunkum about a middle-aged morals offender who pleaded guilty to the violation of the Mann Act and to transporting a nine-year-old girl across state lines for immoral purposes, whatever these are. Dolores darling! You are not nine but almost thirteen, and I would not advise you to consider yourself my cross-country slave, and I deplore the Mann Act as lending itself to a dreadful pun, the revenge that the Gods of Semantics take against tight-zippered Philistines. I am your father, and I *am* speaking English, and I love you.

"Finally, let us see what happens if you, a minor, accused of having impaired the morals of an adult in a respectable inn, what happens if you complain to the police of my having kidnaped and raped you? Let us suppose they believe you. A minor female, who allows a person over twenty-one to know her carnally, involves her victim into statutory rape, or second-degree sodomy, depending on the technique; and the maximum penalty is ten years. So I go to jail. Okay. I go to jail. But what happens to you, my orphan? Well, you are luckier. You become the ward of the Department of Public Welfare—which I am afraid sounds a little bleak. A nice grim matron of the Miss Phalen type, but more rigid and not a drinking woman, will take away your lipstick and fancy clothes. No more gadding about! I don't know if you have ever heard of the laws relating to dependent, neglected, incorrigible and delinquent children. While I stand gripping the bars, you, happy neglected child, will be given a choice of various dwelling places, all more or less the same, the correctional school, the reformatory, the juvenile detention home, or one of those admirable girls' protectories where you knit things, and sing hymns, and have rancid pancakes on Sundays. You will go there, Lolita—*my* Lolita, *this* Lolita will leave her Catullus and go there, as the wayward girl you are. In plainer words, if we two are found out, you will be analyzed and institutionalized, my pet, *c'est tout*. You will dwell, my Lolita will dwell (come here, my brown flower) with thirty-nine other dopes in a dirty dormitory (no, allow me, please) under the supervision of hideous matrons. This is the situation, this is the choice. Don't you think that under the circumstances Dolores Haze had better stick to her old man?''

By rubbing all this in, I succeeded in terrorizing Lo, who despite a certain brash alertness of manner and spurts of wit was not as intelligent a child as her I.Q. might suggest. But if I managed to establish that background of shared secrecy and shared guilt, I was much less successful in keeping her in good humor. Every morning during our yearlong travels I had to devise some expectation, some special point in space and time for her to look forward to, for her to survive till bedtime. Otherwise, deprived of a shaping and sustaining purpose, the skeleton of her day sagged and collapsed. The object in view might be anything—a lighthouse in Virginia, a natural cave in Arkansas converted to a café, a collection of guns and violins somewhere in Oklahoma, a replica of the Grotto of Lourdes in Louisiana, shabby photographs of the bonanza mining period in the local museum of a Rocky Mountains resort, anything whatsoever—but it had to be there, in front of us, like a fixed star, although as likely as not Lo would feign gagging as soon as we got to it.

By putting the geography of the United States into motion, I did my best for hours on end to give her the impression of "going places," of rolling on to some definite destination, to some unusual delight. I have never seen such smooth amiable roads as those that now radiated before us, across the crazy quilt of forty-eight states. Voraciously we consumed those long highways, in rapt silence we glided over their glossy black dance floors. Not only had Lo no eye for scenery but she furiously resented my calling her attention to this or that enchanting detail of landscape; which I myself learned to discern only after being exposed for quite a time to the delicate beauty ever present in the margin of our undeserving journey. By a paradox of pictorial thought, the average lowland North-American countryside had at first seemed to me something I accepted with a shock of amused recognition because of those painted oilcloths which were imported from America in the old days to be hung above washstands in Central-European nurseries, and which fascinated a drowsy child at bed time with the rustic green views they depicted—opaque curly trees, a barn, cattle, a brook, the dull white of vague orchards in bloom, and perhaps a stone fence or hills of greenish gouache. But gradually the models of those elementary rusticities became stranger and stranger to the eye, the nearer I came to know them. Beyond the tilled plain, beyond the toy roofs, there would be a slow suffusion of inutile loveliness, a low sun in a platinum haze with a warm, peeled-peach tinge pervading the upper edge of a two-dimensional, dove-gray cloud fusing with the distant amorous mist. There might be a line of spaced trees silhouetted against the horizon, and hot still noons above a wilderness of clover, and Claude Lorrain clouds inscribed remotely into misty azure with only their cumulus part conspicuous against the neutral swoon of the background. Or again, it might be a stern El Greco horizon, pregnant with inky rain, and a passing glimpse of some mummy-necked farmer, and all around alternating strips of quick-silverish water and harsh green corn, the whole arrangement opening like a fan, somewhere in Kansas.

Now and then, in the vastness of those plains, huge trees would advance toward us to cluster self-consciously by the roadside and provide a bit of humanitarian shade above a picnic table, with sun flecks, flattened paper cups, samaras and discarded ice-cream sticks littering the brown ground. A great user of roadside facilities, my unfastidious Lo would be charmed by toilet signs—Guys-Gals, John-Jane, Jack-Jill and even Buck's-Doe's; while lost in an artist's dream, I would stare at the honest brightness of the gasoline paraphernalia against the splendid green of oaks, or at a distant hill scrambling out—scarred but still untamed—from the wilderness of agriculture that was trying to swallow it.

At night, tall trucks studded with colored lights, like dreadful giant Christmas trees, loomed in the darkness and thundered by the belated little sedan. And again next day a thinly populated sky, losing its blue to the heat, would melt overhead, and Lo would clamor for a drink, and her cheeks would hollow vigorously over the straw, and the car inside would be a furnace when we got in again, and the road shimmered ahead, with a remote car changing its shape mirage-like in the surface glare, and seeming to hang for a moment, old-fashionedly square and high, in the hot haze. And as we pushed westward, patches of what the garage-man called "sage brush" appeared, and then the mysterious outlines of table-like hills, and then red bluffs ink-blotted with junipers, and then a mountain range, dun grading into blue, and blue into dream, and the desert would meet us with a steady gale, dust, gray thorn bushes, and hideous bits of tissue paper mimicking pale flowers among the prickles of wind-tortured withered stalks all along the highway; in the middle of which there sometimes stood simple cows, immobilized in a position (tail left, white eyelashes right) cutting across all human rules of traffic.

My lawyer has suggested I give a clear, frank account of the itinerary we followed, and I suppose I have reached here a point where I cannot avoid that chore. Roughly, during that mad year (August 1947 to August 1948), our route began with a series of wiggles and whorls in New England, then meandered south, up and down, east and west; dipped deep into *ce qu'on appelle* Dixieland, avoided Florida because the Farlows were there, veered west, zigzagged through corn belts and cotton belts (this is not *too* clear I am afraid, Clarence, but I did not keep any notes, and have at my disposal only an atrociously crippled tour book in three volumes, almost a symbol of my torn and tattered past, in which to check these recollections); crossed and recrossed the Rockies, straggled through southern deserts where we wintered; reached the Pacific, turned north through the pale lilac fluff of flowering shrubs along forest roads; almost reached the Canadian border; and proceeded east, across good lands and bad lands, back to agriculture on a grand scale, avoiding, despite little Lo's strident remonstrations, little Lo's birthplace, in a corn, coal and hog producing area; and finally returned to the fold of the East, petering out in the college town of Beardsley.

2

Now, in perusing what follows, the reader should bear in mind not only the general circuit as adumbrated above, with its many sidetrips and tourist traps, secondary circles and skittish deviations, but also the fact that far from being an indolent *partie de plaisir*, our tour was a hard, twisted, teleological growth, whose sole *raison d'être* (these French clichés are symptomatic) was to keep my companion in passable humor from kiss to kiss.

Thumbing through that battered tour book, I dimly evoke that Magnolia Garden in a southern state which cost me four bucks and which, according to the ad in the book, you must visit for three reasons: because John Galsworthy (a stone-dead writer of sorts) acclaimed it as the world's fairest garden; because in 1900 Baedeker's Guide had marked it with a star; and finally, because . . . O, Reader, My Reader, guess! . . . because children (and by Jingo was not my Lolita a child!) will "walk starry-eyed and reverently through this foretaste of Heaven, drinking in beauty that can influence a life." "Not mine," said grim Lo, and settled down on a bench with the fillings of two Sunday papers in her lovely lap.

We passed and re-passed through the whole gamut of American roadside restaurants, from the lowly Eat with its deer head (dark trace of long tear at inner canthus), "humorous" picture post cards of the posterior "Kurort" type, impaled guest checks, life savers, sunglasses, adman visions of celestial sundaes, one half of a chocolate cake under glass, and several horribly experienced flies zigzagging over the sticky sugar-pour on the ignoble counter; and all the way to the expensive place with the subdued lights, preposterously poor table linen, inept waiters (ex-convicts or college boys), the roan back of a screen actress, the sable eyebrows of her male of the moment, and an orchestra of zoot-suiters with trumpets.

We inspected the world's largest stalagmite in a cave where three southeastern states have a family reunion; admission by age; adults one dollar, pubescents sixty cents. A granite obelisk commemorating the Battle of Blue Licks, with old bones and Indian pottery in the museum nearby, Lo a dime, very reasonable. The present log cabin boldly simulating the past log cabin where Lincoln was born. A boulder, with a plaque, in memory of the author of "Trees" (by now we are in Poplar Cove, N.C., reached by what my kind, tolerant, usually so restrained tour book angrily calls "a very narrow road, poorly maintained," to which, though no Kilmerite, I subscribe). From a hired motorboat operated by an elderly, but still repulsively handsome White Russian, a baron they said (Lo's palms were damp, the little fool), who had known in California good old Maximovich and Valeria, we could distinguish the inaccessible "millionaires' colony" on an island, somewhere off the Georgia coast. We inspected further: a collection of European hotel picture post cards in a museum devoted to hobbies at a Mississippi resort, where with a hot wave of pride I discovered a colored photo of my father's Mirana, its striped awnings, its flag flying above the retouched palm trees. "So what?" said Lo, squinting at the bronzed owner of an expensive car who had followed us into the Hobby House. Relics of the cotton era. A forest in Arkansas and, on her brown shoulder, a raised purple-pink swelling (the work of some gnat) which I eased of its beautiful transparent poison between my long thumbnails and then sucked till I was gorged on her spicy blood. Bourbon Street (in a town named New Orleans) whose sidewalks, said the tour book, "may [I liked the "may"] feature entertainment by pickaninnies who will [I liked the "will" even better] tap-dance for pennies" (what fun), while "its numerous small and intimate night clubs are thronged with visitors" (naughty). Collections of frontier lore. Ante-bellum homes with iron-trellis balconies and hand-worked stairs, the kind down which movie ladies with sun-kissed shoulders run in rich Technicolor, holding up the fronts of their flounced skirts with both little hands in that special way, and the devoted Negress shaking her head on the upper landing. The Menninger Foundation, a psychiatric clinic, just for the heck of it. A patch of beautifully eroded clay; and yucca blossoms, so pure, so waxy, but lousy with creeping white flies. Independence, Missouri, the starting point of the Old Oregon Trail; and Abilene, Kansas, the home of the Wild Bill Something Rodeo. Distant mountains. Near mountains. More mountains; bluish beauties never attainable, or ever turning into inhabited hill after hill; south-eastern ranges, altitudinal failures as alps go; heart and sky-piercing snow-veined gray colossi of stone, relentless peaks appearing from nowhere at a turn of the highway; timbered enormities, with a system of neatly overlapping dark firs, interrupted in places by pale puffs of aspen; pink and lilac formations, Pharaonic, phallic, "too prehistoric for words" (blasé Lo); buttes of black lava; early spring mountains with young-elephant lanugo along their spines; end-of-the-summer mountains, all hunched up, their heavy Egyptian limbs folded under folds of tawny moth-eaten plush; oatmeal hills, flecked with green round oaks; a last rufous mountain with a rich rug of lucerne at its foot.

Moreover, we inspected: Little Iceberg Lake, somewhere in Colorado, and the snow banks, and the cushionets of tiny alpine flowers, and more snow; down which Lo in red-peaked cap tried to slide, and squealed, and was snowballed by some youngsters, and retaliated in kind *comme on dit*. Skeletons of burned aspens, patches of spired blue flowers. The various items of a scenic drive. Hundreds of scenic drives, thousands of Bear Creeks, Soda Springs, Painted Canyons. Texas, a drought-struck plain. Crystal Chamber in the longest cave in the world, children under 12 free, Lo a young captive. A collection of a local lady's homemade sculptures, closed on a miserable Monday morning, dust, wind, witherland. Conception Park, in a town on the Mexican border which I dared not cross. There and elsewhere, hundreds of gray hummingbirds in the dusk, probing the throats of dim flowers. Shakespeare, a ghost town in New Mexico, where bad man Russian Bill was colorfully hanged seventy years ago. Fish hatcheries. Cliff dwellings. The mummy of a child (Florentine Bea's Indian contemporary). Our twentieth Hell's Canyon. Our fiftieth Gateway to something or other *fide* that tour book, the cover of which had been lost by that time. A tick in my groin. Always the same three old men, in hats and suspenders, idling away the summer afternoon under the trees near the public fountain. A hazy blue view beyond railings on a mountain pass, and the backs of a family enjoying it (with Lo, in a hot, happy, wild, intense, hopeful, hopeless whisper—"Look, the McCrystals, please, let's talk to them, please"—let's talk to them, reader!—"please! I'll do anything you want, oh, please . . ."). Indian ceremonial dances, strictly commercial. ART: American Refrigerator Transit Company. Obvious Arizona, pueblo dwellings, aboriginal pictographs, a dinosaur track in a desert canyon, printed there thirty million years ago, when I was a child. A lanky, six-foot, pale boy with an active Adam's apple, ogling Lo and her orange-brown bare midriff, which I kissed five minutes later, Jack. Winter in the desert, spring in the foothills, almonds in bloom. Reno, a dreary town in Nevada, with a nightlife said to be "cosmopolitan and mature." A winery in California, with a church built in the shape of a wine barrel. Death Valley. Scotty's Castle. Works of Art collected by one Rogers over a period of years. The ugly villas of handsome actresses. R. L. Stevenson's footprint on an extinct volcano. Mission Dolores: good title for book. Surf-carved sandstone festoons. A man having a lavish epileptic fit on the ground in Russian Gulch State Park. Blue, blue Crater Lake. A fish hatchery in Idaho and the State Penitentiary. Somber Yellowstone Park and its colored hot springs, baby geysers, rainbows of bubbling mud—symbols of my passion. A herd of antelopes in a wildlife refuge. Our hundredth cavern, adults one dollar, Lolita fifty cents. A chateau built by a French marquess in N.D. The Corn Palace in S.D.; and the huge heads of presidents carved in towering granite. The Bearded Woman read our jingle and now she is no longer single. A zoo in Indiana where a large troop of monkeys lived on concrete replica of Christopher Columbus' flagship. Billions of dead, or halfdead, fish-smelling May flies in every window of every eating place all along a dreary sandy shore. Fat gulls on big stones as seen from the ferry *City of Cheboygan*, whose brown woolly smoke arched and dipped over the green shadow it cast on the aquamarine lake. A motel whose ventilator pipe passed under the city sewer. Lincoln's home, largely spurious, with parlor books and period furniture that most visitors reverently accepted as personal belongings.

We had rows, minor and major. The biggest ones we had took place: at Lacework Cabins, Virginia; on Park Avenue, Little Rock, near a school; on Milner Pass, 10,759 feet high, in Colorado; at the corner of Seventh Street and Central Avenue in Phoenix, Arizona; on Third Street, Los Angeles, because the tickets to some studio or other were sold out; at a motel called Poplar Shade in Utah, where six pubescent trees were scarcely taller than my Lolita, and where she asked, *à propos de rien*, how long did I think we were going to live in stuffy cabins, doing filthy things together and never behaving like ordinary people? On N. Broadway, Burns, Oregon, corner of W. Washington, facing Safeway, a grocery. In some little town in the Sun Valley of Idaho, before a brick hotel, pale and flushed bricks nicely mixed, with, opposite, a poplar playing its liquid shadows all over the local Honor Roll. In a sage brush wilderness, between Pinedale and Farson. Somewhere in Nebraska, on Main Street, near the First National Bank, established 1889, with a view of a railway crossing in the vista of the street, and beyond that the white organ pipes of a multiple silo. And on McEwen St., corner of Wheaton Ave., in a Michigan town bearing his first name.

We came to know the curious roadside species, Hitchhiking Man, *Homo pollex* of science, with all its many sub-species and forms: the modest soldier, spic and span, quietly waiting, quietly conscious of khaki's viatic appeal; the schoolboy wishing to go two blocks; the killer wishing to go two thousand miles; the mysterious, nervous, elderly gent, with brand-new suitcase and clipped mustache; a trio of optimistic Mexicans; the college student displaying the grime of vacational outdoor work as proudly as the name of the famous college arching across the front of his sweatshirt; the desperate lady whose battery has just died on her; the clean-cut, glossy-haired, shifty-eyed, white-faced young beasts in loud shirts and coats, vigorously, almost priapically thrusting out tense thumbs to tempt lone women or sad-sack salesmen with fancy cravings.

"Let's take him," Lo would often plead, rubbing her knees together in a way she had, as some particularly disgusting *pollex*, some man of my age and shoulder breadth, with the *face à claques* of an unemployed actor, walked backwards, practically in the path of our car.

Oh, I had to keep a very sharp eye on Lo, little limp Lo! Owing perhaps to constant amorous exercise, she radiated, despite her very childish appearance, some special languorous glow which threw garage fellows, hotel pages, vacationists, goons in luxurious cars, maroon morons near blued pools, into fits of concupiscence which might have tickled my pride, had it not incensed my jealousy. For little Lo was aware of that glow of hers, and I would often catch her *coulant un regard* in the direction of some amiable male, some grease monkey, with a sinewy golden-brown forearm and watch-braceleted wrist, and hardly had I turned my back to go and buy this very Lo a lollipop, than I would hear her and the fair mechanic burst into a perfect love song of wisecracks.

When, during our longer stops, I would relax after a particularly violent morning in bed, and out of the goodness of my lulled heart allow her—indulgent Hum!—to visit the rose garden or children's library across the street with a motor court neighbor's plain little Mary and Mary's eight-year-old brother, Lo would come back an hour late, with barefoot Mary trailing far behind, and the little boy metamorphosed into two gangling, golden-haired high school uglies, all muscles and gonorrhea. The reader may well imagine what I answered my pet when—rather uncertainly, I admit—she would ask me if she could go with Carl and Al here to the roller-skating rink.

I remember the first time, a dusty windy afternoon, I did let her go to one such rink. Cruelly she said it would be no fun if I accompanied her, since that time of day was reserved for teenagers. We wrangled out a compromise: I remained in the car, among other (empty) cars with their noses to the canvas-topped open-air rink, where some fifty young people, many in pairs, were endlessly rolling round and round to mechanical music, and the wind silvered the trees. Dolly wore blue jeans and white high shoes, as most of the other girls did. I kept counting the revolutions of the rolling crowd—and suddenly she was missing. When she rolled past again, she was together with three hoodlums whom I had heard analyze a moment before the girl skaters from the outside—and jeer at a lovely leggy young thing who had arrived clad in red shorts instead of those jeans or slacks.

At inspection stations on highways entering Arizona or California, a policeman's cousin would peer with such intensity at us that my poor heart wobbled. "Any honey?" he would inquire, and every time my sweet fool giggled. I still have, vibrating all along my optic nerve, visions of Lo on horseback, a link in the chain of a guided trip along a bridle trail: Lo bobbing at a walking pace, with an old woman rider in front and a lecherous red-necked dude-rancher behind; and I behind him, hating his fat flowery-shirted back even more fervently than a motorist does a slow truck on a mountain road. Or else, at a ski lodge, I would see her floating away from me, celestial and solitary, in an ethereal chairlift, up and up, to a glittering summit where laughing athletes stripped to the waist were waiting for her, for her.

In whatever town we stopped I would inquire, in my polite European way, anent the whereabouts of natatoriums, museums, local schools, the number of children in the nearest school and so forth; and at school bus time, smiling and twitching a little (I discovered this *tic nerveux* because cruel Lo was the first to mimic it), I would park at a strategic point, with my vagrant schoolgirl beside me in the car, to watch the children leave school—always a pretty sight. This sort of thing soon began to bore my so easily bored Lolita, and, having a childish lack of sympathy for other people's whims, she would insult me and my desire to have her caress me while blue-eyed little brunettes in blue shorts, copperheads in green boleros, and blurred boyish blondes in faded slacks passed by in the sun.

As a sort of compromise, I freely advocated whenever and wherever possible the use of swimming pools with other girl-children. She adored brilliant water and was a remarkably smart diver. Comfortably robed, I would settle down in the rich post-meridian shade after my own demure dip, and there I would sit, with a dummy book or a bag of bonbons, or both, or nothing but my tingling glands, and watch her gambol, rubber-capped, bepearled, smoothly tanned, as glad as an ad, in her trim-fitted satin pants and shirred bra. Pubescent sweetheart! How smugly would I marvel that she was mine, mine, mine, and revise the recent matitudinal swoon to the moan of the mourning doves, and devise the late afternoon one, and slitting my sun-speared eyes, compare Lolita to whatever other nymphets parsimonious chance collected around her for my anthological delectation and judgment; and today, putting my hand on my ailing heart, I really do not think that any of them ever surpassed her in desirability, or if they did, it was so two or three times at the most, in a certain light, with certain perfumes blended in the air—once in the hopeless case of a pale Spanish child, the daughter of a heavy-jawed nobleman, and another time—*mais je divague.*

Naturally, I had to be always wary, fully realizing, in my lucid jealousy, the danger of those dazzling romps. I had only to turn away for a moment—to walk, say, a few steps in order to see if our cabin was at last ready after the morning change of linen—and Lo and Behold, upon returning, I would find the former, *les yeux perdus,* dipping and kicking her long-toed feet in the water on the stone edge of which she lolled, while, on either side of her, there crouched a *brun adolescent* whom her russet beauty and the quicksilver in the baby folds of her stomach were sure to cause to *se tordre*—oh Baudelaire!—in recurrent dreams for months to come.

I tried to teach her to play tennis so we might have more amusements in common; but although I had been a good player in my prime, I proved to be hopeless as a teacher; and so, in California, I got her to take a number of very expensive lessons with a famous coach, a husky, wrinkled old-timer, with a harem of ball boys; he looked an awful wreck off the court, but now and then, when, in the course of a lesson, to keep up the exchange, he would put out as it were an exquisite spring blossom of a stroke and twang the ball back to his pupil, that divine delicacy of absolute power made me recall that, thirty years before, I had seen *him* in Cannes demolish the great Gobbert! Until she began taking those lessons, I thought she would never learn the game. On this or that hotel court I would drill Lo, and try to relive the days when in a hot gale, a daze of dust, and queer lassitude, I fed ball after ball to gay, innocent, elegant Annabel (gleam of bracelet, pleated white skirt, black velvet hair band). With every word of persistent advice I would only augment Lo's sullen fury. To our games, oddly enough, she preferred—at least, before we reached California—formless pat ball approximations—more ball hunting than actual play—with a wispy, weak, wonderfully pretty in an *ange gauche* way coeval. A helpful spectator, I would go up to that other child, and inhale her faint musky fragrance as I touched her forearm and held her knobby wrist, and push this way or that her cool thigh to show her the back-hand stance. In the meantime, Lo, bending forward, would let her sunny-brown curls hang forward as she stuck her racket, like a cripple's stick, into the ground and emitted a tremendous ugh of disgust at my intrusion. I would leave them to their game and look on, comparing their bodies in motion, a silk scarf round my throat; this was in south Arizona, I think—and the days had a lazy lining of warmth, and awkward Lo would slash at the ball and miss it, and curse, and send a simulacrum of a serve into the net, and show the wet glistening young down of her armpit as she brandished her racket in despair, and her even more insipid partner would dutifully rush out after every ball, and retrieve none; but both were enjoying themselves beautifully, and in clear ringing tones kept the exact score of their ineptitudes all the time.

One day, I remember, I offered to bring them cold drinks from the hotel, and went up the gravel path, and came back with two tall glasses of pineapple juice, soda and ice; and then a sudden void within my chest made me stop as I saw that the tennis court was deserted. I stooped to set down the glasses on a bench and for some reason, with a kind of icy vividness, saw Charlotte's face in death, and I glanced around, and noticed Lo in white shorts receding through the speckled shadow of a garden path in the company of a tall man who carried two tennis rackets. I sprang after them, but as I was crashing through the shrubbery, I saw, in an alternate vision, as if life's course constantly branched, Lo, in slacks, and her companion, in shorts, trudging up and down a small weedy area, and beating bushes with their rackets in listless search for their last lost ball.

I itemize these sunny nothings mainly to prove to my judges that I did everything in my power to give my Lolita a really good time. How charming it was to see her, a child herself, showing another child some of her few accomplishments, such as for example a special way of jumping rope. With her right hand holding her left arm behind her untanned back, the lesser nymphet, a diaphanous darling, would be all eyes, as the pavonine sun was all eyes on the gravel under the flowering trees, while in the midst of that oculate paradise, my freckled and raffish lass skipped, repeating the movements of so many others I had gloated over on the sun-shot, watered, damp-smelling sidewalks and ramparts of ancient Europe. Presently, she would hand the rope back to her little Spanish friend, and watch in her turn the repeated lesson, and brush away the hair from her brow, and fold her arms, and step on one toe with the other, or drop her hands loosely upon her still unflared hips, and I would satisfy myself that the damned staff had at last finished cleaning up our cottage; whereupon, flashing a smile to the shy, dark-haired page girl of my princess and thrusting my fatherly fingers deep into Lo's hair from behind, and then gently but firmly clasping them around the nape of her neck, I would lead my reluctant pet to our small home for a quick connection before dinner.

"Whose cat has scratched poor you?" a full-blown fleshy handsome woman of the repulsive type to which I was particularly attractive might ask me at the "lodge," during a table d'hôte dinner followed by dancing promised to Lo. This was one of the reasons why I tried to keep as far away from people as possible, while Lo, on the other hand, would do her utmost to draw as many potential witnesses into her orbit as she could.

She would be, figuratively speaking, wagging her tiny tail, her whole behind in fact as little bitches do—while some grinning stranger accosted us and began a bright conversation with a comparative study of license plates. "Long way from home!" Inquisitive parents, in order to pump Lo about me, would suggest her going to a movie with their children. We had some close shaves. The waterfall nuisance pursued me of course in all our caravansaries. But I never realized how wafery their wall substance was until one evening, after I had loved too loudly, a neighbor's masculine cough filled the pause as clearly as mine would have done; and next morning as I was having breakfast at the milk bar (Lo was a late sleeper, and I liked to bring her a pot of hot coffee in bed), my neighbor of the eve, an elderly fool wearing plain glasses on his long virtuous nose and a convention badge on his lapel, somehow managed to rig up a conversation with me, in the course of which he inquired, if my missus was like his missus a rather reluctant get-upper when not on the farm; and had not the hideous danger I was skirting almost suffocated me, I might have enjoyed the odd look of surprise on his thin-lipped weather-beaten face when I drily answered, as I slithered off my stool, that I was thank God a widower.

How sweet it was to bring that coffee to her, and then deny it until she had done her morning duty. And I was such a thoughtful friend, such a passionate father, such a good pediatrician, attending to all the wants of my little auburn brunette's body! My only grudge against nature was that I could not turn my Lolita inside out and apply voracious lips to her young matrix, her unknown heart, her nacreous liver, the sea-grapes of her lungs, her comely twin kidneys. On especially tropical afternoons, in the sticky closeness of the siesta, I liked the cool feel of armchair leather against my massive nakedness as I held her in my lap. There she would be, a typical kid picking her nose while engrossed in the lighter sections of a newspaper, as indifferent to my ecstasy as if it were something she had sat upon, a shoe, a doll, the handle of a tennis racket, and was too indolent to remove. Her eyes would follow the adventures of her favorite strip characters: there was one well-drawn sloppy bobby-soxer, with high cheekbones and angular gestures, that I was not above enjoying myself; she studied the photographic results of head-on collisions; she never doubted the reality of place, time and circumstance alleged to match the publicity pictures of naked-thighed beauties; and she was curiously fascinated by the photographs of local brides, some in full wedding apparel, holding bouquets and wearing glasses.

A fly would settle and walk in the vicinity of her navel or explore her tender pale areolas. She tried to catch it in her fist (Charlotte's method) and then would turn to the column Let's Explore Your Mind.

"Let's explore your mind. Would sex crimes be reduced if children obeyed a few don'ts? Don't play around public toilets. Don't take candy or rides from strangers. If picked up, mark down the license of the car."

". . . and the brand of the candy," I volunteered.

She went on, her cheek (recedent) against mine (pursuant); and this was a good day, mark, O reader!

"If you don't have a pencil, but are old enough to read—"

"We," I quip-quoted, "medieval mariners, have placed in this bottle—"

"If," she repeated, "you don't have a pencil, but are old enough to read and write—this is what the guy means, isn't it, you dope—scratch the number somehow on the roadside."

"With your little claws, Lolita.' "

3

She had entered my world, umber and black Humberland, with rash curiosity; she surveyed it with a shrug of amused distaste; and it seemed to me now that she was ready to turn away from it with something akin to plain repulsion. Never did she vibrate under my touch, and a strident "what d'you think you are doing?" was all I got for my pains. To the wonderland I had to offer, my fool preferred the corniest movies, the most cloying fudge. To think that between a Hamburger and a Humburger, she would—invariably, with icy precision— plump for the former. There is nothing more atrociously cruel than an adored child. Did I mention the name of that milk bar I visited a moment ago? It was, of all things, The Frigid Queen. Smiling a little sadly, I dubbed her My Frigid Princess. She did not see the wistful joke.

Oh, do not scowl at me, reader, I do not intend to convey the impression that I did not manage to be happy. Reader must understand that in the possession and thralldom of a nymphet the enchanted traveler stands, as it were, *beyond happiness.* For there is no other bliss on earth comparable to that of fondling a nymphet. It is *hors concours*, that bliss, it belongs to another class, another plane of sensitivity. Despite our tiffs, despite her nastiness, despite all the fuss and faces she made, and the vulgarity, and the danger, and the horrible hopelessness of it all, I still dwelled deep in my elected paradise—a paradise whose skies were the color of hell-flames—but still a paradise.

The able psychiatrist who studies my case—and whom by now Dr. Humbert has plunged, I trust, into a state of leporine fascination—is no doubt anxious to have me take my Lolita to the seaside and have me find there, at last, the "gratification" of a lifetime urge, and release from the "subconscious" obsession of an incomplete childhood romance with the initial little Miss Lee.

Well, comrade, let me tell you that I *did* look for a beach, though I also have to confess that by the time we reached its mirage of gray water, so many delights had already been granted me by my traveling companion that the search for a Kingdom by the Sea, a Sublimated Riviera, or whatnot, far from being the impulse of the subconscious, had become the rational pursuit of a purely theoretical thrill. The angels knew it, and arranged things accordingly. A visit to a plausible cove on the Atlantic side was completely messed up by foul weather. A thick damp sky, muddy waves, a sense of boundless but somehow matter-of-fact mist—what could be further re-moved from the crisp charm, the sapphire occasion and rosy contingency of my Riviera romance? A couple of semitropical beaches on the Gulf, though bright enough, were starred and spattered by venomous beasties and swept by hurricane winds. Finally, on a Californian beach, facing the phantom of the Pa-cific, I hit upon some rather perverse privacy in a kind of cave whence you could hear the shrieks of a lot of girl scouts taking their first surf bath on a separate part of the beach, behind rotting trees; but the fog was like a wet blanket, and the sand was gritty and clammy, and Lo was all gooseflesh and grit, and for the first time in my life I had as little desire for her as for a manatee. Perhaps, my learned readers may perk up if I tell them that even had we discovered a piece of sympathetic seaside somewhere, it would have come too late, since my real liberation had occurred much earlier: at the moment, in point of fact, when Annabel Haze, alias Dolores Lee, alias Loleeta, had appeared to me, golden and brown, kneeling, looking up, on that shoddy veranda, in a kind of fictitious, dishonest, but eminently satisfactory seaside arrangement (although there was nothing but a second-rate lake in the neighborhood).

So much for those special sensations, influenced, if not ac-tually brought about, by the tenets of modern psychiatry. Consequently, I turned away—I headed my Lolita away—from beaches which were either too bleak when lone, or too populous when ablaze. However, in recollection, I suppose, of my hopeless hauntings of public parks in Europe, I was still keenly interested in outdoor activities and desirous of finding suitable playgrounds in the open where I had suffered such shameful privations. Here, too, I was to be thwarted. The disappointment I must now register (as I gently grade my story into an expression of the continuous risk and dread that ran through my bliss) should in no wise reflect on the lyrical, epic, tragic but never Arcadian American wilds. They are beautiful, heart-rendingly beautiful, those wilds, with a quality of wide-eyed, unsung, innocent surrender that my lacquered, toy-bright Swiss villages and exhaustively lauded Alps no longer possess. Innumerable lovers have clipped and kissed on the trim turf of old-world mountainsides, on the innerspring moss, by a handy, hygienic rill, on rustic benches under the initialed oaks, and in so many *cabanes* in so many beech forests. But in the Wilds of America the open-air lover will not find it easy to indulge in the most ancient of all crimes and pastimes. Poisonous plants burn his sweetheart's buttocks, nameless insects sting his; sharp items of the forest floor prick his knees, insects hers; and all around there abides a sustained rustle of potential snakes—*que dis-je*, of semi-extinct dragons!—while the crablike seeds of ferocious flowers cling, in a hideous green crust, to gartered black sock and sloppy white sock alike.

I am exaggerating a little. One summer noon, just below timberline, where heavenly-hued blossoms that I would fain call larkspur crowded all along a purly mountain brook, we did find, Lolita and I, a secluded romantic spot, a hundred feet or so above the pass where we had left our car. The slope seemed untrodden. A last panting pine was taking a well-earned breather on the rock it had reached. A marmot whistled at us and withdrew. Beneath the lap-robe I had spread for Lo, dry flowers crepitated softly. Venus came and went. The jagged cliff crowning the upper talus and a tangle of shrubs growing below us seemed to offer us protection from sun and man alike. Alas, I had not reckoned with a faint side trail that curled up in cagey fashion among the shrubs and rocks a few feet from us.

It was then that we came closer to detection than ever before, and no wonder the experience curbed forever my yearning for rural amours.

I remember the operation was over, all over, and she was weeping in my arms;—a salutory storm of sobs after one of the fits of moodiness that had become so frequent with her

in the course of that otherwise admirable year! I had just retracted some silly promise she had forced me to make in a
moment of blind impatient passion, and there she was sprawling and sobbing, and pinching my caressing hand, and I was
laughing happily, and the atrocious, unbelievable, unbearable,
and, I suspect, eternal horror that I know *now* was still but a
dot of blackness in the blue of my bliss; and so we lay, when
with one of those jolts that have ended by knocking my poor
heart out of its groove, I met the unblinking dark eyes of two
strange and beautiful children, faunlet and nymphet, whom
their identical flat dark hair and bloodless cheeks proclaimed
siblings if not twins. They stood crouching and gaping at us,
both in blue playsuits, blending with the mountain blossoms.
I plucked at the lap-robe for desperate concealment—and
within the same instant, something that looked like a polka-
dotted pushball among the undergrowth a few paces away,
went into a turning motion which was transformed into the
gradually rising figure of a stout lady with a raven-black bob,
who automatically added a wild lily to her bouquet, while
staring over her shoulder at us from behind her lovely carved
bluestone children.

Now that I have an altogether different mess on my conscience, I know that I am a courageous man, but in those days
I was not aware of it, and I remember being surprised by my
own coolness. With the quiet murmured order one gives a
sweat-stained distracted cringing trained animal even in the
worst of plights (what mad hope or hate makes the young
beast's flanks pulsate, what black stars pierce the heart of the
tamer!), I made Lo get up, and we decorously walked, and
then indecorously scuttled down to the car. Behind it a nifty
station wagon was parked, and a handsome Assyrian with a
little blue-black beard, *un monsieur très bien*, in silk shirt and
magenta slacks, presumably the corpulent botanist's husband,
was gravely taking the picture of a signboard giving the altitude of the pass. It was well over 10,000 feet and I was quite
out of breath; and with a scrunch and a skid we drove off, Lo
still struggling with her clothes and swearing at me in language that I never dreamed little girls could know, let
alone use.

There were other unpleasant incidents. There was the movie

theatre once, for example. Lo at the time still had for the cinema a veritable passion (it was to decline into tepid condescension during her second high school year). We took in, voluptuously and indiscriminately, oh, I don't know, one hundred and fifty or two hundred programs during that one year, and during some of the denser periods of movie-going we saw many of the newsreels up to half-a-dozen times since the same weekly one went with different main pictures and pursued us from town to town. Her favorite kinds were, in this order: musicals, underworlders, westerners. In the first, real singers and dancers had unreal stage careers in an essentially grief-proof sphere of existence wherefrom death and truth were banned, and where, at the end, white-haired, dewy-eyed, technically deathless, the initially reluctant father of a show-crazy girl always finished by applauding her apotheosis on fabulous Broadway. The underworld was a world apart: there, heroic newspapermen were tortured, telephone bills ran to billions, and, in a robust atmosphere of incompetent marksmanship, villains were chased through sewers and storehouses by pathologically fearless cops (I was to give them less exercise). Finally there was the mahogany landscape, the florid-faced, blue-eyed roughriders, the prim pretty schoolteacher arriving in Roaring Gulch, the rearing horse, the spectacular stampede, the pistol thrust through the shivered windowpane, the stupendous fist fight, the crashing mountain of dusty old-fashioned furniture, the table used as a weapon, the timely somersault, the pinned hand still groping for the dropped bowie knife, the grunt, the sweet crash of fist against chin, the kick in the belly, the flying tackle; and immediately after a plethora of pain that would have hospitalized a Hercules (I should know by now), nothing to show but the rather becoming bruise on the bronzed cheek of the warmed-up hero embracing his gorgeous frontier bride. I remember one matinee in a small airless theatre crammed with children and reeking with the hot breath of popcorn. The moon was yellow above the neckerchiefed crooner, and his finger was on his strumstring, and his foot was on a pine log, and I had innocently encircled Lo's shoulder and approached my jawbone to her temple, when two harpies behind us started muttering the queerest things—I do not know if I understood aright, but what I thought I did, made me withdraw my gentle hand, and of course the rest of the show was fog to me.

Another jolt I remember is connected with a little burg we were traversing at night, during our return journey. Some twenty miles earlier I had happened to tell her that the day school she would attend at Beardsley was a rather high-class, non-coeducational one, with no modern nonsense, where-upon Lo treated me to one of those furious harangues of hers where entreaty and insult, self-assertion and double talk, vicious vulgarity and childish despair, were interwoven in an exasperating semblance of logic which prompted a semblance of explanation from me. Enmeshed in her wild words (swell chance . . . I'd be a sap if I took your opinion seriously . . . Stinker . . . You can't boss me . . . I despise you . . . and so forth), I drove through the slumbering town at a fifty-mile-per-hour pace in continuance of my smooth highway swoosh, and a twosome of patrolmen put their spotlight on the car, and told me to pull over. I shushed Lo who was automatically raving on. The men peered at her and me with malevolent curiosity. Suddenly all dimples, she beamed sweetly at them, as she never did at my orchideous masculinity; for, in a sense, my Lo was even more scared of the law than I—and when the kind officers pardoned us and servilely we crawled on, her eyelids closed and fluttered as she mimicked limp prostration.

At this point I have a curious confession to make. You will laugh—but really and truly I somehow never managed to find out quite exactly what the legal situation was. I do not know it yet. Oh, I have learned a few odds and ends. Alabama prohibits a guardian from changing the ward's residence without an order of the court; Minnesota, to whom I take off my hat, provides that when a relative assumes permanent care and custody of any child under fourteen, the authority of a court does not come into play. Query: is the stepfather of a gaspingly adorable pubescent pet, a stepfather of only one month's standing, a neurotic widower of mature years and small but independent means, with the parapets of Europe, a divorce and a few madhouses behind him, is he to be considered a relative, and thus a natural guardian? And if not, must I, and could I reasonably dare notify some Welfare Board and file a petition (how do you file a petition?), and have a court's agent investigate meek, fishy me and dangerous Dolores Haze? The many books on marriage, rape, adoption and so on, that I guiltily consulted at the public libraries of big and small towns, told me nothing beyond darkly insinuating that the state is the super-guardian of minor children. Pilvin and Zapel, if I remember their names right, in an impressive volume on the legal side of marriage, completely ignored stepfathers with motherless girls on their hands and knees. My best friend, a social service monograph (Chicago, 1936), which was dug out for me at great pains from a dusty storage recess by an innocent old spinster, said "There is no principle that every minor must have a guardian; the court is passive and enters the fray only when the child's situation becomes conspicuously perilous." A guardian, I concluded, was appointed only when he expressed his solemn and formal desire; but months might elapse before he was given notice to appear at a hearing and grow his pair of gray wings, and in the meantime the fair daemon child was legally left to her own devices which, after all, was the case of Dolores Haze. Then came the hearing. A few questions from the bench, a few reassuring answers from the attorney, a smile, a nod, a light drizzle outside, and the appointment was made. And still I dared not. Keep away, be a mouse, curl up in your hole. Courts became extravagantly active only when there was some monetary question involved: two greedy guardians, a robbed orphan, a third, still greedier, party. But here all was in perfect order, an inventory had been made, and her mother's small property was waiting untouched for Dolores Haze to grow up. The best policy seemed to be to refrain from any application. Or would some busybody, some Humane Society, butt in if I kept *too* quiet?

Friend Farlow, who was a lawyer of sorts and ought to have been able to give me some solid advice, was too much occupied with Jean's cancer to do anything more than what he had promised—namely, to look after Charlotte's meager estate while I recovered very gradually from the shock of her death. I had conditioned him into believing Dolores was my natural child, and so could not expect him to bother his head about the situation. I am, as the reader must have gathered by now, a poor businessman; but neither ignorance nor indolence should have prevented me from seeking professional advice elsewhere. What stopped me was the awful feeling that if I meddled with fate in any way and tried to rationalize her fantastic gift, that gift would be snatched away like that palace on the mountain top in the Oriental tale which vanished whenever a prospective owner asked its custodian how come a strip of sunset sky was clearly visible from afar between black rock and foundation.

I decided that at Beardsley (the site of Beardsley College for Women) I would have access to works of reference that I had not yet been able to study, such as Woerner's Treatise "On the American Law of Guardianship" and certain United States Children's Bureau Publications. I also decided that anything was better for Lo than the demoralizing idleness in which she lived. I could persuade her to do so many things—their list might stupefy a professional educator; but no matter how I pleaded or stormed, I could never make her read any other book than the so-called comic books or stories in magazines for American females. Any literature a peg higher smacked to her of school, and though theoretically willing to enjoy *A Girl of the Limberlost* or the *Arabian Nights*, or *Little Women*, she was quite sure she would not fritter away her "vacation" on such highbrow reading matter.

I now think it was a great mistake to move east again and have her go to that private school in Beardsley, instead of somehow scrambling across the Mexican border while the scrambling was good so as to lie low for a couple of years in subtropical bliss, until I could safely marry my little Creole: for I must confess that depending on the condition of my glands and ganglia, I could switch in the course of the same day from one pole of insanity to the other—from the thought that around 1950 I would have to get rid somehow of a difficult adolescent whose magic nymphage had evaporated—to the thought that with patience and luck I might have her produce eventually a nymphet with my blood in her exquisite veins, a Lolita the Second, who would be eight or nine around 1960, when I would still be *dans la force de l'âge*; indeed, the telescopy of my mind, or un-mind, was strong enough to distinguish in the remoteness of time a *vieillard encore vert*—or was

it green rot?—bizarre, tender, salivating Dr. Humbert, practicing on supremely lovely Lolita the Third the art of being a
granddad.

In the days of that wild journey of ours, I doubted not that
as father to Lolita the First I was a ridiculous failure. I did my
best; I read and reread a book with the unintentionally biblical
title *Know Your Own Daughter*, which I got at the same store
where I bought Lo, for her thirteenth birthday, a de luxe
volume with commercially "beautiful" illustrations, of Andersen's *The Little Mermaid*. But even at our very best moments,
when we sat reading on a rainy day (Lo's glance skipping from
the window to her wrist watch and back again), or had a quiet
hearty meal in a crowded diner, or played a childish game of
cards, or went shopping, or silently stared, with other motorists and their children, at some smashed, blood-bespattered
car with a young woman's shoe in the ditch (Lo, as we drove
on: "That was the exact type of moccasin I was trying to
describe to that jerk in the store"); on all those random occasions, I seemed to myself as implausible a father as she
seemed to be a daughter. Was, perhaps, guilty locomotion
instrumental in vitiating our powers of impersonation? Would
improvement be forthcoming with a fixed domicile and a routine schoolgirl's day?

In my choice of Beardsley I was guided not only by the fact
of there being a comparatively sedate school for girls located
there, but also by the presence of the women's college. In my
desire to get myself *casé*, to attach myself somehow to some
patterned surface which my stripes would blend with, I
thought of a man I knew in the department of French at
Beardsley College; he was good enough to use my textbook
in his classes and had attempted to get me over once to deliver
a lecture. I had no intention of doing so, since, as I have once
remarked in the course of these confessions, there are few
physiques I loathe more than the heavy low-slung pelvis, thick
calves and deplorable complexion of the average coed (in
whom I see, maybe, the coffin of coarse female flesh within
which my nymphets are buried alive); but I did crave for a
label, a background, and a simulacrum, and, as presently will
become clear, there was a reason, a rather zany reason, why
old Gaston Godin's company would be particularly safe.

Finally, there was the money question. My income was cracking under the strain of our joy-ride. True, I clung to the cheaper motor courts; but every now and then, there would be a loud hotel de luxe, or a pretentious dude ranch, to mutilate our budget; staggering sums, moreover, were expended on sightseeing and Lo's clothes, and the old Haze bus, although a still vigorous and very devoted machine, necessitated numerous minor and major repairs. In one of our strip maps that has happened to survive among the papers which the authorities have so kindly allowed me to use for the purpose of writing my statement, I find some jottings that help me compute the following. During that extravagant year 1947–1948, August to August, lodgings and food cost us around 5,500 dollars; gas, oil and repairs, 1,234, and various extras almost as much; so that during about 150 days of actual motion (we covered about 27,000 miles!) plus some 200 days of interpolated standstills, this modest *rentier* spent around 8,000 dollars, or better say 10,000 because, unpractical as I am, I have surely forgotten a number of items.

And so we rolled East, I more devastated than braced with the satisfaction of my passion, and she glowing with health, her bi-iliac garland still as brief as a lad's, although she had added two inches to her stature and eight pounds to her weight. We had been everywhere. We had really seen nothing. And I catch myself thinking today that our long journey had only defiled with a sinuous trail of slime the lovely, trustful, dreamy, enormous country that by then, in retrospect, was no more to us than a collection of dog-eared maps, ruined tour books, old tires, and her sobs in the night—every night, every night—the moment I feigned sleep.

4

When, through decorations of light and shade, we drove up to 14 Thayer Street, a grave little lad met us with the keys and a note from Gaston who had rented the house for us. My Lo, without granting her new surroundings one glance, unseeingly turned on the radio to which instinct led her and lay down on the living room sofa with a batch of old magazines which in the same precise and blind manner she landed by dipping her hand into the nether anatomy of a lamp table.

I really did not mind where to dwell provided I could lock my Lolita up somewhere; but I had, I suppose, in the course of my correspondence with vague Gaston, vaguely visualized a house of ivied brick. Actually the place bore a dejected resemblance to the Haze home (a mere 400 miles distant): it was the same sort of dull gray frame affair with a shingled roof and dull green drill awnings; and the rooms, though smaller and furnished in a more consistent plush-and-plate style, were arranged in much the same order. My study turned out to be, however, a much larger room, lined from floor to ceiling with some two thousand books on chemistry which my landlord (on sabbatical leave for the time being) taught at Beardsley College.

I had hoped Beardsley School for girls, an expensive day school, with lunch thrown in and a glamorous gymnasium, would, while cultivating all those young bodies, provide some formal education for their minds as well. Gaston Godin, who was seldom right in his judgment of American habitus, had warned me that the institution might turn out to be one of those where girls are taught, as he put it with a foreigner's love for such things: "not to spell very well, but to smell very well." I don't think they achieved even that.

At my first interview with headmistress Pratt, she approved of my child's "nice blue eyes" (blue! Lolita!) and of my own friendship with that "French genius" (a genius! Gaston!)— and then, having turned Dolly over to a Miss Cormorant, she wrinkled her brow in a kind of *recueillement* and said:

"We are not so much concerned, Mr. Humbird, with having our students become bookworms or be able to reel off all the capitals of Europe which nobody knows anyway, or learn by heart the dates of forgotten battles. What we are concerned with is the adjustment of the child to group life. This is why we stress the four D's: Dramatics, Dance, Debating and Dating. We are confronted by certain facts. Your delightful Dolly will presently enter an age group where dates, dating, date dress, date book, date etiquette, mean as much to her as, say, business, business connections, business success, mean to you, or as much as [smiling] the happiness of my girls means to me. Dorothy Humbird is already involved in a whole system of social life which consists, whether we like it or not, of hot-dog stands, corner drugstores, malts and cokes, movies, square-dancing, blanket parties on beaches, and even hair-fixing parties! Naturally at Beardsley School we disapprove of some of these activities; and we rechannel others into more constructive directions. But we do try to turn our backs on the fog and squarely face the sunshine. To put it briefly, while adopting certain teaching techniques, we are more interested in communication than in composition. That is, with due respect to Shakespeare and others, we want our girls to *communicate* freely with the live world around them rather than plunge into musty old books. We are still groping perhaps, but we grope intelligently, like a gynecologist feeling a tumor. We think, Dr. Humburg, in organismal and organizational terms. We have done away with the mass of irrelevant topics that have traditionally been presented to young girls, leaving no place, in former days, for the knowledges and the skills, and the attitudes they will need in managing their lives and—as the cynic might add—the lives of their husbands. Mr. Humberson, let us put it this way: the position of a star is important, but the most practical spot for an icebox in the kitchen may be even more important to the budding house-wife. You say that all you expect a child to obtain from school is a sound education. But what do we mean by education? In the old days it was in the main a verbal phenomenon; I mean, you could have a child learn by heart a good encyclopedia and he or she would know as much as or more than a school could offer. Dr. Hummer, do you realize that for the modern pre-adolescent child, medieval dates are of less vital value than weekend ones [twinkle]?—to repeat a pun that I heard the Beardsley college psychoanalyst permit herself the other day. We live not only in a world of thoughts, but also in a world of things. Words without experience are meaningless. What on earth can Dorothy Hummerson care for Greece and the Orient with their harems and slaves?"

This program rather appalled me, but I spoke to two intelligent ladies who had been connected with the school, and they affirmed that the girls did quite a bit of sound reading and that the "communication" line was more or less ballyhoo aimed at giving old-fashioned Beardsley School a financially remunerative modern touch, though actually it remained as prim as a prawn.

Another reason attracting me to that particular school may seem funny to some readers, but it was very important to me, for that is the way I am made. Across our street, exactly in front of our house, there was, I noticed, a gap of weedy waste-land, with some colorful bushes and a pile of bricks and a few scattered planks, and the foam of shabby mauve and chrome autumn roadside flowers; and through that gap you could see a shimmery section of School Rd., running parallel to our Thayer St., and immediately beyond that, the playground of the school. Apart from the psychological comfort this general arrangement should afford me by keeping Dolly's day adjacent to mine, I immediately foresaw the pleasure I would have in distinguishing from my study-bedroom, by means of powerful binoculars, the statistically inevitable percentage of nymphets among the other girl-children playing around Dolly during recess; unfortunately, on the very first day of school, workmen arrived and put up a fence some way down the gap, and in no time a construction of tawny wood maliciously arose be-yond that fence utterly blocking my magic vista; and as soon as they had erected a sufficient amount of material to spoil everything, those absurd builders suspended their work and never appeared again.

5

In a street called Thayer Street, in the residential green, fawn, and golden of a mellow academic townlet, one was bound to have a few amiable fine-dayers yelping at you. I prided myself on the exact temperature of my relations with them: never rude, always aloof. My west-door neighbor, who might have been a businessman or a college teacher, or both, would speak to me once in a while as he barbered some late garden blooms or watered his car, or, at a later date, defrosted his driveway (I don't mind if these verbs are all wrong), but my brief grunts, just sufficiently articulate to sound like con-ventional assents or interrogative pause-fillers, precluded any evolution toward chumminess. Of the two houses flanking the bit of scrubby waste opposite, one was closed, and the other contained two professors of English, tweedy and short-haired Miss Lester and fadedly feminine Miss Fabian, whose only subject of brief sidewalk conversation with me was (God bless their tact!) the young loveliness of my daughter and the naïve charm of Gaston Godin. My east-door neighbor was by far the most dangerous one, a sharp-nosed character whose late brother had been attached to the College as Superintendent of Buildings and Grounds. I remember her waylaying Dolly, while I stood at the living-room window, feverishly awaiting my darling's return from school. The odious spinster, trying to conceal her morbid inquisitiveness under a mask of dulcet goodwill, stood leaning on her slim umbrella (the sleet had just stopped, a cold wet sun had sidled out), and Dolly, her brown coat open despite the raw weather, her structural heap of books pressed against her stomach, her knees showing pink above her clumsy wellingtons, a sheepish frightened little smile flitting over and off her snub-nosed face, which—owing perhaps to the pale wintry light—looked almost plain, in a rustic, German, *mägdlein*-like way, as she stood there and dealt with Miss East's questions "And where is your mother, my dear? And what is your poor father's occupation? And where did you live before?" Another time the loathsome creature accosted me with a welcoming whine—but I evaded her; and a few days later there came from her a note in a blue-margined envelope, a nice mixture of poison and treacle, suggesting Dolly come over on a Sunday and curl up in a chair to look through the "loads of beautiful books my dear mother gave me when I was a child, instead of having the radio on at full blast till all hours of the night."

I had also to be careful in regard to a Mrs. Holigan, a charwoman and cook of sorts whom I had inherited with the vacuum cleaner from the previous tenants. Dolly got lunch at school, so that this was no trouble, and I had become adept at providing her with a big breakfast and warming up the dinner that Mrs. Holigan prepared before leaving. That kindly and harmless woman had, thank God, a rather bleary eye that missed details, and I had become a great expert in bedmaking; but still I was continuously obsessed by the feeling that some

fatal stain had been left somewhere, or that, on the rare occasions where Holigan's presence happened to coincide with
Lo's, simple Lo might succumb to buxom sympathy in the
course of a cozy kitchen chat. I often felt we lived in a lighted
house of glass, and that any moment some thin-lipped parchment face would peer through a carelessly unshaded window
to obtain a free glimpse of things that the most jaded *voyeur*
would have paid a small fortune to watch.

6

A word about Gaston Godin. The main reason why I enjoyed—or at least tolerated with relief—his company was the
spell of absolute security that his ample person cast on my
secret. Not that he knew it; I had no special reason to confide
in him, and he was much too self-centered and abstract to
notice or suspect anything that might lead to a frank question
on his part and a frank answer on mine. He spoke well of me
to Beardsleyans, he was my good herald. Had he discovered
mes goûts and Lolita's status, it would have interested him only
insofar as throwing some light on the simplicity of my attitude
toward *him*, which attitude was as free of polite strain as it
was of ribald allusions; for despite his colorless mind and dim
memory, he was perhaps aware that I knew more about him
than the burghers of Beardsley did. He was a flabby, dough-
faced, melancholy bachelor tapering upward to a pair of narrow, not quite level shoulders and a conical pear-head which
had sleek black hair on one side and only a few plastered wisps
on the other. But the lower part of his body was enormous,
and he ambulated with a curious elephantine stealth by means
of phenomenally stout legs. He always wore black, even his
tie was black; he seldom bathed; his English was a burlesque.
And, nonetheless, everybody considered him to be a supremely lovable, lovably freakish fellow! Neighbors pampered
him; he knew by name all the small boys in our vicinity (he
lived a few blocks away from me) and had some of them clean
his sidewalk and burn leaves in his back yard, and bring wood
from his shed, and even perform simple chores about the
house, and he would feed them fancy chocolates, with *real*
liqueurs inside—in the privacy of an orientally furnished den

in his basement, with amusing daggers and pistols arrayed on the moldy, rug-adorned walls among the camouflaged hot-water pipes. Upstairs he had a studio—he painted a little, the old fraud. He had decorated its sloping wall (it was really not more than a garret) with large photographs of pensive André Gide, Tchaïkovsky, Norman Douglas, two other well-known English writers, Nijinsky (all thighs and fig leaves), Harold D. Doublename (a misty-eyed left-wing professor at a Midwest-ern university) and Marcel Proust. All these poor people seemed about to fall on you from their inclined plane. He had also an album with snapshots of all the Jackies and Dickies of the neighborhood, and when I happened to thumb through it and make some casual remark, Gaston would purse his fat lips and murmur with a wistful pout *"Oui, ils sont gentils."* His brown eyes would roam around the various sentimental and artistic bric-a-brac present, and his own banal *toiles* (the conventionally primitive eyes, sliced guitars, blue nipples and geometrical designs of the day), and with a vague gesture to-ward a painted wooden bowl or veined vase, he would say *"Prenez donc une de ces poires. La bonne dame d'en face m'en offre plus que je n'en peux savourer."* Or: *"Missise Taille Lore vient de me donner ces dahlias, belles fleurs que j'exècre."* (Som-ber, sad, full of world-weariness.)

For obvious reasons, I preferred my house to his for the games of chess we had two or three times weekly. He looked like some old battered idol as he sat with his pudgy hands in his lap and stared at the board as if it were a corpse. Wheezing he would meditate for ten minutes—then make a losing move. Or the good man, after even more thought, might utter: *Au roi!* with a slow old-dog woof that had a gargling sound at the back of it which made his jowls wabble; and then he would lift his circumflex eyebrows with a deep sigh as I pointed out to him that he was in check himself.

Sometimes, from where we sat in my cold study I could hear Lo's bare feet practicing dance techniques in the living room downstairs; but Gaston's outgoing senses were com-fortably dulled, and he remained unaware of those naked rhythms—and-one, and-two, and-one, and-two, weight trans-ferred on a straight right leg, leg up and out to the side, and-one, and-two, and only when she started jumping, opening her legs at the height of the jump, and flexing one leg, and extending the other, and flying, and landing on her toes— only then did my pale, pompous, morose opponent rub his head or cheek as if confusing those distant thuds with the awful stabs of my formidable Queen.

Sometimes Lola would slouch in while we pondered the board—and it was every time a treat to see Gaston, his elephant eye still fixed on his pieces, ceremoniously rise to shake hands with her, and forthwith release her limp fingers, and without looking once at her, descend again into his chair to topple into the trap I had laid for him. One day around Christmas, after I had not seen him for a fortnight or so, he asked me *"Et toutes vos fillettes, elles vont bien?"* from which it became evident to me that he had multiplied my unique Lolita by the number of sartorial categories his downcast moody eye had glimpsed during a whole series of her appearances: blue jeans, a skirt, shorts, a quilted robe.

I am loath to dwell so long on the poor fellow (sadly enough, a year later, during a voyage to Europe, from which he did not return, he got involved in a *sale histoire*, in Naples of all places!). I would have hardly alluded to him at all had not his Beardsley existence had such a queer bearing on my case. I need him for my defense. There he was, devoid of any talent whatsoever, a mediocre teacher, a worthless scholar, a glum repulsive fat old invert, highly contemptuous of the American way of life, triumphantly ignorant of the English language—there he was in priggish New England, crooned over by the old and caressed by the young—oh, having a grand time and fooling everybody; and here was I.

7

I am now faced with the distasteful task of recording a definite drop in Lolita's morals. If her share in the ardors she kindled had never amounted to much, neither had pure lucre ever come to the fore. But I was weak, I was not wise, my schoolgirl nymphet had me in thrall. With the human element dwindling, the passion, the tenderness, and the torture only increased; and of this she took advantage.

Her weekly allowance, paid to her under condition she

fulfill her basic obligations, was twenty-one cents at the start
of the Beardsley era—and went up to one dollar five before its
end. This was a more than generous arrangement seeing she
constantly received from me all kinds of small presents and
had for the asking any sweetmeat or movie under the moon—
although, of course, I might fondly demand an additional kiss,
or even a whole collection of assorted caresses, when I knew
she coveted very badly some item of juvenile amusement. She
was, however, not easy to deal with. Only very listlessly did
she earn her three pennies—or three nickels—per day; and she
proved to be a cruel negotiator whenever it was in her power
to deny me certain life-wrecking, strange, slow paradisal philters without which I could not live more than a few days in
a row, and which, because of the very nature of love's languor,
I could not obtain by force. Knowing the magic and might
of her own soft mouth, she managed—during one school-
year!—to raise the bonus price of a fancy embrace to three,
and even four bucks. O Reader! Laugh not, as you imagine
me, on the very rack of joy noisily emitting dimes and quarters, and great big silver dollars like some sonorous, jingly and
wholly demented machine vomiting riches; and in the margin
of that leaping epilepsy she would firmly clutch a handful of
coins in her little fist, which, anyway, I used to pry open afterwards unless she gave me the slip, scrambling away to hide
her loot. And just as every other day I would cruise all around
the school area and on comatose feet visit drugstores, and peer
into foggy lanes, and listen to receding girl laughter in between my heart throbs and the falling leaves, so every now
and then I would burgle her room and scrutinize torn papers
in the wastebasket with the painted roses, and look under the
pillow of the virginal bed I had just made myself. Once I
found eight one-dollar notes in one of her books (fittingly—
Treasure Island), and once a hole in the wall behind Whistler's
Mother yielded as much as twenty-four dollars and some
change—say twenty-four sixty—which I quietly removed,
upon which, next day, she accused, to my face, honest Mrs.
Holigan of being a filthy thief. Eventually, she lived up to her
I.Q. by finding a safer hoarding place which I never discovered; but by that time I had brought prices down drastically
by having her earn the hard and nauseous way permission to

participate in the school's theatrical program; because what I feared most was not that she might ruin me, but that she might accumulate sufficient cash to run away. I believe the poor fierce-eyed child had figured out that with a mere fifty dollars in her purse she might somehow reach Broadway or Hollywood—or the foul kitchen of a diner (Help Wanted) in a dismal ex-prairie state, with the wind blowing, and the stars blinking, and the cars, and the bars, and the barmen, and everything soiled, torn, dead.

8

I did my best, your Honor, to tackle the problem of boys. Oh, I used even to read in the Beardsley *Star* a so-called Column for Teens, to find out how to behave!

A word to fathers. Don't frighten away daughter's friend. Maybe it is a bit hard for you to realize that now the boys are finding her attractive. To you she is still a little girl. To the boys she's charming and fun, lovely and gay. They like her. Today you clinch big deals in an executive's office, but yesterday you were just highschool Jim carrying Jane's school books. Remember? Don't you want your daughter, now that her turn has come, to be happy in the admiration and company of boys she likes? Don't you want them to have wholesome fun together?

Wholesome fun? Good Lord!

Why not treat the young fellows as guests in your house? Why not make conversation with them? Draw them out, make them laugh and feel at ease?

Welcome, fellow, to this bordello.

If she breaks the rules don't explode out loud in front of her partner in crime. Let her take the brunt of your displeasure in private. And stop making the boys feel she's the daughter of an old ogre.

First of all the old ogre drew up a list under "absolutely forbidden" and another under "reluctantly allowed." Absolutely forbidden were dates, single or double or triple—the next step being of course mass orgy. She might visit a candy bar with her girl friends, and there giggle-chat with occasional young males, while I waited in the car at a discreet distance;

and I promised her that if her group were invited by a socially acceptable group in Butler's Academy for Boys for their annual ball (heavily chaperoned, of course), I might consider the question whether a girl of fourteen can don her first "formal" (a kind of gown that makes thin-armed teen-agers look like flamingoes). Moreover, I promised her to throw a party at our house to which she would be allowed to invite her prettier girl friends and the nicer boys she would have met by that time at the Butler dance. But I was quite positive that as long as my regime lasted she would never, never be permitted to go with a youngster in rut to a movie, or neck in a car, or go to boy-girl parties at the houses of schoolmates, or indulge out of my earshot in boy-girl telephone conversations, even if "only discussing his relations with a friend of mine."

Lo was enraged by all this—called me a lousy crook and worse—and I would probably have lost my temper had I not soon discovered, to my sweetest relief, that what really angered her was my depriving her not of a specific satisfaction but of a general right. I was impinging, you see, on the conventional program, the stock pastimes, the "things that are done," the routine of youth; for there is nothing more conservative than a child, especially a girl-child, be she the most auburn and russet, the most mythopoeic nymphet in October's orchard-haze.

Do not misunderstand me. I cannot be absolutely certain that in the course of the winter she did not manage to have, in a casual way, improper contacts with unknown young fellows; of course, no matter how closely I controlled her leisure, there would constantly occur unaccounted-for time leaks with over-elaborate explanations to stop them up in retrospect; of course, my jealousy would constantly catch its jagged claw in the fine fabrics of nymphet falsity; but I did definitely feel— and can now vouchsafe for the accuracy of my feeling—that there was no reason for serious alarm. I felt that way not because I never once discovered any palpable hard young throat to crush among the masculine mutes that flickered somewhere in the background; but because it was to me "overwhelmingly obvious" (a favorite expression with my aunt Sybil) that all varieties of high school boys—from the perspiring nincompoop whom "holding hands" thrills, to the self-sufficient rapist with pustules and a souped-up car—equally bored my sophisticated young mistress. "All this noise about boys gags me," she had scrawled on the inside of a schoolbook, and underneath, in Mona's hand (Mona is due any minute now), there was the sly quip: "What about Rigger?" (due too).

Faceless, then, are the chappies I happened to see in her company. There was for instance Red Sweater who one day, the day we had the first snow—saw her home; from the parlor window I observed them talking near our porch. She wore her first cloth coat with a fur collar; there was a small brown cap on my favorite hairdo—the fringe in front and the swirl at the sides and the natural curls at the back—and her damp-dark moccasins and white socks were more sloppy than ever. She pressed as usual her books to her chest while speaking or listening, and her feet gestured all the time: she would stand on her left instep with her right toe, remove it backward, cross her feet, rock slightly, sketch a few steps, and then start the series all over again. There was Windbreaker who talked to her in front of a restaurant one Sunday afternoon while his mother and sister attempted to walk me away for a chat; I dragged along and looked back at my only love. She had developed more than one conventional mannerism, such as the polite adolescent way of showing one is literally "doubled up" with laughter by inclining one's head, and so (as she sensed my call), still feigning helpless merriment, she walked backward a couple of steps, and then faced about, and walked toward me with a fading smile. On the other hand, I greatly liked—perhaps because it reminded me of her first unforgettable confession—her trick of sighing "oh dear!" in humorous wistful submission to fate, or emitting a long "no-o" in a deep almost growling undertone when the blow of fate had actually fallen. Above all—since we are speaking of movement and youth—I liked to see her spinning up and down Thayer Street on her beautiful young bicycle: rising on the pedals to work on them lustily, then sinking back in a languid posture while the speed wore itself off; and then she would stop at our mailbox and, still astride, would flip through a magazine she found there, and put it back, and press her tongue to one side of her upperlip and push off with her foot, and again sprint through pale shade and sun.

On the whole she seemed to me better adapted to her surroundings than I had hoped she would be when considering
my spoiled slave-child and the bangles of demeanor she naïvely affected the winter before in California. Although I could
never get used to the constant state of anxiety in which the
guilty, the great, the tenderhearted live, I felt I was doing my
best in the way of mimicry. As I lay on my narrow studio bed
after a session of adoration and despair in Lolita's cold bedroom, I used to review the concluded day by checking my
own image as it prowled rather than passed before the mind's
red eye. I watched dark-and-handsome, not un-Celtic, probably high-church, possibly very high-church, Dr. Humbert see
his daughter off to school. I watched him greet with his slow
smile and pleasantly arched thick black ad-eyebrows good
Mrs. Holigan, who smelled of the plague (and would head, I
knew, for master's gin at the first opportunity). With Mr.
West, retired executioner or writer of religious tracts—who
cared?—I saw neighbor what's his name, I think they are
French or Swiss, meditate in his frank-windowed study over a
typewriter, rather gaunt-profiled, an almost Hitlerian cowlick
on his pale brow. Weekends, wearing a well-tailored overcoat
and brown gloves, Professor H. might be seen with his daughter strolling to Walton Inn (famous for its violet-ribboned
china bunnies and chocolate boxes among which you sit and
wait for a "table for two" still filthy with your predecessor's
crumbs). Seen on weekdays, around one P.M., saluting with
dignity Argus-eyed East while maneuvering the car out of the
garage and around the damned evergreens, and down onto
the slippery road. Raising a cold eye from book to clock in
the positively sultry Beardsley College library, among bulky
young women caught and petrified in the overflow of human
knowledge. Walking across the campus with the college clergyman, the Rev. Rigger (who also taught Bible in Beardsley
School). "Somebody told me her mother was a celebrated
actress killed in an airplane accident. Oh? My mistake, I presume. Is that so? I see. How sad." (Sublimating her mother,
eh?) Slowly pushing my little pram through the labyrinth of
the supermarket, in the wake of Professor W., also a slow-
moving and gentle widower with the eyes of a goat. Shoveling
the snow in my shirt-sleeves, a voluminous black and white

muffler around my neck. Following with no show of rapacious haste (even taking time to wipe my feet on the mat) my schoolgirl daughter into the house. Taking Dolly to the dentist—pretty nurse beaming at her—old magazines—*ne montrez pas vos zhambes*. At dinner with Dolly in town, Mr. Edgar H. Humbert was seen eating his steak in the continental knife-and-fork manner. Enjoying, in duplicate, a concert: two marble-faced, becalmed Frenchmen sitting side by side, with Monsieur H. H.'s musical little girl on her father's right, and the musical little boy of Professor W. (father spending a hygienic evening in Providence) on Monsieur G. G.'s left. Opening the garage, a square of light that engulfs the car and is extinguished. Brightly pajamaed, jerking down the window shade in Dolly's bedroom. Saturday morning, unseen, solemnly weighing the winter-bleached lassie in the bathroom. Seen and heard Sunday morning, no churchgoer after all, saying don't be too late, to Dolly who is bound for the covered court. Letting in a queerly observant schoolmate of Dolly's: "First time I've seen a man wearing a smoking jacket, sir—except in movies, of course."

9

Her girl friends, whom I had looked forward to meet, proved on the whole disappointing. There was Opal Something, and Linda Hall, and Avis Chapman, and Eva Rosen, and Mona Dahl (save one, all these names are approximations, of course). Opal was a bashful, formless, bespectacled, be-pimpled creature who doted on Dolly who bullied her. With Linda Hall the school tennis champion, Dolly played singles at least twice a week: I suspect Linda was a true nymphet, but for some unknown reason she did not come—was perhaps not allowed to come—to our house; so I recall her only as a flash of natural sunshine on an indoor court. Of the rest, none had any claims to nymphetry except Eva Rosen. Avis was a plump lateral child with hairy legs, while Mona, though handsome in a coarse sensual way and only a year older than my aging mistress, had obviously long ceased to be a nymphet, if she ever had been one. Eva Rosen, a displaced little person from France, was on the other hand a good example of a not strik-

ingly beautiful child revealing to the perspicacious amateur
some of the basic elements of nymphet charm, such as a perfect pubescent figure and lingering eyes and high cheekbones.
Her glossy copper hair had Lolita's silkiness, and the features
of her delicate milky-white face with pink lips and silverfish
eyelashes were less foxy than those of her likes—the great clan
of intra-racial redheads; nor did she sport their green uniform
but wore, as I remember her, a lot of black or cherry dark—
a very smart black pullover, for instance, and high-heeled
black shoes, and garnet-red fingernail polish. I spoke French
to her (much to Lo's disgust). The child's tonalities were still
admirably pure, but for school words and play words she resorted to current American and then a slight Brooklyn accent
would crop up in her speech, which was amusing in a little
Parisian who went to a select New England school with phoney British aspirations. Unfortunately, despite "that French
kid's uncle" being "a millionaire," Lo dropped Eva for some
reason before I had had time to enjoy in my modest way her
fragrant presence in the Humbert open house. The reader
knows what importance I attached to having a bevy of page
girls, consolation prize nymphets, around my Lolita. For a
while, I endeavored to interest my senses in Mona Dahl who
was a good deal around, especially during the spring term
when Lo and she got so enthusiastic about dramatics. I have
often wondered what secrets outrageously treacherous Dolores Haze had imparted to Mona while blurting out to me
by urgent and well-paid request various really incredible details concerning an affair that Mona had had with a marine at
the seaside. It was characteristic of Lo that she chose for her
closest chum that elegant, cold, lascivious, experienced young
female whom I once heard (misheard, Lo swore) cheerfully
say in the hallway to Lo—who had remarked that her (Lo's)
sweater was of virgin wool: "The only thing about you that
is, kiddo . . ." She had a curiously husky voice, artificially
waved dull dark hair, earrings, amber-brown prominent eyes
and luscious lips. Lo said teachers had remonstrated with her
on her loading herself with so much costume jewelry. Her
hands trembled. She was burdened with a 150 I.Q. And I also
knew she had a tremendous chocolate-brown mole on her
womanish back which I inspected the night Lo and she had

worn low-cut pastel-colored, vaporous dresses for a dance at
the Butler Academy.

I am anticipating a little, but I cannot help running my
memory all over the keyboard of that school year. In meeting
my attempts to find out what kind of boys Lo knew, Miss
Dahl was elegantly evasive. Lo who had gone to play tennis
at Linda's country club had telephoned she might be a full
half hour late, and so, would I entertain Mona who was coming to practice with her a scene from *The Taming of the Shrew*.
Using all the modulations, all the allure of manner and voice
she was capable of and staring at me with perhaps—could I
be mistaken?—a faint gleam of crystalline irony, beautiful
Mona replied: "Well, sir, the fact is Dolly is not much concerned with mere boys. Fact is, we are rivals. She and I have
a crush on the Reverend Rigger." (This was a joke—I have
already mentioned that gloomy giant of a man, with the jaw
of a horse: he was to bore me to near murder with his impressions of Switzerland at a tea party for parents that I am
unable to place correctly in terms of time.)

How had the ball been? Oh, it had been a riot. A what? A
panic. Terrific, in a word. Had Lo danced a lot? Oh, not a
frightful lot, just as much as she could stand. What did she,
languorous Mona, think of Lo? Sir? Did she think Lo was
doing well at school? Gosh, she certainly was quite a kid. But
her general behavior was—? Oh, she was a swell kid. But still?
"Oh, she's a doll," concluded Mona, and sighed abruptly, and
picked up a book that happened to lie at hand, and with a
change of expression, falsely furrowing her brow, inquired:
"Do tell me about Ball Zack, sir. Is he really that good?" She
moved up so close to my chair that I made out through lotions and creams her uninteresting skin scent. A sudden odd
thought stabbed me: was my Lo playing the pimp? If so, she
had found the wrong substitute. Avoiding Mona's cool gaze,
I talked literature for a minute. Then Dolly arrived—and slit
her pale eyes at us. I left the two friends to their own devices.
One of the latticed squares in a small cobwebby casement
window at the turn of the staircase was glazed with ruby, and
that raw wound among the unstained rectangles and its asymmetrical position—a knight's move from the top—always
strangely disturbed me.

Sometimes . . . Come on, how often exactly, Bert? Can
you recall four, five, more such occasions? Or would no human heart have survived two or three? Sometimes (I have
nothing to say in reply to your question), while Lolita would
be haphazardly preparing her homework, sucking a pencil,
lolling sideways in an easy chair with both legs over its arm,
I would shed all my pedagogic restraint, dismiss all our quar-
rels, forget all my masculine pride—and literally crawl on my
knees to your chair, my Lolita! You would give me one look—
a gray furry question mark of a look: "Oh no, not again"
(incredulity, exasperation); for you never deigned to believe that I could, without any specific designs, ever crave to
bury my face in your plaid skirt, my darling! The fragility of
those bare arms of yours—how I longed to enfold them, all
your four limpid lovely limbs, a folded colt, and take your
head between my unworthy hands, and pull the temple-skin
back on both sides, and kiss your chinesed eyes, and—
"Pulease, leave me alone, will you," you would say, "for
Christ's sake leave me alone." And I would get up from the
floor while you looked on, your face deliberately twitching
in imitation of my *tic nerveux.* But never mind, never mind,
I am only a brute, never mind, let us go on with my miserable
story.

11

One Monday forenoon, in December I think, Pratt asked
me to come over for a talk. Dolly's last report had been poor,
I knew. But instead of contenting myself with some such plausible explanation of this summons, I imagined all sorts of
horrors, and had to fortify myself with a pint of my "pin"
before I could face the interview. Slowly, all Adam's apple and
heart, I went up the steps of the scaffold.

A huge woman, gray-haired, frowsy, with a broad flat nose
and small eyes behind black-rimmed glasses— "Sit down,"
she said, pointing to an informal and humiliating hassock,
while she perched with ponderous spryness on the arm of an
oak chair. For a moment or two, she peered at me with smiling

curiosity. She had done it at our first meeting, I recalled, but I could afford then to scowl back. Her eye left me. She lapsed into thought—probably assumed. Making up her mind she rubbed, fold on fold, her dark gray flannel skirt at the knee, dispelling a trace of chalk or something. Then she said, still rubbing, not looking up:

"Let me ask a blunt question, Mr. Haze. You are an old-fashioned Continental father, aren't you?"

"Why, no," I said, "conservative, perhaps, but not what you would call old-fashioned."

She sighed, frowned, then clapped her big plump hands together in a let's-get-down-to-business manner, and again fixed her beady eyes upon me.

"Dolly Haze," she said, "is a lovely child, but the onset of sexual maturing seems to give her trouble."

I bowed slightly. What else could I do?

"She is still shuttling," said Miss Pratt, showing how with her liver-spotted hands, "between the anal and genital zones of development. Basically she is a lovely—"

"I beg your pardon," I said, "what zones?"

"That's the old-fashioned European in you!" cried Pratt delivering a slight tap on my wrist watch and suddenly disclosing her dentures. "All I mean is that biologic and psychologic drives—do you smoke?—are not fused in Dolly, do not fall so to speak into a—into a rounded pattern." Her hands held for a moment an invisible melon.

"She is attractive, bright though careless" (breathing heavily, without leaving her perch, the woman took time out to look at the lovely child's report sheet on the desk at her right). "Her marks are getting worse and worse. Now I wonder, Mr. Haze—" Again the false meditation.

"Well," she went on with zest, "as for me, I do smoke, and, as dear Dr. Pierce used to say: I'm not proud of it but I jeest love it." She lit up and the smoke she exhaled from her nostrils was like a pair of tusks.

"Let me give you a few details, it won't take a moment. Now let me see [rummaging among her papers]. She is defiant toward Miss Redcock and impossibly rude to Miss Cormorant. Now here is one of our special research reports: Enjoys singing with group in class though mind seems to wander.

Crosses her knees and wags left leg to rhythm. Type of by-words: a two-hundred-forty-two word area of the commonest pubescent slang fenced in by a number of obviously European polysyllabics. Sighs a good deal in class. Let me see. Yes. Now comes the last week in November. Sighs a good deal in class. Chews gum vehemently. Does not bite her nails though if she did, this would conform better to her general pattern—scientifically speaking, of course. Menstruation, according to the subject, well established. Belongs at present to no church organization. By the way, Mr. Haze, her mother was—? Oh, I see. And you are—? Nobody's business is, I suppose, God's business. Something else we wanted to know. She has no regular home duties, I understand. Making a princess of your Dolly, Mr. Haze, eh? Well, what else have we got here? Handles books gracefully. Voice pleasant. Giggles rather often. A little dreamy. Has private jokes of her own, transposing for instance the first letters of some of her teachers' names. Hair light and dark brown, lustrous—well [laughing] you are aware of *that*, I suppose. Nose unobstructed, feet high-arched, eyes—let me see, I had here somewhere a still more recent report. Aha, here we are. Miss Gold says Dolly's tennis form is excellent to superb, even better than Linda Hall's, but concentration and point-accumulation are just "poor to fair." Miss Cormorant cannot decide whether Dolly has exceptional emotional control or none at all. Miss Horn reports she—I mean, Dolly—cannot verbalize her emotions, while according to Miss Cole Dolly's metabolic efficiency is superfine. Miss Molar thinks Dolly is myopic and should see a good ophthalmologist, but Miss Redcock insists that the girl simulates eye-strain to get away with scholastic incompetence. And to conclude, Mr. Haze, our researchers are wondering about something really crucial. Now I want to ask you something. I want to know if your poor wife, or yourself, or anyone else in the family—I understand she has several aunts and a maternal grandfather in California?—oh, *had!*—I'm sorry—well, we all wonder if anybody in the family has instructed Dolly in the process of mammalian reproduction. The general impression is that fifteen-year-old Dolly remains morbidly uninterested in sexual matters, or to be exact, represses her curiosity in order to save her ignorance and self-dignity. All right—

fourteen. You see, Mr. Haze, Beardsley School does not believe in bees and blossoms, and storks and love birds, but it
does believe very strongly in preparing its students for mu-
tually satisfactory mating and successful child rearing. We feel
Dolly could make excellent progress if only she would put her
mind to her work. Miss Cormorant's report is significant in
that respect. Dolly is inclined to be, mildly speaking, impudent. But all feel that *primo*, you should have your family
doctor tell her the facts of life and, *secundo*, that you allow
her to enjoy the company of her schoolmates' brothers at the
Junior Club or in Dr. Rigger's organization, or in the lovely
homes of our parents."

"She may meet boys at her own lovely home," I said.

"I hope she will," said Pratt buoyantly. "When we questioned her about her troubles, Dolly refused to discuss the
home situation, but we have spoken to some of her friends
and really—well, for example, we insist you un-veto her non-
participation in the dramatic group. You just must allow her
to take part in *The Hunted Enchanters*. She was such a perfect
little nymph in the try-out, and sometime in spring the author
will stay for a few days at Beardsley College and may attend
a rehearsal or two in our new auditorium. I mean it is all part
of the fun of being young and alive and beautiful. You must
understand—"

"I always thought of myself," I said, "as a very understanding father."

"Oh no doubt, no doubt, but Miss Cormorant thinks, and
I am inclined to agree with her, that Dolly is obsessed by
sexual thoughts for which she finds no outlet, and will tease
and martyrize other girls, or even our younger instructors because *they* do have innocent dates with boys."

Shrugged my shoulders. A shabby *émigré*.

"Let us put our two heads together, Mr. Haze. What on
earth is wrong with that child?"

"She seems quite normal and happy to me," I said (disaster
coming at last? was I found out? had they got some hypnotist?).

"What worries me," said Miss Pratt looking at her watch
and starting to go over the whole subject again, "is that both
teachers and schoolmates find Dolly antagonistic, dissatisfied,

cagey—and everybody wonders why you are so firmly opposed to all the natural recreations of a normal child."

"Do you mean sex play?" I asked jauntily, in despair, a cornered old rat.

"Well, I certainly welcome this civilized terminology," said Pratt with a grin. "But this is not quite the point. Under the auspices of Beardsley School, dramatics, dances and other natural activities are not technically sex play, though girls do meet boys, if that is what you object to."

"All right," I said, my hassock exhaling a weary sigh. "You win. She can take part in that play. Provided male parts are taken by female parts."

"I am always fascinated," said Pratt, "by the admirable way foreigners—or at least naturalized Americans—use our rich language. I'm sure Miss Gold, who conducts the play group, will be overjoyed. I notice she is one of the few teachers that seem to like—I mean who seem to find Dolly manageable. This takes care of general topics, I guess; now comes a special matter. We are in trouble again."

Pratt paused truculently, then rubbed her index finger under her nostrils with such vigor that her nose performed a kind of war dance.

"I'm a frank person," she said, "but conventions are conventions, and I find it difficult . . . Let me put it this way . . . The Walkers, who live in what we call around here the Duke's Manor, you know the great gray house on the hill—they send their two girls to our school, and we have the niece of President Moore with us, a really gracious child, not to speak of a number of other prominent children. Well, under the circumstances, it is rather a jolt when Dolly, who looks like a little lady, uses words which you as a foreigner probably simply do not know or do not understand. Perhaps it might be better— Would you like me to have Dolly come up here right away to discuss things? No? You see—oh well, let's have it out. Dolly has written a most obscene four-letter word which our Dr. Cutler tells me is low-Mexican for urinal with her lipstick on some health pamphlets which Miss Redcock, who is getting married in June, distributed among the girls, and we thought she should stay after hours—another half hour at least. But if you like—"

"No," I said, "I don't want to interfere with rules. I shall talk to her later. I shall thrash it out."

"Do," said the woman rising from her chair arm. "And perhaps we can get together again soon, and if things do not improve we might have Dr. Cutler analyze her."

Should I marry Pratt and strangle her?

". . . And perhaps your family doctor might like to examine her physically—just a routine check-up. She is in Mushroom—the last classroom along that passage."

Beardsley School, it may be explained, copied a famous girls' school in England by having "traditional" nicknames for its various classrooms: Mushroom, Room-In 8, B-room, Room-BA and so on. Mushroom was smelly, with a sepia print of Reynolds' "Age of Innocence" above the chalkboard, and several rows of clumsy-looking pupil desks. At one of these, my Lolita was reading the chapter on "Dialogue" in Baker's *Dramatic Technique*, and all was very quiet, and there was another girl with a very naked, porcelain-white neck and wonderful platinum hair, who sat in front reading too, absolutely lost to the world and interminably winding a soft curl around one finger, and I sat beside Dolly just behind that neck and that hair, and unbuttoned my overcoat and for sixty-five cents plus the permission to participate in the school play, had Dolly put her inky, chalky, red-knuckled hand under the desk. Oh, stupid and reckless of me, no doubt, but after the torture I had been subjected to, I simply had to take advantage of a combination that I knew would never occur again.

12

Around Christmas she caught a bad chill and was examined by a friend of Miss Lester, a Dr. Ilse Tristramson (hi, Ilse, you were a dear, uninquisitive soul, and you touched my dove very gently). She diagnosed bronchitis, patted Lo on the back (all its bloom erect because of the fever) and put her to bed for a week or longer. At first she "ran a temperature" in American parlance, and I could not resist the exquisite caloricity of unexpected delights—Venus febriculosa—though it was a very languid Lolita that moaned and coughed and shivered in my embrace. And as soon as she was well again, I threw a Party with Boys.

Perhaps I had drunk a little too much in preparation for the ordeal. Perhaps I made a fool of myself. The girls had decorated and plugged in a small fir tree—German custom, except that colored bulbs had superseded wax candles. Records were chosen and fed into my landlord's phonograph. Chic Dolly wore a nice gray dress with fitted bodice and flared skirt. Humming, I retired to my study upstairs—and then every ten or twenty minutes I would come down like an idiot just for a few seconds; to pick up ostensibly my pipe from the mantelpiece or hunt for the newspaper; and with every new visit these simple actions became harder to perform, and I was reminded of the dreadfully distant days when I used to brace myself to casually enter a room in the Ramsdale house where Little Carmen was on.

The party was not a success. Of the three girls invited, one did not come at all, and one of the boys brought his cousin Roy, so there was a superfluity of two boys, and the cousins knew all the steps, and the other fellows could hardly dance at all, and most of the evening was spent in messing up the kitchen, and then endlessly jabbering about what card game to play, and sometime later, two girls and four boys sat on the floor of the living room, with all windows open, and played a word game which Opal could not be made to understand, while Mona and Roy, a lean handsome lad, drank ginger ale in the kitchen, sitting on the table and dangling their legs, and hotly discussing Predestination and the Law of Averages. After they had all gone my Lo said ugh, closed her eyes, and dropped into a chair with all four limbs starfished to express the utmost disgust and exhaustion and swore it was the most revolting bunch of boys she had ever seen. I bought her a new tennis racket for that remark.

January was humid and warm, and February fooled the forsythia: none of the townspeople had ever *seen* such weather. Other presents came tumbling in. For her birthday I bought her a bicycle, the doe-like and altogether charming machine already mentioned—and added to this a *History of Modern American Painting*: her bicycle manner, I mean her approach to it, the hip movement in mounting, the grace and so on, afforded me supreme pleasure; but my attempt to refine her pictorial taste was a failure; she wanted to know if the guy noon-napping on Doris Lee's hay was the father of the pseudo-voluptuous hoyden in the foreground, and could not understand why I said Grant Wood or Peter Hurd was good, and Reginald Marsh or Frederick Waugh awful.

13

By the time spring had touched up Thayer Street with yellow and green and pink, Lolita was irrevocably stage-struck. Pratt, whom I chanced to notice one Sunday lunching with some people at Walton Inn, caught my eye from afar and went through the motion of sympathetically and discreetly clapping her hands while Lo was not looking. I detest the theatre as being a primitive and putrid form, historically speaking; a form that smacks of stone-age rites and communal nonsense despite those individual injections of genius, such as, say, Elizabethan poetry which a closeted reader automatically pumps out of the stuff. Being much occupied at the time with my own literary labors, I did not bother to read the complete text of *The Enchanted Hunters*, the playlet in which Dolores Haze was assigned the part of a farmer's daughter who imagines herself to be a woodland witch, or Diana, or something, and who, having got hold of a book on hypnotism, plunges a number of lost hunters into various entertaining trances before falling in her turn under the spell of a vagabond poet (Mona Dahl). That much I gleaned from bits of crumpled and poorly typed script that Lo sowed all over the house. The coincidence of the title with the name of an unforgettable inn was pleasant in a sad little way: I wearily thought I had better not bring it to my own enchantress's notice, lest a brazen accusation of mawkishness hurt me even more than her failure to notice it for herself had done. I assumed the playlet was just another, practically anonymous, version of some banal legend. Nothing prevented one, of course, from supposing that in quest of an attractive name the founder of the hotel had been immediately and solely influenced by the chance fantasy of the second-rate muralist he had hired, and that subsequently the hotel's name had suggested the play's title. But in my credulous, simple, benevolent mind I happened to twist it the other way round, and without giving the whole matter much thought really, supposed that mural, name and title had all been derived from a common source, from some local tradition, which I, an alien unversed in New England lore, would not be supposed to know. In consequence I was under the impression (all this quite casually, you understand, quite outside any orbit of importance) that the accursed playlet belonged to the type of whimsey for juvenile consumption, arranged and rearranged many times, such as *Hansel and Gretel* by Richard Roe, or *The Sleeping Beauty* by Dorothy Doe, or *The Emperor's New Clothes* by Maurice Vermont and Marion Rumpelmeyer—all this to be found in any *Plays for School Actors* or *Let's Have a Play!* In other words, I did not know—and would not have cared, if I did—that actually *The Enchanted Hunters* was a quite recent and technically original composition which had been produced for the first time only three or four months ago by a highbrow group in New York. To me—inasmuch as I could judge from my charmer's part—it seemed to be a pretty dismal kind of fancy work, with echoes from Lenormand and Maeterlinck and various quiet British dreamers. The red-capped, uniformly attired hunters, of which one was a banker, another a plumber, a third a policeman, a fourth an undertaker, a fifth an underwriter, a sixth an escaped convict (you see the possibilities!), went through a complete change of mind in Dolly's Dell, and remembered their real lives only as dreams or nightmares from which little Diana had aroused them; but a seventh Hunter (in a *green* cap, the fool) was a Young Poet, and he insisted, much to Diana's annoyance, that she and the entertainment provided (dancing nymphs, and elves, and monsters) were his, the Poet's, invention. I understand that finally, in utter disgust at this cocksureness, barefooted Dolores was to lead check-trousered Mona to the paternal farm behind the Perilous Forest to prove to the braggard she was not a poet's fancy, but a rustic, down-to-brown-earth lass—and a last-minute kiss was to enforce the play's profound message, namely, that mirage and reality merge in love. I considered it wiser not to criticize the thing in front of Lo: she was so healthily engrossed in "problems of expression," and so charmingly did she put her narrow Florentine hands together, batting her eyelashes and pleading with me not to come to rehearsals as some ridiculous parents did because she wanted to dazzle me with a perfect First Night—and because I was, anyway, always butting in and saying the wrong thing, and cramping her style in the presence of other people.

There was one very special rehearsal . . . my heart, my heart . . . there was one day in May marked by a lot of gay flurry—it all rolled past, beyond my ken, immune to my memory, and when I saw Lo next, in the late afternoon, balancing on her bike, pressing the palm of her hand to the damp bark of a young birch tree on the edge of our lawn, I was so struck by the radiant tenderness of her smile that for an instant I believed all our troubles gone. "Can you remember," she said, "what was the name of that hotel, *you* know [nose puckered], come on, you know—with those white columns and the marble swan in the lobby? Oh, you know [noisy exhalation of breath]—the hotel where you raped me. Okay, skip it. I mean, was it [almost in a whisper] The Enchanted Hunters? Oh, it was? [musingly] Was it?"—and with a yelp of amorous vernal laughter she slapped the glossy bole and tore uphill, to the end of the street, and then rode back, feet at rest on stopped pedals, posture relaxed, one hand dreaming in her print-flowered lap.

14

Because it supposedly tied up with her interest in dance and dramatics, I had permitted Lo to take piano lessons with a Miss Emperor (as we French scholars may conveniently call her) to whose blue-shuttered little white house a mile or so beyond Beardsley Lo would spin off twice a week. One Friday night toward the end of May (and a week or so after the very special rehearsal Lo had not had me attend) the telephone in my study, where I was in the act of mopping up Gustave's—I mean Gaston's—king's side, rang and Miss Emperor asked if Lo was coming next Tuesday because she had missed last Tuesday's and today's lessons. I said she would by all means—and went on with the game. As the reader may well imagine, my faculties were now impaired, and a move or two later, with

Gaston to play, I noticed through the film of my general distress that he could collect my queen; he noticed it too, but
thinking it might be a trap on the part of his tricky opponent,
he demurred for quite a minute, and puffed and wheezed,
and shook his jowls, and even shot furtive glances at me, and
made hesitating half-thrusts with his pudgily bunched fingers—dying to take that juicy queen and not daring—and all
of a sudden he swooped down upon it (who knows if it did
not teach him certain later audacities?), and I spent a dreary
hour in achieving a draw. He finished his brandy and presently
lumbered away, quite satisfied with this result (*mon pauvre
ami, je ne vous ai jamais revu et quoiqu'il y ait bien peu de
chance que vous voyiez mon livre, permettez-moi de vous dire
que je vous serre la main bien cordialement, et que toutes mes
fillettes vous saluent*). I found Dolores Haze at the kitchen
table, consuming a wedge of pie, with her eyes fixed on her
script. They rose to meet mine with a kind of celestial vapidity.
She remained singularly unruffled when confronted with my
discovery, and said *d'un petit air faussement contrit* that she
knew she was a very wicked kid, but simply had not been able
to resist the enchantment, and had used up those music
hours—O Reader, My Reader!—in a nearby public park rehearsing the magic forest scene with Mona. I said "fine"—
and stalked to the telephone. Mona's mother answered: "Oh
yes, she's in" and retreated with a mother's neutral laugh of
polite pleasure to shout off stage "Roy calling!" and the very
next moment Mona rustled up, and forthwith, in a low monotonous not untender voice started berating Roy for something he had said or done and I interrupted her, and presently
Mona was saying in her humblest, sexiest contralto, "yes, sir,"
"surely, sir," "I am alone to blame, sir, in this unfortunate
business," (what elocution! what poise!) "honest, I feel very
bad about it"—and so on and so forth as those little harlots
say.

So downstairs I went clearing my throat and holding my
heart. Lo was now in the living room, in her favorite overstuffed chair. As she sprawled there, biting at a hangnail and
mocking me with her heartless vaporous eyes, and all the time
rocking a stool upon which she had placed the heel of an
outstretched shoeless foot, I perceived all at once with a sick-

ening qualm how much she had changed since I first met her two years ago. Or had this happened during those last two weeks? *Tendresse?* Surely that was an exploded myth. She sat right in the focus of my incandescent anger. The fog of all lust had been swept away leaving nothing but this dreadful lucidity. Oh, she had changed! Her complexion was now that of any vulgar untidy highschool girl who applies shared cosmetics with grubby fingers to an unwashed face and does not mind what soiled texture, what pustulate epidermis comes in contact with her skin. Its smooth tender bloom had been so lovely in former days, so bright with tears, when I used to roll, in play, her tousled head on my knee. A coarse flush had now replaced that innocent fluorescence. What was locally known as a "rabbit cold" had painted with flaming pink the edges of her contemptuous nostrils. As in terror I lowered my gaze, it mechanically slid along the underside of her tensely stretched bare thigh—how polished and muscular her legs had grown! She kept her wide-set eyes, clouded-glass gray and slightly bloodshot, fixed upon me, and I saw the stealthy thought showing through them that perhaps after all Mona was right, and she, orphan Lo, could expose me without getting penalized herself. How wrong I was. How mad I was! Everything about her was of the same exasperating impenetrable order—the strength of her shapely legs, the dirty sole of her white sock, the thick sweater she wore despite the closeness of the room, her wenchy smell, and especially the dead end of her face with its strange flush and freshly made-up lips. Some of the red had left stains on her front teeth, and I was struck by a ghastly recollection—the evoked image not of Monique, but of another young prostitute in a bell-house, ages ago, who had been snapped up by somebody else before I had time to decide whether her mere youth warranted my risking some appalling disease, and who had just such flushed prominent *pommettes* and a dead *maman*, and big front teeth, and a bit of dingy red ribbon in her country-brown hair.

"Well, speak," said Lo. "Was the corroboration satisfactory?"

"Oh, yes," I said. "Perfect. Yes. And I do not doubt you two made it up. As a matter of fact, I do not doubt you have told her everything about us."

"Oh, yah?"

I controlled my breath and said: "Dolores, this must stop right away. I am ready to yank you out of Beardsley and lock you up you know where, but this must stop. I am ready to take you away the time it takes to pack a suitcase. This must stop or else anything may happen."

"Anything may happen, huh?"

I snatched away the stool she was rocking with her heel and her foot fell with a thud on the floor.

"Hey," she cried, "take it easy."

"First of all you go upstairs," I cried in my turn,—and simultaneously grabbed at her and pulled her up. From that moment, I stopped restraining my voice, and we continued yelling at each other, and she said unprintable things. She said she loathed me. She made monstrous faces at me, inflating her cheeks and producing a diabolical plopping sound. She said I had attempted to violate her several times when I was her mother's roomer. She said she was sure I had murdered her mother. She said she would sleep with the very first fellow who asked her and I could do nothing about it. I said she was to go upstairs and show me all her hiding places. It was a strident and hateful scene. I held her by her knobby wrist and she kept turning and twisting it this way and that, surreptitiously trying to find a weak point so as to wrench herself free at a favorable moment, but I held her quite hard and in fact hurt her rather badly for which I hope my heart may rot, and once or twice she jerked her arm so violently that I feared her wrist might snap, and all the while she stared at me with those unforgettable eyes where cold anger and hot tears struggled, and our voices were drowning the telephone, and when I grew aware of its ringing she instantly escaped.

With people in movies I seem to share the services of the machina telephonica and its sudden god. This time it was an irate neighbor. The east window happened to be agape in the living room, with the blind mercifully down, however; and behind it the damp black night of a sour New England spring had been breathlessly listening to us. I had always thought that type of haddocky spinster with the obscene mind was the result of considerable literary inbreeding in modern fiction; but now I am convinced that prude and prurient Miss East—

or to explode her incognito, Miss Fenton Lebone—had been probably protruding three-quarter-way from her bedroom window as she strove to catch the gist of our quarrel.

". . . This racket . . . lacks all sense of . . ." quacked the receiver, "we do not live in a tenement here. I must emphatically . . ."

I apologized for my daughter's friends being so loud. Young people, you know—and cradled the next quack and a half.

Downstairs the screen door banged. Lo? Escaped?

Through the casement on the stairs I saw a small impetuous ghost slip through the shrubs; a silvery dot in the dark—hub of bicycle wheel—moved, shivered, and she was gone.

It so happened that the car was spending the night in a repair shop downtown. I had no other alternative than to pursue on foot the winged fugitive. Even now, after more than three years have heaved and elapsed, I cannot visualize that spring-night street, that already so leafy street, without a gasp of panic. Before their lighted porch Miss Lester was promenading Miss Fabian's dropsical dackel. Mr. Hyde almost knocked it over. Walk three steps and run three. A tepid rain started to drum on the chestnut leaves. At the next corner, pressing Lolita against an iron railing, a blurred youth held and kissed—no, not her, mistake. My talons still tingling, I flew on.

Half a mile or so east of number fourteen, Thayer Street tangles with a private lane and a cross street; the latter leads to the town proper; in front of the first drugstore, I saw—with what melody of relief!—Lolita's fair bicycle waiting for her. I pushed instead of pulling, pulled, pushed, pulled, and entered. Look out! Some ten paces away Lolita, through the glass of a telephone booth (membranous god still with us), cupping the tube, confidentially hunched over it, slit her eyes at me, turned away with her treasure, hurriedly hung up, and walked out with a flourish.

"Tried to reach you at home," she said brightly. "A great decision has been made. But first buy me a drink, dad."

She watched the listless pale fountain girl put in the ice, pour in the coke, add the cherry syrup—and my heart was bursting with love-ache. That childish wrist. My lovely child.

You have a lovely child, Mr. Humbert. We always admire her as she passes by. Mr. Pim watched Pippa suck in the concoction.

J'ai toujours admiré l'œuvre ormonde du sublime Dublinois. And in the meantime the rain had become a voluptuous shower.

"Look," she said as she rode the bike beside me, one foot scraping the darkly glistening sidewalk, "look, I've decided something. I want to leave school. I hate that school. I hate the play, I really do! Never go back. Find another. Leave at once. Go for a long trip again. But *this* time we'll go wherever *I* want, won't we?"

I nodded. My Lolita.

"I choose? *C'est entendu?*" she asked wobbling a little beside me. Used French only when she was a very good little girl.

"Okay. *Entendu.* Now hop-hop-hop, Lenore, or you'll get soaked." (A storm of sobs was filling my chest.)

She bared her teeth and after her adorable school-girl fashion, leaned forward, and away she sped, my bird.

Miss Lester's finely groomed hand held a porch-door open for a waddling old dog *qui prenait son temps.*

Lo was waiting for me near the ghostly birch tree.

"I am drenched," she declared at the top of her voice. "Are you glad? To hell with the play! See what I mean?"

An invisible hag's claw slammed down an upper-floor window.

In our hallway, ablaze with welcoming lights, my Lolita peeled off her sweater, shook her gemmed hair, stretched towards me two bare arms, raised one knee:

"Carry me upstairs, please. I feel sort of romantic to-night."

It may interest physiologists to learn, at this point, that I have the ability—a most singular case, I presume—of shedding torrents of tears throughout the other tempest.

15

The brakes were relined, the waterpipes unclogged, the valves ground, and a number of other repairs and improve-

ments were paid for by not very mechanically-minded but prudent papa Humbert, so that the late Mrs. Humbert's car was
in respectable shape when ready to undertake a new journey.

We had promised Beardsley School, good old Beardsley
School, that we would be back as soon as my Hollywood
engagement came to an end (inventive Humbert was to be, I
hinted, chief consultant in the production of a film dealing
with "existentialism," still a hot thing at the time). Actually I
was toying with the idea of gently trickling across the Mexican
border—I was braver now than last year—and there deciding
what to do with my little concubine who was now sixty inches
tall and weighed ninety pounds. We had dug out our tour
books and maps. She had traced our route with immense zest.
Was it thanks to those theatricals that she had now outgrown
her juvenile jaded airs and was so adorably keen to explore
rich reality? I experienced the queer lightness of dreams that
pale but warm Sunday morning when we abandoned Professor
Chem's puzzled house and sped along Main Street toward the
four-lane highway. My Love's striped, black-and-white, cotton frock, jaunty blue cap, white socks and brown moccasins
were not quite in keeping with the large beautifully cut
aquamarine on a silver chainlet, which gemmed her throat: a
spring rain gift from me. We passed the New Hotel, and she
laughed. "A penny for your thoughts," I said and she
stretched out her palm at once, but at that moment I had to
apply the brakes rather abruptly at a red light. As we pulled
up, another car came to a gliding stop alongside, and a very
striking looking, athletically lean young woman (where had I
seen her?) with a high complexion and shoulder-length brilliant bronze hair, greeted Lo with a ringing "Hi!"—and then,
addressing me, effusively, edusively, (placed!), stressing certain
words, said: "What a *shame* it was to *tear* Dolly away from
the play—you should have *heard* the author *raving* about her
after that rehearsal—" "Green light, you dope," said Lo under her breath, and simultaneously, waving in bright adieu a
bangled arm, Joan of Arc (in a performance we saw at the
local theatre) violently outdistanced us to swerve into Campus
Avenue.

"Who was it exactly? Vermont or Rumpelmeyer?"

"No—Edusa Gold—the gal who coaches us."

"I was not referring to her. Who exactly concocted that play?"

"Oh! Yes, of course. Some old woman, Clare Something, I guess. There was quite a crowd of them there."

"So she complimented you?"

"Complimented my eye—she kissed me on my pure brow"—and my darling emitted that new yelp of merriment which—perhaps in connection with her theatrical mannerisms—she had lately begun to affect.

"You are a funny creature, Lolita," I said—or some such words. "Naturally, I am overjoyed you gave up that absurd stage business. But what is curious is that you dropped the whole thing only a week before its natural climax. Oh, Lolita, you should be careful of those surrenders of yours. I remember you gave up Ramsdale for camp, and camp for a joyride, and I could list other abrupt changes in your disposition. You must be careful. There are things that should never be given up. You must persevere. You should try to be a little nicer to me, Lolita. You should also watch your diet. The tour of your thigh, you know, should not exceed seventeen and a half inches. More might be fatal (I was kidding, of course). We are now setting out on a long happy journey. I remember—"

16

I remember as a child in Europe gloating over a map of North America that had "Appalachian Mountains" boldly running from Alabama up to New Brunswick, so that the whole region they spanned—Tennessee, the Virginias, Pennsylvania, New York, Vermont, New Hampshire and Maine, appeared to my imagination as a gigantic Switzerland or even Tibet, all mountain, glorious diamond peak upon peak, giant conifers, *le montagnard émigré* in his bear skin glory, and *Felis tigris goldsmithi*, and Red Indians under the catalpas. That it all boiled down to a measly suburban lawn and a smoking garbage incinerator, was appalling. Farewell, Appalachia! Leaving it, we crossed Ohio, the three states beginning with "I," and Nebraska—ah, that first whiff of the West! We

travelled very leisurely, having more than a week to reach
Wace, Continental Divide, where she passionately desired to
see the Ceremonial Dances marking the seasonal opening of
Magic Cave, and at least three weeks to reach Elphinstone,
gem of a western State where she yearned to climb Red Rock
from which a mature screen star had recently jumped to her
death after a drunken row with her gigolo.

Again we were welcomed to wary motels by means of inscriptions that read:

"We wish you to feel at home while here. *All* equipment
was carefully checked upon your arrival. Your license number
is on record here. Use hot water sparingly. We reserve the
right to eject without notice any objectionable person. Do not
throw waste material of *any* kind in the toilet bowl. Thank
you. Call again. The Management. P.S. We consider our
guests the Finest People of the World."

In these frightening places we paid ten for twins, flies
queued outside at the screenless door and successfully scrambled in, the ashes of our predecessors still lingered in the ashtrays, a woman's hair lay on the pillow, one heard one's
neighbor hanging his coat in his closet, the hangers were in-
geniously fixed to their bars by coils of wire so as to thwart
theft, and, in crowning insult, the pictures above the twin beds
were identical twins. I also noticed that commercial fashion
was changing. There was a tendency for cabins to fuse and
gradually form the caravansary, and, lo (she was not interested
but the reader may be), a second story was added, and a lobby
grew in, and cars were removed to a communal garage, and
the motel reverted to the good old hotel.

I now warn the reader not to mock me and my mental daze.
It is easy for him and me to decipher *now* a past destiny; but
a destiny in the making is, believe me, not one of those honest
mystery stories where all you have to do is keep an eye on the
clues. In my youth I once read a French detective tale where
the clues were actually in italics; but that is not McFate's
way—even if one does learn to recognize certain obscure in-
dications.

For instance: I would not swear that there was not at least
one occasion, prior to, or at the very beginning of, the Mid-
west lap of our journey, when she managed to convey some

information to, or otherwise get into contact with, a person or persons unknown. We had stopped at a gas station, under the sign of Pegasus, and she had slipped out of her seat and escaped to the rear of the premises while the raised hood, under which I had bent to watch the mechanic's manipulations, hid her for a moment from my sight. Being inclined to be lenient, I only shook my benign head though strictly speaking such visits were taboo, since I felt instinctively that toilets—as also telephones—happened to be, for reasons unfathomable, the points where my destiny was liable to catch. We all have such fateful objects—it may be a recurrent landscape in one case, a number in another—carefully chosen by the gods to attract events of special significance for us: here shall John always stumble; there shall Jane's heart always break.

Well—my car had been attended to, and I had moved it away from the pumps to let a pickup truck be serviced—when the growing volume of her absence began to weigh upon me in the windy grayness. Not for the first time, and not for the last, had I stared in such dull discomfort of mind at those stationary trivialities that look almost surprised, like staring rustics, to find themselves in the stranded traveller's field of vision: that green garbage can, those very black, very white-walled tires for sale, those bright cans of motor oil, that red icebox with assorted drinks, the four, five, seven discarded bottles within the incompleted crossword puzzle of their wooden cells, that bug patiently walking up the inside of the window of the office. Radio music was coming from its open door, and because the rhythm was not synchronized with the heave and flutter and other gestures of wind-animated vegetation, one had the impression of an old scenic film living its own life while piano or fiddle followed a line of music quite outside the shivering flower, the swaying branch. The sound of Charlotte's last sob incongruously vibrated through me as, with her dress fluttering athwart the rhythm, Lolita veered from a totally unexpected direction. She had found the toilet occupied and had crossed over to the sign of the Conche in the next block. They said there they were proud of their home-clean restrooms. These prepaid postcards, they said, had been provided for your comments. No postcards. No soap. Nothing. No comments.

That day or the next, after a tedious drive through a land of food crops, we reached a pleasant little burg and put up at Chestnut Court—nice cabins, damp green grounds, apple trees, an old swing—and a tremendous sunset which the tired child ignored. She had wanted to go through Kasbeam because it was only thirty miles north from her home town but on the following morning I found her quite listless, with no desire to see again the sidewalk where she had played hopscotch some five years before. For obvious reasons I had rather dreaded that side trip, even though we had agreed not to make ourselves conspicuous in any way—to remain in the car and not look up old friends. My relief at her abandoning the project was spoiled by the thought that had she felt I were totally against the nostalgic possibilities of Pisky, as I had been last year, she would not have given up so easily. On my mentioning this with a sigh, she sighed too and complained of being out of sorts. She wanted to remain in bed till teatime at least, with lots of magazines, and then if she felt better she suggested we just continue westward. I must say she was very sweet and languid, and craved for fresh fruits, and I decided to go and fetch her a toothsome picnic lunch in Kasbeam. Our cabin stood on the timbered crest of a hill, and from our window you could see the road winding down, and then running as straight as a hair parting between two rows of chestnut trees, towards the pretty town, which looked singularly distinct and toylike in the pure morning distance. One could make out an elf-like girl on an insect-like bicycle, and a dog, a bit too large proportionately, all as clear as those pilgrims and mules winding up wax-pale roads in old paintings with blue hills and red little people. I have the European urge to use my feet when a drive can be dispensed with, so I leisurely walked down, eventually meeting the cyclist—a plain plump girl with pigtails, followed by a huge St. Bernard dog with orbits like pansies. In Kasbeam a very old barber gave me a very mediocre haircut: he babbled of a baseball-playing son of his, and, at every explodent, spat into my neck, and every now and then wiped his glasses on my sheet-wrap, or interrupted his tremulous scissor work to produce faded newspaper clippings, and so inattentive was I that it came as a shock to realize as he pointed to an easeled photograph among the ancient gray lotions, that the mustached young ball player had been dead for the last thirty years.

I had a cup of hot flavorless coffee, bought a bunch of bananas for my monkey, and spent another ten minutes or so in a delicatessen store. At least an hour and a half must have elapsed when this homeward-bound little pilgrim appeared on the winding road leading to Chestnut Castle.

The girl I had seen on my way to town was now loaded with linen and engaged in helping a misshapen man whose big head and coarse features reminded me of the "Bertoldo" character in low Italian comedy. They were cleaning the cabins of which there was a dozen or so on Chestnut Crest, all pleasantly spaced amid the copious verdure. It was noon, and most of them, with a final bang of their screen doors, had already got rid of their occupants. A very elderly, almost mummy-like couple in a very new model were in the act of creeping out of one of the contiguous garages; from another a red hood protruded in somewhat cod-piece fashion; and nearer to our cabin, a strong and handsome young man with a shock of black hair and blue eyes was putting a portable refrigerator into a station wagon. For some reason he gave me a sheepish grin as I passed. On the grass expanse opposite, in the many-limbed shade of luxuriant trees, the familiar St. Bernard dog was guarding his mistress' bicycle, and nearby a young woman, far gone in the family way, had seated a rapt baby on a swing and was rocking it gently, while a jealous boy of two or three was making a nuisance of himself by trying to push or pull the swing board; he finally succeeded in getting himself knocked down by it, and bawled loudly as he lay supine on the grass while his mother continued to smile gently at neither of her present children. I recall so clearly these minutiae probably because I was to check my impressions so thoroughly only a few minutes later; and besides, something in me had been on guard ever since that awful night in Beardsley. I now refused to be diverted by the feeling of well-being that my walk had engendered—by the young summer breeze that enveloped the nape of my neck, the giving crunch of the

damp gravel, the juicy tidbit I had sucked out at last from a
hollow tooth, and even the comfortable weight of my provisions which the general condition of my heart should not have
allowed me to carry; but even that miserable pump of mine
seemed to be working sweetly, and I felt *adolori d'amoureuse
langueur*, to quote dear old Ronsard, as I reached the cottage
where I had left my Dolores.

To my surprise I found her dressed. She was sitting on the
edge of the bed in slacks and T-shirt, and was looking at me
as if she could not quite place me. The frank soft shape of her
small breasts was brought out rather than blurred by the limpness of her thin shirt, and this frankness irritated me. She had
not washed; yet her mouth was freshly though smudgily
painted, and her broad teeth glistened like wine-tinged ivory,
or pinkish poker chips. And there she sat, hands clasped in
her lap, and dreamily brimmed with a diabolical glow that had
no relation to me whatever.

I plumped down my heavy paper bag and stood staring at
the bare ankles of her sandaled feet, then at her silly face, then
again at her sinful feet. "You've been out," I said (the sandals
were filthy with gravel).

"I just got up," she replied, and added upon intercepting
my downward glance: "Went out for a sec. Wanted to see if
you were coming back."

She became aware of the bananas and uncoiled herself
tableward.

What special suspicion could I have? None indeed—but
those muddy, moony eyes of hers, that singular warmth em-
anating from her! I said nothing. I looked at the road meandering so distinctly within the frame of the window . . .
Anybody wishing to betray my trust would have found it a
splendid lookout. With rising appetite, Lo applied herself to
the fruit. All at once I remembered the ingratiating grin of
the Johnny nextdoor. I stepped out quickly. All cars had disappeared except his station wagon; his pregnant young wife
was now getting into it with her baby and the other, more or
less cancelled, child.

"What's the matter, where are you going?" cried Lo from
the porch.

I said nothing. I pushed her softness back into the room

and went in after her. I ripped her shirt off. I unzipped the rest of her. I tore off her sandals. Wildly, I pursued the shadow of her infidelity; but the scent I travelled upon was so slight as to be practically undistinguishable from a madman's fancy.

17

Gros Gaston, in his prissy way, had liked to make presents— presents just a prissy wee bit out of the ordinary, or so he prissily thought. Noticing one night that my box of chessmen was broken, he sent me next morning, with a little lad of his, a copper case: it had an elaborate Oriental design over the lid and could be securely locked. One glance sufficed to assure me that it was one of those cheap money boxes called for some reason "luizettas" that you buy in Algiers and else- where, and wonder what to do with afterwards. It turned out to be much too flat for holding my bulky chessmen, but I kept it—using it for a totally different purpose.

In order to break some pattern of fate in which I obscurely felt myself being enmeshed, I had decided—despite Lo's vis- ible annoyance—to spend another night at Chestnut Court; definitely waking up at four in the morning, I ascertained that Lo was still sound asleep (mouth open, in a kind of dull amazement at the curiously inane life we all had rigged up for her) and satisfied myself that the precious contents of the "luizetta" were safe. There, snugly wrapped in a white woollen scarf, lay a pocket automatic: caliber .32, capacity of magazine 8 cartridges, length a little under one ninth of Lolita's length, stock checked walnut, finish full blued. I had inherited it from the late Harold Haze, with a 1938 catalog which cheerily said in part: "Particularly well adapted for use in the home and car as well as on the person." There it lay, ready for instant service on the person or persons, loaded and fully cocked with the slide lock in safety position, thus precluding any accidental discharge. We must remember that a pistol is the Freudian symbol of the Ur-father's central forelimb.

I was now glad I had it with me—and even more glad that I had learned to use it two years before, in the pine forest around my and Charlotte's glass lake. Farlow, with whom I had roamed those remote woods, was an admirable marks-

man, and with his .38 actually managed to hit a hummingbird,
though I must say not much of it could be retrieved for
proof—only a little iridescent fluff. A burley ex-policeman
called Krestovski, who in the twenties had shot and killed two
escaped convicts, joined us and bagged a tiny woodpecker—
completely out of season, incidentally. Between those two
sportsmen I of course was a novice and kept missing everything, though I did wound a squirrel on a later occasion when
I went out alone. "You lie here," I whispered to my lightweight compact little chum, and then toasted it with a dram
of gin.

18

The reader must now forget Chestnuts and Colts, and accompany us further west. The following days were marked by
a number of great thunderstorms—or perhaps, there was but
one single storm which progressed across country in ponderous frog-leaps and which we could not shake off just as we
could not shake off detective Trapp: for it was during those
days that the problem of the Aztec Red convertible presented
itself to me, and quite overshadowed the theme of Lo's lovers.

Queer! I who was jealous of every male we met—queer,
how I misinterpreted the designations of doom. Perhaps I had
been lulled by Lo's modest behavior in winter, and anyway it
would have been too foolish even for a lunatic to suppose
another Humbert was avidly following Humbert and Humbert's nymphet with Jovian fireworks, over the great and ugly
plains. I surmised, *donc*, that the Red Yak keeping behind us
at a discreet distance mile after mile was operated by a detective whom some busybody had hired to see what exactly
Humbert Humbert was doing with that minor stepdaughter
of his. As happens with me at periods of electrical disturbance
and crepitating lightnings, I had hallucinations. Maybe they
were more than hallucinations. I do not know what she or he,
or both had put into my liquor but one night I felt sure somebody was tapping on the door of our cabin, and I flung it
open, and noticed two things—that I was stark naked and
that, white-glistening in the rain-dripping darkness, there
stood a man holding before his face the mask of Jutting Chin,

a grotesque sleuth in the funnies. He emitted a muffled guffaw and scurried away, and I reeled back into the room, and fell asleep again, and am not sure even to this day that the visit was not a drug-provoked dream: I have thoroughly studied Trapp's type of humor, and this might have been a plausible sample. Oh, crude and absolutely ruthless! Somebody, I imagined, was making money on those masks of popular monsters and morons. Did I see next morning two urchins rummaging in a garbage can and trying on Jutting Chin? I wonder. It may all have been a coincidence—due to atmospheric conditions, I suppose.

Being a murderer with a sensational but incomplete and unorthodox memory, I cannot tell you, ladies and gentlemen, the exact day when I first knew with utter certainty that the red convertible was following us. I do remember, however, the first time I saw its driver quite clearly. I was proceeding slowly one afternoon through torrents of rain and kept seeing that red ghost swimming and shivering with lust in my mirror, when presently the deluge dwindled to a patter, and then was suspended altogether. With a swishing sound a sunburst swept the highway, and needing a pair of new sunglasses, I pulled up at a filling station. What was happening was a sickness, a cancer, that could not be helped, so I simply ignored the fact that our quiet pursuer, in his converted state, stopped a little behind us at a café or bar bearing the idiotic sign: The Bustle: A Deceitful Seatful. Having seen to the needs of my car, I walked into the office to get those glasses and pay for the gas. As I was in the act of signing a traveller's check and wondered about my exact whereabouts, I happened to glance through a side window, and saw a terrible thing. A broad-backed man, baldish, in an oatmeal coat and dark-brown trousers, was listening to Lo who was leaning out of the car and talking to him very rapidly, her hand with outspread fingers going up and down as it did when she was very serious and emphatic. What struck me with sickening force was—how should I put it?—the voluble familiarity of her way, as if they had known each other—oh, for weeks and weeks. I saw him scratch his cheek and nod, and turn, and walk back to his convertible, a broad and thickish man of my age, somewhat resembling Gustave Trapp, a cousin of my father's in Switzerland—same smoothly tanned face, fuller than mine, with a small dark mustache and a rosebud degenerate mouth. Lolita was studying a road map when I got back into the car.

"What did that man ask you, Lo?"

"Man? Oh, that man. Oh yes. Oh, I don't know. He wondered if I had a map. Lost his way, I guess."

We drove on, and I said:

"Now listen, Lo. I do not know whether you are lying or not, and I do not know whether you are insane or not, and I do not care for the moment; but that person has been following us all day, and his car was at the motel yesterday, and I think he is a cop. You know perfectly well what will happen and where you will go if the police find out about things. Now I want to know exactly what he said to you and what you told him."

She laughed.

"If he's really a cop," she said shrilly but not illogically, "the worst thing we could do, would be to show him we are scared. Ignore him, *Dad*."

"Did he ask where we were going?"

"Oh, he knows *that*" (mocking me).

"Anyway," I said, giving up, "I have seen his face now. He is not pretty. He looks exactly like a relative of mine called Trapp."

"Perhaps he is Trapp. If I were you— Oh, look, all the nines are changing into the next thousand. When I was a little kid," she continued unexpectedly, "I used to think they'd stop and go back to nines, if only my mother agreed to put the car in reverse."

It was the first time, I think, she spoke spontaneously of her pre-Humbertian childhood; perhaps, the theatre had taught her that trick; and silently we travelled on, unpursued.

But next day, like pain in a fatal disease that comes back as the drug and hope wear off, there it was again behind us, that glossy red beast. The traffic on the highway was light that day; nobody passed anybody; and nobody attempted to get in between our humble blue car and its imperious red shadow—as if there were some spell cast on that interspace, a zone of evil mirth and magic, a zone whose very precision and stability had a glass-like virtue that was almost artistic. The driver behind me, with his stuffed shoulders and Trappish mustache, looked like a display dummy, and his convertible seemed to move only because an invisible rope of silent silk connected it with our shabby vehicle. We were many times weaker than his splendid, lacquered machine, so that I did not even attempt to outspeed him. *O lente currite noctis equi!* O softly run, nightmares! We climbed long grades and rolled downhill again, and heeded speed limits, and spared slow children, and reproduced in sweeping terms the black wiggles of curves on their yellow shields, and no matter how and where we drove, the enchanted interspace slid on intact, mathematical, mirage-like, the viatic counterpart of a magic carpet. And all the time I was aware of a private blaze on my right: her joyful eye, her flaming cheek.

A traffic policeman, deep in the nightmare of crisscross streets—at half-past-four P.M. in a factory town—was the hand of chance that interrupted the spell. He beckoned me on, and then with the same hand cut off my shadow. A score of cars were launched in between us, and I sped on, and deftly turned into a narrow lane. A sparrow alighted with a jumbo bread crumb, was tackled by another, and lost the crumb.

When after a few grim stoppages and a bit of deliberate meandering, I returned to the highway, our shadow had dis-appeared.

Lola snorted and said: "If he is what you think he is, how silly to give him the slip."

"I have other notions by now," I said.

"You should—ah—check them by—ah—keeping in touch with him, fahther deah," said Lo, writhing in the coils of her own sarcasm. "Gee, you *are* mean," she added in her ordinary voice.

We spent a grim night in a very foul cabin, under a sonorous amplitude of rain, and with a kind of prehistorically loud thun-der incessantly rolling above us.

"I am not a lady and do not like lightning," said Lo, whose dread of electric storms gave me some pathetic solace.

We had breakfast in the township of Soda, pop. 1001.

"Judging by the terminal figure," I remarked, "Fatface is already here."

"Your humor," said Lo, "is sidesplitting, deah fahther."

We were in sage-brush country by that time, and there was a day or two of lovely release (I had been a fool, all was well, that discomfort was merely a trapped flatus), and presently the mesas gave way to real mountains, and, on time, we drove into Wace.

Oh, disaster. Some confusion had occurred, she had mis-read a date in the Tour Book, and the Magic Cave ceremonies were over! She took it bravely, I must admit—and, when we discovered there was in kurortish Wace a summer theatre in full swing, we naturally drifted toward it one fair mid-June evening. I really could not tell you the plot of the play we saw. A trivial affair, no doubt, with self-conscious light effects and a mediocre leading lady. The only detail that pleased me was a garland of seven little graces, more or less immobile, prettily painted, bare-limbed—seven bemused pubescent girls in colored gauze that had been recruited locally (judging by the partisan flurry here and there among the audience) and were supposed to represent a living rainbow, which lingered throughout the last act, and rather teasingly faded behind a series of multiplied veils. I remember thinking that this idea of children-colors had been lifted by authors Clare Quilty and Vivian Darkbloom from a passage in James Joyce, and that two of the colors were quite exasperatingly lovely—Orange who kept fidgeting all the time, and Emerald who, when her eyes got used to the pitch-black pit where we all heavily sat, suddenly smiled at her mother or her protector.

As soon as the thing was over, and manual applause—a sound my nerves cannot stand—began to crash all around me, I started to pull and push Lo toward the exit, in my so natural amorous impatience to get her back to our neon-blue cottage in the stunned, starry night: I always say nature is stunned by the sights she sees. Dolly-Lo, however, lagged behind, in a rosy daze, her pleased eyes narrowed, her sense of vision swamping the rest of her senses to such an extent that her limp hands hardly came together at all in the mechanical ac-tion of clapping they still went through. I had seen that kind of thing in children before but, by God, this was a special child, myopically beaming at the already remote stage where

I glimpsed something of the joint authors—a man's tuxedo and the bare shoulders of a hawk-like, black-haired, strikingly tall woman.

"You've again hurt my wrist, you brute," said Lolita in a small voice as she slipped into her car seat.

"I am dreadfully sorry, my darling, my own ultraviolet darling," I said, unsuccessfully trying to catch her elbow, and I added, to change the conversation—to change the direction of fate, oh God, oh God: "Vivian is quite a woman. I am sure we saw her yesterday in that restaurant, in Soda pop."

"Sometimes," said Lo, "you are quite revoltingly dumb. First, Vivian is the male author, the gal author is Clare; and second, she is forty, married and has Negro blood."

"I thought," I said kidding her, "Quilty was an ancient flame of yours, in the days when you loved me, in sweet old Ramsdale."

"What?" countered Lo, her features working. "That fat dentist? You must be confusing me with some other fast little article."

And I thought to myself how those fast little articles forget everything, everything, while we, old lovers, treasure every inch of their nymphancy.

19

With Lo's knowledge and assent, the two post offices given to the Beardsley postmaster as forwarding addresses were P.O. Wace and P.O. Elphinstone. Next morning we visited the former and had to wait in a short but slow queue. Serene Lo studied the rogues' gallery. Handsome Bryan Bryanski, alias Anthony Bryan, alias Tony Brown, eyes hazel, complexion fair, was wanted for kidnaping. A sad-eyed old gentleman's faux-pas was mail fraud, and, as if that were not enough, he was cursed with deformed arches. Sullen Sullivan came with a caution: Is believed armed, and should be considered extremely dangerous. If you want to make a movie out of my book, have one of these faces gently melt into my own, while I look. And moreover there was a smudgy snapshot of a Missing Girl, age fourteen, wearing brown shoes when last seen, rhymes. Please notify Sheriff Buller.

I forget my letters; as to Dolly's, there was her report and a very special-looking envelope. This I deliberately opened and perused its contents. I concluded I was doing the foreseen since she did not seem to mind and drifted toward the news-stand near the exit.

"Dolly-Lo: Well, the play was a grand success. All three hounds lay quiet having been slightly drugged by Cutler, I suspect, and Linda knew all your lines. She was fine, she had alertness and control, but lacked somehow the *responsiveness*, the *relaxed vitality*, the charm of *my*—and the author's— Diana; but there was no author to applaud us as last time, and the terrific electric storm outside interfered with our own modest off-stage thunder. Oh dear, life does fly. Now that everything is over, school, play, the Roy mess, mother's con-finement (our baby, alas, did not live!), it all seems such a long time ago, though practically I still bear traces of the paint.

"We are going to New York after to-morrow, and I guess I can't manage to wriggle out of accompanying my parents to Europe. I have even worse news for you. Dolly-Lo! I may not be back at Beardsley if and when you return. With one thing and another, one being you know who, and the other not being who you think you know, Dad wants me to go to school in Paris for one year while he and Fullbright are around.

"As expected, poor Poet stumbled in Scene III when arriv-ing at the bit of French nonsense. Remember? *Ne manque pas de dire à ton amant, Chimène, comme le lac est beau car il faut qu'il t'y mène.* Lucky beau! *Qu'il t'y*— What a tongue-twister! Well, be good, Lollikins. Best love from your Poet, and best regards to the Governor. Your Mona. P.S. Because of one thing and another, my correspondence happens to be rigidly controlled. So better wait till I write you from Eu-rope." (She never did as far as I know. The letter contained an element of mysterious nastiness that I am too tired to-day to analyze. I found it later preserved in one of the Tour Books, and give it here *à titre documentaire*. I read it twice.)

I looked up from the letter and was about to— There was no Lo to behold. While I was engrossed in Mona's witchery, Lo had shrugged her shoulders and vanished. "Did you hap-pen to see—" I asked of a hunchback sweeping the floor near

the entrance. He had, the old lecherer. He guessed she had
seen a friend and had hurried out. I hurried out too. I
stopped—she had not. I hurried on. I stopped again. It had
happened at last. She had gone for ever.

In later years I have often wondered why she did *not* go for
ever that day. Was it the retentive quality of her new summer
clothes in my locked car? Was it some unripe particle in some
general plan? Was it simply because, all things considered, I
might as well be used to convey her to Elphinstone—the secret terminus, anyway? I only know I was quite certain she
had left me for ever. The noncommittal mauve mountains half
encircling the town seemed to me to swarm with panting,
scrambling, laughing, panting Lolitas who dissolved in their
haze. A big W made of white stones on a steep talus in the
far vista of a cross street seemed the very initial of woe.

The new and beautiful post office I had just emerged from
stood between a dormant movie house and a conspiracy of
poplars. The time was 9 A.M. mountain time. The street was
Main Street. I paced its blue side peering at the opposite
one: charming it into beauty, was one of those fragile young
summer mornings with flashes of glass here and there and a
general air of faltering and almost fainting at the prospect of
an intolerably torrid noon. Crossing over, I loafed and leafed,
as it were, through one long block: Drugs, Real Estate, Fashions, Auto Parts, Cafe, Sporting Goods, Real Estate, Furniture, Appliances, Western Union, Cleaners, Grocery. Officer,
officer, my daughter has run away. In collusion with a detective; in love with a blackmailer. Took advantage of my utter
helplessness. I peered into all the stores. I deliberated inly if
I should talk to any of the sparse foot-passengers. I did not.
I sat for a while in the parked car. I inspected the public garden on the east side. I went back to Fashions and Auto Parts.
I told myself with a burst of furious sarcasm—*un ricane-
ment*—that I was crazy to suspect her, that she would turn up
in a minute.

She did.

I wheeled around and shook off the hand she had placed
on my sleeve with a timid and imbecile smile.

"Get into the car," I said.

She obeyed, and I went on pacing up and down, struggling

with nameless thoughts, trying to plan some way of tackling her duplicity.

Presently she left the car and was at my side again. My sense of hearing gradually got tuned in to station Lo again, and I became aware she was telling me that she had met a former girl friend.

"Yes? Whom?"

"A Beardsley girl."

"Good. I know every name in your group. Alice Adams?"

"This girl was not in my group."

"Good. I have a complete student list with me. Her name please."

"She was not in my school. She is just a town girl in Beardsley."

"Good. I have the Beardsley directory with me too. We'll look up all the Browns."

"I only know her first name."

"Mary or Jane?"

"No—Dolly, like me."

"So that's the dead end" (the mirror you break your nose against). "Good. Let us try another angle. You have been absent twenty-eight minutes. What did the two Dollys do?"

"We went to a drugstore."

"And you had there—?"

"Oh, just a couple of cokes."

"Careful, Dolly. We can check that, you know."

"At least, she had. I had a glass of water."

"Good. Was it that place there?"

"Sure."

"Good, come on, we'll grill the soda jerk."

"Wait a sec. Come to think it might have been further down—just around the corner."

"Come on all the same. Go in please. Well, let's see." (Opening a chained telephone book.) "Dignified Funeral Service. No, not yet. Here we are: Druggists-Retail. Hill Drug Store. Larkin's Pharmacy. And two more. That's all Wace seems to have in the way of soda fountains—at least in the business section. Well, we will check them all."

"Go to hell," she said.

"Lo, rudeness will get you nowhere."

"Okay," she said. "But you're not going to trap me. Okay, so we did not have a pop. We just talked and looked at dresses in show windows."

"Which? That window there for example?"

"Yes, that one there, for example."

"Oh Lo! Let's look closer at it."

It was indeed a pretty sight. A dapper young fellow was vacuum-cleaning a carpet of sorts upon which stood two figures that looked as if some blast had just worked havoc with them. One figure was stark naked, wigless and armless. Its comparatively small stature and smirking pose suggested that when clothed it had represented, and would represent when clothed again, a girl-child of Lolita's size. But in its present state it was sexless. Next to it, stood a much taller veiled bride, quite perfect and *intacta* except for the lack of one arm. On the floor, at the feet of these damsels, where the man crawled about laboriously with his cleaner, there lay a cluster of three slender arms, and a blond wig. Two of the arms happened to be twisted and seemed to suggest a clasping gesture of horror and supplication.

"Look, Lo," I said quietly. "Look well. Is not that a rather good symbol of something or other? However"—I went on as we got back into the car—"I have taken certain precautions. Here (delicately opening the glove compartment), on this pad, I have our boy friend's car number."

As the ass I was I had not memorized it. What remained of it in my mind were the initial letter and the closing figure as if the whole amphitheatre of six signs receded concavely behind a tinted glass too opaque to allow the central series to be deciphered, but just translucent enough to make out its extreme edges—a capital P and a 6. I have to go into those details (which in themselves can interest only a professional psychologue) because otherwise the reader (ah, if I could visualize him as a blond-bearded scholar with rosy lips sucking *la pomme de sa canne* as he quaffs my manuscript!) might not understand the quality of the shock I experienced upon noticing that the P had acquired the bustle of a B and that the 6 had been deleted altogether. The rest, with erasures revealing the hurried shuttle smear of a pencil's rubber end, and with parts of numbers obliterated or reconstructed in a child's

hand, presented a tangle of barbed wire to any logical interpretation. All I knew was the state—one adjacent to the state
Beardsley was in.

I said nothing. I put the pad back, closed the compartment,
and drove out of Wace. Lo had grabbed some comics from
the back seat and, mobile-white-bloused, one brown elbow
out of the window, was deep in the current adventure of some
clout or clown. Three or four miles out of Wace, I turned into
the shadow of a picnic ground where the morning had
dumped its litter of light on an empty table; Lo looked up
with a semi-smile of surprise and without a word I delivered
a tremendous backhand cut that caught her smack on her hot
hard little cheekbone.

And then the remorse, the poignant sweetness of sobbing
atonement, groveling love, the hopelessness of sensual reconciliation. In the velvet night, at Mirana Motel (Mirana!) I
kissed the yellowish soles of her long-toed feet, I immolated
myself . . . But it was all of no avail. Both doomed were we.
And soon I was to enter a new cycle of persecution.

In a street of Wace, on its outskirts . . . Oh, I am quite
sure it was not a delusion. In a street of Wace, I had glimpsed
the Aztec Red convertible, or its identical twin. Instead of
Trapp, it contained four or five loud young people of several
sexes—but I said nothing. After Wace a totally new situation
arose. For a day or two, I enjoyed the mental emphasis with
which I told myself that we were not, and never had been
followed; and then I became sickeningly conscious that Trapp
had changed his tactics and was still with us, in this or that
rented car.

A veritable Proteus of the highway, with bewildering ease
he switched from one vehicle to another. This technique implied the existence of garages specializing in "stage-automo-
bile" operations, but I never could discover the remises he
used. He seemed to patronize at first the Chevrolet genus,
beginning with a Campus Cream convertible, then going on
to a small Horizon Blue sedan, and thenceforth fading into
Surf Gray and Driftwood Gray. Then he turned to other
makes and passed through a pale dull rainbow of paint shades,
and one day I found myself attempting to cope with the subtle
distinction between our own Dream Blue Melmoth and the

Crest Blue Oldsmobile he had rented; grays, however, remained his favorite cryptochromism, and, in agonizing nightmares, I tried in vain to sort out properly such ghosts as
Chrysler's Shell Gray, Chevrolet's Thistle Gray, Dodge's
French Gray . . .

The necessity of being constantly on the lookout for his
little moustache and open shirt—or for his baldish pate and
broad shoulders—led me to a profound study of all cars on
the road—behind, before, alongside, coming, going, every vehicle under the dancing sun: the quiet vacationist's automobile with the box of Tender-Touch tissues in the back
window; the recklessly speeding jalopy full of pale children
with a shaggy dog's head protruding, and a crumpled mud-
guard; the bachelor's tudor sedan crowded with suits on
hangers; the huge fat house trailer weaving in front, immune
to the Indian file of fury boiling behind it; the car with the
young female passenger politely perched in the middle of the
front seat to be closer to the young male driver; the car carrying on its roof a red boat bottom up . . . The gray car
slowing up before us, the gray car catching up with us.

We were in mountain country, somewhere between Snow
and Champion, and rolling down an almost imperceptible
grade, when I had my next distinct view of Detective Para-
mour Trapp. The gray mist behind us had deepened and concentrated into the compactness of a Dominion Blue sedan. All
of a sudden, as if the car I drove responded to my poor heart's
pangs, we were slithering from side to side, with something
making a helpless plap-plap-plap under us.

"You got a flat, mister," said cheerful Lo.

I pulled up—near a precipice. She folded her arms and put
her foot on the dashboard. I got out and examined the right
rear wheel. The base of its tire was sheepishly and hideously
square. Trapp had stopped some fifty yards behind us. His
distant face formed a grease spot of mirth. This was my
chance. I started to walk towards him—with the brilliant idea
of asking him for a jack though I had one. He backed a little.
I stubbed my toe against a stone—and there was a sense of
general laughter. Then a tremendous truck loomed from behind Trapp and thundered by me—and immediately after, I
heard it utter a convulsive honk. Instinctively I looked back—

and saw my own car gently creeping away. I could make out
Lo ludicrously at the wheel, and the engine was certainly running—though I remembered I had cut it but had not applied
the emergency brake; and during the brief space of throb-time
that it took me to reach the croaking machine which came to
a standstill at last, it dawned upon me that during the last two
years little Lo had had ample time to pick up the rudiments
of driving. As I wrenched the door open, I was goddam sure
she had started the car to prevent me from walking up to
Trapp. Her trick proved useless, however, for even while I was
pursuing her he had made an energetic U-turn and was gone.
I rested for a while. Lo asked wasn't I going to thank her—
the car had started to move by itself and— Getting no answer,
she immersed herself in a study of the map. I got out again
and commenced the "ordeal of the orb," as Charlotte used
to say. Perhaps, I was losing my mind.

We continued our grotesque journey. After a forlorn and
useless dip, we went up and up. On a steep grade I found
myself behind the gigantic truck that had overtaken us. It was
now groaning up a winding road and was impossible to pass.
Out of its front part a small oblong of smooth silver—the
inner wrapping of chewing gum—escaped and flew back into
our windshield. It occurred to me that if I were really losing
my mind, I might end by murdering somebody. In fact—said
high-and-dry Humbert to floundering Humbert—it might be
quite clever to prepare things—to transfer the weapon from
box to pocket—so as to be ready to take advantage of the
spell of insanity when it does come.

20

By permitting Lolita to study acting I had, fond fool, suffered her to cultivate deceit. It now appeared that it had not
been merely a matter of learning the answers to such questions
as what is the basic conflict in "Hedda Gabler," or where are
the climaxes in "Love Under the Lindens," or analyze the
prevailing mood of "Cherry Orchard"; it was really a matter
of learning to betray me. How I deplored now the exercises
in sensual simulation that I had so often seen her go through

in our Beardsley parlor when I would observe her from some
strategic point while she, like a hypnotic subject or a performer in a mystic rite, produced sophisticated versions of
infantile make-believe by going through the mimetic actions
of hearing a moan in the dark, seeing for the first time a
brand new young stepmother, tasting something she hated,
such as buttermilk, smelling crushed grass in a lush orchard,
or touching mirages of objects with her sly, slender, girl-child
hands. Among my papers I still have a mimeographed sheet
suggesting:

Tactile drill. Imagine yourself picking up and holding: a pingpong
ball, an apple, a sticky date, a new flannel-fluffed tennis ball, a hot
potato, an ice cube, a kitten, a puppy, a horseshoe, a feather, a flashlight.
    Knead with your fingers the following imaginary things: a piece of
bread, india rubber, a friend's aching temple, a sample of velvet, a
rose petal.
    You are a blind girl. Palpate the face of: a Greek youth, Cyrano,
Santa Claus, a baby, a laughing faun, a sleeping stranger, your father.

But she had been so pretty in the weaving of those delicate
spells, in the dreamy performance of her enchantments and
duties! On certain adventurous evenings, in Beardsley, I also
had her dance for me with the promise of some treat or gift,
and although these routine leg-parted leaps of hers were more
like those of a football cheerleader than like the languorous
and jerky motions of a Parisian *petit rat*, the rhythms of her
not quite nubile limbs had given me pleasure. But all that was
nothing, absolutely nothing, to the indescribable itch of rapture that her tennis game produced in me—the teasing delirious feeling of teetering on the very brink of unearthly order
and splendor.
    Despite her advanced age, she was more of a nymphet than
ever, with her apricot-colored limbs, in her sub-teen tennis
togs! Winged gentlemen! No hereafter is acceptable if it does
not produce her as she was then, in that Colorado resort between Snow and Elphinstone, with everything right: the white
wide little-boy shorts, the slender waist, the apricot midriff,
the white breast-kerchief whose ribbons went up and encircled
her neck to end behind in a dangling knot leaving bare her

gaspingly young and adorable apricot shoulder blades with that pubescence and those lovely gentle bones, and the smooth, downward-tapering back. Her cap had a white peak. Her racket had cost me a small fortune. Idiot, triple idiot! I could have filmed her! I would have had her now with me, before my eyes, in the projection room of my pain and despair!

She would wait and relax for a bar or two of white-lined time before going into the act of serving, and often bounced the ball once or twice, or pawed the ground a little, always at ease, always rather vague about the score, always cheerful as she so seldom was in the dark life she led at home. Her tennis was the highest point to which I can imagine a young creature bringing the art of make-believe, although I daresay, for her it was the very geometry of basic reality.

The exquisite clarity of all her movements had its auditory counterpart in the pure ringing sound of her every stroke. The ball when it entered her aura of control became somehow whiter, its resilience somehow richer, and the instrument of precision she used upon it seemed inordinately prehensile and deliberate at the moment of clinging contact. Her form was, indeed, an absolutely perfect imitation of absolutely top-notch tennis—without any utilitarian results. As Edusa's sister, Electra Gold, a marvelous young coach, said to me once while I sat on a pulsating hard bench watching Dolores Haze toying with Linda Hall (and being beaten by her): "Dolly has a magnet in the center of her racket guts, but why the heck is she so polite?" Ah, Electra, what did it matter, with such grace! I remember at the very first game I watched being drenched with an almost painful convulsion of beauty assimilation. My Lolita had a way of raising her bent left knee at the ample and springy start of the service cycle when there would develop and hang in the sun for a second a vital web of balance between toed foot, pristine armpit, burnished arm and far back-flung racket, as she smiled up with gleaming teeth at the small globe suspended so high in the zenith of the powerful and graceful cosmos she had created for the express purpose of falling upon it with a clean resounding crack of her golden whip.

It had, that serve of hers, beauty, directness, youth, a classical purity of trajectory, and was, despite its spanking pace, fairly easy to return, having as it did no twist or sting to its long elegant hop.

That I could have had all her strokes, all her enchantments, immortalized in segments of celluloid, makes me moan to-day with frustration. They would have been so much more than the snapshots I burned! Her overhead volley was related to her service as the envoy is to the ballade; for she had been trained, my pet, to patter up at once to the net on her nimble, vivid, white-shod feet. There was nothing to choose between her forehand and backhand drives: they were mirror images of one another—my very loins still tingle with those pistol reports repeated by crisp echoes and Electra's cries. One of the pearls of Dolly's game was a short half-volley that Ned Litam had taught her in California.

She preferred acting to swimming, and swimming to tennis; yet I insist that had not something within her been broken by me—not that I realized it then!—she would have had on the top of her perfect form the will to win, and would have become a real girl champion. Dolores, with two rackets under her arm, in Wimbledon. Dolores endorsing a Dromedary. Dolores turning professional. Dolores acting a girl champion in a movie. Dolores and her gray, humble, hushed husband-coach, old Humbert.

There was nothing wrong or deceitful in the spirit of her game—unless one considered her cheerful indifference toward its outcome as the feint of a nymphet. She who was so cruel and crafty in everyday life, revealed an innocence, a frankness, a kindness of ball-placing, that permitted a second-rate but determined player, no matter how uncouth and incompetent, to poke and cut his way to victory. Despite her small stature, she covered the one thousand and fifty-three square feet of her half of the court with wonderful ease, once she had entered into the rhythm of a rally and as long as she could direct that rhythm; but any abrupt attack, or sudden change of tactics on her adversary's part, left her helpless. At match point, her second serve, which—rather typically—was even stronger and more stylish than her first (for she had none of the inhibitions that cautious winners have), would strike vibrantly the harp-cord of the net—and ricochet out of court. The polished gem of her dropshot was snapped up and put away by an opponent who seemed four-legged and wielded a crooked paddle. Her dramatic drives and lovely volleys would candidly fall at his feet. Over and over again she would land an easy one into the net—and merrily mimic dismay by drooping in a ballet attitude, with her forelocks hanging. So sterile were her grace and whipper that she could not even win from panting me and my old-fashioned lifting drive.

I suppose I am especially susceptible to the magic of games. In my chess sessions with Gaston I saw the board as a square pool of limpid water with rare shells and stratagems rosily visible upon the smooth tessellated bottom, which to my confused adversary was all ooze and squid-cloud. Similarly, the initial tennis coaching I had inflicted on Lolita—prior to the revelations that came to her through the great Californian's lessons—remained in my mind as oppressive and distressful memories—not only because she had been so hopelessly and irritatingly irritated by every suggestion of mine—but because the precious symmetry of the court instead of reflecting the harmonies latent in her was utterly jumbled by the clumsiness and lassitude of the resentful child I mistaught. Now things were different, and on that particular day, in the pure air of Champion, Colorado, on that admirable court at the foot of steep stone stairs leading up to Champion Hotel where we had spent the night, I felt I could rest from the nightmare of unknown betrayals within the innocence of her style, of her soul, of her essential grace.

She was hitting hard and flat, with her usual effortless sweep, feeding me deep skimming balls—all so rhythmically coordinated and overt as to reduce my footwork to, practically, a swinging stroll—crack players will understand what I mean. My rather heavily cut serve that I had been taught by my father who had learned it from Decugis or Borman, old friends of his and great champions, would have seriously troubled my Lo, had I really tried to trouble her. But who would upset such a lucid dear? Did I ever mention that her bare arm bore the 8 of vaccination? That I loved her hopelessly? That she was only fourteen?

An inquisitive butterfly passed, dipping, between us.

Two people in tennis shorts, a red-haired fellow only about

eight years my junior, with sunburnt bright pink shins, and an indolent dark girl with a moody mouth and hard eyes, about two years Lolita's senior, appeared from nowhere. As is common with dutiful tyros, their rackets were sheathed and framed, and they carried them not as if they were the natural and comfortable extensions of certain specialized muscles, but hammers or blunderbusses or wimbles, or my own dreadful cumbersome sins. Rather unceremoniously seating themselves near my precious coat, on a bench adjacent to the court, they fell to admiring very vocally a rally of some fifty exchanges that Lo innocently helped me to foster and uphold—until there occurred a syncope in the series causing her to gasp as her overhead smash went out of court, whereupon she melted into winsome merriment, my golden pet.

I felt thirsty by then, and walked to the drinking fountain; there Red approached me and in all humility suggested a mixed double. "I am Bill Mead," he said. "And that's Fay Page, actress. Maffy On Say"—he added (pointing with his ridiculously hooded racket at polished Fay who was already talking to Dolly). I was about to reply "Sorry, but—" (for I hate to have my filly involved in the chops and jabs of cheap bunglers), when a remarkably melodious cry diverted my attention: a bellboy was tripping down the steps from the hotel to our court and making me signs. I was wanted, if you please, on an urgent long distance call—so urgent in fact that the line was being held for me. Certainly. I got into my coat (inside pocket heavy with pistol) and told Lo I would be back in a minute. She was picking up a ball—in the continental foot-racket way which was one of the few nice things I had taught her,—and smiled—she smiled at me!

An awful calm kept my heart afloat as I followed the boy up to the hotel. This, to use an American term, in which discovery, retribution, torture, death, eternity appear in the shape of a singularly repulsive nutshell, was *it*. I had left her in mediocre hands, but it hardly mattered now. I would fight, of course. Oh, I would fight. Better destroy everything than surrender her. Yes, quite a climb.

At the desk, a dignified, Roman-nosed man, with, I suggest, a very obscure past that might reward investigation, handed me a message in his own hand. The line had not been held after all. The note said:

"Mr. Humbert. The head of Birdsley (sic!) School called. Summer residence—Birdsley 2-8282. Please call back immediately. Highly important."

I folded myself into a booth, took a little pill, and for about twenty minutes tussled with space-spooks. A quartet of propositions gradually became audible: soprano, there was no such number in Beardsley; alto, Miss Pratt was on her way to England; tenor, Beardsley School had not telephoned; bass, they could not have done so, since nobody knew I was, that particular day, in Champion, Colo. Upon my stinging him, the Roman took the trouble to find out if there had been a long distance call. There had been none. A fake call from some local dial was not excluded. I thanked him. He said: You bet. After a visit to the purling men's room and a stiff drink at the bar, I started on my return march. From the very first terrace I saw, far below, on the tennis court which seemed the size of a school child's ill-wiped slate, golden Lolita playing in a double. She moved like a fair angel among three horrible Boschian cripples. One of these, her partner, while changing sides, jocosely slapped her on her behind with his racket. He had a remarkably round head and wore incongruous brown trousers. There was a momentary flurry—he saw me, and throwing away his racket—mine!—scuttled up the slope. He waved his wrists and elbows in would-be comical imitation of rudimentary wings, as he climbed, bow-legged, to the street, where his gray car awaited him. Next moment he and the grayness were gone. When I came down, the remaining trio were collecting and sorting out the balls.

"Mr. Mead, who was that person?"

Bill and Fay, both looking very solemn, shook their heads.

That absurd intruder had butted in to make up a double, hadn't he, Dolly?

Dolly. The handle of my racket was still disgustingly warm. Before returning to the hotel, I ushered her into a little alley half-smothered in fragrant shrubs, with flowers like smoke, and was about to burst into ripe sobs and plead with her imperturbed dream in the most abject manner for clarification, no matter how meretricious, of the slow awfulness enveloping me, when we found ourselves behind the convulsed Mead twosome—assorted people, you know, meeting among idyllic settings in old comedies. Bill and Fay were both weak with laughter—we had come at the end of their private joke. It did not really matter.

Speaking as if it really did not really matter, and assuming, apparently, that life was automatically rolling on with all its routine pleasures, Lolita said she would like to change into her bathing things, and spend the rest of the afternoon at the swimming pool. It was a gorgeous day. Lolita!

21

"Lo! Lola! Lolita!" I hear myself crying from a doorway into the sun, with the acoustics of time, domed time, endowing my call and its tell-tale hoarseness with such a wealth of anxiety, passion and pain that really it would have been instrumental in wrenching open the zipper of her nylon shroud had she been dead. Lolita! In the middle of a trim turfed terrace I found her at last—she had run out before I was ready. Oh Lolita! There she was playing with a damned dog, not me. The animal, a terrier of sorts, was losing and snapping up again and adjusting between his jaws a wet little red ball; he took rapid chords with his front paws on the resilient turf, and then would bounce away. I had only wanted to see where she was, I could not swim with my heart in that state, but who cared—and there she was, and there was I, in my robe— and so I stopped calling; but suddenly something in the pattern of her motions, as she dashed this way and that in her Aztec Red bathing briefs and bra, struck me . . . there was an ecstasy, a madness about her frolics that was too much of a glad thing. Even the dog seemed puzzled by the extravagance of her reactions. I put a gentle hand to my chest as I surveyed the situation. The turquoise blue swimming pool some distance behind the lawn was no longer behind that lawn, but within my thorax, and my organs swam in it like excrements in the blue sea water in Nice. One of the bathers had left the pool and, half-concealed by the peacocked shade of trees, stood quite still, holding the ends of the towel around

his neck and following Lolita with his amber eyes. There he
stood, in the camouflage of sun and shade, disfigured by them
and masked by his own nakedness, his damp black hair or
what was left of it, glued to his round head, his little mustache
a humid smear, the wool on his chest spread like a symmetrical
trophy, his naval pulsating, his hirsute thighs dripping with
bright droplets, his tight wet black bathing trunks bloated and
bursting with vigor where his great fat bullybag was pulled up
and back like a padded shield over his reversed beasthood.
And as I looked at his oval nut-brown face, it dawned upon
me that what I had recognized him by was the reflection of
my daughter's countenance—the same beatitude and grimace
but made hideous by his maleness. And I also knew that the
child, my child, knew he was looking, enjoyed the lechery of
his look and was putting on a show of gambol and glee, the
vile and beloved slut. As she made for the ball and missed it,
she fell on her back, with her obscene young legs madly ped-
alling in the air; I could sense the musk of her excitement
from where I stood, and then I saw (petrified with a kind of
sacred disgust) the man close his eyes and bare his small, horribly small and even, teeth as he leaned against a tree in which
a multitude of dappled Priaps shivered. Immediately afterwards a marvelous transformation took place. He was no
longer the satyr but a very good-natured and foolish Swiss
cousin, the Gustave Trapp I have mentioned more than once,
who used to counteract his "sprees" (he drank beer with milk,
the good swine) by feats of weight-lifting—tottering and
grunting on a lake beach with his otherwise very complete
bathing suit jauntily stripped from one shoulder. *This* Trapp
noticed me from afar and working the towel on his nape
walked back with false insouciance to the pool. And as if the
sun had gone out of the game, Lo slackened and slowly got
up ignoring the ball that the terrier placed before her. Who
can say what heartbreaks are caused in a dog by our discon-
tinuing a romp? I started to say something, and then sat down
on the grass with a quite monstrous pain in my chest and
vomited a torrent of browns and greens that I had never remembered eating.

I saw Lolita's eyes, and they seemed to be more calculating
than frightened. I heard her saying to a kind lady that her

father was having a fit. Then for a long time I lay in a lounge chair swallowing pony upon pony of gin. And next morning I felt strong enough to drive on (which in later years no doctor believed).

22

The two-room cabin we had ordered at Silver Spur Court, Elphinstone, turned out to belong to the glossily browned pine-log kind that Lolita used to be so fond of in the days of our carefree first journey; oh, how different things were now! I am not referring to Trapp or Trapps. After all—well, really . . . After all, gentlemen, it was becoming abundantly clear that all those identical detectives in prismatically changing cars were figments of my persecution mania, recurrent images based on coincidence and chance resemblance. *Soyons logiques*, crowed the cocky Gallic part of my brain—and proceeded to rout the notion of a Lolita-maddened salesman or comedy gangster, with stooges, persecuting me, and hoaxing me, and otherwise taking riotous advantage of my strange relations with the law. I remember humming my panic away. I remember evolving even an explanation of the "Birdsley" telephone call . . . But if I could dismiss Trapp, as I had dismissed my convulsions on the lawn at Champion, I could do nothing with the anguish of knowing Lolita to be so tantalizingly, so miserably unattainable and beloved on the very eve of a new era, when my alembics told me she should stop being a nymphet, stop torturing me.

An additional, abominable, and perfectly gratuitous worry was lovingly prepared for me in Elphinstone. Lo had been dull and silent during the last lap—two hundred mountainous miles uncontaminated by smoke-gray sleuths or zigzagging zanies. She hardly glanced at the famous, oddly shaped, splendidly flushed rock which jutted above the mountains and had been the take-off for nirvana on the part of a temperamental show girl. The town was newly built, or rebuilt, on the flat floor of a seven-thousand-foot-high valley; it would soon bore Lo, I hoped, and we would spin on to California, to the Mexican border, to mythical bays, saguaro deserts, fatamorganas. José Lizzarrabengoa, as you remember, planned to take his

Carmen to the *Etats Unis.* I conjured up a Central American tennis competition in which Dolores Haze and various Californian schoolgirl champions would dazzlingly participate. Good-will tours on that smiling level eliminate the distinction between passport and sport. Why did I hope we would be happy abroad? A change of environment is the traditional fallacy upon which doomed loves, and lungs, rely.

Mrs. Hays, the brisk, brickly rouged, blue-eyed widow who ran the motor court, asked me if I were Swiss perchance, because her sister had married a Swiss ski instructor. I was, whereas my daughter happened to be half Irish. I registered, Hays gave me the key and a twinkling smile, and, still twinkling, showed me where to park the car; Lo crawled out and shivered a little: the luminous evening air was decidedly crisp. Upon entering the cabin, she sat down on a chair at a card table, buried her face in the crook of her arm and said she felt awful. Shamming, I thought, shamming, no doubt, to evade my caresses; I was passionately parched; but she began to whimper in an unusually dreary way when I attempted to fondle her. Lolita ill. Lolita dying. Her skin was scalding hot! I took her temperature, orally, then looked up a scribbled formula I fortunately had in a jotter and after laboriously reducing the, meaningless to me, degrees Fahrenheit to the intimate centigrade of my childhood, found she had 40.4, which at least made sense. Hysterical little nymphs might, I knew, run up all kinds of temperature—even exceeding a fatal count. And I would have given her a sip of hot spiced wine, and two aspirins, and kissed the fever away, if, upon an examination of her lovely uvula, one of the gems of her body, I had not seen that it was a burning red. I undressed her. Her breath was bittersweet. Her brown rose tasted of blood. She was shaking from head to toe. She complained of a painful stiffness in the upper vertebrae—and I thought of poliomyelitis as any American parent would. Giving up all hope of intercourse, I wrapped her up in a laprobe and carried her into the car. Kind Mrs. Hays in the meantime had alerted the local doctor. "You are lucky it happened here," she said; for not only was Blue the best man in the district, but the Elphinstone hospital was as modern as modern could be, despite its limited capacity. With a heterosexual Erlkönig in pursuit, thither I drove, half-

blinded by a royal sunset on the lowland side and guided by
a little old woman, a portable witch, perhaps his daughter,
whom Mrs. Hays had lent me, and whom I was never to see
again. Dr. Blue, whose learning, no doubt, was infinitely inferior to his reputation, assured me it was a virus infection,
and when I alluded to her comparatively recent flu, curtly said
this was another bug, he had forty such cases on his hands;
all of which sounded like the "ague" of the ancients. I wondered if I should mention, with a casual chuckle, that my fifteen-year-old daughter had had a minor accident while
climbing an awkward fence with her boy friend, but knowing
I was drunk, I decided to withhold the information till later
if necessary. To an unsmiling blond bitch of a secretary I gave
my daughter's age as "practically sixteen." While I was not
looking, my child was taken away from me! In vain I insisted
I be allowed to spend the night on a "welcome" mat in a
corner of their damned hospital. I ran up constructivistic
flights of stairs, I tried to trace my darling so as to tell her she
had better not babble, especially if she felt as lightheaded as
we all did. At one point, I was rather dreadfully rude to a very
young and very cheeky nurse with overdeveloped gluteal parts
and blazing black eyes—of Basque descent, as I learned. Her
father was an imported shepherd, a trainer of sheep dogs. Finally, I returned to the car and remained in it for I do not
know how many hours, hunched up in the dark, stunned by
my new solitude, looking out openmouthed now at the dimly
illumed, very square and low hospital building squatting in the
middle of its lawny block, now up at the wash of stars and
the jagged silvery ramparts of the *haute montagne* where at
the moment Mary's father, lonely Joseph Lore, was dreaming
of Oloron, Lagore, Rolas—*que sais-je!*—or seducing a ewe.
Such-like fragrant vagabond thoughts have been always a solace to me in times of unusual stress, and only when, despite
liberal libations, I felt fairly numbed by the endless night, did
I think of driving back to the motel. The old woman had
disappeared, and I was not quite sure of my way. Wide gravel
roads criss-crossed drowsy rectangular shadows. I made out
what looked like the silhouette of gallows on what was probably a school playground; and in another wastelike block there
rose in domed silence the pale temple of some local sect. I

found the highway at last, and then the motel, where millions of so-called "millers," a kind of insect, were swarming around the neon contours of "No Vacancy"; and, when, at 3 A.M., after one of those untimely hot showers which like some mordant only help to fix a man's despair and weariness, I lay on her bed that smelled of chestnuts and roses, and peppermint, and the very delicate, very special French perfume I latterly allowed her to use, I found myself unable to assimilate the simple fact that for the first time in two years I was separated from my Lolita. All at once it occurred to me that her illness was somehow the development of a theme—that it had the same taste and tone as the series of linked impressions which had puzzled and tormented me during our journey; I imagined that secret agent, or secret lover, or prankster, or hallucination, or whatever he was, prowling around the hospital—and Aurora had hardly "warmed her hands," as the pickers of lavender say in the country of my birth, when I found myself trying to get into that dungeon again, knocking upon its green doors, breakfast-less, stool-less, in despair.

This was Tuesday, and Wednesday or Thursday, splendidly reacting like the darling she was to some "serum" (sparrow's sperm or dugong's dung), she was much better, and the doctor said that in a couple of days she would be "skipping" again.

Of the eight times I visited her, the last one alone remains sharply engraved on my mind. It had been a great feat to come for I felt all hollowed out by the infection that by then was at work on me too. None will know the strain it was to carry that bouquet, that load of love, those books that I had traveled sixty miles to buy: Browning's *Dramatic Works, The History of Dancing, Clowns and Columbines, The Russian Ballet, Flowers of the Rockies, The Theatre Guild Anthology, Tennis* by Helen Wills, who had won the National Junior Girl Singles at the age of fifteen. As I was staggering up to the door of my daughter's thirteen-dollar-a-day private room, Mary Lore, the beastly young part-time nurse who had taken an unconcealed dislike to me, emerged with a finished breakfast tray, placed it with a quick crash on a chair in the corridor, and, fundament jigging, shot back into the room—probably to warn her poor little Dolores that the tyrannic old father was creeping up on

crepe soles, with books and bouquet: the latter I had composed of wild flowers and beautiful leaves gathered with my
own gloved hands on a mountain pass at sunrise (I hardly slept
at all that fateful week).

Feeding my Carmencita well? Idly I glanced at the tray. On
a yolk-stained plate there was a crumpled envelope. It had
contained something, since one edge was torn, but there was
no address on it—nothing at all, save a phony armorial design
with "Ponderosa Lodge" in green letters; thereupon I performed a *chassé-croisé* with Mary, who was in the act of bustling out again—wonderful how fast they move and how little
they do, those rumpy young nurses. She glowered at the envelope I had put back, uncrumpled.

"You better not touch," she said, nodding directionally:
"Could burn your fingers."

Below my dignity to rejoin. All I said was:

"Je croyais que c'était un bill—not a *billet doux."* Then,
entering the sunny room, to Lolita: *"Bonjour, mon petit."*

"Dolores," said Mary Lore, entering with me, past me,
through me, the plump whore, and blinking, and starting to
fold very rapidly a white flannel blanket as she blinked: "Dolores, your pappy thinks you are getting letters from my boy
friend. It's me (smugly tapping herself on the small gilt cross
she wore) gets them. And my pappy can parlay-voo as well as
yours."

She left the room. Dolores, so rosy and russet, lips freshly
painted, hair brilliantly brushed, bare arms straightened out
on neat coverlet, lay innocently beaming at me or nothing.
On the bed table, next to a paper napkin and a pencil, her
topaz ring burned in the sun.

"What gruesome funeral flowers," she said. "Thanks all the
same. But do you mind very much cutting out the French? It
annoys everybody."

Back at the usual rush came the ripe young hussy, reeking
of urine and garlic, with the *Deseret News,* which her fair patient eagerly accepted, ignoring the sumptuously illustrated
volumes I had brought.

"My sister Ann," said Mary (topping information with
afterthought), "works at the Ponderosa place."

Poor Bluebeard. Those brutal brothers. *Est-ce que tu ne*

m'aimes plus, ma Carmen? She never had. At the moment I knew my love was as hopeless as ever—and I also knew the two girls were conspirators, plotting in Basque, or Zemfirian, against my hopeless love. I shall go further and say that Lo was playing a double game since she was also fooling sentimental Mary whom she had told, I suppose, that she wanted to dwell with her fun-loving young uncle and not with cruel melancholy me. And another nurse whom I never identified, and the village idiot who carted cots and coffins into the elevator, and the idiotic green love birds in a cage in the waiting room—all were in the plot, the sordid plot. I suppose Mary thought comedy father Professor Humbertoldi was interfering with the romance between Dolores and her father-substitute, roly-poly Romeo (for you *were* rather lardy, you know, Rom, despite all that "snow" and "joy juice").

My throat hurt. I stood, swallowing, at the window and stared at the mountains, at the romantic rock high up in the smiling plotting sky.

"My Carmen," I said (I used to call her that sometimes), "we shall leave this raw sore town as soon as you get out of bed."

"Incidentally, I want all my clothes," said the gitanilla, humping up her knees and turning to another page.

". . . Because, really," I continued, "there is no point in staying here."

"There is no point in staying anywhere," said Lolita.

I lowered myself into a cretonne chair and, opening the attractive botanical work, attempted, in the fever-humming hush of the room, to identify my flowers. This proved impossible. Presently a musical bell softly sounded somewhere in the passage.

I do not think they had more than a dozen patients (three or four were lunatics, as Lo had cheerfully informed me earlier) in that show place of a hospital, and the staff had too much leisure. However—likewise for reasons of show—regulations were rigid. It is also true that I kept coming at the wrong hours. Not without a secret flow of dreamy *malice*, visionary Mary (next time it will be *une belle dame toute en bleu* floating through Roaring Gulch) plucked me by the sleeve to lead me out. I looked at her hand; it dropped. As I

was leaving, leaving voluntarily, Dolores Haze reminded me
to bring her next morning . . . She did not remember where
the various things she wanted were . . . "Bring me," she cried
(out of sight already, door on the move, closing, closed), "the
new gray suitcase and Mother's trunk"; but by next morning
I was shivering, and boozing, and dying in the motel bed she
had used for just a few minutes, and the best I could do under
the circular and dilating circumstances was to send the two
bags over with the widow's beau, a robust and kindly trucker.
I imagined Lo displaying her treasures to Mary . . . No
doubt, I was a little delirious—and on the following day I was
still a vibration rather than a solid, for when I looked out of
the bathroom window at the adjacent lawn, I saw Dolly's
beautiful young bicycle propped up there on its support, the
graceful front wheel looking away from me, as it always did,
and a sparrow perched on the saddle—but it was the landlady's bike, and smiling a little, and shaking my poor head
over my fond fancies, I tottered back to my bed, and lay as
quiet as a saint—

> *Saint*, forsooth! While brown Dolores,
> On a patch of sunny green
> With Sanchicha reading stories
> In a movie magazine—

—which was represented by numerous specimens wherever
Dolores landed, and there was some great national celebration
in town judging by the firecrackers, veritable bombs, that exploded all the time, and at five minutes to two P.M. I heard
the sound of whistling lips nearing the half-opened door of
my cabin, and then a thump upon it.

It was big Frank. He remained framed in the opened door,
one hand on its jamb, leaning forward a little.

Howdy. Nurse Lore was on the telephone. She wanted to
know was I better and would I come today?

At twenty paces Frank used to look a mountain of health;
at five, as now, he was a ruddy mosaic of scars—had been
blown through a wall overseas; but despite nameless injuries
he was able to man a tremendous truck, fish, hunt, drink, and
buoyantly dally with roadside ladies. That day, either because
it was such a great holiday, or simply because he wanted to

divert a sick man, he had taken off the glove he usually wore on his left hand (the one pressing against the side of the door) and revealed to the fascinated sufferer not only an entire lack of fourth and fifth fingers, but also a naked girl, with cinnabar nipples and indigo delta, charmingly tattooed on the back of his crippled hand, its index and middle digit making her legs while his wrist bore her flower-crowned head. Oh, delicious . . . reclining against the woodwork, like some sly fairy.

I asked him to tell Mary Lore I would stay in bed all day and would get into touch with my daughter sometime tomorrow if I felt probably Polynesian.

He noticed the direction of my gaze and made her right hip twitch amorously.

"Okey-dokey," big Frank sang out, slapped the jamb, and whistling, carried my message away, and I went on drinking, and by morning the fever was gone, and although I was as limp as a toad, I put on the purple dressing gown over my maize yellow pajamas, and walked over to the office telephone. Everything was fine. A bright voice informed me that yes, everything was fine, my daughter had checked out the day before, around two, her uncle, Mr. Gustave, had called for her with a cocker spaniel pup and a smile for everyone, and a black Caddy Lack, and had paid Dolly's bill in cash, and told them to tell me I should not worry, and keep warm, they were at Grandpa's ranch as agreed.

Elphinstone was, and I hope still is, a very cute little town. It was spread like a maquette, you know, with its neat green-wool trees and red-roofed houses over the valley floor and I think I have alluded earlier to its model school and temple and spacious rectangular blocks, some of which were, curiously enough, just unconventional pastures with a mule or a unicorn grazing in the young July morning mist. Very amusing: at one gravel-groaning sharp turn I sideswiped a parked car but said to myself telestically—and, telephathically (I hoped), to its gesticulating owner—that I would return later, address Bird School, Bird, New Bird, the gin kept my heart alive but bemazed my brain, and after some lapses and losses common to dream sequences, I found myself in the reception room, trying to beat up the doctor, and roaring at people under chairs, and clamoring for Mary who luckily for her was

not there; rough hands plucked at my dressing gown, ripping
off a pocket, and somehow I seem to have been sitting on a
bald brown-headed patient, whom I had mistaken for Dr.
Blue, and who eventually stood up, remarking with a preposterous accent: "Now, who is nevrotic, I ask?"—and then a
gaunt unsmiling nurse presented me with seven beautiful,
beautiful books and the exquisitely folded tartan lap robe, and
demanded a receipt; and in the sudden silence I became aware
of a policeman in the hallway, to whom my fellow motorist
was pointing me out, and meekly I signed the very symbolic
receipt, thus surrendering my Lolita to all those apes. But
what else could I do? One simple and stark thought stood out
and this was: "Freedom for the moment is everything." One
false move—and I might have been made to explain a life of
crime. So I simulated a coming out of a daze. To my fellow
motorist I paid what he thought was fair. To Dr. Blue, who
by then was stroking my hand, I spoke in tears of the liquor
I bolstered too freely a tricky but not necessarily diseased heart
with. To the hospital in general I apologized with a flourish
that almost bowled me over, adding however that I was not
on particularly good terms with the rest of the Humbert clan.
To myself I whispered that I still had my gun, and was still a
free man—free to trace the fugitive, free to destroy my
brother.

23

A thousand-mile stretch of silk-smooth road separated Kasbeam, where, to the best of my belief, the red fiend had been
scheduled to appear for the first time, and fateful Elphinstone
which we had reached about a week before Independence
Day. The journey had taken up most of June for we had seldom made more than a hundred and fifty miles per traveling
day, spending the rest of the time, up to five days in one case,
at various stopping places, all of them also prearranged, no
doubt. It was that stretch, then, along which the fiend's spoor
should be sought; and to this I devoted myself, after several
unmentionable days of dashing up and down the relentlessly
radiating roads in the vicinity of Elphinstone.

Imagine me, reader, with my shyness, my distaste for any

ostentation, my inherent sense of the *comme il faut*, imagine
me masking the frenzy of my grief with a trembling ingratiating smile while devising some casual pretext to flip through
the hotel register: "Oh," I would say, "I am almost positive
that I stayed here once—let me look up the entries for mid-
June—no, I see I'm wrong after all—what a very quaint name
for a home town, Kawtagain. Thanks very much." Or: "I had
a customer staying here—I mislaid his address—may I . . . ?"
And every once in a while, especially if the operator of the
place happened to be a certain type of gloomy male, personal
inspection of the books was denied me.

I have a memo here: between July 5 and November 18, when
I returned to Beardsley for a few days, I registered, if not
actually stayed, at 342 hotels, motels and tourist homes. This
figure includes a few registrations between Chestnut and
Beardsley, one of which yielded a shadow of the fiend ("N.
Petit, Larousse, Ill."); I had to space and time my inquiries
carefully so as not to attract undue attention; and there must
have been at least fifty places where I merely inquired at the
desk—but that was a futile quest, and I preferred building up
a foundation of verisimilitude and good will by first paying
for an unneeded room. My survey showed that of the 300 or
so books inspected, at least 20 provided me with a clue: the
loitering fiend had stopped even more often than we, or else—
he was quite capable of that—he had thrown in additional
registrations in order to keep me well furnished with derisive
hints. Only in one case had he actually stayed at the same
motor court as we, a few paces from Lolita's pillow. In some
instances he had taken up quarters in the same or in a neighboring block; not infrequently he had lain in wait at an intermediate spot between two bespoken points. How vividly I
recalled Lolita, just before our departure from Beardsley,
prone on the parlor rug, studying tour books and maps, and
marking laps and stops with her lipstick!

I discovered at once that he had foreseen my investigations
and had planted insulting pseudonyms for my special benefit.
At the very first motel office I visited, Ponderosa Lodge, his
entry, among a dozen obviously human ones, read: Dr. Gratiano Forbeson, Mirandola, NY. Its Italian Comedy connotations could not fail to strike me, of course. The landlady

deigned to inform me that the gentleman had been laid up for five days with a bad cold, that he had left his car for repairs in some garage or other and that he had checked out on the 4th of July. Yes, a girl called Ann Lore had worked formerly at the Lodge, but was now married to a grocer in Cedar City. One moonlit night I waylaid white-shoed Mary on a solitary street; an automaton, she was about to shriek, but I managed to humanize her by the simple act of falling on my knees and with pious yelps imploring her to help. She did not know a thing, she swore. Who was this Gratiano Forbeson? She seemed to waver. I whipped out a hundred-dollar bill. She lifted it to the light of the moon. "He is your brother," she whispered at last. I plucked the bill out of her moon-cold hand, and spitting out a French curse turned and ran away. This taught me to rely on myself alone. No detective could discover the clues Trapp had tuned to my mind and manner. I could not hope, of course, he would ever leave his correct name and address; but I did hope he might slip on the glaze of his own subtlety, by daring, say, to introduce a richer and more personal shot of color than was strictly necessary, or by revealing too much through a qualitative sum of quantitative parts which revealed too little. In one thing he succeeded: he succeeded in thoroughly enmeshing me and my thrashing anguish in his demoniacal game. With infinite skill, he swayed and staggered, and regained an impossible balance, always leaving me with the sportive hope—if I may use such a term in speaking of betrayal, fury, desolation, horror and hate— that he might give himself away next time. He never did— though coming damn close to it. We all admire the spangled acrobat with classical grace meticulously walking his tight rope in the talcum light; but how much rarer art there is in the sagging rope expert wearing scarecrow clothes and impersonating a grotesque drunk! *I* should know.

The clues he left did not establish his identity but they reflected his personality, or at least a certain homogenous and striking personality; his genre, his type of humor—at its best at least—the tone of his brain, had affinities with my own. He mimed and mocked me. His allusions were definitely highbrow. He was well-read. He knew French. He was versed in logodaedaly and logomancy. He was an amateur of sex lore.

He had a feminine handwriting. He would change his name but he could not disguise, no matter how he slanted them, his very peculiar t's, w's and l's. Quelquepart Island was one of his favorite residences. He did not use a fountain pen which fact, as any psychoanalyst will tell you, meant that the patient was a repressed undinist. One mercifully hopes there are water nymphs in the Styx.

His main trait was his passion for tantalization. Goodness, what a tease the poor fellow was! He challenged my scholarship. I am sufficiently proud of my knowing something to be modest about my not knowing all; and I daresay I missed some elements in that cryptogrammic paper chase. What a shiver of triumph and loathing shook my frail frame when, among the plain innocent names in the hotel recorder, his fiendish conundrum would ejaculate in my face! I noticed that whenever he felt his enigmas were becoming too recondite, even for such a solver as I, he would lure me back with an easy one. "Arsène Lupin" was obvious to a Frenchman who remembered the detective stories of his youth; and one hardly had to be a Coleridgian to appreciate the trite poke of "A. Person, Porlock, England." In horrible taste but basically suggestive of a cultured man—not a policeman, not a common goon, not a lewd salesman—were such assumed names as "Arthur Rainbow"—plainly the travestied author of *Le Bateau Bleu*—let me laugh a little too, gentlemen—and "Morris Schmetterling," of *L'Oiseau Ivre* fame (*touché*, reader!). The silly but funny "D. Orgon, Elmira, NY," was from Molière, of course, and because I had quite recently tried to interest Lolita in a famous 18th-century play, I welcomed as an old friend "Harry Bumper, Sheridan, Wyo." An ordinary encyclopedia informed me who the peculiar looking "Phineas Quimby, Lebanon, NH" was; and any good Freudian, with a German name and some interest in religious prostitution, should recognize at a glance the implication of "Dr. Kitzler, Eryx, Miss." So far so good. That sort of fun was shoddy but on the whole impersonal and thus innocuous. Among entries that arrested my attention as undoubtable clues *per se* but baffled me in respect to their finer points I do not care to mention many since I feel I am groping in a border-land mist with verbal phantoms turning, perhaps, into living vacationists.

Who was "Johnny Randall, Ramble, Ohio"? Or was he a real person who just happened to write a hand similar to "N.S. Aristoff, Catagela, NY"? What was the sting in "Catagela"? And what about "James Mavor Morell, Hoaxton, England"? "Aristophanes," "hoax"—fine, but what was I missing?

There was one strain running through all that pseud-onymity which caused me especially painful palpitations when I came across it. Such things as "G. Trapp, Geneva, NY." was the sign of treachery on Lolita's part. "Aubrey Beardsley, Quelquepart Island" suggested more lucidly than the garbled telephone message had that the starting point of the affair should be looked for in the East. "Lucas Picador, Merrymay, Pa." insinuated that my Carmen had betrayed my pathetic endearments to the impostor. Horribly cruel, forsooth, was "Will Brown, Dolores, Colo." The gruesome "Harold Haze, Tombstone, Arizona" (which at another time would have ap-pealed to my sense of humor) implied a familiarity with the girl's past that in nightmare fashion suggested for a moment that my quarry was an old friend of the family, maybe an old flame of Charlotte's, maybe a redresser of wrongs ("Donald Quix, Sierra, Nev."). But the most penetrating bodkin was the anagramtailed entry in the register of Chestnut Lodge "Ted Hunter, Cane, NH.".

The garbled license numbers left by all these Persons and Orgons and Morells and Trapps only told me that motel keep-ers omit to check if guests' cars are accurately listed. Refer-ences—incompletely or incorrectly indicated—to the cars the fiend had hired for short laps between Wace and Elphinstone were of course useless; the license of the initial Aztec was a shimmer of shifting numerals, some transposed, others altered or omitted, but somehow forming interrelated combinations (such as "WS 1564" and "SH 1616," and "Q32888" or "CU 88322") which however were so cunningly contrived as to never reveal a common denominator.

It occurred to me that after he had turned that convertible over to accomplices at Wace and switched to the stage-motor car system, his successors might have been less careful and might have inscribed at some hotel office the archtype of those interrelated figures. But if looking for the fiend along a road I knew he had taken was such a complicated vague and un-

profitable business, what could I expect from any attempt to
trace unknown motorists traveling along unknown routes?

24

By the time I reached Beardsley, in the course of the har-
rowing recapitulation I have now discussed at sufficient
length, a complete image had formed in my mind; and
through the—always risky—process of elimination I had reduced this image to the only concrete source that morbid
cerebration and torpid memory could give it.

Except for the Rev. Rigor Mortis (as the girls called him),
and an old gentleman who taught non-obligatory German
and Latin, there were no regular male teachers at Beardsley
School. But on two occasions an art instructor on the Beardsley College faculty had come over to show the schoolgirls
magic lantern pictures of French castles and nineteenth-cen-
tury paintings. I had wanted to attend those projections and
talks, but Dolly, as was her wont, had asked me not to, period.
I also remembered that Gaston had referred to that particular
lecturer as a brilliant *garçon*; but that was all; memory refused
to supply me with the name of the chateau-lover.

On the day fixed for the execution, I walked through the
sleet across the campus to the information desk in Maker Hall,
Beardsley College. There I learned that the fellow's name was
Riggs (rather like that of the minister), that he was a bachelor,
and that in ten minutes he would issue from the "Museum"
where he was having a class. In the passage leading to the
auditorium I sat on a marble bench of sorts donated by Cecilia
Dalrymple Ramble. As I waited there, in prostatic discomfort,
drunk, sleep-starved, with my gun in my fist in my raincoat
pocket, it suddenly occurred to me that I was demented and
was about to do something stupid. There was not one chance
in a million that Albert Riggs, Ass. Prof., was hiding my Lolita
at his Beardsley home, 24 Pritchard Road. He could not be
the villain. It was absolutely preposterous. I was losing my
time and my wits. He and she were in California and not here
at all.

Presently, I noticed a vague commotion behind some white
statues; a door—not the one I had been staring at—opened

briskly, and amid a bevy of women students a baldish head and two bright brown eyes bobbed, advanced.

He was a total stranger to me but insisted we had met at a lawn party at Beardsley School. How was my delightful tennis-playing daughter? He had another class. He would be seeing me.

Another attempt at identification was less speedily resolved: through an advertisement in one of Lo's magazines I dared to get in touch with a private detective, an ex-pugilist, and merely to give him some idea of the *method* adopted by the fiend, I acquainted him with the kind of names and addresses I had collected. He demanded a goodish deposit and for two years—two years, reader!—that imbecile busied himself with checking those nonsense data. I had long severed all monetary relations with him when he turned up one day with the triumphant information that an eighty-year-old Indian by the name of Bill Brown lived near Dolores, Colo.

25

This book is about Lolita; and now that I have reached the part which (had I not been forestalled by another internal combustion martyr) might be called *"Dolorès Disparue,"* there would be little sense in analyzing the three empty years that followed. While a few pertinent points have to be marked, the general impression I desire to convey is of a side door crashing open in life's full flight, and a rush of roaring black time drowning with its whipping wind the cry of lone disaster.

Singularly enough, I seldom if ever dreamed of Lolita as I remembered her—as I saw her constantly and obsessively in my conscious mind during my daymares and insomnias. More precisely: she did haunt my sleep but she appeared there in strange and ludicrous disguises as Valeria or Charlotte, or a cross between them. That complex ghost would come to me, shedding shift after shift, in an atmosphere of great melancholy and disgust, and would recline in dull invitation on some narrow board or hard settee, with flesh ajar like the rubber valve of a soccer ball's bladder. I would find myself, dentures fractured or hopelessly mislaid, in horrible *chambres garnies* where I would be entertained at tedious vivisecting parties that generally ended with Charlotte or Valeria weeping

in my bleeding arms and being tenderly kissed by my broth-
erly lips in a dream disorder of auctioneered Viennese bric-à-
brac, pity, impotence and the brown wigs of tragic old women
who had just been gassed.

One day I removed from the car and destroyed an accumulation of teen-magazines. You know the sort. Stone age at
heart; up to date, or at least Mycenaean, as to hygiene. A
handsome, very ripe actress with huge lashes and a pulpy red
underlip, endorsing a shampoo. Ads and fads. Young scholars
dote on plenty of pleats—*que c'était loin, tout cela!* It is your
hostess' duty to provide robes. Unattached details take all the
sparkle out of your conversation. All of us have known "pickers"—one who picks her cuticle at the office party. Unless he
is very elderly or very important, a man should remove his
gloves before shaking hands with a woman. Invite Romance by
wearing the Exciting New Tummy Flattener. Trims tums, nips
hips. Tristram in Movielove. Yessir! The Joe-Roe marital enigma
is making yaps flap. Glamourize yourself quickly and inexpen-
sively. Comics. Bad girl dark hair fat father cigar; good girl red
hair handsome daddums clipped mustache. Or that repulsive
strip with the big gagoon and his wife, a kiddoid gnomide. *Et
moi qui t'offrais mon génie . . .* I recalled the rather charming
nonsense verse I used to write her when she was a child: "nonsense," she used to say mockingly, "is correct."

The Squirl and his Squirrel, the Rabs and their Rabbits
Have certain obscure and peculiar habits.
Male hummingbirds make the most exquisite rockets.
The snake when he walks holds his hands in his pockets . . .

Other things of hers were harder to relinquish. Up to the
end of 1949, I cherished and adored, and stained with my
kisses and merman tears, a pair of old sneakers, a boy's shirt
she had worn, some ancient blue jeans I found in the trunk
compartment, a crumpled school cap, suchlike wanton treasures. Then, when I understood my mind was cracking, I collected these sundry belongings, added to them what had been
stored in Beardsley—a box of books, her bicycle, old coats,
galoshes—and on her fifteenth birthday mailed everything as
an anonymous gift to a home for orphaned girls on a windy
lake, on the Canadian border.

It is just possible that had I gone to a strong hypnotist he might have extracted from me and arrayed in a logical pattern certain chance memories that I have threaded through my book with considerably more ostentation than they present themselves with to my mind even now when I know what to seek in the past. At the time I felt I was merely losing contact with reality; and after spending the rest of the winter and most of the following spring in a Quebec sanatorium where I had stayed before, I resolved first to settle some affairs of mine in New York and then to proceed to California for a thorough search there.

Here is something I composed in my retreat:

> Wanted, wanted: Dolores Haze.
> Hair: brown. Lips: scarlet.
> Age: five thousand three hundred days.
> Profession: none, or "starlet."
>
> Where are you hiding, Dolores Haze?
> *Why* are you hiding, darling?
> (I talk in a daze, I walk in a maze,
> I cannot get out, said the starling.)
>
> Where are you riding, Dolores Haze?
> What make is the magic carpet?
> Is a Cream Cougar the present craze?
> And where are you parked, my car pet?
>
> Who is your hero, Dolores Haze?
> Still one of those blue-caped star-men?
> Oh the balmy days and the palmy bays,
> And the cars, and the bars, my Carmen!
>
> Oh Dolores, that juke-box hurts!
> Are you still dancin', darlin'?
> (Both in worn levis, both in torn T-shirts,
> And I, in my corner, snarlin'.)
>
> Happy, happy is gnarled McFate
> Touring the States with a child wife,
> Plowing his Molly in every State
> Among the protected wild life.

My Dolly, my folly! Her eyes were *vair*,
And never closed when I kissed her.
Know an old perfume called *Soleil Vert*?
Are you from Paris, mister?

L'autre soir un air froid d'opéra m'alita:
Son félé—bien fol est qui s'y fie!
Il neige, le décor s'écroule, Lolita!
Lolita, qu'ai-je fait de ta vie?

Dying, dying, Lolita Haze,
Of hate and remorse, I'm dying.
And again my hairy fist I raise,
And again I hear you crying.

Officer, officer, there they go—
In the rain, where that lighted store is!
And her socks are white, and I love her so,
And her name is Haze, Dolores.

Officer, officer, there they are—
Dolores Haze and her lover!
Whip out your gun and follow that car.
Now tumble out, and take cover.

Wanted, wanted: Dolores Haze.
Her dream-gray gaze never flinches.
Ninety pounds is all she weighs
With a height of sixty inches.

My car is limping, Dolores Haze,
And the last long lap is the hardest,
And I shall be dumped where the weed decays,
And the rest is rust and stardust.

By psychoanalyzing this poem, I notice it is really a maniac's masterpiece. The stark, stiff, lurid rhymes correspond very exactly to certain perspectiveless and terrible landscapes and figures, and magnified parts of landscapes and figures, as drawn by psychopaths in tests devised by their astute trainers. I wrote many more poems. I immersed myself in the poetry of others. But not for a second did I forget the load of revenge.

I would be a knave to say, and the reader a fool to believe, that the shock of losing Lolita cured me of pederosis. My accursed nature could not change, no matter how my love for her did. On playgrounds and beaches, my sullen and stealthy eye, against my will, still sought out the flash of a nymphet's limbs, the sly tokens of Lolita's handmaids and rosegirls. But one essential vision in me had withered: never did I dwell now on possibilities of bliss with a little maiden, specific or synthetic, in some out-of-the-way place; never did my fancy sink its fangs into Lolita's sisters, far far away, in the coves of evoked islands. *That* was all over, for the time being at least. On the other hand, alas, two years of monstrous indulgence had left me with certain habits of lust: I feared lest the void I lived in might drive me to plunge into the freedom of sudden insanity when confronted with a chance temptation in some lane between school and supper. Solitude was corrupting me. I needed company and care. My heart was a hysterical unreliable organ. This is how Rita enters the picture.

26

She was twice Lolita's age and three quarters of mine: a very slight, dark-haired, pale-skinned adult, weighing a hundred and five pounds, with charmingly asymmetrical eyes, an angular, rapidly sketched profile, and a most appealing *ensellure* to her supple back—I think she had some Spanish or Babylonian blood. I picked her up one depraved May evening somewhere between Montreal and New York, or more narrowly, between Toylestown and Blake, at a darkishly burning bar under the sign of the Tigermoth, where she was amiably drunk: she insisted we had gone to school together, and she placed her trembling little hand on my ape paw. My senses were very slightly stirred but I decided to give her a try; I did—and adopted her as a constant companion. She was so kind, was Rita, such a good sport, that I daresay she would have given herself to any pathetic creature or fallacy, an old broken tree or a bereaved porcupine, out of sheer chumminess and compassion.

When I first met her she had but recently divorced her third husband—and a little more recently had been abandoned by her seventh *cavalier servant*—the others, the mutables, were too numerous and mobile to tabulate. Her brother was—and no doubt still is—a prominent, pasty-faced, suspenders-and-painted-tie-wearing politician, mayor and booster of his ball-playing, Bible-reading, grain-handling home town. For the last eight years he had been paying his great little sister several hundred dollars per month under the stringent condition that she would never never enter great little Grainball City. She told me, with wails of wonder, that for some God-damn reason every new boy friend of hers would first of all take her Grainball-ward: it was a fatal attraction; and before she knew what was what, she would find herself sucked into the lunar orbit of the town, and would be following the flood-lit drive that encircled it—"going round and round," as she phrased it, "like a God-damn mulberry moth."

She had a natty little coupé; and in it we traveled to California so as to give my venerable vehicle a rest. Her natural speed was ninety. Dear Rita! We cruised together for two dim years, from summer 1950 to summer 1952, and she was the sweetest, simplest, gentlest, dumbest Rita imaginable. In comparison to her, Valechka was a Schlegel, and Charlotte a Hegel. There is no earthly reason why I should dally with her in the margin of this sinister memoir, but let me say (hi, Rita—wherever you are, drunk or hangoverish, Rita, hi!) that she was the most soothing, the most comprehending companion that I ever had, and certainly saved me from the madhouse. I told her I was trying to trace a girl and plug that girl's bully. Rita solemnly approved of the plan—and in the course of some investigation she undertook on her own (without really knowing a thing), around San Humbertino, got entangled with a pretty awful crook herself; I had the devil of a time retrieving her—used and bruised but still cocky. Then one day she proposed playing Russian roulette with my sacred automatic; I said you couldn't, it was not a revolver, and we struggled for it, until at last it went off, touching off a very thin and very comical spurt of hot water from the hole it made in the wall of the cabin room; I remember her shrieks of laughter.

The oddly prepubescent curve of her back, her ricey skin, her slow languorous columbine kisses kept me from mischief. It is not the artistic aptitudes that are secondary sexual char-

acters as some shams and shamans have said; it is the other
way around: sex is but the ancilla of art. One rather mysterious
spree that had interesting repercussions I must notice. I had
abandoned the search: the fiend was either in Tartary or burning away in my cerebellum (the flames fanned by my fancy
and grief) but certainly not having Dolores Haze play champion tennis on the Pacific Coast. One afternoon, on our way
back East, in a hideous hotel, the kind where they hold conventions and where labeled, fat, pink men stagger around, all
first names and business and booze—dear Rita and I awoke
to find a third in our room, a blond, almost albino, young
fellow with white eyelashes and large transparent ears, whom
neither Rita nor I recalled having ever seen in our sad lives.
Sweating in thick dirty underwear, and with old army boots
on, he lay snoring on the double bed beyond my chaste Rita.
One of his front teeth was gone, amber pustules grew on his
forehead. Ritochka enveloped her sinuous nudity in my raincoat—the first thing at hand; I slipped on a pair of candy-
striped drawers; and we took stock of the situation. Five
glasses had been used, which, in the way of clues, was an
embarrassment of riches. The door was not properly closed.
A sweater and a pair of shapeless tan pants lay on the floor.
We shook their owner into miserable consciousness. He was
completely amnesic. In an accent that Rita recognized as pure
Brooklynese, he peevishly insinuated that somehow we had
purloined his (worthless) identity. We rushed him into his
clothes and left him at the nearest hospital, realizing on the
way that somehow or other after forgotten gyrations, we were
in Grainball. Half a year later Rita wrote the doctor for news.
Jack Humbertson as he had been tastelessly dubbed was still
isolated from his personal past. Oh Mnemosyne, sweetest and
most mischievous of muses!

I would not have mentioned this incident had it not started
a chain of ideas that resulted in my publishing in the *Cantrip
Review* an essay on "Mimir and Memory," in which I suggested among other things that seemed original and important to that splendid review's benevolent readers, a theory of
perceptual time based on the circulation of the blood and
conceptually depending (to fill up this nutshell) on the mind's
being conscious not only of matter but also of its own self,

thus creating a continuous spanning of two points (the stor-
able future and the stored past). In result of this venture—
and in culmination of the impression made by my previous
travaux—I was called from New York, where Rita and I were
living in a little flat with a view of gleaming children taking
shower baths far below in a fountainous arbor of Central Park,
to Cantrip College, four hundred miles away, for one year. I
lodged there, in special apartments for poets and philosophers,
from September 1951 to June 1952, while Rita whom I preferred not to display vegetated—somewhat indecorously, I am
afraid—in a roadside inn where I visited her twice a week.
Then she vanished—more humanly than her predecessor had
done: a month later I found her in the local jail. She was *très
digne*, had had her appendix removed, and managed to convince me that the beautiful bluish furs she had been accused
of stealing from a Mrs. Roland MacCrum had really been a
spontaneous, if somewhat alcoholic, gift from Roland himself.
I succeeded in getting her out without appealing to her
touchy brother, and soon afterwards we drove back to Central
Park West, by way of Briceland, where we had stopped for a
few hours the year before.

A curious urge to relive my stay there with Lolita had got
hold of me. I was entering a phase of existence where I had
given up all hope of tracing her kidnaper and her. I now attempted to fall back on old settings in order to save what still
could be saved in the way of *souvenir, souvenir que me veux-
tu?* Autumn was ringing in the air. To a post card requesting
twin beds Professor Hamburg got a prompt expression of regret in reply. They were full up. They had one bathless basement room with four beds which they thought I would not
want. Their note paper was headed:

THE ENCHANTED HUNTERS

NEAR CHURCHES   NO DOGS

All legal beverages

I wondered if the last statement was true. All? Did they have
for instance sidewalk grenadine? I also wondered if a hunter,
enchanted or otherwise, would not need a pointer more than
a pew, and with a spasm of pain I recalled a scene worthy of
a great artist: *petite nymphe accroupie*; but that silky cocker

spaniel had perhaps been a baptized one. No—I felt I could not endure the throes of revisiting that lobby. There was a much better possibility of retrievable time elsewhere in soft, rich-colored, autumnal Briceland. Leaving Rita in a bar, I made for the town library. A twittering spinster was only too glad to help me disinter mid-August 1947 from the bound *Briceland Gazette*, and presently, in a secluded nook under a naked light, I was turning the enormous and fragile pages of a coffin-black volume almost as big as Lolita.

Reader! *Bruder!* What a foolish Hamburg that Hamburg was! Since his supersensitive system was loath to face the actual scene, he thought he could at least enjoy a secret part of it—which reminds one of the tenth or twentieth soldier in the raping queue who throws the girl's black shawl over her white face so as not to see those impossible eyes while taking his military pleasure in the sad, sacked village. What *I* lusted to get was the printed picture that had chanced to absorb my trespassing image while the *Gazette*'s photographer was concentrating on Dr. Braddock and his group. Passionately I hoped to find preserved the portrait of the artist as a younger brute. An innocent camera catching me on my dark way to Lolita's bed—what a magnet for Mnemosyne! I cannot well explain the true nature of that urge of mine. It was allied, I suppose, to that swooning curiosity which impels one to examine with a magnifying glass bleak little figures—still life practically, and everybody about to throw up—at an early morning execution, and the patient's expression impossible to make out in the print. Anyway, I was literally gasping for breath, and one corner of the book of doom kept stabbing me in the stomach while I scanned and skimmed . . . *Brute Force* and *Possessed* were coming on Sunday, the 24th, to both theaters. Mr. Purdom, independent tobacco auctioneer, said that ever since 1925 he had been an Omen Faustum smoker. Husky Hank and his petite bride were to be the guests of Mr. and Mrs. Reginald G. Gore, 58 Inchkeith Ave. The size of certain parasites is one sixth of the host. Dunkerque was fortified in the tenth century. Misses' socks, 39 c. Saddle Oxfords 3.98. Wine, wine, wine, quipped the author of *Dark Age* who refused to be photographed, may suit a Persian bubble bird, but I say give me rain, rain, rain on the shingle roof for roses

and inspiration every time. Dimples are caused by the adher-
ence of the skin to the deeper tissues. Greeks repulse a heavy
guerilla assault—and, ah, at last, a little figure in white, and
Dr. Braddock in black, but whatever spectral shoulder was
brushing against his ample form—nothing of myself could I
make out.

I went to find Rita who introduced me with her *vin triste*
smile to a pocket-sized wizened truculently tight old man saying this was—what was that name again, son?—a former
schoolmate of hers. He tried to retain her, and in the slight
scuffle that followed I hurt my thumb against his hard head.
In the silent painted park where I walked her and aired her a
little, she sobbed and said I would soon, soon leave her as
everybody had, and I sang her a wistful French ballad, and
strung together some fugitive rhymes to amuse her:

> The place was called *Enchanted Hunters.* Query:
> What Indian dyes, Diana, did thy dell
> endorse to make of Picture Lake a very
> blood bath of trees before the blue hotel?

She said: "Why blue when it is white, why blue for heaven's
sake?" and started to cry again, and I marched her to the car,
and we drove on to New York, and soon she was reasonably
happy again high up in the haze on the little terrace of our
flat. I notice I have somehow mixed up two events, my visit
with Rita to Briceland on our way to Cantrip, and our passing
through Briceland again on our way back to New York, but
such suffusions of swimming colors are not to be disdained
by the artist in recollection.

27

My letterbox in the entrance hall belonged to the type that
allows one to glimpse something of its contents through a
glassed slit. Several times already, a trick of harlequin light that
fell through the glass upon an alien handwriting had twisted
it into a semblance of Lolita's script causing me almost to
collapse as I leant against an adjacent urn, almost my own.
Whenever that happened—whenever her lovely, loopy, childish scrawl was horribly transformed into the dull hand of one

of my few correspondents—I used to recollect, with anguished amusement, the times in my trustful, pre-dolorian past when I would be misled by a jewel-bright window opposite wherein my lurking eye, the ever alert periscope of my shameful vice, would make out from afar a half-naked nymphet stilled in the act of combing her Alice-in-Wonderland hair. There was in the fiery phantasm a perfection which made my wild delight also perfect, just because the vision was out of reach, with no possibility of attainment to spoil it by the awareness of an appended taboo; indeed, it may well be that the very attraction immaturity has for me lies not so much in the limpidity of pure young forbidden fairy child beauty as in the security of a situation where infinite perfections fill the gap between the little given and the great promised—the great rosegray never-to-be-had. *Mes fenêtres!* Hanging above blotched sunset and welling night, grinding my teeth, I would crowd all the demons of my desire against the railing of a throbbing balcony: it would be ready to take off in the apricot and black humid evening; did take off—whereupon the lighted image would move and Eve would revert to a rib, and there would be nothing in the window but an obese partly clad man reading the paper.

Since I sometimes won the race between my fancy and nature's reality, the deception was bearable. Unbearable pain began when chance entered the fray and deprived me of the smile meant for me. *"Savez-vous qu'à dix ans ma petite était folle de vous?"* said a woman I talked to at a tea in Paris, and the *petite* had just married, miles away, and I could not even remember if I had ever noticed her in that garden, next to those tennis courts, a dozen years before. And now likewise, the radiant foreglimpse, the promise of reality, a promise not only to be simulated seductively but also to be nobly held— all this, chance denied me—chance and a change to smaller characters on the pale beloved writer's part. My fancy was both Proustianized and Procrusteanized; for that particular morning, late in September 1952, as I had come down to grope for my mail, the dapper and bilious janitor with whom I was on execrable terms started to complain that a man who had seen Rita home recently had been "sick like a dog" on the front steps. In the process of listening to him and tipping him, and then listening to a revised and politer version of the incident, I had the impression that one of the two letters which that blessed mail brought was from Rita's mother, a crazy little woman, whom we had once visited on Cape Cod and who kept writing me to my various addresses, saying how wonderfully well matched her daughter and I were, and how wonderful it would be if we married; the other letter which I opened and scanned rapidly in the elevator was from John Farlow.

I have often noticed that we are inclined to endow our friends with the stability of type that literary characters acquire in the reader's mind. No matter how many times we reopen "King Lear," never shall we find the good king banging his tankard in high revelry, all woes forgotten, at a jolly reunion with all three daughters and their lapdogs. Never will Emma rally, revived by the sympathetic salts in Flaubert's father's timely tear. Whatever evolution this or that popular character has gone through between the book covers, his fate is fixed in our minds, and, similarly, we expect our friends to follow this or that logical and conventional pattern we have fixed for them. Thus X will never compose the immortal music that would clash with the second-rate symphonies he has accustomed us to. Y will never commit murder. Under no circumstances can Z ever betray us. We have it all arranged in our minds, and the less often we see a particular person the more satisfying it is to check how obediently he conforms to our notion of him every time we hear of him. Any deviation in the fates we have ordained would strike us as not only anomalous but unethical. We would prefer not to have known at all our neighbor, the retired hot-dog stand operator, if it turns out he has just produced the greatest book of poetry his age has seen.

I am saying all this in order to explain how bewildered I was by Farlow's hysterical letter. I knew his wife had died but I certainly expected him to remain, throughout a devout widowhood, the dull, sedate and reliable person he had always been. Now he wrote that after a brief visit to the U.S. he had returned to South America and had decided that whatever affairs he had controlled at Ramsdale he would hand over to Jack Windmuller of that town, a lawyer whom we both knew.

He seemed particularly relieved to get rid of the Haze "complications." He had married a Spanish girl. He had stopped smoking and had gained thirty pounds. She was very young and a ski champion. They were going to India for their honeymonsoon. Since he was "building a family" as he put it, he would have no time henceforth for my affairs which he termed "very strange and very aggravating." Busybodies—a whole committee of them, it appeared—had informed him that the whereabouts of little Dolly Haze were unknown, and that I was living with a notorious divorcee in California. His father-in-law was a count, and exceedingly wealthy. The people who had been renting the Haze house for some years now wished to buy it. He suggested that I better produce Dolly quick. He had broken his leg. He enclosed a snapshot of himself and a brunette in white wool beaming at each other among the snows of Chile.

I remember letting myself into my flat and starting to say: Well, at least we shall now track them down—when the other letter began talking to me in a small matter-of-fact voice:

DEAR DAD:

How's everything? I'm married. I'm going to have a baby. I guess he's going to be a big one. I guess he'll come right for Christmas. This is a hard letter to write. I'm going nuts because we don't have enough to pay our debts and get out of here. Dick is promised a big job in Alaska in his very specialized corner of the mechanical field, that's all I know about it but it's really grand. Pardon me for withholding our home address but you may still be mad at me, and Dick must not know. This town is something. You can't see the morons for the smog. Please do send us a check, Dad. We could manage with three or four hundred or even less, anything is welcome, you might sell my old things, because once we get there the dough will just start rolling in. Write, please. I have gone through much sadness and hardship.

Yours expecting,
DOLLY (MRS. RICHARD F. SCHILLER)

28

I was again on the road, again at the wheel of the old blue sedan, again alone. Rita had still been dead to the world when I read that letter and fought the mountains of agony it raised

within me. I had glanced at her as she smiled in her sleep and
had kissed her on her moist brow, and had left her forever,
with a note of tender adieu which I taped to her navel—otherwise she might not have found it.

"Alone" did I say? *Pas tout à fait.* I had my little black
chum with me, and as soon as I reached a secluded spot, I
rehearsed Mr. Richard F. Schiller's violent death. I had found
a very old and very dirty gray sweater of mine in the back of
the car, and this I hung up on a branch, in a speechless glade,
which I had reached by a wood road from the now remote
highway. The carrying out of the sentence was a little marred
by what seemed to me a certain stiffness in the play of the
trigger, and I wondered if I should get some oil for the mysterious thing but decided I had no time to spare. Back into
the car went the old dead sweater, now with additional per-
forations, and having reloaded warm Chum, I continued my
journey.

The letter was dated September 18, 1952 (this was September
22), and the address she gave was "General Delivery, Coalmont" (not "Va.," not "Pa.," not "Tenn."—and not Coalmont, anyway—I have camouflaged everything, my love).
Inquiries showed this to be a small industrial community some
eight hundred miles from New York City. At first I planned
to drive all day and all night, but then thought better of it
and rested for a couple of hours around dawn in a motor court
room, a few miles before reaching the town. I had made up
my mind that the fiend, this Schiller, had been a car salesman
who had perhaps got to know my Lolita by giving her a ride
in Beardsley—the day her bike blew a tire on the way to Miss
Emperor—and that he had got into some trouble since then.
The corpse of the executed sweater, no matter how I changed
its contours as it lay on the back seat of the car, had kept
revealing various outlines pertaining to Trapp-Schiller—the
grossness and obscene bonhommie of his body, and to counteract this taste of coarse corruption I resolved to make myself
especially handsome and smart as I pressed home the nipple
of my alarm clock before it exploded at the set hour of six
A.M. Then, with the stern and romantic care of a gentleman
about to fight a duel, I checked the arrangement of my papers,
bathed and perfumed my delicate body, shaved my face and

chest, selected a silk shirt and clean drawers, pulled on transparent taupe socks, and congratulated myself for having with me in my trunk some very exquisite clothes—a waistcoat with nacreous buttons, for instance, a pale cashmere tie and so on.

I was not able, alas, to hold my breakfast, but dismissed that physicality as a trivial contretemps, wiped my mouth with a gossamer handkerchief produced from my sleeve, and, with a blue block of ice for heart, a pill on my tongue and solid death in my hip pocket, I stepped neatly into a telephone booth in Coalmont (Ah-ah-ah, said its little door) and rang up the only Schiller—Paul, Furniture—to be found in the battered book. Hoarse Paul told me he did know a Richard, the son of a cousin of his, and his address was, let me see, 10 Killer Street (I am not going very far for my pseudonyms). Ah-ah-ah, said the little door.

At 10 Killer Street, a tenement house, I interviewed a number of dejected old people and two long-haired strawberry-blond incredibly grubby nymphets (rather abstractly, just for the heck of it, the ancient beast in me was casting about for some lightly clad child I might hold against me for a minute, after the killing was over and nothing mattered any more, and everything was allowed). Yes, Dick Skiller had lived there, but had moved when he married. Nobody knew his address. "They might know at the store," said a bass voice from an open manhole near which I happened to be standing with the two thin-armed, barefoot little girls and their dim grandmothers. I entered the wrong store and a wary old Negro shook his head even before I could ask anything. I crossed over to a bleak grocery and there, summoned by a customer at my request, a woman's voice from some wooden abyss in the floor, the manhole's counterpart, cried out: Hunter Road, last house.

Hunter Road was miles away, in an even more dismal district, all dump and ditch, and wormy vegetable garden, and shack, and gray drizzle, and red mud, and several smoking stacks in the distance. I stopped at the last "house"—a clapboard shack, with two or three similar ones farther away from the road and a waste of withered weeds all around. Sounds of hammering came from behind the house, and for several minutes I sat quite still in my old car, old and frail, at the end of my journey, at my gray goal, *finis*, my friends, *finis*, my fiends. The time was around two. My pulse was 40 one minute and 100 the next. The drizzle crepitated against the hood of the car. My gun had migrated to my right trouser pocket. A nondescript cur came out from behind the house, stopped in surprise, and started good-naturedly woof-woofing at me, his eyes slit, his shaggy belly all muddy, and then walked about a little and woofed once more.

29

I got out of the car and slammed its door. How matter-of-fact, how square that slam sounded in the void of the sunless day! *Woof*, commented the dog perfunctorily. I pressed the bell button, it vibrated through my whole system. *Personne. Je resonne. Repersonne.* From what depth this re-nonsense? Woof, said the dog. A rush and a shuffle, and woosh-woof went the door.

Couple of inches taller. Pink-rimmed glasses. New, heaped-up hairdo, new ears. How simple! The moment, the death I had kept conjuring up for three years was as simple as a bit of dry wood. She was frankly and hugely pregnant. Her head looked smaller (only two seconds had passed really, but let me give them as much wooden duration as life can stand), and her pale-freckled cheeks were hollowed, and her bare shins and arms had lost all their tan, so that the little hairs showed. She wore a brown, sleeveless cotton dress and sloppy felt slippers.

"We—e—ell!" she exhaled after a pause with all the emphasis of wonder and welcome.

"Husband at home?" I croaked, fist in pocket.

I could not kill *her*, of course, as some have thought. You see, I loved her. It was love at first sight, at last sight, at ever and ever sight.

"Come in," she said with a vehement cheerful note. Against the splintery deadwood of the door, Dolly Schiller flattened herself as best she could (even rising on tiptoe a little) to let me pass, and was crucified for a moment, looking down, smiling down at the threshold, hollow-cheeked with round *pommettes*, her watered-milk-white arms outspread on the wood.

I passed without touching her bulging babe. Dolly-smell, with a faint fried addition. My teeth chattered like an idiot's. "No, you stay out" (to the dog). She closed the door and followed me and her belly into the dollhouse parlor.

"Dick's down there," she said pointing with an invisible tennis racket, inviting my gaze to travel from the drab parlor-bedroom where we stood, right across the kitchen, and through the back-doorway where, in a rather primitive vista, a dark-haired young stranger in overalls, instantaneously reprieved, was perched with his back to me on a ladder fixing something near or upon the shack of his neighbor, a plumper fellow with only one arm, who stood looking up.

This pattern she explained from afar, apologetically ("Men will be men"); should she call him in?

No.

Standing in the middle of the slanting room and emitting questioning "hm's," she made familiar Javanese gestures with her wrists and hands, offering me, in a brief display of humorous courtesy, to choose between a rocker and the divan (their bed after ten P.M.). I say "familiar" because one day she had welcomed me with the same wrist dance to her party in Beardsley. We both sat down on the divan. Curious: although actually her looks had faded, I definitely realized, so hopelessly late in the day, how much she looked—had always looked—like Botticelli's russet Venus—the same soft nose, the same blurred beauty. In my pocket my fingers gently let go and repacked a little at the tip, within the handkerchief it was nested in, my unused weapon.

"That's not the fellow I want," I said.

The diffuse look of welcome left her eyes. Her forehead puckered as in the old bitter days:

"Not *who*?"

"Where is he? Quick!"

"Look," she said, inclining her head to one side and shaking it in that position. "Look, you are not going to bring that up."

"I certainly am," I said, and for a moment—strangely enough the only merciful, endurable one in the whole interview—we were bristling at each other as if she were still mine.

A wise girl, she controlled herself.

Dick did not know a thing of the whole mess. He thought I was her father. He thought she had run away from an upper-class home just to wash dishes in a diner. He believed anything. Why should I want to make things harder than they were by raking up all that muck?

But, I said, she must be sensible, she must be a sensible girl (with her bare drum under that thin brown stuff), she must understand that if she expected the help I had come to give, I must have at least a clear comprehension of the situation.

"Come, his name!"

She thought I had guessed long ago. It was (with a mischievous and melancholy smile) such a sensational name. I would never believe it. She could hardly believe it herself.

His name, my fall nymph.

It was so unimportant, she said. She suggested I skip it. Would I like a cigarette?

No. His name.

She shook her head with great resolution. She guessed it was too late to raise hell and I would never believe the unbelievably unbelievable—

I said I had better go, regards, nice to have seen her.

She said really it was useless, she would never tell, but on the other hand, after all— "Do you really want to know who it was? Well, it was—"

And softly, confidentially, arching her thin eyebrows and puckering her parched lips, she emitted, a little mockingly, somewhat fastidiously, not untenderly, in a kind of muted whistle, the name that the astute reader has guessed long ago.

Waterproof. Why did a flash from Hourglass Lake cross my consciousness? I, too, had known it, without knowing it, all along. There was no shock, no surprise. Quietly the fusion took place, and everything fell into order, into the pattern of branches that I have woven throughout this memoir with the express purpose of having the ripe fruit fall at the right moment; yes, with the express and perverse purpose of rendering—she was talking but I sat melting in my golden peace—of rendering that golden and monstrous peace through the satisfaction of logical recognition, which my most inimical reader should experience now.

She was, as I say, talking. It now came in a relaxed flow.

He was the only man she had ever been crazy about. What about Dick? Oh, Dick was a lamb, they were quite happy together, but she meant something different. And *I* had never counted, of course?

She considered me as if grasping all at once the incredible— and somehow tedious, confusing and unnecessary—fact that the distant, elegant, slender, forty-year-old valetudinarian in velvet coat sitting beside her had known and adored every pore and follicle of her pubescent body. In her washed-out gray eyes, strangely spectacled, our poor romance was for a moment reflected, pondered upon, and dismissed like a dull party, like a rainy picnic to which only the dullest bores had come, like a humdrum exercise, like a bit of dry mud caking her childhood.

I just managed to jerk my knee out of the range of a sketchy tap—one of her acquired gestures.

She asked me not to be dense. The past was the past. I had been a good father, she guessed—granting me *that*. Proceed, Dolly Schiller.

Well, did I know that he had known her mother? That he was practically an old friend? That he had visited with his uncle in Ramsdale?—oh, years ago—and spoken at Mother's club, and had tugged and pulled her, Dolly, by her bare arm onto his lap in front of everybody, and kissed her face, she was ten and furious with him? Did I know he had seen me and her at the inn where he was writing the very play she was to rehearse in Beardsley, two years later? Did I know— It had been horrid of her to sidetrack me into believing that Clare was an old female, maybe a relative of his or a sometime lifemate—and oh, what a close shave it had been when the Wace *Journal* carried his picture.

The *Briceland Gazette* had not. Yes, very amusing.

Yes, she said, this world was just one gag after another, if somebody wrote up her life nobody would ever believe it.

At this point, there came brisk homey sounds from the kitchen into which Dick and Bill had lumbered in quest of beer. Through the doorway they noticed the visitor, and Dick entered the parlor.

"Dick, this is my Dad!" cried Dolly in a resounding violent voice that struck me as totally strange, and new, and cheerful,

and old, and sad, because the young fellow, veteran of a remote war, was hard of hearing.

Arctic blue eyes, black hair, ruddy cheeks, unshaven chin.
We shook hands. Discreet Bill, who evidently took pride in
working wonders with one hand, brought in the beer cans he
had opened. Wanted to withdraw. The exquisite courtesy of
simple folks. Was made to stay. A beer ad. In point of fact, I
preferred it that way, and so did the Schillers. I switched to
the jittery rocker. Avidly munching, Dolly plied me with
marshmallows and potato chips. The men looked at her fragile, *frileux*, diminutive, old-world, youngish but sickly, father
in velvet coat and beige vest, maybe a viscount.

They were under the impression I had come to stay, and
Dick with a great wrinkling of brows that denoted difficult
thought, suggested Dolly and he might sleep in the kitchen
on a spare mattress. I waved a light hand and told Dolly who
transmitted it by means of a special shout to Dick that I had
merely dropped in on my way to Readsburg where I was to
be entertained by some friends and admirers. It was then noticed that one of the few thumbs remaining to Bill was bleeding (not such a wonder-worker after all). How womanish and
somehow never seen that way before was the shadowy division
between her pale breasts when she bent down over the man's
hand! She took him for repairs to the kitchen. For a few
minutes, three or four little eternities which positively welled
with artificial warmth, Dick and I remained alone. He sat on
a hard chair rubbing his forelimbs and frowning. I had an idle
urge to squeeze out the blackheads on the wings of his perspiring nose with my long agate claws. He had nice sad eyes
with beautiful lashes, and very white teeth. His Adam's apple
was large and hairy. Why don't they shave better, those young
brawny chaps? He and his Dolly had had unrestrained intercourse on that couch there, at least a hundred and eighty
times, probably much more; and before that—how long had
she known him? No grudge. Funny—no grudge at all, nothing except grief and nausea. He was now rubbing his nose. I
was sure that when finally he would open his mouth, he would
say (slightly shaking his head): "Aw, she's a swell kid, Mr.
Haze. She sure is. And she's going to make a swell mother."
He opened his mouth—and took a sip of beer. This gave him

countenance—and he went on sipping till he frothed at the mouth. He was a lamb. He had cupped her Florentine breasts. His fingernails were black and broken, but the phalanges, the whole carpus, the strong shapely wrist were far, far finer than mine: I have hurt too much too many bodies with my twisted poor hands to be proud of them. French epithets, a Dorset yokel's knuckles, an Austrian tailor's flat finger tips—that's Humbert Humbert.

Good. If he was silent I could be silent too. Indeed, I could very well do with a little rest in this subdued, frightened-to-death rocking chair, before I drove to wherever the beast's lair was—and then pulled the pistol's foreskin back, and then enjoyed the orgasm of the crushed trigger: I was always a good little follower of the Viennese medicine man. But presently I became sorry for poor Dick whom, in some hypnotoid way, I was horribly preventing from making the only remark he could think up ("She's a swell kid . . .").

"And so," I said, "you are going to Canada?"

In the kitchen, Dolly was laughing at something Bill had said or done.

"And so," I shouted, "you are going to Canada? Not Canada"—I re-shouted—"I mean Alaska, of course."

He nursed his glass and, nodding sagely, replied: "Well, he cut it on a jagger, I guess. Lost his right arm in Italy."

Lovely mauve almond trees in bloom. A blown-off surrealistic arm hanging up there in the pointillistic mauve. A flowergirl tattoo on the hand. Dolly and band-aided Bill reappeared. It occurred to me that her ambiguous, brown and pale beauty excited the cripple. Dick, with a grin of relief stood up. He guessed Bill and he would be going back to fix those wires. He guessed Mr. Haze and Dolly had loads of things to say to each other. He guessed he would be seeing me before I left. Why do those people guess so much and shave so little, and are so disdainful of hearing aids?

"Sit down," she said, audibly striking her flanks with her palms. I relapsed into the black rocker.

"So you betrayed me? Where did you go? Where is he now?"

She took from the mantelpiece a concave glossy snapshot. Old woman in white, stout, beaming, bowlegged, very short dress; old man in his shirtsleeves, drooping mustache, watch chain. Her in-laws. Living with Dick's brother's family in Juneau.

"Sure you don't want to smoke?"

She was smoking herself. First time I saw her doing it. *Streng verboten* under Humbert the Terrible. Gracefully, in a blue mist, Charlotte Haze rose from her grave. I would find him through Uncle Ivory if she refused.

"Betrayed you? No." She directed the dart of her cigarette, index rapidly tapping upon it, toward the hearth exactly as her mother used to do, and then, like her mother, oh my God, with her fingernail scratched and removed a fragment of cigarette paper from her underlip. No. She had not betrayed me. I was among friends. Edusa had warned her that Cue liked little girls, had been almost jailed once, in fact (nice fact), and he knew she knew. Yes . . . Elbow in palm, puff, smile, exhaled smoke, darting gesture. Waxing reminiscent. He saw—smiling—through everything and everybody, because he was not like me and her but a genius. A great guy. Full of fun. Had rocked with laughter when she confessed about me and her, and said he had thought so. It was quite safe, under the circumstances, to tell him . . .

Well, Cue—they all called him Cue—

Her camp five years ago. Curious coincidence.

— . . . took her to a dude ranch about a day's drive from Elephant (Elphinstone). Named? Oh, some silly name—Duk Duk Ranch—*you* know just plain silly—but it did not matter now, anyway, because the place had vanished and disintegrated. Really, she meant, I could not imagine how utterly lush that ranch was, she meant it had everything but everything, even an indoor waterfall. Did I remember the redhaired guy we ("we" was good) had once had some tennis with? Well, the place really belonged to Red's brother, but he had turned it over to Cue for the summer. When Cue and she came, the others had them actually go through a coronation ceremony and then—a terrific ducking, as when you cross the Equator. *You* know.

Her eyes rolled in synthetic resignation.

"Go on, please."

Well. The idea was he would take her in September to Hollywood and arrange a tryout for her, a bit part in the tennis-match scene of a movie picture based on a play of his—*Golden Guts*—and perhaps even have her double one of its sensational starlets on the Kleig-struck tennis court. Alas, it never came to that.

"Where is the hog now?"

He was not a hog. He was a great guy in many respects. But it was all drink and drugs. And, of course, he was a complete freak in sex matters, and his friends were his slaves. I just could not imagine (I, Humbert, could not imagine!) what they all did at Duk Duk Ranch. She refused to take part because she loved him, and he threw her out.

"What things?"

"Oh, weird, filthy, fancy things. I mean, he had two girls and two boys, and three or four men, and the idea was for all of us to tangle in the nude while an old woman took movie pictures." (Sade's Justine was twelve at the start.)

"What things exactly?"

"Oh, things . . . Oh, I—really I"—she uttered the "I" as a subdued cry while she listened to the source of the ache, and for lack of words spread the five fingers of her angularly up-and-down-moving hand. No, she gave it up, she refused to go into particulars with that baby inside her.

That made sense.

"It is of no importance now," she said pounding a gray cushion with her fist and then lying back, belly up, on the divan. "Crazy things, filthy things. I said no, I'm just not going to [she used, in all insouciance really, a disgusting slang term which, in a literal French translation, would be *souffler*] your beastly boys, because I want only you. Well, he kicked me out."

There was not much else to tell. That winter 1949, Fay and she had found jobs. For almost two years she had—oh, just drifted, oh, doing some restaurant work in small places, and then she had met Dick. No, she did not know where the other was. In New York, she guessed. Of course, he was so famous she would have found him at once if she had wanted. Fay had tried to get back to the Ranch—and it just was not there any more—it had burned to the ground, *nothing* remained, just a charred heap of rubbish. It was so *strange*, so *strange*—

She closed her eyes and opened her mouth, leaning back

on the cushion, one felted foot on the floor. The wooden floor slanted, a little steel ball would have rolled into the kitchen. I knew all I wanted to know. I had no intention of torturing my darling. Somewhere beyond Bill's shack an afterwork radio had begun singing of folly and fate, and there she was with her ruined looks and her adult, rope-veined narrow hands and her gooseflesh white arms, and her shallow ears, and her unkempt armpits, there she was (my Lolita!), hopelessly worn at seventeen, with that baby, dreaming already in her of becoming a big shot and retiring around 2020 A.D.—and I looked and looked at her, and knew as clearly as I know I am to die, that I loved her more than anything I had ever seen or imagined on earth, or hoped for anywhere else. She was only the faint violet whiff and dead leaf echo of the nymphet I had rolled myself upon with such cries in the past; an echo on the brink of a russet ravine, with a far wood under a white sky, and brown leaves choking the brook, and one last cricket in the crisp weeds . . . but thank God it was not that echo alone that I worshiped. What I used to pamper among the tangled vines of my heart, *mon grand péché radieux*, had dwindled to its essence: sterile and selfish vice, all *that* I canceled and cursed. You may jeer at me, and threaten to clear the court, but until I am gagged and half-throttled, I will shout my poor truth. I insist the world know how much I loved my Lolita, *this* Lolita, pale and polluted, and big with another's child, but still gray-eyed, still sooty-lashed, still auburn and almond, still Carmencita, still mine; *Changeons de vie, ma Carmen, allons vivre quelque part où nous ne serons jamais séparés;* Ohio? The wilds of Massachusetts? No matter, even if those eyes of hers would fade to myopic fish, and her nipples swell and crack, and her lovely young velvety delicate delta be tainted and torn—even then I would go mad with tenderness at the mere sight of your dear wan face, at the mere sound of your raucous young voice, my Lolita.

"Lolita," I said, "this may be neither here nor there but I have to say it. Life is very short. From here to that old car you know so well there is a stretch of twenty, twenty-five paces. It is a very short walk. Make those twenty-five steps. Now. Right now. Come just as you are. And we shall live happily ever after."

Carmen, voulez-vous venir avec moi?

"You mean," she said opening her eyes and raising herself slightly, the snake that may strike, "you mean you will give us [us] that money only if I go with you to a motel. Is *that* what you mean?"

"No," I said, "you got it all wrong. I want you to leave your incidental Dick, and this awful hole, and come to live with me, and die with me, and everything with me" (words to that effect).

"You're crazy," she said, her features working.

"Think it over, Lolita. There are no strings attached. Except, perhaps—well, no matter." (A reprieve, I wanted to say but did not.) "Anyway, if you refuse you will still get your . . . *trousseau.*"

"No kidding?" asked Dolly.

I handed her an envelope with four hundred dollars in cash and a check for three thousand six hundred more.

Gingerly, uncertainly, she received *mon petit cadeau*; and then her forehead became a beautiful pink. "You mean," she said, with agonized emphasis, "you are giving us *four thousand bucks?*" I covered my face with my hand and broke into the hottest tears I had ever shed. I felt them winding through my fingers and down my chin, and burning me, and my nose got clogged, and I could not stop, and then she touched my wrist.

"I'll die if you touch me," I said. "You are sure you are not coming with me? Is there no hope of your coming? Tell me only this."

"No," she said. "No, honey, no."

She had never called me honey before.

"No," she said, "it is quite out of the question. I would sooner go back to Cue. I mean—"

She groped for words. I supplied them mentally ("*He* broke my heart. *You* merely broke my life").

"I think," she went on—"oops"—the envelope skidded to the floor—she picked it up—"I think it's oh utterly *grand* of you to give us all that dough. It settles everything, we can start next week. Stop crying, please. You should understand. Let me get you some more beer. Oh, don't cry, I'm so sorry I cheated so much, but that's the way things are."

I wiped my face and my fingers. She smiled at the *cadeau.*

She exulted. She wanted to call Dick. I said I would have to leave in a moment, did not want to see him at all, at all. We tried to think of some subject of conversation. For some reason, I kept seeing—it trembled and silkily glowed on my damp retina—a radiant child of twelve, sitting on a threshold, "pinging" pebbles at an empty can. I almost said—trying to find some casual remark—"I wonder sometimes what has become of the little McCoo girl, did she ever get better?"—but stopped in time lest she rejoin: "I wonder sometimes what has become of the little Haze girl . . ." Finally, I reverted to money matters. That sum, I said, represented more or less the net rent from her mother's house; she said: "Had it not been sold years ago?" No (I admit I *had* told her this in order to sever all connections with R.); a lawyer would send a full account of the financial situation later; it was rosy; some of the small securities her mother had owned had gone up and up. Yes, I was quite sure I had to go. I had to go, and find him, and destroy him.

Since I would not have survived the touch of her lips, I kept retreating in a mincing dance, at every step she and her belly made toward me.

She and the dog saw me off. I was surprised (this a rhetorical figure, I was not) that the sight of the old car in which she had ridden as a child and a nymphet, left her so very indifferent. All she remarked was it was getting sort of purplish about the gills. I said it was hers, I could go by bus. She said don't be silly, they would fly to Jupiter and buy a car there. I said I would buy this one from her for five hundred dollars.

"At this rate we'll be millionnaires next," she said to the ecstatic dog.

Carmencita, lui demandais-je . . . "One last word," I said in my horrible careful English, "are you quite, quite sure that—well, not tomorrow, of course, and not after tomorrow, but—well—some day, any day, you will not come to live with me? I will create a brand new God and thank him with piercing cries, if you give me that microscopic hope" (to that effect).

"No," she said smiling, "no."

"It would have made all the difference," said Humbert Humbert.

Then I pulled out my automatic—I mean, this is the kind of fool thing a reader might suppose I did. It never even occurred to me to do it.

"Good by-aye!" she chanted, my American sweet immortal dead love; for she is dead and immortal if you are reading this. I mean, such is the formal agreement with the so-called authorities.

Then, as I drove away, I heard her shout in a vibrant voice to her Dick; and the dog started to lope alongside my car like a fat dolphin, but he was too heavy and old, and very soon gave up.

And presently I was driving through the drizzle of the dying day, with the windshield wipers in full action but unable to cope with my tears.

30

Leaving as I did Coalmont around four in the afternoon (by Route X—I do not remember the number), I might have made Ramsdale by dawn had not a short-cut tempted me. I had to get onto Highway Y. My map showed quite blandly that just beyond Woodbine, which I reached at nightfall, I could leave paved X and reach paved Y by means of a transverse dirt road. It was only some forty miles long according to my map. Otherwise I would have to follow X for another hundred miles and then use leisurely looping Z to get to Y and my destination. However, the short-cut in question got worse and worse, bumpier and bumpier, muddier and muddier, and when I attempted to turn back after some ten miles of purblind, tortuous and tortoise-slow progress, my old and weak Melmoth got stuck in deep clay. All was dark and muggy, and hopeless. My headlights hung over a broad ditch full of water. The surrounding country, if any, was a black wilderness. I sought to extricate myself but my rear wheels only whined in slosh and anguish. Cursing my plight, I took off my fancy clothes, changed into slacks, pulled on the bullet-riddled sweater, and waded four miles back to a roadside farm. It started to rain on the way but I had not the strength to go back for a mackintosh. Such incidents have convinced me that my heart is basically sound despite recent diagnoses. Around midnight, a wrecker dragged my car out. I navigated back to Highway X and traveled on. Utter weariness overtook me an hour later, in an anonymous little town. I pulled up at the curb and in darkness drank deep from a friendly flask.

The rain had been cancelled miles before. It was a black warm night, somewhere in Appalachia. Now and then cars passed me, red tail-lights receding, white headlights advancing, but the town was dead. Nobody strolled and laughed on the sidewalks as relaxing burghers would in sweet, mellow, rotting Europe. I was alone to enjoy the innocent night and my terrible thoughts. A wire receptacle on the curb was very particular about acceptable contents: Sweepings. Paper. No Garbage. Sherry-red letters of light marked a Camera Shop. A large thermometer with the name of a laxative quietly dwelt on the front of a drugstore. Rubinov's Jewelry Company had a display of artificial diamonds reflected in a red mirror. A lighted green clock swam in the linenish depths of Jiffy Jeff Laundry. On the other side of the street a garage said in its sleep—genuflexion lubricity; and corrected itself to Gulflex Lubrication. An airplane, also gemmed by Rubinov, passed, droning, in the velvet heavens. How many small dead-of-night towns I had seen! This was not yet the last.

Let me dally a little, he is as good as destroyed. Some way further across the street, neon lights flickered twice slower than my heart: the outline of a restaurant sign, a large coffee-pot, kept bursting, every full second or so, into emerald life, and every time it went out, pink letters saying Fine Foods relayed it, but the pot could still be made out as a latent shadow teasing the eye before its next emerald resurrection. We made shadowgraphs. This furtive burg was not far from The Enchanted Hunters. I was weeping again, drunk on the impossible past.

31

At this solitary stop for refreshments between Coalmont and Ramsdale (between innocent Dolly Schiller and jovial Uncle Ivor), I reviewed my case. With the utmost simplicity and clarity I now saw myself and my love. Previous attempts seemed out of focus in comparison. A couple of years before, under the guidance of an intelligent French-speaking confessor, to whom, in a moment of metaphysical curiosity, I had turned over a Protestant's drab atheism for an old-fashioned popish cure, I had hoped to deduce from my sense of sin the existence of a Supreme Being. On those frosty mornings in rime-laced Quebec, the good priest worked on me with the finest tenderness and understanding. I am infinitely obliged to him and the great Institution he represented. Alas, I was unable to transcend the simple human fact that whatever spiritual solace I might find, whatever lithophanic eternities might be provided for me, nothing could make my Lolita forget the foul lust I had inflicted upon her. Unless it can be proven to me—to me as I am now, today, with my heart and my beard, and my putrefaction—that in the infinite run it does not matter a jot that a North American girl-child named Dolores Haze had been deprived of her childhood by a maniac, unless this can be proven (and if it can, then life is a joke), I see nothing for the treatment of my misery but the melancholy and very local palliative of articulate art. To quote an old poet:

> The moral sense in mortals is the duty
> We have to pay on mortal sense of beauty.

32

There was the day, during our first trip—our first circle of paradise—when in order to enjoy my phantasms in peace I firmly decided to ignore what I could not help perceiving, the fact that I was to her not a boy friend, not a glamour man, not a pal, not even a person at all, but just two eyes and a foot of engorged brawn—to mention only mentionable matters. There was the day when having withdrawn the functional promise I had made her on the eve (whatever she had set her funny little heart on—a roller rink with some special plastic floor or a movie matinee to which she wanted to go alone), I happened to glimpse from the bathroom, through a chance combination of mirror aslant and door ajar, a look on her face . . . that look I cannot exactly describe . . . an expression of helplessness so perfect that it seemed to grade into one of rather comfortable inanity just because this was the very limit of injustice and frustration—and every limit presupposes something beyond it—hence the neutral illumination. And when you bear in mind that these were the raised eyebrows and parted lips of a child, you may better appreciate what depths of calculated carnality, what reflected despair, restrained me from falling at her dear feet and dissolving in human tears, and sacrificing my jealousy to whatever pleasure Lolita might hope to derive from mixing with dirty and dangerous children in an outside world that was real to her.

And I have still other smothered memories, now unfolding themselves into limbless monsters of pain. Once, in a sunset-ending street of Beardsley, she turned to little Eva Rosen (I was taking both nymphets to a concert and walking behind them so close as almost to touch them with my person), she turned to Eva, and so very serenely and seriously, in answer to something the other had said about its being better to die than hear Milton Pinski, some local schoolboy she knew, talk about music, my Lolita remarked:

"You know, what's so dreadful about dying is that you are completely on your own"; and it struck me, as my automaton knees went up and down, that I simply did not know a thing about my darling's mind and that quite possibly, behind the awful juvenile clichés, there was in her a garden and a twilight, and a palace gate—dim and adorable regions which happened to be lucidly and absolutely forbidden to me, in my polluted rags and miserable convulsions; for I often noticed that living as we did, she and I, in a world of total evil, we would become strangely embarrassed whenever I tried to discuss something she and an older friend, she and a parent, she and a real healthy sweetheart, I and Annabel, Lolita and a sublime, purified, analyzed, deified Harold Haze, might have discussed—an abstract idea, a painting, stippled Hopkins or shorn Baudelaire, God or Shakespeare, anything of a genuine kind. Good will! She would mail her vulnerability in trite brashness and boredom, whereas I, using for my desperately detached comments an artificial tone of voice that set my own last teeth on edge, provoked my audience to such outbursts of rudeness as made any further conversation impossible, oh my poor, bruised child.

I loved you. I was a pentapod monster, but I loved you. I was despicable and brutal, and turpid, and everything, *mais je t'aimais, je t'aimais!* And there were times when I knew how you felt, and it was hell to know it, my little one. Lolita girl, brave Dolly Schiller.

I recall certain moments, let us call them icebergs in paradise, when after having had my fill of her—after fabulous, insane exertions that left me limp and azure-barred—I would gather her in my arms with, at last, a mute moan of human tenderness (her skin glistening in the neon light coming from the paved court through the slits in the blind, her soot-black lashes matted, her grave gray eyes more vacant than ever—for all the world a little patient still in the confusion of a drug after a major operation)—and the tenderness would deepen to shame and despair, and I would lull and rock my lone light Lolita in my marble arms, and moan in her warm hair, and caress her at random and mutely ask her blessing, and at the peak of this human agonized selfless tenderness (with my soul actually hanging around her naked body and ready to repent), all at once, ironically, horribly, lust would swell again—and "oh, *no*," Lolita would say with a sigh to heaven, and the next moment the tenderness and the azure—all would be shattered.

Mid-twentieth century ideas concerning child-parent relationship have been considerably tainted by the scholastic rigmarole and standardized symbols of the psychoanalytic racket, but I hope I am addressing myself to unbiased readers. Once when Avis's father had honked outside to signal papa had come to take his pet home, I felt obliged to invite him into the parlor, and he sat down for a minute, and while we conversed, Avis, a heavy, unattractive, affectionate child, drew up to him and eventually perched plumply on his knee. Now, I do not remember if I have mentioned that Lolita always had an absolutely enchanting smile for strangers, a tender furry slitting of the eyes, a dreamy sweet radiance of all her features which did not mean a thing of course but was so beautiful, so endearing that one found it hard to reduce such sweetness to but a magic gene automatically lighting up her face in at-

avistic token of some ancient rite of welcome—hospitable
prostitution, the coarse reader may say. Well, there she stood
while Mr. Byrd twirled his hat and talked, and—yes, look how
stupid of me, I have left out the main characteristic of the
famous Lolita smile, namely: while the tender, nectared, dimpled brightness played, it was never directed at the stranger
in the room but hung in its own remote flowered void, so to
speak, or wandered with myopic softness over chance objects—and this is what was happening now: while fat Avis sidled up to her papa, Lolita gently beamed at a fruit knife that
she fingered on the edge of the table, whereon she leaned,
many miles away from me. Suddenly, as Avis clung to her
father's neck and ear while, with a casual arm, the man enveloped his lumpy and large offspring, I saw Lolita's smile lose
all its light and become a frozen little shadow of itself, and
the fruit knife slipped off the table and struck her with its
silver handle a freak blow on the ankle which made her gasp, and
crouch head forward, and then, jumping on one leg, her face
awful with the preparatory grimace which children hold till
the tears gush, she was gone—to be followed at once and
consoled in the kitchen by Avis, who had such a wonderful fat
pink dad, and a small chubby brother, and a brand-new baby
sister, and a home, and two grinning dogs, and Lolita had
nothing. And I have a neat pendant to that little scene—also
in a Beardsley setting. Lolita, who had been reading near the
fire, stretched herself, and then inquired, her elbow up, with
a grunt: "Where is she buried anyway?" "Who?" "Oh, you
know, my murdered mummy." "And *you* know where her
grave is," I said controlling myself, whereupon I named the
cemetery—just outside Ramsdale, between the railway tracks
and Lakeview Hill. "Moreover," I added, "the tragedy of
such an accident is somewhat cheapened by the epithet you
saw fit to apply to it. If you really wish to triumph in your
mind over the idea of death—" "Ray," said Lo for hurray,
and languidly left the room, and for a long while I stared with
smarting eyes into the fire. Then I picked up her book. It was
some trash for young people. There was a gloomy girl Marion,
and there was her stepmother who turned out to be, against
all expectations, a young, gay, understanding redhead who
explained to Marion that Marion's dead mother had really

been a heroic woman since she had deliberately dissimulated her great love for Marion because she was dying, and did not want her child to miss her. I did not rush up to her room with cries. I always preferred the mental hygiene of noninterference. Now, squirming and pleading with my own memory, I recall that on this and similar occasions, it was always my habit and method to ignore Lolita's states of mind while comforting my own base self. When my mother, in a livid wet dress, under the tumbling mist (so I vividly imagined her), had run panting ecstatically up that ridge above Moulinet to be felled there by a thunderbolt, I was but an infant, and in retrospect no yearnings of the accepted kind could I ever graft upon any moment of my youth, no matter how savagely psychotherapists heckled me in my later periods of depression. But I admit that a man of my power of imagination cannot plead personal ignorance of universal emotions. I may also have relied too much on the abnormally chill relations between Charlotte and her daughter. But the awful point of the whole argument is this. It had become gradually clear to my conventional Lolita during our singular and bestial cohabitation that even the most miserable of family lives was better than the parody of incest, which, in the long run, was the best I could offer the waif.

33

Ramsdale revisited. I approached it from the side of the lake. The sunny noon was all eyes. As I rode by in my mud-flecked car, I could distinguish scintillas of diamond water between the far pines. I turned into the cemetery and walked among the long and short stone monuments. *Bonzhur*, Charlotte. On some of the graves there were pale, transparent little national flags slumped in the windless air under the evergreens. Gee, Ed, that was bad luck—referring to G. Edward Grammar, a thirty-five-year-old New York office manager who had just been arrayed on a charge of murdering his thirty-three-year-old wife, Dorothy. Bidding for the perfect crime, Ed had bludgeoned his wife and put her into a car. The case came to light when two county policemen on patrol saw Mrs. Grammar's new big blue Chrysler, an anniversary present from her husband, speeding crazily down a hill, just inside their jurisdiction (God bless our good cops!). The car sideswiped a pole, ran up an embankment covered with beard grass, wild strawberry and cinquefoil, and overturned. The wheels were still gently spinning in the mellow sunlight when the officers removed Mrs. G's body. It appeared to be a routine highway accident at first. Alas, the woman's battered body did not match up with only minor damage suffered by the car. I did better.

I rolled on. It was funny to see again the slender white church and the enormous elms. Forgetting that in an American suburban street a lone pedestrian is more conspicuous than a lone motorist, I left the car in the avenue to walk unobtrusively past 342 Lawn Street. Before the great bloodshed, I was entitled to a little relief, to a cathartic spasm of mental regurgitation. Closed were the white shutters of the Junk mansion, and somebody had attached a found black velvet hair ribbon to the white FOR SALE sign which was leaning toward the sidewalk. No dog barked. No gardener telephoned. No Miss Opposite sat on the vined porch—where to the lone pedestrian's annoyance two pony-tailed young women in identical polka-dotted pinafores stopped doing whatever they were doing to stare at him: she was long dead, no doubt, these might be her twin nieces from Philadelphia.

Should I enter my old house? As in a Turgenev story, a torrent of Italian music came from an open window—that of the living room: what romantic soul was playing the piano where no piano had plunged and plashed on that bewitched Sunday with the sun on her beloved legs? All at once I noticed that from the lawn I had mown a golden-skinned, brown-haired nymphet of nine or ten, in white shorts, was looking at me with wild fascination in her large blue-black eyes. I said something pleasant to her, meaning no harm, an old-world compliment, what nice eyes you have, but she retreated in haste and the music stopped abruptly, and a violent-looking dark man, glistening with sweat, came out and glared at me. I was on the point of identifying myself when, with a pang of dream-embarrassment, I became aware of my mud-caked dungarees, my filthy and torn sweater, my bristly chin, my bum's bloodshot eyes. Without saying a word, I turned and plodded back the way I had come. An aster-like anemic flower grew out of a remembered chink in the sidewalk. Quietly resurrected, Miss Opposite was being wheeled out by her nieces onto her porch, as if it were a stage and I the star performer. Praying she would not call to me, I hurried to my car. What a steep little street. What a profound avenue. A red ticket showed between wiper and windshield; I carefully tore it into two, four, eight pieces.

Feeling I was losing my time, I drove energetically to the downtown hotel where I had arrived with a new bag more than five years before. I took a room, made two appointments by telephone, shaved, bathed, put on black clothes and went down for a drink in the bar. Nothing had changed. The barroom was suffused with the same dim, impossible garnet-red light that in Europe years ago went with low haunts, but here meant a bit of atmosphere in a family hotel. I sat at the same little table where at the very start of my stay, immediately after becoming Charlotte's lodger, I had thought fit to celebrate the occasion by suavely sharing with her half a bottle of champagne, which had fatally conquered her poor brimming heart. As then, a moon-faced waiter was arranging with stellar care fifty sherries on a round tray for a wedding party. Murphy-Fantasia, this time. It was eight minutes to three. As I walked through the lobby, I had to skirt a group of ladies who with *mille grâces* were taking leave of each other after a luncheon party. With a harsh cry of recognition, one pounced upon me. She was a stout, short woman in pearl-gray, with a long, gray, slim plume to her small hat. It was Mrs. Chatfield. She attacked me with a fake smile, all aglow with evil curiosity. (Had I done to Dolly, perhaps, what Frank Lasalle, a fifty-year-old mechanic, had done to eleven-year-old Sally Horner in 1948?) Very soon I had that avid glee well under control. She thought I was in California. How was—? With exquisite pleasure I informed her that my stepdaughter had just married a brilliant young mining engineer with a hush-hush job in the Northwest. She said she disapproved of such early marriages, she would never let her Phyllis, who was now eighteen—

"Oh yes, of course," I said quietly. "I remember Phyllis. Phyllis and Camp Q. Yes, of course. By the way, did she ever tell you how Charlie Holmes debauched there his mother's little charges?"

Mrs. Chatfield's already broken smile now disintegrated completely.

"For shame," she cried, "for shame, Mr. Humbert! The poor boy has just been killed in Korea."

I said didn't she think *"vient de,"* with the infinitive, expressed recent events so much more neatly than the English "just," with the past? But I had to be trotting off, I said.

There were only two blocks to Windmuller's office. He greeted me with a very slow, very enveloping, strong, searching grip. He thought I was in California. Had I not lived at one time at Beardsley? His daughter had just entered Beardsley College. And how was—? I gave all necessary information about Mrs. Schiller. We had a pleasant business conference. I walked out into the hot September sunshine a contented pauper.

Now that everything had been put out of the way, I could dedicate myself freely to the main object of my visit to Ramsdale. In the methodical manner on which I have always prided myself, I had been keeping Clare Quilty's face masked in my dark dungeon, where he was waiting for me to come with barber and priest: *"Réveillez-vous, Laqueue, il est temps de mourir!"* I have no time right now to discuss the mnemonics of physiognomization—I am on my way to his uncle and walking fast—but let me jot down this: I had preserved in the alcohol of a clouded memory the toad of a face. In the course of a few glimpses, I had noticed its slight resemblance to a cheery and rather repulsive wine dealer, a relative of mine in Switzerland. With his dumbbells and stinking tricot, and fat hairy arms, and bald patch, and pig-faced servant-concubine, he was on the whole a harmless old rascal. Too harmless, in fact, to be confused with my prey. In the state of mind I now found myself, I had lost contact with Trapp's image. It had become completely engulfed by the face of Clare Quilty—as represented, with artistic precision, by an easeled photograph of him that stood on his uncle's desk.

In Beardsley, at the hands of charming Dr. Molnar, I had undergone a rather serious dental operation, retaining only a few upper and lower front teeth. The substitutes were de-

pendent on a system of plates with an inconspicuous wire affair running along my upper gums. The whole arrangement
was a masterpiece of comfort, and my canines were in perfect
health. However, to garnish my secret purpose with a plausible pretext, I told Dr. Quilty that, in hope of alleviating facial
neuralgia, I had decided to have all my teeth removed. What
would a complete set of dentures cost? How long would the
process take, assuming we fixed our first appointment for
some time in November? Where was his famous nephew now?
Would it be possible to have them all out in one dramatic
session?

A white-smocked, gray-haired man, with a crew cut and the
big flat cheeks of a politician, Dr. Quilty perched on the corner of his desk, one foot dreamily and seductively rocking as
he launched on a glorious long-range plan. He would first
provide me with provisional plates until the gums settled.
Then he would make me a permanent set. He would like to
have a look at that mouth of mine. He wore perforated pied
shoes. He had not visited with the rascal since 1946, but supposed he could be found at his ancestral home, Grimm Road,
not far from Parkington. It was a noble dream. His foot
rocked, his gaze was inspired. It would cost me around six
hundred. He suggested he take measurements right away, and
make the first set before starting operations. My mouth was
to him a splendid cave full of priceless treasures, but I denied
him entrance.

"No," I said. "On second thoughts, I shall have it all done
by Dr. Molnar. His price is higher, but he is of course a much
better dentist than you."

I do not know if any of my readers will ever have a chance
to say that. It is a delicious dream feeling. Clare's uncle remained sitting on the desk, still looking dreamy, but his foot
had stopped push-rocking the cradle of rosy anticipation. On
the other hand, his nurse, a skeleton-thin, faded girl, with the
tragic eyes of unsuccessful blondes, rushed after me so as to
be able to slam the door in my wake.

Push the magazine into the butt. Press home until you
hear or feel the magazine catch engage. Delightfully snug.
Capacity: eight cartridges. Full Blued. Aching to be discharged.

34

A gas station attendant in Parkington explained to me very
clearly how to get to Grimm Road. Wishing to be sure Quilty
would be at home, I attempted to ring him up but learned
that his private telephone had recently been disconnected. Did
that mean he was gone? I started to drive to Grimm Road,
twelve miles north of the town. By that time night had eliminated most of the landscape and as I followed the narrow
winding highway, a series of short posts, ghostly white, with
reflectors, borrowed my own lights to indicate this or that
curve. I could make out a dark valley on one side of the road
and wooded slopes on the other, and in front of me, like
derelict snowflakes, moths drifted out of the blackness into
my probing aura. At the twelfth mile, as foretold, a curiously
hooded bridge sheathed me for a moment and, beyond it, a
white-washed rock loomed on the right, and a few car lengths
further, on the same side, I turned off the highway up gravelly
Grimm Road. For a couple of minutes all was dank, dark,
dense forest. Then, Pavor Manor, a wooden house with a turret, arose in a circular clearing. Its windows glowed yellow
and red; its drive was cluttered with half a dozen cars. I
stopped in the shelter of the trees and abolished my lights to
ponder the next move quietly. He would be surrounded by
his henchmen and whores. I could not help seeing the inside
of that festive and ramshackle castle in terms of "Troubled
Teens," a story in one of her magazines, vague "orgies," a
sinister adult with penele cigar, drugs, bodyguards. At least,
he was there. I would return in the torpid morning.

Gently I rolled back to town, in that old faithful car of mine
which was serenely, almost cheerfully working for me. My
Lolita! There was still a three-year-old bobby pin of hers in
the depths of the glove compartment. There was still that
stream of pale moths siphoned out of the night by my headlights. Dark barns still propped themselves up here and there
by the roadside. People were still going to the movies. While
searching for night lodgings, I passed a drive-in. In a selenian
glow, truly mystical in its contrast with the moonless and massive night, on a gigantic screen slanting away among dark
drowsy fields, a thin phantom raised a gun, both he and his

arm reduced to tremulous dishwater by the oblique angle of that receding world,—and the next moment a row of trees shut off the gesticulation.

35

I left Insomnia Lodge next morning around eight and spent some time in Parkington. Visions of bungling the execution kept obsessing me. Thinking that perhaps the cartridges in the automatic had gone stale during a week of inactivity, I removed them and inserted a fresh batch. Such a thorough oil bath did I give Chum that now I could not get rid of the stuff. I bandaged him up with a rag, like a maimed limb, and used another rag to wrap up a handful of spare bullets.

A thunderstorm accompanied me most of the way back to Grimm Road, but when I reached Pavor Manor, the sun was visible again, burning like a man, and the birds screamed in the drenched and steaming trees. The elaborate and decrepit house seemed to stand in a kind of daze, reflecting as it were my own state, for I could not help realizing, as my feet touched the springy and insecure ground, that I had overdone the alcoholic stimulation business.

A guardedly ironic silence answered my bell. The garage, however, was loaded with his car, a black convertible for the nonce. I tried the knocker. Re-nobody. With a petulant snarl, I pushed the front door—and, how nice, it swung open as in a medieval fairy tale. Having softly closed it behind me, I made my way across a spacious and very ugly hall; peered into an adjacent drawing room; noticed a number of used glasses growing out of the carpet; decided that master was still asleep in the master bedroom.

So I trudged upstairs. My right hand clutched muffled Chum in my pocket, my left patted the sticky banisters. Of the three bedrooms I inspected, one had obviously been slept in that night. There was a library full of flowers. There was a rather bare room with ample and deep mirrors and a polar bear skin on the slippery floor. There were still other rooms. A happy thought struck me. If and when master returned from his constitutional in the woods, or emerged from some secret lair, it might be wise for an unsteady gunman with a long job before him to prevent his playmate from locking himself up in a room. Consequently, for at least five minutes I went about—lucidly insane, crazily calm, an enchanted and very tight hunter—turning whatever keys in whatever locks there were and pocketing them with my free left hand. The house, being an old one, had more planned privacy than have modern glamour-boxes, where the bathroom, the only lock-able locus, has to be used for the furtive needs of planned parenthood.

Speaking of bathrooms—I was about to visit a third one when master came out of it, leaving a brief waterfall behind him. The corner of a passage did not quite conceal me. Gray-faced, baggy-eyed, fluffily disheveled in a scanty balding way, but still perfectly recognizable, he swept by me in a purple bathrobe, very like one I had. He either did not notice me, or else dismissed me as some familiar and innocuous halluci-nation—and, showing me his hairy calves, he proceeded, sleepwalker-wise, downstairs. I pocketed my last key and followed him into the entrance hall. He had half opened his mouth and the front door, to peer out through a sunny chink as one who thinks he has heard a half-hearted visitor ring and recede. Then, still ignoring the raincoated phantasm that had stopped in midstairs, master walked into a cozy boudoir across the hall from the drawing room, through which—taking it easy, knowing he was safe—I now went away from him, and in a bar-adorned kitchen gingerly unwrapped dirty Chum, tak-ing care not to leave any oil stains on the chrome—I think I got the wrong product, it was black and awfully messy. In my usual meticulous way, I transferred naked Chum to a clean recess about me and made for the little boudoir. My step, as I say, was springy—too springy perhaps for success. But my heart pounded with tiger joy, and I crunched a cocktail glass underfoot.

Master met me in the Oriental parlor.

"Now who are you?" he asked in a high hoarse voice, his hands thrust into his dressing-gown pockets, his eyes fixing a point to the northeast of my head. "Are you by any chance Brewster?"

By now it was evident to everybody that he was in a fog and completely at my so-called mercy. I could enjoy myself.

"That's right," I answered suavely. "*Je suis Monsieur Brus-tère*. Let us chat for a moment before we start."

He looked pleased. His smudgy mustache twitched. I removed my raincoat. I was wearing a black suit, a black shirt, no tie. We sat down in two easy chairs.

"You know," he said, scratching loudly his fleshy and gritty gray cheek and showing his small pearly teeth in a crooked grin, "you don't *look* like Jack Brewster. I mean, the resemblance is not particularly striking. Somebody told me he had a brother with the same telephone company."

To have him trapped, after those years of repentance and rage . . . To look at the black hairs on the back of his pudgy hands . . . To wander with a hundred eyes over his purple silks and hirsute chest foreglimpsing the punctures, and mess, and music of pain . . . To know that this semi-animated, subhuman trickster who had sodomized my darling—oh, my darling, this was intolerable bliss!

"No, I am afraid I am neither of the Brewsters."

He cocked his head, looking more pleased than ever.

"Guess again, Punch."

"Ah," said Punch, "so you have not come to bother me about those long-distance calls?"

"You do make them once in a while, don't you?"

"Excuse me?"

I said I had said I thought he had said he had never—

"People," he said, "people in general, I'm not accusing you, Brewster, but you know it's absurd the way people invade this damned house without even knocking. They use the *va-terre*, they use the kitchen, they use the telephone. Phil calls Philadelphia. Pat calls Patagonia. I refuse to pay. You have a funny accent, Captain."

"Quilty," I said, "do you recall a little girl called Dolores Haze, Dolly Haze? Dolly called Dolores, Colo?"

"Sure, she may have made those calls, sure. Any place. Paradise, Wash., Hell Canyon. Who cares?"

"I do, Quilty. You see, I am her father."

"Nonsense," he said. "You are not. You are some foreign literary agent. A Frenchman once translated my *Proud Flesh* as *La Fierté de la Chair*. Absurd."

"She was my child, Quilty."

In the state he was in he could not really be taken aback by anything, but his blustering manner was not quite convincing. A sort of wary inkling kindled his eyes into a semblance of life. They were immediately dulled again.

"I'm very fond of children myself," he said, "and fathers are among my best friends."

He turned his head away, looking for something. He beat his pockets. He attempted to rise from his seat.

"Down!" I said—apparently much louder than I intended.

"You need not roar at me," he complained in his strange feminine manner. "I just wanted a smoke. I'm dying for a smoke."

"You're dying anyway."

"Oh, chucks," he said. "You begin to bore me. What do you want? Are you French, mister? Woolly-woo-boo-are? Let's go to the barroomette and have a stiff—"

He saw the little dark weapon lying in my palm as if I were offering it to him.

"Say!" he drawled (now imitating the underworld numbskull of movies), "that's a swell little gun you've got there. What d'you want for her?"

I slapped down his outstretched hand and he managed to knock over a box on a low table near him. It ejected a handful of cigarettes.

"Here they are," he said cheerfully. "You recall Kipling: *une femme est une femme, mais un Caporal est une cigarette?* Now we need matches."

"Quilty," I said, "I want you to concentrate. You are going to die in a moment. The hereafter for all we know may be an eternal state of excruciating insanity. You smoked your last cigarette yesterday. Concentrate. Try to understand what is happening to you."

He kept taking the Drome cigarette apart and munching bits of it.

"I am willing to try," he said. "You are either Australian, or a German refugee. Must you talk to me? This is a Gentile's house, you know. Maybe, you'd better run along. And do stop demonstrating that gun. I've an old Stern-Luger in the music room."

I pointed Chum at his slippered foot and crushed the

trigger. It clicked. He looked at his foot, at the pistol, again at his foot. I made another awful effort, and, with a ridiculously feeble and juvenile sound, it went off. The bullet entered the thick pink rug, and I had the paralyzing impression that it had merely trickled in and might come out again.

"See what I mean?" said Quilty. "You should be a little more careful. Give me that thing for Christ's sake."

He reached for it. I pushed him back into the chair. The rich joy was waning. It was high time I destroyed him, but he must understand why he was being destroyed. His condition infected me, the weapon felt limp and clumsy in my hand.

"Concentrate," I said, "on the thought of Dolly Haze whom you kidnaped—"

"I did not!" he cried. "You're all wet. I saved her from a beastly pervert. Show me your badge instead of shooting at my foot, you ape, you. Where is that badge? I'm not responsible for the rapes of others. Absurd! That joy ride, I grant you, was a silly stunt but you got her back, didn't you? Come, let's have a drink."

I asked him whether he wanted to be executed sitting or standing.

"Ah, let me think," he said. "It is not an easy question. Incidentally—I made a mistake. Which I sincerely regret. You see, I had no fun with your Dolly. I am practically impotent, to tell the melancholy truth. And I gave her a splendid vacation. She met some remarkable people. Do you happen to know—"

And with a tremendous lurch he fell all over me, sending the pistol hurtling under a chest of drawers. Fortunately he was more impetuous than vigorous, and I had little difficulty in shoving him back into his chair.

He puffed a little and folded his arms on his chest.

"Now you've done it," he said. *"Vous voilà dans de beaux draps, mon vieux."*

His French was improving.

I looked around. Perhaps, if— Perhaps I could— On my hands and knees? Risk it?

"Alors, que fait-on?" he asked watching me closely.

I stooped. He did not move. I stooped lower.

"My dear sir," he said, "stop trifling with life and death. I am a playwright. I have written tragedies, comedies, fantasies. I have made private movies out of *Justine* and other eighteenth-century sexcapades. I'm the author of fifty-two successful scenarios. I know all the ropes. Let me handle this. There should be a poker somewhere, why don't I fetch it, and then we'll fish out your property."

Fussily, busybodily, cunningly, he had risen again while he talked. I groped under the chest trying at the same time to keep an eye on him. All of a sudden I noticed that he had noticed that I did not seem to have noticed Chum protruding from beneath the other corner of the chest. We fell to wrestling again. We rolled all over the floor, in each other's arms, like two huge helpless children. He was naked and goatish under his robe, and I felt suffocated as he rolled over me. I rolled over him. We rolled over me. They rolled over him. We rolled over us.

In its published form, this book is being read, I assume, in the first years of 2000 A.D. (1935 plus eighty or ninety, live long, my love); and elderly readers will surely recall at this point the obligatory scene in the Westerns of their childhood. Our tussle, however, lacked the ox-stunning fisticuffs, the flying furniture. He and I were two large dummies, stuffed with dirty cotton and rags. It was a silent, soft, formless tussle on the part of two literati, one of whom was utterly disorganized by a drug while the other was handicapped by a heart condition and too much gin. When at last I had possessed myself of my precious weapon, and the scenario writer had been reinstalled in his low chair, both of us were panting as the cowman and the sheepman never do after their battle.

I decided to inspect the pistol—our sweat might have spoiled something—and regain my wind before proceeding to the main item in the program. To fill in the pause, I proposed he read his own sentence—in the poetical form I had given it. The term "poetical justice" is one that may be most happily used in this respect. I handed him a neat typescript.

"Yes," he said, "splendid idea. Let me fetch my reading glasses" (he attempted to rise).

"No."

"Just as you say. Shall I read out loud?"

"Yes."

"Here goes. I see it's in verse."

> Because you took advantage of a sinner
> because you took advantage
> because you took
> because you took advantage of my disadvantage . . .

"That's good, you know. That's damned good."

> . . . when I stood Adam-naked
> before a federal law and all its stinging stars

"Oh, grand stuff!"

> . . . Because you took advantage of a sin
> when I was helpless moulting moist and tender
> hoping for the best
> dreaming of marriage in a mountain state
> aye of a litter of Lolitas . . .

"Didn't get that."

> Because you took advantage of my inner
> essential innocence
> because you cheated me—

"A little repetitious, what? Where was I?"

> Because you cheated me of my redemption
> because you took
> her at the age when lads
> play with erector sets

"Getting smutty, eh?"

> a little downy girl still wearing poppies
> still eating popcorn in the colored gloam
> where tawny Indians took paid croppers
> because you stole her
> from her wax-browed and dignified protector
> spitting into his heavy-lidded eye
> ripping his flavid toga and at dawn
> leaving the hog to roll upon his new discomfort
> the awfulness of love and violets
> remorse despair while you

took a dull doll to pieces
and threw its head away
because of all you did
because of all I did not
you have to die

"Well, sir, this is certainly a fine poem. Your best as far as I am concerned."

He folded and handed it back to me.

I asked him if he had anything serious to say before dying. The automatic was again ready for use on the person. He looked at it and heaved a big sigh.

"Now look here, Mac," he said. "You are drunk and I am a sick man. Let us postpone the matter. I need quiet. I have to nurse my impotence. Friends are coming in the afternoon to take me to a game. This pistol-packing farce is becoming a frightful nuisance. We are men of the world, in everything— sex, free verse, marksmanship. If you bear me a grudge, I am ready to make unusual amends. Even an old-fashioned *ren-contre*, sword or pistol, in Rio or elsewhere—is not excluded. My memory and my eloquence are not at their best today but really, my dear Mr. Humbert, you were not an ideal stepfa-ther, and I did not force your little protégée to join me. It was she made me remove her to a happier home. This house is not as modern as that ranch we shared with dear friends. But it is roomy, cool in summer and winter, and in a word comfortable, so, since I intend retiring to England or Florence forever, I suggest you move in. It is yours, gratis. Under the condition you stop pointing at me that [he swore disgust-ingly] gun. By the way, I do not know if you care for the bizarre, but if you do, I can offer you, also gratis, as house pet, a rather exciting little freak, a young lady with three breasts, one a dandy, this is a rare and delightful marvel of nature. Now, *soyons raisonnables.* You will only wound me hideously and then rot in jail while I recuperate in a tropical setting. I promise you, Brewster, you will be happy here, with a magnificent cellar, and all the royalties from my next play— I have not much at the bank right now but I propose to borrow—you know, as the Bard said, with that cold in his head, to borrow and to borrow and to borrow. There are other advantages. We have here a most reliable and bribable charwoman, a Mrs. Vibrissa—curious name—who comes from the village twice a week, alas not today, she has daughters, granddaughters, a thing or two I know about the chief of police makes him my slave. I am a playwright. I have been called the American Maeterlinck. Maeterlinck-Schmetterling, says I. Come on! All this is very humiliating, and I am not sure I am doing the right thing. Never use herculanita with rum. Now drop that pistol like a good fellow. I knew your dear wife slightly. You may use my wardrobe. Oh, another thing—you are going to like this. I have an absolutely unique collection of erotica upstairs. Just to mention one item: the in folio de-luxe *Bagration Island* by the explorer and psychoanalyst Melanie Weiss, a remarkable lady, a remarkable work—drop that gun—with photographs of eight hundred and something male organs she examined and measured in 1932 on Bagration, in the Barda Sea, very illuminating graphs, plotted with love under pleasant skies—drop that gun—and moreover I can arrange for you to attend executions, not everybody knows that the chair is painted yellow—"

Feu. This time I hit something hard. I hit the back of a black rocking chair, not unlike Dolly Schiller's—my bullet hit the inside surface of its back whereupon it immediately went into a rocking act, so fast and with such zest that any one coming into the room might have been flabbergasted by the double miracle: that chair rocking in a panic all by itself, and the armchair, where my purple target had just been, now void of all live content. Wiggling his fingers in the air, with a rapid heave of his rump, he flashed into the music room and the next second we were tugging and gasping on both sides of the door which had a key I had overlooked. I won again, and with another abrupt movement Clare the Impredictable sat down before the piano and played several atrociously vigorous, fundamentally hysterical, plangent chords, his jowls quivering, his spread hands tensely plunging, and his nostrils emitting the soundtrack snorts which had been absent from our fight. Still singing those impossible sonorities, he made a futile attempt to open with his foot a kind of seaman's chest near the piano. My next bullet caught him somewhere in the side, and he rose from his chair higher and higher, like old, gray, mad Nijinski, like Old Faithful, like some old nightmare of mine, to a phenomenal altitude, or so it seemed, as he rent the air—still shaking with the rich black music—head thrown back in a howl, hand pressed to his brow, and with his other hand clutching his armpit as if stung by a hornet, down he came on his heels and, again a normal robed man, scurried out into the hall.

I see myself following him through the hall, with a kind of double, triple, kangaroo jump, remaining quite straight on straight legs while bouncing up twice in his wake, and then bouncing between him and the front door in a ballet-like stiff bounce, with the purpose of heading him off, since the door was not properly closed.

Suddenly dignified, and somewhat morose, he started to walk up the broad stairs, and, shifting my position, but not actually following him up the steps, I fired three or four times in quick succession, wounding him at every blaze; and every time I did it to him, that horrible thing to him, his face would twitch in an absurd clownish manner, as if he were exaggerating the pain; he slowed down, rolled his eyes half closing them and made a feminine "ah!" and he shivered every time a bullet hit him as if I were tickling him, and every time I got him with those slow, clumsy, blind bullets of mine, he would say under his breath, with a phoney British accent—all the while dreadfully twitching, shivering, smirking, but withal talking in a curiously detached and even amiable manner: "Ah, that hurts, sir, enough! Ah, that hurts atrociously, my dear fellow. I pray you, desist. Ah—very painful, very painful, indeed . . . God! Hah! This is abominable, you should really not—" His voice trailed off as he reached the landing, but he steadily walked on despite all the lead I had lodged in his bloated body—and in distress, in dismay, I understood that far from killing him I was injecting spurts of energy into the poor fellow, as if the bullets had been capsules wherein a heady elixir danced.

I reloaded the thing with hands that were black and bloody—I had touched something he had anointed with his thick gore. Then I rejoined him upstairs, the keys jangling in my pockets like gold.

He was trudging from room to room, bleeding majestically,

trying to find an open window, shaking his head, and still trying to talk me out of murder. I took aim at his head, and he retired to the master bedroom with a burst of royal purple where his ear had been.

"Get out, get out of here," he said coughing and spitting; and in a nightmare of wonder, I saw this blood-spattered but still buoyant person get into his bed and wrap himself up in the chaotic bedclothes. I hit him at very close range through the blankets, and then he lay back, and a big pink bubble with juvenile connotations formed on his lips, grew to the size of a toy balloon, and vanished.

I may have lost contact with reality for a second or two— oh, nothing of the I-just-blacked-out sort that your common criminal enacts; on the contrary, I want to stress the fact that I was responsible for every shed drop of his bubbleblood; but a kind of momentary shift occurred as if I were in the connubial bedroom, and Charlotte were sick in bed. Quilty was a very sick man. I held one of his slippers instead of the pistol—I was sitting on the pistol. Then I made myself a little more comfortable in the chair near the bed, and consulted my wrist watch. The crystal was gone but it ticked. The whole sad business had taken more than an hour. He was quiet at last. Far from feeling any relief, a burden even weightier than the one I had hoped to get rid of was with me, upon me, over me. I could not bring myself to touch him in order to make sure he was really dead. He looked it: a quarter of his face gone, and two flies beside themselves with a dawning sense of unbelievable luck. My hands were hardly in better condition than his. I washed up as best I could in the adjacent bathroom. Now I could leave. As I emerged on the landing, I was amazed to discover that a vivacious buzz I had just been dismissing as a mere singing in my ears was really a medley of voices and radio music coming from the downstairs drawing room.

I found there a number of people who apparently had just arrived and were cheerfully drinking Quilty's liquor. There was a fat man in an easy chair; and two dark-haired pale young beauties, sisters no doubt, big one and small one (almost a child), demurely sat side by side on a davenport. A florid-faced fellow with sapphire-blue eyes was in the act of bringing two glasses out of the bar-like kitchen, where two or three women were chatting and chinking ice. I stopped in the doorway and said: "I have just killed Clare Quilty." "Good for you," said the florid fellow as he offered one of the drinks to the elder girl. "Somebody ought to have done it long ago," remarked the fat man. "What does he say, Tony?" asked a faded blonde from the bar. "He says," answered the florid fellow, "he has killed Cue." "Well," said another unidentified man rising in a corner where he had been crouching to inspect some records, "I guess we all should do it to him some day." "Anyway," said Tony, "he'd better come down. We can't wait for him much longer if we want to go to that game." "Give this man a drink somebody," said the fat person. "Want a beer?" said a woman in slacks, showing it to me from afar.

Only the two girls on the davenport, both wearing black, the younger fingering a bright something about her white neck, only they said nothing, but just smiled on, so young, so lewd. As the music paused for a moment, there was a sudden noise on the stairs. Tony and I stepped out into the hall. Quilty of all people had managed to crawl out onto the landing, and there we could see him, flapping and heaving, and then subsiding, forever this time, in a purple heap.

"Hurry up, Cue," said Tony with a laugh. "I believe, he's still—" He returned to the drawing room, music drowned the rest of the sentence.

This, I said to myself, was the end of the ingenious play staged for me by Quilty. With a heavy heart I left the house and walked through the spotted blaze of the sun to my car. Two other cars were parked on both sides of it, and I had some trouble squeezing out.

36

The rest is a little flattish and faded. Slowly I drove down-hill, and presently found myself going at the same lazy pace in a direction opposite to Parkington. I had left my raincoat in the boudoir and Chum in the bathroom. No, it was not a house I would have liked to live in. I wondered idly if some surgeon of genius might not alter his own career, and perhaps the whole destiny of mankind, by reviving quilted Quilty,

Clare Obscure. Not that I cared; on the whole I wished to forget the whole mess—and when I did learn he was dead, the only satisfaction it gave me was the relief of knowing I need not mentally accompany for months a painful and disgusting convalescence interrupted by all kinds of unmentionable operations and relapses, and perhaps an actual visit from him, with trouble on my part to rationalize him as not being a ghost. Thomas had something. It is strange that the tactile sense, which is so infinitely less precious to men than sight, becomes at critical moments our main, if not only, handle to reality. I was all covered with Quilty—with the feel of that tumble before the bleeding.

The road now stretched across open country, and it occurred to me—not by way of protest, not as a symbol, or anything like that, but merely as a novel experience—that since I had disregarded all laws of humanity, I might as well disregard the rules of traffic. So I crossed to the left side of the highway and checked the feeling, and the feeling was good. It was a pleasant diaphragmal melting, with elements of diffused tactility, all this enhanced by the thought that nothing could be nearer to the elimination of basic physical laws than deliberately driving on the wrong side of the road. In a way, it was a very spiritual itch. Gently, dreamily, not exceeding twenty miles an hour, I drove on that queer mirror side. Traffic was light. Cars that now and then passed me on the side I had abandoned to them, honked at me brutally. Cars coming towards me wobbled, swerved, and cried out in fear. Presently I found myself approaching populated places. Passing through a red light was like a sip of forbidden Burgundy when I was a child. Meanwhile complications were arising. I was being followed and escorted. Then in front of me I saw two cars placing themselves in such a manner as to completely block my way. With a graceful movement I turned off the road, and after two or three big bounces, rode up a grassy slope, among surprised cows, and there I came to a gentle rocking stop. A kind of thoughtful Hegelian synthesis linking up two dead women.

I was soon to be taken out of the car ('Bye, Melmoth, thanks a lot, old fellow)—and was, indeed, looking forward to surrender myself to many hands, without doing anything to cooperate, while they moved and carried me, relaxed, comfortable, surrendering myself lazily, like a patient, and deriving an eerie enjoyment from my limpness and the absolutely reliable support given me by the police and the ambulance people. And while I was waiting for them to run up to me on the high slope, I evoked a last mirage of wonder and hopelessness. One day, soon after her disappearance, an attack of abominable nausea forced me to pull up on the ghost of an old mountain road that now accompanied, now traversed a brand new highway, with its population of asters bathing in the detached warmth of a pale-blue afternoon in late summer. After coughing myself inside out, I rested a while on a boulder, and then, thinking the sweet air might do me good, walked a little way toward a low stone parapet on the precipice side of the highway. Small grasshoppers spurted out of the withered roadside weeds. A very light cloud was opening its arms and moving toward a slightly more substantial one belonging to another, more sluggish, heavenlogged system. As I approached the friendly abyss, I grew aware of a melodious unity of sounds rising like vapor from a small mining town that lay at my feet, in a fold of the valley. One could make out the geometry of the streets between blocks of red and gray roofs, and green puffs of trees, and a serpentine stream, and the rich, ore-like glitter of the city dump, and beyond the town, roads crisscrossing the crazy quilt of dark and pale fields, and behind it all, great timbered mountains. But even brighter than those quietly rejoicing colors—for there are colors and shades that seem to enjoy themselves in good company—both brighter and dreamier to the ear than they were to the eye, was that vapory vibration of accumulated sounds that never ceased for a moment, as it rose to the lip of granite where I stood wiping my foul mouth. And soon I realized that all these sounds were of one nature, that no other sounds but these came from the streets of the transparent town, with the women at home and the men away. Reader! What I heard was but the melody of children at play, nothing but that, and so limpid was the air that within this vapor of blended voices —majestic and minute, remote and magically near, frank and divinely enigmatic—one could hear now and then, as if released, an almost articulate spurt of vivid laughter, or the crack of a bat, or the clatter of a toy wagon, but it was all really too far for the eye to distinguish any movement in the lightly etched streets. I stood listening to that musical vibration from my lofty slope, to those flashes of separate cries with a kind of demure murmur for background, and then I knew that the hopelessly poignant thing was not Lolita's absence from my side, but the absence of her voice from that concord.

This then is my story. I have reread it. It has bits of marrow sticking to it, and blood, and beautiful bright-green flies. At this or that twist of it I feel my slippery self eluding me, gliding into deeper and darker waters than I care to probe. I have camouflaged what I could so as not to hurt people. And I have toyed with many pseudonyms for myself before I hit on a particularly apt one. There are in my notes "Otto Otto" and "Mesmer Mesmer" and "Lambert Lambert," but for some reason I think my choice expresses the nastiness best.

When I started, fifty-six days ago, to write *Lolita*, first in the psychopathic ward for observation, and then in this well-heated, albeit tombal, seclusion, I thought I would use these notes in toto at my trial, to save not my head, of course, but my soul. In mid-composition, however, I realized that I could not parade living Lolita. I still may use parts of this memoir in hermetic sessions, but publication is to be deferred.

For reasons that may appear more obvious than they really are, I am opposed to capital punishment; this attitude will be, I trust, shared by the sentencing judge. Had I come before myself, I would have given Humbert at least thirty-five years for rape, and dismissed the rest of the charges. But, even so, Dolly Schiller will probably survive me by many years. The following decision I make with all the legal impact and support of a signed testament: I wish this memoir to be published only when Lolita is no longer alive.

Thus, neither of us is alive when the reader opens this book. But while the blood still throbs through my writing hand, you are still as much part of blessed matter as I am, and I can still talk to you from here to Alaska. Be true to your Dick. Do not let other fellows touch you. Do not talk to strangers. I hope you will love your baby. I hope it will be a boy. That husband of yours, I hope, will always treat you well, because otherwise my specter shall come at him, like black smoke, like a demented giant, and pull him apart nerve by nerve. And do not pity C. Q. One had to choose between him and H. H., and one wanted H. H. to exist at least a couple of months longer, so as to have him make you live in the minds of later generations. I am thinking of aurochs and angels, the secret of durable pigments, prophetic sonnets, the refuge of art. And this is the only immortality you and I may share, my Lolita.

VLADIMIR NABOKOV
ON A BOOK ENTITLED *LOLITA*

After doing my impersonation of suave John Ray, the character in *Lolita* who pens the Foreword, any comments coming straight from me may strike one—may strike me, in fact—as an impersonation of Vladimir Nabokov talking about his own book. A few points, however, have to be discussed; and the autobiographic device may induce mimic and model to blend.

Teachers of Literature are apt to think up such problems as "What is the author's purpose?" or still worse "What is the guy trying to say?" Now, I happen to be the kind of author who in starting to work on a book has no other purpose than to get rid of that book and who, when asked to explain its origin and growth, has to rely on such ancient terms as Interreaction of Inspiration and Combination—which, I admit, sounds like a conjurer explaining one trick by performing another.

The first little throb of *Lolita* went through me late in 1939 or early in 1940, in Paris, at a time when I was laid up with a severe attack of intercostal neuralgia. As far as I can recall, the initial shiver of inspiration was somehow prompted by a newspaper story about an ape in the Jardin des Plantes who, after months of coaxing by a scientist, produced the first drawing ever charcoaled by an animal: this sketch showed the bars of the poor creature's cage. The impulse I record had no textual connection with the ensuing train of thought, which resulted, however, in a prototype of my present novel, a short story some thirty pages long. I wrote it in Russian, the language in which I had been writing novels since 1924 (the best of these are not translated into English, and all are prohibited for political reasons in Russia). The man was a Central European, the anonymous nymphet was French, and the loci were Paris and Provence. I had him marry the little girl's sick mother who soon died, and after a thwarted attempt to take advantage of the orphan in a hotel room, Arthur (for that was his name) threw himself under the wheels of a truck. I read the story one blue-papered wartime night to a group of friends—Mark Aldanov, two social revolutionaries, and a woman doctor; but I was not pleased with the thing and destroyed it sometime after moving to America in 1940.

Around 1949, in Ithaca, upstate New York, the throbbing, which had never quite ceased, began to plague me again. Combination joined inspiration with fresh zest and involved me in a new treatment of the theme, this time in English—the language of my first governess in St. Petersburg, circa 1903, a Miss Rachel Home. The nymphet, now with a dash of Irish blood, was really much the same lass, and the basic marrying-her-mother idea also subsisted; but otherwise the thing was new and had grown in secret the claws and wings of a novel.

The book developed slowly, with many interruptions and asides. It had taken me some forty years to invent Russia and Western Europe, and now I was faced by the task of inventing America. The obtaining of such local ingredients as would allow me to inject a modicum of average "reality" (one of the few words which mean nothing without quotes) into the brew of individual fancy, proved at fifty a much more difficult process than it had been in the Europe of my youth when receptiveness and retention were at their automatic best. Other books intervened. Once or twice I was on the point of burning the unfinished draft and had carried my Juanita Dark as far as the shadow of the leaning incinerator on the innocent lawn, when I was stopped by the thought that the ghost of the destroyed book would haunt my files for the rest of my life.

Every summer my wife and I go butterfly hunting. The specimens are deposited at scientific institutions, such as the Museum of Comparative Zoology at Harvard or the Cornell University collection. The locality labels pinned under these butterflies will be a boon to some twenty-first-century scholar with a taste for recondite biography. It was at such of our headquarters as Telluride, Colorado; Afton, Wyoming; Portal, Arizona; and Ashland, Oregon, that *Lolita* was energetically resumed in the evenings or on cloudy days. I finished copying the thing out in longhand in the spring of 1954, and at once began casting around for a publisher.

At first, on the advice of a wary old friend, I was meek enough to stipulate that the book be brought out anonymously. I doubt that I shall ever regret that soon afterwards, realizing how likely a mask was to betray my own cause, I decided to sign *Lolita*. The four American publishers, W, X, Y, Z, who in turn were offered the typescript and had their readers glance at it, were shocked by *Lolita* to a degree that even my wary old friend F.P. had not expected.

While it is true that in ancient Europe, and well into the eighteenth century (obvious examples come from France), deliberate lewdness was not inconsistent with flashes of comedy, or vigorous satire, or even the verve of a fine poet in a wanton mood, it is also true that in modern times the term "pornography" connotes mediocrity, commercialism, and certain strict rules of narration. Obscenity must be mated with banality because every kind of aesthetic enjoyment has to be entirely replaced by simple sexual stimulation which demands the traditional word for direct action upon the patient. Old rigid rules must be followed by the pornographer in order to have his patient feel the same security of satisfaction as, for example, fans of detective stories feel—stories where, if you do not watch out, the real murderer may turn out to be, to the fan's disgust, artistic originality (who for instance would want a detective story without a single dialogue in it?). Thus, in pornographic novels, action has to be limited to the copulation of clichés. Style, structure, imagery should never distract the reader from his tepid lust. The novel must consist of an alternation of sexual scenes. The passages in between must be reduced to sutures of sense, logical bridges of the simplest design, brief expositions and explanations, which the reader will probably skip but must know they exist in order not to feel cheated (a mentality stemming from the routine of "true" fairy tales in childhood). Moreover, the sexual scenes in the book must follow a crescendo line, with new variations, new combinations, new sexes, and a steady increase in the number of participants (in a Sade play they call the gardener in), and therefore the end of the book must be more replete with lewd lore than the first chapters.

Certain techniques in the beginning of *Lolita* (Humbert's Journal, for example) misled some of my first readers into assuming that this was going to be a lewd book. They expected the rising succession of erotic scenes; when these stopped, the readers stopped, too, and felt bored and let down. This, I suspect, is one of the reasons why not all the four firms read the typescript to the end. Whether they found it pornographic or not did not interest me. Their refusal to buy the book was based not on my treatment of the theme but on the theme itself, for there are at least three themes which are utterly taboo as far as most American publishers are concerned. The two others are: a Negro-White marriage which is a complete and glorious success resulting in lots of children and grandchildren; and the total atheist who lives a happy and useful life, and dies in his sleep at the age of 106.

Some of the reactions were very amusing: one reader suggested that his firm might consider publication if I turned my Lolita into a twelve-year-old lad and had him seduced by Humbert, a farmer, in a barn, amidst gaunt and arid surroundings, all this set forth in short, strong, "realistic" sentences ("He acts crazy. We all act crazy, I guess. I guess God acts crazy." Etc.). Although everybody should know that I detest symbols and allegories (which is due partly to my old feud with Freudian voodooism and partly to my loathing of generalizations devised by literary mythists and sociologists), an otherwise intelligent reader who flipped through the first part described *Lolita* as "Old

Europe debauching young America," while another flipper saw in it "Young America debauching old Europe." Publisher X, whose advisers got so bored with Humbert that they never got beyond page 188, had the naïveté to write me that Part Two was too long. Publisher Y, on the other hand, regretted there were no good people in the book. Publisher Z said if he printed *Lolita*, he and I would go to jail.

No writer in a free country should be expected to bother about the exact demarcation between the sensuous and the sensual; this is preposterous; I can only admire but cannot emulate the accuracy of judgment of those who pose the fair young mammals photographed in magazines where the general neckline is just low enough to provoke a past master's chuckle and just high enough not to make a postmaster frown. I presume there exist readers who find titillating the display of mural words in those hopelessly banal and enormous novels which are typed out by the thumbs of tense mediocrities and called "powerful" and "stark" by the reviewing hack. There are gentle souls who would pronounce *Lolita* meaningless because it does not teach them anything. I am neither a reader nor a writer of didactic fiction, and, despite John Ray's assertion, *Lolita* has no moral in tow. For me a work of fiction exists only insofar as it affords me what I shall bluntly call aesthetic bliss, that is a sense of being somehow, somewhere, connected with other states of being where art (curiosity, tenderness, kindness, ecstasy) is the norm. There are not many such books. All the rest is either topical trash or what some call the Literature of Ideas, which very often is topical trash coming in huge blocks of plaster that are carefully transmitted from age to age until somebody comes along with a hammer and takes a good crack at Balzac, at Gorki, at Mann.

Another charge which some readers have made is that *Lolita* is anti-American. This is something that pains me considerably more than the idiotic accusation of immorality. Considerations of depth and perspective (a suburban lawn, a mountain meadow) led me to build a number of North American sets. I needed a certain exhilarating milieu. Nothing is more exhilarating than philistine vulgarity. But in regard to philistine vulgarity there is no intrinsic difference between Palearctic manners and Nearctic manners. Any proletarian from Chicago can be as bourgeois (in the Flaubertian sense) as a duke. I chose American motels instead of Swiss hotels or English inns only because I am trying to be an American writer and claim only the same rights that other American writers enjoy. On the other hand, my creature Humbert is a foreigner and an anarchist, and there are many things, besides nymphets, in which I disagree with him. And all my Russian readers know that my old worlds—Russian, British, German, French—are just as fantastic and personal as my new one is.

Lest the little statement I am making here seem an airing of grudges, I must hasten to add that besides the lambs who read the typescript of *Lolita* or its Olympia Press edition in a spirit of "Why did he have to write it?" or "Why should I read about maniacs?" there have been a number of wise, sensitive, and staunch people who understood my book much better than I can explain its mechanism here.

Every serious writer, I dare say, is aware of this or that published book of his as of a constant comforting presence. Its pilot light is steadily burning somewhere in the basement and a mere touch applied to one's private thermostat instantly results in a quiet little explosion of familiar warmth. This presence, this glow of the book in an ever accessible remoteness is a most companionable feeling, and the better the book has conformed to its prefigured contour and color the ampler and smoother it glows. But even so, there are certain points, byroads, favorite hollows that one evokes more eagerly and enjoys more tenderly than the rest of one's book. I have not reread *Lolita* since I went through the proofs in the spring of 1955 but I find it to be a delightful presence now that it quietly hangs about the house like a summer day which one knows to be bright behind the haze. And when I thus think of *Lolita*, I seem always to pick out for special delectation such images as Mr. Taxovich, or that class list of Ramsdale School, or Charlotte saying "waterproof," or Lolita in slow motion advancing toward Humbert's gifts, or the pictures decorating the stylized garret of Gaston Godin, or the Kasbeam barber (who cost me a month of work), or Lolita playing tennis, or the hospital at Elphinstone, or pale, pregnant, beloved, irretrievable Dolly Schiller dying in Gray Star (the capital town of the book), or the tinkling sounds of the valley town coming up the mountain trail (on which I caught the first known female of *Lycaeides sublivens* Nabokov). These are the nerves of the novel. These are the secret points, the subliminal co-ordinates by means of which the book is plotted—although I realize very clearly that these and other scenes will be skimmed over or not noticed, or never even reached, by those who begin reading the book under the impression that it is something on the lines of *Memoirs of a Woman of Pleasure* or *Les Amours de Milord Grosvit.* That my novel does contain various allusions to the physiological urges of a pervert is quite true. But after all we are not children, not illiterate juvenile delinquents, not English public school boys who after a night of homosexual romps have to endure the paradox of reading the Ancients in expurgated versions.

It is childish to study a work of fiction in order to gain information about a country or about a social class or about the author. And yet one of my very few intimate friends, after reading *Lolita*, was sincerely worried that I (I!) should be living "among such depressing people"—when the only discomfort I really experienced was to live in my workshop among discarded limbs and unfinished torsos.

After Olympia Press, in Paris, published the book, an American critic suggested that *Lolita* was the record of my love affair with the romantic novel. The substitution "English language" for "romantic novel" would make this elegant formula more correct. But here I feel my voice rising to a much too strident pitch. None of my American friends have read my Russian books and thus every appraisal on the strength of my English ones is bound to be out of focus. My private tragedy, which cannot, and indeed should not, be anybody's concern, is that I had to abandon my natural idiom, my untrammeled, rich, and infinitely docile Russian tongue for a second-rate brand of English, devoid of any of those apparatuses—the baffling mirror, the black velvet backdrop, the implied associations and traditions—which the native illusionist, frac-tails flying, can magically use to transcend the heritage in his own way.

November 12, 1956

PNIN

to Véra

Chapter One

THE ELDERLY PASSENGER sitting on the north-window side of that inexorably moving railway coach, next to an empty seat and facing two empty ones, was none other than Professor Timofey Pnin. Ideally bald, sun-tanned, and clean-shaven, he began rather impressively with that great brown dome of his, tortoise-shell glasses (masking an infantile absence of eyebrows), apish upper lip, thick neck, and strong-man torso in a tightish tweed coat, but ended, somewhat disappointingly, in a pair of spindly legs (now flanneled and crossed) and frail-looking, almost feminine feet.

His sloppy socks were of scarlet wool with lilac lozenges; his conservative black oxfords had cost him about as much as all the rest of his clothing (flamboyant goon tie included). Prior to the nineteen-forties, during the staid European era of his life, he had always worn long underwear, its terminals tucked into the tops of neat silk socks, which were clocked, soberly colored, and held up on his cotton-clad calves by garters. In those days, to reveal a glimpse of that white underwear by pulling up a trouser leg too high would have seemed to Pnin as indecent as showing himself to ladies minus collar and tie; for even when decayed Mme. Roux, the concierge of the squalid apartment house in the Sixteenth Arrondissement of Paris—where Pnin, after escaping from Leninized Russia and completing his college education in Prague, had spent fifteen years—happened to come up for the rent while he was without his *faux col*, prim Pnin would cover his front stud with a chaste hand. All this underwent a change in the heady atmosphere of the New World. Nowadays, at fifty-two, he was crazy about sun-bathing, wore sport shirts and slacks, and when crossing his legs would carefully, deliberately, brazenly display a tremendous stretch of bare shin. Thus he might have appeared to a fellow passenger; but except for a soldier asleep at one end and two women absorbed in a baby at the other, Pnin had the coach to himself.

Now a secret must be imparted. Professor Pnin was on the wrong train. He was unaware of it, and so was the conductor, already threading his way through the train to Pnin's coach. As a matter of fact, Pnin at the moment felt very well satisfied with himself. When inviting him to deliver a Friday-evening lecture at Cremona—some two hundred versts west of Waindell, Pnin's academic perch since 1945—the vice-president of the Cremona Women's Club, a Miss Judith Clyde, had advised our friend that the most convenient train left Waindell at 1:52 P.M., reaching Cremona at 4:17; but Pnin—who, like so many Russians, was inordinately fond of everything in the line of timetables, maps, catalogues, collected them, helped himself freely to them with the bracing pleasure of getting something for nothing, and took especial pride in puzzling out schedules for himself—had discovered, after some study, an inconspicuous reference mark against a still more convenient train (Lv. Waindell 2:19 P.M., Ar. Cremona 4:32 P.M.); the mark indicated that Fridays, and Fridays only, the two-nineteen stopped at Cremona on its way to a distant and much larger city, graced likewise with a mellow Italian name. Unfortunately for Pnin, his timetable was five years old and in part obsolete.

He taught Russian at Waindell College, a somewhat provincial institution characterized by an artificial lake in the middle of a landscaped campus, by ivied galleries connecting the various halls, by murals displaying recognizable members of the faculty in the act of passing on the torch of knowledge from Aristotle, Shakespeare, and Pasteur to a lot of monstrously built farm boys and farm girls, and by a huge, active, buoyantly thriving German Department which its Head, Dr. Hagen, smugly called (pronouncing every syllable very distinctly) "a university within a university."

In the Fall Semester of that particular year (1950), the enrollment in the Russian Language courses consisted of one student, plump and earnest Betty Bliss, in the Transitional Group, one, a mere name (Ivan Dub, who never materialized) in the Advanced, and three in the flourishing Elementary: Josephine Malkin, whose grandparents had been born in Minsk; Charles McBeth, whose prodigious memory had already disposed of ten languages and was prepared to entomb ten more; and languid Eileen Lane, whom somebody had told that by the time one had mastered the Russian alphabet one could practically read "Anna Karamazov" in the original. As a teacher, Pnin was far from being able to compete with those stupendous Russian ladies, scattered all over academic America, who, without having had any formal training at all, manage somehow, by dint of intuition, loquacity, and a kind of maternal bounce, to infuse a magic knowledge of their difficult and beautiful tongue into a group of innocent-eyed students in an atmosphere of Mother Volga songs, red caviar, and tea; nor did Pnin, as a teacher, ever presume to approach the lofty halls of modern scientific linguistics, that ascetic fraternity of phonemes, that temple wherein earnest young people are taught not the language itself, but the method of teaching others to teach that method; which method, like a waterfall splashing from rock to rock, ceases to be a medium of rational navigation but perhaps in some fabulous future may become instrumental in evolving esoteric dialects—Basic Basque and so forth—spoken only by certain elaborate machines. No doubt Pnin's approach to his work was amateurish and lighthearted, depending as it did on exercises in a grammar brought out by the Head of a Slavic Department in a far greater college than Waindell—a venerable fraud whose Russian was a joke but who would generously lend his dignified name to the products of anonymous drudgery. Pnin, despite his many shortcomings, had about him a disarming, old-fashioned charm which Dr. Hagen, his staunch protector, insisted before morose trustees was a delicate imported article worth paying for in domestic cash. Whereas the degree in sociology and political economy that Pnin had obtained with some pomp at the University of Prague around 1925 had become by mid-century a doctorate in desuetude, he was not altogether miscast as a teacher of Russian. He was beloved not for any essential ability but for those unforgettable digressions of his, when he would remove his glasses to beam at the past while massaging the lenses of the present. Nostalgic excursions in broken English. Autobiographical tidbits. How Pnin came to the *Soedinyonnïe Shtatï* (the United States). "Examination on ship before landing. Very well! 'Nothing to declare?' 'Nothing.' Very well! Then political questions. He asks: 'Are you anarchist?' I answer"—time out on the part of the narrator for a spell of cozy mute mirth— " 'First what do we understand

under "Anarchism"? Anarchism practical, metaphysical, theoretical, mystical, abstractical, individual, social? When I was
young,' I say, 'all this had for me signification.' So we had a
very interesting discussion, in consequence of which I passed
two whole weeks on Ellis Island"—abdomen beginning to
heave; heaving; narrator convulsed.

But there were still better sessions in the way of humor.
With an air of coy secrecy, benevolent Pnin, preparing the
children for the marvelous treat he had once had himself, and
already revealing, in an uncontrollable smile, and incomplete
but formidable set of tawny teeth, would open a dilapidated
Russian book at the elegant leatherette marker he had carefully placed there; he would open the book, whereupon as
often as not a look of the utmost dismay would alter his plastic
features; agape, feverishly, he would flip right and left through
the volume, and minutes might pass before he found the right
page—or satisfied himself that he had marked it correctly after
all. Usually the passage of his choice would come from some
old and naïve comedy of merchant-class habitus rigged up by
Ostrovski almost a century ago, or from an equally ancient
but even more dated piece of trivial Leskovian jollity dependent on verbal contortions. He delivered these stale goods with
the rotund gusto of the classical Alexandrinka (a theater in
Petersburg), rather than with the crisp simplicity of the Moscow Artists; but since to appreciate whatever fun those passages still retained one had to have not only a sound
knowledge of the vernacular but also a good deal of literary
insight, and since his poor little class had neither, the performer would be alone in enjoying the associative subtleties
of his text. The heaving we have already noted in another
connection would become here a veritable earthquake. Directing his memory, with all the lights on and all the masks
of the mind a-miming, toward the days of his fervid and receptive youth (in a brilliant cosmos that seemed all the fresher
for having been abolished by one blow of history), Pnin would
get drunk on his private wines as he produced sample after
sample of what his listeners politely surmised was Russian humor. Presently the fun would become too much for him; pear-
shaped tears would trickle down his tanned cheeks. Not only
his shocking teeth but also an astonishing amount of pink

upper-gum tissue would suddenly pop out, as if a jack-in-the-box had been sprung, and his hand would fly to his mouth, while his big shoulders shook and rolled. And although the speech he smothered behind his dancing hand was now doubly unintelligible to the class, his complete surrender to his own merriment would prove irresistible. By the time he was helpless with it he would have his students in stitches, with abrupt barks of clockwork hilarity coming from Charles and a dazzling flow of unsuspected lovely laughter transfiguring Josephine, who was not pretty, while Eileen, who was, dissolved in a jelly of unbecoming giggles.

All of which does not alter the fact that Pnin was on the wrong train.

How should we diagnose his sad case? Pnin, it should be particularly stressed, was anything but the type of that good-natured German platitude of last century, *der zerstreute Professor*. On the contrary, he was perhaps too wary, too persistently on the lookout for diabolical pitfalls, too painfully on the alert lest his erratic surroundings (unpredictable America) inveigle him into some bit of preposterous oversight. It was the world that was absent-minded and it was Pnin whose business it was to set it straight. His life was a constant war with insensate objects that fell apart, or attacked him, or refused to function, or viciously got themselves lost as soon as they entered the sphere of his existence. He was inept with his hands to a rare degree; but because he could manufacture in a twinkle a one-note mouth organ out of a pea pod, make a flat pebble skip ten times on the surface of a pond, shadowgraph with his knuckles a rabbit (complete with blinking eye), and perform a number of other tame tricks that Russians have up their sleeves, he believed himself endowed with considerable manual and mechanical skill. On gadgets he doted with a kind of dazed, superstitious delight. Electric devices enchanted him. Plastics swept him off his feet. He had a deep admiration for the zipper. But the devoutly plugged-in clock would make nonsense of his mornings after a storm in the middle of the night had paralyzed the local power station. The frame of his spectacles would snap in mid-bridge, leaving him with two identical pieces, which he would vaguely attempt to unite, in the hope, perhaps, of some organic marvel of

restoration coming to the rescue. The zipper a gentleman depends on most would come loose in his puzzled hand at some
nightmare moment of haste and despair.

And he still did not know that he was on the wrong train.

A special danger area in Pnin's case was the English language. Except for such not very helpful odds and ends as "the
rest is silence," "nevermore," "weekend," "who's who," and
a few ordinary words like "eat," "street," "fountain pen,"
"gangster," "Charleston," "marginal utility," he had had no
English at all at the time he left France for the States. Stub-
bornly he sat down to the task of learning the language of
Fenimore Cooper, Edgar Poe, Edison, and thirty-one Presidents. In 1941, at the end of one year of study, he was profi-
cient enough to use glibly terms like "wishful thinking" and
"okey-dokey." By 1942 he was able to interrupt his narration
with the phrase, "To make a long story short." By the time
Truman entered his second term, Pnin could handle practically any topic; but otherwise progress seemed to have stopped
despite all his efforts, and by 1950 his English was still full of
flaws. That autumn he supplemented his Russian courses by
delivering a weekly lecture in a so-called symposium ("Wing-
less Europe: A Survey of Contemporary Continental Culture") directed by Dr. Hagen. All our friend's lectures,
including sundry ones he gave out of town, were edited by
one of the younger members of the German Department. The
procedure was somewhat complicated. Professor Pnin laboriously translated his own Russian verbal flow, teeming with
idiomatic proverbs, into patchy English. This was revised by
young Miller. Then Dr. Hagen's secretary, a Miss Eisenbohr,
typed it out. Then Pnin deleted the passages he could not
understand. Then he read it to his weekly audience. He was
utterly helpless without the prepared text, nor could he use
the ancient system of dissimulating his infirmity by moving his
eyes up and down—snapping up an eyeful of words, reeling
them off to his audience, and drawing out the end of the
sentence while diving for the next. Pnin's worried eye would
be bound to lose its bearings. Therefore he preferred reading
his lectures, his gaze glued to his text, in a slow, monotonous
baritone that seemed to climb one of those interminable
flights of stairs used by people who dread elevators.

The conductor, a gray-headed fatherly person with steel spectacles placed rather low on his simple, functional nose and a bit of soiled adhesive tape on his thumb, had now only three coaches to deal with before reaching the last one, where Pnin rode.

Pnin in the meantime had yielded to the satisfaction of a special Pninian craving. He was in a Pninian quandary. Among other articles indispensable for a Pninian overnight stay in a strange town, such as shoe trees, apples, dictionaries, and so on, his Gladstone bag contained a relatively new black suit he planned to wear that night for the lecture ("Are the Russian People Communist?") before the Cremona ladies. It also contained next Monday's symposium lecture ("Don Quixote and Faust"), which he intended to study the next day, on his way back to Waindell, and a paper by the graduate student, Betty Bliss ("Dostoevski and Gestalt Psychology"), that he had to read for Dr. Hagen, who was her main director of cerebration. The quandary was as follows: If he kept the Cremona manuscript—a sheaf of typewriter-size pages, carefully folded down the center—on his person, in the security of his body warmth, the chances were, theoretically, that he would forget to transfer it from the coat he was wearing to the one he would wear. On the other hand, if he placed the lecture in the pocket of the suit in the bag *now*, he would, he knew, be tortured by the possibility of his luggage being stolen. On the third hand (these mental states sprout additional forelimbs all the time), he carried in the inside pocket of his present coat a precious wallet with two ten-dollar bills, the newspaper clipping of a letter he had written, with my help, to the New York Times in 1945 anent the Yalta conference, and his certificate of naturalization; and it was physically possible to pull out the wallet, if needed, in such a way as fatally to dislodge the folded lecture. During the twenty minutes he had been on the train, our friend had already opened his bag twice to play with his various papers. When the conductor reached the car, diligent Pnin was perusing with difficulty Betty's last effort, which began, "When we consider the mental climate wherein we all live, we cannot but notice——"

The conductor entered; did not awake the soldier; promised the women he would let them know when they would be about to arrive; and presently was shaking his head over Pnin's ticket. The Cremona stop had been abolished two years before.

"Important lecture!" cried Pnin. "What to do? It is a catastroph!"

Gravely, comfortably, the gray-headed conductor sank into the opposite seat and consulted in silence a tattered book full of dog-eared insertions. In a few minutes, namely at 3:08, Pnin would have to get off at Whitchurch; this would enable him to catch the four-o'clock bus that would deposit him, around six, at Cremona.

"I was thinking I gained twelve minutes, and now I have lost nearly two whole hours," said Pnin bitterly. Upon which, clearing his throat and ignoring the consolation offered by the kind gray-head ("You'll make it."), he took off his reading glasses, collected his stone-heavy bag, and repaired to the vestibule of the car so as to wait there for the confused greenery skimming by to be cancelled and replaced by the definite station he had in mind.

2

Whitchurch materialized as scheduled. A hot, torpid expanse of cement and sun lay beyond the geometrical solids of various clean-cut shadows. The local weather was unbelievably summery for October. Alert, Pnin entered a waiting room of sorts, with a needless stove in the middle, and looked around. In a solitary recess, one could make out the upper part of a perspiring young man who was filling out forms on the broad wooden counter before him.

"Information, please," said Pnin. "Where stops four-o'clock bus to Cremona?"

"Right across the street," briskly answered the employee without looking up.

"And where possible to leave baggage?"

"That bag? I'll take care of it."

And with the national informality that always nonplused Pnin, the young man shoved the bag into a corner of his nook.

"Quittance?" queried Pnin, Englishing the Russian for "receipt" (*kvitantsiya*).

"What's that?"

"Number?" tried Pnin.

"You don't need a number," said the fellow, and resumed his writing.

Pnin left the station, satisfied himself about the bus stop, and entered a coffee shop. He consumed a ham sandwich, ordered another, and consumed that too. At exactly five minutes to four, having paid for the food but not for an excellent toothpick which he carefully selected from a neat little cup in the shape of a pine cone near the cash register, Pnin walked back to the station for his bag.

A different man was now in charge. The first had been called home to drive his wife in all haste to the maternity hospital. He would be back in a few minutes.

"But I must obtain my valise!" cried Pnin.

The substitute was sorry but could not do a thing.

"It is there!" cried Pnin, leaning over and pointing.

This was unfortunate. He was still in the act of pointing when he realized that he was claiming the wrong bag. His index finger wavered. That hesitation was fatal.

"My bus to Cremona!" cried Pnin.

"There is another at eight," said the man.

What was our poor friend to do? Horrible situation! He glanced streetward. The bus had just come. The engagement meant an extra fifty dollars. His hand flew to his right side. *It* was there, *slava Bogu* (thank God)! Very well! He would not wear his black suit—*vot i vsyo* (that's all). He would retrieve it on his way back. He had lost, dumped, shed many more valuable things in his day. Energetically, almost lightheartedly, Pnin boarded the bus.

He had endured this new stage of his journey only for a few city blocks when an awful suspicion crossed his mind. Ever since he had been separated from his bag, the tip of his left forefinger had been alternating with the proximal edge of his right elbow in checking a precious presence in his inside coat pocket. All of a sudden he brutally yanked it out. It was Betty's paper.

Emitting what he thought were international exclamations of anxiety and entreaty, Pnin lurched out of his seat. Reeling, he reached the exit. With one hand the driver grimly milked out a handful of coins from his little machine, refunded him the price of the ticket, and stopped the bus. Poor Pnin landed in the middle of a strange town.

He was less strong than his powerfully puffed-out chest might imply, and the wave of hopeless fatigue that suddenly submerged his topheavy body, detaching him, as it were, from reality, was a sensation not utterly unknown to him. He found himself in a damp, green, purplish park, of the formal and funereal type, with the stress laid on somber rhododendrons, glossy laurels, sprayed shade trees and closely clipped lawns; and hardly had he turned into an alley of chestnut and oak, which the bus driver had curtly told him led back to the railway station, than that eerie feeling, that tingle of unreality overpowered him completely. Was it something he had eaten? That pickle with the ham? Was it a mysterious disease that none of his doctors had yet detected? My friend wondered, and I wonder, too.

I do not know if it has ever been noted before that one of the main characteristics of life is discreteness. Unless a film of flesh envelops us, we die. Man exists only insofar as he is separated from his surroundings. The cranium is a space-traveler's helmet. Stay inside or you perish. Death is divestment, death is communion. It may be wonderful to mix with the landscape, but to do so is the end of the tender ego. The sensation poor Pnin experienced was something very like that divestment, that communion. He felt porous and pregnable. He was sweating. He was terrified. A stone bench among the laurels saved him from collapsing on the sidewalk. Was his seizure a heart attack? I doubt it. For the nonce I am his physician, and let me repeat, I doubt it. My patient was one of those singular and unfortunate people who regard their heart ("a hollow, muscular organ," according to the gruesome definition in *Webster's New Collegiate Dictionary*, which Pnin's orphaned bag contained) with a queasy dread, a nervous repulsion, a sick hate, as if it were some strong slimy untouchable monster that one had to be parasitized with, alas. Occasionally, when puzzled by his tumbling and tottering pulse, doctors examined him more thoroughly, the cardiograph outlined fabulous mountain ranges and indicated a dozen fatal diseases that excluded one another. He was afraid of touching his own wrist.

He never attempted to sleep on his left side, even in those dismal hours of the night when the insomniac longs for a third side after trying the two he has.

And now, in the park of Whitchurch, Pnin felt what he had felt already on August 10, 1942, and February 15 (his birthday), 1937, and May 18, 1929, and July 4, 1920—that the repulsive automaton he lodged had developed a consciousness of its own and not only was grossly alive but was causing him pain and panic. He pressed his poor bald head against the stone back of the bench and recalled all the past occasions of similar discomfort and despair. Could it be pneumonia this time? He had been chilled to the bone a couple of days before in one of those hearty American drafts that a host treats his guests to after the second round of drinks on a windy night. And suddenly Pnin (was he dying?) found himself sliding back into his own childhood. This sensation had the sharpness of retrospective detail that is said to be the dramatic privilege of drowning individuals, especially in the former Russian Navy— a phenomenon of suffocation that a veteran psychoanalyst, whose name escapes me, has explained as being the subconsciously evoked shock of one's baptism which causes an explosion of intervening recollections between the first immersion and the last. It all happened in a flash but there is no way of rendering it in less than so many consecutive words.

Pnin came from a respectable, fairly well-to-do, St. Petersburg family. His father, Dr. Pavel Pnin, an eye specialist of considerable repute, had once had the honor of treating Leo Tolstoy for a case of conjunctivitis. Timofey's mother, a frail, nervous little person with a waspy waist and bobbed hair, was the daughter of the once famous revolutionary Umov (rhymes with "zoom off") and of a German lady from Riga. Through his half swoon, he saw his mother's approaching eyes. It was a Sunday in midwinter. He was eleven. He had been preparing lessons for his Monday classes at the First Gymnasium when a strange chill pervaded his body. His mother took his temperature, looked at her child with a kind of stupefaction, and immediately called her husband's best friend, the pediatrician Belochkin. He was a small, beetle-browed man, with a short beard and cropped hair. Easing the skirts of his frock coat, he sat down on the edge of Timofey's bed. A race was run between the doctor's fat golden watch and Timofey's pulse (an easy winner). Then Timofey's torso was bared, and to it Belochkin pressed the icy nudity of his ear and the sandpapery side of his head. Like the flat sole of some monopode, the ear ambulated all over Timofey's back and chest, gluing itself to this or that patch of skin and stomping on to the next. No sooner had the doctor left than Timofey's mother and a robust servant girl with safety pins between her teeth encased the distressed little patient in a strait-jacket-like compress. It consisted of a layer of soaked linen, a thicker layer of absorbent cotton, and another of tight flannel, with a sticky diabolical oilcloth—the hue of urine and fever—coming between the clammy pang of the linen next to his skin and the excruciating squeak of the cotton around which the outer layer of flannel was wound. A poor cocooned pupa, Timosha (Tim) lay under a mass of additional blankets; they were of no avail against the branching chill that crept up his ribs from both sides of his frozen spine. He could not close his eyes because his eyelids stung so. Vision was but oval pain with oblique stabs of light; familiar shapes became the breeding places of evil delusions. Near his bed was a four-section screen of polished wood, with pyrographic designs representing a bridle path felted with fallen leaves, a lily pond, an old man hunched up on a bench, and a squirrel holding a reddish object in its front paws. Timosha, a methodical child, had often wondered what that object could be (a nut? a pine cone?), and now that he had nothing else to do, he set himself to solve this dreary riddle, but the fever that hummed in his head drowned every effort in pain and panic. Still more oppressive was his tussle with the wallpaper. He had always been able to see that in the vertical plane a combination made up of three different clusters of purple flowers and seven different oak leaves was repeated a number of times with soothing exactitude; but now he was bothered by the undismissable fact that he could not find what system of inclusion and circumscription governed the horizontal recurrence of the pattern; that such a recurrence existed was proved by his being able to pick out here and there, all along the wall from bed to wardrobe and from stove to door, the reappearance of this or that element of the series, but when he tried traveling right or left from any chosen set of three inflorescences and seven leaves, he forthwith lost himself in a meaningless tangle of rhododendron and oak. It stood to reason that if the evil designer—the destroyer of minds, the friend of fever—had concealed the key of the pattern with such monstrous care, that key must be as precious as life itself and, when found, would regain for Timofey Pnin his everyday health, his everyday world; and this lucid—alas, too lucid—thought forced him to persevere in the struggle.

A sense of being late for some appointment as odiously exact as school, dinner, or bedtime added the discomfort of awkward haste to the difficulties of a quest that was grading into delirium. The foliage and the flowers, with none of the intricacies of their warp disturbed, appeared to detach themselves in one undulating body from their pale-blue background which, in its turn, lost its papery flatness and dilated in depth till the spectator's heart almost burst in response to the expansion. He could still make out through the autonomous garlands certain parts of the nursery more tenacious of life than the rest, such as the lacquered screen, the gleam of a tumbler, the brass knobs of his bedstead, but these interfered even less with the oak leaves and rich blossoms than would the reflection of an inside object in a windowpane with the outside scenery perceived through the same glass. And although the witness and victim of these phantasms was tucked up in bed, he was, in accordance with the twofold nature of his surroundings, simultaneously seated on a bench in a green and purple park. During one melting moment, he had the sensation of holding at last the key he had sought; but, coming from very far, a rustling wind, its soft volume increasing as it ruffled the rhododendrons—now blossomless, blind—confused whatever rational pattern Timofey Pnin's surroundings had once had. He was alive and that was sufficient. The back of the bench against which he still sprawled felt as real as his clothes, or his wallet, or the date of the Great Moscow Fire—1812.

A gray squirrel sitting on comfortable haunches on the ground before him was sampling a peach stone. The wind paused, and presently stirred the foliage again.

The seizure had left him a little frightened and shaky, but he argued that had it been a real heart attack, he would have surely felt a good deal more unsettled and concerned, and this roundabout piece of reasoning completely dispelled his fear. It was now four-twenty. He blew his nose and trudged to the station.

The initial employee was back. "Here's your bag," he said cheerfully. "Sorry you missed the Cremona bus."

"At least"—and what dignified irony our unfortunate friend tried to inject into that "at least"—"I hope everything is good with your wife?"

"She'll be all right. Have to wait till tomorrow, I guess."

"And now," said Pnin, "where is located the public telephone?"

The man pointed with his pencil as far out and sideways as he could without leaving his lair. Pnin, bag in hand, started to go, but he was called back. The pencil was now directed streetward.

"Say, see those two guys loading that truck? They're going to Cremona right now. Just tell them Bob Horn sent you. They'll take you."

3

Some people—and I am one of them—hate happy ends. We feel cheated. Harm is the norm. Doom should not jam. The avalanche stopping in its tracks a few feet above the cowering village behaves not only unnaturally but unethically. Had I been reading about this mild old man, instead of writing about him, I would have preferred him to discover, upon his arrival to Cremona, that his lecture was not this Friday but the next. Actually, however, he not only arrived safely but was in time for dinner—a fruit cocktail, to begin with, mint jelly with the anonymous meat course, chocolate syrup with the vanilla ice cream. And soon afterwards, surfeited with sweets, wearing his black suit, and juggling three papers, all of which he had stuffed into his coat so as to have the one he wanted among the rest (thus thwarting mischance by mathematical necessity), he sat on a chair near the lectern, while, at the lectern, Judith Clyde, an ageless blonde in aqua rayon, with large, flat cheeks stained a beautiful candy pink and two bright eyes basking in blue lunacy behind a rimless pince-nez, presented the speaker:

"Tonight," she said, "the speaker of the evening—— This, by the way, is our third Friday night; last time, as you all remember, we all enjoyed hearing what Professor Moore had to say about agriculture in China. Tonight we have here, I am proud to say, the Russian-born, and citizen of this country, Professor—now comes a difficult one, I am afraid—Professor Pun-neen. I hope I have it right. He hardly needs any introduction, of course, and we are all happy to have him. We have a long evening before us, a long and rewarding evening, and I am sure you would all like to have time to ask him questions afterwards. Incidentally, I am told his father was Dostoevski's family doctor, and he has traveled quite a bit on both sides of the Iron Curtain. Therefore I will not take up your precious time any longer and will only add a few words about our next Friday lecture in this program. I am sure you will all be delighted to know that there is a grand surprise in store for all of us. Our next lecturer is the distinguished poet and prose writer, Miss Linda Lacefield. We all know she has written poetry, prose, and some short stories. Miss Lacefield was born in New York. Her ancestors on both sides fought on both sides in the Revolutionary War. She wrote her first poem before graduation. Many of her poems—three of them, at least—have been published in *Response, A Hundred Love Lyrics by American Women.* In 1922 she received the cash prize offered by——"

But Pnin was not listening. A faint ripple stemming from his recent seizure was holding his fascinated attention. It lasted only a few heartbeats, with an additional systole here and there—last, harmless echoes—and was resolved in demure reality as his distinguished hostess invited him to the lectern; but while it lasted, how limpid the vision was! In the middle of the front row of seats he saw one of his Baltic aunts, wearing the pearls and the lace and the blond wig she had worn at all the performances given by the great ham actor Khodotov, whom she had adored from afar before drifting into insanity. Next to her, shyly smiling, sleek dark head inclined, gentle brown gaze shining up at Pnin from under velvet eyebrows, sat a dead sweetheart of his, fanning herself with a program. Murdered, forgotten, unrevenged, incorrupt, immortal, many old friends were scattered throughout the dim hall among more recent people, such as Miss Clyde, who had modestly regained a front seat. Vanya Bednyashkin, shot by the Reds in 1919 in Odessa because his father had been a Liberal, was gaily signaling to his former schoolmate from the back of the hall. And in an inconspicuous situation Dr. Pavel Pnin and his anxious wife, both a little blurred but on the whole wonderfully recovered from their obscure dissolution, looked at their son with the same life-consuming passion and pride that they had looked at him with that night in 1912 when, at a school festival, commemorating Napoleon's defeat, he had recited (a bespectacled lad all alone on the stage) a poem by Pushkin.

The brief vision was gone. Old Miss Herring, retired Professor of History, author of *Russia Awakes* (1922), was bending across one or two intermediate members of the audience to compliment Miss Clyde on her speech, while from behind that lady another twinkling old party was thrusting into her field of vision a pair of withered, soundlessly clapping hands.

Chapter Two

THE FAMOUS Waindell College bells were in the midst of their morning chimes.

Laurence G. Clements, a Waindell scholar, whose only popular course was the Philosophy of Gesture, and his wife Joan, Pendelton '30, had recently parted with their daughter, her father's best student: Isabel had married in her junior year a Waindell graduate with an engineering job in a remote Western State.

The bells were musical in the silvery sun. Framed in the picture window, the little town of Waindell—white paint, black pattern of twigs—was projected, as if by a child, in primitive perspective devoid of aerial depth, into the slate-gray hills; everything was prettily frosted with rime; the shiny parts of parked cars shone; Miss Dingwall's old Scotch terrier, a cylindrical small boar of sorts, had started upon his rounds up Warren Street and down Spelman Avenue and back again; but no amount of neighborliness, landscaping, and change ringing could soften the season; in a fortnight, after a ruminant pause, the academic year would enter its most winterly phase, the Spring Term, and the Clementses felt dejected, apprehensive, and lonely in their nice old drafty house that now seemed to hang about them like the flabby skin and flapping clothes of some fool who had gone and lost a third of his weight. Isabel was so young after all, and so vague, and they really knew nothing about her in-laws beyond that wedding selection of marchpane faces in a hired hall with the vaporous bride so helpless without her glasses.

The bells, under the enthusiastic direction of Dr. Robert Trebler, active member of the Music Department, were still going strong in the angelic sky, and over a frugal breakfast of oranges and lemons Laurence, blondish, baldish, and unwholesomely fat, was criticizing the head of the French Department, one of the people Joan had invited to meet Professor Entwistle of Goldwin University at their house that evening. "Why on earth," he fumed, "did you have to ask

317

that fellow Blorenge, a mummy, a bore, one of the stucco pillars of education?"

"I *like* Ann Blorenge," said Joan, stressing her affirmation and affection with nods. "A vulgar old cat!" cried Laurence. "A pathetic old cat," murmured Joan—and it was then that Dr. Trebler stopped and the hallway telephone took over.

Technically speaking, the narrator's art of integrating telephone conversations still lags far behind that of rendering dialogues conducted from room to room, or from window to window across some narrow blue alley in an ancient town with water so precious, and the misery of donkeys, and rugs for sale, and minarets, and foreigners and melons, and the vibrant morning echoes. When Joan, in her brisk long-limbed way, got to the compelling instrument before it gave up, and said hullo (eyebrows up, eyes roaming), a hollow quiet greeted her; all she could hear was the informal sound of a steady breathing; presently the breather's voice said, with a cozy foreign accent: "One moment, excuse me"—this was quite casual, and he continued to breathe and perhaps hem and hum or even sigh a little to the accompaniment of a crepitation that evoked the turning over of small pages.

"Hullo!" she repeated.

"You are," suggested the voice warily, "Mrs. Fire?"

"No," said Joan, and hung up. "And besides," she went on, swinging back into the kitchen and addressing her husband who was sampling the bacon she had prepared for herself, "you cannot deny that Jack Cockerell considers Blorenge to be a first-rate administrator."

"What was that telephone call?"

"Somebody wanting Mrs. Feuer or Fayer. Look here, if you deliberately neglect everything George——" [Dr. O. G. Helm, their family doctor]

"Joan," said Laurence, who felt much better after that opalescent rasher, "Joan, my dear, you are aware, aren't you, that you told Margaret Thayer yesterday you wanted a roomer?"

"Oh, gosh," said Joan—and obligingly the telephone rang again.

"It is evident," said the same voice, comfortably resuming the conversation, "that I employed by mistake the name of the informer. I am connected with Mrs. Clement?"

"Yes, this is Mrs. Clements," said Joan.

"Here speaks Professor——" There followed a preposterous little explosion. "I conduct the classes in Russian. Mrs. Fire, who is now working at the library part time——"

"Yes—Mrs. Thayer, I know. Well, do you want to see that room?"

He did. Could he come to inspect it in approximately half an hour? Yes, she would be in. Untenderly she cradled the receiver.

"What was it this time?" asked her husband, looking back, pudgy freckled hand on banister, on his way upstairs to the security of his study.

"A cracked ping-pong ball. Russian."

"Professor Pnin, by God!" cried Laurence. " 'I know him well: he is the brooch——' Well, I flatly refuse to have that freak in my house."

He trudged up, truculently. She called after him:

"Lore, did you finish writing that article last night?"

"Almost." He had turned the corner of the stairs—she heard his hand squeaking on the banisters, then striking them. "I will today. First I have that damned EOS examination to prepare."

This stood for the Evolution of Sense, his greatest course (with an enrollment of twelve, none even remotely apostolic) which had opened and would close with the phrase destined to be overquoted one day: The evolution of sense is, in a sense, the evolution of nonsense.

2

Half an hour later, Joan glanced over the moribund cactuses in the sun-porch window and saw a raincoated, hatless man, with a head like a polished globe of copper, optimistically ringing at the front door of her neighbor's beautiful brick house. The old Scotty stood beside him in much the same candid attitude as he. Miss Dingwall came out with a mop, let the slowpoke, dignified dog in, and directed Pnin to the Clements' clapboard residence.

Timofey Pnin settled down in the living room, crossed his legs *po amerikanski* (the American way), and entered into some unnecessary detail. It was a curriculum vitae in a nut-shell—a coconut shell. Born in St. Petersburg in 1898. Both parents died of typhus in 1917. Left for Kiev in 1918. Was with the White Army five months, first as a "field telephonist," then at the Military Information Office. Escaped from Red-invaded Crimea to Constantinople in 1919. Completed university education——

"Say, I was there as a child exactly the same year," said pleased Joan. "My father went to Turkey on a government mission and took us along. We might have met! I remember the word for water. And there was a rose garden——"

"Water in Turkish is 'su,'" said Pnin, a linguist by neces-sity, and went on with his fascinating past: Completed university education in Prague. Was connected with various scientific insti-tutions. Then—— "Well, to make a long story very short: habi-tated in Paris from 1925, abandoned France at beginning of Hitler war. Is now here. Is American citizen. Is teaching Russian and such like subjects at Vandal College. From Hagen, Head of German Department, obtainable all references. Or from the College Home for Single Instructors."

Hadn't he been comfortable there?

"Too many people," said Pnin. "Inquisitive people. Whereas special privacy is now to me absolutely necessary." He coughed into his fist with an unexpected cavernous sound (which somehow reminded Joan of a professional Don Cos-sack she had once met) and then took the plunge: "I must warn: will have all my teeth pulled out. It is a repulsive operation."

"Well, come upstairs," said Joan brightly.

Pnin peered into Isabel's pink-walled, white-flounced room. It had suddenly begun to snow, though the sky was pure plat-inum, and the slow scintillant downcome got reflected in the silent looking glass. Methodically Pnin inspected Hoecker's "Girl with a Cat" above the bed, and Hunt's "The Belated Kid" above the bookshelf. Then he held his hand at a little distance from the window.

"Is temperature uniform?"

Joan dashed to the radiator.

"Piping hot," she reported.

"I am asking—are there currents of air?"

"Oh yes, you will have plenty of air. And here is the bathroom—small, but all yours."

"No *douche*?" inquired Pnin, looking up. "Maybe it is better so. My friend, Professor Chateau of Columbia, once broke his leg in two places. Now I must think. What price are you prepared to demand? I ask it, because I will not give more than a dollar per day—not including, of course, nootrition."

"All right," said Joan with that pleasant, quick laugh of hers.

The same afternoon, one of Pnin's students, Charles McBeth ("A madman, I think, judging by his compositions," Pnin used to say), zestfully brought over Pnin's luggage in a pathologically purplish car with no fenders on the left side, and after an early dinner at The Egg and We, a recently inaugurated and not very successful little restaurant which Pnin frequented from sheer sympathy with failure, our friend applied himself to the pleasant task of Pninizing his new quarters. Isabel's adolescence had gone with her, or, if not, had been eradicated by her mother, but traces of the girl's childhood somehow had been allowed to remain, and before finding the most advantageous situations for his elaborate sun lamp, huge Russian-alphabet typewriter in a broken coffin fixed with Scotch tape, five pairs of handsome, curiously small shoes with ten shoe trees rooted in them, a coffee grinding-and-boiling contraption which was not quite as good as the one that had exploded last year, a couple of alarm clocks running the same race every night, and seventy-four library books, mainly old Russian periodicals solidly bound by WCL, Pnin delicately exiled to a chair on the landing half a dozen forlorn volumes, such as *Birds at Home*, *Happy Days in Holland*, and *My First Dictionary* ("With more than 600 illustrations depicting zoos, the human body, farms, fires—all scientifically chosen"), and also a lone wooden bead with a hole through the center.

Joan, who used the word "pathetic" perhaps a little too often, declared she would ask that pathetic savant for a drink with their guests, to which her husband replied he was also a pathetic savant and would go to a movie if she carried out her threat. However, when Joan went up to Pnin with her offer he declined the invitation, saying, rather simply, he had resolved not to use alcohol any more. Three couples and

Entwistle arrived around nine, and by ten the little party was in full swing, when suddenly Joan, while talking to pretty Gwen Cockerell, noticed Pnin, in a green sweater, standing in the doorway that led to the foot of the stairs and holding aloft, for her to see, a tumbler. She sped toward him—and simultaneously her husband almost collided with her as he trotted across the room to stop, choke, abolish Jack Cockerell, head of the English Department, who, with his back to Pnin, was entertaining Mrs. Hagen and Mrs. Blorenge with his famous act—he being one of the greatest, if not the greatest, mimics of Pnin on the campus. His model, in the meantime, was saying to Joan: "This is not a clean glass in the bathroom, and there exist other troubles. It blows from the floor, and it blows from the walls——" But Dr. Hagen, a pleasant, rectangular old man, had noticed Pnin, too, and was greeting him joyfully, and the next moment Pnin, his tumbler replaced by a highball, was being introduced to Professor Entwistle.

"Zdrastvuyte kak pozhivaete horosho spasibo," Entwistle rattled off in excellent imitation of Russian speech—and indeed he rather resembled a genial Tsarist colonel in mufti. "One night in Paris," he went on, his eyes twinkling, "at the *Ougolok* cabaret, this demonstration convinced a group of Russian revelers that I was a compatriot of theirs—posing as an American, don't you know."

"In two-three years," said Pnin, missing one bus but boarding the next, "I will also be taken for an American," and everybody roared except Professor Blorenge.

"We'll get you an electric heater," Joan told Pnin confidentially, as she offered him some olives.

"What make heater?" asked Pnin suspiciously.

"That remains to be seen. Any other complaints?"

"Yes—sonic disturbance," said Pnin. "I hear every, every sound from downstairs, but now it is not the place to discuss it, I think."

3

The guests started to leave. Pnin trudged upstairs, a clean glass in his hand. Entwistle and his host were the last to come out on the porch. Wet snow drifted in the black night.

"It's such a pity," said Professor Entwistle, "that we cannot tempt you to come to Goldwin for good. We have Schwarz and old Crates, who are among your greatest admirers. We have a real lake. We have everything. We even have a Professor Pnin on our staff."

"I know, I know," said Clements, "but these offers I keep getting are coming too late. I plan to retire soon, and till then I prefer to remain in the musty but familiar hole. How did you like"—he lowered his voice—"Monsieur Blorenge?"

"Oh, he struck me as a capital fellow. In some ways, however, I must say he reminded me of that probably legendary figure, the Chairman of French, who thought Chateaubriand was a famous *chef*."

"Careful," said Clements. "That story was first told about Blorenge, and is true."

4

Next morning heroic Pnin marched to town, walking a cane in the European manner (up-down, up-down) and letting his gaze dwell upon various objects in a philosophical effort to imagine what it would be to see them again after the ordeal and then recall what it had been to perceive them through the prism of its expectation. Two hours later he was trudging back, leaning on his cane and not looking at anything. A warm flow of pain was gradually replacing the ice and wood of the anesthetic in his thawing, still half-dead, abominably martyred mouth. After that, during a few days he was in mourning for an intimate part of himself. It surprised him to realize how fond he had been of his teeth. His tongue, a fat sleek seal, used to flop and slide so happily among the familiar rocks, checking the contours of a battered but still secure kingdom, plunging from cave to cove, climbing this jag, nuzzling that notch, finding a shred of sweet seaweed in the same old cleft; but now not a landmark remained, and all there existed was a great dark wound, a terra incognita of gums which dread and disgust forbade one to investigate. And when the plates were thrust in, it was like a poor fossil skull being fitted with the grinning jaws of a perfect stranger.

There were, as per plan, no lectures, nor did he attend the

examinations given for him by Miller. Ten days passed—and suddenly he began to enjoy the new gadget. It was a revelation, it was a sunrise, it was a firm mouthful of efficient, alabastrine, humane America. At night he kept his treasure in a special glass of special fluid where it smiled to itself, pink and pearly, as perfect as some lovely representative of deep-sea flora. The great work on Old Russia, a wonderful dream mixture of folklore, poetry, social history, and *petite histoire*, which for the last ten years or so he had been fondly planning, now seemed accessible at last, with headaches gone, and this new amphitheater of translucid plastics implying, as it were, a stage and a performance. When the spring term began his class could not help noticing the sea change, as he sat coquettishly tapping with the rubber end of a pencil upon those even, too even, incisors and canines while some student translated some sentence in old and ruddy Professor Oliver Bradstreet Mann's *Elementary Russian* (actually written from beginning to end by two frail drudges, John and Olga Krotki, both dead today), such as "The boy is playing with his nurse and his uncle." And one evening he waylaid Laurence Clements, who was in the act of scuttling up to his study, and with incoherent exclamations of triumph started to demonstrate the beauty of the thing, the ease with which it could be taken out and put in again, and urged surprised but not unfriendly Laurence to have all his teeth out first thing tomorrow.

"You will be a reformed man like I," cried Pnin.

It should be said for both Laurence and Joan that rather soon they began to appreciate Pnin at his unique Pninian worth, and this despite the fact that he was more of a poltergeist than a lodger. He did something fatal to his new heater and gloomily said never mind, it would soon be spring now. He had an irritating way of standing on the landing and assiduously brushing his clothes there, the brush clinking against the buttons, for at least five minutes every blessed morning. He had a passionate intrigue with Joan's washing machine. Although forbidden to come near it, he would be caught trespassing again and again. Casting aside all decorum and caution, he would feed it anything that happened to be at hand, his handkerchief, kitchen towels, a heap of shorts and shirts smuggled down from his room, just for the joy of watching

through the porthole what looked like an endless tumble of
dolphins with the staggers. One Sunday, after checking the
solitude, he could not resist, out of sheer scientific curiosity,
giving the mighty machine a pair of rubber-soled canvas shoes
stained with clay and chlorophyll to play with; the shoes
tramped away with a dreadful arhythmic sound, like an army
going over a bridge, and came back without their soles, and
Joan appeared from her little sitting room behind the pantry
and said in sadness, "Again, Timofey?" But she forgave him,
and liked to sit with him at the kitchen table, both cracking
nuts or drinking tea. Desdemona, the old colored charwoman,
who came on Fridays and with whom at one time God had
gossiped daily ("'Desdemona,' the Lord would say to me,
'that man George is no good.'"), happened to glimpse Pnin
basking in the unearthly lilac light of his sun lamp, wearing
nothing but shorts, dark glasses, and a dazzling Greek-Cath-
olic cross on his broad chest, and insisted thereafter that he
was a saint. Laurence, on going up to his study one day, a
secret and sacred lair cunningly carved out of the attic, was
incensed to find the mellow lights on and fat-naped Pnin
braced on his thin legs serenely browsing in a corner: "Excuse
me, I only am grazing," as the gentle intruder (whose English
was growing richer at a surprising pace) remarked, glancing
over the higher of his two shoulders; but somehow that very
afternoon a chance reference to a rare author, a passing allusion tacitly recognized in the middle distance of an idea, an
adventurous sail descried on the horizon, led insensibly to a
tender mental concord between the two men, both of whom
were really at ease only in their warm world of natural scholarship. There are human solids and there are human surds,
and Clements and Pnin belonged to the latter variety. Thenceforth they would often "devise," as they met and stopped on
thresholds, on landings, on two different levels of staircase
steps (exchanging altitudes and turning to each other anew),
or as they walked in opposite directions up and down a room
which at the moment existed for them only as an *espace meublé*, to use a Pninian term. It soon transpired that Timofey
was a veritable encyclopedia of Russian shrugs and shakes, had
tabulated them, and could add something to Laurence's files
on the philosophical interpretation of pictorial and non-pic-

torial, national and environmental gestures. It was very pleasant to see the two men discuss a legend or a religion, Timofey
blossoming out in amphoric motion, Laurence chopping away
with one hand. Laurence even made a film of what Timofey
considered to be the essentials of Russian "carpalistics," with
Pnin in a polo shirt, a Gioconda smile on his lips, demonstrating the movements underlying such Russian verbs—used
in reference to hands—as *mahnut'*, *vsplesnut'*, *razvesti*: the
one-hand downward loose shake of weary relinquishment;
the two-hand dramatic splash of amazed distress; and the "dis-
junctive" motion—hands traveling apart to signify helpless
passivity. And in conclusion, very slowly, Pnin showed how,
in the international "shaking the finger" gesture, a half turn,
as delicate as the switch of the wrist in fencing, metamorphosed the Russian solemn symbol of pointing up, "the Judge
in Heaven sees you!" into a German air picture of the stick—
"something is coming to you!" "However," added objective
Pnin, "Russian metaphysical police can break physical bones
also very well."

With apologies for his "negligent toilet," Pnin showed the
film to a group of students—and Betty Bliss, a graduate working in Comparative Literature where Pnin was assisting Dr.
Hagen, announced that Timofey Pavlovich looked exactly like
Buddha in an oriental moving picture she had seen in the
Asiatic Department. This Betty Bliss, a plump maternal girl of
some twenty-nine summers, was a soft thorn in Pnin's aging
flesh. Ten years before she had had a handsome heel for a
lover, who had jilted her for a little tramp, and later she had
had a dragging, hopelessly complicated, Chekhovian rather
than Dostoevskian affair with a cripple who was now married
to his nurse, a cheap cutie. Poor Pnin hesitated. In principle,
marriage was not excluded. In his new dental glory, he went
so far one seminar session, after the rest had gone, as to hold
her hand on his palm and pat it while they were sitting together and discussing Turgenev's poem in prose: "How fair,
how fresh were the roses." She could hardly finish reading,
her bosom bursting with sighs, the held hand aquiver. "Turgenev," said Pnin, putting the hand back on the table, "was
made by the ugly, but adored by him, singer Pauline Viardot
to play the idiot in charades and *tableaux vivants*, and Madam

Pushkin said: 'You annoy me with your verses, Pushkin'—and
in old age—to think only!—the wife of colossus, colossus Tolstoy liked much better than him a stoopid moozishan with a
red noz!''

Pnin had nothing against Miss Bliss. In trying to visualize
a serene senility, he saw her with passable clarity bringing him
his lap robe or refilling his fountain pen. He liked her all
right—but his heart belonged to another woman.

The cat, as Pnin would say, cannot be hid in a bag. In order
to explain my poor friend's abject excitement one evening in
the middle of the term—when he received a certain telegram
and then paced his room for at least forty minutes—it should
be stated that Pnin had not always been single. The Clementses were playing Chinese checkers among the reflections
of a comfortable fire when Pnin came clattering downstairs,
slipped, and almost fell at their feet like a supplicant in some
ancient city full of injustice, but retrieved his balance—only
to crash into the poker and tongs.

"I have come," he said, panting, "to inform, or more correctly ask you, if I can have a female visitor Saturday—in the
day, of course. She is my former wife, now Dr. Liza Wind—
maybe you have heard in psychiatric circles."

5

There are some beloved women whose eyes, by a chance
blend of brilliancy and shape, affect us not directly, not at the
moment of shy perception, but in a delayed and cumulative
burst of light when the heartless person is absent, and the
magic agony abides, and its lenses and lamps are installed in
the dark. Whatever eyes Liza Pnin, now Wind, had, they
seemed to reveal their essence, their precious-stone water,
only when you evoked them in thought, and then a blank,
blind, moist aquamarine blaze shivered and stared as if a spat-
ter of sun and sea had got between your own eyelids. Actually
her eyes were of a light transparent blue with contrasting black
lashes and bright pink canthus, and they slightly stretched up
templeward, where a set of feline little lines fanned out from
each. She had a sweep of dark brown hair above a lustrous
forehead, and a snow-and-rose complexion, and she used a

very light red lipstick, and save for a certain thickness of ankle
and wrist, there was hardly a flaw to her full-blown, animated,
elemental, not particularly well-groomed beauty.

Pnin, then a rising young scholar and she, a more limpid
mermaid than now but practically the same person, had met
around 1925, in Paris. He wore a sparse auburn beard (today
only white bristles would sprout if he did not shave—poor
Pnin, poor albino porcupine!), and this divided monastic
growth, topped by a fat glossy nose and innocent eyes, nicely
epitomized the physique of old-fashioned intellectual Russia.
A small job at the Aksakov Institute, rue Vert-Vert, combined
with another at Saul Bagrov's Russian book shop, rue Gresset,
supplied him with a livelihood. Liza Bogolepov, a medical student just turned twenty, and perfectly charming in her black
silk jumper and tailor-made skirt, was already working at the
Meudon sanatorium directed by that remarkable and formidable old lady, Dr. Rosetta Stone, one of the most destructive
psychiatrists of the day; and, moreover, Liza wrote verse—
mainly in halting anapaest; indeed, Pnin saw her for the first
time at one of those literary soirees where young émigré poets,
who had left Russia in their pale, unpampered pubescence,
chanted nostalgic elegies dedicated to a country that could be
little more to them than a sad stylized toy, a bauble found in
the attic, a crystal globe which you shake to make a soft luminous snowstorm inside over a minuscule fir tree and a log
cabin of papier mâché. Pnin wrote her a tremendous love letter—now safe in a private collection—and she read it with
tears of self pity while recovering from a pharmacopoeial attempt at suicide because of a rather silly affair with a littérateur
who is now—— But no matter. Five analysts, intimate friends
of hers, all said: "Pnin—and a baby at once."

Marriage hardly changed their manner of life except that
she moved into Pnin's dingy apartment. He went on with his
Slavic studies, she with her psychodramatics and her lyrical
ovipositing, laying all over the place like an Easter rabbit, and
in those green and mauve poems—about the child she wanted
to bear, and the lovers she wanted to have, and St. Petersburg
(courtesy Anna Akhmatov)—every intonation, every image,
every simile had been used before by other rhyming rabbits.
One of her admirers, a banker, and straightforward patron of

the arts, selected among the Parisian Russians an influential literary critic, Zhorzhik Uranski, and for a champagne dinner at the *Ougolok* had the old boy devote his next *feuilleton* in one of the Russian-language newspapers to an appreciation of Liza's muse on whose chestnut curls Zhorzhik calmly placed Anna Akhmatov's coronet, whereupon Liza burst into happy tears—for all the world like little Miss Michigan or the Oregon Rose Queen. Pnin, who was not in the know, carried about a folded clipping of that shameless rave in his honest pocketbook, naïvely reading out passages to this or that amused friend until it got quite frayed and smudgy. Nor was he in the know concerning graver matters, and in fact was actually pasting the remnants of the review in an album when, on a December day in 1938, Liza telephoned from Meudon, saying that she was going to Montpellier with a man who understood her "organic ego," a Dr. Eric Wind, and would never see Timofey again. An unknown French woman with red hair called for Liza's things and said, well, you cellar rat, there is no more any poor lass to *taper dessus*—and a month or two later there dribbled in from Dr. Wind a German letter of sympathy and apology assuring *lieber Herr Pnin* that he, Dr. Wind, was eager to marry "the woman who has come out of your life into mine." Pnin of course would have given her a divorce as readily as he would his life, with the wet stems cut and a bit of fern, and all of it wrapped up as crisply as at the earth-smelling florist's when the rain makes gray and green mirrors of Easter day; but it transpired that in South America Dr. Wind had a wife with a tortuous mind and a phony passport, who did not wish to be bothered until certain plans of her own took shape. Meanwhile the New World had started to beckon Pnin too: from New York a great friend of his, Professor Konstantin Chateau, offered him every assistance for a migratory voyage. Pnin informed Dr. Wind of his plans and sent Liza the last issue of an émigré magazine where she was mentioned on page 202. He was halfway through the dreary hell that had been devised by European bureaucrats (to the vast amusement of the Soviets) for holders of that miserable thing, the Nansen Passport (a kind of parolee's card issued to Russian émigrés), when one damp April day in 1940 there was a vigorous ring at his door and Liza tramped in, puffing and carrying before her like a chest of drawers a seven-month pregnancy, and announced, as she tore off her hat and kicked off her shoes, that it had all been a mistake, and from now on she was again Pnin's faithful and lawful wife, ready to follow him wherever he went—even beyond the ocean if need be. Those days were probably the happiest in Pnin's life—it was a permanent glow of weighty, painful felicity—and the vernalization of the visas, and the preparations, and the medical examination, with a deaf-and-dumb doctor applying a dummy stethoscope to Pnin's jammed heart through all his clothes, and the kind Russian lady (a relative of mine) who was so helpful at the American Consulate, and the journey to Bordeaux, and the beautiful clean ship—everything had a rich fairy-tale tinge to it. He was not only ready to adopt the child when it came but was passionately eager to do so, and she listened with a satisfied, somewhat cowish expression to the pedagogical plans he unfolded, for he actually seemed to forehear the babe's vagitus, and its first word in the near future. She had always been fond of sugar-coated almonds, but now she consumed fabulous quantities of them (two pounds between Paris and Bordeaux), and ascetic Pnin contemplated her greed with shakes and shrugs of delighted awe, and something about the smooth silkiness of those *dragées* remained in his mind, forever mingled with the memory of her taut skin, her complexion, her flawless teeth.

It was a little disappointing that as soon as she came aboard she gave one glance at the swelling sea, said: "*Nu, eto izvinite* (Nothing doing)," and promptly retired into the womb of the ship, within which, for most of the crossing, she kept lying on her back in the cabin she shared with the loquacious wives of the three laconic Poles—a wrestler, a gardener, and a barber—whom Pnin got as cabin mates. On the third evening of the voyage, having remained in the lounge long after Liza had gone to sleep, he cheerfully accepted a game of chess proposed by the former editor of a Frankfurt newspaper, a melancholy baggy-eyed patriarch in a turtle-neck sweater and plus fours. Neither was a good player; both were addicted to spectacular but quite unsound sacrifices of pieces; each was overanxious to win; and the proceedings were furthermore enlivened by Pnin's fantastic brand of German (*"Wenn Sie so, dann ich so, und Pferd fliegt"*). Presently another passenger came up, said *entschuldigen Sie*, could he watch their game? And sat down beside them. He had reddish hair cropped close and long pale eyelashes resembling fish moths, and he wore a shabby double-breasted coat, and soon he was clucking under his breath and shaking his head every time the patriarch, after much dignified meditation, lurched forward to make a wild move. Finally this helpful spectator, obviously an expert, could not resist pushing back a pawn his compatriot had just moved, and pointing with a vibrating index to a rook instead—which the old Frankfurter incontinently drove into the armpit of Pnin's defense. Our man lost, of course, and was about to leave the lounge when the expert overtook him, saying *entschuldigen Sie*, could he talk for a moment to Herr Pnin? ("You see, I know your name," he remarked parenthetically, lifting his useful index)—and suggested a couple of beers at the bar. Pnin accepted, and when the tankards were placed before them the polite stranger continued thus: "In life, as in chess, it is always better to analyze one's motives and intentions. The day we came on board I was like a playful child. Next morning, however, I began already to fear that an astute husband—this is not a compliment, but a hypothesis in retrospection—would sooner or later study the passenger list. Today my conscience has tried me and found me guilty. I can endure the deception no longer. Your health. This is not at all our German nectar but it is better than Coca-Cola. My name is Dr. Eric Wind; alas, it is not unknown to you."

Pnin, in silence, his face working, one palm still on the wet bar, had started to slither clumsily off his uncomfortable mushroom seat, but Wind put five long sensitive fingers on his sleeve.

"Lasse mich, lasse mich," wailed Pnin, trying to beat off the limp fawning hand.

"Please!" said Dr. Wind. "Be just. The prisoner has always the last word; it is his right. Even the Nazis admit it. And first of all—I want you to allow me to pay at least one half of the lady's passage."

"Ach nein, nein, nein," said Pnin. "Let us finish this nightmare conversation (*diese koschmarische Sprache*)."

"As you like," said Dr. Wind, and proceeded to impress

upon pinned Pnin the following points: That it had all been
Liza's idea—"simplifying matters, you know, for the sake of
our child" (the "our" sounded tripersonal); that Liza should
be treated as a very sick woman (pregnancy being really the
sublimation of a death wish); that he (Dr. Wind) would marry
her in America—"where I am also going," Dr. Wind added
for clarity; and that he (Dr. Wind) should at least be permitted
to pay for the beer. From then on to the end of the voyage
that had turned from green and silver to a uniform gray, Pnin
busied himself overtly with his English-language manuals, and
although immutably meek with Liza, tried to see her as little
as he could without awakening her suspicions. Every now and
then Dr. Wind would appear from nowhere and make from
afar signs of recognition and reassurance. And at last, when
the great statue arose from the morning haze where, ready to
be ignited by the sun, pale, spellbound buildings stood like
those mysterious rectangles of unequal height that you see in
bar graph representations of compared percentages (natural
resources, the frequency of mirages in different deserts), Dr.
Wind resolutely walked up to the Pnins and identified himself—"because all three of us must enter the land of liberty
with pure hearts." And after a bathetic sojourn on Ellis Island,
Timofey and Liza parted.

There were complications—but at last Wind married her.
In the course of the first five years in America, Pnin glimpsed
her on several occasions in New York; he and the Winds were
naturalized on the same day; then, after his removal to Waindell in 1945, half a dozen years passed without any meetings
or correspondence. He heard of her, however, from time to
time. Recently (in December 1951) his friend Chateau had sent
him an issue of a journal of psychiatry with an article written
by Dr. Albina Dunkelberg, Dr. Eric Wind, and Dr. Liza Wind
on "Group Psychotherapy Applied to Marriage Counseling."
Pnin used to be always embarrassed by Liza's *"psihooslinïe"*
("psychoasinine") interests, and even now, when he ought to
have been indifferent, he felt a twinge of revulsion and pity.
Eric and she were working under the great Bernard Maywood,
a genial giant of a man—referred to as "The Boss" by over-
adaptive Eric—at a Research Bureau attached to a Planned
Parenthood Center. Encouraged by his and his wife's protec-

tor, Eric evolved the ingenious idea (possibly not his own) of sidetracking some of the more plastic and stupid clients of the Center into a psychotherapeutic trap—a "tension-releasing" circle on the lines of a quilting bee, where young married women in groups of eight relaxed in a comfortable room amid an atmosphere of cheerful first-name informality, with doctors at a table facing the group, and a secretary unobtrusively taking notes, and traumatic episodes floating out of everybody's childhood like corpses. At these sessions, the ladies were made to discuss among themselves with absolute frankness their problems of marital maladjustment, which entailed, of course, comparing notes on their mates, who later were interviewed, too, in a special "husband group," likewise very informal, with a great passing around of cigars and anatomic charts. Pnin skipped the actual reports and case histories—and there is no need to go here into those hilarious details. Suffice it to say that already at the third session of the female group, after this or that lady had gone home and seen the light and come back to describe the newly discovered sensation to her still blocked but rapt sisters, a ringing note of revivalism pleasingly colored the proceedings ("Well, girls, when George last night——"). And this was not all. Dr. Eric Wind hoped to work out a technique that would allow bringing all those husbands and wives together in a joint group. Incidentally it was deadening to hear him and Liza smacking their lips over the word "group." In a long letter to distressed Pnin, Professor Chateau affirmed that Dr. Wind even called Siamese twins "a group." And indeed progressive, idealistic Wind dreamed of a happy world consisting of Siamese centuplets, anatomically conjoined communities, whole nations built around a communicating liver. "It is nothing but a kind of microcosmos of communism—all that psychiatry," rumbled Pnin, in his answer to Chateau. "Why not leave their private sorrows to people? Is sorrow not, one asks, the only thing in the world people really possess?"

6

"Look," said Joan Saturday morning to her husband, "I have decided to tell Timofey they will have the house to them-

selves today from two to five. We must give those pathetic
creatures every possible chance. There are things I can do in
town, and you will be dropped at the library."

"It so happens," answered Laurence, "that I have not the
least intention to be dropped or otherwise moved anywhere
today. Besides, it is highly improbable they will need eight
rooms for their reunion."

Pnin put on his new brown suit (paid for by the Cremona
lecture) and, after a hurried lunch at The Egg and We, walked
through the snow-patched park to the Waindell bus station,
arriving there almost an hour too early. He did not bother to
puzzle out why exactly Liza had felt the urgent need to see
him on her way back from visiting St. Bartholomew's, the
preparatory school near Boston that her son would go to next
fall: all he knew was that a flood of happiness foamed and rose
behind the invisible barrier that was to burst open any moment now. He met five buses, and in each of them clearly
made out Liza waving to him through a window as she and
the other passengers started to file out, and then one bus after
another was drained and she had not turned up. Suddenly he
heard her sonorous voice (*"Timofey, zdrastvuy!"*) behind him,
and, wheeling around, saw her emerge from the only Greyhound he had decided would not bring her. What change
could our friend discern in her? What change could there be,
good God! There she was. She always felt hot and buoyant,
no matter the cold, and now her sealskin coat was wide open
on her frilled blouse as she hugged Pnin's head and he felt
the grapefruit fragrance of her neck, and kept muttering: *"Nu,
nu, vot i horosho, nu vot"*—mere verbal heart props—and she
cried out: "Oh, he has splendid new teeth!" He helped her
into a taxi, her bright diaphanous scarf caught on something,
and Pnin slipped on the pavement, and the taximan said
"Easy," and took her bag from him, and everything had happened before, in this exact sequence.

It was, she told him as they drove up Park Street, a school
in the English tradition. No, she did not want to eat anything,
she had had a big lunch at Albany. It was a "very fancy"
school—she said this in English—the boys played a kind of
indoor tennis with their hands, between walls, and there
would be in his form a —— (she produced with false noncha-

lance a well-known American name which meant nothing to Pnin because it was not that of a poet or a president). "By the way," interrupted Pnin, ducking and pointing, "you can just see a corner of the campus from here." All this was due ("Yes, I see, *vizhu, vizhu, kampus kak kampus.* The usual kind of thing"), all this, including a scholarship, was due to the influence of Dr. Maywood ("You know, Timofey, some day you should write him a word, just a little sign of courtesy"). The Principal, a clergyman, had shown her the trophies Bernard had won there as a boy. Eric of course had wanted Victor to go to a public school but had been overruled. The Reverend Hopper's wife was the niece of an English Earl.

"Here we are. This is my *palazzo*," said jocose Pnin, who had not been able to concentrate on her rapid speech.

They entered—and he suddenly felt that this day which he had been looking forward to with such fierce longing was passing much too quickly—was going, going, would be gone in a few minutes. Perhaps, he thought, if she said right away what she wanted of him the day might slow down and be really enjoyed.

"What a gruesome place, *kakoy zhutkiy dom*," she said, sitting on the chair near the telephone and taking off her galoshes—such familiar movements! "Look at that aquarelle with the minarets. They must be terrible people."

"No," said Pnin, "they are my friends."

"My dear Timofey," she said, as he escorted her upstairs, "you have had some pretty awful friends in your time."

"And here is my room," said Pnin.

"I think I'll lie on your virgin bed, Timofey. And I'll recite you some verses in a minute. That hellish headache of mine is seeping back again. I felt so splendid all day."

"I have some aspirin."

"Uhn-uhn," she said, and this acquired negative stood out strangely against her native speech.

He turned away as she started to take off her shoes, and the sound they made toppling to the floor reminded him of very old days.

She lay back, black-skirted, white-bloused, brown-haired, with one pink hand over her eyes.

"How is everything with you?" asked Pnin (have her say

what she wants of me, quick!) as he sank into the white rocker near the radiator.

"Our work is very interesting," she said, still shielding her eyes, "but I must tell you I don't love Eric any more. Our relations have disintegrated. Incidentally Eric dislikes his child. He says he is the land father and you, Timofey, are the water father."

Pnin started to laugh: he rolled with laughter, the rather juvenile rocker fairly cracking under him. His eyes were like stars and quite wet.

She looked at him curiously for an instant from under her plump hand—and went on:

"Eric is one hard emotional block in his attitude toward Victor. I don't know how many times the boy must have killed him in his dreams. And, with Eric, verbalization—I have long noticed—confuses problems instead of clarifying them. He is a very difficult person. What is your salary, Timofey?"

He told her.

"Well," she said, "it is not grand. But I suppose you can even lay something aside—it is more than enough for your needs, for your microscopic needs, Timofey."

Her abdomen tightly girdled under the black skirt jumped up two or three times with mute, cozy, good-natured reminiscential irony—and Pnin blew his nose, shaking his head the while, in voluptuous, rapturous mirth.

"Listen to my latest poem," she said, her hands now along her sides as she lay perfectly straight on her back, and she sang out rhythmically, in long-drawn, deep-voiced tones:

> "*Ya nadela tyomnoe plat'e,*
> *I monashenki ya skromney;*
> *Iz slonovoy kosti raspyat'e*
> *Nad holodnoy postel'yu moey.*
>
> *No ogni nabivalïh orgiy*
> *Prozhigayut moyo zabïtyo*
> *I shepchu ya imya Georgiy—*
> *Zolotoe imya tvoyo!*
>
> (*I have put on a dark dress*
> *And am more modest than a nun;*

An ivory crucifix
Is over my cold bed.

But the lights of fabulous orgies
Burn through my oblivion,
And I whisper the name George—
Your golden name!)"

"He is a very interesting man," she went on, without any interval. "Practically English, in fact. He flew a bomber in the war and now he is with a firm of brokers who have no sympathy with him and do not understand him. He comes from an ancient family. His father was a dreamer, had a floating casino, you know, and all that, but was ruined by some Jewish gangsters in Florida and voluntarily went to prison for another man; it is a family of heroes."

She paused. The silence in the little room was punctuated rather than broken by the throbbing and tinkling in those whitewashed organ pipes.

"I made Eric a complete report," Liza continued with a sigh. "And now he keeps assuring me he can cure me if I co-operate. Unfortunately I am also co-operating with George."

She pronounced George as in Russian—both *g*'s hard, both *e*'s longish.

"Well, *c'est la vie*, as Eric so originally says. How can you sleep with that string of cobweb hanging from the ceiling?" She looked at her wrist watch. "Goodness, I must catch the bus at four-thirty. You must call a taxi in a minute. I have something to say to you of the utmost importance."

Here it was coming at last—so late.

She wanted Timofey to lay aside every month a little money for the boy—because she could not ask Bernard Maywood now—and she might die—and Eric did not care what happened—and somebody ought to send the lad a small sum now and then, as if coming from his mother—pocket money, you know—he would be among rich boys. She would write Timofey giving him an address and some more details. Yes—she never doubted that Timofey was a darling (*"Nu kakoy zhe ti dushka"*). And now where was the bathroom? And would he please telephone for the taxi?

"Incidentally," she said, as he was helping her into her coat and as usual searching with a frown for the fugitive armhole while she pawed and groped, "you know, Timofey, this brown suit of yours is a mistake: a gentleman does not wear brown."

He saw her off, and walked back through the park. To hold her, to keep her—just as she was—with her cruelty, with her vulgarity, with her blinding blue eyes, with her miserable poetry, with her fat feet, with her impure, dry, sordid, infantile soul. All of a sudden he thought: If people are reunited in Heaven (I don't believe it, but suppose), then how shall I stop it from creeping upon me, over me, that shriveled, helpless, lame thing, her soul? But this is the earth, and I am, curiously enough, alive, and there is something in me and in life——

He seemed to be quite unexpectedly (for human despair seldom leads to great truths) on the verge of a simple solution of the universe but was interrupted by an urgent request. A squirrel under a tree had seen Pnin on the path. In one sinuous tendril-like movement, the intelligent animal climbed up to the brim of a drinking fountain and, as Pnin approached, thrust its oval face toward him with a rather coarse spluttering sound, its cheeks puffed out. Pnin understood and after some fumbling he found what had to be pressed for the necessary results. Eying him with contempt, the thirsty rodent forthwith began to sample the stocky sparkling pillar of water, and went on drinking for a considerable time. "She has fever, perhaps," thought Pnin, weeping quietly and freely, and all the time politely pressing the contraption down while trying not to meet the unpleasant eye fixed upon him. Its thirst quenched, the squirrel departed without the least sign of gratitude.

The water father continued upon his way, came to the end of the path, then turned into a side street where there was a small bar of log-cabin design with garnet glass in its casement windows.

7

When Joan with a bagful of provisions, two magazines, and three parcels, came home at a quarter past five, she found in the porch mailbox a special-delivery air-mail letter from her daughter. More than three weeks had elapsed since Isabel had briefly written her parents to say that, after a honeymoon in Arizona, she had safely reached her husband's home town. Juggling with her packages, Joan tore the envelope open. It was an ecstatically happy letter, and she gulped it down, everything swimming a little in the radiance of her relief. On the outside of the front door she felt, then saw with brief surprise, Pnin's keys, like a bit of his fondest viscera, dangling with their leathern case from the lock; she used them to open the door, and as soon as she had entered she heard, coming from the pantry, a loud anarchistic knocking—cupboards being opened and shut one after the other.

She put her bag and parcels down on the sideboard in the kitchen and asked in the direction of the pantry: "What are you looking for, Timofey?"

He came out of there, darkly flushed, wild-eyed, and she was shocked to see that his face was a mess of unwiped tears.

"I search, John, for the viscous and sawdust," he said tragically.

"I am afraid there is no soda," she answered with her lucid Anglo-Saxon restraint. "But there is plenty of whisky in the dining-room cabinet. However, I suggest we both have some nice hot tea instead."

He made the Russian "relinquishing" gesture.

"No, I don't want anything at all," he said, and sat down at the kitchen table with an awful sigh.

She sat down next to him and opened one of the magazines she had bought.

"We are going to look at some pictures, Timofey."

"I do not want, John. You know I do not understand what is advertisement and what is not advertisement."

"You just relax, Timofey, and I'll do the explaining. Oh, look—I like this one. Oh, this is very clever. We have here a combination of two ideas—the Desert Island and the Girl in the Puff. Now, look, Timofey—please"—he reluctantly put on his reading glasses—"this is a desert island with a lone palm, and this is a bit of broken raft, and this is a shipwrecked mariner, and this is the ship's cat he saved, and this here, on that rock——"

"Impossible," said Pnin. "So small island, moreover with palm, cannot exist in such big sea."

"Well, it exists here."

"Impossible isolation," said Pnin.

"Yes, but—— Really, you are not playing fair, Timofey. You know perfectly well you agree with Lore that the world of the mind is based on a compromise with logic."

"I have reservations," said Pnin. "First of all, logic herself——"

"All right, I'm afraid we are wandering away from our little joke. Now, you look at the picture. So this is the mariner, and this is the pussy, and this is a rather wistful mermaid hanging around, and now look at the puffs right above the sailor and the pussy."

"Atomic bomb explosion," said Pnin sadly.

"No, not at all. It is something much funnier. You see, these round puffs are supposed to be the projections of their thoughts. And now at last we are getting to the amusing part. The sailor imagines the mermaid as having a pair of legs, and the cat imagines her as all fish."

"Lermontov," said Pnin, lifting two fingers, "has expressed everything about mermaids in only two poems. I cannot understand American humor even when I am happy, and I must say——" He removed his glasses with trembling hands, elbowed the magazine aside, and, resting his head on his arm, broke into muffled sobs.

She heard the front door open and close, and a moment later Laurence peeped into the kitchen with facetious furtiveness. Joan's right hand waved him away; her left directed him to the rainbow-rimmed envelope on top of the parcels. The private smile she flashed was a summary of Isabel's letter; he grabbed it and, no more in jest, tiptoed out again.

Pnin's unnecessarily robust shoulders continued to shake. She closed the magazine and for a minute studied its cover: toy-bright school tots, Isabel and the Hagen child, shade trees still off duty, a white spire, the Waindell bells.

"Doesn't she want to come back?" asked Joan softly.

Pnin, his head on his arm, started to beat the table with his loosely clenched fist.

"I haf nofing," wailed Pnin between loud, damp sniffs, "I haf nofing left, nofing, nofing!"

Chapter Three

DURING the eight years Pnin had taught at Waindell College he had changed his lodgings—for one reason or another, mainly sonic—about every semester. The accumulation of consecutive rooms in his memory now resembled those displays of grouped elbow chairs on show, and beds, and lamps, and inglenooks which, ignoring all space-time distinctions, commingle in the soft light of a furniture store beyond which it snows, and the dusk deepens, and nobody really loves anybody. The rooms of his Waindell period looked especially trim in comparison with one he had had in uptown New York, midway between Tsentral Park and Reeverside, on a block memorable for the wastepaper along the curb, the bright pat of dog dirt somebody had already slipped upon, and a tireless boy pitching a ball against the steps of the high brown porch; and even that room became positively dapper in Pnin's mind (where a small ball still rebounded) when compared with the old, now dust-blurred lodgings of his long Central-European, Nansen-passport period.

With age, however, Pnin had become choosy. Pretty fixtures no longer sufficed. Waindell was a quiet townlet, and Waindellville, in a notch of the hills, was yet quieter; but nothing was quiet enough for Pnin. There had been, at the start of his life here, that studio in the thoughtfully furnished College Home for Single Instructors, a very nice place despite certain gregarious drawbacks ("Ping-pong, Pnin?" "I don't any more play at games of infants"), until workmen came and started to drill holes in the street—Brainpan Street, Pningrad—and patch them up again, and this went on and on, in fits of shivering black zigzags and stunned pauses, for weeks, and it did not seem likely they would ever find again the precious tool they had entombed by mistake. There had been (to pick out here and there only special offenders) that room in the eminently hermetic-looking Duke's Lodge, Waindellville: a delightful *kabinet*, above which, however, every evening, among crashing bathroom cascades and banging doors, two monstrous statues on primitive legs of stone would grimly tramp—shapes hard to reconcile with the slender build of his actual upstairs neighbors, who turned out to be the Starrs, of the Fine Arts Department ("I am Christopher, and this is Louise"), an angelically gentle couple keenly interested in Dostoevski and Shostakovich. There had been—in yet another rooming house—a still cozier bedroom-study, with nobody butting in for a free lesson in Russian; but as soon as the formidable Waindell winter began to penetrate the coziness by means of sharp little drafts, coming not only from the window but even from the closet and the base plugs, the room had developed something like a streak of madness or mystic delusion—namely, a tenacious murmur of music, more or less classical, oddly located in Pnin's silver-washed radiator. He tried to muffle it up with a blanket, as if it were a caged songbird, but the song persisted until Mrs. Thayer's old mother was removed to the hospital where she died, upon which the radiator switched to Canadian French.

He tried habitats of another type: rooms for rent in private houses which, although differing from each other in many respects (not all, for instance, were clapboard ones; a few were stucco, or at least partly stucco), had one generic characteristic in common: in their parlor or stair-landing bookcases Hendrik Willem van Loon and Dr. Cronin were inevitably present; they might be separated by a flock of magazines, or by some glazed and buxom historical romance, or even by Mrs. Garnett impersonating somebody (and in such houses there would be sure to hang somewhere a Toulouse-Lautrec poster), but you found the pair without fail, exchanging looks of tender recognition, like two old friends at a crowded party.

2

He had returned for a spell to the College Home, but so had the pavement drillers, and there had cropped up other nuisances besides. At present Pnin was still renting the pink-walled, white-flounced second-floor bedroom in the Clements' house, and this was the first house he really liked and the first room he had occupied for more than a year. By now he had weeded out all trace of its former occupant; or so he thought, for he did not notice, and probably never would, a

funny face scrawled on the wall just behind the headboard of
the bed and some half-erased height-level marks penciled on
the doorjamb, beginning from a four-foot altitude in 1940.

For more than a week now, Pnin had had the run of the
house: Joan Clements had left by plane for a Western state to
visit her married daughter, and a couple of days later, at the
very beginning of his spring course in philosophy, Professor
Clements, summoned by a telegram, had flown West too.

Our friend had a leisurely breakfast, pleasantly based on the
milk that had not been discontinued, and at half-past nine
prepared for his usual walk to the campus.

It warmed my heart, the Russian-intelligentski way he had
of getting into his overcoat: his inclined head would demonstrate its ideal baldness, and his large, Duchess of Wonderland chin would firmly press against the crossed ends of his
green muffler to hold it in place on his chest while, with a
jerk of his broad shoulders, he contrived to get into both
armholes at once; another heave and the coat was on.

He picked up his *portfel'* (briefcase), checked its contents,
and walked out.

He was still at a newspaper's throw from his porch when
he remembered a book the college library had urgently requested him to return, for the use of another reader. For a
moment he struggled with himself; he still needed the volume;
but kindly Pnin sympathized too much with the passionate
clamor of another (unknown) scholar not to go back for the
stout and heavy tome: It was Volume 18—mainly devoted to
Tolstoyana—of *Sovetskiy Zolotoy Fond Literaturï* (Soviet Gold
Fund of Literature), *Moskva-Leningrad, 1940*.

3

The organs concerned in the production of English speech
sounds are the larynx, the velum, the lips, the tongue (that
punchinello in the troupe), and, last but not least, the lower
jaw; mainly upon its overenergetic and somewhat ruminant
motion did Pnin rely when translating in class passages in the
Russian grammar or some poem by Pushkin. If his Russian
was music, his English was murder. He had enormous difficulty ("dzeefeecooltsee" in Pninian English) with depalati-

zation, never managing to remove the extra Russian moisture from *t*'s and *d*'s before the vowels he so quaintly softened. His explosive "hat" ("I never go in a hat even in winter") differed from the common American pronunciation of "hot" (typical of Waindell townspeople, for example) only by its briefer duration, and thus sounded very much like the German verb *hat* (has). Long *o*'s with him inevitably became short ones: his "no" sounded positively Italian, and this was accentuated by his trick of triplicating the simple negative ("May I give you a lift, Mr. Pnin?" "No-no-no, I have only two paces from here"). He did not possess (nor was he aware of this lack) any long *oo*: all he could muster when called upon to utter "noon" was the lax vowel of the German "*nun* " ("I have no classes in after*nun* on Tuesday. Today is Tuesday.")

Tuesday—true; but what day of the month, we wonder. Pnin's birthday for instance fell on February 3, by the Julian calendar into which he had been born in St. Petersburg in 1898. He never celebrated it nowadays, partly because, after his departure from Russia, it sidled by in a Gregorian disguise (thirteen—no, twelve days late), and partly because during the academic year he existed mainly on a motuweth frisas basis.

On the chalk-clouded blackboard, which he wittily called the grayboard, he now wrote a date. In the crook of his arm he still felt the bulk of *Zol. Fond Lit.* The date he wrote had nothing to do with the day this was in Waindell:

December 26, 1829

He carefully drilled in a big white full stop, and added underneath:

3:03 P.M. St. Petersburg

Dutifully this was taken down by Frank Backman, Rose Balsamo, Frank Carroll, Irving D. Herz, beautiful, intelligent Marilyn Hohn, John Mead, Jr., Peter Volkov, and Allan Bradbury Walsh.

Pnin, rippling with mute mirth, sat down again at his desk: he had a tale to tell. That line in the absurd Russian grammar, "*Brozhu li ya vdol' ulits shumnih* (Whether I wander along noisy streets)," was really the opening of a famous poem. Although Pnin was supposed in this Elementary Russian class to

stick to language exercises (*"Mama, telefon! Brozhu li ya vdol'*
ulits shumnih. Ot Vladivostoka do Vashingtona 5000 mil'."), he
took every opportunity to guide his students on literary and
historical tours.

In a set of eight tetrametric quatrains Pushkin described the
morbid habit he always had—wherever he was, whatever he
was doing—of dwelling on thoughts of death and of closely
inspecting every passing day as he strove to find in its cryptogram a certain "future anniversary": the day and month that
would appear, somewhere, sometime upon his tombstone.

" 'And where will fate send me', imperfective future,
'death,' " declaimed inspired Pnin, throwing his head back
and translating with brave literality, " 'in fight, in travel, or in
waves? Or will the neighboring dale'—*dolina*, same word,
'valley' we would now say—'accept my refrigerated ashes',
poussière, 'cold dust' perhaps more correct. 'And though it is
indifferent to the insensible body . . .' "

Pnin went on to the end and then, dramatically pointing
with the piece of chalk he still held, remarked how carefully
Pushkin had noted the day and even the minute of writing
down that poem.

"But," exclaimed Pnin in triumph, "he died on a quite,
quite different day! He died——" The chair back against
which Pnin was vigorously leaning emitted an ominous crack,
and the class resolved a pardonable tension in loud young
laughter.

(Sometime, somewhere—Petersburg? Prague?—one of the
two musical clowns pulled out the piano stool from under the
other, who remained, however, playing on, in a seated,
though seatless, position, with his rhapsody unimpaired.
Where? Circus Busch, Berlin!)

4

Pnin did not bother to leave the classroom between his
dismissed Elementary and the Advanced that was trickling in.
The office where *Zol. Fond Lit.* now lay, partly enveloped in
Pnin's green muffler, on the filing case, was on another floor,
at the end of a resonant passage and next to the faculty lavatory. Till 1950 (this was 1953—how time flies!) he had shared

an office in the German Department with Miller, one of the younger instructors, and then was given for his exclusive use Office R, which formerly had been a lumber room but had now been completely renovated. During the spring he had lovingly Pninized it. It had come with two ignoble chairs, a cork bulletin board, a can of floor wax forgotten by the janitor, and a humble pedestal desk of indeterminable wood. He wangled from the Administration a small steel file with an entrancing locking device. Young Miller, under Pnin's direction, embraced and brought over Pnin's part of a sectional bookcase. From old Mrs. McCrystal, in whose white frame house he had spent a mediocre winter (1949–50), Pnin purchased for three dollars a faded, once Turkish rug. With the help of the janitor he screwed onto the side of the desk a pencil sharpener—that highly satisfying, highly philosophical implement that goes ticonderoga-ticonderoga, feeding on the yellow finish and sweet wood, and ends up in a kind of soundlessly spinning ethereal void as we all must. He had other, even more ambitious plans, such as an armchair and a tall lamp. When, after a summer spent teaching in Washington, Pnin returned to his office, an obese dog lay asleep on his rug, and his furniture had been moved to a darker part of the office, so as to make room for a magnificent stainless-steel desk and a swivel chair to match, in which sat writing and smiling to himself the newly imported Austrian scholar, Dr. Bodo von Falternfels; and thenceforth, so far as Pnin was concerned, Office R had gone to seed.

5

At noon, as usual, Pnin washed his hands and head.

He picked up in Office R his overcoat, muffler, book, and brief case. Dr. Falternfels was writing and smiling; his sandwich was half unwrapped; his dog was dead. Pnin walked down the gloomy stairs and through the Museum of Sculpture. Humanities Hall, where, however, Ornithology and Anthropology also lurked, was connected with another brick building, Frieze Hall, which housed the dining rooms and the Faculty Club, by means of a rather rococo openwork gallery: it went up a slope, then turned sharply and wandered down toward a routine smell of potato chips and the sadness of balanced meals. In summer its trellis was alive with quivering flowers; but now through its nakedness an icy wind blew, and someone had placed a found red mitten upon the spout of the dead fountain that stood where one branch of the gallery led to the President's House.

President Poore, a tall, slow, elderly man wearing dark glasses, had started to lose his sight a couple of years before and was now almost totally blind. With solar regularity, however, he would be led every day by his niece and secretary to Frieze Hall; he came, a figure of antique dignity, moving in his private darkness to an invisible luncheon, and although everybody had long grown accustomed to his tragic entrance, there was invariably the shadow of a hush while he was being steered to his carved chair and while he groped for the edge of the table; and it was strange to see, directly behind him on the wall, his stylized likeness in a mauve double-breasted suit and mahogany shoes, gazing with radiant magenta eyes at the scrolls handed him by Richard Wagner, Dostoevski, and Confucius, a group that Oleg Komarov, of the Fine Arts Department, had painted a decade ago into Lang's celebrated mural of 1938, which carried all around the dining room a pageant of historical figures and Waindell faculty members.

Pnin, who wanted to ask his compatriot something, sat down beside him. This Komarov, a Cossack's son, was a very short man with a crew cut and a death's-head's nostrils. He and Serafima, his large, cheerful, Moscow-born wife, who wore a Tibetan charm on a long silver chain that hung down to her ample, soft belly, would throw Russki parties every now and then, with Russki hors d'oeuvres and guitar music and more or less phony folk songs—occasions at which shy graduate students would be taught vodka-drinking rites and other stale Russianisms; and after such feasts, upon meeting gruff Pnin, Serafima and Oleg (she raising her eyes to heaven, he covering his with one hand) would murmur in awed self-gratitude: "*Gospodi, skol'ko mï im dayom!* (My, what a lot we give them!)"—"them" being the benighted American people. Only another Russian could understand the reactionary and Sovietophile blend presented by the pseudo-colorful Komarovs, for whom an ideal Russia consisted of the Red Army, an anointed monarch, collective farms, anthroposophy, the Russian Church and the Hydro-Electric Dam. Pnin and Oleg Komarov were usually in a subdued state of war, but meetings were inevitable, and such of their American colleagues as deemed the Komarovs "grand people" and mimicked droll Pnin were sure the painter and Pnin were excellent friends.

It would be hard to say, without applying some very special tests, which of them, Pnin or Komarov, spoke the worse English; probably Pnin; but for reasons of age, general education, and a slightly longer stage of American citizenship, he found it possible to correct Komarov's frequent English interpolations, and Komarov resented this even more than he did Pnin's *antikvarniy liberalizm.*

"Look here, Komarov (*Poslushayte, Komarov*"—a rather discourteous manner of address)—said Pnin. "I cannot understand who else here might want this book; certainly none of my students; and if it is you, I cannot understand why you should want it anyway."

"I don't," answered Komarov, glancing at the volume. "Not interested," he added in English.

Pnin moved his lips and lower jaw mutely once or twice, wanted to say something, did not, and went on with his salad.

6

This being Tuesday, he could walk over to his favorite haunt immediately after lunch and stay there till dinner time. No gallery connected Waindell College Library with any other buildings, but it was intimately and securely connected with Pnin's heart. He walked past the great bronze figure of the first president of the college, Alpheus Frieze, in sports cap and knickerbockers, holding by its horns the bronze bicycle he was eternally about to mount, judging by the position of his left foot, forever glued to the left pedal. There was snow on the saddle and snow in the absurd basket that recent pranksters had attached to the handle bars. *"Huligani,"* fumed Pnin, shaking his head—and slipped slightly on a flag of the path that meandered down a turfy slope among the leafless elms. Besides the big book under his right arm, he carried in his left hand his brief case, an old, Central European-looking, black *portfel'*, and this he swung rhythmically by its leathern grip as he marched to his books, to his scriptorium in the stacks, to his paradise of Russian lore.

An elliptic flock of pigeons, in circular volitation, soaring gray, flapping white, and then gray again, wheeled across the limpid, pale sky, above the College Library. A train whistled afar as mournfully as in the steppes. A skimpy squirrel dashed over a patch of sunlit snow, where a tree trunk's shadow, olive-green on the turf, became grayish blue for a stretch, while the tree itself, with a brisk, scrabbly sound, ascended, naked, into the sky, where the pigeons swept by for a third and last time. The squirrel, invisible now in a crotch, chattered, scolding the delinquents who would pot him out of his tree. Pnin, on the dirty black ice of the flagged path, slipped again, threw up one arm in an abrupt convulsion, regained his balance, and, with a solitary smile, stooped to pick up *Zol. Fond Lit.*, which lay wide open to a snapshot of a Russian pasture with Lyov Tolstoy trudging across it toward the camera and some long-maned horses behind him, their innocent heads turned toward the photographer too.

V boyu li, v stranstvii, v volnah? In fight, in travel, or in waves? Or on the Waindell campus? Gently champing his dentures, which retained a sticky layer of cottage cheese, Pnin went up the slippery library steps.

Like so many aging college people, Pnin had long ceased to notice the existence of students on the campus, in the corridors, in the library—anywhere, in brief, save in functional classroom concentrations. In the beginning, he had been much upset by the sight of some of them, their poor young heads on their forearms, fast asleep among the ruins of knowledge; but now, except for a girl's comely nape here and there, he saw nobody in the Reading Room.

Mrs. Thayer was at the circulation desk. Her mother and Mrs. Clements' mother had been first cousins.

"How are you today, Professor Pnin?"

"I am very well, Mrs. Fire."

"Laurence and Joan aren't back yet, are they?"

"No. I have brought this book back because I received this card——"

"I wonder if poor Isabel will really get divorced."

"I have not heard. Mrs. Fire, permit me to ask——"

"I suppose we'll have to find you another room, if they bring her back with them."

"Mrs. Fire, permit me to ask something or other. This card which I received yesterday—could you maybe tell me who is the other reader?"

"Let me check."

She checked. The other reader proved to be Timofey Pnin; Volume 18 had been requested by him the Friday before. It was also true that this Volume 18 was already charged to this Pnin, who had had it since Christmas and now stood with his hands upon it, like an ancestral picture of a magistrate.

"It can't be!" cried Pnin. "I requested on Friday Volume 19, year 1947, not 18, year 1940."

"But look—you wrote Volume 18. Anyway, 19 is still being processed. Are you keeping this?"

"Eighteen, 19," muttered Pnin. "There is not great difference! I put the year correctly, *that* is important! Yes, I still need 18—and send to me a more effishant card when 19 available."

Growling a little, he took the unwieldy, abashed book to his favorite alcove and laid it down there, wrapped in his muffler.

They can't read, these women. The year was plainly inscribed.

As usual he marched to the Periodicals Room and there glanced at the news in the latest (Saturday, February 12—and this was Tuesday, O Careless Reader!) issue of the Russian-language daily published, since 1918, by an émigré group in Chicago. As usual, he carefully scanned the advertisements. Dr. Popov, photographed in his new white smock, promised elderly people new vigor and joy. A music corporation listed Russian phonograph records for sale, such as "Broken Life, a Waltz" and "The Song of a Front-Line Chauffeur." A somewhat Gogolian mortician praised his hearses de luxe, which were also available for picnics. Another Gogolian person, in Miami, offered "a two-room apartment for non-drinkers (*dlya trezvih*), among fruit trees and flowers," while in Hammond a room was wistfully being let "in a small quiet family"—and for no special reason the reader suddenly saw, with passionate and ridiculous lucidity, his parents, Dr. Pavel Pnin and Valeria Pnin, he with a medical journal, she with a political review, sitting in two armchairs, facing each other in a small, cheerfully lighted drawing room on Galernaya Street, St. Petersburg, forty years ago.

He also perused the current item in a tremendously long and tedious controversy between three émigré factions. It had started by Faction A's accusing Faction B of inertia and illustrating it by the proverb, "He wishes to climb the fir tree but is afraid to scrape his shins." This had provoked an acid Letter to the Editor from "An Old Optimist," entitled "Fir Trees and Inertia" and beginning: "There is an old American saying 'He who lives in a glass house should not try to kill two birds with one stone.'" In the present issue, there was a two-thousand-word *feuilleton* contributed by a representative of Faction C and headed "On Fir Trees, Glass Houses, and Optimism," and Pnin read this with great interest and sympathy.

He then returned to his carrell for his own research.

He contemplated writing a *Petite Histoire* of Russian culture, in which a choice of Russian Curiosities, Customs, Literary Anecdotes, and so forth would be presented in such a way as to reflect in miniature *la Grande Histoire*—Major Concatenations of Events. He was still at the blissful stage of collecting his material; and many good young people considered it a treat and an honor to see Pnin pull out a catalogue drawer from the comprehensive bosom of a card cabinet and take it, like a big nut, to a secluded corner and there make a quiet mental meal of it, now moving his lips in soundless comment, critical, satisfied, perplexed, and now lifting his rudimentary eyebrows and forgetting them there, left high upon his spacious brow where they remained long after all trace of displeasure or doubt had gone. He was lucky to be at Waindell. Sometime in the nineties the eminent bibliophile and Slavist John Thurston Todd (his bearded bust presided over the drinking fountain), had visited hospitable Russia, and after his death the books he had amassed there quietly chuted into a remote stack. Wearing rubber gloves so as to avoid being stung by the *amerikanski* electricity in the metal of the shelving, Pnin would go to those books and gloat over them: obscure magazines of the Roaring Sixties in marbled boards; century-old historical monographs, their somnolent pages foxed with fungus spots; Russian classics in horrible and pathetic cameo bindings, whose molded profiles of poets reminded dewy-eyed Timofey of his boyhood, when he could idly palpate on the book cover Pushkin's slightly chafed side whisker or Zhukovski's smudgy nose.

Today from Kostromskoy's voluminous work (Moscow, 1855), on Russian myths—a rare book, not to be removed from the library—Pnin, with a not unhappy sigh, started to copy out a passage referring to the old pagan games that were still practiced at the time, throughout the woodlands of the Upper Volga, in the margins of Christian ritual. During a festive week in May—the so-called Green Week which graded into Whitsuntide—peasant maidens would make wreaths of buttercups and frog orchises; then, singing snatches of ancient love chants, they hung these garlands on riverside willows; and on Whitsunday the wreaths were shaken down into the river, where, unwinding, they floated like so many serpents while the maidens floated and chanted among them.

A curious verbal association struck Pnin at this point; he could not catch it by its mermaid tail but made a note on his index card and plunged back into Kostromskoy.

When Pnin raised his eyes again, it was dinnertime.

Doffing his spectacles, he rubbed with the knuckles of the hand that held them his naked and tired eyes and, still in thought, fixed his mild gaze on the window above, where, gradually, through his dissolving meditation, there appeared the violet-blue air of dusk, silver-tooled by the reflection of the fluorescent lights of the ceiling, and, among spidery black twigs, a mirrored row of bright book spines.

Before leaving the library, he decided to look up the correct pronunciation of "interested," and discovered that Webster, or at least the battered 1930 edition lying on a table in the Browsing Room, did not place the stress accent on the third syllable, as he did. He sought a list of errata at the back, failed to find one, and, upon closing the elephantine lexicon, realized with a pang that he had immured somewhere in it the index card with notes that he had been holding all this time.

Must now search and search through 2500 thin pages, some torn! On hearing his interjection, suave Mr. Case, a lank, pink-faced librarian with sleek white hair and a bow tie, strolled up, took up the colossus by both ends, inverted it, and gave it a slight shake, whereupon it shed a pocket comb, a Christmas card, Pnin's notes, and a gauzy wraith of tissue paper, which descended with infinite listlessness to Pnin's feet and was replaced by Mr. Case on the Great Seals of the United States and Territories.

Pnin pocketed his index card and, while doing so, recalled without any prompting what he had not been able to recall a while ago:

. . . *plila i pela, pela i plila* . . .
. . . she floated and she sang, she sang and floated . . .

Of course! Ophelia's death! *Hamlet!* In good old Andrey Kroneberg's Russian translation, 1844—the joy of Pnin's youth, and of his father's and grandfather's young days! And here, as in the Kostromskoy passage, there is, we recollect, also a willow and also wreaths. But where to check properly? Alas, *"Gamlet" Vil'yama Shekspira* had not been acquired by Mr. Todd, was not represented in Waindell College Library, and whenever you were reduced to look up something in the English version, you never found this or that beautiful, noble, sonorous line that you remembered all your life from Kroneberg's text in Vengerov's splendid edition. Sad!

It was getting quite dark on the sad campus. Above the distant, still sadder hills there lingered, under a cloud bank, a depth of tortoise-shell sky. The heart-rending lights of Waindellville, throbbing in a fold of those dusky hills, were putting on their usual magic, though actually, as Pnin well knew, the place, when you got there, was merely a row of brick houses, a service station, a skating rink, a supermarket. As he walked to the little tavern in Library Lane for a large portion of Virginia ham and a good bottle of beer, Pnin suddenly felt very tired. Not only had the *Zol. Fond* tome become even heavier after its unnecessary visit to the library, but something that Pnin had half heard in the course of the day, and had been reluctant to follow up, now bothered and oppressed him, as does, in retrospection, a blunder we have made, a piece of rudeness we have allowed ourselves, or a threat we have chosen to ignore.

7

Over an unhurried second bottle, Pnin debated with himself his next move or, rather, mediated in a debate between weary-brained Pnin, who had not been sleeping well lately, and an insatiable Pnin, who wished to continue reading at home, as always, till the 2 A.M. freight train moaned its way up the valley. It was decided at last that he would go to bed immediately after attending the program presented by intense Christopher and Louise Starr every second Tuesday at New Hall, rather high-brow music and unusual movie offerings which President Poore, in answer to some absurd criticism last year, had termed "probably the most inspiring and inspired venture in the entire academic community."

ZFL was now asleep in Pnin's lap. To his left sat two Hindu students. At his right there was Professor Hagen's daughter, a hoydenish Drama major. Komarov, thank goodness, was too far behind for his scarcely interesting remarks to carry.

The first part of the program, three ancient movie shorts, bored our friend: that cane, that bowler, that white face, those black, arched eyebrows, those twitchy nostrils meant nothing to him. Whether the incomparable comedian danced in the sun with chapleted nymphs near a waiting cactus, or was a prehistoric man (the supple cane now a supple club), or was glared at by burly Mack Swain at a hectic night club, old-fashioned, humorless Pnin remained indifferent. "Clown," he snorted to himself. "Even Glupishkin and Max Linder used to be more comical."

The second part of the program consisted of an impressive Soviet documentary film, made in the late forties. It was supposed to contain not a jot of propaganda, to be all sheer art, merrymaking, and the euphoria of proud toil. Handsome, unkempt girls marched in an immemorial Spring Festival with banners bearing snatches of old Russian ballads such as *"Ruki proch ot Korei," "Bas les mains devant la Corée," "La paz vencera a la guerra," "Der Friede besiegt den Krieg."* A flying ambulance was shown crossing a snowy range in Tajikistan. Kirghiz actors visited a sanatorium for coal miners among palm trees and staged there a spontaneous performance. In a mountain pasture somewhere in legendary Ossetia, a herdsman reported by portable radio to the local Republic's Ministry of Agriculture on the birth of a lamb. The Moscow Metro shimmered, with its columns and statues, and six would-be travelers seated on three marble benches. A factory worker's family spent a quiet evening at home, all dressed up, in a parlor choked with ornamental plants, under a great silk lampshade. Eight thousand soccer fans watched a match between Torpedo and Dynamo. Eight thousand citizens at Moscow's Electrical Equipment Plant unanimously nominated Stalin candidate from the Stalin Election District of Moscow. The latest Zim passenger model started out with the factory worker's family and a few other people for a picnic in the country. And then——

"I must not, I must not, oh it is idiotical," said Pnin to himself as he felt—unaccountably, ridiculously, humiliatingly —his tear glands discharge their hot, infantine, uncontrollable fluid.

In a haze of sunshine—sunshine projecting in vaporous shafts between the white boles of birches, drenching the pendulous foliage, trembling in eyelets upon the bark, dripping onto the long grass, shining and smoking among the ghosts of racemose bird cherries in scumbled bloom—a Russian wildwood enveloped the rambler. It was traversed by an old forest road with two soft furrows and a continuous traffic of mushrooms and daisies. The rambler still followed in mind that road as he trudged back to his anachronistic lodgings; was again the youth who had walked through those woods with a fat book under his arm; the road emerged into the romantic, free, beloved radiance of a great field unmowed by time (the horses galloping away and tossing their silvery manes among the tall flowers), as drowsiness overcame Pnin, who was now fairly snug in bed with two alarm clocks alongside, one set at 7:30, the other at 8, clicking and clucking on his night table.

Komarov, in a sky-blue shirt, bent over the guitar he was tuning. A birthday party was in progress, and calm Stalin cast with a thud his ballot in the election of governmental pall-

bearers. In fight, in travel . . . waves or Waindell. . . .
"Wonderful!" said Dr. Bodo von Falternfels, raising his head
from his writing.

Pnin had all but lapsed into velvety oblivion when some
frightful accident happened outside: groaning and clutching
at its brow, a statue was making an extravagant fuss over a
broken bronze wheel—and then Pnin was awake, and a car-
avan of lights and of shadowy humps progressed across the
window shade. A car door slammed, a car drove off, a key
unlocked the brittle, transparent house, three vibrant voices
spoke; the house, and the chink under Pnin's door, lit up with
a shiver. It was a fever, it was an infection. In fear and helplessness, toothless, nightshirted Pnin heard a suitcase one-leg-
gedly but briskly stomping upstairs, and a pair of young feet
tripping up steps so familiar to them, and one could already
make out the sound of eager breathing. . . . In fact, the automatic revival of happy homecomings from dismal summer
camps would have actually had Isabel kick open—Pnin's—
door, had not her mother's warning yelp stopped her in time.

Chapter Four

THE KING, his father, wearing a very white sports shirt open at the throat and a very black blazer, sat at a spacious desk whose highly polished surface twinned his upper half in reverse, making of him a kind of court card. Ancestral portraits darkened the walls of the vast paneled room. Otherwise, it was not unlike the headmaster's study at St. Bart's School, on the Atlantic seaboard, some three thousand miles west of the imagined Palace. A copious spring shower kept lashing at the french windows, beyond which young greenery, all eyes, shivered and streamed. Nothing but this sheet of rain seemed to separate and protect the Palace from the revolution that for several days had been rocking the city. . . . Actually, Victor's father was a cranky refugee doctor, whom the lad had never much liked and had not seen now for almost two years.

The King, his more plausible father, had decided not to abdicate. No newspapers were coming out. The Orient Express was stranded, with all its transient passengers, at a suburban station, on the platform of which, reflected in puddles, picturesque peasants stood and gaped at the curtained windows of the long, mysterious cars. The Palace, and its terraced gardens, and the city below the palatial hill, and the main city square, where decapitations and folk dances had already started, despite the weather—all this was at the heart of a cross whose arms terminated in Trieste, Graz, Budapest, and Zagreb, as designated in *Rand McNally's Ready Reference Atlas of the World*. And at the heart of that heart sat the King, pale and calm, and on the whole closely resembling his son as that underformer imagined he would look at forty himself. Pale and calm, a cup of coffee in his hand, his back to the emerald-and-gray window, the King sat listening to a masked messenger, a corpulent old nobleman in a wet cloak, who had managed to make his way through the rebellion and the rain from the besieged Council Hall to the isolated Palace.

"Abdication! One third of the alphabet!" coldly quipped the King, with the trace of an accent. "The answer is no. I prefer the unknown quantity of exile."

Saying this, the King, a widower, glanced at the desk photograph of a beautiful dead woman, at those great blue eyes, that carmine mouth (it was a colored photo, not fit for a king, but no matter). The lilacs, in sudden premature bloom, wildly beat, like shut-out maskers, at the dripping panes. The old messenger bowed and walked backward through the wilderness of the study, wondering secretly whether it would not be wiser for him to leave history alone and make a dash for Vienna where he had some property. . . . Of course, Victor's mother was not really dead; she had left his everyday father, Dr. Eric Wind (now in South America), and was about to be married in Buffalo to a man named Church.

Victor indulged night after night in these mild fancies, trying to induce sleep in his cold cubicle which was exposed to every noise in the restless dorm. Generally he did not reach that crucial flight episode when the King alone—*solus rex* (as chess problem makers term royal solitude)—paced a beach on the Bohemian Sea, at Tempest Point, where Percival Blake, a cheerful American adventurer, had promised to meet him with a powerful motorboat. Indeed, the very act of postponing that thrilling and soothing episode, the very protraction of its lure, coming as it did on top of the repetitive fancy, formed the main mechanism of its soporific effect.

An Italian film made in Berlin for American consumption, with a wild-eyed youngster in rumpled shorts, pursued through slums and ruins and a brothel or two by a multiple agent; a version of *The Scarlet Pimpernel*, recently staged at St. Martha's, the nearest girls' school; an anonymous Kafkaesque story in a *ci-devant* avant-garde magazine read aloud in class by Mr. Pennant, a melancholy Englishman with a past; and, not least, the residue of various family allusions of long standing to the flight of Russian intellectuals from Lenin's regime thirty-five years ago—these were the obvious sources of Victor's fantasies; they may have been, at one time, intensely affecting; by now they had become frankly utilitarian, as a simple and pleasant drug.

2

He was now fourteen but looked two or three years older—not because of his lanky height, close on six feet, but because of a casual ease of demeanor, an expression of amiable aloofness about his plain but clean-cut features, and a complete lack of clumsiness or constraint which, far from precluding modesty and reserve, lent a sunny something to his shyness and a detached blandness to his quiet ways. Under his left eye a brown mole almost the size of a cent punctuated the pallor of his cheek. I do not think he loved anybody.

In his attitude toward his mother, passionate childhood affection had long since been replaced by tender condescension, and all he permitted himself was an inward sigh of amused submission to fate when, in her fluent and flashy New York English, with brash metallic nasalities and soft lapses into furry Russianisms, she regaled strangers in his presence with stories that he had heard countless times and that were either over-embroidered or untrue. It was more trying when among such strangers Dr. Eric Wind, a completely humorless pedant who believed that his English (acquired in a German high school) was impeccably pure, would mouth a stale facetious phrase, saying "the pond" for the ocean, with the confidential and arch air of one who makes his audience the precious gift of a fruity colloquialism. Both parents, in their capacity of psychotherapists, did their best to impersonate Laius and Jocasta, but the boy proved to be a very mediocre little Oedipus. In order not to complicate the modish triangle of Freudian romance (father, mother, child), Liza's first husband had never been mentioned. Only when the Wind marriage started to disintegrate, about the time that Victor was enrolled at St. Bart's, Liza informed him that she had been Mrs. Pnin before she left Europe. She told him that this former husband of hers had migrated to America too—that in fact he would soon see Victor; and since everything Liza alluded to (opening wide her radiant black-lashed blue eyes) invariably took on a veneer of mystery and glamour, the figure of the great Timofey Pnin, scholar and gentleman, teaching a practically dead language at the famous Waindell College some three hundred miles northwest of St. Bart's, acquired in Victor's hospitable mind a curious charm, a family resemblance to those Bulgarian kings or Mediterranean princes who used to be world-famous experts in butterflies or sea shells. He therefore experienced pleasure when Professor Pnin entered into a staid and decorous correspondence with him; a first letter, couched in beautiful French but very indifferently typed, was followed by a picture postcard representing the Gray Squirrel. The card belonged to an educational series depicting Our Mammals and Birds; Pnin had acquired the whole series specially for the purpose of this correspondence. Victor was glad to learn that "squirrel" came from a Greek word which meant "shadowtail." Pnin invited Victor to visit him during the next vacation and informed the boy that he would meet him at the Waindell bus station. "To be recognized," he wrote, in English, "I will appear in dark spectacles and hold a black brief case with my monogram in silver."

3

Both Eric and Liza Wind were morbidly concerned with heredity, and instead of delighting in Victor's artistic genius, they used to worry gloomily about its genetic cause. Art and science had been represented rather vividly in the ancestral past. Should one trace Victor's passion for pigments back to Hans Andersen (no relation to the bedside Dane), who had been a stained-glass artist in Lübeck before losing his mind (and believing himself to be a cathedral) soon after his beloved daughter married a gray-haired Hamburg jeweler, author of a monograph on sapphires and Eric's maternal grandfather? Or was Victor's almost pathological precision of pencil and pen a by-product of Bogolepov's science? For Victor's mother's great-grandfather, the seventh son of a country pope, had been no other than that singular genius, Feofilakt Bogolepov, whose only rival for the title of greatest Russian mathematician was Nikolay Lobachevski. One wonders.

Genius is non-conformity. At two, Victor did not make little spiral scribbles to express buttons or portholes, as a million tots do, why not you? Lovingly he made his circles perfectly round and perfectly closed. A three-year-old child, when asked to copy a square, shapes one recognizable corner and then is content to render the rest of the outline as wavy or circular; but Victor at three not only copied the researcher's (Dr. Liza Wind's) far from ideal square with contemptuous accuracy but added a smaller one beside the copy. He never went through that initial stage of graphic activity when infants draw *Kopf-füsslers* (tadpole people), or humpty dumpties with L-like legs, and arms ending in rake prongs; in fact, he avoided the human form altogether and when pressed by Papa (Dr. Eric Wind) to draw Mama (Dr. Liza Wind), responded with a lovely un-dulation, which he said was her shadow on the new refriger-ator. At four, he evolved an individual stipple. At five, he began to draw objects in perspective—a side wall nicely fore-shortened, a tree dwarfed by distance, one object half masking another. And at six, Victor already distinguished what so many adults never learn to see—the colors of shadows, the differ-ence in tint between the shadow of an orange and that of a plum or of an avocado pear.

To the Winds, Victor was a problem child insofar as he refused to be one. From the Wind point of view, every male child had an ardent desire to castrate his father and a nostalgic urge to re-enter his mother's body. But Victor did not reveal any behavior disorder, did not pick his nose, did not suck his thumb, was not even a nail biter. Dr. Wind, with the object of eliminating what he, a radiophile, termed "the static of personal relationship," had his impregnable child tested psy-chometrically at the Institute by a couple of outsiders, young Dr. Stern and his smiling wife (I am Louis and this is Christina). But the results were either monstrous or nil: the seven-year-old subject scored on the so-called Godunov Drawing-of-an-Animal Test a sensational mental age of seventeen, but on being given a Fairview Adult Test promptly sank to the mentality of a two-year-old. How much care, skill, inventiveness have gone to devise those marvelous techniques! What a shame that certain patients refuse to co-operate! There is, for instance, the Kent-Rosanoff Absolutely Free Association Test, in which little Joe or Jane is asked to respond to a Stim-ulus Word, such as table, duck, music, sickness, thickness, low, deep, long, happiness, fruit, mother, mushroom. There is the charming Bièvre Interest-Attitude Game (a blessing on rainy afternoons), in which little Sam or Ruby is asked to put a little mark in front of the things about which he or she feels sort of fearful, such as dying, falling, dreaming, cyclones, funerals, father, night, operation, bedroom, bathroom, converge, and so forth; there is the Augusta Angst Abstract Test in which the little one (*das Kleine*) is made to express a list of terms ("groaning," "pleasure," "darkness") by means of unlifted lines. And there is, of course, the Doll Play, in which Patrick or Patricia is given two identical rubber dolls and a cute little bit of clay which Pat must fix on one of them before he or she starts playing, and oh the lovely doll house, with so many rooms and lots of quaint miniature objects, including a chamber pot no bigger than a cupule, and a medicine chest, and a poker, and a double bed, and even a pair of teeny-weeny rubber gloves in the kitchen, and you may be as mean as you like and do anything you want to Papa doll if you think he is beating Mama doll when they put out the lights in the bedroom. But bad Victor would not play with Lou and Tina, ignored the dolls, struck out all the listed words (which was against the rules), and made drawings that had no subhuman significance whatever.

Nothing of the slightest interest to therapists could Victor be made to discover in those beautiful, *beautiful* Rorschach ink blots, wherein children see, or should see, all kinds of things, seascapes, escapes, capes, the worms of imbecility, neurotic tree trunks, erotic galoshes, umbrellas, and dumbbells. Nor did any of Victor's casual sketches represent the so-called mandala—a term supposedly meaning (in Sanskrit) a magic ring, and applied by Dr. Jung and others to any doodle in the shape of a more or less fourfold spreading structure, such as a halved mangosteen, or a cross, or the wheel on which egos are broken like Morphos, or more exactly, the molecule of carbon, with its four valences—that main chemical component of the brain, automatically magnified and reflected on paper.

The Sterns reported that "unfortunately the psychic value of Victor's Mind Pictures and Word Associations is completely obscured by the boy's artistic inclinations." And thenceforth the Winds' little patient, who had trouble in going to sleep and lacked appetite, was allowed to read in bed till after midnight and evade oatmeal in the morning.

4

In planning her boy's education, Liza had been torn between two libidos: to endow him with the latest benefits of Modern Child Psychotherapy, and to find, among American frames of religious reference, the nearest approach to the melodious and wholesome amenities of the Greek Catholic Church, that mild communion whose demands on one's conscience are so small in comparison with the comforts it offers.

Little Victor at first went to a progressive kindergarten in New Jersey, and then, upon the advice of some Russian friends, attended a day school there. The school was directed by an Episcopal clergyman who proved to be a wise and gifted educator, sympathetic to superior children, no matter how bizarre or rowdy they might be; Victor was certainly a little peculiar, but on the other hand very quiet. At twelve, he went to St. Bartholomew's.

Physically, St. Bart's was a great mass of self-conscious red brick, erected in 1869 on the outskirts of Cranton, Massachusetts. Its main building formed three sides of a large quadrangle, the fourth being a cloistered passage. Its gabled gatehouse was glossily coated on one side with American ivy and tipped somewhat top-heavily with a Celtic cross of stone. The ivy rippled in the wind like the back skin of a horse. The hue of red brick is fondly supposed to grow richer with time; that of good old St. Bart's had only grown dirty. Under the cross and immediately over the sonorous-looking but really echoless arc of the entrance was carved a dagger of sorts, an attempt to represent the butcher's knife so reproachfully held (in the Vienna Missal) by St. Bartholomew, one of the Apostles—the one, namely, who had been flayed alive and exposed to the flies in the summer of 65 A.D. or thereabouts, in Albanopolis, now Derbent, southeastern Russia. His coffin, when cast by a furious king into the Caspian Sea, had blandly sailed all the way to Lipari Island off the coast of Sicily—probably a legend, seeing that the Caspian had been strictly an inland affair ever since the Pleistocene. Beneath this heraldic weapon—which rather resembled a carrot pointing upward—an inscription in burnished church text read: "*Sursum*." Two gentle English shepherd dogs belonging to one of the masters and greatly attached to each other could generally be found drowsing in their private Arcadia on a lawn before the gate.

Liza on her first visit to the school had greatly admired everything about it from the fives courts and the chapel to the plaster casts in the corridors and the photographs of cathedrals in the classrooms. The three lower forms were assigned to dormitories with windowed alcoves; there was a master's room at the end. Visitors could not help admiring the fine gymnasium. Very evocative, too, were the oaken seats and hammer-beamed roof of the chapel, a Romanesque structure that had been donated half a century ago by Julius Schonberg, wool manufacturer, brother of the world-famous Egyptologist Samuel Schonberg who perished in the Messina earthquake. There were twenty-five masters and the headmaster, the Reverend Archibald Hopper, who on warm days wore elegant clerical gray and performed his duties in radiant ignorance of the intrigue that was on the point of dislodging him.

5

Although Victor's eye was his supreme organ, it was rather by smells and sounds that the neutral notion of St. Bart's impressed itself on his consciousness. There was the musty, dull reek of old varnished wood in the dorms, and the night sounds in the alcoves—loud gastric explosions and a special squeaking of bed springs, accentuated for effect—and the bell in the hallway, in the hollow of one's headache, at 6:45 A.M. There was the odor of idolatry and incense coming from the burner that hung on chains and on shadows of chains from the ribbed ceiling of the chapel; and there was the Reverend Hopper's mellow voice, nicely blending vulgarity with refinement; and Hymn 166, "Sun of My Soul," which new boys were required to learn by heart; and there was, in the locker room, the immemorial sweat of the hamper on wheels, which held a communal supply of athletic supporters—a beastly gray tangle, from which one had to untwist a strap for oneself to put on at the start of the sport period—and how harsh and sad the clusters of cries from each of the four playing fields!

With an intelligence quotient of about a hundred and eighty and an average grade of ninety, Victor easily ranked first in a class of thirty-six and was, in fact, one of the three best scholars in the school. He had little respect for most of his teachers; but he revered Lake, a tremendously obese man with shaggy eyebrows and hairy hands and an attitude of somber embarrassment in the presence of athletic, rosy-cheeked lads (Victor was neither). Lake was enthroned, Buddhalike, in a curiously neat studio that looked more like a reception room in an art gallery than a workshop. Nothing adorned its pale gray walls except two identically framed pictures: a copy of Gertrude Käsebier's photographic masterpiece "Mother and Child" (1897), with the wistful, angelic infant looking up and away (at what?); and a similarly toned reproduction of the head of Christ from Rembrandt's "The Pilgrims of Emmaus," with the same, though slightly less celestial, expression of eyes and mouth.

He had been born in Ohio, had studied in Paris and Rome, had taught in Ecuador and Japan. He was a recognized art expert, and it puzzled people why, during the past ten winters, Lake chose to bury himself at St. Bart's. While endowed with the morose temper of genius, he lacked originality and was aware of that lack; his own paintings always seemed beautifully clever imitations, although one could never quite tell whose manner he mimicked. His profound knowledge of innumerable techniques, his indifference to "schools" and "trends," his detestation of quacks, his conviction that there was no difference whatever between a genteel aquarelle of yesterday and, say, conventional neo-plasticism or banal non-objectivism of today, and that nothing but individual talent mattered—these views made of him an unusual teacher. St. Bart's was not particularly pleased either with Lake's methods or with their results, but kept him on because it was fashionable to have at least one distinguished freak on the staff. Among the many exhilarating things Lake taught was that the order of the solar spectrum is not a closed circle but a spiral of tints from cadmium red and oranges through a strontian yellow and a pale paradisal green to cobalt blues and violets, at which point the sequence does not grade into red again but passes into another spiral, which starts with a kind of lavender gray and goes on to Cinderella shades transcending human perception. He taught that there is no such thing as the Ashcan

School or the Cache Cache School or the Cancan School.
That the work of art created with string, stamps, a Leftist
newspaper, and the droppings of doves is based on a series of
dreary platitudes. That there is nothing more banal and more
bourgeois than paranoia. That Dali is really Norman Rock-
well's twin brother kidnaped by gypsies in babyhood. That
Van Gogh is second-rate and Picasso supreme, despite his
commercial foibles; and that if Degas could immortalize a
calèche, why could not Victor Wind do the same to a motor
car?

One way to do it might be by making the scenery penetrate
the automobile. A polished black sedan was a good subject,
especially if parked at the intersection of a tree-bordered street
and one of those heavyish spring skies whose bloated gray
clouds and amoeba-shaped blotches of blue seem more physical than the reticent elms and evasive pavement. Now break
the body of the car into separate curves and panels; then put
it together in terms of reflections. These will be different for
each part: the top will display inverted trees with blurred
branches growing like roots into a washily photographed sky,
with a whalelike building swimming by—an architectural afterthought; one side of the hood will be coated with a band
of rich celestial cobalt; a most delicate pattern of black twigs
will be mirrored in the outside surface of the rear window;
and a remarkable desert view, a distended horizon, with a remote house here and a lone tree there, will stretch along the
bumper. This mimetic and integrative process Lake called the
necessary "naturalization" of man-made things. In the streets
of Cranton, Victor would find a suitable specimen of car and
loiter around it. Suddenly the sun, half masked but dazzling,
would join him. For the sort of theft Victor was contemplating
there could be no better accomplice. In the chrome plating,
in the glass of a sun-rimmed headlamp, he would see a view
of the street and himself comparable to the microcosmic version of a room (with a dorsal view of diminutive people) in
that very special and very magical small convex mirror that,
half a millennium ago, Van Eyck and Petrus Christus and Mem-
ling used to paint into their detailed interiors, behind the sour
merchant or the domestic Madonna.

To the latest issue of the school magazine Victor had contributed a poem about painters, over the *nom de guerre* Moinet, and under the motto "Bad reds should all be avoided; even if carefully manufactured, they are still bad" (quoted from an old book on the technique of painting but smacking of a political aphorism). The poem began:

> Leonardo! Strange diseases
> strike at madders mixed with lead:
> nun-pale now are Mona Lisa's
> lips that you had made so red.

He dreamed of mellowing his pigments as the Old Masters had done—with honey, fig juice, poppy oil, and the slime of pink snails. He loved water colors and he loved oils, but was wary of the too fragile pastel and the too coarse distemper. He studied his mediums with the care and patience of an insatiable child—one of those painter's apprentices (it is now Lake who is dreaming!), lads with bobbed hair and bright eyes who would spend years grinding colors in the workshop of some great Italian skiagrapher, in a world of amber and paradisal glazes. At eight, he had once told his mother that he wanted to paint air. At nine, he had known the sensuous delight of a graded wash. What did it matter to him that gentle chiaroscuro, offspring of veiled values and translucent undertones, had long since died behind the prison bars of abstract art, in the poorhouse of hideous primitivism? He placed various objects in turn—an apple, a pencil, a chess pawn, a comb—behind a glass of water and peered through it at each studiously: the red apple became a clear-cut red band bounded by a straight horizon, half a glass of Red Sea, Arabia Felix. The short pencil, if held obliquely, curved like a stylized snake, but if held vertically became monstrously fat—almost pyramidal. The black pawn, if moved to and fro, divided into a couple of black ants. The comb, stood on end, resulted in the glass's seeming to fill with beautifully striped liquid, a zebra cocktail.

6

On the eve of the day on which Victor had planned to arrive, Pnin entered a sport shop in Waindell's Main Street and asked for a football. The request was unseasonable but he was offered one.

"No, no," said Pnin, "I do not wish an egg or, for example, a torpedo. I want a simple football ball. Round!"

And with wrists and palms he outlined a portable world. It was the same gesture he used in class when speaking of the "harmonical wholeness" of Pushkin.

The salesman lifted a finger and silently fetched a soccer ball.

"Yes, this I will buy," said Pnin with dignified satisfaction.

Carrying his purchase, wrapped in brown paper and Scotch-taped, he entered a bookstore and asked for *Martin Eden.*

"Eden, Eden, Eden," the tall dark lady in charge repeated rapidly, rubbing her forehead. "Let me see, you don't mean a book on the British statesman? Or do you?"

"I mean," said Pnin, "a celebrated work by the celebrated American writer Jack London."

"London, London, London," said the woman, holding her temples.

Pipe in hand, her husband, a Mr. Tweed, who wrote topical poetry, came to the rescue. After some search he brought from the dusty depths of his not very prosperous store an old edition of *The Son of the Wolf.*

"I'm afraid," he said, "that's all we have by this author."

"Strange!" said Pnin. "The vicissitudes of celebrity! In Russia, I remember, everybody—little children, full-grown people, doctors, advocates—everybody read and reread him. This is not his best book but O.K., O.K., I will take it."

On coming home to the house where he roomed that year, Professor Pnin laid out the ball and the book on the desk of the guest room upstairs. Cocking his head, he surveyed these gifts. The ball did not look nice in its shapeless wrapping; he disrobed it. Now it showed its handsome leather. The room was tidy and cozy. A schoolboy should like that picture of a snowball knocking off a professor's top hat. The bed had just been made by the cleaning woman; old Bill Sheppard, the landlord, had come up from the first floor and had gravely screwed a new bulb into the desk lamp. A warm humid wind pressed through the open window, and one could hear the noise of an exuberant creek that ran below. It was going to rain. Pnin closed the window.

In his own room, on the same floor, he found a note. A laconic wire from Victor had been transmitted by phone: it said that he would be exactly twenty-four hours late.

7

Victor and five other boys were being held over one precious day of Easter vacation for smoking cigars in the attic. Victor, who had a queasy stomach and no dearth of olefactory phobias (all of which had been lovingly concealed from the Winds), had not actually participated in the smoking, beyond a couple of wry puffs; several times he had dutifully followed to the forbidden attic two of his best friends—adventurous, boisterous boys, Tony Brade, Jr., and Lance Boke. You penetrated there through the trunk room and then up an iron ladder, which emerged upon a catwalk right under the roof. Here the fascinating, strangely brittle skeleton of the building became both visible and tangible, with all its beams and boards, maze of partitions, sliced shadows, flimsy laths through which the foot collapsed to a crepitation of plaster dislodged from unseen ceilings beneath. The labyrinth ended in a small platform hooded within a recess at the very peak of the gable, among a motley mess of old comic books and recent cigar ashes. The ashes were discovered; the boys confessed. Tony Brade, the grandson of a famous St. Bart's headmaster, was given permission to leave, for family reasons; a fond cousin wished to see him before sailing for Europe. Wisely, Tony begged to be detained with the rest.

The headmaster in Victor's time was, as I have already said, the Reverend Mr. Hopper, a dark-haired, fresh-faced pleasant nonentity, greatly admired by Bostonian matrons. As Victor and his fellow culprits were at dinner with the entire Hopper family, various crystalline hints were dropped here and there, especially by sweet-voiced Mrs. Hopper, an Englishwoman whose aunt had married an earl; the Reverend might relent and the six boys be taken that last evening to a movie in town instead of being sent early to bed. And after dinner, with a kindly wink, she bade them accompany the Reverend, who briskly walked hallward.

Old-fashioned trustees might find it proper to condone the floggings that Hopper had inflicted on special offenders once or twice in the course of his brief and undistinguished career; but what no boy could stomach was the little mean smirk which crooked the headmaster's red lips as he paused on his way to the hall to pick up a neatly folded square of cloth—his cassock and surplice; the station wagon was at the door, and "putting the clinch on the punishment," as the boys expressed it, the false clergyman treated them to a guest performance at Rudbern, twelve miles away, in a cold brick church, before a meager congregation.

8

Theoretically, the simplest way to reach Waindell from Cranton was to get by taxi to Framingham, catch a fast train to Albany, and then a local for a shorter stretch in a northwestern direction; actually, the simplest way was also the most unpractical one. Whether there was some old solemn feud between those railways, or whether both had united to grant a sporting chance to other means of conveyance, the fact remained that no matter how you juggled with timetables, a three-hour wait at Albany between trains was the briefest you could hope to achieve.

There was a bus leaving Albany at 11 A.M. and arriving at Waindell at around 3 P.M. but that meant taking the 6:31 A.M. train from Framingham; Victor felt he could not get up in time; he took, instead, a slightly later and considerably slower train that allowed him to catch at Albany the last bus to Waindell, which deposited him there at half past eight in the evening.

It rained all the way. It was raining when he arrived at the Waindell terminal. Because of a streak of dreaminess and a gentle abstraction in his nature, Victor in any queue was always at its very end. He had long since grown used to this handicap, as one grows used to weak sight or a limp. Stooping a little because of his height, he followed without impatience the passengers that filed out through the bus onto the shining asphalt: two lumpy old ladies in semitransparent raincoats, like potatoes in cellophane; a small boy of seven or eight with a crew cut and a frail, hollowed nape; a many-angled, diffident, elderly cripple, who declined all assistance and came out in parts; three rosy-kneed Waindell coeds in shorts; the small boy's exhausted mother; a number of other passengers; and then—Victor, with a grip in his hand and two magazines under his arm.

In an archway of the bus station a totally bald man with a brownish complexion, wearing dark glasses and carrying a black brief case, was bending in amiable interrogatory welcome over the thin-necked little boy, who, however, kept shaking his head and pointing to his mother, who was waiting for her luggage to emerge from the Greyhound's belly. Shyly and gaily Victor interrupted the *quid pro quo*. The brown-domed gentleman took off his glasses and, unbending himself, looked up, up, up at tall, tall, tall Victor, at his blue eyes and reddish-brown hair. Pnin's well-developed zygomatic muscles raised and rounded his tanned cheeks; his forehead, his nose, and even his large beautiful ears took part in the smile. All in all, it was an extremely satisfactory meeting.

Pnin suggested leaving the luggage and walking one block—if Victor was not afraid of the rain (it was pouring hard, and the asphalt glistened in the darkness, tarnlike, under large, noisy trees). It would be, Pnin conjectured, a treat for the boy to have a late meal in a diner.

"You arrived well? You had no disagreeable adventures?"

"None, sir."

"You are very hungry?"

"No, sir. Not particularly."

"My name is Timofey," said Pnin, as they made themselves comfortable at a window table in the shabby old diner. "Second syllable pronounced as 'muff,' ahksent on last syllable, 'ey' as in 'prey' but a little more protracted. 'Timofey Pavlovich Pnin,' which means 'Timothy the son of Paul.' The pahtronymic has the ahksent on the first syllable and the rest is sloored—Timofey Pahlch. I have a long time debated with myself—let us wipe these knives and these forks—and have concluded that you must call me simply Mr. Tim or, even shorter, Tim, as do some of my extremely sympathetic colleagues. It is—what do you want to eat? Veal cutlet? O.K., I will also eat veal cutlet—it is naturally a concession to America, my new country, wonderful America which sometimes surprises me but always provokes respect. In the beginning I was greatly embarrassed——"

In the beginning Pnin was greatly embarrassed by the ease with which first names were bandied about in America: after a single party, with an iceberg in a drop of whisky to start and with a lot of whisky in a little tap water to finish, you were supposed to call a gray-templed stranger "Jim," while he called you "Tim" for ever and ever. If you forgot and called him next morning Professor Everett (his real name to you) it was (for him) a horrible insult. In reviewing his Russian friends throughout Europe and the United States, Timofey Pahlch could easily count at least sixty dear people whom he had intimately known since, say, 1920, and whom he never called anything but Vadim Vadimich, Ivan Hristoforovich, or Samuil Izrailevich, as the case might be, and who called him by his name and patronymic with the same effusive sympathy, over a strong warm handshake, whenever they met: "Ah, Timofey Pahlch! *Nu kak?* (Well how?) *A vï, baten'ka, zdorovo postareli* (Well, well, old boy, you certainly don't look any younger)!"

Pnin talked. His talk did not amaze Victor, who had heard many Russians speak English, and he was not bothered by the fact that Pnin pronounced the word "family" as if the first syllable were the French for "woman."

"I speak in French with much more facility than in English," said Pnin, "but you—*vous comprenez le français? Bien? Assez bien? Un peu?*"

"*Très un peu*," said Victor.

"Regrettable, but nothing to be done. I will now speak to you about sport. The first description of box in Russian literature we find in a poem by Mihail Lermontov, born 1814, killed 1841—easy to remember. The first description of tennis, on the other hand, is found in *Anna Karenina*, Tolstoy's novel, and is related to year 1875. In youth one day, in the Russian countryside, latitude of Labrador, a racket was given to me to play with the family of the Orientalist Gotovtsev, perhaps you have heard. It was, I recollect, a splendid summer day and we played, played, played until all the twelve balls were lost. You also will recollect the past with interest when old.

"Another game," continued Pnin, lavishly sugaring his coffee, "was naturally *kroket*. I was a champion of *kroket*. However, the favorite national recreation was so-called *gorodki*, which means "little towns." One remembers a place in the garden and the wonderful atmosphere of youth: I was strong, I wore an embroidered Russian shirt, nobody plays now such healthy games."

He finished his cutlet and proceeded with the subject:

"One drew," said Pnin, "a big square on the ground, one placed there, like columns, cylindrical pieces of wood, you know, and then from some distance one threw at them a thick stick, very hard, like a boomerang, with a wide, wide development of the arm—excuse me—fortunately it is sugar, not salt."

"I still hear," said Pnin, picking up the sprinkler and shaking his head a little at the surprising persistence of memory, "I still hear the *trakh!*, the crack when one hit the wooden pieces and they jumped in the air. Will you not finish the meat? You do not like it?"

"It's awfully good," said Victor, "but I am not very hungry."

"Oh, you must eat more, much more if you want to be a footballist."

"I'm afraid I don't care much for football. In fact, I hate football. I'm not very good at any game, really."

"You are not a lover of football?" said Pnin, and a look of dismay crept over his large expressive face. He pursed his lips. He opened them—but said nothing. In silence he ate his vanilla ice cream, which contained no vanilla and was not made of cream.

"We will now take your luggage and a taxi," said Pnin.

As soon as they reached the Sheppard house, Pnin ushered Victor into the parlor and rapidly introduced him to his landlord, old Bill Sheppard, formerly superintendent of the college grounds (who was totally deaf and wore a white button in one ear), and to his brother, Bob Sheppard, who had recently come from Buffalo to live with Bill after the latter's wife died. Leaving Victor with them for a minute, Pnin hastily stomped upstairs. The house was a vulnerable construction, and objects in the rooms downstairs reacted with various vibrations to the vigorous footsteps on the upper landing and to the sudden rasp of a window sash in the guest room.

"Now that picture there," deaf Mr. Sheppard was saying, pointing with a didactic finger at a large muddy water color on the wall, "represents the farm where my brother and I used to spend summers fifty years ago. It was painted by my mother's schoolmate, Grace Wells: her son, Charlie Wells, owns that hotel in Waindellville—I am sure Dr. Neen has met him—a very very fine man. My late wife was an artist too. I shall show you some works of hers in a moment. Well, that tree there, behind that barn—you can just make it out——"

A terrible clatter and crash came from the stairs: Pnin, on his way down, had lost his footing.

"In the spring of 1905," said Mr. Sheppard, wagging his index at the picture, "under that cottonwood tree——"

He noticed that his brother and Victor had hurried out of the room to the foot of the stairs. Poor Pnin had come down the last steps on his back. He lay supine for a moment, his eyes moving to and fro. He was helped to his feet. No bones were broken.

Pnin smiled and said: "It is like the splendid story of Tolstoy—you must read one day, Victor—about Ivan Ilyich Golovin who fell and got in consequence kidney of the cancer. Victor will now come upstairs with me."

Victor followed, with grip. There was a reproduction of Van Gogh's "La Berceuse" on the landing and Victor, in passing, acknowledged it with a nod of ironic recognition. The guest room was full of the noise of the rain falling on fragrant branches in the framed blackness of the open window. On the desk lay a wrapped-up book and a ten-dollar bill. Victor beamed and bowed to his gruff but kindly host. "Unwrap," said Pnin.

With courteous eagerness, Victor obeyed. Then he sat down on the edge of the bed and, his auburn hair coming down in glossy lanks over his right temple, his striped tie dangling out of the front of his gray jacket, his bulky gray-flanneled knees parted, zestfully opened the book. He intended to praise it— first, because it was a gift, and second, because he believed it

to be a translation from Pnin's mother tongue. He remembered there had been at the Psychotherapeutic Institute a Dr.
Yakov London from Russia. Rather unfortunately, Victor lit
upon a passage about Zarinska, the Yukon Indian Chief's
daughter, and lightheartedly mistook her for a Russian
maiden. "Her great black eyes were fixed upon her tribesmen
in fear and in defiance. So extreme the tension, she had forgotten to breathe . . ."

"I think I'm going to like this," said polite Victor. "Last
summer I read *Crime and*——. A young yawn distended his
staunchly smiling mouth. With sympathy, with approval, with
heartache Pnin looked at Liza yawning after one of those long
happy parties at the Arbenins' or the Polyanskis' in Paris, fifteen, twenty, twenty-five years ago.

"No more reading today," said Pnin. "I know that it is a
very exciting book but you will read and read tomorrow. I
wish you good night. The bathroom is across the landing."

He shook hands with Victor and marched to his own room.

9

It still rained. All the lights in the Sheppard house were out.
The brook in the gully behind the garden, a trembling trickle
most of the time, was tonight a loud torrent that tumbled
over itself in its avid truckling to gravity, as it carried through
corridors of beech and spruce last year's leaves, and some leafless twigs, and a brand-new, unwanted soccer ball that had
recently rolled into the water from the sloping lawn after Pnin
disposed of it by defenestration. He had fallen asleep at last,
despite the discomfort in his back, and in the course of one
of those dreams that still haunt Russian fugitives, even when
a third of a century has elapsed since their escape from the
Bolsheviks, Pnin saw himself fantastically cloaked, fleeing
through great pools of ink under a cloud-barred moon from
a chimerical palace, and then pacing a desolate strand with his
dead friend Ilya Isidorovich Polyanski as they waited for some
mysterious deliverance to arrive in a throbbing boat from beyond the hopeless sea. The Sheppard brothers were both
awake in their adjacent beds, on their Beautyrest mattresses;
the younger listened in the dark to the rain and wondered if

after all they should sell the house with its audible roof and wet garden; the elder lay thinking of silence, of a green damp churchyard, of an old farm, of a poplar that years ago lightning had struck, killing John Head, a dim, distant relation. Victor had, for once, fallen asleep as soon as he put his head under his pillow—a recently evolved method about which Dr. Eric Wind (sitting on a bench, near a fountain, in Quito, Ecuador) would never learn. Around half past one the Sheppards started to snore, the deaf one doing it with a rattle at the end of each exhalation and many volumes louder than the other, a modest and melancholy wheezer. On the sandy beach where Pnin was still pacing (his worried friend had gone home for a map), there appeared before him a set of approaching footprints, and he awoke with a gasp. His back hurt. It was now past four. The rain had stopped.

Pnin sighed a Russian "okh-okh-okh" sigh, and sought a more comfortable position. Old Bill Sheppard trudged to the downstairs bathroom, brought down the house, then trudged back.

Presently all were asleep again. It was a pity nobody saw the display in the empty street, where the auroral breeze wrinkled a large luminous puddle, making of the telephone wires reflected in it illegible lines of black zigzags.

Chapter Five

F ROM the top platform of an old, seldom used lookout
tower—a "prospect tower" as it was formerly termed—
that stood on a wooded hill eight hundred feet high, called
Mount Ettrick, in one of the fairest of New England's fair
states, the adventurous summer tourist (Miranda or Mary,
Tom or Jim, whose penciled names were almost obliterated
on the balustrade) might observe a vast sea of greenery,
composed mainly of maple, beech, tacamahac, and pine.
Some five miles west, a slender white church steeple marked
the spot where nestled the small town of Onkwedo, once famous for its springs. Three miles north, in a riverside clearing at the foot of a grassy knoll, one could distinguish the
gables of an ornate house (variously known as Cook's,
Cook's Place, Cook's Castle, or The Pines—its initial ap-
pellation). Along the south side of Mount Ettrick, a state
highway continued east after passing through Onkwedo. Numerous dirt roads and foot trails crisscrossed the timbered
plain within the triangle of land limited by the somewhat tortuous hypotenuse of a rural paved road that weaved northeast
from Onkwedo to The Pines, the long cathetus of the state
highway just mentioned, and the short cathetus of a river
spanned by a steel bridge near Mount Ettrick and a wooden
one near Cook's.

On a dull warm day in the summer of 1954, Mary or Almira,
or, for that matter, Wolfgang von Goethe, whose name had
been carved in the balustrade by some old-fashioned wag,
might have noticed an automobile that had turned off the
highway just before reaching the bridge and was now nosing
and poking this way and that in a maze of doubtful roads. It
moved warily and unsteadily, and whenever it changed its
mind, it would slow down and raise dust behind like a back-
kicking dog. At times it might seem, to a less sympathetic soul
than our imagined observer, that this pale blue, egg-shaped
two-door sedan, of uncertain age and in mediocre condition,
was manned by an idiot. Actually its driver was Professor
Timofey Pnin, of Waindell College.

Pnin had started taking lessons at the Waindell Driving
School early in the year, but "true understanding," as he put
it, had come to him only when, a couple of months later, he
had been laid up with a sore back and had done nothing but
study with deep enjoyment the forty-page *Driver's Manual*,
issued by the State Governor in collaboration with another
expert, and the article on "Automobile" in the *Encyclopedia
Americana*, with illustrations of Transmissions, and Carbu-
retors, and Brakes, and a Member of the Glidden Tour, *circa*
1905, stuck in the mud of a country road among depressing
surroundings. Then and only then was the dual nature of his
initial inklings transcended at last as he lay on his sickbed,
wiggling his toes and shifting phantom gears. During actual
lessons with a harsh instructor who cramped his style, issued
unnecessary directives in yelps of technical slang, tried to wres-
tle the wheel from him at corners, and kept irritating a calm,
intelligent pupil with expressions of vulgar detraction, Pnin
had been totally unable to combine perceptually the car he
was driving in his mind and the car he was driving on the
road. Now the two fused at last. If he failed the first time he
took his driver's-license test, it was mainly because he started
an argument with the examiner in an ill-timed effort to prove
that nothing could be more humiliating to a rational creature
than being required to encourage the development of a base
conditional reflex by stopping at a red light when there was
not an earthly soul around, heeled or wheeled. He was more
circumspect the next time, and passed. An irresistible senior,
enrolled in his Russian Language course, Marilyn Hohn, sold
him for a hundred dollars her humble old car: she was getting
married to the owner of a far grander machine. The trip from
Waindell to Onkwedo, with an overnight stop at a tourist
home, had been slow and difficult but uneventful. Just before
entering Onkwedo, he had pulled up at a gas station and had
got out for a breath of country air. An inscrutable white sky
hung over a clover field, and from a pile of firewood near a
shack came a rooster's cry, jagged and gaudy—a vocal cox-
comb. Some chance intonation on the part of this slightly
hoarse bird, combined with the warm wind pressing itself
against Pnin in search of attention, recognition, anything,
briefly reminded him of a dim dead day when he, a Petrograd

University freshman, had arrived at the small station of a Baltic summer resort, and the sounds, and the smells, and the sadness——

"Kind of muggy," said the hairy-armed attendant, as he started to wipe the windshield.

Pnin took a letter out of his wallet, unfolded the tiny mimeographed-sketch map attached to it, and asked the attendant how far was the church at which one was supposed to turn left to reach Cook's Place. It was really striking how the man resembled Pnin's colleague at Waindell College, Dr. Hagen—one of those random likenesses as pointless as a bad pun.

"Well, there is a better way to get there," said the false Hagen. "The trucks have messed up that road, and besides you won't like the way it winds. Now you just drive on. Drive through the town. Five miles out of Onkwedo, just after you have passed the trail to Mount Ettrick on your left, and just before reaching the bridge, take the first left turn. It's a good gravel road."

He stepped briskly around the hood and lunged with his rag at the windshield from the other side.

"You turn north and go on bearing north at each crossing—there are quite a few logging trails in those woods but you just bear north and you'll get to Cook's in twelve minutes flat. You can't miss it."

Pnin had now been in that maze of forest roads for about an hour and had come to the conclusion that "bear north," and in fact the word "north" itself, meant nothing to him. He also could not explain what had compelled him, a rational being, to listen to a chance busybody instead of firmly following the pedantically precise instructions that his friend, Alexandr Petrovich Kukolnikov (known locally as Al Cook) had sent him when inviting him to spend the summer at his large and hospitable country house. Our luckless car operator had by now lost himself too thoroughly to be able to go back to the highway, and since he had little experience in maneuvering on rutty narrow roads, with ditches and even ravines gaping on either side, his various indecisions and gropings took those bizarre visual forms that an observer on the lookout tower might have followed with a compassionate eye; but there was no living creature in that forlorn and listless upper region except for an ant who had his own troubles, having, after hours of inept perseverance, somehow reached the upper platform and the balustrade (his *autostrada*) and was getting all bothered and baffled much in the same way as that preposterous toy car progressing below. The wind had subsided. Under the pale sky the sea of tree tops seemed to harbor no life. Presently, however, a gun shot popped, and a twig leaped into the sky. The dense upper boughs in that part of the otherwise stirless forest started to move in a receding sequence of shakes or jumps, with a swinging lilt from tree to tree, after which all was still again. Another minute passed, and then everything happened at once: the ant found an upright beam leading to the roof of the tower and started to ascend it with renewed zest; the sun appeared; and Pnin at the height of hopelessness, found himself on a paved road with a rusty but still glistening sign directing wayfarers "To The Pines."

2

Al Cook was a son of Piotr Kukolnikov, wealthy Moscow merchant of Old-Believers antecedents, self-made man, Maecenas and philanthropist—the famous Kukolnikov who under the last Tsar had been twice imprisoned in a fairly comfortable fortress for giving financial assistance to Social-Revolutionary groups (terrorists, mainly), and under Lenin had been put to death as an "Imperialistic spy" after almost a week of medieval tortures in a Soviet jail. His family reached America via Harbin, around 1925, and young Cook by dint of quiet perseverance, practical acumen, and some scientific training, rose to a high and secure position in a great chemical concern. A kindly, very reserved man of stocky build, with a large immobile face that was tied up in the middle by a neat little pince-nez, he looked what he was—a Business Executive, a Mason, a Golfer, a prosperous and cautious man. He spoke beautifully correct, neutral English, with only the softest shadow of a Slavic accent, and was a delightful host, of the silent variety, with a twinkling eye, and a highball in each hand; and only when some very old and beloved Russian friend was his midnight guest would Alexandr Petrovich suddenly start to discuss God, Lermontov, Liberty, and divulge a hereditary streak of rash

idealism that would have greatly confused a Marxist eaves-
dropper.

He married Susan Marshall, the attractive, voluble, blond
daughter of Charles G. Marshall, the inventor, and because
one could not imagine Alexandr and Susan otherwise than
raising a huge healthy family, it came as a shock to me and
other well-wishers to learn that as the result of an operation
Susan would remain childless all her life. They were still
young, loved each other with a sort of old-world simplicity
and integrity very soothing to observe, and instead of popu-
lating their country place with children and grandchildren,
they collected, every even-year summer, elderly Russians
(Cook's fathers or uncles, as it were); on odd-year summers
they would have *amerikantsï* (Americans), Alexandr's business
acquaintances or Susan's relatives and friends.

This was the first time Pnin was coming to The Pines but
I had been there before. Émigré Russians—liberals and intellectuals who had left Russia around 1920—could be found
swarming all over the place. You would find them in every
patch of speckled shade, sitting on rustic benches and discussing émigré writers—Bunin, Aldanov, Sirin; lying suspended in hammocks, with the Sunday issue of a Russian-
language newspaper over their faces in traditional defense
against flies; sipping tea with jam on the veranda; walking
in the woods and wondering about the edibility of local toad-
stools.

Samuil Lvovich Shpolyanski, a large majestically calm old
gentleman, and small, excitable, stuttering Count Fyodor Ni-
kitich Poroshin, both of whom, around 1920, had been members of one of those heroic Regional Governments that were
formed in the Russian provinces by democratic groups to
withstand Bolshevik dictatorship, would pace the avenue of
pines and discuss the tactics to be adopted at the next joint
meeting of the Free Russia Committee (which they had
founded in New York) with another, younger, anti-Commu-
nist organization. From a pavilion half smothered by locust
trees came fragments of a heated exchange between Professor
Bolotov, who taught the History of Philosophy, and Professor
Chateau, who taught the Philosophy of History: "Reality is
Duration," one voice, Bolotov's, would boom. "It is not!"

the other would cry. "A soap bubble is as real as a fossil tooth!"

Pnin and Chateau, both born in the late nineties of the nineteenth century, were comparative youngsters. Most of the other men had seen sixty and had trudged on. On the other hand, a few of the ladies, such as Countess Poroshin and Madam Bolotov, were still in their late forties and, thanks to the hygienic atmosphere of the New World, had not only preserved, but improved, their good looks. Some parents brought their offspring with them—healthy, tall, indolent, difficult American children of college age, with no sense of nature, and no Russian, and no interest whatsoever in the niceties of their parents' backgrounds and pasts. They seemed to live at The Pines on a physical and mental plane entirely different from that of their parents: now and then passing from their own level to ours through a kind of interdimensional shimmer; responding curtly to a well-meaning Russian joke or anxious piece of advice, and then fading away again; keeping always aloof (so that one felt one had engendered a brood of elves), and preferring any Onkwedo store product, any sort of canned goods to the marvelous Russian foods provided by the Kukolnikov household at loud, long dinners on the screened porch. With great distress Poroshin would say of his children (Igor and Olga, college sophomores) "My twins are exasperating. When I see them at home during breakfast or dinner and try to tell them most interesting, most exciting things—for instance, about local elective self-government in the Russian Far North in the seventeenth century or, say, something about the history of the first medical schools in Russia—there is, by the way, an excellent monograph by Chistovich on the subject, published in 1883—they simply wander off and turn on the radio in their rooms." Both young people were around the summer Pnin was invited to The Pines. But they stayed invisible; they would have been hideously bored in this out-of-the-way place, had not Olga's admirer, a college boy whose surname nobody seemed to know, arrived from Boston for the weekend in a spectacular car, and had not Igor found a congenial companion in Nina, the Bolotov girl, a handsome slattern with Egyptian eyes and brown limbs, who went to a dancing school in New York.

The household was looked after by Praskovia, a sturdy, sixty-year-old woman of the people with the vivacity of one a score of years younger. It was an exhilarating sight to watch her as she stood on the back porch surveying the chickens, knuckles on hips, dressed in baggy homemade shorts and a matronly blouse with rhinestones. She had nursed Alexandr and his brother when both were children in Harbin and now she was helped in her household duties by her husband, a gloomy and stolid old Cossack whose main passions in life were amateur bookbinding—a self-taught and almost pathological process that he was impelled to inflict upon any old catalogue or pulp magazine that came his way; the making of fruit liqueurs; and the killing of small forest animals.

Of that season's guests, Pnin knew well Professor Chateau, a friend of his youth, with whom he had attended the University of Prague in the early twenties, and he was also well acquainted with the Bolotovs, whom he had last seen in 1949 when he welcomed them with a speech at a formal dinner given them by the Association of Russian Émigré Scholars at the Barbizon-Plaza, upon the occasion of Bolotov's arrival from France. Personally, I never cared much for Bolotov and his philosophical works, which so oddly combine the obscure and the trite; the man's achievement is perhaps a mountain— but a mountain of platitudes; I have always liked, however, Varvara, the seedy philosopher's exuberant buxom wife. When she first visited The Pines, in 1951, she had never seen the New England countryside before. Its birches and bilberries deceived her into placing mentally Lake Onkwedo, not on the parallel of, say, Lake Ohrida in the Balkans, where it belonged, but on that of Lake Onega in northern Russia, where she had spent her first fifteen summers, before fleeing from the Bolsheviks to western Europe, with her aunt Lidia Vinogradov, the well-known feminist and social worker. Consequently the sight of a hummingbird in probing flight, or a catalpa in ample bloom, produced upon Varvara the effect of some unnatural or exotic vision. More fabulous than pictures in a bestiary were to her the tremendous porcupines that came to gnaw at the delicious, gamy old wood of the house, or the elegant, eerie little skunks that sampled the cat's milk in the backyard. She was nonplused and enchanted by the number of plants and creatures she could not identify, mistook Yellow Warblers for stray canaries, and on the occasion of Susan's birthday was known to have brought, with pride and panting enthusiasm, for the ornamentation of the dinner table, a profusion of beautiful poison-ivy leaves, hugged to her pink, freckled breast.

3

The Bolotovs and Madam Shpolyanski, a little lean woman in slacks, were the first people to see Pnin as he cautiously turned into a sandy avenue, bordered with wild lupines, and, sitting very straight, stiffly clutching the steering wheel as if he were a farmer more used to his tractor than to his car, entered, at ten miles an hour and in first gear, the grove of old, disheveled, curiously authentic-looking pines that separated the paved road from Cook's Castle.

Varvara buoyantly rose from the seat of the pavilion—where she and Roza Shpolyanski had just discovered Bolotov reading a battered book and smoking a forbidden cigarette. She greeted Pnin with a clapping of hands, while her husband showed as much geniality as he was capable of by slowly waving the book he had closed on his thumb to mark the place. Pnin killed the motor and sat beaming at his friends. The collar of his green sport shirt was undone; his partly unzipped windbreaker seemed too tight for his impressive torso; his bronzed bald head, with the puckered brow and conspicuous vermicular vein on the temple, bent low as he wrestled with the door handle and finally dived out of the car.

"*Avtomobil', kostyum—nu pryamo amerikanets* (a veritable American), *pryamo Ayzenhauer!*" said Varvara, and introduced Pnin to Roza Abramovna Shpolyanski.

"We had some mutual friends forty years ago," remarked that lady, peering at Pnin with curiosity.

"Oh, let us not mention such astronomical figures," said Bolotov, approaching and replacing with a grass blade the thumb he had been using as a bookmarker. "You know," he continued, shaking Pnin's hand, "I am rereading *Anna Karenin* for the seventh time and I derive as much rapture as I did, not forty, but sixty, years ago, when I was a lad of seven.

And, every time, one discovers new things—for instance I notice now that Lyov Nikolaich does not know on what day his novel starts: it seems to be Friday because that is the day the clockman comes to wind up the clocks in the Oblonski house, but it is also Thursday as mentioned in the conversation at the skating rink between Lyovin and Kitty's mother.''

''What on earth does it matter,'' cried Varvara. ''Who on earth wants to know the exact day?''

''I can tell you the exact day,'' said Pnin, blinking in the broken sunlight and inhaling the remembered tang of northern pines. ''The action of the novel starts in the beginning of 1872, namely on Friday, February the twenty-third by the New Style. In his morning paper Oblonski reads that Beust is rumored to have proceeded to Wiesbaden. This is of course Count Friedrich Ferdinand von Beust, who had just been appointed Austrian Ambassador to the Court of St. James's. After presenting his credentials, Beust had gone to the continent for a rather protracted Christmas vacation—had spent there two months with his family, and was now returning to London, where, according to his own memoirs in two volumes, preparations were under way for the thanksgiving service to be held in St. Paul's on February the twenty-seventh for the recovering from typhoid fever of the Prince of Wales. However (*odnako*), it really is hot here (*i zharko zhe u vas*)! I think I shall now present myself before the most luminous orbs (*presvetlïe ochi*, jocular) of Alexandr Petrovich and then go for a dip (*okupnutsya*, also jocular) in the river he so vividly describes in his letter.''

''Alexandr Petrovich is away till Monday, on business or pleasure,'' said Varvara Bolotov, ''but I think you will find Susanna Karlovna sun-bathing on her favorite lawn behind the house. Shout before you approach too near.''

4

Cook's Castle was a three-story brick-and-timber mansion built around 1860 and partly rebuilt half a century later, when Susan's father purchased it from the Dudley-Greene family in order to make of it a select resort hotel for the richer patrons of the curative Onkwedo Springs. It was an elaborate and ugly

building in a mongrel style, with the Gothic bristling through
remnants of French and Florentine, and when originally designed might have belonged to the variety which Samuel
Sloan, an architect of the time, classified as An Irregular
Northern Villa "well adapted to the highest requirements of
social life" and called "Northern" because of "the aspiring
tendency of its roof and towers." The piquancy of these pin-
nacles and the merry, somewhat even inebriated air the mansion had of having been composed of several smaller Northern
Villas, hoisted into mid-air and knocked together anyhow,
with parts of unassimilated roofs, half-hearted gables, cornices,
rustic quoins, and other projections sticking out on all sides,
had, alas, but briefly attracted tourists. By 1920, the Onkwedo
waters had mysteriously lost whatever magic they had contained, and after her father's death Susan had vainly tried to
sell The Pines, since they had another more comfortable house
in the residential quarter of the industrial city where her husband worked. However, now that they had got accustomed
to use the Castle for entertaining their numerous friends, Susan was glad that the meek beloved monster had found no
purchaser.

Within, the diversity was as great as without. Four spacious
rooms opened from the large hall that retained something of
its hostelic stage in the generous dimensions of the grate. The
hand rail of the stairs, and at least one of its spindles, dated
from 1720, having been transferred to the house, while it was
being built, from a far older one, whose very site was no
longer exactly known. Very ancient, too, were the beautiful
sideboard panels of game and fish in the dining room. In the
half dozen rooms of which each of the upper floors consisted,
and in the two wings in the rear, one could discover, among
disparate pieces of furniture, some charming satinwood bureau, some romantic rosewood sofa, but also all kinds of bulky
and miserable articles, broken chairs, dusty marble-topped tables, morose *étagères* with bits of dark-looking glass in the
back as mournful as the eyes of old apes. The chamber Pnin
got was a pleasant southeast one on the upper floor: it had
remnants of gilt paper on the walls, an army cot, a plain wash-
stand, and all kinds of shelves, brackets, and scrollwork

moldings. Pnin shook open the casement, smiled at the smiling forest, again remembered a distant first day in the country,
and presently walked down, clad in a new navy-blue bathrobe
and wearing on his bare feet a pair of ordinary rubber over-
shoes, a sensible precaution if one intends to walk through
damp and, perhaps, snake-infested grass. On the garden terrace he found Chateau.

Konstantin Ivanich Chateau, a subtle and charming scholar
of pure Russian lineage despite his surname (derived, I am
told, from that of a Russianized Frenchman who adopted orphaned Ivan), taught at a large New York university and had
not seen his very dear Pnin for at least five years. They embraced with a warm rumble of joy. I confess to have been
myself, at one time, under the spell of angelic Konstantin
Ivanich, namely, when we used to meet every day in the winter of 1935 or 1936 for a morning stroll under the laurels and
nettle trees of Grasse, southern France, where he then shared
a villa with several other Russian expatriates. His soft voice,
the gentlemanly St. Petersburgan burr of his *r*'s, his mild, melancholy caribou eyes, the auburn goatee he continuously
twiddled, with a shredding motion of his long, frail fingers—
everything about Chateau (to use a literary formula as old-
fashioned as he) produced a rare sense of well-being in his
friends. Pnin and he talked for a while, comparing notes. As
not unusual with firm-principled exiles, every time they met
after a separation they not only endeavored to catch up with
a personal past, but also to sum up by means of a few rapid
passwords—allusions, intonations impossible to render in a
foreign language—the course of recent Russian history, thirty-
five years of hopeless injustice following a century of struggling justice and glimmering hope. Next, they switched to the
usual shop talk of European teachers abroad, sighing and
shaking heads over the "typical American college student"
who does not know geography, is immune to noise, and
thinks education is but a means to get eventually a remunerative job. Then they inquired about each other's work in progress, and both were extremely modest and reticent about
their respective researches. Finally, as they walked along a
meadow path, brushing against the goldenrod, toward the

wood where a rocky river ran, they spoke of their healths:
Chateau, who looked so jaunty, with one hand in the pocket
of his white flannel trousers and his lustring coat rather rak-
ishly opened on a flannel waistcoat, cheerfully said that in the
near future he would have to undergo an exploratory operation of the abdomen, and Pnin said, laughing, that every time
he was X-rayed, doctors vainly tried to puzzle out what they
termed "a shadow behind the heart."

"Good title for a bad novel," remarked Chateau.

As they were passing a grassy knoll just before entering the
wood, a pink-faced venerable man in a seersucker suit, with a
shock of white hair and a tumefied purple nose resembling a
huge raspberry, came striding toward them down the sloping
field, a look of disgust contorting his features.

"I have to go back for my hat," he cried dramatically as he
drew near.

"Are you acquainted?" murmured Chateau, fluttering his
hands introductively. "Timofey Pavlich Pnin, Ivan Ilyich Gramineev."

"*Moyo pochtenie* (My respects)," said both men, bowing to
each other over a powerful handshake.

"I thought," resumed Gramineev, a circumstantial narrator,
"that the day would continue as overcast as it had begun. By
stupidity (*po gluposti*) I came out with an unprotected head.
Now the sun is roasting my brains. I have to interrupt my
work."

He gestured toward the top of the knoll. There his easel
stood in delicate silhouette against the blue sky. From that
crest he had been painting a view of the valley beyond, complete with quaint old barn, gnarled apple tree, and kine.

"I can offer you my panama," said kind Chateau, but Pnin
had already produced from his bathrobe pocket a large red
handkerchief: he expertly twisted each of its corners into a
knot.

"Admirable. . . . Most grateful," said Gramineev, adjusting this headgear.

"One moment," said Pnin. "You must tuck in the knots."

This done, Gramineev started walking up the field toward
his easel. He was a well-known, frankly academic painter,
whose soulful oils—"Mother Volga," "Three Old Friends"

(lad, nag, dog), "April Glade," and so forth—still graced a museum in Moscow.

"Somebody told me," said Chateau, as he and Pnin continued to progress riverward, "that Liza's boy has an extraordinary talent for painting. Is that correct?"

"Yes," answered Pnin. "All the more vexing (*tem bolee obidno*) that his mother, who I think is about to marry a third time, took Victor suddenly to California for the rest of the summer, whereas if he had accompanied me here, as had been planned, he would have had the splendid opportunity of being coached by Gramineev."

"You exaggerate the splendor," softly rejoined Chateau.

They reached the bubbling and glistening stream. A concave ledge between higher and lower diminutive cascades formed a natural swimming pool under the alders and pines. Chateau, a non-bather, made himself comfortable on a boulder. Throughout the academic year Pnin had regularly exposed his body to the radiation of a sun lamp; hence, when he stripped down to his bathing trunks, he glowed in the dappled sunlight of the riverside grove with a rich mahogany tint. He removed his cross and his rubbers.

"Look, how pretty," said observant Chateau.

A score of small butterflies, all of one kind, were settled on a damp patch of sand, their wings erect and closed, showing their pale undersides with dark dots and tiny orange-rimmed peacock spots along the hindwing margins; one of Pnin's shed rubbers disturbed some of them and, revealing the celestial hue of their upper surface, they fluttered around like blue snowflakes before settling again.

"Pity Vladimir Vladimirovich is not here," remarked Chateau. "He would have told us all about these enchanting insects."

"I have always had the impression that his entomology was merely a pose."

"Oh no," said Chateau. "You will lose it some day," he added, pointing to the Greek Catholic cross on a golden chainlet that Pnin had removed from his neck and hung on a twig. Its glint perplexed a cruising dragonfly.

"Perhaps I would not mind losing it," said Pnin. "As you well know, I wear it merely from sentimental reasons. And the

sentiment is becoming burdensome. After all, there is too
much of the physical about this attempt to keep a particle of
one's childhood in contact with one's breastbone."

"You are not the first to reduce faith to a sense of touch,"
said Chateau, who was a practicing Greek Catholic and deplored his friend's agnostic attitude.

A horsefly applied itself, blind fool, to Pnin's bald head, and
was stunned by a smack of his meaty palm.

From a smaller boulder than the one upon which Chateau
was perched, Pnin gingerly stepped down into the brown and
blue water. He noticed he still had his wrist watch—removed
it and left it inside one of his rubbers. Slowly swinging his
tanned shoulders, Pnin waded forth, the loopy shadows of
leaves shivering and slipping down his broad back. He stopped
and breaking the glitter and shade around him, moistened his
inclined head, rubbed his nape with wet hands, soused in turn
each armpit, and then, joining both palms, glided into the
water, his dignified breast stroke sending off ripples on either
side. Around the natural basin, Pnin swam in state. He swam
with a rhythmical splutter—half gurgle, half puff. Rhythmically he opened his legs and widened them out at the knees
while flexing and straightening out his arms like a giant frog.
After two minutes of this, he waded out and sat on the boulder to dry. Then he put on his cross, his wrist watch, his
rubbers, and his bathrobe.

5

Dinner was served on the screened porch. As he sat down
next to Bolotov and began to stir the sour cream in his red
botvinia (chilled beet soup), wherein pink ice cubes tinkled,
Pnin automatically resumed an earlier conversation.

"You will notice," he said, "that there is a significant difference between Lyovin's spiritual time and Vronski's physical
one. In mid-book, Lyovin and Kitty lag behind Vronski and
Anna by a whole year. When, on a Sunday evening in May
1876, Anna throws herself under that freight train, she has
existed more than four years since the beginning of the novel,
but in the case of the Lyovins, during the same period, 1872

to 1876, hardly three years have elapsed. It is the best example of relativity in literature that is known to me.''

After dinner, a game of croquet was suggested. These people favored the time-honored but technically illegal setting of hoops, where two of the ten are crossed at the center of the ground to form the so-called Cage or Mousetrap. It became immediately clear that Pnin, who teamed with Madam Bolotov against Shpolyanski and Countess Poroshin, was by far the best player of the lot. As soon as the pegs were driven in and the game started, the man was transfigured. From his habitual, slow, ponderous, rather rigid self, he changed into a terrifically mobile, scampering, mute, sly-visaged hunchback. It seemed to be always his turn to play. Holding his mallet very low and daintily swinging it between his parted spindly legs (he had created a minor sensation by changing into Bermuda shorts expressly for the game), Pnin foreshadowed every stroke with nimble aim-taking oscillations of the mallet head, then gave the ball an accurate tap, and forthwith, still hunched, and with the ball still rolling, walked rapidly to the spot where he had planned for it to stop. With geometrical gusto, he ran it through hoops, evoking cries of admiration from the onlookers. Even Igor Poroshin, who was passing by like a shadow with two cans of beer he was carrying to some private banquet, stopped for a second and shook his head appreciatively before vanishing in the shrubbery. Plaints and protests, however, would mingle with the applause when Pnin, with brutal indifference, croqueted, or rather rocketed, an adversary's ball. Placing in contact with it his own ball, and firmly putting his curiously small foot upon the latter, he would bang at his ball so as to drive the other up the country by the shock of the stroke. When appealed to, Susan said it was completely against the rules, but Madam Shpolyanski insisted it was perfectly acceptable and said that when she was a child her English governess used to call it a Hong Kong.

After Pnin had tolled the stake and all was over, and Varvara accompanied Susan to get the evening tea ready, Pnin quietly retired to a bench under the pines. A certain extremely unpleasant and frightening cardiac sensation, which he had experienced several times throughout his adult life, had come upon him again. It was not pain or palpitation, but rather an

awful feeling of sinking and melting into one's physical surroundings—sunset, red boles of trees, sand, still air. Meanwhile Roza Shpolyanski, noticing Pnin sitting alone, and
taking advantage of this, walked over to him (*"sidite, sidite!"*
don't get up) and sat down next to him on the bench.

"In 1916 or 1917," she said, "you may have had occasion to
hear my maiden name—Geller—from some great friends of
yours."

"No, I don't recollect," said Pnin.

"It is of no importance, anyway. I don't think we ever met.
But you knew well my cousins, Grisha and Mira Belochkin.
They constantly spoke of you. He is living in Sweden, I
think—and, of course, you have heard of his poor sister's terrible end. . . ."

"Indeed, I have," said Pnin.

"Her husband," said Madam Shpolyanski, "was a most
charming man. Samuil Lvovich and I knew him and his first
wife, Svetlana Chertok, the pianist, very intimately. He was
interned by the Nazis separately from Mira, and died in the
same concentration camp as did my elder brother Misha. You
did not know Misha, did you? He was also in love with Mira
once upon a time."

"*Tshay gotoff* (tea's ready)," called Susan from the porch in
her funny functional Russian. "Timofey, Rozochka! *Tshay!*"

Pnin told Madam Shpolyanski he would follow her in a
minute, and after she had gone he continued to sit in the first
dusk of the arbor, his hands clasped on the croquet mallet he
still held.

Two kerosene lamps cozily illuminated the porch of the
country house. Dr. Pavel Antonovich Pnin, Timofey's father,
an eye specialist, and Dr. Yakov Grigorievich Belochkin,
Mira's father, a pediatrician, could not be torn away from their
chess game in a corner of the veranda, so Madam Belochkin
had the maid serve them there—on a special small Japanese
table, near the one they were playing at—their glasses of tea
in silver holders, the curd and whey with black bread, the
Garden Strawberries, *zemlyanika,* and the other cultivated
species, *klubnika* (Hautbois or Green Strawberries), and the
radiant golden jams, and the various biscuits, wafers, pretzels,
zwiebacks—instead of calling the two engrossed doctors to

the main table at the other end of the porch, where sat the rest of the family and guests, some clear, some grading into a luminous mist.

Dr. Belochkin's blind hand took a pretzel; Dr. Pnin's seeing hand took a rook. Dr. Belochkin munched and stared at the hole in his ranks; Dr. Pnin dipped an abstract zwieback into the hole of his tea.

The country house that the Belochkins rented that summer was in the same Baltic resort near which the widow of General N—— let a summer cottage to the Pnins on the confines of her vast estate, marshy and rugged, with dark woods hemming in a desolate manor. Timofey Pnin was again the clumsy, shy, obstinate, eighteen-year-old boy, waiting in the dark for Mira—and despite the fact that logical thought put electric bulbs into the kerosene lamps and reshuffled the people, turning them into aging émigrés and securely, hopelessly, forever wire-netting the lighted porch, my poor Pnin, with hallucinatory sharpness, imagined Mira slipping out of there into the garden and coming toward him among tall tobacco flowers whose dull white mingled in the dark with that of her frock. This feeling coincided somehow with the sense of diffusion and dilation within his chest. Gently he laid his mallet aside and, to dissipate the anguish, started walking away from the house, through the silent pine grove. From a car which was parked near the garden tool house and which contained presumably at least two of his fellow guests' children, there issued a steady trickle of radio music.

"Jazz, jazz, they always must have their jazz, those youngsters," muttered Pnin to himself, and turned into the path that led to the forest and river. He remembered the fads of his and Mira's youth, the amateur theatricals, the gypsy ballads, the passion she had for photography. Where were they now, those artistic snapshots she used to take—pets, clouds, flowers, an April glade with shadows of birches on wet-sugar snow, soldiers posturing on the roof of a boxcar, a sunset skyline, a hand holding a book? He remembered the last day they had met, on the Neva embankment in Petrograd, and the tears, and the stars, and the warm rose-red silk lining of her karakul muff. The Civil War of 1918–22 separated them: history broke their engagement. Timofey wandered south-

ward, to join briefly the ranks of Denikin's army, while Mira's
family escaped from the Bolsheviks to Sweden and then settled
down in Germany, where eventually she married a fur dealer
of Russian extraction. Sometime in the early thirties, Pnin, by
then married too, accompanied his wife to Berlin, where she
wished to attend a congress of psychotherapists, and one
night, at a Russian restaurant on the Kurfürstendamm, he saw
Mira again. They exchanged a few words, she smiled at him
in the remembered fashion, from under her dark brows, with
that bashful slyness of hers; and the contour of her prominent
cheekbones, and the elongated eyes, and the slenderness of
arm and ankle were unchanged, were immortal, and then she
joined her husband who was getting his overcoat at the cloak-
room, and that was all—but the pang of tenderness remained,
akin to the vibrating outline of verses you know you know
but cannot recall.

What chatty Madam Shpolyanski mentioned had conjured
up Mira's image with unusual force. This was disturbing. Only
in the detachment of an incurable complaint, in the sanity of
near death, could one cope with this for a moment. In order
to exist rationally, Pnin had taught himself, during the last ten
years, never to remember Mira Belochkin—not because, in
itself, the evocation of a youthful love affair, banal and brief,
threatened his peace of mind (alas, recollections of his marriage to Liza were imperious enough to crowd out any former
romance), but because, if one were quite sincere with oneself,
no conscience, and hence no consciousness, could be expected
to subsist in a world where such things as Mira's death were
possible. One had to forget—because one could not live with
the thought that this graceful, fragile, tender young woman
with those eyes, that smile, those gardens and snows in the
background, had been brought in a cattle car to an extermi-
nation camp and killed by an injection of phenol into the
heart, into the gentle heart one had heard beating under one's
lips in the dusk of the past. And since the exact form of her
death had not been recorded, Mira kept dying a great number
of deaths in one's mind, and undergoing a great number of
resurrections, only to die again and again, led away by a
trained nurse, inoculated with filth, tetanus bacilli, broken
glass, gassed in a sham shower bath with prussic acid, burned

alive in a pit on a gasoline-soaked pile of beechwood. According to the investigator Pnin had happened to talk to in
Washington, the only certain thing was that being too weak
to work (though still smiling, still able to help other Jewish
women), she was selected to die and was cremated only a few
days after her arrival in Buchenwald, in the beautifully wooded
Grosser Ettersberg, as the region is resoundingly called. It is
an hour's stroll from Weimar, where walked Goethe, Herder,
Schiller, Wieland, the inimitable Kotzebue and others. "*Aber
warum*—but why—" Dr. Hagen, the gentlest of souls alive,
would wail, "why had one to put that horrid camp so near!"
for indeed, it was near—only five miles from the cultural heart
of Germany—"that nation of universities," as the President
of Waindell College, renowned for his use of the *mot juste*,
had so elegantly phrased it when reviewing the European situation in a recent Commencement speech, along with the
compliment he paid another torture house, "Russia—the
country of Tolstoy, Stanislavski, Raskolnikov, and other great
and good men."

Pnin slowly walked under the solemn pines. The sky was
dying. He did not believe in an autocratic God. He did believe, dimly, in a democracy of ghosts. The souls of the dead,
perhaps, formed committees, and these, in continuous session,
attended to the destinies of the quick.

The mosquitoes were getting bothersome. Time for tea.
Time for a game of chess with Chateau. That strange spasm
was over, one could breathe again. On the distant crest of the
knoll, at the exact spot where Gramineev's easel had stood a
few hours before, two dark figures in profile were silhouetted
against the ember-red sky. They stood there closely, facing
each other. One could not make out from the road whether
it was the Poroshin girl and her beau, or Nina Bolotov and
young Poroshin, or merely an emblematic couple placed with
easy art on the last page of Pnin's fading day.

Chapter Six

THE 1954 FALL TERM had begun. Again the marble neck of a homely Venus in the vestibule of Humanities Hall received the vermilion imprint, in applied lipstick, of a mimicked kiss. Again the *Waindell Recorder* discussed the Parking Problem. Again in the margins of library books earnest freshmen inscribed such helpful glosses as "Description of nature," or "Irony"; and in a pretty edition of Mallarmé's poems an especially able scholiast had already underlined in violet ink the difficult word *oiseaux* and scrawled above it "birds." Again autumn gales plastered dead leaves against one side of the latticed gallery leading from Humanities to Frieze Hall. Again, on serene afternoons, huge, amber-brown Monarch butterflies flapped over asphalt and lawn as they lazily drifted south, their incompletely retracted black legs hanging rather low beneath their polka-dotted bodies.

And still the College creaked on. Hard-working graduates, with pregnant wives, still wrote dissertations on Dostoevski and Simone de Beauvoir. Literary departments still labored under the impression that Stendhal, Galsworthy, Dreiser, and Mann were great writers. Word plastics like "conflict" and "pattern" were still in vogue. As usual, sterile instructors successfully endeavored to "produce" by reviewing the books of more fertile colleagues, and, as usual, a crop of lucky faculty members were enjoying or about to enjoy various awards received earlier in the year. Thus, an amusing little grant was affording the versatile Starr couple—baby-faced Christopher Starr and his child-wife Louise of the Fine Arts Department— the unique opportunity of recording postwar folk songs in East Germany, into which these amazing young people had somehow obtained permission to penetrate. Tristram W. Thomas ("Tom" to his friends), Professor of Anthropology, had obtained ten thousand dollars from the Mandeville Foundation for a study of the eating habits of Cuban fishermen and palm climbers. Another charitable institution had come to the assistance of Dr. Bodo von Falternfels, to enable him to complete "a bibliography concerned with such published and

manuscript material as has been devoted in recent years to a
critical appraisal of the influence of Nietzsche's disciples on
Modern Thought." And, last but not least, the bestowal of a
particularly generous grant was allowing the renowned Waindell psychiatrist, Dr. Rudolph Aura, to apply to ten thousand
elementary school pupils the so-called Fingerbowl Test, in
which the child is asked to dip his index in cups of colored fluids
whereupon the proportion between length of digit and wetted
part is measured and plotted in all kinds of fascinating graphs.

The Fall Term had begun, and Dr. Hagen was faced with
a complicated situation. During the summer, he had been in-
formally approached by an old friend about whether he might
consider accepting next year a delightfully lucrative professorship at Seaboard, a far more important university than Waindell. This part of the problem was comparatively easy to solve.
On the other hand, there remained the chilling fact that the
department he had so lovingly built, with which Blorenge's
French Department, although far richer in funds, could not
vie in cultural impact, would be relinquished into the claws of
treacherous Falternfels, whom he, Hagen, had obtained from
Austria and who had turned against him—had actually managed to appropriate by underhand methods the direction of
Europa Nova, an influential quarterly Hagen had founded in
1945. Hagen's proposed departure—of which, as yet, he had
divulged nothing to his colleagues—would have a still more
heart-rending consequence: Assistant Professor Pnin must be
left in the lurch. There had never been any regular Russian
Department at Waindell and my poor friend's academic existence had always depended on his being employed by the
eclectic German Department in a kind of Comparative Literature extension of one of its branches. Out of pure spite, Bodo
was sure to lop off that limb, and Pnin, who had no life tenure
at Waindell, would be forced to leave—unless some other lit-
erature-and-language Department agreed to adopt him. The
only departments that seemed flexible enough to do so were
those of English and French. But Jack Cockerell, Chairman
of English, disapproved of everything Hagen did, considered
Pnin a joke, and was, in fact, unofficially but hopefully haggling for the services of a prominent Anglo-Russian writer
who, if necessary, could teach all the courses that Pnin must

keep in order to survive. As a last resort, Hagen turned to Blorenge.

2

Two interesting characteristics distinguished Leonard Blorenge, Chairman of French Literature and Language; he disliked Literature and he had no French. This did not prevent him from traveling tremendous distances to attend Modern Language conventions, at which he would flaunt his ineptitude as if it were some majestic whim, and parry with great thrusts of healthy lodge humor any attempt to inveigle him into the subtleties of the parley-voo. A highly esteemed money-getter, he had recently induced a rich old man, whom three great universities had courted in vain, to promote with a fantastic endowment a riot of research conducted by graduates under the direction of Dr. Slavski, a Canadian, toward the erection on a hill near Waindell, of a "French Village," two streets and a square, to be copied from those of the ancient little burg of Vandel in the Dordogne. Despite the grandiose element always present in his administrative illuminations, Blorenge personally was a man of ascetic tastes. He had happened to go to school with Sam Poore, Waindell's President, and for many years, regularly, even after the latter had lost his sight, the two would go fishing together on a bleak, wind-raked lake, at the end of a gravel road lined with fireweed, seventy miles north of Waindell, in the kind of dreary brush country—scrub oak and nursery pine—that, in terms of nature, is the counterpart of a slum. His wife, a sweet woman of simple antecedents, referred to him at her club as "Professor Blorenge." He gave a course entitled "Great Frenchmen," which he had had his secretary copy out from a set of *The Hastings Historical and Philosophical Magazine* for 1882–94, discovered by him in an attic and not represented in the College Library.

3

Pnin had just rented a small house, and had invited the Hagens and the Clementses, and the Thayers, and Betty Bliss to a housewarming party. On the morning of that day, good Dr. Hagen made a desperate visit to Blorenge's office and revealed to him, and to him alone, the whole situation. When he told Blorenge that Falternfels was a strong anti-Pninist, Blorenge drily rejoined that so was he; in fact, after meeting Pnin socially, he "definitely felt" (it is truly a wonder how prone these practical people are to feel rather than to think) that Pnin was not fit even to loiter in the vicinity of an American college. Staunch Hagen said that for several terms Pnin had been admirably dealing with the Romantic Movement and might surely handle Chateaubriand and Victor Hugo under the auspices of the French Department.

"Dr. Slavski takes care of that crowd," said Blorenge. "In fact, I sometimes think we overdo literature. Look, this week Miss Mopsuestia begins the Existentialists, your man Bodo does Romain Rolland, I lecture on General Boulanger and De Béranger. No, we have definitely enough of the stuff."

Hagen, playing his last card, suggested Pnin could teach a French language course: like many Russians, our friend had had a French governess as a child, and after the Revolution he lived in Paris for more than fifteen years.

"You mean," asked Blorenge sternly, "he can *speak* French?"

Hagen, who was well aware of Blorenge's special requirements, hesitated.

"Out with it, Herman! Yes or no?"

"I am sure he could adapt himself."

"He does speak it, eh?"

"Well, yes."

"In that case," said Blorenge, "we can't use him in First-Year French. It would be unfair to our Mr. Smith, who gives the elementary course this term and, naturally, is required to be only one lesson ahead of his students. Now it so happens that Mr. Hashimoto needs an assistant for his overflowing group in Intermediate French. Does your man *read* French as well as speak it?"

"I repeat, he can adapt himself," hedged Hagen.

"I know what adaptation means," said Blorenge, frowning. "In 1950, when Hash was away, I engaged that Swiss skiing instructor and he smuggled in mimeo copies of some old

French anthology. It took us almost a year to bring the class back to its initial level. Now, if what's-his-name does not read French——"

"I'm afraid he does," said Hagen with a sigh.

"Then we can't use him at all. As you know, we believe only in speech records and other mechanical devices. No books are allowed."

"There still remains Advanced French," murmured Hagen.

"Carolina Slavski and I take care of that," answered Blorenge.

4

For Pnin, who was totally unaware of his protector's woes, the new Fall Term began particularly well: he had never had so few students to bother about, or so much time for his own research. This research had long entered the charmed stage when the quest overrides the goal, and a new organism is formed, the parasite so to speak of the ripening fruit. Pnin averted his mental gaze from the end of his work, which was so clearly in sight that one could make out the rocket of an asterisk, the flare of a "sic!" This line of land was to be shunned as the doom of everything that determined the rapture of endless approximation. Index cards were gradually loading a shoe box with their compact weight. The collation of two legends; a precious detail in manners or dress; a reference checked and found to be falsified by incompetence, carelessness, or fraud; the spine thrill of a felicitous guess; and all the innumerable triumphs of *bezkorïstnïy* (disinterested, devoted) scholarship—this had corrupted Pnin, this had made of him a happy, footnote-drugged maniac who disturbs the book mites in a dull volume, a foot thick, to find in it a reference to an even duller one. And on another, more human, plane there was the little brick house that he had rented on Todd Road, at the corner of Cliff Avenue.

It had lodged the family of the late Martin Sheppard, an uncle of Pnin's previous landlord in Creek Street and for many years the caretaker of the Todd property, which the town of Waindell had now acquired for the purpose of turning its rambling mansion into a modern nursing home. Ivy and spruce muffled its locked gate, whose top Pnin could see on the far side of Cliff Avenue from a north window of his new home. This avenue was the crossbar of a T, in the left crotch of which he dwelt. Opposite the front of his house, immediately across Todd Road (the upright of the T) old elms screened the sandy shoulder of its patched-up asphalt from a cornfield east of it, while along its west side a regiment of young fir trees, identical upstarts, walked, campusward, behind a fence, for almost the whole distance to the next residence—the Varsity Football Coach's magnified cigar box, which stood half a mile south from Pnin's house.

The sense of living in a discrete building all by himself was to Pnin something singularly delightful and amazingly satisfying to a weary old want of his innermost self, battered and stunned by thirty-five years of homelessness. One of the sweetest things about the place was the silence—angelic, rural, and perfectly secure, thus in blissful contrast to the persistent cacophonies that had surrounded him from six sides in the rented rooms of his former habitations. And the tiny house was so spacious! With grateful surprise, Pnin thought that had there been no Russian Revolution, no exodus, no expatriation in France, no naturalization in America, everything—at the best, at the best, Timofey!—would have been much the same: a professorship in Kharkov or Kazan, a suburban house such as this, old books within, late blooms without. It was—to be more precise—a two-story house of cherry-red brick, with white shutters and a shingle roof. The green plat on which it stood had a frontage of about fifty arshins and was limited at the back by a vertical stretch of mossy cliff with tawny shrubs on its crest. A rudimentary driveway along the south side of the house led to a small whitewashed garage for the poor man's car Pnin owned. A curious basketlike net, somewhat like a glorified billiard pocket—lacking, however, a bottom— was suspended for some reason above the garage door, upon the white of which it cast a shadow as distinct as its own weave but larger and in a bluer tone. Pheasants visited the weedy ground between the garage and the cliff. Lilacs—those Russian garden graces, to whose springtime splendor, all honey and hum, my poor Pnin greatly looked forward—crowded in sapless ranks along one wall of the house. And a tall deciduous tree, which Pnin, a birch-lime-willow-aspen-poplar-oak man, was unable to identify, cast its large, heart-shaped, rust-colored leaves and Indian-summer shadows upon the wooden steps of the open porch.

A cranky-looking oil furnace in the basement did its best to send up its weak warm breath through registers in the floors. The kitchen looked healthy and gay, and Pnin had a great time with all kinds of cookware, kettles and pans, toasters and skillets, all of which came with the house. The living room was scantily and dingily furnished, but had a rather attractive bay harboring a huge old globe, where Russia was painted a pale blue, with a discolored or scrubbed patch all over Poland. In a very small dining room, where Pnin contemplated arranging a buffet supper for his guests, a pair of crystal candlesticks with pendants was responsible in the early mornings for iridescent reflections, which glowed charmingly on the sideboard and reminded my sentimental friend of the stained-glass casements that colored the sunlight orange and green and violet on the verandas of Russian country houses. A china closet, every time he passed by it, went into a rumbling act that also was somehow familiar from dim back rooms of the past. The second floor consisted of two bedrooms, both of which had been the abode of many small children, with incidental adults. The floors were chafed by tin toys. From the wall of the chamber Pnin decided to sleep in he had untacked a pennant-shaped red cardboard with the enigmatic word "Cardinals" daubed on it in white; but a tiny rocker for a three-year-old Pnin, painted pink, was allowed to remain in its corner. A disabled sewing machine occupied a passageway leading to the bathroom, where the usual short tub, made for dwarfs by a nation of giants, took as long to fill as the tanks and basins of the arithmetic in Russian school books.

He was now ready to give that party. The living room had a sofa that could seat three, there were two wing-back chairs, an overstuffed easy chair, a chair with a rush seat, one hassock, and two footstools. All of a sudden he experienced an odd feeling of dissatisfaction as he checked the little list of his guests. It had body but it lacked bouquet. Of course, he was tremendously fond of the Clementses (real people—not like most of the campus dummies), with whom he had had such exhilarating talks in the days when he was their roomer; of course, he felt very grateful to Herman Hagen for many a good turn, such as that raise Hagen had recently arranged; of course, Mrs. Hagen was, in Waindell parlance, "a lovely person"; of course, Mrs. Thayer was always so helpful at the library, and her husband had such a soothing capacity for showing how silent a man could be if he strictly avoided comments on the weather. But there was nothing extraordinary, nothing original, about this combination of people, and old Pnin recalled those birthday parties in his boyhood—the half a dozen children invited who were somehow always the same, and the pinching shoes, and the aching temples, and the kind of heavy, unhappy, constraining dullness that would settle on him after all the games had been played and a rowdy cousin had started putting nice new toys to vulgar and stupid uses; and he also recalled the lone buzz in his ears when, in the course of a protracted hide-and-seek routine, after an hour of uncomfortable concealment, he emerged from a dark and stuffy wardrobe in the maid's chamber, only to find that all his playmates had already gone home.

While visiting a famous grocery between Waindelville and Isola, he ran into Betty Bliss, asked her, and she said she still remembered Turgenev's prose poem about roses, with its refrain "*Kak horoshi, kak svezhi* (How fair, how fresh)," and would certainly be delighted to come. He asked the celebrated mathematician, Professor Idelson, and his wife, the sculptress, and they said they would come with joy but later telephoned to say they were tremendously sorry—they had overlooked a previous engagement. He asked young Miller, by now an Associate Professor, and Charlotte, his pretty, freckled wife, but it turned out she was on the point of having a baby. He asked old Carrol, the Frieze Hall head janitor, with his son Frank, who had been my friend's only talented student and had written a brilliant doctor's thesis for him on the relationship between Russian, English, and German iambics; but Frank was in the army, and old Carrol confessed that "the missus and I do not mix much with the profs." He rang up the residence of President Poore, whom he had once talked to (about improving the curriculum) at a lawn function, until it started to rain, and asked him to come, but President Poore's niece answered that her uncle nowadays "never visits with anybody except a few personal friends." He was about to give up the notion of enlivening his list, when a perfectly new and really admirable idea occurred to him.

5

Pnin and I had long since accepted the disturbing but seldom discussed fact that on any given college staff one could find not only a person who was uncommonly like one's dentist or the local postmaster, but also a person who had a twin within the same professional group. I know, indeed, of a case of triplets at a comparatively small college where, according to its sharp-eyed president, Frank Reade, the radix of the troika was, absurdly enough, myself; and I recall the late Olga Krotki once telling me that among the fifty or so faculty members of a wartime Intensive Language School, at which the poor, one-lunged lady had to teach Lethean and Fenugreek, there were as many as six Pnins, besides the genuine and, to me, unique article. It should not be deemed surprising, therefore, that even Pnin, not a very observant man in everyday life, could not help becoming aware (sometime during his ninth year at Waindell) that a lanky, bespectacled old fellow with scholarly strands of steel-gray hair falling over the right side of his small but corrugated brow, and with a deep furrow descending from each side of his sharp nose to each corner of his long upper-lip—a person whom Pnin knew as Professor Thomas Wynn, Head of the Ornithology Department, having once talked to him at some party about gay golden orioles, melancholy cuckoos, and other Russian countryside birds—was not always Professor Wynn. At times he graded, as it were, into somebody else, whom Pnin did not know by name but whom he classified, with a bright foreigner's fondness for puns as "Twynn" (or, in Pninian, "Tvin"). My friend and compatriot soon realized that he could never be sure whether the owlish, rapidly stalking gentleman, whose path he would cross every other day at different points of progress, between office and classroom, between classroom and stairs, between drinking fountain and lavatory, was really his chance acquaintance, the ornithologist, whom he felt bound to greet in passing, or the Wynn-like stranger, who acknowledged that somber salute with exactly the same degree of automatic politeness as any chance acquaintance would. The moment of meeting would be very brief, since both Pnin and Wynn (or Twynn) walked fast; and sometimes Pnin, in order to avoid the exchange of urbane barks, would feign reading a letter on the run, or would manage to dodge his rapidly advancing colleague and tormentor by swerving into a stairway and then continuing along a lower-floor corridor; but no sooner had he begun to rejoice in the smartness of the device than upon using it one day he almost collided with Tvin (or Vin) pounding along the subjacent passage. When the new Fall Term (Pnin's tenth) began, the nuisance was aggravated by the fact that Pnin's class hours had been changed, thus abolishing certain trends on which he had been learning to rely in his efforts to elude Wynn and Wynn's simulator. It seemed he would have to endure it always. For recalling certain other duplications in the past—disconcerting likenesses he alone had seen—bothered Pnin told himself it would be useless to ask anybody's assistance in unraveling the T. Wynns.

On the day of his party, as he was finishing a late lunch in Frieze Hall, Wynn, or his double, neither of whom had ever appeared there before, suddenly sat down beside him and said:

"I have long wanted to ask you something—you teach Russian, don't you? Last summer I was reading a magazine article on birds——"

("Vin! This is Vin!" said Pnin to himself, and forthwith perceived a decisive course of action.)

"—well, the author of that article—I don't remember his name, I think it was a Russian one—mentioned that in the Skoff region, I hope I pronounce it right, a local cake is baked in the form of a bird. Basically, of course, the symbol is phallic, but I was wondering if you knew of such a custom?"

It was then that the brilliant idea flashed in Pnin's mind.

"Sir, I am at your service," he said with a note of exultation quivering in his throat—for he now saw his way to pin down definitely the personality of at least the initial Wynn who liked birds. "Yes, sir. I know all about those *zhavoronki*, those *alouettes*, those—we must consult a dictionary for the English name. So I take the opportunity to extend a cordial invitation to you to visit me this evening. Half past eight, postmeridian. A little house-heating soirée, nothing more. Bring also your spouse—or perhaps you are a Bachelor of Hearts?"

(Oh, punster Pnin!)

His interlocutor said he was not married. He would love to come. What was the address?

"It is nine hundred ninety nine, Todd Rodd, very simple! At the very very end of the rodd, where it unites with Cleef Ahvnue. A leetle breek house and a beeg blahk cleef."

6

That afternoon Pnin could hardly wait to start culinary operations. He began them soon after five and only interrupted them to don, for the reception of his guests, a sybaritic smoking jacket of blue silk, with tasseled belt and satin lapels, won at an émigré charity bazaar in Paris twenty years ago—how the time flies! This jacket he wore with a pair of old tuxedo trousers, likewise of European origin. Peering at himself in the cracked mirror of the medicine chest, he put on his heavy tortoiseshell reading glasses, from under the saddle of which his Russian potato nose smoothly bulged. He bared his synthetic teeth. He inspected his cheeks and chin to see if his morning shave still held. It did. With finger and thumb he grasped a long nostril hair, plucked it out after a second hard tug, and sneezed lustily, an "Ah!" of well-being rounding out the explosion.

At half past seven Betty arrived to help with final arrangements. Betty now taught English and History at Isola High School. She had not changed since the days when she was a buxom graduate student. Her pink-rimmed myopic gray eyes peered at you with the same ingenuous sympathy. She wore the same Gretchen-like coil of thick hair around her head. There was the same scar on her soft throat. But an engagement ring with a diminutive diamond had appeared on her plump hand, and this she displayed with coy pride to Pnin, who vaguely experienced a twinge of sadness. He reflected that there was a time he might have courted her—would have done so, in fact, had she not had a servant maid's mind, which had remained unaltered too. She could still relate a long story on a "she said–I said–she said" basis. Nothing on earth could make her disbelieve in the wisdom and wit of her favorite woman's magazine. She still had the curious trick—shared by two or three other small-town young women within Pnin's limited ken—of giving you a delayed little tap on the sleeve in acknowledgment of, rather than in retaliation for, any remark reminding her of some minor lapse: you would say, "Betty, you forgot to return that book," or "I thought, Betty, you said you would never marry," and before she actually answered, there it would come, that demure gesture, retracted at the very moment her stubby fingers came into contact with your wrist.

"He is a biochemist and is now in Pittsburgh," said Betty as she helped Pnin to arrange buttered slices of French bread around a pot of glossy-gray fresh caviar and to rinse three large bunches of grapes. There was also a large plate of cold cuts, real German pumpernickel, and a dish of very special vinaigrette, where shrimps hobnobbed with pickles and peas, and some miniature sausages in tomato sauce, and hot *pirozhki* (mushroom tarts, meat tarts, cabbage tarts), and four kinds of nuts, and various interesting Oriental sweets. Drinks were to be represented by whisky (Betty's contribution), *ryabinovka* (a rowanberry liqueur), brandy-and-grenadine cocktails, and of course Pnin's Punch, a heady mixture of chilled Chateau Yquem, grapefruit juice, and maraschino, which the solemn host had already started to stir in a large bowl of brilliant aquamarine glass with a decorative design of swirled ribbing and lily pads.

"My, what a lovely thing!" cried Betty.

Pnin eyed the bowl with pleased surprise as if seeing it for the first time. It was, he said, a present from Victor. Yes, how was he, how did he like St. Bart's? He liked it so-so. He had passed the beginning of the summer in California with his mother, then had worked two months at a Yosemite hotel. A *what*? A hotel in the Californian mountains. Well, he had returned to his school and had suddenly sent this.

By some tender coincidence the bowl had come on the very day Pnin had counted the chairs and started to plan this party. It had come enclosed in a box within another box inside a third one, and wrapped up in an extravagant mass of excelsior and paper that had spread all over the kitchen like a carnival storm. The bowl that emerged was one of those gifts whose first impact produces in the recipient's mind a colored image, a blazoned blur, reflecting with such emblematic force the sweet nature of the donor that the tangible attributes of the thing are dissolved, as it were, in this pure inner blaze, but suddenly and forever leap into brilliant being when praised by an outsider to whom the true glory of the object is unknown.

7

A musical tinkle reverberated through the small house, and the Clementses entered with a bottle of French champagne and a cluster of dahlias.

Dark-blue-eyed, long-lashed, bob-haired Joan wore an old black silk dress that was smarter than anything other faculty wives could devise, and it was always a pleasure to watch good old bald Tim Pnin bend slightly to touch with his lips the light hand that Joan, alone of all the Waindell ladies, knew how to raise to exactly the right level for a Russian gentleman to kiss. Laurence, fatter than ever, dressed in nice gray flannels, sank into the easy chair and immediately grabbed the first book at hand, which happened to be an English-Russian and Russian-English pocket dictionary. Holding his glasses in one hand, he looked away, trying to recall something he had always wished to check but now could not remember, and his attitude accentuated his striking resemblance, somewhat *en jeune*, to Jan van Eyck's ample-jowled, fluff-haloed Canon van der Paele, seized by a fit of abstraction in the presence of the puzzled Virgin to whom a super, rigged up as St. George, is directing the good Canon's attention. Everything was there—the knotty temple, the sad, musing gaze, the folds and furrows of facial flesh, the thin lips, and even the wart on the left cheek.

Hardly had the Clementses settled down than Betty let in the man interested in bird-shaped cakes. Pnin was about to say "Professor Vin" but Joan—rather unfortunately, perhaps—interrupted the introduction with "Oh, we know Thomas!

Who does not know Tom?" Tim Pnin returned to the kitchen, and Betty handed around some Bulgarian cigarettes.

"I thought, Thomas," remarked Clements, crossing his fat legs, "you were out in Havana interviewing palm-climbing fishermen?"

"Well, I'll be on my way after midyears," said Professor Thomas. "Of course, most of the actual field work has been done already by others."

"Still, it was nice to get that grant, wasn't it?"

"In our branch," replied Thomas with perfect composure, "we have to undertake many difficult journeys. In fact, I may push on to the Windward Islands. If," he added with a hollow laugh, "Senator McCarthy does not crack down on foreign travel."

"He received a grant of ten thousand dollars," said Joan to Betty, whose face dropped a curtsy as she made that special grimace consisting of a slow half-bow and tensing of chin and lower lip that automatically conveys, on the part of Bettys, a respectful, congratulatory, and slightly awed recognition of such grand things as dining with one's boss, being in *Who's Who*, or meeting a duchess.

The Thayers, who came in a new station wagon, presented their host with an elegant box of mints. Dr. Hagen, who came on foot, triumphantly held aloft a bottle of vodka.

"Good evening, good evening, good evening," said hearty Hagen.

"Dr. Hagen," said Thomas as he shook hands with him. "I hope the Senator did not see you walking about with that stuff."

The good Doctor had perceptibly aged since last year but was as sturdy and square-shaped as ever with his well-padded shoulders, square chin, square nostrils, leonine glabella, and rectangular brush of grizzled hair that had something topiary about it. He wore a black suit over a white nylon shirt, and a black tie with a red thunderbolt streaking down it. Mrs. Hagen had been prevented from coming, at the very last moment, by a dreadful migraine, alas.

Pnin served the cocktails "or better to say flamingo tails— specially for ornithologists," as he slyly quipped.

"Thank you!" chanted Mrs. Thayer, as she received her

glass, raising her linear eyebrows, on that bright note of genteel inquiry which is meant to combine the notions of surprise,
unworthiness, and pleasure. An attractive, prim, pink-faced
lady of forty or so, with pearly dentures and wavy goldenized
hair, she was the provincial cousin of the smart, relaxed Joan
Clements, who had been all over the world, even in Turkey
and Egypt, and was married to the most original and least
liked scholar on the Waindell campus. A good word should
be also put in at this point for Margaret Thayer's husband,
Roy, a mournful and mute member of the Department of
English, which, except for its ebullient chairman, Cockerell,
was an aerie of hypochondriacs. Outwardly, Roy was an obvious figure. If you drew a pair of old brown loafers, two beige
elbow patches, a black pipe, and two baggy eyes under heavy
eyebrows, the rest was easy to fill out. Somewhere in the middle distance hung an obscure liver ailment, and somewhere in
the background there was Eighteenth-Century Poetry, Roy's
particular field, an overgrazed pasture, with the trickle of a
brook and a clump of initialed trees; a barbed-wire arrangement on either side of this field separated it from Professor
Stowe's domain, the preceding century, where the lambs were
whiter, the turf softer, the rill purlier, and from Dr. Shapiro's
early nineteenth century, with its glen mists, sea fogs, and
imported grapes. Roy Thayer avoided talking of his subject,
avoided, in fact, talking of any subject, had squandered a decade of gray life on an erudite work dealing with a forgotten
group of unnecessary poetasters, and kept a detailed diary, in
cryptogrammed verse, which he hoped posterity would some-
day decipher and, in sober backcast, proclaim the greatest literary achievement of our time—and for all I know, Roy
Thayer, you might be right.

When everybody was comfortably lapping and lauding the
cocktails, Professor Pnin sat down on the wheezy hassock near
his newest friend and said:

"I have to report, sir, on the skylark, *zhavoronok* in Russian,
about which you made me the honor to interrogate me. Take
this with you to your home. I have here tapped on the type-
writing machine a condensed account with bibliography. I
think we will now transport ourselves to the other room where
a supper *à la fourchette* is, I think, awaiting us."

8

Presently, guests with full plates drifted back into the parlor. The punch was brought in.

"Gracious, Timofey, where on earth did you get that perfectly divine bowl!" exclaimed Joan.

"Victor presented it to me."

"But where did he *get* it?"

"Antiquaire store in Cranton, I think."

"Gosh, it must have cost a fortune."

"One dollar? Ten dollars? Less maybe?"

"Ten dollars—nonsense! Two hundred, I should say. *Look* at it! Look at this writhing pattern. You know, you should show it to the Cockerells. They know everything about old glass. In fact, they have a Lake Dunmore pitcher that looks like a poor relation of this."

Margaret Thayer admired it in her turn, and said that when she was a child, she imagined Cinderella's glass shoes to be exactly of that greenish blue tint; whereupon Professor Pnin remarked that, *primo*, he would like everybody to say if contents were as good as container, and, *secundo*, that Cendrillon's shoes were not made of glass but of Russian squirrel fur—*vair*, in French. It was, he said, an obvious case of the survival of the fittest among words, *verre* being more evocative than *vair* which, he submitted, came not from *varius*, variegated, but from *veveritsa*, Slavic for a certain beautiful, pale, winter-squirrel fur, having a bluish, or better say *sizyy*, columbine, shade—from *columba*, Latin for "pigeon," as somebody here well knows—so you see, Mrs. Fire, you were, in general, correct."

"The contents are fine," said Laurence Clements.

"This beverage is certainly delicious," said Margaret Thayer.

("I always thought 'columbine' was some sort of flower," said Thomas to Betty, who lightly acquiesced.)

The respective ages of several children were then passed in review. Victor would be fifteen soon. Eileen, the granddaughter of Mrs. Thayer's eldest sister, was five. Isabel was twenty-three and greatly enjoying a secretarial job in New York. Dr. Hagen's daughter was twenty-four, and about to return from

Europe, where she had spent a wonderful summer touring Bavaria and Switzerland with a very gracious old lady, Dorianna Karen, famous movie star of the twenties.

The telephone rang. Somebody wanted to talk to Mrs. Sheppard. With a precision quite unusual for him in such matters, unpredictable Pnin not only rattled off the woman's new address and telephone number, but also supplied those of her eldest son.

9

By ten o'clock, Pnin's Punch and Betty's scotch were causing some of the guests to talk louder than they thought they did. A carmine flush had spread over one side of Mrs. Thayer's neck, under the little blue star of her left earring, and, sitting very straight, she regaled her host with an account of the feud between two of her co-workers at the library. It was a simple office story, but her changes of tone from Miss Shrill to Mr. Basso, and the consciousness of the soiree going on so nicely, made Pnin bend his head and guffaw ecstatically behind his hand. Roy Thayer was weakly twinkling to himself as he looked into his punch, down his gray porous nose, and politely listened to Joan Clements who, when she was a little high as she was now, had a fetching way of rapidly blinking, or even completely closing her black-lashed blue eyes, and of interrupting her sentences, to punctuate a clause or gather new momentum, by deep hawing pants: "But don't you think—haw—that what he is trying to do—haw—practically in all his novels—haw—is—haw—to express the fantastic recurrence of certain situations?" Betty remained her controlled little self, and expertly looked after the refreshments. In the bay end of the room, Clements kept morosely revolving the slow globe as Hagen, carefully avoiding the traditional intonations he would have used in more congenial surroundings, told him and grinning Thomas the latest story about Mrs. Idelson, communicated by Mrs. Blorenge to Mrs. Hagen. Pnin came up with a plate of nougat.

"This is not quite for your chaste ears, Timofey," said Hagen to Pnin, who always confessed he never could see the point of any "scabrous anecdote." "However—"

Clements moved away to rejoin the ladies. Hagen began to retell the story, and Thomas began to re-grin. Pnin waved a hand at the raconteur in a Russian disgusted "oh-go-on-with-you" gesture and said:

"I have heard quite the same anecdote thirty-five years ago in Odessa, and even then I could not understand what is comical in it."

10

At a still later stage of the party, certain rearrangements had again taken place. In a corner of the davenport, bored Clements was flipping through an album of *Flemish Masterpieces* that Victor had been given by his mother and had left with Pnin. Joan sat on a footstool, at her husband's knee, a plate of grapes in the lap of her wide skirt, wondering when would it be time to go without hurting Timofey's feelings. The others were listening to Hagen discussing modern education:

"You may laugh," he said, casting a sharp glance at Clements—who shook his head, denying the charge, and then passed the album to Joan, pointing out something in it that had suddenly provoked his glee.

"You may laugh, but I affirm that the only way to escape from the morass—just a drop, Timofey: that will do—is to lock up the student in a soundproof cell and eliminate the lecture room."

"Yes, that's it," said Joan to her husband under her breath, handing the album back to him.

"I am glad you agree, Joan," continued Hagen. "However, I have been called an *enfant terrible* for expounding this theory, and perhaps you will not go on agreeing so easily when you hear me out. Phonograph records on every possible subject will be at the isolated student's disposal . . ."

"But the personality of the lecturer," said Margaret Thayer. "Surely that counts for something."

"It does not!" shouted Hagen. "That is the tragedy! Who, for example, wants *him*"—he pointed to radiant Pnin—"who wants his personality? Nobody! They will reject Timofey's wonderful personality without a quaver. The world wants a machine, not a Timofey."

"One could have Timofey televised," said Clements.

"Oh, I would love that," said Joan, beaming at her host, and Betty nodded vigorously. Pnin bowed deeply to them with an "I-am-disarmed" spreading of both hands.

"And what do *you* think of my controversial plan?" asked Hagen of Thomas.

"I can tell you what Tom thinks," said Clements, still contemplating the same picture in the book that lay open on his knees. "Tom thinks that the best method of teaching anything is to rely on discussion in class, which means letting twenty young blockheads and two cocky neurotics discuss for fifty minutes something that neither their teacher nor they know. Now, for the last three months," he went on, without any logical transition, "I have been looking for this picture, and here it is. The publisher of my new book on the Philosophy of Gesture wants a portrait of me, and Joan and I knew we had seen somewhere a stunning likeness by an Old Master but could not even recall his period. Well, here it is, here it is. The only retouching needed would be the addition of a sport shirt and the deletion of this warrior's hand."

"I must really protest," began Thomas.

Clements passed the open book to Margaret Thayer, and she burst out laughing.

"I must protest, Laurence," said Tom. "A relaxed discussion in an atmosphere of broad generalizations is a more realistic approach to education than the old-fashioned formal lecture."

"Sure, sure," said Clements.

Joan scrambled up to her feet and covered her glass with her narrow palm when Pnin offered to replenish it. Mrs. Thayer looked at her wrist watch, and then at her husband. A soft yawn distended Laurence's mouth. Betty asked Thomas if he knew a man called Fogelman, an expert in bats, who lived in Santa Clara, Cuba. Hagen asked for a glass of water or beer. Whom does he remind me of? thought Pnin suddenly. Eric Wind? Why? They are quite different physically.

The setting of the final scene was the hallway. Hagen could not find the cane he had come with (it had fallen behind a trunk in the closet).

"And *I* think I left my purse where I was sitting," said Mrs. Thayer, pushing her pensive husband ever so slightly toward the living room.

Pnin and Clements, in last-minute discourse, stood on either side of the living-room doorway, like two well-fed caryatids, and drew in their abdomens to let the silent Thayer pass. In the middle of the room Professor Thomas and Miss Bliss—he with his hands behind his back and rising up every now and then on his toes, she holding a tray—were standing and talking of Cuba, where a cousin of Betty's fiancé had lived for quite a while, Betty understood. Thayer blundered from chair to chair, and found himself with a white bag, not knowing really where he picked it up, his mind being occupied by the adumbrations of lines he was to write down later in the night:

> *We sat and drank, each with a separate past locked up*
> *in him, and fate's alarm clocks set at unrelated futures*
> *—when, at last, a wrist was cocked, and eyes of consorts*
> *met . . .*

Meanwhile Pnin asked Joan Clements and Margaret Thayer if they would care to see how he had embellished the upstairs rooms. The idea enchanted them. He led the way. His so-called *kabinet* now looked very cozy, its scratched floor snugly covered with the more or less Pakistan rug which he had once acquired for his office and had recently removed in drastic silence from under the feet of the surprised Falternfels. A tartan lap robe, under which Pnin had crossed the ocean from Europe in 1940, and some endemic cushions disguised the unremovable bed. The pink shelves, which he had found supporting several generations of children's books—from *Tom the Bootblack, or the Road to Success* by Horatio Alger, Jr., 1889, through *Rolf in the Woods* by Ernest Thompson Seton, 1911, to a 1928 edition of *Compton's Pictured Encyclopedia* in ten volumes with foggy little photographs—were now loaded with three hundred sixty-five items from the Waindell College Library.

"And to think I have stamped all these," sighed Mrs. Thayer, rolling her eyes in mock dismay.

"Some stamped Mrs. Miller," said Pnin, a stickler for historical truth.

What struck the visitors most in the bedroom was a large folding screen that cut off the fourposter bed from insidious drafts, and the view from the row of small windows: a dark rock wall rising abruptly some fifty feet away, with a stretch of pale starry sky above the black growth of its crest. On the back lawn, across the reflection of a window, Laurence strolled into the shadows.

"At last you are really comfortable," said Joan.

"And you know what I will say to you," replied Pnin in a confidential undertone vibrating with triumph. "Tomorrow morning, under the curtain of mysteree, I will see a gentleman who is wanting to help me to buy this house!"

They came down again. Roy handed his wife Betty's bag. Herman found his cane. Margaret's bag was sought. Laurence reappeared.

"Good-by, good-by, Professor Vin!" sang out Pnin, his cheeks ruddy and round in the lamplight of the porch.

(Still in the hallway, Betty and Margaret Thayer admired proud Dr. Hagen's walking stick, recently sent him from Germany, a gnarled cudgel, with a donkey's head for knob. The head could move one ear. The cane had belonged to Dr. Hagen's Bavarian grandfather, a country clergyman. The mechanism of the other ear had broken down in 1914, according to a note the pastor had left. Hagen carried it, he said, in defense against a certain Alsatian in Greenlawn Lane. American dogs were not used to pedestrians. He always preferred walking to driving. The ear could not be repaired. At least, in Waindell.)

"Now I wonder why he called me that," said T. W. Thomas, Professor of Anthropology, to Laurence and Joan Clements as they walked through blue darkness toward four cars parked under the elms on the other side of the road.

"Our friend," answered Clements, "employs a nomenclature all his own. His verbal vagaries add a new thrill to life.

His mispronunciations are mythopeic. His slips of the tongue are oracular. He calls my wife John."

"Still I find it a little disturbing," said Thomas.

"He probably mistook you for somebody else," said Clements. "And for all I know you *may* be somebody else."

Before they had crossed the street they were overtaken by Dr. Hagen. Professor Thomas, still looking puzzled, took his leave.

"Well," said Hagen.

It was a fair fall night, velvet below, steel above.

Joan asked:

"You're sure you don't want us to give you a lift?"

"It's a ten-minute walk. And a walk is a must on such a wonderful night."

The three of them stood for a moment gazing at the stars.

"And all these are worlds," said Hagen.

"Or else," said Clements with a yawn, "a frightful mess. I suspect it is really a fluorescent corpse, and we are inside it."

From the lighted porch came Pnin's rich laughter as he finished recounting to the Thayers and Betty Bliss how he, too, had once retrieved the wrong reticule.

"Come, my fluorescent corpse, let's be moving," said Joan. "It was so nice to see you, Herman. Give my love to Irmgard. What a delightful party. I have never seen Timofey so happy."

"Yes, thank you," answered Hagen absent-mindedly.

"You should have seen his face," said Joan, "when he told us he was going to talk to a real-estate man tomorrow about buying that dream house."

"He did? You're sure he said that?" Hagen asked sharply.

"Quite sure," said Joan. "And if anybody needs a house, it is certainly Timofey."

"Well, good night," said Hagen. "Glad you could come. Good night."

He waited for them to reach their car, hesitated, and then marched back to the lighted porch, where, standing as on a stage, Pnin was shaking hands a second or third time with the Thayers and Betty.

("I would never," said Joan, as she backed the car and worked on the wheel, "but *never* have allowed my child to go abroad with that old Lesbian." "Careful," said Laurence, "he may be drunk but he is not out of earshot.")

"I shall not forgive you," said Betty to her merry host, "for not letting me do the dishes."

"I'll help him," said Hagen, ascending the porch steps and thumping upon them with his cane. "You, children, run along now."

There was a final round of handshakes, and the Thayers and Betty left.

12

"First," said Hagen, as he and Pnin re-entered the living room, "I guess I'll have a last cup of wine with you."

"Perfect. Perfect!" cried Pnin. "Let us finish my *cruchon*."

They made themselves comfortable, and Dr. Hagen said:

"You are a wonderful host, Timofey. This is a very delightful moment. My grandfather used to say that a glass of good wine should be always sipped and savored as if it were the last one before the execution. I wonder what you put into this punch. I also wonder if, as our charming Joan affirms, you are really contemplating buying this house?"

"Not contemplating—peeping a little at possibilities," replied Pnin with a gurgling laugh.

"I question the wisdom of it," continued Hagen, nursing his goblet.

"Naturally, I am expecting that I will get tenure at last," said Pnin rather slyly. "I am now Assistant Professor nine years. Years run. Soon I will be Assistant Emeritus. Hagen, why are you silent?"

"You place me in a very embarrassing position, Timofey. I hoped you would not raise this particular question."

"I do not raise the question. I say that I only expect—oh, not next year, but example given, at hundredth anniversary of Liberation of Serfs—Waindell will make me Associate."

"Well, you see, my dear friend, I must tell you a sad secret. It is not official yet, and you must promise not to mention it to anyone."

"I swear," said Pnin, raising his hand.

"You cannot but know," continued Hagen, "with what

loving care I built our great department. I, too, am no longer young. You say, Timofey, you have been here for nine years. But I have been giving my all for *twenty-nine* years to this university! My modest all. As my friend, Dr. Kraft, wrote me the other day: you, Herman Hagen, have done alone more for Germany in America than all our missions have done in Germany for America. And what happens now? I have nursed this Falternfels, this dragon, in my bosom, and he has now worked himself into a key position. I spare you the details of the intrigue!"

"Yes," said Pnin with a sigh, "intrigue is horrible, horrible. But, on the other side, honest work will always prove its advantage. You and I will give next year some splendid new courses which I have planned long ago. On Tyranny. On the Boot. On Nicholas the First. On all the precursors of modern atrocity. Hagen, when we speak of injustice, we forget Armenian massacres, tortures which Tibet invented, colonists in Africa. . . . The history of man is the history of pain!"

Hagen bent over to his friend and patted him on his knobby knee.

"You are a wonderful romantic, Timofey, and under happier circumstances . . . However, I can tell you that in the Spring Term we *are* going to do something unusual. We are going to stage a Dramatic Program—scenes from Kotzebue to Hauptmann. I see it as a sort of apotheosis. . . . But let us not anticipate. I, too, am a romantic, Timofey, and therefore cannot work with people like Bodo, as our trustees wish me to do. Kraft is retiring at Seaboard, and it has been offered to me that I replace him, beginning next fall."

"I congratulate you," said Pnin warmly.

"Thanks, my friend. It is certainly a very fine and prominent position. I shall apply to a wider field of scholarship and administration the invaluable experience I have gained here. Of course, since I know Bodo will not continue you in the German Department, my first move was to suggest you come with me, but they tell me they have enough Slavists at Seaboard without you. So I spoke to Blorenge, but the French Department here is also full up. This is unfortunate, because Waindell feels that it would be too much of a financial burden to pay you for two or three Russian courses that have ceased to attract students. Political trends in America, as we all know, discourage interest in things Russian. On the other hand, you'll be glad to know that the English Department is inviting one of your most brilliant compatriots, a really fascinating lecturer—I have heard him once; I think he's an old friend of yours."

Pnin cleared his throat and asked:

"It signifies that they are firing me?"

"Now, don't take it too hard, Timofey. I'm sure your old friend—"

"Who is old friend?" queried Pnin, slitting his eyes.

Hagen named the fascinating lecturer.

Leaning forward, his elbows propped on his knees, clasping and unclasping his hands, Pnin said:

"Yes, I know him thirty years or more. We are friends, but there is one thing perfectly certain. I will never work under him."

"Well, I guess you should sleep on it. Perhaps some solution may be found. Anyway, we'll have ample opportunity to discuss these matters. We shall just go on teaching, you and I, as if nothing had happened, *nicht wahr*? We must be brave, Timofey!"

"So they have fired me," said Pnin, clasping his hands and nodding his head.

"Yes, we are in the same boat, in the same boat," said jovial Hagen, and he stood up. It was getting very late.

"I go now," said Hagen, who, though a lesser addict of the present tense than Pnin, also held it in favor. "It has been a wonderful party, and I would never have allowed myself to spoil the merriment if our mutual friend had not informed me of your optimistic intentions. Good night. Oh, by the way . . . Naturally, you will get your salary for the Fall Term in full, and then we shall see how much we can obtain for you in the Spring Term, especially if you will agree to take off some stupid office work from my poor old shoulders, and also if you will participate vitally in the Dramatic Program in New Hall. I think you should actually play in it, under my daughter's direction; it would distract you from sad thoughts. Now go to bed at once, and put yourself to sleep with a good mystery story."

On the porch he pumped Pnin's unresponsive hand with enough vigor for two. Then he flourished his cane and merrily marched down the wooden steps.

The screen door banged behind him.

"Der arme Kerl," muttered kindhearted Hagen to himself as he walked homeward. "At least, I have sweetened the pill."

13

From the sideboard and dining-room table Pnin removed to the kitchen sink the used china and silverware. He put away what food remained into the bright Arctic light of the refrigerator. The ham and tongue had all gone, and so had the little sausages; but the vinaigrette had not been a success, and enough caviar and meat tarts were left over for a meal or two tomorrow. "Boom-boom-boom," said the china closet as he passed by. He surveyed the living room and started to tidy it up. A last drop of Pnin's Punch glistened in its beautiful bowl. Joan had crooked a lipstick-stained cigarette butt in her saucer; Betty had left no trace and had taken all the glasses back to the kitchen. Mrs. Thayer had forgotten a booklet of pretty multicolored matches on her plate, next to a bit of nougat. Mr. Thayer had twisted into all kinds of weird shapes half a dozen paper napkins; Hagen had quenched a messy cigar in an uneaten bunchlet of grapes.

In the kitchen, Pnin prepared to wash up the dishes. He removed his silk coat, his tie, and his dentures. To protect his shirt front and tuxedo trousers, he donned a soubrette's dappled apron. He scraped various tidbits off the plates into a brown paper bag, to be given eventually to a mangy little white dog, with pink patches on its back, that visited him sometimes in the afternoon—there was no reason a human's misfortune should interfere with a canine's pleasure.

He prepared a bubble bath in the sink for the crockery, glass, and silverware, and with infinite care lowered the aquamarine bowl into the tepid foam. Its resonant flint glass emitted a sound full of muffled mellowness as it settled down to soak. He rinsed the amber goblets and the silverware under the tap, and submerged them in the same foam. Then he fished out the knives, forks, and spoons, rinsed them, and began to wipe them. He worked very slowly, with a certain vagueness of manner that might have been taken for a mist of abstraction in a less methodical man. He gathered the wiped spoons into a posy, placed them in a pitcher which he had washed but not dried, and then took them out one by one and wiped them all over again. He groped under the bubbles, around the goblets, and under the melodious bowl, for any piece of forgotten silver—and retrieved a nutcracker. Fastidious Pnin rinsed it, and was wiping it, when the leggy thing somehow slipped out of the towel and fell like a man from a roof. He almost caught it—his fingertips actually came into contact with it in mid-air, but this only helped to propel it into the treasure-concealing foam of the sink, where an excruciating crack of broken glass followed upon the plunge.

Pnin hurled the towel into a corner and, turning away, stood for a moment staring at the blackness beyond the threshold of the open back door. A quiet, lacy-winged little green insect circled in the glare of a strong naked lamp above Pnin's glossy bald head. He looked very old, with his toothless mouth half open and a film of tears dimming his blank, unblinking eyes. Then, with a moan of anguished anticipation, he went back to the sink and, bracing himself, dipped his hand deep into the foam. A jagger of glass stung him. Gently he removed a broken goblet. The beautiful bowl was intact. He took a fresh dish towel and went on with his household work.

When everything was clean and dry, and the bowl stood aloof and serene on the safest shelf of a cupboard, and the little bright house was securely locked up in the large dark night, Pnin sat down at the kitchen table and, taking a sheet of yellow scrap paper from its drawer, unclipped his fountain pen and started to compose the draft of a letter:

"Dear Hagen," he wrote in his clear firm hand, "permit me to recaputilate (crossed out) recapitulate the conversation we had tonight. It, I must confess, somewhat astonished me. If I had the honor to correctly understand you, you said——"

Chapter Seven

MY FIRST recollection of Timofey Pnin is connected with a speck of coal dust that entered my left eye on a spring Sunday in 1911.

It was one of those rough, gusty, and lustrous mornings in St. Petersburg, when the last transparent piece of Ladoga ice has been carried away to the gulf by the Neva, and her indigo waves heave and lap the granite of the embankment, and the tugboats and huge barges, moored along the quay, creak and scrape rhythmically, and the mahogany and brass of anchored steam yachts shine in the skittish sun. I had been trying out a beautiful new English bicycle given me for my twelfth birthday, and, as I rode home to our rosy-stone house in the Morskaya, over parquet-smooth wooden pavements, the consciousness of having gravely disobeyed my tutor was less bothersome than the granule of smarting pain in the far north of my eyeball. Home remedies, such as the application of wads of cotton wool soaked in cool tea and the *tri-k-nosu* (rub-noseward) device, only made matters worse; and when I awoke next morning, the object lurking under my upper eyelid felt like a solid polygon that became more deeply embedded at every watery wink. In the afternoon I was taken to a leading ophthalmologist, Dr. Pavel Pnin.

One of those silly incidents that remain forever in a child's receptive mind marked the space of time my tutor and I spent in Dr. Pnin's sundust-and-plush waiting room, where the blue dab of a window in miniature was reflected in the glass dome of an ormolu clock on the mantelpiece, and two flies kept describing slow quadrangles around the lifeless chandelier. A lady, wearing a plumed hat, and her dark-spectacled husband were sitting in connubial silence on the davenport; then a cavalry officer entered and sat near the window reading a newspaper; then the husband repaired to Dr. Pnin's study; and then I noticed an odd expression on my tutor's face.

With my good eye I followed his stare. The officer was leaning toward the lady. In rapid French he berated her for something she had done or not done the day before. She gave him

423

her gloved hand to kiss. He glued himself to its eyelet—and forthwith left, cured of whatever had ailed him.

In softness of features, body bulk, leanness of leg, apish shape of ear and upper lip, Dr. Pavel Pnin looked very like Timofey, as the latter was to look three or four decades later. In the father, however, a fringe of straw-colored hair relieved a waxlike calvity; he wore a black-rimmed pince-nez on a black ribbon like the late Dr. Chekhov; he spoke in a gentle stutter, very unlike his son's later voice. And what a divine relief it was when, with a tiny instrument resembling an elf's drumstick, the tender doctor removed from my eyeball the offending black atom! I wonder where that speck is now? The dull, mad fact is that it *does* exist somewhere.

Perhaps because on my visits to schoolmates I had seen other middle-class apartments, I unconsciously retained a picture of the Pnin flat that probably corresponds to reality. I can report therefore that as likely as not it consisted of two rows of rooms divided by a long corridor; on one side was the waiting room, the doctor's office, presumably a dining room and a drawing room further on; and on the other side were two or three bedrooms, a schoolroom, a bathroom, a maid's room, and a kitchen. I was about to leave with a phial of eye lotion, and my tutor was taking the opportunity to ask Dr. Pnin if eyestrain might cause gastric trouble, when the front door opened and shut. Dr. Pnin nimbly walked into the passage, voiced a query, received a quiet answer, and returned with his son Timofey, a thirteen-year-old *gimnazist* (classical school pupil) in his *gimnazicheskiy* uniform—black blouse, black pants, shiny black belt (I attended a more liberal school where we wore what we liked).

Do I really remember his crew cut, his puffy pale face, his red ears? Yes, distinctly. I even remember the way he imperceptibly removed his shoulder from under the proud paternal hand, while the proud paternal voice was saying: "This boy has just got a Five Plus (A+) in the Algebra examination." From the end of the corridor there came a steady smell of hashed-cabbage pie, and through the open door of the schoolroom I could see a map of Russia on the wall, books on a shelf, a stuffed squirrel, and a toy monoplane with linen wings and a rubber motor. I had a similar one but twice as big, bought in Biarritz. After one had wound up the propeller for some time, the rubber would change its manner of twist and develop fascinating thick whorls which predicted the end of its tether.

2

Five years later, after spending the beginning of the summer on our estate near St. Petersburg, my mother, my young brother, and I happened to visit a dreary old aunt at her curiously desolate country seat not far from a famous resort on the Baltic coast. One afternoon, as in concentrated ecstasy I was spreading, underside up, an exceptionally rare aberration of the Paphia Fritillary, in which the silver stripes ornamenting the lower surface of its hindwings had fused into an even expanse of metallic gloss, a footman came up with the information that the old lady requested my presence. In the reception hall I found her talking to two self-conscious youths in university student uniforms. One, with the blond fuzz, was Timofey Pnin, the other, with the russet down, was Grigoriy Belochkin. They had come to ask my grandaunt the permission to use an empty barn on the confines of her property for the staging of a play. This was a Russian translation of Arthur Schnitzler's three-act *Liebelei*. Ancharov, a provincial semiprofessional actor, with a reputation consisting mainly of faded newspaper clippings, was helping to rig up the thing. Would I participate? But at sixteen I was as arrogant as I was shy, and declined to play the anonymous gentleman in Act One. The interview ended in mutual embarrassment, not alleviated by Pnin or Belochkin overturning a glass of pear *kvas*, and I went back to my butterfly. A fortnight later I was somehow or other compelled to attend the performance. The barn was full of *dachniki* (vacationists) and disabled soldiers from a nearby hospital. I came with my brother, and next to me sat the steward of my aunt's estate, Robert Karlovich Horn, a cheerful plump person from Riga with bloodshot, porcelain-blue eyes, who kept applauding heartily at the wrong moments. I remember the odor of decorative fir branches, and the eyes of peasant children glistening through the chinks in the walls. The front seats were so close to the stage that when the be-

trayed husband produced a packet of love letters written to
his wife by Fritz Lobheimer, dragoon and college student, and
flung them into Fritz's face, you could see perfectly well that
they were old postcards with the stamp corners cut off. I am
perfectly sure that the small role of this irate Gentleman was
taken by Timofey Pnin (though, of course, he might also have
appeared as somebody else in the following acts); but a buff
overcoat, bushy mustachios, and a dark wig with a median
parting disguised him so thoroughly that the minuscule interest I took in his existence might not have warranted any
conscious assurance on my part. Fritz, the young lover
doomed to die in a duel, not only has that mysterious affair
backstage with the Lady in Black Velvet, the Gentleman's
wife, but toys with the heart of Christine, a naïve Viennese
maiden. Fritz was played by stocky, forty-year-old Ancharov,
who wore a warm-taupe make-up, thumped his chest with the
sound of rug beating, and by his impromptu contributions
to the role he had not deigned to learn almost paralyzed
Fritz's pal, Theodor Kaiser (Grigoriy Belochkin). A mon-
eyed old maid in real life, whom Ancharov humored, was
miscast as Christine Weiring, the violinist's daughter. The
role of the little milliner, Theodor's amoretta, Mizi Schlager,
was charmingly acted by a pretty, slender-necked, velvet-
eyed girl, Belochkin's sister, who got the greatest ovation of
the night.

3

It is improbable that during the years of Revolution and
Civil War which followed I had occasion to recall Dr. Pnin
and his son. If I have reconstructed in some detail the prec-
edent impressions, it is merely to fix what flashed through my
mind when, on an April night in the early twenties, at a Paris
cafe, I found myself shaking hands with auburn-bearded, in-
fantine-eyed Timofey Pnin, erudite young author of several
admirable papers on Russian culture. It was the custom
among émigré writers and artists to gather at the Three Fountains after the recitals or lectures that were so popular among
Russian expatriates; and it was on such an occasion that, still
hoarse from my reading, I tried not only to remind Pnin of

former meetings, but also to amuse him and other people around us with the unusual lucidity and strength of my memory. However, he denied everything. He said he vaguely recalled my grandaunt but had never met me. He said that his marks in algebra had always been poor and that, anyway, his father never displayed him to patients; he said that in *Zabava* (*Liebelei*) he had only acted the part of Christine's father. He repeated that we had never seen each other before. Our little discussion was nothing more than good-natured banter, and everybody laughed; and noticing how reluctant he was to recognize his own past, I switched to another, less personal, topic.

Presently I grew aware that a striking-looking young girl in a black silk sweater, with a golden band around her brown hair, had become my chief listener. She stood before me, right elbow resting on left palm, right hand holding cigarette between finger and thumb as a gypsy would, cigarette sending up its smoke; bright blue eyes half closed because of the smoke. She was Liza Bogolepov, a medical student who also wrote poetry. She asked me if she could send me for appraisal a batch of her poems. A little later at the same party, I noticed her sitting next to a repulsively hairy young composer, Ivan Nagoy; they were drinking *auf Bruderschaft*, which is performed by intertwining arms with one's co-drinker, and some chairs away Dr. Barakan, a talented neurologist and Liza's latest lover, was watching her with quiet despair in his dark almond-shaped eyes.

A few days later she sent me those poems; a fair sample of her production is the kind of stuff that émigré rhymsterettes wrote after Akhmatova: lackadaisical little lyrics that tiptoed in more or less anapaestic trimeter and sat down rather heavily with a wistful sigh:

> *Samotsvétov króme ochéy*
> *Net u menyá nikakíh,*
> *No est' róza eshchó nezhnéy*
> *Rózovih gúb moíh.*
> *I yúnosha tíhiy skazál:*
> *"Vashe sérdtse vsegó nezhnéy . . ."*
> *I yá opustíla glazá . . .*

I have marked the stress accents, and transliterated the Russian with the usual understanding that *u* is pronounced like a short "oo," *i* like a short "ee," and *zh* like a French "j." Such incomplete rhymes as *skazal-glaza* were considered very elegant. Note also the erotic undercurrents and *cour d'amour* implications. A prose translation would go: "No jewels, save my eyes, do I own, but I have a rose which is even softer than my rosy lips. And a quiet youth said: 'There is nothing softer than your heart.' And I lowered my gaze. . . ."

I wrote back telling Liza that her poems were bad and she ought to stop composing. Sometime later I saw her in another café, sitting at a long table, abloom and ablaze among a dozen young Russian poets. She kept her sapphire glance on me with a mocking and mysterious persistence. We talked. I suggested she let me see those poems again in some quieter place. She did. I told her they struck me as being even worse than they had seemed at the first reading. She lived in the cheapest room of a decadent little hotel with no bath and a pair of twittering young Englishmen for neighbors.

Poor Liza! She had of course her artistic moments when she would stop, entranced, on a May night in a squalid street to admire—nay, to adore—the motley remains of an old poster on a wet black wall in the light of a street lamp, and the translucent green of linden leaves where they drooped next to the lamp, but she was one of those women who combine healthy good looks with hysterical sloppiness; lyrical outbursts with a very practical and very commonplace mind; a vile temper with sentimentality; and languorous surrender with a robust capacity for sending people on wild-goose errands. In the result of emotions and in the course of events, the narration of which would be of no public interest whatsoever, Liza swallowed a handful of sleeping pills. As she tumbled into unconsciousness she knocked over an open bottle of the deep-red ink which she used to write down her verses, and that bright trickle coming from under her door was noticed by Chris and Lew just in time to have her saved.

I had not seen her for a fortnight after that contretemps when, on the eve of my leaving for Switzerland and Germany, she waylaid me in the little garden at the end of my street, looking svelt and strange in a charming new dress as dove-gray as Paris, and wearing a really enchanting new hat with a blue bird's wing, and handed me a folded paper. "I want a last piece of advice from you," said Liza in what the French call a "white" voice. "This is an offer of marriage that I have received. I shall wait till midnight. If I don't hear from you, I shall accept it." She hailed a taxi and was gone.

The letter has by chance remained among my papers. Here it is:

"I am afraid you will be pained by my confession, my dear Lise" (the writer, though using Russian, called her through-out by this French form of her name, in order, I presume, to avoid both the too familiar 'Liza' and the too formal 'Eliza-veta Innokentievna'). "It is always painful for a sensitive (*chut-kiy*) person to see another in an awkward position. And I am definitely in an awkward position.

"You, Lise, are surrounded by poets, scientists, artists, dan-dies. The celebrated painter who made your portrait last year is now, it is said, drinking himself to death (*govoryat, spilsya*) in the wilds of Massachusetts. Rumor proclaims many other things. And here I am, daring to write to you.

"I am not handsome, I am not interesting, I am not tal-ented. I am not even rich. But, Lise, I offer you everything I have, to the last blood corpuscle, to the last tear, everything. And, believe me, this is more than any genius can offer you because a genius needs to keep so much in store, and thus cannot offer you the whole of himself as I do. I may not achieve happiness, but I know I shall do everything to make you happy. I want you to write poems. I want you to go on with your psychotherapeutic research—in which I do not un-derstand much, while questioning the validity of what I can understand. Incidentally, I am sending you under separate cover a pamphlet published in Prague by my friend Professor Chateau, which brilliantly refutes your Dr. Halp's theory of birth being an act of suicide on the part of the infant. I have permitted myself to correct an obvious misprint on page 48 of Chateau's excellent paper. I await your" (probably "deci-sion," the bottom of the page with the signature had been cut off by Liza).

4

When half a dozen years later I revisited Paris, I learned that Timofey Pnin had married Liza Bogolepov soon after my departure. She sent me a published collection of her poems *Suhie Gubï* (Dry Lips) with the inscription in dark-red ink: "To a Stranger from a Stranger" (*neznakomtsu ot neznakomki*). I saw Pnin and her at an evening tea in the apartment of a famous émigré, a social revolutionary, one of those informal gatherings where old-fashioned terrorists, heroic nuns, gifted hedonists, liberals, adventurous young poets, elderly novelists and artists, publishers and publicists, free-minded philosophers and scholars would represent a kind of special knighthood, the active and significant nucleus of an exiled society which during the third of a century it flourished remained practically unknown to American intellectuals, for whom the notion of Russian emigration was made to mean by astute communist propaganda a vague and perfectly fictitious mass of so-called Trotskiites (whatever these are), ruined reactionaries, reformed or disguised Cheka men, titled ladies, professional priests, restaurant keepers, and White Russian military groups, all of them of no cultural importance whatever.

Taking advantage of Pnin's being engaged in a political discussion with Kerenski at the other end of the table, Liza informed me—with her usual crude candor—that she had "told Timofey everything"; that he was "a saint" and had "pardoned" me. Fortunately, she did not often accompany him to later receptions where I had the pleasure of sitting next to him, or opposite him, in the company of dear friends, on our small lone planet, above the black and diamond city, with the lamplight on this or that Socratic cranium and a slice of lemon revolving in the glass of stirred tea. One night, as Dr. Barakan, Pnin, and I were sitting at the Bolotovs, I happened to be talking to the neurologist about a cousin of his, Ludmila, now Lady D——, whom I had known in Yalta, Athens, and London, when suddenly Pnin cried to Dr. Barakan across the table: "Now, don't believe a word he says, Georgiy Aramovich. He makes up everything. He once invented that we were schoolmates in Russia and cribbed at examinations. He is a dreadful inventor (*on uzhasnïy vïdumshchik*)." Barakan and I were so astounded by this outburst that we just sat and looked at each other in silence.

5

In the rememoration of old relationships, later impressions often tend to be dimmer than earlier ones. I recall talking to Liza and her new husband, Dr. Eric Wind, in between two acts of a Russian play in New York sometime in the early forties. He said he had a "really tender feeling for Herr Professor Pnin" and gave me some bizarre details of their voyage together from Europe in the beginning of World War II. I ran into Pnin several times during those years at various social and academic functions in New York; but the only vivid recollection I have is of our ride together on a west-side bus, on a very festive and very wet night in 1952. We had come from our respective colleges to participate in a literary and artistic program before a large émigré audience in downtown New York on the occasion of the hundredth anniversay of a great writer's death. Pnin had been teaching at Waindell since the mid-forties and never had I seen him look healthier, more prosperous, and more self-assertive. He and I turned out to be, as he quipped, *vos'midesyatniki* (men of the Eighties), that is, we both happened to have lodgings for the night in the West Eighties; and as we hung from adjacent straps in the crowded and spasmodic vehicle, my good friend managed to combine a vigorous ducking and twisting of the head (in his continuous attempts to check and recheck the numbers of cross streets) with a magnificent account of all he had not had sufficient time to say at the celebration on Homer's and Gogol's use of the Rambling Comparison.

6

When I decided to accept a professorship at Waindell, I stipulated that I could invite whomever I wanted for teaching in the special Russian Division I planned to inaugurate. With this confirmed, I wrote to Timofey Pnin offering him in the most cordial terms I could muster to assist me in any way and to any extent he desired. His answer surprised me and hurt me. Curtly he wrote that he was through with teaching and would not even bother to wait till the end of the spring term. Then he turned to other subjects. Victor (about whom I had politely inquired) was in Rome with his mother; she had divorced her third husband and married an Italian art dealer. Pnin concluded his letter by saying that to his great regret he would be leaving Waindell two or three days before the public lecture that I was to give there Tuesday, February the fifteenth. He did not specify his destination.

The Greyhound that brought me to Waindell on Monday the fourteenth arrived after nightfall. I was met by the Cockerells, who treated me to a late supper at their house, where I discovered I was to spend the night, instead of sleeping at a hotel as I had hoped. Gwen Cockerell turned out to be a very pretty woman in her late thirties, with a kitten's profile and graceful limbs. Her husband, whom I had once met in New Haven and remembered as a rather limp, moon-faced, neutrally blond Englishman, had acquired an unmistakable resemblance to the man he had now been mimicking for almost ten years. I was tired and not overanxious to be entertained throughout the supper with a floor show, but I must admit that Jack Cockerell impersonated Pnin to perfection. He went on for at least two hours, showing me everything—Pnin teaching, Pnin eating, Pnin ogling a coed, Pnin narrating the epic of the electric fan which he had imprudently set going on a glass shelf right above the bathtub into which its own vibration had almost caused it to fall; Pnin trying to convince Professor Wynn, the ornithologist who hardly knew him, that they were old pals, Tim and Tom—and Wynn leaping to the conclusion that this was somebody impersonating Professor Pnin. It was all built of course around the Pninian gesture and the Pninian wild English, but Cockerell also managed to imitate such things as the subtle degree of difference between the silence of Pnin and the silence of Thayer, as they sat motionlessly ruminating in adjacent chairs at the Faculty Club. We got Pnin in the Stacks, and Pnin on the Campus Lake. We heard Pnin criticize the various rooms he had successively rented. We listened to Pnin's account of his learning to drive a car, and of his dealing with his first puncture on the way back from "the chicken farm of some Privy Counselor of the Tsar," where Cockerell supposed Pnin spent the summers. We arrived at last to Pnin's declaration one day that he had been "shot" by which, according to the impersonator, the poor fellow meant "fired"—(a mistake I doubt my friend could have made). Brilliant Cockerell also told of the strange feud between Pnin and his compatriot Komarov—the mediocre muralist who had kept adding fresco portraits of faculty members in the college dining hall to those already depicted there by the great Lang. Although Komarov belonged to another political faction than Pnin, the patriotic artist had seen in Pnin's dismissal an anti-Russian gesture and had started to delete a sulky Napoleon that stood between young, plumpish (now gaunt) Blorenge and young, mustached (now shaven) Hagen, in order to paint in Pnin; and there was the scene between Pnin and President Poore at lunch—an enraged, spluttering Pnin losing all control over what English he had, pointing a shaking forefinger at the preliminary outlines of a ghostly muzhik on the wall, and shouting that he would sue the college if his face appeared above that blouse; and there was his audience, imperturbable Poore, trapped in the dark of his total blindness, waiting for Pnin to peter out and then asking at large: "Is that foreign gentleman on our staff?" Oh, the impersonation was deliciously funny, and although Gwen Cockerell must have heard the program many times before, she laughed so loud that their old dog Sobakevich, a brown cocker with a tearstained face, began to fidget and sniff at me. The performance, I repeat, was magnificent, but it was too long. By midnight the fun began to thin; the smile I was keeping afloat began to develop, I felt, symptoms of labial cramp. Finally the whole thing grew to be such a bore that I fell wondering if by some poetical vengeance this Pnin business had not become with Cockerell the kind of fatal obsession which substitutes its own victim for that of the initial ridicule.

We had been having a good deal of Scotch, and sometime after midnight Cockerell made one of those sudden decisions that seem so bright and gay at a certain stage of intoxication. He said he was sure foxy old Pnin had not really left yesterday, but was lying low. So why not telephone and find out? He made the call, and although there was no answer to the series of compelling notes which simulate the far sound of actual ringing in an imaginary hallway, it stood to reason that this perfectly healthy telephone would have been probably disconnected, had Pnin really vacated the house. I was foolishly eager to say something friendly to my good Timofey Pahlich, and so after a little while I attempted to reach him too. Suddenly there was a click, a sonic vista, the response of a heavy breathing, and then a poorly disguised voice said: "He is not at home, he has gone, he has quite gone"—after which the speaker hung up; but none save my old friend, not even his best imitator, could rhyme so emphatically "at" with the German *"hat,"* "home" with the French *"homme,"* and "gone" with the head of "Goneril." Cockerell then proposed driving over to 999 Todd Road and serenading its burrowed tenant, but here Mrs. Cockerell intervened; and after an evening that somehow left me with the mental counterpart of a bad taste in the mouth, we all went to bed.

7

I spent a poor night in a charming, airy, prettily furnished room where neither window nor door closed properly, and where an omnibus edition of Sherlock Holmes which had pursued me for years supported a bedside lamp, so weak and wan that the set of galleys I had brought with me to correct could not sweeten insomnia. The thunder of trucks rocked the house every two minutes or so; I kept dozing off and sitting up with a gasp, and through the parody of a window shade some light from the street reached the mirror and dazzled me into thinking I was facing a firing squad.

I am so constituted that I absolutely must gulp down the juice of three oranges before confronting the rigors of day. So at seven-thirty I took a quick shower, and five minutes later was out of the house in the company of the long-eared and dejected Sobakevich.

The air was keen, the sky clear and burnished. Southward the empty road could be seen ascending a gray-blue hill among patches of snow. A tall leafless poplar, as brown as a broom, rose on my right, and its long morning shadow

crossing to the opposite side of the street reached there a crenulated, cream-colored house which, according to Cockerell,
had been thought by my predecessor to be the Turkish Consulate on account of crowds of fez wearers he had seen entering. I turned left, northward, and walked a couple of blocks
downhill to a restaurant that I had noted on the eve; but the
place had not opened yet, and I turned back. Hardly had I
taken a couple of steps when a great truck carrying beer rumbled up the street, immediately followed by a small pale blue
sedan with the white head of a dog looking out, after which
came another great truck, exactly similar to the first. The
humble sedan was crammed with bundles and suitcases; its
driver was Pnin. I emitted a roar of greeting, but he did not
see me, and my only hope was that I might walk uphill fast
enough to catch him while the red light one block ahead kept
him at bay.

I hurried past the rear truck, and had another glimpse of
my old friend, in tense profile, wearing a cap with ear flaps
and a storm coat; but next moment the light turned green,
the little white dog leaning out yapped at Sobakevich, and
everything surged forward—truck one, Pnin, truck two. From
where I stood I watched them recede in the frame of the
roadway, between the Moorish house and the Lombardy poplar. Then the little sedan boldly swung past the front truck
and, free at last, spurted up the shining road, which one could
make out narrowing to a thread of gold in the soft mist where
hill after hill made beauty of distance, and where there was
simply no saying what miracle might happen.

Cockerell, brown-robed and sandaled, let in the cocker and
led me kitchenward, to a British breakfast of depressing kidney
and fish.

"And now," he said, "I am going to tell you the story of
Pnin rising to address the Cremona Women's Club and discovering he had brought the wrong lecture."

PALE FIRE

To Véra

This reminds me of the ludicrous account he gave Mr. Langton, of the despicable state of a young gentleman of good family. "Sir, when I heard of him last, he was running about town shooting cats." And then in a sort of kindly reverie, he bethought himself of his own favorite cat, and said, "But Hodge shan't be shot: no, no, Hodge shall not be shot."

JAMES BOSWELL, the Life of Samuel Johnson

Contents

Foreword

[443]

Pale Fire

A POEM IN FOUR CANTOS

[457]

Commentary

[486]

Index

[659]

Foreword

Pale Fire, a poem in heroic couplets, of nine hundred ninety-nine lines, divided into four cantos, was composed by John Francis Shade (born July 5, 1898, died July 21, 1959) during the last twenty days of his life, at his residence in New Wye, Appalachia, U.S.A. The manuscript, mostly a Fair Copy, from which the present text has been faithfully printed, consists of eighty medium-sized index cards, on each of which Shade reserved the pink upper line for headings (canto number, date) and used the fourteen light-blue lines for writing out with a fine nib in a minute, tidy, remarkably clear hand, the text of his poem, skipping a line to indicate double space, and always using a fresh card to begin a new canto.

The short (166 lines) Canto One, with all those amusing birds and parhelia, occupies thirteen cards. Canto Two, your favorite, and that shocking tour de force, Canto Three, are identical in length (334 lines) and cover twenty-seven cards each. Canto Four reverts to One in length and occupies again thirteen cards, of which the last four used on the day of his death give a Corrected Draft instead of a Fair Copy.

A methodical man, John Shade usually copied out his daily quota of completed lines at midnight but even if he recopied them again later, as I suspect he sometimes did, he marked his card or cards not with the date of his final adjustments, but with that of his Corrected Draft or first Fair Copy. I mean, he preserved the date of actual creation rather than that of second or third thoughts. There is a very loud amusement park right in front of my present lodgings.

We possess in result a complete calendar of his work. Canto One was begun in the small hours of July 2 and completed on July 4. He started the next canto on his birthday and finished it on July 11. Another week was devoted to Canto Three. Canto Four was begun on July 19, and as already noted, the last third of its text (lines 949–999) is supplied by a Corrected Draft. This is extremely rough in appearance, teeming with devastating erasures and cataclysmic insertions, and does not follow the lines of the card as rigidly as the Fair Copy does.

Actually, it turns out to be beautifully accurate when you once make the plunge and compel yourself to open your eyes in the limpid depths under its confused surface. It contains not one gappy line, not one doubtful reading. This fact would be sufficient to show that the imputations made (on July 24, 1959) in a newspaper interview with one of our professed Shadeans—who affirmed *without having seen the manuscript of the poem* that it "consists of disjointed drafts none of which yields a definite text"—is a malicious invention on the part of those who would wish not so much to deplore the state in which a great poet's work was interrupted by death as to asperse the competence, and perhaps honesty, of its present editor and commentator.

Another pronouncement publicly made by Prof. Hurley and his clique refers to a structural matter. I quote from the same interview: "None can say how long John Shade planned his poem to be, but it is not improbable that what he left represents only a small fraction of the composition he saw in a glass, darkly." Nonsense again! Aside from the veritable clarion of internal evidence ringing throughout Canto Four, there exists Sybil Shade's affirmation (in a document dated July 25, 1959) that her husband "never intended to go beyond four parts." For him the third canto was the penultimate one, and thus I myself have heard him speak of it, in the course of a sunset ramble, when, as if thinking aloud, he reviewed the day's work and gesticulated in pardonable self-approbation while his discreet companion kept trying in vain to adapt the swing of a long-limbed gait to the disheveled old poet's jerky shuffle. Nay, I shall even assert (as our shadows still walk without us) that there remained to be written only *one* line of the poem (namely verse 1000) which would have been identical to line 1 and would have completed the symmetry of the structure, with its two identical central parts, solid and ample, forming together with the shorter flanks twin wings of five hundred verses each, and damn that music. Knowing Shade's combinational turn of mind and subtle sense of harmonic balance, I cannot imagine that he intended to deform the faces of his crystal by meddling with its predictable growth. And if all this were not enough—and it is, it is enough—I have had the dramatic occasion of hearing my poor friend's own voice proclaim on the evening of July 21 the end, or almost the end, of his labors. (See my note to line 991.)

This batch of eighty cards was held by a rubber band which I now religiously put back after examining for the last time their precious contents. Another, much thinner, set of a dozen cards, clipped together and enclosed in the same manila envelope as the main batch, bears some additional couplets running their brief and sometimes smudgy course among a chaos of first drafts. As a rule, Shade destroyed drafts the moment he ceased to need them: well do I recall seeing him from my porch, on a brilliant morning, burning a whole stack of them in the pale fire of the incinerator before which he stood with bent head like an official mourner among the wind-borne black butterflies of that backyard auto-da-fé. But he saved those twelve cards because of the unused felicities shining among the dross of used draftings. Perhaps, he vaguely expected to replace certain passages in the Fair Copy with some of the lovely rejections in his files, or, more probably, a sneaking fondness for this or that vignette, suppressed out of architectonic considerations, or because it had annoyed Mrs. S., urged him to put off its disposal till the time when the marble finality of an immaculate typescript would have confirmed it or made the most delightful variant seem cumbersome and impure. And perhaps, let me add in all modesty, he intended to ask my advice after reading his poem to me as I know he planned to do.

In my notes to the poem the reader will find these canceled readings. Their places are indicated, or at least suggested, by the draftings of established lines in their immediate neighborhood. In a sense, many of them are more valuable artistically and historically than some of the best passages in the final text. I must now explain how *Pale Fire* came to be edited by me.

Immediately after my dear friend's death I prevailed on his distraught widow to forelay and defeat the commercial passions and academic intrigues that were bound to come swirling around her husband's manuscript (transferred by me to a safe spot even before his body had reached the grave) by signing an agreement to the effect that he had turned over the manuscript to me; that I would have it published without delay, with my commentary, by a firm of my choice; that all profits, except the publisher's percentage, would accrue to her; and that on publication day the manuscript would be handed over to the Library of Congress for permanent preservation. I defy any serious critic to find this contract unfair. Nevertheless, it has been called (by Shade's former lawyer) "a fantastic farrago of evil," while another person (his former literary agent) has wondered with a sneer if Mrs. Shade's tremulous signature might not have been penned "in some peculiar kind of red ink." Such hearts, such brains, would be unable to comprehend that one's attachment to a masterpiece may be utterly overwhelming, especially when it is the underside of the weave that entrances the beholder and only begetter, whose own past intercoils there with the fate of the innocent author.

As mentioned, I think, in my last note to the poem, the depth charge of Shade's death blasted such secrets and caused so many dead fish to float up, that I was forced to leave New Wye soon after my last interview with the jailed killer. The writing of the commentary had to be postponed until I could find a new incognito in quieter surroundings, but practical matters concerning the poem had to be settled at once. I took a plane to New York, had the manuscript photographed, came to terms with one of Shade's publishers, and was on the point of clinching the deal when, quite casually, in the midst of a vast sunset (we sat in a cell of walnut and glass fifty stories above the progression of scarabs), my interlocutor observed: "You'll be happy to know, Dr. Kinbote, that Professor So-and-so [one of the members of the Shade committee] has consented to act as our adviser in editing the stuff."

Now "happy" is something extremely subjective. One of our sillier Zemblan proverbs says: *the lost glove is happy.* Promptly I refastened the catch of my briefcase and betook myself to another publisher.

Imagine a soft, clumsy giant; imagine a historical personage whose knowledge of money is limited to the abstract billions of a national debt; imagine an exiled prince who is unaware of the Golconda in his cuff links! This is to say—oh, hyperbolically—that I am the most impractical fellow in the world. Between such a person and an old fox in the book publishing business, relations are at first touchingly carefree and chummy, with expansive banterings and all sorts of amiable tokens. I have no reason to suppose that anything will ever happen to prevent this initial relationship with good old Frank, my present publisher, from remaining a permanent fixture.

Frank has acknowledged the safe return of the galleys I had been sent here and has asked me to mention in my Preface— and this I willingly do—that I alone am responsible for any mistakes in my commentary. Insert before a professional. A professional proofreader has carefully rechecked the printed text of the poem against the phototype of the manuscript, and has found a few trivial misprints I had missed; that has been all in the way of outside assistance. Needless to say how much I had been looking forward to Sybil Shade's providing me with abundant biographical data; unfortunately she left New Wye even before I did, and is dwelling now with relatives in Quebec. We might have had, of course, a most fruitful correspondence, but the Shadeans were not to be shaken off. They headed for Canada in droves to pounce on the poor lady as soon as I had lost contact with her and her changeful moods. Instead of answering a month-old letter from my cave in Cedarn, listing some of my most desperate queries, such as the real name of "Jim Coates" etc., she suddenly shot me a wire, requesting me to accept Prof. H. (!) and Prof. C. (!!) as co-editors of her husband's poem. How deeply this surprised and pained me! Naturally, it precluded collaboration with my friend's misguided widow.

And he was a very dear friend indeed! The calendar says I had known him only for a few months but there exist friendships which develop their own inner duration, their own eons of transparent time, independent of rotating, malicious music. Never shall I forget how elated I was upon learning, as mentioned in a note my reader shall find, that the suburban house (rented for my use from Judge Goldsworth who had gone on his Sabbatical to England) into which I moved on February 5, 1959, stood next to that of the celebrated American poet whose verses I had tried to put into Zemblan two decades earlier! Apart from this glamorous neighborhood, the Goldsworthian château, as I was soon to discover, had little to recommend it. The heating system was a farce, depending as it did on registers in the floor wherefrom the tepid exhalations

of a throbbing and groaning basement furnace were transmitted to the rooms with the faintness of a moribund's last
breath. By occluding the apertures upstairs I attempted to give
more energy to the register in the living room but its climate
proved to be incurably vitiated by there being nothing between it and the arctic regions save a sleezy front door without
a vestige of vestibule—either because the house had been built
in midsummer by a naïve settler who could not imagine the
kind of winter New Wye had in store for him, or because old-
time gentility required that a chance caller at the open door
could satisfy himself from the threshold that nothing unseemly
was going on in the parlor.

February and March in Zembla (the two last of the four
"white-nosed months," as we call them) used to be pretty
rough too, but even a peasant's room there presented a solid
of uniform warmth—not a reticulation of deadly drafts. It is
true that, as usually happens to newcomers, I was told I had
chosen the worst winter in years—and this at the latitude of
Palermo. On one of my first mornings there, as I was preparing to leave for college in the powerful red car I had just
acquired, I noticed that Mr. and Mrs. Shade, neither of whom
I had yet met socially (I was to learn later that they assumed
I wished to be left alone), were having trouble with their old
Packard in the slippery driveway where it emitted whines of
agony but could not extricate one tortured rear wheel out of
a concave inferno of ice. John Shade busied himself clumsily
with a bucket from which, with the gestures of a sower, he
distributed handfuls of brown sand over the blue glaze. He
wore snowboots, his vicuña collar was up, his abundant gray
hair looked berimed in the sun. I knew he had been ill a few
months before, and thinking to offer my neighbors a ride to
the campus in my powerful machine, I hurried out toward
them. A lane curving around the slight eminence on which
my rented castle stood separated it from my neighbors' driveway, and I was about to cross that lane when I lost my footing
and sat down on the surprisingly hard snow. My fall acted as
a chemical reagent on the Shades' sedan, which forthwith
budged and almost ran over me as it swung into the lane with
John at the wheel strenuously grimacing and Sybil fiercely
talking to him. I am not sure either saw me.

A few days later, however, namely on Monday, February 16, I was introduced to the old poet at lunch time in the faculty club. "At last presented credentials," as noted, a little ironically, in my agenda. I was invited to join him and four or five other eminent professors at his usual table, under an enlarged photograph of Wordsmith College as it was, stunned and shabby, on a remarkably gloomy summer day in 1903. His laconic suggestion that I "try the pork" amused me. I am a strict vegetarian, and I like to cook my own meals. Consuming something that had been handled by a fellow creature was, I explained to the rubicund convives, as repulsive to me as eating any creature, and that would include—lowering my voice—the pulpous pony-tailed girl student who served us and licked her pencil. Moreover, I had already finished the fruit brought with me in my briefcase, so I would content myself, I said, with a bottle of good college ale. My free and simple demeanor set everybody at ease. The usual questions were fired at me about eggnogs and milkshakes being or not being acceptable to one of my persuasion. Shade said that with him it was the other way around: he must make a definite effort to partake of a vegetable. Beginning a salad, was to him like stepping into sea water on a chilly day, and he had always to brace himself in order to attack the fortress of an apple. I was not yet used to the rather fatiguing jesting and teasing that goes on among American intellectuals of the inbreeding academic type and so abstained from telling John Shade in front of all those grinning old males how much I admired his work lest a serious discussion of literature degenerate into mere facetiation. Instead I asked him about one of my newly acquired students who also attended his course, a moody, delicate, rather wonderful boy; but with a resolute shake of his hoary forelock the old poet answered that he had ceased long ago to memorize faces and names of students and that the only person in his poetry class whom he could visualize was an extramural lady on crutches. "Come, come," said Professor Hurley, "do you mean, John, you really don't have a mental or visceral picture of that stunning blonde in the black leotard who haunts Lit. 202?" Shade, all his wrinkles beaming, benignly tapped Hurley on the wrist to make him stop. Another tormentor inquired if it was true that I had installed two ping-pong tables in my basement. I asked, was it a crime? No, he said, but why two? "Is *that* a crime?" I countered, and they all laughed.

Despite a wobbly heart (see line 735), a slight limp, and a certain curious contortion in his method of progress, Shade had an inordinate liking for long walks, but the snow bothered him, and he preferred, in winter, to have his wife call for him after classes with the car. A few days later, as I was about to leave Parthenocissus Hall—or Main Hall (or now Shade Hall, alas), I saw him waiting outside for Mrs. Shade to fetch him. I stood beside him for a minute, on the steps of the pillared porch, while pulling my gloves on, finger by finger, and looking away, as if waiting to review a regiment: "That was a thorough job," commented the poet. He consulted his wrist watch. A snowflake settled upon it. "Crystal to crystal," said Shade. I offered to take him home in my powerful Kramler. "Wives, Mr. Shade, are forgetful." He cocked his shaggy head to look at the library clock. Across the bleak expanse of snow-covered turf two radiant lads in colorful winter clothes passed, laughing and sliding. Shade glanced at his watch again and, with a shrug, accepted my offer.

I wanted to know if he did not mind being taken the longer way, with a stop at Community Center where I wanted to buy some chocolate-coated cookies and a little caviar. He said it was fine with him. From the inside of the supermarket, through a plate-glass window, I saw the old chap pop into a liquor store. When I returned with my purchases, he was back in the car, reading a tabloid newspaper which I had thought no poet would deign to touch. A comfortable burp told me he had a flask of brandy concealed about his warmly coated person. As we turned into the driveway of his house, we saw Sybil pulling up in front of it. I got out with courteous vivacity. She said: "Since my husband does not believe in introducing people, let us do it ourselves: You are Dr. Kinbote, aren't you? And I am Sybil Shade." Then she addressed her husband saying he might have waited in his office another minute: she had honked and called, and walked all the way up, et cetera. I turned to go, not wishing to listen to a marital scene, but she called me back: "Have a drink with us," she said, "or rather with me, because John is forbidden to touch alcohol." I explained I could not stay long as I was about to have a kind of little seminar at home followed by some table tennis, with two charming identical twins and another boy, another boy.

Henceforth I began seeing more and more of my celebrated neighbor. The view from one of my windows kept providing me with first-rate entertainment, especially when I was on the wait for some tardy guest. From the second story of my house the Shades' living-room window remained clearly visible so long as the branches of the deciduous trees between us were still bare, and almost every evening I could see the poet's slippered foot gently rocking. One inferred from it that he was sitting with a book in a low chair but one never managed to glimpse more than that foot and its shadow moving up and down to the secret rhythm of mental absorption, in the concentrated lamplight. Always at the same time the brown morocco slipper would drop from the wool-socked foot which continued to oscillate, with, however, a slight slackening of pace. One knew that bedtime was closing in with all its terrors; that in a few minutes the toe would prod and worry the slipper, and then disappear with it from my golden field of vision traversed by the black bendlet of a branch. And sometimes Sybil Shade would trip by with the velocity and swinging arms of one flouncing out in a fit of temper, and would return a little later, at a much slower gait, having, as it were, pardoned her husband for his friendship with an eccentric neighbor; but the riddle of her behavior was entirely solved one night when by dialing their number and watching their window at the same time I magically induced her to go through the hasty and quite innocent motions that had puzzled me.

Alas, my peace of mind was soon to be shattered. The thick venom of envy began squirting at me as soon as academic suburbia realized that John Shade valued my society above that of all other people. Your snicker, my dear Mrs. C., did not escape our notice as I was helping the tired old poet to find his galoshes after that dreary get-together party at your house. One day I happened to enter the English Literature office in quest of a magazine with the picture of the Royal Palace in Onhava, which I wanted my friend to see, when I overheard a young instructor in a green velvet jacket, whom

I shall mercifully call Gerald Emerald, carelessly saying in answer to something the secretary had asked: "I guess Mr. Shade
has already left with the Great Beaver." Of course, I am quite
tall, and my brown beard is of a rather rich tint and texture;
the silly cognomen evidently applied to me, but was not worth
noticing, and after calmly taking the magazine from a pam-
phlet-cluttered table, I contented myself on my way out with
pulling Gerald Emerald's bow-tie loose with a deft jerk of my
fingers as I passed by him. There was also the morning when
Dr. Nattochdag, head of the department to which I was attached, begged me in a formal voice to be seated, then closed
the door, and having regained, with a downcast frown, his
swivel chair, urged me "to be more careful." In what sense,
careful? A boy had complained to his adviser. Complained of
what, good Lord? That I had criticized a literature course he
attended ("a ridiculous survey of ridiculous works, conducted
by a ridiculous mediocrity"). Laughing in sheer relief, I embraced my good Netochka, telling him I would never be
naughty again. I take this opportunity to salute him. He always behaved with such exquisite courtesy toward me that I
sometimes wondered if he did not suspect what Shade suspected, and what only three people (two trustees and the president of the college) definitely knew.

   Oh, there were many such incidents. In a skit performed
by a group of drama students I was pictured as a pompous
woman hater with a German accent, constantly quoting
Housman and nibbling raw carrots; and a week before Shade's
death, a certain ferocious lady at whose club I had refused to
speak on the subject of "The Hally Vally" (as she put it, confusing Odin's Hall with the title of a Finnish epic), said to me
in the middle of a grocery store, "You are a remarkably disagreeable person. I fail to see how John and Sybil can stand
you," and, exasperated by my polite smile, she added:
"What's more, you are insane."

   But let me not pursue the tabulation of nonsense. Whatever
was thought, whatever was said, I had my full reward in John's
friendship. This friendship was the more precious for its tenderness being intentionally concealed, especially when we
were not alone, by that gruffness which stems from what can
be termed the dignity of the heart. His whole being consti-

tuted a mask. John Shade's physical appearance was so little in keeping with the harmonies hiving in the man, that one felt inclined to dismiss it as a coarse disguise or passing fashion; for if the fashions of the Romantic Age subtilized a poet's manliness by baring his attractive neck, pruning his profile and reflecting a mountain lake in his oval gaze, present-day bards, owing perhaps to better opportunities of aging, look like gorillas or vultures. My sublime neighbor's face had something about it that might have appealed to the eye, had it been only leonine or only Iroquoian; but unfortunately, by combining the two it merely reminded one of a fleshy Hogarthian tippler of indeterminate sex. His misshapen body, that gray mop of abundant hair, the yellow nails of his pudgy fingers, the bags under his lusterless eyes, were only intelligible if regarded as the waste products eliminated from his intrinsic self by the same forces of perfection which purified and chiseled his verse. He was his own cancellation.

I have one favorite photograph of him. In this color snapshot taken by a onetime friend of mine, on a brilliant spring day, Shade is seen leaning on a sturdy cane that had belonged to his aunt Maud (see line 86). I am wearing a white windbreaker acquired in a local sports shop and a pair of lilac slacks hailing from Cannes. My left hand is half raised—not to pat Shade on the shoulder as seems to be the intention, but to remove my sunglasses which, however, it never reached in *that* life, the life of the picture; and the library book under my right arm is a treatise on certain Zemblan calisthenics in which I proposed to interest that young roomer of mine who snapped the picture. A week later he was to betray my trust by taking sordid advantage of my absence on a trip to Washington whence I returned to find he had been entertaining a fiery-haired whore from Exton who had left her combings and reek in all three bathrooms. Naturally, we separated at once, and through a chink in the window curtains I saw bad Bob standing rather pathetically, with his crewcut, and shabby valise, and the skis I had given him, all forlorn on the roadside, waiting for a fellow student to drive him away forever. I can forgive everything save treason.

We never discussed, John Shade and I, any of my personal misfortunes. Our close friendship was on that higher, exclusively intellectual level where one can rest from emotional troubles, not share them. My admiration for him was for me a sort of alpine cure. I experienced a grand sense of wonder whenever I looked at him, especially in the presence of other people, inferior people. This wonder was enhanced by my awareness of their not feeling what I felt, of their not seeing what I saw, of their taking Shade for granted, instead of drenching every nerve, so to speak, in the romance of his presence. Here he is, I would say to myself, that is his head, containing a brain of a different brand than that of the synthetic jellies preserved in the skulls around him. He is looking from the terrace (of Prof. C.'s house on that March evening) at the distant lake. I am looking at him. I am witnessing a unique physiological phenomenon: John Shade perceiving and transforming the world, taking it in and taking it apart, re-combining its elements in the very process of storing them up so as to produce at some unspecified date an organic miracle, a fusion of image and music, a line of verse. And I experienced the same thrill as when in my early boyhood I once watched across the tea table in my uncle's castle a conjurer who had just given a fantastic performance and was now quietly consuming a vanilla ice. I stared at his powdered cheeks, at the magical flower in his buttonhole where it had passed through a succession of different colors and had now become fixed as a white carnation, and especially at his marvelous fluid-looking fingers which could if he chose make his spoon dissolve into a sunbeam by twiddling it, or turn his plate into a dove by tossing it up in the air.

Shade's poem is, indeed, that sudden flourish of magic: my gray-haired friend, my beloved old conjurer, put a pack of index cards into his hat—and shook out a poem.

To this poem we now must turn. My Foreword has been, I trust, not too skimpy. Other notes, arranged in a running commentary, will certainly satisfy the most voracious reader. Although those notes, in conformity with custom, come after the poem, the reader is advised to consult them first and then study the poem with their help, rereading them of course as he goes through its text, and perhaps, after having done with the poem, consulting them a third time so as to complete the picture. I find it wise in such cases as this to eliminate the bother of back-and-forth leafings by either cutting out and clipping together the pages with the text of the thing, or, even more simply, purchasing two copies of the same work which can then be placed in adjacent positions on a comfortable table—not like the shaky little affair on which my typewriter is precariously enthroned now, in this wretched motor lodge, with that carrousel inside and outside my head, miles away from New Wye. Let me state that without my notes Shade's text simply has no human reality at all since the human reality of such a poem as his (being too skittish and reticent for an autobiographical work), with the omission of many pithy lines carelessly rejected by him, has to depend entirely on the reality of its author and his surroundings, attachments and so forth, a reality that only my notes can provide. To this statement my dear poet would probably not have subscribed, but, for better or worse, it is the commentator who has the last word.

CHARLES KINBOTE

Oct. 19, 1959, Cedarn, Utana

Pale Fire

A Poem in Four Cantos

1 I was the shadow of the waxwing slain
By the false azure in the windowpane;
I was the smudge of ashen fluff—and I
Lived on, flew on, in the reflected sky.
And from the inside, too, I'd duplicate
Myself, my lamp, an apple on a plate:
Uncurtaining the night, I'd let dark glass
Hang all the furniture above the grass,
And how delightful when a fall of snow
10 Covered my glimpse of lawn and reached up so
As to make chair and bed exactly stand
Upon that snow, out in that crystal land!

Retake the falling snow: each drifting flake
Shapeless and slow, unsteady and opaque,
A dull dark white against the day's pale white
And abstract larches in the neutral light.
And then the gradual and dual blue
As night unites the viewer and the view,
And in the morning, diamonds of frost
20 Express amazement: Whose spurred feet have crossed
From left to right the blank page of the road?
Reading from left to right in winter's code:
A dot, an arrow pointing back; repeat:
Dot, arrow pointing back . . . A pheasant's feet!
Torquated beauty, sublimated grouse,
Finding your China right behind my house.
Was he in *Sherlock Holmes*, the fellow whose
Tracks pointed back when he reversed his shoes?

All colors made me happy: even gray.
30 My eyes were such that literally they

457

Took photographs. Whenever I'd permit,
Or, with a silent shiver, order it,
Whatever in my field of vision dwelt—
An indoor scene, hickory leaves, the svelte
Stilettos of a frozen stillicide—
Was printed on my eyelids' nether side
Where it would tarry for an hour or two,
And while this lasted all I had to do
Was close my eyes to reproduce the leaves,
40   Or indoor scene, or trophies of the eaves.

I cannot understand why from the lake
I could make out our front porch when I'd take
Lake Road to school, whilst now, although no tree
Has intervened, I look but fail to see
Even the roof. Maybe some quirk in space
Has caused a fold or furrow to displace
The fragile vista, the frame house between
Goldsworth and Wordsmith on its square of green.

I had a favorite young shagbark there
50   With ample dark jade leaves and a black, spare,
Vermiculated trunk. The setting sun
Bronzed the black bark, around which, like undone
Garlands, the shadows of the foliage fell.
It is now stout and rough; it has done well.
White butterflies turn lavender as they
Pass through its shade where gently seems to sway
The phantom of my little daughter's swing.

The house itself is much the same. One wing
We've had revamped. There's a solarium. There's
60   A picture window flanked with fancy chairs.
TV's huge paperclip now shines instead
Of the stiff vane so often visited
By the naïve, the gauzy mockingbird
Retelling all the programs she had heard;
Switching from *chippo-chippo* to a clear
To-wee, to-wee; then rasping out: *come here,*
Come here, come herrr; flirting her tail aloft,

Or gracefully indulging in a soft
Upward hop-flop, and instantly (*to-wee!*)
70 Returning to her perch—the new TV.

I was an infant when my parents died.
They both were ornithologists. I've tried
So often to evoke them that today
I have a thousand parents. Sadly they
Dissolve in their own virtues and recede,
But certain words, chance words I hear or read,
Such as "bad heart" always to him refer,
And "cancer of the pancreas" to her.

A preterist: one who collects cold nests.
80 Here was my bedroom, now reserved for guests.
Here, tucked away by the Canadian maid,
I listened to the buzz downstairs and prayed
For everybody to be always well,
Uncles and aunts, the maid, her niece Adèle
Who'd seen the Pope, people in books, and God.

I was brought up by dear bizarre Aunt Maud,
A poet and a painter with a taste
For realistic objects interlaced
With grotesque growths and images of doom.
90 She lived to hear the next babe cry. Her room
We've kept intact. Its trivia create
A still life in her style: the paperweight
Of convex glass enclosing a lagoon,
The verse book open at the Index (Moon,
Moonrise, Moor, Moral), the forlorn guitar,
The human skull; and from the local *Star*
A curio: *Red Sox Beat Yanks 5–4
On Chapman's Homer*, thumbtacked to the door.

My God died young. Theolatry I found
100 Degrading, and its premises, unsound.
No free man needs a God; but was I free?
How fully I felt nature glued to me
And how my childish palate loved the taste
Half-fish, half-honey, of that golden paste!

My picture book was at an early age
The painted parchment papering our cage:
Mauve rings around the moon; blood-orange sun;
Twinned Iris; and that rare phenomenon
The iridule—when, beautiful and strange,
110 In a bright sky above a mountain range
One opal cloudlet in an oval form
Reflects the rainbow of a thunderstorm
Which in a distant valley has been staged—
For we are most artistically caged.

And there's the wall of sound: the nightly wall
Raised by a trillion crickets in the fall.
Impenetrable! Halfway up the hill
I'd pause in thrall of their delirious trill.
That's Dr. Sutton's light. That's the Great Bear.
120 A thousand years ago five minutes were
Equal to forty ounces of fine sand.
Outstare the stars. Infinite foretime and
Infinite aftertime: above your head
They close like giant wings, and you are dead.

The regular vulgarian, I daresay,
Is happier: he sees the Milky Way
Only when making water. Then as now
I walked at my own risk: whipped by the bough,
Tripped by the stump. Asthmatic, lame and fat,
130 I never bounced a ball or swung a bat.

I was the shadow of the waxwing slain
By feigned remoteness in the windowpane.
I had a brain, five senses (one unique),
But otherwise I was a cloutish freak.
In sleeping dreams I played with other chaps
But really envied nothing—save perhaps
The miracle of a lemniscate left
Upon wet sand by nonchalantly deft
Bicycle tires.
                    A thread of subtle pain,

140 Tugged at by playful death, released again,
But always present, ran through me. One day,
When I'd just turned eleven, as I lay
Prone on the floor and watched a clockwork toy—
A tin wheelbarrow pushed by a tin boy—
Bypass chair legs and stray beneath the bed,
There was a sudden sunburst in my head.

And then black night. That blackness was sublime.
I felt distributed through space and time:
One foot upon a mountaintop, one hand
150 Under the pebbles of a panting strand,
One ear in Italy, one eye in Spain,
In caves, my blood, and in the stars, my brain.
There were dull throbs in my Triassic; green
Optical spots in Upper Pleistocene,
An icy shiver down my Age of Stone,
And all tomorrows in my funnybone.

During one winter every afternoon
I'd sink into that momentary swoon.
And then it ceased. Its memory grew dim.
160 My health improved. I even learned to swim.
But like some little lad forced by a wench
With his pure tongue her abject thirst to quench,
I was corrupted, terrified, allured,
And though old doctor Colt pronounced me cured
Of what, he said, were mainly growing pains,
The wonder lingers and the shame remains.

CANTO TWO

There was a time in my demented youth
When somehow I suspected that the truth
About survival after death was known
170 To every human being: I alone
Knew nothing, and a great conspiracy
Of books and people hid the truth from me.

There was the day when I began to doubt
Man's sanity: How could he live without
Knowing for sure what dawn, what death, what doom
Awaited consciousness beyond the tomb?

And finally there was the sleepless night
When I decided to explore and fight
The foul, the inadmissible abyss,
180 Devoting all my twisted life to this
One task. Today I'm sixty-one. Waxwings
Are berry-pecking. A cicada sings.

The little scissors I am holding are
A dazzling synthesis of sun and star.
I stand before the window and I pare
My fingernails and vaguely am aware
Of certain flinching likenesses: the thumb,
Our grocer's son; the index, lean and glum
College astronomer Starover Blue;
190 The middle fellow, a tall priest I knew;
The feminine fourth finger, an old flirt;
And little pinky clinging to her skirt.
And I make mouths as I snip off the thin
Strips of what Aunt Maud used to call "scarf-skin."

Maud Shade was eighty when a sudden hush
Fell on her life. We saw the angry flush
And torsion of paralysis assail
Her noble cheek. We moved her to Pinedale,
Famed for its sanitarium. There she'd sit
200 In the glassed sun and watch the fly that lit
Upon her dress and then upon her wrist.
Her mind kept fading in the growing mist.
She still could speak. She paused, and groped, and found
        found
What seemed at first a serviceable sound,
But from adjacent cells impostors took
The place of words she needed, and her look
Spelt imploration as she sought in vain
To reason with the monsters in her brain.

What moment in the gradual decay
210 Does resurrection choose? What year? What day?
Who has the stopwatch? Who rewinds the tape?
Are some less lucky, or do all escape?
A syllogism: *other men die; but I*
Am not another; therefore I'll not die.
Space is a swarming in the eyes; and time,
A singing in the ears. In this hive I'm
Locked up. Yet, *if* prior to life we had
Been able to imagine life, what mad,
Impossible, unutterably weird,
220 Wonderful nonsense it might have appeared!

So why join in the vulgar laughter? Why
Scorn a hereafter none can verify:
The Turk's delight, the future lyres, the talks
With Socrates and Proust in cypress walks,
The seraph with his six flamingo wings,
And Flemish hells with porcupines and things?
It isn't that we dream too wild a dream:
The trouble is we do not make it seem
Sufficiently unlikely; for the most
230 We can think up is a domestic ghost.

How ludicrous these efforts to translate
Into one's private tongue a public fate!
Instead of poetry divinely terse,
Disjointed notes, Insomnia's mean verse!

Life is a message scribbled in the dark.
Anonymous.
     Espied on a pine's bark,
As we were walking home the day she died,
An empty emerald case, squat and frog-eyed,
Hugging the trunk; and its companion piece,
240 A gum-logged ant.
      That Englishman in Nice,
A proud and happy linguist: *je nourris*
Les pauvres cigales—meaning that he
Fed the poor sea gulls!

                    Lafontaine was wrong:
Dead is the mandible, alive the song.

And so I pare my nails, and muse, and hear
Your steps upstairs, and all is right, my dear.

Sybil, throughout our high-school days I knew
Your loveliness, but fell in love with you
During an outing of the senior class
250 To New Wye Falls. We luncheoned on damp grass.
Our teacher of geology discussed
The cataract. Its roar and rainbow dust
Made the tame park romantic. I reclined
In April's haze immediately behind
Your slender back and watched your neat small head
Bend to one side. One palm with fingers spread,
Between a star of trillium and a stone,
Pressed on the turf. A little phalange bone
Kept twitching. Then you turned and offered me
260 A thimbleful of bright metallic tea.

Your profile has not changed. The glistening teeth
Biting the careful lip; the shade beneath
The eye from the long lashes; the peach down
Rimming the cheekbone; the dark silky brown
Of hair brushed up from temple and from nape;
The very naked neck; the Persian shape
Of nose and eyebrow, you have kept it all—
And on still nights we hear the waterfall.

Come and be worshiped, come and be caressed,
270 My dark Vanessa, crimson-barred, my blest
My Admirable butterfly! Explain
How could you, in the gloom of Lilac Lane,
Have let uncouth, hysterical John Shade
Blubber your face, and ear, and shoulder blade?

We have been married forty years. At least
Four thousand times your pillow has been creased
By our two heads. Four hundred thousand times

The tall clock with the hoarse Westminster chimes
Has marked our common hour. How many more
280   Free calendars shall grace the kitchen door?

I love you when you're standing on the lawn
Peering at something in a tree: "It's gone.
It was so small. It might come back" (all this
Voiced in a whisper softer than a kiss).
I love you when you call me to admire
A jet's pink trail above the sunset fire.
I love you when you're humming as you pack
A suitcase or the farcical car sack
With round-trip zipper. And I love you most
290   When with a pensive nod you greet her ghost
And hold her first toy on your palm, or look
At a postcard from her, found in a book.

She might have been you, me, or some quaint blend:
Nature chose me so as to wrench and rend
Your heart and mine. At first we'd smile and say:
"All little girls are plump" or "Jim McVey
(The family oculist) will cure that slight
Squint in no time." And later: "She'll be quite
Pretty, you know"; and, trying to assuage
300   The swelling torment: "That's the awkward age."
"She should take riding lessons," you would say
(Your eyes and mine not meeting). "She should play
Tennis, or badminton. Less starch, more fruit!
She may not be a beauty, but she's cute."

It was no use, no use. The prizes won
In French and history, no doubt, were fun;
At Christmas parties games were rough, no doubt,
And one shy little guest might be left out;
But let's be fair: while children of her age
310   Were cast as elves and fairies on the stage
That *she*'d helped paint for the school pantomime,
My gentle girl appeared as Mother Time,
A bent charwoman with slop pail and broom,
And like a fool I sobbed in the men's room.

Another winter was scrape-scooped away.
The Toothwort White haunted our woods in May.
Summer was power-mowed, and autumn, burned.
Alas, the dingy cygnet never turned
Into a wood duck. And again your voice:
320 "But this is prejudice! You should rejoice
That she is innocent. Why overstress
The physical? She *wants* to look a mess.
Virgins have written some *resplendent* books.
Lovemaking is not everything. Good looks
Are not *that* indispensable!" And still
Old Pan would call from every painted hill,
And still the demons of our pity spoke:
No lips would share the lipstick of her smoke;
The telephone that rang before a ball
330 Every two minutes in Sorosa Hall
For her would never ring; and, with a great
Screeching of tires on gravel, to the gate
Out of the lacquered night, a white-scarfed beau
Would never come for her; she'd never go,
A dream of gauze and jasmine, to that dance.
We sent her, though, to a château in France.

And she returned in tears, with new defeats,
New miseries. On days when all the streets
Of College Town led to the game, she'd sit
340 On the library steps, and read or knit;
Mostly alone she'd be, or with that nice
Frail roommate, now a nun; and, once or twice,
With a Korean boy who took my course.
She had strange fears, strange fantasies, strange force
Of character—as when she spent three nights
Investigating certain sounds and lights
In an old barn. She twisted words: pot, top,
Spider, redips. And "powder" was "red wop."
She called you a didactic katydid.
350 She hardly ever smiled, and when she did,
It was a sign of pain. She'd criticize
Ferociously our projects, and with eyes
Expressionless sit on her tumbled bed

Spreading her swollen feet, scratching her head
With psoriatic fingernails, and moan,
Murmuring dreadful words in monotone.

She was my darling: difficult, morose—
But still my darling. You remember those
Almost unruffled evenings when we played
360 Mah-jongg, or she tried on your furs, which made
Her almost fetching; and the mirrors smiled,
The lights were merciful, the shadows mild.
Sometimes I'd help her with a Latin text,
Or she'd be reading in her bedroom, next
To my fluorescent lair, and you would be
In your own study, twice removed from me,
And I would hear both voices now and then:
"Mother, what's *grimpen*?" "What is what?"
                                        "Grim Pen."
Pause, and your guarded scholium. Then again:
370 "Mother, what's *chtonic*?" That, too, you'd explain,
Appending: "Would you like a tangerine?"
"No. Yes. And what does *sempiternal* mean?"
You'd hesitate. And lustily I'd roar
The answer from my desk through the closed door.

It does not matter what it was she read
(some phony modern poem that was said
In English Lit to be a document
"Engazhay and compelling"—what this meant
Nobody cared); the point is that the three
380 Chambers, *then* bound by you and her and me,
Now form a tryptich or a three-act play
In which portrayed events forever stay.

I think she always nursed a small mad hope.

I'd finished recently my book on Pope.
Jane Dean, my typist, offered her one day
To meet Pete Dean, a cousin. Jane's fiancé
Would then take all of them in his new car
A score of miles to a Hawaiian bar.

The boy was picked up at a quarter past
390   Eight in New Wye. Sleet glazed the roads. At last
They found the place—when suddenly Pete Dean
Clutching his brow exclaimed that he had clean
Forgotten an appointment with a chum
Who'd land in jail if he, Pete, did not come,
Et cetera. She said she understood.
After he'd gone the three young people stood
Before the azure entrance for awhile.
Puddles were neon-barred; and with a smile
She said she'd be *de trop*, she'd much prefer
400   Just going home. Her friends escorted her
To the bus stop and left; but she, instead
Of riding home, got off at Lochanhead.

You scrutinized your wrist: "It's eight fifteen.
[And here time forked.] I'll turn it on." The screen
In its blank broth evolved a lifelike blur,
And music welled.
                    He took one look at her,
And shot a death ray at well-meaning Jane.

A male hand traced from Florida to Maine
The curving arrows of Aeolian wars.
410   You said that later a quartet of bores,
Two writers and two critics, would debate
The Cause of Poetry on Channel 8.
A nymph came pirouetting, under white
Rotating petals, in a vernal rite
To kneel before an altar in a wood
Where various articles of toilet stood.
I went upstairs and read a galley proof,
And heard the wind roll marbles on the roof.
"See the blind beggar dance, the cripple sing"
420   Has unmistakably the vulgar ring
Of its preposterous age. Then came your call,
My tender mockingbird, up from the hall.
I was in time to overhear brief fame
And have a cup of tea with you: my name
Was mentioned twice, as usual just behind

(one oozy footstep) Frost.
                              "Sure you don't mind?
I'll catch the Exton plane, because you know
If I don't come by midnight with the dough—"

And then there was a kind of travelog:
430   A host narrator took us through the fog
Of a March night, where headlights from afar
Approached and grew like a dilating star,
To the green, indigo and tawny sea
Which we had visited in thirty-three,
Nine months before her birth. Now it was all
Pepper-and-salt, and hardly could recall
That first long ramble, the relentless light,
The flock of sails (one blue among the white
Clashed queerly with the sea, and two were red),
440   The man in the old blazer, crumbing bread,
The crowding gulls insufferably loud,
And one dark pigeon waddling in the crowd.

"Was that the phone?" You listened at the door.
Nothing. Picked up the program from the floor.
More headlights in the fog. There was no sense
In window-rubbing: only some white fence
And the reflector poles passed by unmasked.

"Are we quite sure she's acting right?" you asked.
"It's technically a blind date, of course.
450   Well, shall we try the preview of *Remorse*?"
And we allowed, in all tranquillity,
The famous film to spread its charmed marquee;
The famous face flowed in, fair and inane:
The parted lips, the swimming eyes, the grain
Of beauty on the cheek, odd gallicism,
And the soft form dissolving in the prism
Of corporate desire.
                              "I think," she said,
"I'll get off here." "It's only Lochanhead."
"Yes, that's okay." Gripping the stang, she peered
460   *At ghostly trees. Bus stopped. Bus disappeared.*

Thunder above the Jungle. "No, not that!"
Pat Pink, our guest (antiatomic chat).
Eleven struck. You sighed. "Well, I'm afraid
There's nothing else of interest." You played
Network roulette: the dial turned and trk'ed.
Commercials were beheaded. Faces flicked.
An open mouth in midsong was struck out.
An imbecile with sideburns was about
To use his gun, but you were much too quick.
470   A jovial Negro raised his trumpet. Trk.
Your ruby ring made life and laid the law.
Oh, switch it off! And as life snapped we saw
A pinhead light dwindle and die in black
Infinity.

> *Out of his lakeside shack*
> *A watchman, Father Time, all gray and bent,*
> *Emerged with his uneasy dog and went*
> *Along the reedy bank. He came too late.*

You gently yawned and stacked away your plate.
We heard the wind. We heard it rush and throw
480   Twigs at the windowpane. Phone ringing? No.
I helped you with the dishes. The tall clock
Kept on demolishing young root, old rock.

"Midnight," you said. What's midnight to the young?
And suddenly a festive blaze was flung
Across five cedar trunks, snowpatches showed,
And a patrol car on our bumpy road
Came to a crunching stop. Retake, retake!

People have thought she tried to cross the lake
At Lochan Neck where zesty skaters crossed
490   From Exe to Wye on days of special frost.
Others supposed she might have lost her way
By turning left from Bridgeroad; and some say
She took her poor young life. I know. You know.

It was a night of thaw, a night of blow,
With great excitement in the air. Black spring

Stood just around the corner, shivering
In the wet starlight and on the wet ground.
The lake lay in the mist, its ice half drowned.
A blurry shape stepped off the reedy bank
500 Into a crackling, gulping swamp, and sank.

CANTO THREE

L'if, lifeless tree! Your great Maybe, Rabelais:
The grand potato.
                          I.P.H., a lay
Institute (I) of Preparation (P)
For the Hereafter (H), or If, as we
Called it—big if!—engaged me for one term
To speak on death ("to lecture on the Worm,"
Wrote President McAber).
                                    You and I,
And she, then a mere tot, moved from New Wye
To Yewshade, in another, higher state.
510 I love great mountains. From the iron gate
Of the ramshackle house we rented there
One saw a snowy form, so far, so fair,
That one could only fetch a sigh, as if
It might assist assimilation.
                                      Iph
Was a larvorium and a violet:
A grave in Reason's early spring. And yet
It missed the gist of the whole thing; it missed
What mostly interests the preterist;
For we die every day; oblivion thrives
520 Not on dry thighbones but on blood-ripe lives,
And our best yesterdays are now foul piles
Of crumpled names, phone numbers and foxed files.
I'm ready to become a floweret
Or a fat fly, but never, to forget.
And I'll turn down eternity unless
The melancholy and the tenderness

Of mortal life; the passion and the pain;
The claret taillight of that dwindling plane
Off Hesperus; your gesture of dismay
530   On running out of cigarettes; the way
You smile at dogs; the trail of silver slime
Snails leave on flagstones; this good ink, this rhyme,
This index card, this slender rubber band
Which always forms, when dropped, an ampersand,
Are found in Heaven by the newlydead
Stored in its strongholds through the years.
                                        Instead

The Institute assumed it might be wise
Not to expect too much of paradise:
What if there's nobody to say hullo
To the newcomer, no reception, no
540   Indoctrination? What if you are tossed
Into a boundless void, your bearings lost,
Your spirit stripped and utterly alone,
Your task unfinished, your despair unknown,
Your body just beginning to putresce,
A non-undressable in morning dress,
Your widow lying prone on a dim bed,
Herself a blur in your dissolving head!

While snubbing gods, including the big G,
550   Iph borrowed some peripheral debris
From mystic visions; and it offered tips
(The amber spectacles for life's eclipse)—
How not to panic when you're made a ghost:
Sidle and slide, choose a smooth surd, and coast,
Meet solid bodies and glissade right through,
Or let a person circulate through you.
How to locate in blackness, with a gasp,
Terra the Fair, an orbicle of jasp.
How to keep sane in spiral types of space.
560   Precautions to be taken in the case
Of freak reincarnation: what to do
On suddenly discovering that you
Are now a young and vulnerable toad
Plump in the middle of a busy road,

Or a bear cub beneath a burning pine,
Or a book mite in a revived divine.

Time means succession, and succession, change:
Hence timelessness is bound to disarrange
Schedules of sentiment. We give advice
570   To widower. He has been married twice:
He meets his wives; both loved, both loving, both
Jealous of one another. Time means growth,
And growth means nothing in Elysian life.
Fondling a changeless child, the flax-haired wife
Grieves on the brink of a remembered pond
Full of a dreamy sky. And, also blond,
But with a touch of tawny in the shade,
Feet up, knees clasped, on a stone balustrade
The other sits and raises a moist gaze
580   Toward the blue impenetrable haze.
How to begin? Which first to kiss? What toy
To give the babe? Does that small solemn boy
Know of the head-on crash which on a wild
March night killed both the mother and the child?
And she, the second love, with instep bare
In ballerina black, why does she wear
The earrings from the other's jewel case?
And why does she avert her fierce young face?

For as we know from dreams it is so hard
590   To speak to our dear dead! They disregard
Our apprehension, queaziness and shame—
The awful sense that they're not quite the same.
And our school chum killed in a distant war
Is not surprised to see us at his door,
And in a blend of jauntiness and gloom
Points at the puddles in his basement room.

But who can teach the thoughts we should roll-call
When morning finds us marching to the wall
Under the stage direction of some goon
600   Political, some uniformed baboon?
We'll think of matters only known to us—

Empires of rhyme, Indies of calculus;
Listen to distant cocks crow, and discern
Upon the rough gray wall a rare wall fern;
And while our royal hands are being tied,
Taunt our inferiors, cheerfully deride
The dedicated imbeciles, and spit
Into their eyes just for the fun of it.

Nor can one help the exile, the old man
610   Dying in a motel, with the loud fan
Revolving in the torrid prairie night
And, from the outside, bits of colored light
Reaching his bed like dark hands from the past
Offering gems; and death is coming fast.
He suffocates and conjures in two tongues
The nebulae dilating in his lungs.

A wrench, a rift—that's all one can foresee.
Maybe one finds *le grand néant*; maybe
Again one spirals from the tuber's eye.

620   As you remarked the last time we went by
The Institute: "I really could not tell
The difference between this place and Hell."

We heard cremationists guffaw and snort
At Grabermann's denouncing the Retort
As detrimental to the birth of wraiths.
We all avoided criticizing faiths.
The great Starover Blue reviewed the role
Planets had played as landfalls of the soul.
The fate of beasts was pondered. A Chinese
630   Discanted on the etiquette at teas
With ancestors, and how far up to go.
I tore apart the fantasies of Poe,
And dealt with childhood memories of strange
Nacreous gleams beyond the adults' range.
Among our auditors were a young priest
And an old Communist. Iph could at least
Compete with churches and the party line.

In later years it started to decline:
Buddhism took root. A medium smuggled in
640   Pale jellies and a floating mandolin.
Fra Karamazov, mumbling his inept
All is allowed, into some classes crept;
And to fulfill the fish wish of the womb,
A school of Freudians headed for the tomb.

That tasteless venture helped me in a way.
I learnt what to ignore in my survey
Of death's abyss. And when we lost our child
I knew there would be nothing: no self-styled
Spirit would touch a keyboard of dry wood
650   To rap out her pet name; no phantom would
Rise gracefully to welcome you and me
In the dark garden, near the shagbark tree.

"What is that funny creaking—do you hear?"
"It is the shutter on the stairs, my dear."

"If you're not sleeping, let's turn on the light.
I hate that wind! Let's play some chess." "All right."

"I'm sure it's not the shutter. There—again."
"It is a tendril fingering the pane."

"What glided down the roof and made that thud?"
660   "It is old winter tumbling in the mud."

"And now what shall I do? My knight is pinned."

Who rides so late in the night and the wind?
It is the writer's grief. It is the wild
March wind. It is the father with his child.

Later came minutes, hours, whole days at last,
When she'd be absent from our thoughts, so fast
Did life, the woolly caterpillar run.
We went to Italy. Sprawled in the sun
On a white beach with other pink or brown

670   Americans. Flew back to our small town.
       Found that my bunch of essays *The Untamed
       Seahorse* was "universally acclaimed"
       (It sold three hundred copies in one year).
       Again school started, and on hillsides, where
       Wound distant roads, one saw the steady stream
       Of carlights all returning to the dream
       Of college education. You went on
       Translating into French Marvell and Donne.
       It was a year of Tempests: Hurricane
680   Lolita swept from Florida to Maine.
       Mars glowed. Shahs married. Gloomy Russians spied.
       Lang made your portrait. And one night I died.

       The Crashaw Club had paid me to discuss
       Why Poetry Is Meaningful to Us.
       I gave my sermon, a dull thing but short.
       As I was leaving in some haste, to thwart
       The so-called "question period" at the end,
       One of those peevish people who attend
       Such talks only to say they disagree
690   Stood up and pointed with his pipe at me.

       And then it happened—the attack, the trance,
       Or one of my old fits. There sat by chance
       A doctor in the front row. At his feet
       Patly I fell. My heart had stopped to beat,
       It seems, and several moments passed before
       It heaved and went on trudging to a more
       Conclusive destination. Give me now
       Your full attention.
                             I can't tell you how
       I knew—but I did know that I had crossed
700   The border. Everything I loved was lost
       But no aorta could report regret.
       A sun of rubber was convulsed and set;
       And blood-black nothingness began to spin
       A system of cells interlinked within
       Cells interlinked within cells interlinked

Within one stem. And dreadfully distinct
Against the dark, a tall white fountain played.

I realized, of course, that it was made
Not of our atoms; that the sense behind
710   The scene was not our sense. In life, the mind
Of any man is quick to recognize
Natural shams, and then before his eyes
The reed becomes a bird, the knobby twig
An inchworm, and the cobra head, a big
Wickedly folded moth. But in the case
Of my white fountain what it did replace
Perceptually was something that, I felt,
Could be grasped only by whoever dwelt
In the strange world where I was a mere stray.

720   And presently I saw it melt away:
Though still unconscious, I was back on earth.
The tale I told provoked my doctor's mirth.
He doubted very much that in the state
He found me in "one could hallucinate
Or dream in any sense. Later, perhaps,
But not during the actual collapse.
No, Mr. Shade."
               But, Doctor, I was dead!
He smiled. "Not quite: just half a shade," he said.

However, I demurred. In mind I kept
730   Replaying the whole thing. Again I stepped
Down from the platform, and felt strange and hot,
And saw that chap stand up, and toppled, not
Because a heckler pointed with his pipe,
But probably because the time was ripe
For just that bump and wobble on the part
Of a limp blimp, an old unstable heart.

My vision reeked with truth. It had the tone,
The quiddity and quaintness of its own
Reality. It *was*. As time went on,
740   Its constant vertical in triumph shone.

Often when troubled by the outer glare
Of street and strife, inward I'd turn, and there,
There in the background of my soul it stood,
Old Faithful! And its presence always would
Console me wonderfully. Then, one day,
I came across what seemed a twin display.

It was a story in a magazine
About a Mrs. Z. whose heart had been
Rubbed back to life by a prompt surgeon's hand.
750   She told her interviewer of "The Land
Beyond the Veil" and the account contained
A hint of angels, and a glint of stained
Windows, and some soft music, and a choice
Of hymnal items, and her mother's voice;
But at the end she mentioned a remote
Landscape, a hazy orchard—and I quote:
"Beyond that orchard through a kind of smoke
I glimpsed a tall white fountain—and awoke."

If on some nameless island Captain Schmidt
760   Sees a new animal and captures it,
And if, a little later, Captain Smith
Brings back a skin, that island is no myth.
Our fountain was a signpost and a mark
Objectively enduring in the dark,
Strong as a bone, substantial as a tooth,
And almost vulgar in its robust truth!

The article was by Jim Coates. To Jim
Forthwith I wrote. Got her address from him.
Drove west three hundred miles to talk to her.
770   Arrived. Was met by an impassioned purr.
Saw that blue hair, those freckled hands, that rapt
Orchideous air—and knew that I was trapped.

"Who'd miss the opportunity to meet
A poet so distinguished?" It was sweet
Of me to come! I desperately tried
To ask my questions. They were brushed aside:

"Perhaps some other time." The journalist
Still had her scribblings. I should not insist.
She plied me with fruit cake, turning it all
780   Into an idiotic social call.
"I can't believe," she said, "that it is *you*!
I loved your poem in the *Blue Review*.
That one about *Mon Blon*. I have a niece
Who's climbed the Matterhorn. The other piece
I could not understand. I mean the sense.
Because, of course, the sound—But I'm so dense!"

She was. I might have persevered. I might
Have made her tell me more about the white
Fountain we both had seen "beyond the veil"
790   But if (I thought) I mentioned that detail
She'd pounce upon it as upon a fond
Affinity, a sacramental bond,
Uniting mystically her and me,
And in a jiffy our two souls would be
Brother and sister trembling on the brink
Of tender incest. "Well," I said, "I think
It's getting late. . . ."
                         I also called on Coates.
He was afraid he had mislaid her notes.
He took his article from a steel file:
800   "It's accurate. I have not changed her style.
There's one misprint—not that it matters much:
Mountain, not *fountain*. The majestic touch."

Life Everlasting—based on a misprint!
I mused as I drove homeward: take the hint,
And stop investigating my abyss?
But all at once it dawned on me that *this*
Was the real point, the contrapuntal theme;
Just this: not text, but texture; not the dream
But topsy-turvical coincidence,
810   Not flimsy nonsense, but a web of sense.
Yes! It sufficed that I in life could find
Some kind of link-and-bobolink, some kind
Of correlated pattern in the game,

Plexed artistry, and something of the same
Pleasure in it as they who played it found.

It did not matter who they were. No sound,
No furtive light came from their involute
Abode, but there they were, aloof and mute,
Playing a game of worlds, promoting pawns
To ivory unicorns and ebon fauns;
Kindling a long life here, extinguishing
A short one there; killing a Balkan king;
Causing a chunk of ice formed on a high-
Flying airplane to plummet from the sky
And strike a farmer dead; hiding my keys,
Glasses or pipe. Coordinating these
Events and objects with remote events
And vanished objects. Making ornaments
Of accidents and possibilities.

Stormcoated, I strode in: Sybil, it is
My firm conviction—"Darling, shut the door.
Had a nice trip?" Splendid—but what is more
I have returned convinced that I can grope
My way to some—to some—"Yes, dear?" Faint hope.

CANTO FOUR

Now I shall spy on beauty as none has
Spied on it yet. Now I shall cry out as
None has cried out. Now I shall try what none
Has tried. Now I shall do what none has done.
And speaking of this wonderful machine:
I'm puzzled by the difference between
Two methods of composing: *A*, the kind
Which goes on solely in the poet's mind,
A testing of performing words, while he
Is soaping a third time one leg, and *B*,
The other kind, much more decorous, when
He's in his study writing with a pen.

In method *B* the hand supports the thought,
The abstract battle is concretely fought.
The pen stops in mid-air, then swoops to bar
850   A canceled sunset or restore a star,
And thus it physically guides the phrase
Toward faint daylight through the inky maze.

But method *A* is agony! The brain
Is soon enclosed in a steel cap of pain.
A muse in overalls directs the drill
Which grinds and which no effort of the will
Can interrupt, while the automaton
Is taking off what he has just put on
Or walking briskly to the corner store
860   To buy the paper he has read before.

Why is it so? Is it, perhaps, because
In penless work there is no pen-poised pause
And one must use three hands at the same time,
Having to choose the necessary rhyme,
Hold the completed line before one's eyes,
And keep in mind all the preceding tries?
Or is the process deeper with no desk
To prop the false and hoist the poetesque?
For there are those mysterious moments when
870   Too weary to delete, I drop my pen;
I ambulate—and by some mute command
The right word flutes and perches on my hand.

My best time is the morning; my preferred
Season, midsummer. I once overheard
Myself awakening while half of me
Still slept in bed. I tore my spirit free,
And caught up with myself—upon the lawn
Where clover leaves cupped the topaz of dawn,
And where Shade stood in nightshirt and one shoe.
880   And then I realized that *this* half too
Was fast asleep; both laughed and I awoke
Safe in my bed as day its eggshell broke,
And robins walked and stopped, and on the damp

Gemmed turf a brown shoe lay! My secret stamp,
The Shade impress, the mystery inborn.
Mirages, miracles, midsummer morn.

Since my biographer may be too staid
Or know too little to affirm that Shade
Shaved in his bath, here goes:
                              "He'd fixed a sort
890   Of hinge-and-screw affair, a steel support
Running across the tub to hold in place
The shaving mirror right before his face
And with his toe renewing tap-warmth, he'd
Sit like a king there, and like Marat bleed."

The more I weigh, the less secure my skin;
In places it's ridiculously thin;
Thus near the mouth: the space between its wick
And my grimace, invites the wicked nick.
Or this dewlap: some day I must set free
900   The Newport Frill inveterate in me.
My Adam's apple is a prickly pear:
Now I shall speak of evil and despair
As none has spoken. Five, six, seven, eight,
Nine strokes are not enough. Ten. I palpate
Through strawberry-and-cream the gory mess
And find unchanged that patch of prickliness.

I have my doubts about the one-armed bloke
Who in commercials with one gliding stroke
Clears a smooth path of flesh from ear to chin,
910   Then wipes his face and fondly tries his skin.
I'm in the class of fussy bimanists.
As a discreet ephebe in tights assists
A female in an acrobatic dance,
My left hand helps, and holds, and shifts its stance.

Now I shall speak . . . Better than any soap
Is the sensation for which poets hope
When inspiration and its icy blaze,
The sudden image, the immediate phrase

Over the skin a triple ripple send
920 Making the little hairs all stand on end
As in the enlarged animated scheme
Of whiskers mowed when held up by Our Cream.

Now I shall speak of evil as none has
Spoken before. I loathe such things as jazz;
The white-hosed moron torturing a black
Bull, rayed with red; abstractist bric-a-brac;
Primitivist folk-masks; progressive schools;
Music in supermarkets; swimming pools;
Brutes, bores, class-conscious Philistines, Freud, Marx,
930 Fake thinkers, puffed-up poets, frauds and sharks.

And while the safety blade with scrape and screak
Travels across the country of my cheek,
Cars on the highway pass, and up the steep
Incline big trucks around my jawbone creep,
And now a silent liner docks, and now
Sunglassers tour Beirut, and now I plough
Old Zembla's fields where my gray stubble grows,
And slaves make hay between my mouth and nose.

Man's life as commentary to abstruse
940 *Unfinished poem.* Note for further use.

Dressing in all the rooms, I rhyme and roam
Throughout the house with, in my fist, a comb
Or a shoehorn, which turns into the spoon
I eat my egg with. In the afternoon
You drive me to the library. We dine
At half past six. And that odd muse of mine,
My versipel, is with me everywhere,
In carrel and in car, and in my chair.

And all the time, and all the time, my love,
950 You too are there, beneath the word, above
The syllable, to underscore and stress
The vital rhythm. One heard a woman's dress
Rustle in days of yore. I've often caught

The sound and sense of your approaching thought.
And all in you is youth, and you make new,
By quoting them, old things I made for you.

Dim Gulf was my first book (free verse); *Night Rote*
Came next; then *Hebe's Cup*, my final float
In that damp carnival, for now I term
960   Everything "Poems," and no longer squirm.
(But *this* transparent thingum does require
Some moondrop title. Help me, Will! *Pale Fire*.)

Gently the day has passed in a sustained
Low hum of harmony. The brain is drained
And a brown ament, and the noun I meant
To use but did not, dry on the cement.
Maybe my sensual love for the *consonne
D'appui*, Echo's fey child, is based upon
A feeling of fantastically planned,
970   Richly rhymed life.
                      I feel I understand
Existence, or at least a minute part
Of my existence, only through my art,
In terms of combinational delight;
And if my private universe scans right,
So does the verse of galaxies divine
Which I suspect is an iambic line.
I'm reasonably sure that we survive
And that my darling somewhere is alive,
As I am reasonably sure that I
980   Shall wake at six tomorrow, on July
The twenty-second, nineteen fifty-nine,
And that the day will probably be fine;
So this alarm clock let me set myself,
Yawn, and put back Shade's "Poems" on their shelf.

But it's not bedtime yet. The sun attains
Old Dr. Sutton's last two windowpanes.
The man must be—what? Eighty? Eighty-two?
Was twice my age the year I married you.
Where are you? In the garden. I can see

990 Part of your shadow near the shagbark tree.
     Somewhere horseshoes are being tossed. Click. Clunk.
     (Leaning against its lamppost like a drunk.)
     A dark Vanessa with a crimson band
     Wheels in the low sun, settles on the sand
     And shows its ink-blue wingtips flecked with white.
     And through the flowing shade and ebbing light
     A man, unheedful of the butterfly—
     Some neighbor's gardener, I guess—goes by
     Trundling an empty barrow up the lane.

Commentary

Lines 1–4:   I was the shadow of the waxwing slain, etc.

The image in these opening lines evidently refers to a bird knocking itself out, in full flight, against the outer surface of a glass pane in which a mirrored sky, with its slightly darker tint and slightly slower cloud, presents the illusion of continued space. We can visualize John Shade in his early boyhood, a physically unattractive but otherwise beautifully developed lad, experiencing his first eschatological shock, as with incredulous fingers he picks up from the turf that compact ovoid body and gazes at the wax-red streaks ornamenting those gray-brown wings and at the graceful tail feathers tipped with yellow as bright as fresh paint. When in the last year of Shade's life I had the fortune of being his neighbor in the idyllic hills of New Wye (see Foreword), I often saw those particular birds most convivially feeding on the chalk-blue berries of junipers growing at the corner of his house. (See also lines 181–182.)

My knowledge of garden Aves had been limited to those of northern Europe but a young New Wye gardener, in whom I was interested (see note to line 998), helped me to identify the profiles of quite a number of tropical-looking little strangers and their comical calls; and, naturally, every tree top plotted its dotted line toward the ornithological work on my desk to which I would gallop from the lawn in nomenclatorial agitation. How hard I found to fit the name "robin" to the suburban impostor, the gross fowl, with its untidy dull-red livery and the revolting gusto it showed when consuming long, sad, passive worms!

Incidentally, it is curious to note that a crested bird called in Zemblan *sampel* ("silktail"), closely resembling a waxwing in shape and shade, is the model of one of the three heraldic creatures (the other two being respectively a reindeer proper and a merman azure, crined or) in the armorial bearings of the Zemblan King, Charles the Beloved (born 1915), whose glorious misfortunes I discussed so often with my friend.

The poem was begun at the dead center of the year, a few

486

minutes after midnight July 1, while I played chess with a young Iranian enrolled in our summer school; and I do not doubt that our poet would have understood his annotator's temptation to synchronize a certain fateful fact, the departure from Zembla of the would-be regicide Gradus, with that date. Actually, Gradus left Onhava on the Copenhagen plane on July 5.

Line 12: that crystal land

Perhaps an allusion to Zembla, my dear country. After this, in the disjointed, half-obliterated draft which I am not at all sure I have deciphered properly:

> Ah, I must not forget to say something
> That my friend told me of a certain king.

Alas, he would have said a great deal more if a domestic anti-Karlist had not controlled every line he communicated to her! Many a time have I rebuked him in bantering fashion: "You really should promise to use all that wonderful stuff, you bad gray poet, you!" And we would both giggle like boys. But then, after the inspiring evening stroll, we had to part, and grim night lifted the drawbridge between his impregnable fortress and my humble home.

That King's reign (1936–1958) will be remembered by at least a few discerning historians as a peaceful and elegant one. Owing to a fluid system of judicious alliances, Mars in his time never marred the record. Internally, until corruption, betrayal, and Extremism penetrated it, the People's Place (parliament) worked in perfect harmony with the Royal Council. Harmony, indeed, was the reign's password. The polite arts and pure sciences flourished. Technicology, applied physics, industrial chemistry and so forth were suffered to thrive. A small skyscraper of ultramarine glass was steadily rising in Onhava. The climate seemed to be improving. Taxation had become a thing of beauty. The poor were getting a little richer, and the rich a little poorer (in accordance with what may be known some day as Kinbote's Law). Medical care was spreading to the confines of the state: less and less often, on his tour of the country, every autumn, when the rowans hung coral-heavy, and the puddles tinkled with Muscovy glass, the friendly and eloquent monarch would be interrupted by a pertussal "back-draucht" in a crowd of schoolchildren. Parachuting had become a popular sport. Everybody, in a word, was content—even the political mischiefmakers who were contentedly making mischief paid by a contented *Sosed* (Zembla's gigantic neighbor). But let us not pursue this tiresome subject.

To return to the King: take for instance the question of personal culture. How often is it that kings engage in some special research? Conchologists among them can be counted on the fingers of one maimed hand. The last king of Zembla—partly under the influence of his uncle Conmal, the great translator of Shakespeare (see notes to lines 39–40 and 962), had become, despite frequent migraines, passionately addicted to the study of literature. At forty, not long before the collapse of his throne, he had attained such a degree of scholarship that he dared accede to his venerable uncle's raucous dying request: "Teach, Karlik!" Of course, it would have been unseemly for a monarch to appear in the robes of learning at a university lectern and present to rosy youths *Finnegans Wake* as a monstrous extension of Angus MacDiarmid's "incoherent transactions" and of Southey's Lingo-Grande ("Dear Stumparumper," etc.) or discuss the Zemblan variants, collected in 1798 by Hodinski, of the *Kongs-skugg-sio* (*The Royal Mirror*), an anonymous masterpiece of the twelfth century. Therefore he lectured under an assumed name and in a heavy make-up, with wig and false whiskers. All brown-bearded, apple-cheeked, blue-eyed Zemblans look alike, and I who have not shaved now for a year, resemble my disguised king (see also note to line 894).

During these periods of teaching, Charles Xavier made it a rule to sleep at a *pied-à-terre* he had rented, as any scholarly citizen would, in Coriolanus Lane: a charming, central-heated studio with adjacent bathroom and kitchenette. One recalls with nostalgic pleasure its light gray carpeting and pearl-gray walls (one of them graced with a solitary copy of Picasso's *Chandelier, pot et casserole émaillée*), a shelfful of calf-bound poets, and a virginal-looking daybed under its rug of imitation panda fur. How far from this limpid simplicity seemed the palace and the odious Council Chamber with its unsolvable problems and frightened councilors!

Line 17:   And then the gradual;   *Line 29:*   gray

By an extraordinary coincidence (inherent perhaps in the contrapuntal nature of Shade's art) our poet seems to name here (gradual, gray) a man, whom he was to see for one fatal moment three weeks later, but of whose existence at the time (July 2) he could not have known. Jakob Gradus called himself variously Jack Degree or Jacques de Grey, or James de Gray, and also appears in police records as Ravus, Ravenstone, and d'Argus. Having a morbid affection for the ruddy Russia of the Soviet era, he contended that the real origin of his name should be sought in the Russian word for grape, *vinograd*, to which a Latin suffix had adhered, making it Vinogradus. His father, Martin Gradus, had been a Protestant minister in Riga, but except for him and a maternal uncle (Roman Tselovalni-kov, police officer and part-time member of the Social-Revo-lutionary party), the whole clan seems to have been in the liquor business. Martin Gradus died in 1920, and his widow moved to Strasbourg where she soon died, too. Another Gra-dus, an Alsatian merchant, who oddly enough was totally un-related to our killer but had been a close business friend of his kinsmen for years, adopted the boy and raised him with his own children. It would seem that at one time young Gra-dus studied pharmacology in Zurich, and at another, traveled to misty vineyards as an itinerant wine taster. We find him next engaging in petty subversive activities—printing peevish pam-phlets, acting as messenger for obscure syndicalist groups, or-ganizing strikes at glass factories, and that sort of thing. Sometime in the forties he came to Zembla as a brandy sales-man. There he married a publican's daughter. His connection with the Extremist party dates from its first ugly writhings, and when the revolution broke out, his modest organizational gifts found some appreciation in various offices. His departure for Western Europe, with a sordid purpose in his heart and a loaded gun in his pocket, took place on the very day that an innocent poet in an innocent land was beginning Canto Two of *Pale Fire*. We shall accompany Gradus in constant thought, as he makes his way from distant dim Zembla to green Appalachia, through the entire length of the poem, following the road of its rhythm, riding past in a rhyme, skidding around the corner of a run-on, breathing with the caesura, swinging down to the foot of the page from line to line as from branch to branch, hiding between two words (see note to line 596), reappearing on the horizon of a new canto, steadily marching nearer in iambic motion, crossing streets, moving up with his valise on the escalator of the pentameter, stepping off, boarding a new train of thought, entering the hall of a hotel, putting out the bedlight, while Shade blots out a word, and falling asleep as the poet lays down his pen for the night.

Line 27:   Sherlock Holmes

A hawk-nosed, lanky, rather likable private detective, the main character in various stories by Conan Doyle. I have no means to ascertain at the present time which of these is referred to here but suspect that our poet simply made up this Case of the Reversed Footprints.

Lines 34–35:   Stilettos of a frozen stillicide

How persistently our poet evokes images of winter in the beginning of a poem which he started composing on a balmy summer night! The mechanism of the associations is easy to make out (glass leading to crystal and crystal to ice) but the prompter behind it retains his incognito. One is too modest to suppose that the fact that the poet and his future commentator first met on a winter day somehow impinges here on the actual season. In the lovely line heading this comment the reader should note the last word. My dictionary defines it as "a succession of drops falling from the eaves, eavesdrop, cavesdrop." I remember having encountered it for the first time in a poem by Thomas Hardy. The bright frost has eternalized the bright eavesdrop. We should also note the cloak-

and-dagger hint-glint in the "svelte stilettos" and the shadow
of regicide in the rhyme.

Lines 39–40: Was close my eyes, etc.

These lines are represented in the drafts by a variant reading:

39 . . . . and home would haste my thieves,
40 The sun with stolen ice, the moon with leaves

One cannot help recalling a passage in *Timon of Athens* (Act
IV, Scene 3) where the misanthrope talks to the three ma-
rauders. Having no library in the desolate log cabin where I
live like Timon in his cave, I am compelled for the purpose
of quick citation to retranslate this passage into English prose
from a Zemblan poetical version of *Timon* which, I hope, sufficiently approximates the text, or is at least faithful to its
spirit:

> The sun is a thief: she lures the sea
> and robs it. The moon is a thief:
> he steals his silvery light from the sun.
> The sea is a thief: it dissolves the moon.

For a prudent appraisal of Conmal's translations of Shakespeare's works, see note to line 962.

Line 42: I could make out

By the end of May I could make out the outlines of some
of my images in the shape his genius might give them; by
mid-June I felt sure at last that he would recreate in a poem
the dazzling Zembla burning in my brain. I mesmerized him
with it, I saturated him with my vision, I pressed upon him,
with a drunkard's wild generosity, all that I was helpless myself
to put into verse. Surely, it would not be easy to discover in
the history of poetry a similar case—that of two men, different
in origin, upbringing, thought associations, spiritual intona-

tion and mental mode, one a cosmopolitan scholar, the other a fireside poet, entering into a secret compact of this kind. At length I knew he was ripe with my Zembla, bursting with suitable rhymes, ready to spurt at the brush of an eyelash. I kept urging him at every opportunity to surmount his habitual sloth and start writing. My little pocket diary contains such jottings as: "Suggested to him the heroic measure"; "retold the escape"; "offered the use of a quiet room in my house"; "discussed making recordings of my voice for his use"; and finally, under date of July 3: "poem begun!"

Although I realize only too clearly, alas, that the result, in its pale and diaphanous final phase, cannot be regarded as a direct echo of my narrative (of which, incidentally, only a few fragments are given in my notes—mainly to Canto One), one can hardly doubt that the sunset glow of the story acted as a catalytic agent upon the very process of the sustained creative effervescence that enabled Shade to produce a 1000-line poem in three weeks. There is, moreover, a symptomatic family resemblance in the coloration of both poem and story. I have reread, not without pleasure, my comments to his lines, and in many cases have caught myself borrowing a kind of opalescent light from my poet's fiery orb, and unconsciously aping the prose style of his own critical essays. But his widow, and his colleagues, may stop worrying and enjoy in full the fruit of whatever advice they gave my good-natured poet. Oh yes, the final text of the poem is entirely his.

If we discount, as I think we should, three casual allusions to royalty (605, 822, and 894) and the Popian "Zembla" in line 937, we may conclude that the final text of *Pale Fire* has been deliberately and drastically drained of every trace of the material I contributed; but we also find that despite the control exercised upon my poet by a domestic censor and God knows whom else, he has given the royal fugitive a refuge in the vaults of the variants he has preserved; for in his draft as many as thirteen verses, superb singing verses (given by me in note to lines 70, 79, and 130, all in Canto One, which he obviously worked at with a greater degree of creative freedom than he enjoyed afterwards) bear the specific imprint of my theme, a minute but genuine star ghost of my discourse on Zembla and her unfortunate king.

Lines 47–48: the frame house between Goldsworth and Wordsmith

The first name refers to the house in Dulwich Road that I rented from Hugh Warren Goldsworth, authority on Roman Law and distinguished judge. I never had the pleasure of meeting my landlord but I came to know his handwriting almost as well as I do Shade's. The second name denotes, of course, Wordsmith University. In seeming to suggest a midway situation between the two places, our poet is less concerned with spatial exactitude than with a witty exchange of syllables invoking the two masters of the heroic couplet, between whom he embowers his own muse. Actually, the "frame house on its square of green" was five miles west of the Wordsmith campus but only fifty yards or so distant from my east windows.

In the Foreword to this work I have had occasion to say something about the amenities of my habitation. The charming, charmingly vague lady (see note to line 691), who secured it for me, sight unseen, meant well, no doubt, especially since it was widely admired in the neighborhood for its "old-world spaciousness and graciousness." Actually, it was an old, dismal, white-and-black, half-timbered house, of the type termed *wodnaggen* in my country, with carved gables, drafty bow windows and a so-called "semi-noble" porch, surmounted by a hideous veranda. Judge Goldsworth had a wife and four daughters. Family photographs met me in the hallway and pursued me from room to room, and although I am sure that Alphina (9), Betty (10), Candida (12), and Dee (14) will soon change from horribly cute little schoolgirls to smart young ladies and superior mothers, I must confess that their pert pictures irritated me to such an extent that finally I gathered them one by one and dumped them all in a closet under the gallows row of their cellophane-shrouded winter clothes. In the study I found a large picture of their parents, with sexes reversed, Mrs. G. resembling Malenkov, and Mr. G. a Medusa-locked hag, and this I replaced by the reproduction of a beloved early Picasso: earth boy leading raincloud horse. I did not bother, though, to do much about the family books which were also all over the house—four sets of different Children's

Encyclopedias, and a stolid grown-up one that ascended all
the way from shelf to shelf along a flight of stairs to burst an
appendix in the attic. Judging by the novels in Mrs. Goldsworth's boudoir, her intellectual interests were fully developed, going as they did from Amber to Zen. The head of this
alphabetic family had a library too, but this consisted mainly
of legal works and a lot of conspicuously lettered ledgers. All
the layman could glean for instruction and entertainment was
a morocco-bound album in which the judge had lovingly
pasted the life histories and pictures of people he had sent to
prison or condemned to death: unforgettable faces of imbecile
hoodlums, last smokes and last grins, a strangler's quite or-
dinary-looking hands, a self-made widow, the close-set merciless eyes of a homicidal maniac (somewhat resembling, I
admit, the late Jacques d'Argus), a bright little parricide aged
seven ("Now, sonny, we want you to tell us—"), and a sad
pudgy old pederast who had blown up his blackmailer. What
rather surprised me was that he, my learned landlord, and not
his "missus," directed the household. Not only had he left
me a detailed inventory of all such articles as cluster around
a new tenant like a mob of menacing natives, but he had taken
stupendous pains to write out on slips of paper recommen-
dations, explanations, injunctions and supplementary lists.
Whatever I touched on the first day of my stay yielded a specimen of Goldsworthiana. I unlocked the medicine chest in the
second bathroom, and out fluttered a message advising me
that the slit for discarded safety blades was too full for use. I
opened the icebox, and it warned me with a bark that "no
national specialties with odors hard to get rid of" should be
placed therein. I pulled out the middle drawer of the desk in
the study—and discovered a *catalogue raisonné* of its meager
contents which included an assortment of ashtrays, a damask
paperknife (described as "one ancient dagger brought by Mrs.
Goldsworth's father from the Orient"), and an old but unused
pocket diary optimistically maturing there until its calendric
correspondencies came around again. Among various detailed
notices affixed to a special board in the pantry, such as plumbing instructions, dissertations on electricity, discourses on cactuses and so forth, I found the diet of the black cat that came
with the house:

Mon, Wed, Fri: Liver
Tue, Thu, Sat: Fish
Sun: Ground meat

(All it got from me was milk and sardines; it was a likable
little creature but after a while its movements began to grate
on my nerves and I farmed it out to Mrs. Finley, the cleaning
woman.) But perhaps the funniest note concerned the manipulations of the window curtains which had to be drawn in
different ways at different hours to prevent the sun from getting at the upholstery. A description of the position of the
sun, daily and seasonal, was given for the several windows,
and if I had heeded all this I would have been kept as busy
as a participant in a regatta. A footnote, however, generously
suggested that instead of manning the curtains, I might prefer
to shift and reshift out of sun range the more precious pieces
of furniture (two embroidered armchairs and a heavy "royal
console") but should do it carefully lest I scratch the wall
moldings. I cannot, alas, reproduce the meticulous schedule
of these transposals but seem to recall that I was supposed to
castle the long way before going to bed and the short way
first thing in the morning. My dear Shade roared with laughter when I led him on a tour of inspection and had him find
some of those bunny eggs for himself. Thank God, his robust
hilarity dissipated the atmosphere of *damnum infectum* in
which I was supposed to dwell. On his part, he regaled me
with a number of anecdotes concerning the judge's dry wit
and courtroom mannerisms; most of these anecdotes were
doubtless folklore exaggerations, a few were evident inventions, and all were harmless. He did not bring up, my sweet
old friend never did, ridiculous stories about the terrifying
shadows that Judge Goldsworth's gown threw across the underworld, or about this or that beast lying in prison and positively dying of *raghdirst* (thirst for revenge)—crass banalities
circulated by the scurrilous and the heartless—by all those for
whom romance, remoteness, sealskin-lined scarlet skies, the
darkening dunes of a fabulous kingdom, simply do not exist.
But enough of this. Let us turn to our poet's windows. I have
no desire to twist and batter an unambiguous *apparatus cri-
ticus* into the monstrous semblance of a novel.

Today it would be impossible for me to describe Shade's house in terms of architecture or indeed in any term other than those of peeps and glimpses, and window-framed opportunities. As previously mentioned (see Foreword), the coming of summer presented a problem in optics: the encroaching foliage did not always see eye to eye with me: it confused a green monocle with an opaque occludent, and the idea of protection with that of obstruction. Meanwhile (on July 3 according to my agenda) I had learned—not from John but from Sybil—that my friend had started to work on a long poem. After not having seen him for a couple of days, I happened to be bringing him some third-class mail from his box on the road, adjacent to Goldsworth's (which I used to ignore, crammed as it was with leaflets, local advertisements, commercial catalogues, and that kind of trash) and ran into Sybil whom a shrub had screened from my falcon eye. Straw-hatted and garden-gloved, she was squatting on her hams in front of a flower bed and pruning or tying up something, and her close-fitting brown trousers reminded me of the mandolin tights (as I jokingly called them) that my own wife used to wear. She said not to bother him with those ads and added the information about his having "begun a really big poem." I felt the blood rush to my face and mumbled something about his not having shown any of it to me yet, and she straightened herself, and swept the black and gray hair off her forehead, and stared at me, and said: "What do you mean—shown any of it? He never shows anything unfinished. Never, never. He will not even discuss it with you until it is quite, quite finished." I could not believe it, but soon discovered on talking to my strangely reticent friend that he had been well coached by his lady. When I endeavored to draw him out by means of good-natured sallies such as: "People who live in glass houses should not write poems," he would only yawn and shake his head, and retort that "foreigners ought to keep away from old saws." Nevertheless the urge to find out what he was doing with all the live, glamorous, palpitating, shimmering material I had lavished upon him, the itching desire to see him at work (even if the fruit of his work was denied me), proved to be utterly agonizing and uncontrollable and led me to indulge in an orgy of spying which no considerations of pride could stop.

Windows, as well known, have been the solace of first-person literature throughout the ages. But this observer never could emulate in sheer luck the eavesdropping *Hero of Our Time* or the omnipresent one of *Time Lost*. Yet I was granted now and then scraps of happy hunting. When my casement window ceased to function because of an elm's gross growth, I found, at the end of the veranda, an ivied corner from which I could view rather amply the front of the poet's house. If I wanted to see its south side I could go down to the back of my garage and look from behind a tulip tree across the curving downhill road at several precious bright windows, for he never pulled down the shades (*she* did). If I yearned for the opposite side, all I had to do was walk uphill to the top of my garden where my bodyguard of black junipers watched the stars, and the omens, and the patch of pale light under the lone street-lamp on the road below. By the onset of the season here conjured up, I had surmounted the very special and very private fears that are discussed elsewhere (see note to line 62) and rather enjoyed following in the dark a weedy and rocky easterly projection of my grounds ending in a locust grove on a slightly higher level than the north side of the poet's house.

Once, three decades ago, in my tender and terrible boyhood, I had the occasion of seeing a man in the act of making contact with God. I had wandered into the so-called Rose Court at the back of the Ducal Chapel in my native Onhava, during an interval in hymnal practice. As I mooned there, lifting and cooling my bare calves by turns against a smooth column, I could hear the distant sweet voices interblending in subdued boyish merriment which some chance grudge, some jealous annoyance with one particular lad, prevented me from joining. The sound of rapid steps made me raise my morose gaze from the sectile mosaic of the court—realistic rose petals cut out of rodstein and large, almost palpable thorns cut out of green marble. Into these roses and thorns there walked a black shadow: a tall, pale, long-nosed, dark-haired young minister whom I had seen around once or twice strode out of the vestry and without seeing me stopped in the middle of the

court. Guilty disgust contorted his thin lips. He wore spectacles. His clenched hands seemed to be gripping invisible
prison bars. But there is no bound to the measure of grace
which man may be able to receive. All at once his look
changed to one of rapture and reverence. I had never seen
such a blaze of bliss before but was to perceive something of
that splendor, of that spiritual energy and divine vision, now,
in another land, reflected upon the rugged and homely face
of old John Shade. How glad I was that the vigils I had kept
all through the spring had prepared me to observe him at his
miraculous midsummer task! I had learned exactly when and
where to find the best points from which to follow the contours of his inspiration. My binoculars would seek him out
and focus upon him from afar in his various places of labor:
at night, in the violet glow of his upstairs study where a
kindly mirror reflected for me his hunched-up shoulders and
the pencil with which he kept picking his ear (inspecting
now and then the lead, and even tasting it); in the forenoon, lurking in the ruptured shadows of his first-floor
study where a bright goblet of liquor quietly traveled from
filing cabinet to lectern, and from lectern to bookshelf,
there to hide if need be behind Dante's bust; on a hot day,
among the vines of a small arborlike portico, through the
garlands of which I could glimpse a stretch of oilcloth, his
elbow upon it, and the plump cherubic fist propping and
crimpling his temple. Incidents of perspective and lighting,
interference by framework or leaves, usually deprived me of
a clear view of his face; and perhaps nature arranged it that
way so as to conceal from a possible predator the mysteries
of generation; but sometimes when the poet paced back and
forth across his lawn, or sat down for a moment on the bench
at the end of it, or paused under his favorite hickory tree, I
could distinguish the expression of passionate interest, rapture
and reverence, with which he followed the images wording
themselves in his mind, and I knew that whatever my agnostic
friend might say in denial, at *that* moment Our Lord was with
him.

On certain nights, when long before its inhabitants' usual
bedtime the house would be dark on the three sides I could
survey from my three vantage points, that very darkness kept

telling me they were at home. Their car stood near its garage—but I could not believe they had gone out on foot, since
in that case they would have left the porch light turned on.
Later considerations and deductions have persuaded me that
the night of great need on which I decided to check the matter was July 11, the date of Shade's completing his Second
Canto. It was a hot, black, blustery night. I stole through the
shrubbery to the rear of their house. At first I thought that
this fourth side was also dark, thus clinching the matter, and
had time to experience a queer sense of relief before noticing
a faint square of light under the window of a little back parlor
where I had never been. It was wide open. A tall lamp with a
parchment-like shade illuminated the bottom of the room
where I could see Sybil and John, her on the edge of a divan,
sidesaddle, with her back to me, and him on a hassock near
the divan upon which he seemed to be slowly collecting and
stacking scattered playing cards left after a game of patience.
Sybil was alternatively huddle-shaking and blowing her nose;
John's face was all blotchy and wet. Not being aware at the
time of the exact type of writing paper my friend used, I could
not help wondering what on earth could be so tear-provoking
about the outcome of a game of cards. As I strained to see
better, standing up to my knees in a horribly elastic box
hedge, I dislodged the sonorous lid of a garbage can. This of
course might have been mistaken for the work of the wind,
and Sybil hated the wind. She at once left her perch, closed
the window with a great bang, and pulled down its strident
blind.

I crept back to my cheerless domicile with a heavy heart
and a puzzled mind. The heart remained heavy but the puzzle
was solved a few days later, very probably on St. Swithin's
Day, for I find in my little diary under that date the antici-
patory *"promnad vespert mid J.S.,"* crossed out with a petu-
lance that broke the lead in midstroke. Having waited and
waited for my friend to join me in the lane, until the red of
the sunset had turned to the ashes of dusk, I walked over to
his front door, hesitated, assessed the gloom and the silence,
and started to walk around the house. This time not a glint
came from the back parlor, but by the bright prosaic light in
the kitchen I distinguished one end of a whitewashed table

and Sybil sitting at it with so rapt a look on her face that one might have supposed she had just thought up a new recipe. The back door was ajar, and as I tapped it open and launched upon some gay airy phrase, I realized that Shade, sitting at the other end of the table, was in the act of reading to her something that I guessed to be a part of his poem. They both started. An unprintable oath escaped from him and he slapped down on the table the stack of index cards he had in his hand. Later he was to attribute this temperamental outburst to his having mistaken, with his reading glasses on, a welcome friend for an intruding salesman; but I must say it shocked me, it shocked me greatly, and disposed me at the time to read a hideous meaning into everything that followed. "Well, sit down," said Sybil, "and have some coffee" (victors are generous). I accepted, as I wanted to see if the recitation would be continued in my presence. It was not. "I thought," I said to my friend, "you were coming out with me for a stroll." He excused himself saying he felt out of sorts, and continued to clean the bowl of his pipe as fiercely as if it were my heart he was hollowing out.

Not only did I understand *then* that Shade regularly read to Sybil cumulative parts of his poem but it also dawns upon me *now* that, just as regularly, she made him tone down or remove from his Fair Copy everything connected with the magnificent Zemblan theme with which I kept furnishing him and which, without knowing much about the growing work, I fondly believed would become the main rich thread in its weave!

Higher up on the same wooded hill stood, and still stands I trust, Dr. Sutton's old clapboard house and, at the very top, eternity shall not dislodge Professor C.'s ultramodern villa from whose terrace one can glimpse to the south the larger and sadder of the three conjoined lakes called Omega, Ozero, and Zero (Indian names garbled by early settlers in such a way as to accommodate specious derivations and commonplace allusions). On the northern side of the hill Dulwich Road joins the highway leading to Wordsmith University to which I shall devote here only a few words partly because all kinds of descriptive booklets should be available to the reader by writing to the University's Publicity Office, but mainly because I wish to convey, in making this reference to Wordsmith briefer than the notes on the Goldsworth and Shade houses, the fact that the college was considerably farther from them than they were from one another. It is probably the first time that the dull pain of distance is rendered through an effect of style and that a topographical idea finds its verbal expression in a series of foreshortened sentences.

After winding for about four miles in a general eastern direction through a beautifully sprayed and irrigated residential section with variously graded lawns sloping down on both sides, the highway bifurcates: one branch goes left to New Wye and its expectant airfield; the other continues to the campus. Here are the great mansions of madness, the impeccably planned dormitories—bedlams of jungle music—the magnificent palace of the Administration, the brick walls, the archways, the quadrangles blocked out in velvet green and chrysoprase, Spencer House and its lily pond, the Chapel, New Lecture Hall, the Library, the prisonlike edifice containing our classrooms and offices (to be called from now on Shade Hall), the famous avenue of all the trees mentioned by Shakespeare, a distant droning sound, the hint of a haze, the turquoise dome of the Observatory, wisps and pale plumes of cirrus, and the poplar-curtained Roman-tiered football field, deserted on summer days except for a dreamy-eyed youngster flying—on a long control line in a droning circle—a motor-powered model plane.

Dear Jesus, do something.

Line 49: shagbark

A hickory. Our poet shared with the English masters the noble knack of transplanting trees into verse with their sap and shade. Many years ago Disa, our King's Queen, whose favorite trees were the jacaranda and the maidenhair, copied out in her album a quatrain from John Shade's collection of short poems *Hebe's Cup*, which I cannot refrain from quoting here (from a letter I received on April 6, 1959, from southern France):

THE SACRED TREE
The ginkgo leaf, in golden hue, when shed,
   A muscat grape,
   Is an old-fashioned butterfly, ill-spread,
   In shape.

When the new Episcopal church in New Wye (see note to line 549) was built, the bulldozers spared an arc of those sacred trees planted by a landscaper of genius (Repburg) at the end of the so-called Shakespeare Avenue, on the campus. I do not know if it is relevant or not but there is a cat-and-mouse game in the second line, and "tree" in Zemblan is *grados.*

Line 57:   The phantom of my little daughter's swing

After this Shade crossed out lightly the following lines in the draft:

   The light is good; the reading lamps, long-necked;
   All doors have keys. Your modern architect
   Is in collusion with psychanalysts:
   When planning parents' bedrooms, he insists
   On lockless doors so that, when looking back,
   The future patient of the future quack
   May find, all set for him, the Primal Scene.

Line 61:   TV's huge paperclip

In the otherwise empty, and pretty fatuous, obituary mentioned in my notes to lines 71–72, there happens to be quoted a manuscript poem (received from Sybil Shade) which is said to have been "composed by our poet apparently at the end of June, thus less than a month before our poet's death, thus being the last short piece that our poet wrote."
Here it is:

THE SWING
The setting sun that lights the tips
Of TV's giant paperclips
   Upon the roof;

The shadow of the doorknob that
At sundown is a baseball bat
    Upon the door;

The cardinal that likes to sit
And make chip-wit, chip-wit, chip-wit
    Upon the tree;

The empty little swing that swings
Under the tree: these are the things
    That break my heart.

I leave *my* poet's reader to decide whether it is likely he would have written this only a few days before he repeated its miniature themes in this part of the poem. I suspect it to be a much earlier effort (it has no year subscript but should be dated soon after his daughter's death) which Shade dug out from among his old papers to see what he could use for *Pale Fire* (the poem our necrologist does not know).

Line 62: often

Often, almost nightly, throughout the spring of 1959, I had feared for my life. Solitude is the playfield of Satan. I cannot describe the depths of my loneliness and distress. There was naturally my famous neighbor just across the lane, and at one time I took in a dissipated young roomer (who generally came home long after midnight). Yet I wish to stress that cold hard core of loneliness which is not good for a displaced soul. Everybody knows how given to regicide Zemblans are: two Queens, three Kings, and fourteen Pretenders died violent deaths, strangled, stabbed, poisoned, and drowned, in the course of only one century (1700–1800). The Goldsworth castle became particularly solitary after that turning point at dusk which resembles so much the nightfall of the mind. Stealthy rustles, the footsteps of yesteryear leaves, an idle breeze, a dog touring the garbage cans—everything sounded to me like a bloodthirsty prowler. I kept moving from window to window, my silk nightcap drenched with sweat, my bared breast a thawing pond, and sometimes, armed with the judge's shotgun, I dared beard the terrors of the terrace. I suppose it was then, on those masquerading spring nights with the sounds of new life in the trees cruelly mimicking the cracklings of old death in my brain, I suppose it was then, on those dreadful nights, that I got used to consulting the windows of my neighbor's house in the hope for a gleam of comfort (see notes to lines 47–48). What would I not have given for the poet's suffering another heart attack (see line 691 and note) leading to my being called over to their house, all windows ablaze, in the middle of the night, in a great warm burst of sympathy, coffee, telephone calls, Zemblan herbal receipts (they work wonders!), and a resurrected Shade weeping in my arms ("There, there, John"). But on those March nights their house was as black as a coffin. And when physical exhaustion and the sepulchral cold drove me at last upstairs to my solitary double bed, I would lie awake and breathless—as if only now living consciously through those perilous nights in my country, where at any moment, a company of jittery revolutionists might enter and hustle me off to a moonlit wall. The sound of a rapid car or a groaning truck would come as a strange mixture of friendly life's relief and death's fearful shadow: would that shadow pull up at my door? Were those phantom thugs coming for me? Would they shoot me at once—or would they smuggle the chloroformed scholar back to Zembla, Rodnaya Zembla, to face there a dazzling decanter and a row of judges exulting in their inquisitorial chairs?

At times I thought that only by self-destruction could I hope to cheat the relentlessly advancing assassins who were in me, in my eardrums, in my pulse, in my skull, rather than on that constant highway looping up over me and around my heart as I dozed off only to have my sleep shattered by that drunken, impossible, unforgettable Bob's return to Candida's or Dee's former bed. As briefly mentioned in the foreword, I finally threw him out; after which for several nights neither wine, nor music, nor prayer could allay my fears. On the other hand, those mellowing spring days were quite sufferable, my lectures pleased everybody, and I made it a point of attending all the social functions available to me. But after the gay evening there came again the insidious approach, the oblique shuffle, that creeping up, and that pause, and the resumed crepitation.

The Goldsworth château had many outside doors, and no matter how thoroughly I inspected them and the window shutters downstairs at bedtime, I never failed to discover next morning something unlocked, unlatched, a little loose, a little ajar, something sly and suspicious-looking. One night the black cat, which a few minutes before I had seen rippling down into the basement where I had arranged toilet facilities for it in an attractive setting, suddenly reappeared on the threshold of the music room, in the middle of my insomnia and a Wagner record, arching its back and sporting a neck bow of white silk which it could certainly never have put on all by itself. I telephoned 11111 and a few minutes later was discussing possible culprits with a policeman who relished greatly my cherry cordial, but whoever had broken in had left no trace. It is so easy for a cruel person to make the victim of his ingenuity believe that he has persecution mania, or is really being stalked by a killer, or is suffering from hallucinations. Hallucinations! Well did I know that among certain youthful instructors whose advances I had rejected there was at least one evil practical joker; I knew it ever since the time I came home from a very enjoyable and successful meeting of students and teachers (at which I had exuberantly thrown off my coat and shown several willing pupils a few of the amusing holds employed by Zemblan wrestlers) and found in my coat pocket a brutal anonymous note saying: "You have hal . . . . . s real bad, chum," meaning evidently "hallucinations," although a malevolent critic might infer from the insufficient number of dashes that little Mr. Anon, despite teaching Freshman English, could hardly spell.

I am happy to report that soon after Easter my fears disappeared never to return. Into Alphina's or Betty's room another lodger moved, Balthasar, Prince of Loam, as I dubbed him, who with elemental regularity fell asleep at nine and by six in the morning was planting heliotropes (*Heliotropium turgenevi*). This is the flower whose odor evokes with timeless intensity the dusk, and the garden bench, and a house of painted wood in a distant northern land.

Line 70:   The new TV

After this, in the draft (dated July 3), come a few unnumbered lines that may have been intended for some later parts of the poem. They are not actually deleted but are accompanied by a question mark in the margin and encircled with a wavy line encroaching upon some of the letters:

> There are events, strange happenings, that strike
> The mind as emblematic. They are like
> Lost similes adrift without a string,
> Attached to nothing. Thus that northern king,
> Whose desperate escape from prison was
> Brought off successfully only because
> Some forty of his followers that night
> Impersonated him and aped his flight—

He never would have reached the western coast had not a fad spread among his secret supporters, romantic, heroic daredevils, of impersonating the fleeing king. They rigged themselves out to look like him in red sweaters and red caps, and popped up here and there, completely bewildering the revolutionary police. Some of the pranksters were much younger than the King, but this did not matter since his pictures in the huts of mountain folks and in the myopic shops of hamlets, where you could buy worms, ginger bread and *zhiletka* blades, had not aged since his coronation. A charming cartoon touch was added on the famous occasion when from the terrace of the Kronblik Hotel, whose chairlift takes tourists to the Kron glacier, one merry mime was seen floating up, like a red moth, with a hapless, and capless, policeman riding two seats behind him in dream-slow pursuit. It gives one pleasure to add that before reaching the staging point, the false king managed to escape by climbing down one of the pylons that supported the traction cable (see also notes to lines 149 and 171).

Line 71:   parents

With commendable alacrity, Professor Hurley produced an Appreciation of John Shade's published works within a month after the poet's death. It came out in a skimpy literary review, whose name momentarily escapes me, and was shown to me in Chicago where I interrupted for a couple of days my automobile journey from New Wye to Cedarn, in these grim autumnal mountains.

A Commentary where placid scholarship should reign is not the place for blasting the preposterous defects of that little obituary. I have only mentioned it because that is where I gleaned a few meager details concerning the poet's parents. His father, Samuel Shade, who died at fifty, in 1902, had studied medicine in his youth and was vice-president of a firm of surgical instruments in Exton. His chief passion, however, was what our eloquent necrologist calls "the study of the feathered tribe," adding that "a bird had been named for him: *Bombycilla Shadei*" (this should be *"shadei,"* of course). The poet's mother, nee Caroline Lukin, assisted him in his work and drew the admirable figures of his *Birds of Mexico*, which I remember having seen in my friend's house. What the obituarist does not know is that Lukin comes from Luke, as also do Locock and Luxon and Lukashevich. It represents one of the many instances when the amorphous-looking but live and personal hereditary patronymic grows, sometimes in fantastic shapes, around the common pebble of a Christian name. The Lukins are an old Essex family. Other names derive from professions such as Rymer, Scrivener, Limner (one who illuminates parchments), Botkin (one who makes bottekins, fancy footwear) and thousands of others. My tutor, a Scotsman, used to call any old tumble-down building "a hurley-house." But enough of this.

A few other items concerning John Shade's university studies and the middle years of his singularly uneventful life can be looked up by his reader in the professor's article. It would have been on the whole a dull piece had it not been enlivened, if that is the term, by certain special features. Thus, there is only one allusion to my friend's masterpiece (the neatly stacked batches of which, as I write this, lie in the sun on my table as so many ingots of fabulous metal) and this I transcribe with morbid delight: "Just before our poet's untimely death he seems to have been working on an autobiographical poem." The circumstances of this death are completely distorted by the professor, a faithful follower of the gentlemen of the daily press who—perhaps for political reasons—had falsified the culprit's motives and intentions without awaiting his trial—which unfortunately was not to take place in this world (see eventually my ultimate note). But, of course, the most striking characteristic of the little obituary is that it contains *not one reference* to the glorious friendship that brightened the last months of John's life.

My friend could not evoke the image of his father. Similarly the King, who also was not quite three when his father, King Alfin, died, was unable to recall his face, although oddly he did remember perfectly well the little monoplane of chocolate that he, a chubby babe, happened to be holding in that very last photograph (Christmas 1918) of the melancholy, riding-breeched aviator in whose lap he reluctantly and uncomfortably sprawled.

Alfin the Vague (1873–1918; regnal dates 1900–1918, but 1900–1919 in most biographical dictionaries, a fumble due to the coincident calendar change from Old Style to New) was given his cognomen by Amphitheatricus, a not unkindly writer of fugitive poetry in the liberal gazettes (who was also responsible for dubbing my capital Uranograd!). King Alfin's absent-mindedness knew no bounds. He was a wretched linguist having at his disposal only a few phrases of French and Danish, but every time he had to make a speech to his subjects—to a group of gaping Zemblan yokels in some remote valley where he had crash-landed—some uncontrollable switch went into action in his mind, and he reverted to those phrases, flavoring them for topical sense with a little Latin. Most of the anecdotes relating to his naïve fits of abstraction are too silly and indecent to sully these pages; but one of them that I do not think especially funny induced such guffaws from Shade (and returned to me, via the Common Room, with such obscene accretions) that I feel inclined to give it here as a sample (and as a corrective). One summer before the first world war, when the emperor of a great foreign realm (I realize how few there are to choose from) was paying an extremely unusual and flattering visit to our little hard country, my father took him and a young Zemblan interpreter (whose sex I leave open) in a newly purchased custom-built car on a jaunt in the countryside. As usual, King Alfin traveled without a vestige of escort, and this, and his brisk driving, seemed to trouble his guest. On their way back, some twenty miles from Onhava, King Alfin decided to stop for repairs. While he tinkered with the motor, the emperor and the interpreter sought the shade of some pines by the highway, and only when King Alfin was back in Onhava, did he gradually realize from a re-iteration of rather frantic questions that he had left somebody behind ("What emperor?" has remained his only memorable *mot*). Generally speaking, in respect of any of my contributions (or what I thought to be contributions) I repeatedly enjoined my poet to record them in writing, by all means, but not to spread them in idle speech; even poets, however, are human.

King Alfin's absent-mindedness was strangely combined with a passion for mechanical things, especially for flying apparatuses. In 1912, he managed to rise in an umbrella-like Fabre "hydroplane" and almost got drowned in the sea between Nitra and Indra. He smashed two Farmans, three Zemblan machines, and a beloved Santos Dumont *Demoiselle*. A very special monoplane, Blenda IV, was built for him in 1916 by his constant "aerial adjutant," Colonel Peter Gusev (later a pioneer parachutist and, at seventy, one of the greatest jumpers of all time), and this was his bird of doom. On the serene, and not too cold, December morning that the angels chose to net his mild pure soul, King Alfin was in the act of trying solo a tricky vertical loop that Prince Andrey Kachurin, the famous Russian stunter and War One hero, had shown him in Gatchina. Something went wrong, and the little Blenda was seen to go into an uncontrolled dive. Behind and above him, in a Caudron biplane, Colonel Gusev (by then Duke of Rahl) and the Queen snapped several pictures of what seemed at first a noble and graceful evolution but then turned into something else. At the last moment, King Alfin managed to straighten out his machine and was again master of gravity when, immediately afterwards, he flew smack into the scaffolding of a huge hotel which was being constructed in the middle of a coastal heath as if for the special purpose of standing in a king's way. This uncompleted and badly gutted building was ordered razed by Queen Blenda who had it replaced

by a tasteless monument of granite surmounted by an improbable type of aircraft made of bronze. The glossy prints of
the enlarged photographs depicting the entire catastrophe
were discovered one day by eight-year-old Charles Xavier in
the drawer of a secretary bookcase. In some of these ghastly
pictures one could make out the shoulders and leathern
casque of the strangely unconcerned aviator, and in the penultimate one of the series, just before the white-blurred shat-
tering crash, one distinctly saw him raise one arm in triumph
and reassurance. The boy had hideous dreams after that but
his mother never found out that he had seen those infernal
records.

Her he remembered—more or less: a horsewoman, tall,
broad, stout, ruddy-faced. She had been assured by a royal
cousin that her son would be safe and happy under the tute-
lage of admirable Mr. Campbell who had taught several
dutiful little princesses to spread butterflies and enjoy *Lord
Ronald's Coronach.* He had immolated his life, so to speak, at
the portable altars of a vast number of hobbies, from the study
of book mites to bear hunting, and could reel off *Macbeth*
from beginning to end during hikes; but he did not give a
damn for his charges' morals, preferred ladies to laddies, and
did not meddle in the complexities of Zemblan ingledom. He
left, for some exotic court, after a ten-year stay, in 1932 when
our Prince, aged seventeen, had begun dividing his time between the University and his regiment. It was the nicest period
in his life. He never could decide what he enjoyed more: the
study of poetry—especially English poetry—or attending pa-
rades, or dancing in masquerades with boy-girls and girl-boys.
His mother died suddenly on July 21, 1936, from an obscure
blood ailment that had also afflicted her mother and grandmother. She had been much better on the day before—and
Charles Xavier had gone to an all-night ball in the so-called
Ducal Dome in Grindelwod: for the nonce, a formal heterosexual affair, rather refreshing after some previous sport. At
about four in the morning, with the sun enflaming the tree
crests and Mt. Falk, a pink cone, the King stopped his powerful car at one of the gates of the palace. The air was so
delicate, the light so lyrical, that he and the three friends he
had with him decided to walk through the linden bosquet the

rest of the distance to the Pavonian Pavilion where guests were lodged. He and Otar, a platonic pal, wore tails but they had lost their top hats to the highway winds. A strange something struck all four of them as they stood under the young limes in the prim landscape of scarp and counterscarp fortified by shadow and countershadow. Otar, a pleasant and cultured adeling with a tremendous nose and sparse hair, had his two mistresses with him, eighteen-year-old Fifalda (whom he later married) and seventeen-year-old Fleur (whom we shall meet in two other notes), daughters of Countess de Fyler, the Queen's favorite lady in waiting. One involuntarily lingers over that picture, as one does when standing at a vantage point of time and knowing in retrospect that in a moment one's life would undergo a complete change. So here was Otar, looking with a puzzled expression at the distant windows of the Queen's quarters, and there were the two girls, side by side, thin-legged, in shimmering wraps, their kitten noses pink, their eyes green and sleepy, their earrings catching and loosing the fire of the sun. There were a few people around, as there always were, no matter the hour, at this gate, along which a road, connecting with the Eastern highway, ran. A peasant woman with a small cake she had baked, doubtlessly the mother of the sentinel who had not yet come to relieve the unshaven dark young *nattdett* (child of night) in his dreary sentry box, sat on a spur stone watching in feminine fascination the luciola-like tapers that moved from window to window; two workmen, holding their bicycles, stood staring too at those strange lights; and a drunk with a walrus mustache kept staggering around and patting the trunks of the lindens. One picks up minor items at such slowdowns of life. The King noticed that some reddish mud flecked the frames of the two bicycles and that their front wheels were both turned in the same direction, parallel to one another. Suddenly, down a steep path among the lilac bushes—a short cut from the Queen's quarters—the Countess came running and tripping over the hem of her quilted robe, and at the same moment, from another side of the palace, all seven councilors, dressed in their formal splendor and carrying like plum cakes replicas of various regalia, came striding down the stairs of stone, in dignified haste, but she beat them by one alin and spat out the news. The drunk started to sing a ribald ballad about "Karlie-Garlie" and fell into the demilune ditch. It is not easy to describe lucidly in short notes to a poem the various approaches to a fortified castle, and so, in my awareness of this problem, I prepared for John Shade, some time in June, when narrating to him the events briefly noticed in some of my comments (see note to line 130, for example), a rather handsomely drawn plan of the chambers, terraces, bastions and pleasure grounds of the Onhava Palace. Unless it has been destroyed or stolen, this careful picture in colored inks on a large (thirty by twenty inches) piece of cardboard might still be where I last saw it in mid-July, on the top of the big black trunk, opposite the old mangle, in a niche of the little corridor leading to the so-called fruit room. If it is not there, it might be looked for in his upper-floor study. I have written about this to Mrs. Shade but she does not reply to my letters. In case it still exists, I wish to beg her, without raising my voice, and very humbly, as humbly as the lowliest of the King's subjects might plead for an immediate restitution of his rights (the plan is mine and is clearly signed with a black chess-king crown after "Kinbote"), to send it, well packed, marked *not to be bent* on the wrapper, and by registered mail, to my publisher for reproduction in later editions of this work. Whatever energy I possessed has quite ebbed away lately, and these excruciating headaches now make impossible the mnemonic effort and eye strain that the drawing of another such plan would demand. The black trunk stands on another brown or brownish even larger one, and there is I think a stuffed fox or coyote next to them in their dark corner.

Line 79: a preterist

Written against this in the margin of the draft are two lines of which only the first can be deciphered. It reads:

The evening is the time to praise the day

I feel pretty sure that my friend was trying to incorporate here something he and Mrs. Shade had heard me quote in my lighter-hearted moments, namely a charming quatrain from our Zemblan counterpart of the Elder Edda, in an anonymous English translation (Kirby's?):

> The wise at nightfall praise the day,
> The wife when she has passed away,
> The ice when it is crossed, the bride
> When tumbled, and the horse when tried.

Line 80: my bedroom

Our Prince was fond of Fleur as of a sister but with no soft shadow of incest or secondary homosexual complications. She had a small pale face with prominent cheekbones, luminous eyes, and curly dark hair. It was rumored that after going about with a porcelain cup and Cinderella's slipper for months, the society sculptor and poet Arnor had found in her what he sought and had used her breasts and feet for his *Lilith Calling Back Adam*; but I am certainly no expert in these tender matters. Otar, her lover, said that when you walked behind her, and she knew you were walking behind her, the swing and play of those slim haunches was something intensely artistic, something Arab girls were taught in special schools by special Parisian panders who were afterwards strangled. Her fragile ankles, he said, which she placed very close together in her dainty and wavy walk, were the "careful jewels" in Arnor's poem about a *miragarl* ("mirage girl"), for which "a dream king in the sandy wastes of time would give three hundred camels and three fountains."

On ságaren wérem trémkin tri stána
Verbálala wod gév ut tri phantána

(I have marked the stress accents).

The Prince did not heed this rather kitschy prattle (all, probably, directed by her mother) and, let it be repeated, regarded her merely as a sibling, fragrant and fashionable, with a painted pout and a *maussade*, blurry, Gallic way of expressing the little she wished to express. Her unruffled rudeness toward the nervous and garrulous Countess amused him. He liked dancing with her—and only with her. He hardly squirmed at all when she stroked his hand or applied herself soundlessly with open lips to his cheek which the haggard after-the-ball dawn had already sooted. She did not seem to mind when he abandoned her for manlier pleasures; and she met him again in the dark of a car or in the half-glow of a cabaret with the subdued and ambiguous smile of a kissing cousin.

The forty days between Queen Blenda's death and his coronation was perhaps the most trying stretch of time in his life. He had had no love for his mother, and the hopeless and helpless remorse he now felt degenerated into a sickly physical fear of her phantom. The Countess, who seemed to be near him, to be rustling at his side, all the time, had him attend table-turning séances with an experienced American medium, séances at which the Queen's spirit, operating the same kind of planchette she had used in her lifetime to chat with Thormodus Torfaeus and A. R. Wallace, now briskly wrote in English: "Charles take take cherish love flower flower flower." An old psychiatrist so thoroughly bribed by the Countess as to look, even on the outside, like a putrid pear, assured him that his vices had subconsciously killed his mother and would continue "to kill her in him" if he did not renounce sodomy. A palace intrigue is a spectral spider that entangles you more nastily at every desperate jerk you try. Our Prince was young, inexperienced, and half-frenzied with insomnia. He hardly struggled at all. The Countess spent a fortune on buying his *kamergrum* (groom of the chamber), his bodyguard, and even the greater part of the Court Chamberlain. She took to sleeping in a small antechamber next to his bachelor bedroom, a splendid spacious circular apartment at the top of the high and massive South West Tower. This had been his father's retreat and was still connected by a jolly chute in the wall with a round swimming pool in the hall below, so that the young Prince could start the day as his father used to start it by slipping open a panel beside his army cot and rolling into the shaft whence he whizzed down straight into bright water. For other needs than sleep Charles Xavier had installed in the middle of the Persian rug-covered floor a so-called patifolia, that is, a huge, oval, luxuriously flounced, swansdown pillow the size of a triple bed. It was in this ample nest that Fleur now slept, curled up in its central hollow, under a coverlet of genuine giant panda fur that had just been rushed from Tibet by a group of Asiatic well-wishers on the occasion of his ascension to the throne. The antechamber, where the Countess was ensconced, had its own inner staircase and bathroom, but also communicated by means of a sliding door with the West Gallery. I do not know what advice or command her mother had given Fleur; but the little thing proved a poor seducer. She kept trying, as one quietly insane, to mend a broken viola d'amore or sat in dolorous attitudes comparing two ancient flutes, both sad-tuned and feeble. Meantime, in Turkish garb, he lolled in his father's ample chair, his legs over its arm, flipping through a volume of *Historia Zemblica*, copying out passages and occasionally fishing out of the nether recesses of his seat a pair of old-fashioned motoring goggles, a black opal ring, a ball of silver chocolate wrapping, or the star of a foreign order.

It was warm in the evening sun. She wore on the second day of their ridiculous cohabitation nothing except a kind of buttonless and sleeveless pajama top. The sight of her four bare limbs and three mousepits (Zemblan anatomy) irritated him, and while pacing about and pondering his coronation speech, he would toss towards her, without looking, her shorts or a terrycloth robe. Sometimes, upon returning to the comfortable old chair he would find her in it contemplating sorrowfully the picture of a *bogtur* (ancient warrior) in the history book. He would sweep her out of his chair, his eyes still on his writing pad, and stretching herself she would move over to the window seat and its dusty sunbeam; but after a while she tried to cuddle up to him, and he had to push away her burrowing dark curly head with one hand while writing with the other or detach one by one her little pink claws from his sleeve or sash.

Her presence at night did not kill insomnia, but at least kept at bay the strong ghost of Queen Blenda. Between exhaustion and drowsiness, he trifled with paltry fancies, such as getting up and pouring out a little cold water from a decanter onto Fleur's naked shoulder so as to extinguish upon it the weak gleam of a moonbeam. Stentoriously the Countess snored in her lair. And beyond the vestibule of his vigil (here he began falling asleep), in the dark cold gallery, lying all over the painted marble and piled three or four deep against the locked door, some dozing, some whimpering, were his new boy pages, a whole mountain of gift boys from Troth, and Tuscany, and Albanoland.

He awoke to find her standing with a comb in her hand before his—or rather, his grandfather's—cheval glass, a trip-tych of bottomless light, a really fantastic mirror, signed with a diamond by its maker, Sudarg of Bokay. She turned about before it: a secret device of reflection gathered an infinite number of nudes in its depths, garlands of girls in graceful and sorrowful groups, diminishing in the limpid distance, or breaking into individual nymphs, some of whom, she mur-mured, must resemble her ancestors when they were young—little peasant *garlien* combing their hair in shallow water as far as the eye could reach, and then the wistful mermaid from an old tale, and then nothing.

On the third night a great stomping and ringing of arms came from the inner stairs, and there burst in the Prime Coun-cilor, three Representatives of the People, and the chief of a new bodyguard. Amusingly, it was the Representatives of the People whom the idea of having for queen the granddaughter of a fiddler infuriated the most. That was the end of Charles Xavier's chaste romance with Fleur, who was pretty yet not repellent (as some cats are less repugnant than others to the good-natured dog told to endure the bitter effluvium of an alien genus). With their white suitcases and obsolete musical instruments the two ladies wandered back to the annex of the Palace. There followed a sweet twang of relief—and then the door of the anteroom slid open with a merry crash and the whole heap of *putti* tumbled in.

He was to go through a far more dramatic ordeal thirteen years later with Disa, Duchess of Payn, whom he married in 1949, as described in notes to lines 275 and 433–434, which the student of Shade's poem will reach in due time; there is no hurry. A series of cool summers ensued. Poor Fleur was still around, though indistinctly so. Disa befriended her after the old Countess perished in the crowded vestibule of the 1950

Exposition of Glass Animals, when part of it was almost destroyed by fire, Gradus helping the fire brigade to clear a space in the square for the lynching of the non-union incendiaries, or at least of the persons (two baffled tourists from Denmark) who had been mistaken for them. Our young Queen may have felt some subtle sympathy for her pale lady in waiting whom from time to time the King glimpsed illuminating a concert program by the diagonal light of an ogival window, or heard making tinny music in Bower B. The beautiful bedroom of his bachelor days is alluded to again in a note to line 130, as the place of his "luxurious captivity" in the beginning of the tedious and unnecessary Zemblan Revolution.

Line 85: Who'd seen the Pope

Pius X, Giuseppe Melchiorre Sarto, 1835–1914; Pope 1903–1914.

Lines 86–90: Aunt Maud

Maud Shade, 1869–1950, Samuel Shade's sister. At her death, Hazel (born 1934) was not exactly a "babe" as implied in line 90. I found her paintings unpleasant but interesting. Aunt Maud was far from spinsterish, and the extravagant and sardonic turn of her mind must have shocked sometimes the genteel dames of New Wye.

Lines 90–93: Her room, etc.

In the draft, instead of the final text:

. . . . her room
We've kept intact. Her trivia for us
Retrace her style: the leaf sarcophagus
(A Luna's dead and shriveled-up cocoon)

The reference is to what my dictionary defines as "a large,

tailed, pale green moth, the caterpillar of which feeds on the hickory." I suspect Shade altered this passage because his moth's name clashed with "Moon" in the next line.

Line 91: trivia

Among these was a scrapbook in which over a period of years (1937–1949) Aunt Maud had been pasting clippings of an involuntarily ludicrous or grotesque nature. John Shade allowed me one day to memorandum the first and the last of the series; they happened to intercommunicate most pleasingly, I thought. Both stemmed from the same family magazine *Life*, so justly famed for its pudibundity in regard to the mysteries of the male sex; hence one can well imagine how startled or titillated those families were. The first comes from the issue of May 10, 1937, p. 67, and advertises the Talon Trouser Fastener (a rather grasping and painful name, by the way). It shows a young gent radiating virility among several ecstatic lady-friends, and the inscription reads: *You'll be amazed that the fly of your trousers could be so dramatically improved.* The second comes from the issue of March 28, 1949, p. 126, and advertises Hanes Fig Leaf Brief. It shows a modern Eve worshipfully peeping from behind a potted tree of knowledge at a leering young Adam in rather ordinary but clean underwear, with the front of his advertised brief conspicuously and compactly shaded, and the inscription reads: *Nothing beats a fig leaf.*

I think there must exist a special subversive group of pseudo-cupids—plump hairless little devils whom Satan commissions to make disgusting mischief in sacrosanct places.

Line 92: the paperweight

The image of those old-fashioned horrors strangely haunted our poet. I have clipped from a newspaper that recently reprinted it an old poem of his where the souvenir shop also preserves a landscape admired by the tourist:

MOUNTAIN VIEW
Between the mountain and the eye
The spirit of the distance draws
A veil of blue amorous gauze,
The very texture of the sky.
A breeze reaches the pines, and I
Join in the general applause.

But we all know it cannot last,
The mountain is too weak to wait—
Even if reproduced and glassed
In me as in a paperweight.

Line 98:   On Chapman's Homer

A reference to the title of Keats' famous sonnet (often quoted in America) which, owing to a printer's absent-mindedness, has been drolly transposed, from some other article, into the account of a sports event. For other vivid misprints see note to line 802.

Line 101:   No free man needs a God

When one considers the numberless thinkers and poets in the history of human creativity whose freedom of mind was enhanced rather than stunted by Faith, one is bound to question the wisdom of this easy aphorism (see also note to line 549).

Line 109:   iridule

An iridescent cloudlet, Zemblan *muderperlwelk.* The term "iridule" is, I believe, Shade's own invention. Above it, in the Fair Copy (card 9, July 4) he has written in pencil "peacock-herl." The peacock-herl is the body of a certain sort of artificial fly also called "alder." So the owner of this motor court, an ardent fisherman, tells me. (See also the "strange nacreous gleams" in line 634.)

Line 119:   Dr. Sutton

This is a recombination of letters taken from two names, one beginning in "Sut," the other ending in "ton." Two distinguished medical men, long retired from practice, dwelt on our hill. Both were very old friends of the Shades; one had a daughter, president of Sybil's club—and this is the Dr. Sutton I visualize in my notes to lines 181 and 1000. He is also mentioned in Line 986.

Lines 120–121:   five minutes were equal to forty ounces, etc.

In the left margin, and parallel to it: "In the Middle Ages an hour was to 480 ounces of fine sand or 22,560 atoms."

I am unable to check either this statement or the poet's calculations in regard to five minutes, i.e., three hundred seconds, since I do not see how 480 can be divided by 300 or vice versa, but perhaps I am only tired. On the day (July 4) John Shade wrote this, Gradus the Gunman was getting ready to leave Zembla for his steady blunderings through two hemispheres (see note to line 181).

Line 130:   I never bounced a ball or swung a bat

Frankly I too never excelled in soccer and cricket; I am a passable horseman, a vigorous though unorthodox skier, a good skater, a tricky wrestler, and an enthusiastic rock-climber.

Line 130 is followed in the draft by four verses which Shade discarded in favor of the Fair Copy continuation (line 131 etc.). This false start goes:

> As children playing in a castle find
> In some old closet full of toys, behind
> The animals and masks, a sliding door
> [four words heavily crossed out] a secret corridor—

The comparison has remained suspended. Presumably our

poet intended to attach it to the account of his stumbling
upon some mysterious truth in the fainting fits of his boyhood. I cannot say how sorry I am that he rejected these lines.
I regret it not only because of their intrinsic beauty, which is
great, but also because the image they contain was suggested
by something Shade had from me. I have already alluded in
the course of these notes to the adventures of Charles Xavier,
last King of Zembla, and to the keen interest my friend took
in the many stories I told him about that king. The index card
on which the variant has been preserved is dated July 4 and
is a direct echo of our sunset rambles in the fragrant lanes of
New Wye and Dulwich. "Tell me more," he would say as he
knocked his pipe empty against a beech trunk, and while the
colored cloud lingered, and while far away in the lighted
house on the hill Mrs. Shade sat quietly enjoying a video
drama, I gladly acceded to my friend's request.

In simple words I described the curious situation in which
the King found himself during the first months of the rebellion. He had the amusing feeling of his being the only black
piece in what a composer of chess problems might term a
king-in-the-corner waiter of the *solus rex* type. The Royalists,
or at least the Modems (Moderate Democrats), might have
still prevented the state from turning into a commonplace
modern tyranny, had they been able to cope with the tainted
gold and the robot troops that a powerful police state from
its vantage ground a few sea miles away was pouring into the
Zemblan Revolution. Despite the hopelessness of the situation, the King refused to abdicate. A haughty and morose
captive, he was caged in his rose-stone palace from a corner
turret of which one could make out with the help of field
glasses lithe youths diving into the swimming pool of a fairy
tale sport club, and the English ambassador in old-fashioned
flannels playing tennis with the Basque coach on a clay court
as remote as paradise. How serene were the mountains, how
tenderly painted on the western vault of the sky!

Somewhere in the mist of the city there occurred every day
disgusting outbursts of violence, arrests and executions, but
the great city rolled on as smoothly as ever, the cafés were
full, splendid plays were being performed at the Royal Theater, and it was really the palace which contained the strongest

concentrate of gloom. Stone-faced, square-shouldered *komizars* enforced strict discipline among the troops on duty within and without. Puritan prudence had sealed up the wine cellars and removed all the maid servants from the southern wing. The ladies in waiting had, of course, left long before, at the time the King exiled his Queen to her villa on the French Riviera. Thank heavens, she was spared those dreadful days in the polluted palace!

The door of every room was guarded. The banqueting hall had three custodians and as many as four loafed in the library whose dark recesses seemed to harbor all the shadows of treason. The bedrooms of the few remaining palace attendants had each its armed parasite, drinking forbidden rum with an old footman or taking liberties with a young page. And in the great Heralds' Hall one could always be sure of finding ribald jokers trying to squeeze into the steel panoply of its hollow knights. And what a smell of leather and goat in the spacious chambers once redolent of carnations and lilacs!

This tremendous company consisted of two main groups: ignorant, ferocious-looking but really quite harmless conscripts from Thule, and taciturn, very polite Extremists from the famous Glass Factory where the revolution had flickered first. One can now reveal (since he is safe in Paris) that this contingent included at least one heroic royalist so virtuosically disguised that he made his unsuspecting fellow guards look like mediocre imitators. Actually Odon happened to be one of the most prominent actors in Zembla and was winning applause in the Royal Theater on his off-duty nights. Through him the King kept in touch with numerous adherents, young nobles, artists, college athletes, gamblers, Black Rose Paladins, members of fencing clubs, and other men of fashion and adventure. Rumors rumbled. It was said that the captive would soon be tried by a special court; but it was also said that he would be shot while ostensibly being transported to another place of confinement. Although flight was discussed daily, the schemes of the conspirators had more aesthetic than practical value. A powerful motorboat had been prepared in a coastal cave near Blawick (Blue Cove) in western Zembla, beyond the chain of tall mountains which separated the city from the sea; the imagined reflections of the trembling transparent water on rock wall and boat were tantalizing, but none of the schemers could suggest how the King could escape from his castle and pass safely through its fortifications.

One August day, at the beginning of his third month of luxurious captivity in the South West Tower, he was accused of using a fop's hand mirror and the sun's cooperative rays to flash signals from his lofty casement. The vastness of the view it commanded was denounced not only as conducive to treachery but as producing in the surveyor an airy sense of superiority over his low-lodged jailers. Accordingly, one evening the King's cot-and-pot were transferred to a dismal lumber room on the same side of the palace but on its first floor. Many years before, it had been the dressing room of his grandfather, Thurgus the Third. After Thurgus died (in 1900) his ornate bedroom was transformed into a kind of chapel and the adjacent chamber, shorn of its full-length multiple mirror and green silk sofa, soon degenerated into what it had now remained for half a century, and old hole of a room with a locked trunk in one corner and an obsolete sewing machine in another. It was reached from a marble-flagged gallery, running along its north side and sharply turning immediately west of it to form a vestibule in the southwest corner of the Palace. The only window gave on an inner court on the south side. This window had once been a glorious dreamway of stained glass, with a firebird and a dazzled huntsman, but a football had recently shattered the fabulous forest scene and now its new ordinary pane was barred from the outside. On the west-side wall, above a whitewashed closet door, hung a large photograph in a frame of black velvet. The fleeting and faint but thousands of times repeated action of the same sun that was accused of sending messages from the tower, had gradually patinated this picture which showed the romantic profile and broad bare shoulders of the forgotten actress Iris Acht, said to have been for several years, ending with her sudden death in 1888, the mistress of Thurgus. In the opposite, east-side wall a frivolous-looking door, similar in turquoise coloration to the room's only other one (opening into the gallery) but securely hasped, had once led to the old rake's bed-chamber; it had now lost its crystal knob, and was flanked on the east-side wall by two banished engravings belonging to the room's period of decay. They were of the sort that is not really supposed to be looked at, pictures that exist merely as general notions of pictures to meet the humble ornamental needs of some corridor or waiting room: one was a shabby and lugubrious *Fête Flamande* after Teniers; the other had once hung in the nursery whose sleepy denizens had always taken it to depict foamy waves in the foreground instead of the blurry shapes of melancholy sheep that it now revealed.

The King sighed and began to undress. His camp bed and a bedtable had been placed, facing the window, in the northeast corner. East was the turquoise door; north, the door of the gallery; west, the door of the closet; south, the window. His black blazer and white trousers were taken away by his former valet's valet. The King sat down on the edge of the bed in his pajamas. The man returned with a pair of morocco bed slippers, pulled them on his master's listless feet, and was off with the discarded pumps. The King's wandering gaze stopped at the casement which was half open. One could see part of the dimly lit court where under an enclosed poplar two soldiers on a stone bench were playing lansquenet. The summer night was starless and stirless, with distant spasms of silent lightning. Around the lantern that stood on the bench a batlike moth blindly flapped—until the punter knocked it down with his cap. The King yawned, and the illumined card players shivered and dissolved in the prism of his tears. His bored glance traveled from wall to wall. The gallery door stood slightly ajar, and one could hear the steps of the guard coming and going. Above the closet, Iris Acht squared her shoulders and looked away. A cricket cricked. The bedside light was just strong enough to put a bright gleam on the gilt key in the lock of the closet door. And all at once that spark on that key caused a wonderful conflagration to spread in the prisoner's mind.

We shall now go back from mid-August 1958 to a certain afternoon in May three decades earlier when he was a dark strong lad of thirteen with a silver ring on the forefinger of his sun-tanned hand. Queen Blenda, his mother, had recently left for Vienna and Rome. He had several dear playmates but none could compete with Oleg, Duke of Rahl. In those days growing boys of high-born families wore on festive occasions—of which we had so many during our long northern spring—sleeveless jerseys, white anklesocks with black buckle shoes, and very tight, very short shorts called *hotinguens*. I wish I could provide the reader with cut-out figures and parts of attire as given in paper-doll charts for children armed with scissors. It would brighten a little these dark evenings that are destroying my brain. Both lads were handsome, long-legged specimens of Varangian boyhood. At twelve, Oleg was the best center forward at the Ducal School. When stripped and shiny in the mist of the bath house, his bold virilia contrasted harshly with his girlish grace. He was a regular faunlet. On that particular afternoon a copious shower lacquered the spring foliage of the palace garden, and oh, how the Persian lilacs in riotous bloom tumbled and tossed behind the green-streaming, amethyst-blotched windowpanes! One would have to play indoors. Oleg was late. Would he come at all?

It occurred to the young Prince to disinter a set of precious toys (the gift of a foreign potentate who had recently been assassinated) which had amused Oleg and him during a pre-vious Easter, and then had been laid aside as happens with those special, artistic playthings which allow their bubble of pleasure to yield all its tang at once before retreating into museum oblivion. What he particularly desired to rediscover now was an elaborate toy circus contained in a box as big as a croquet case. He craved for it; his eyes, his brain, and that in his brain which corresponded to the ball of his thumb, vividly remembered the brown boy acrobats with spangled nates, an elegant and melancholy clown with a ruff, and es-pecially three pup-sized elephants of polished wood with such versatile joints that you could make the sleek jumbo stand upright on one foreleg or rear up solidly on the top of a small white barrel ringed with red. Less than a fortnight had passed since Oleg's last visit, when for the first time the two boys had been allowed to share the same bed, and the tingle of their misbehavior, and the foreglow of another such night, were now mixed in our young Prince with an embarrassment that suggested refuge in earlier, more innocent games.

His English tutor who, after a picnic in Mandevil Forest, was laid up with a sprained ankle, did not know where that circus might be; he advised looking for it in an old lumber room at the end of the West Gallery. Thither the Prince betook himself. That dusty black trunk? It looked grimly negative. The rain was more audible here owing to the proximity of a prolix gutter pipe. What about the closet? Its gilt key turned reluctantly. All three shelves and the space beneath were stuffed with disparate objects: a palette with the dregs of many sunsets; a cupful of counters; an ivory backscratcher; a thirty-twomo edition of *Timon of Athens* translated into Zemblan by his uncle Conmal, the Queen's brother; a seaside *situla* (toy pail); a sixty-five-carat blue diamond accidentally added in his childhood, from his late father's knickknackatory, to the pebbles and shells in that pail; a finger of chalk; and a square board with a design of interlaced figures for some long-forgotten game. He was about to look elsewhere in the closet when on trying to dislodge a piece of black velvet, one corner of which had unaccountably got caught behind the shelf, something gave, the shelf budged, proved removable, and revealed just under its farther edge, in the back of the closet, a keyhole to which the same gilt key was found to fit.

Impatiently he cleared the other two shelves of all they held (mainly old clothes and shoes), removed them as he had done with the middle one, and unlocked the sliding door at the back of the closet. The elephants were forgotten, he stood on the threshold of a secret passage. Its deep darkness was total but something about its speluncar acoustics foretold, clearing its throat hollowly, great things, and he hurried to his own quarters to fetch a couple of flashlights and a pedometer. As he was returning, Oleg arrived. He carried a tulip. His soft blond locks had been cut since his last visit to the palace, and the young Prince thought: Yes, I knew he would be different. But when Oleg knitted his golden brows and bent close to hear about the discovery, the young Prince knew by the downy warmth of that crimson ear and by the vivacious nod greeting the proposed investigation, that no change had occurred in his dear bedfellow.

As soon as Monsieur Beauchamp had sat down for a game of chess at the bedside of Mr. Campbell and had offered his raised fists to choose from, the young Prince took Oleg to the magical closet. The wary, silent, green-carpeted steps of an *escalier dérobé* led to a stone-paved underground passage.

Strictly speaking it was "underground" only in brief spells
when, after burrowing under the southwest vestibule next to
the lumber room, it went under a series of terraces, under the
avenue of birches in the royal park, and then under the three
transverse streets, Academy Boulevard, Coriolanus Lane and
Timon Alley, that still separated it from its final destination.
Otherwise, in its angular and cryptic course it adapted itself
to the various structures which it followed, here availing itself
of a bulwark to fit in its side like a pencil in the pencil hold
of a pocket diary, there running through the cellars of a great
mansion too rich in dark passageways to notice the stealthy
intrusion. Possibly, in the intervening years, certain arcane
connections had been established between the abandoned passage and the outer world by the random repercussions of work
in surrounding layers of masonry or by the blind pokings of
time itself; for here and there magic apertures and penetrations, so narrow and deep as to drive one insane, could be
deduced from a pool of sweet, foul ditch water, bespeaking a
moat, or from a dusky odor of earth and turf, marking the
proximity of a glacis slope overhead; and at one point, where
the passage crept through the basement of a huge ducal villa,
with hothouses famous for their collections of desert flora, a
light spread of sand momentarily changed the sound of one's
tread. Oleg walked in front: his shapely buttocks encased in
tight indigo cotton moved alertly, and his own erect radiance,
rather than his flambeau, seemed to illume with leaps of light
the low ceiling and crowding walls. Behind him the young
Prince's electric torch played on the ground and gave a coat-
ing of flour to the back of Oleg's bare thighs. The air was
musty and cold. On and on went the fantastic burrow. It developed a slight ascending grade. The pedometer had tocked
off 1,888 yards, when at last they reached the end. The magic
key of the lumber room closet slipped with gratifying ease into
the keyhole of a green door confronting them, and would
have accomplished the act promised by its smooth entrance,
had not a burst of strange sounds coming from behind the
door caused our explorers to pause. Two terrible voices, a
man's and a woman's, now rising to a passionate pitch, now
sinking to raucous undertones, were exchanging insults in
Gutnish as spoken by the fisherfolk of Western Zembla. An

abominable threat made the woman shriek out in fright. Sudden silence ensued, presently broken by the man's murmuring some brief phrase of casual approval ("Perfect, my dear," or "Couldn't be better") that was more eerie than anything that had come before.

Without consulting each other, the young Prince and his friend veered in absurd panic and, with the pedometer beating wildly, raced back the way they had come. "Ouf!" said Oleg once the last shelf had been replaced. "You're all chalky behind," said the young Prince as they swung upstairs. They found Beauchamp and Campbell ending their game in a draw. It was near dinner time. The two lads were told to wash their hands. The recent thrill of adventure had been superseded already by another sort of excitement. They locked themselves up. The tap ran unheeded. Both were in a manly state and moaning like doves.

This detailed recollection, whose structure and maculation have taken some time to describe in this note, skimmed through the King's memory in one instant. Certain creatures of the past, and this was one of them, may lie dormant for thirty years as this one had, while their natural habitat undergoes calamitous alterations. Soon after the discovery of the secret passage he almost died of pneumonia. In his delirium he would strive one moment to follow a luminous disk probing an endless tunnel and try the next to clasp the melting haunches of his fair ingle. To recuperate he was sent for a couple of seasons to southern Europe. The death of Oleg at fifteen, in a toboggan accident, helped to obliterate the reality of their adventure. A national revolution was needed to make that secret passage real again.

Having satisfied himself that the guard's creaky steps had moved some distance away, the King opened the closet. It was empty now, save for the tiny volume of *Timon Afinsken* still lying in one corner, and for some old sport clothes and gymnasium shoes crammed into the bottom compartment. The footfalls were now coming back. He did not dare pursue his examination and relocked the closet door.

It was evident he would need a few moments of perfect security to perform with a minimum of noise a succession of small actions: enter the closet, lock it from the inside, remove the shelves, open the secret door, replace the shelves, slip into the yawning darkness, close the secret door and lock it. Say ninety seconds.

He stepped out into the gallery, and the guard, a rather handsome but incredibly stupid Extremist, immediately advanced towards him. "I have a certain urgent desire," said the King. "I want, Hal, to play the piano before going to bed." Hal (if that was his name) led the way to the music room where, as the King knew, Odon kept vigil over the shrouded harp. He was a fox-browed, burly Irishman, with a pink head now covered by the rakish cap of a Russki factory worker. The King sat down at the Bechstein and, as soon as they were left alone, explained briefly the situation while taking tinkling notes with one hand: "Never heard of any passage," muttered Odon with the annoyance of a chess player who is shown how he might have saved the game he has lost. Was His Majesty absolutely sure? His Majesty was. Did he suppose it took one out of the Palace? Definitely out of the Palace.

Anyway, Odon had to leave in a few moments, being due to act that night in *The Merman*, a fine old melodrama which had not been performed, he said, for at least three decades. "I'm quite satisfied with my own melodrama," remarked the King. "Alas," said Odon. Furrowing his forehead, he slowly got into his leathern coat. One could do nothing tonight. If he asked the commandant to be left on duty, it would only provoke suspicion, and the least suspicion might be fatal. Tomorrow he would find some opportunity to inspect that new avenue of escape, *if* it was that and not a dead end. Would Charlie (His Majesty) promise not to attempt anything until then? "But they are moving closer and closer," said the King alluding to the noise of rapping and ripping that came from the Picture Gallery. "Not really," said Odon, "one inch per hour, maybe two. I must be going now," he added indicating with a twitch of the eyelid the solemn and corpulent guard who was coming to relieve him.

Under the unshakable but quite erroneous belief that the crown jewels were concealed somewhere in the Palace, the new administration had engaged a couple of foreign experts (see note to line 681) to locate them. The good work had been going on for a month. The two Russians, after practically dismantling the Council Chamber and several other rooms of state, had transferred their activities to that part of the gallery where the huge oils of Eystein had fascinated several generations of Zemblan princes and princesses. While unable to catch a likeness, and therefore wisely limiting himself to a conventional style of complimentary portraiture, Eystein showed himself to be a prodigious master of the trompe l'oeil in the depiction of various objects surrounding his dignified dead models and making them look even deader by contrast to the fallen petal or the polished panel that he rendered with such love and skill. But in some of those portraits Eystein had also resorted to a weird form of trickery: among his decorations of wood or wool, gold or velvet, he would insert one which was really made of the material elsewhere imitated by paint. This device which was apparently meant to enhance the effect of his tactile and tonal values had, however, something ignoble about it and disclosed not only an essential flaw in Eystein's talent, but the basic fact that "reality" is neither the subject nor the object of true art which creates its own special reality having nothing to do with the average "reality" perceived by the communal eye. But to return to our technicians whose tapping is approaching along the gallery toward the bend where the King and Odon stand ready to part. At this spot hung a portrait representing a former Keeper of the Treasure, decrepit Count Kernel, who was painted with fingers resting lightly on an embossed and emblazoned box whose side facing the spectator consisted of an inset oblong made of real bronze, while upon the shaded top of the box, drawn in perspective, the artist had pictured a plate with the beautifully executed, twin-lobed, brainlike, halved kernel of a walnut.

"They are in for a surprise," murmured Odon in his mother tongue, while in a corner the fat guard was going through some dutiful, rather lonesome, rifle-butt-banging formalities.

The two Soviet professionals could be excused for assuming they would find a real receptacle behind the real metal. At the present moment they were about to decide whether to pry out the plaque or take down the picture; but we can anticipate a little and assure the reader that the receptacle, an oblong hole in the wall, was there all right; it contained nothing, however, except the broken bits of a nutshell.

Somewhere an iron curtain had gone up, baring a painted one, with nymphs and nenuphars. "I shall bring you your flute tomorrow," cried Odon meaningfully in the vernacular, and smiled, and waved, already bemisted, already receding into the remoteness of his Thespian world.

The fat guard led the King back to his room and turned him over to handsome Hal. It was half past nine. The King went to bed. The valet, a moody rascal, brought him his usual milk and cognac nightcap and took away his slippers and dressing gown. The man was practically out of the room when the King commanded him to put out the light, upon which an arm re-entered and a gloved hand found and turned the switch. Distant lightning still throbbed now and then in the window. The King finished his drink in the dark and replaced the empty tumbler on the night table where it knocked with a subdued ring against a steel flashlight prepared by the thoughtful authorities in case electricity failed as it lately did now and then.

He could not sleep. Turning his head he watched the line of light under the door. Presently it was gently opened and his handsome young jailer peeped in. A bizarre little thought danced through the King's mind; but all the youth wanted was to warn his prisoner that he intended to join his companions in the adjacent court, and that the door would be locked until he returned. If, however, the ex-King needed anything, he could call from his window. "How long will you be absent?" asked the King. "*Yeg ved ik* [I know not]," answered the guard. "Good night, bad boy," said the King.

He waited for the guard's silhouette to enter the light in the courtyard where the other Thuleans welcomed him to their game. Then, in secure darkness, the King rummaged for some clothes on the floor of the closet and pulled on, over his pajamas, what felt like skiing trousers and something that smelled like an old sweater. Further gropings yielded a pair of sneakers and a woolen headgear with flaps. He then went through the actions mentally rehearsed before. As he was removing the second shelf, an object fell with a miniature thud; he guessed what it was and took it with him as a talisman.

He dared not press the button of his torch until properly engulfed, nor could he afford a noisy stumble, and therefore negotiated the eighteen invisible steps in a more or less sitting position like a timid novice bum-scraping down the lichened rocks of Mt. Kron. The dim light he discharged at last was now his dearest companion, Oleg's ghost, the phantom of freedom. He experienced a blend of anguish and exultation, a kind of amorous joy, the like of which he had last known on the day of his coronation, when, as he walked to his throne, a few bars of incredibly rich, deep, plenteous music (whose authorship and physical source he was never able to ascertain) struck his ear, and he inhaled the hair oil of the pretty page who had bent to brush a rose petal off the footstool, and by the light of his torch the King now saw that he was hideously garbed in bright red.

The secret passage seemed to have grown more squalid. The intrusion of its surroundings was even more evident than on the day when two lads shivering in thin jerseys and shorts had explored it. The pool of opalescent ditch water had grown in length; along its edge walked a sick bat like a cripple with a broken umbrella. A remembered spread of colored sand bore the thirty-year-old patterned imprint of Oleg's shoe, as immortal as the tracks of an Egyptian child's tame gazelle made thirty centuries ago on blue Nilotic bricks drying in the sun. And, at the spot where the passage went through the foundations of a museum, there had somehow wandered down, to exile and disposal, a headless statue of Mercury, conductor of souls to the Lower World, and a cracked krater with two black figures shown dicing under a black palm.

The last bend of the passage, ending in the green door, contained an accumulation of loose boards across which the fugitive stepped not without stumbling. He unlocked the door and upon pulling it open was stopped by a heavy black drapery. As he began fumbling among its vertical folds for some sort of ingress, the weak light of his torch rolled its hopeless eye and went out. He dropped it: it fell into muffled nothingness. The King thrust both arms into the deep folds of the chocolate-smelling cloth and, despite the uncertainty and the danger of the moment, was, as it were, physically reminded by his own movement of the comical, at first controlled, then frantic undulations of a theatrical curtain through which a nervous actor tries vainly to pass. This grotesque sensation, at this diabolical instant, solved the mystery of the passage even before he wriggled at last through the drapery into the dimly lit, dimly cluttered *lumbarkamer* which had once been Iris Acht's dressing room in the Royal Theater. It still was what it had become after her death: a dusty hole of a room communicating with a kind of hall whither performers would sometimes wander during rehearsals. Pieces of mythological scenery leaning against the wall half concealed a large dusty velvet-framed photograph of King Thurgus—bushy mustache, pince-nez, medals—as he was at the time when the mile-long corridor provided an extravagant means for his trysts with Iris.

The scarlet-clothed fugitive blinked and made for the hall. It led to a number of dressing rooms. Somewhere beyond it a tempest of plaudits grew in volume before petering out. Other distant sounds marked the beginning of the intermission. Several costumed performers passed by the King, and in one of them he recognized Odon. He was wearing a velvet jacket with brass buttons, knickerbockers and striped stockings, the Sunday attire of Gutnish fishermen, and his fist still clutched the cardboard knife with which he had just dispatched his sweetheart. "Good God," he said on seeing the King.

Plucking a couple of cloaks from a heap of fantastic raiments, Odon pushed the King toward a staircase leading to the street. Simultaneously there was a commotion among a group of people smoking on the landing. An old intriguer who by dint of fawning on various Extremist officials had obtained the post of Scenic Director, suddenly pointed a vibrating finger at the King, but being afflicted with a bad stammer could not utter the words of indignant recognition which were making his dentures clack. The King tried to pull the front flap of his cap over his face—and almost lost his footing at the bottom of the narrow stairs. Outside it was raining. A puddle reflected his scarlet silhouette. Several vehicles stood in a transverse lane. It was there that Odon usually left his racing car. For one dreadful second he thought it was gone, but then recalled with exquisite relief that he had parked it that night in an adjacent alley. (See the interesting note to line 149.)

Lines 131–132: I was the shadow of the waxwing slain by feigned remoteness in the windowpane.

The exquisite melody of the two lines opening the poem is picked up here. The repetition of that long-drawn note is saved from monotony by the subtle variation in line 132 where the assonance between its second word and the rhyme gives the ear a kind of languorous pleasure as would the echo of some half-remembered sorrowful song whose strain is more meaningful than its words. Today, when the "feigned remoteness" has indeed performed its dreadful duty, and the poem we have is the only "shadow" that remains, we cannot help reading into these lines something more than mirrorplay and mirage shimmer. We feel doom, in the image of Gradus, eating away the miles and miles of "feigned remoteness" between him and poor Shade. He, too, is to meet, in his urgent and blind flight, a reflection that will shatter him.

Although Gradus availed himself of all varieties of locomotion—rented cars, local trains, escalators, airplanes—somehow the eye of the mind sees him, and the muscles of the mind feel him, as always streaking across the sky with black traveling bag in one hand and loosely folded umbrella in the other, in a sustained glide high over sea and land. The force propelling him is the magic action of Shade's poem itself, the very mechanism and sweep of verse, the powerful iambic motor. Never before has the inexorable advance of fate received such a sensuous form (for other images of that transcendental tramp's approach see note to line 17).

Line 137: lemniscate

"A unicursal bicircular quartic" says my weary old dictionary. I cannot understand what this has to do with bicycling and suspect that Shade's phrase has no real meaning. As other poets before him, he seems to have fallen here under the spell of misleading euphony.

To take a striking example: what can be more resounding, more resplendent, more suggestive of choral and sculptured beauty, than the word *coramen*? In reality, however, it merely denotes the rude strap with which a Zemblan herdsman at-taches his humble provisions and ragged blanket to the meekest of his cows when driving them up to the *vebodar* (upland pastures).

Line 143: a clockwork toy

By a stroke of luck I have seen it! One evening in May or June I dropped in to remind my friend about a collection of pamphlets, by his grandfather, an eccentric clergyman, that he had once said was stored in the basement. I found him gloom-ily waiting for some people (members of his department, I believe, and their wives) who were coming for a formal dinner. He willingly took me down into the basement but after rum-maging among piles of dusty books and magazines, said he would try to find them some other time. It was then that I saw it on a shelf, between a candlestick and a handless alarm clock. He, thinking I might think it had belonged to his dead daughter, hastily explained it was as old as he. The boy was a little Negro of painted tin with a keyhole in his side and no breadth to speak of, just consisting of two more or less fused profiles, and his wheelbarrow was now all bent and broken. He said, brushing the dust off his sleeves, that he kept it as a kind of *memento mori*—he had had a strange fainting fit one day in his childhood while playing with that toy. We were interrupted by Sybil's voice calling from above; but never mind, now the rusty clockwork shall work again, for I have the key.

Line 149: one foot upon a mountain

The Bera Range, a two-hundred-mile-long chain of rugged mountains, not quite reaching the northern end of the Zem-blan peninsula (cut off basally by an impassable canal from the mainland of madness), divides it into two parts, the flourishing eastern region of Onhava and other townships, such as Aros and Grindelwod, and the much narrower western strip with its quaint fishing hamlets and pleasant beach resorts. The two coasts are connected by two asphalted highways: the older one shirks difficulties by running first along the eastern slopes northward to Odevalla, Yeslove and Embla, and only then turning west at the northmost point of the peninsula; the newer one, an elaborate, twisting, marvelously graded road, traverses the range westward from just north of Onhava to Bregberg, and is termed in tourist booklets a "scenic drive." Several trails cross the mountains at various points and lead to passes none of which exceeds an altitude of five thousand feet; a few peaks rise some two thousand feet higher and retain their snow in midsummer; and from one of them, the highest and hardest, Mt. Glitterntin, one can distinguish on clear days, far out to the east, beyond the Gulf of Surprise, a dim iridescence which some say is Russia.

After escaping from the theater, our friends planned to follow the old highway for twenty miles northward, and then turn left on an unfrequented dirt road that would have brought them eventually to the main hideout of the Karlists, a baronial castle in a fir wood on the eastern slope of the Bera Range. But the vigilant stutterer had finally exploded in spasmodic speech; telephones had frantically worked; and the fugitives had hardly covered a dozen miles, when a confused blaze in the darkness before them, at the intersection of the old and new highways, revealed a roadblock that at least had the merit of canceling both routes at one stroke.

Odon spun the car around and at the first opportunity swerved westward into the mountains. The narrow and bumpy lane that engulfed them passed by a woodshed, arrived at a torrent, crossed it with a great clacking of boards, and presently degenerated into a stump-cluttered cutting. They were at the edge of Mandevil Forest. Thunder was rumbling in the terrible brown sky.

For a few seconds both men stood looking upward. The night and the trees concealed the acclivity. From this point a good climber might reach Bregberg Pass by dawn—if he managed to hit a regular trail after pushing through the black wall of the forest. It was decided to part, Charlie proceeding toward the remote treasure in the sea cave, and Odon remaining behind as a decoy. He would, he said, lead them a merry chase, assume sensational disguises, and get into touch with the rest of the gang. His mother was an American, from New Wye in New England. She is said to have been the first woman in the world to shoot wolves, and, I believe, other animals, from an airplane.

A handshake, a flash of lightning. As the King waded into the damp, dark bracken, its odor, its lacy resilience, and the mixture of soft growth and steep ground reminded him of the times he had picnicked hereabouts—in another part of the forest but on the same mountainside, and higher up, as a boy, on the boulderfield where Mr. Campbell had once twisted an ankle and had to be carried down, smoking his pipe, by two husky attendants. Rather dull memories, on the whole. Wasn't there a hunting box nearby—just beyond Silfhar Falls? Good capercaillie and woodcock shooting—a sport much enjoyed by his late mother, Queen Blenda, a tweedy and horsy queen. Now as then, the rain seethed in the black trees, and if you paused you heard your heart thumping, and the distant roar of the torrent. What is the time, *kot or*? He pressed his repeater and, undismayed, it hissed and tinkled out ten twenty-one.

Anyone who has tried to struggle up a steep slope, on a dark night, through a tangle of inimical vegetation, knows what a formidable task our mountaineer had before him. For more than two hours he kept at it, stumbling against stumps, falling into ravines, clutching at invisible bushes, fighting off an army of conifers. He lost his cloak. He wondered if he had not better curl up in the undergrowth and wait for daybreak. All at once a pinhead light gleamed ahead and presently he found himself staggering up a slippery, recently mown meadow. A dog barked. A stone rolled underfoot. He realized he was near a mountainside *bore* (farmhouse). He also realized that he had toppled into a deep muddy ditch.

The gnarled farmer and his plump wife who, like personages in an old tedious tale offered the drenched fugitive a welcome shelter, mistook him for an eccentric camper who had got detached from his group. He was allowed to dry himself in a warm kitchen where he was given a fairy-tale meal of bread and cheese, and a bowl of mountain mead. His feelings (gratitude, exhaustion, pleasant warmth, drowsiness and so on) were too obvious to need description. A fire of larch roots crackled in the stove, and all the shadows of his lost kingdom gathered to play around his rocking chair as he dozed off between that blaze and the tremulous light of a little earthenware cresset, a beaked affair rather like a Roman lamp, hanging above a shelf where poor beady baubles and bits of nacre became microscopic soldiers swarming in desperate battle. He woke up with a crimp in the neck at the first full cowbell of dawn, found his host outside, in a damp corner consigned to the humble needs of nature, and bade the good *grunter* (mountain farmer) show him the shortest way to the pass. "I'll rouse lazy Garh," said the farmer.

A rude staircase led up to a loft. The farmer placed his gnarled hand on the gnarled balustrade and directed toward the upper darkness a guttural call: "Garh! Garh!" Although given to both sexes, the name is, strictly speaking, a masculine one, and the King expected to see emerge from the loft a bare-kneed mountain lad like a tawny angel. Instead there appeared a disheveled young hussy wearing only a man's shirt that came down to her pink shins and an oversized pair of brogues. A moment later, as in a transformation act, she reappeared, her yellow hair still hanging lank and loose, but the dirty shirt replaced by a dirty pullover, and her legs sheathed in corduroy pants. She was told to conduct the stranger to a spot from which he could easily reach the pass. A sleepy and sullen expression blurred whatever appeal her snub-nosed round face might have had for the local shepherds; but she complied readily enough with her father's wish. His wife was crooning an ancient song as she busied herself with pot and pan.

Before leaving, the King asked his host, whose name was Griff, to accept an old gold piece he chanced to have in his pocket, the only money he possessed. Griff vigorously refused and, still remonstrating, started the laborious business of unlocking and unbolting two or three heavy doors. The King glanced at the old woman, received a wink of approval, and put the muted ducat on the mantelpiece, next to a violet seashell against which was propped a color print representing an elegant guardsman with his bare-shouldered wife—Karl the Beloved, as he was twenty odd years before, and his young queen, an angry young virgin with coal-black hair and ice-blue eyes.

The stars had just faded. He followed the girl and a happy

sheepdog up the overgrown trail that glistened with the ruby dew in the theatrical light of an alpine dawn. The very air seemed tinted and glazed. A sepulchral chill emanated from the sheer cliff along which the trail ascended; but on the opposite precipitous side, here and there between the tops of fir trees growing below, gossamer gleams of sunlight were beginning to weave patterns of warmth. At the next turning this warmth enveloped the fugitive, and a black butterfly came dancing down a pebbly rake. The path narrowed still more and gradually deteriorated amidst a jumble of boulders. The girl pointed to the slopes beyond it. He nodded. "Now go home," he said. "I shall rest here and then continue alone."

He sank down on the grass near a patch of matted elfinwood and inhaled the bright air. The panting dog lay down at his feet. Garh smiled for the first time. Zemblan mountain girls are as a rule mere mechanisms of haphazard lust, and Garh was no exception. As soon as she had settled beside him, she bent over and pulled over and off her tousled head the thick gray sweater, revealing her naked back and *blanc-mangé* breasts, and flooded her embarrassed companion with all the acridity of ungroomed womanhood. She was about to proceed with her stripping but he stopped her with a gesture and got up. He thanked her for all her kindness. He patted the innocent dog; and without turning once, with a springy step, the King started to walk up the turfy incline.

He was still chuckling over the wench's discomfiture when he came to the tremendous stones amassed around a small lake which he had reached once or twice from the rocky Kronberg side many years ago. Now he glimpsed the flash of the pool through the aperture of a natural vault, a masterpiece of erosion. The vault was low and he bent his head to step down toward the water. In its limpid tintarron he saw his scarlet reflection but, oddly enough, owing to what seemed to be at first blush an optical illusion, this reflection was not at his feet but much further; moreover, it was accompanied by the ripple-warped reflection of a ledge that jutted high above his present position. And finally, the strain on the magic of the image caused it to snap as his red-sweatered, red-capped doubleganger turned and vanished, whereas he, the observer, remained immobile. He now advanced to the very lip of the water and was met there by a genuine reflection, much larger and clearer than the one that had deceived him. He skirted the pool. High up in the deep-blue sky jutted the empty ledge whereon a counterfeit king had just stood. A shiver of *alfear* (uncontrollable fear caused by elves) ran between his shoulder-blades. He murmured a familiar prayer, crossed himself, and resolutely proceeded toward the pass. At a high point upon an adjacent ridge a *steinmann* (a heap of stones erected as a memento of an ascent) had donned a cap of red wool in his honor. He trudged on. But his heart was a conical ache poking him from below in the throat, and after a while he stopped again to take stock of conditions and decide whether to scramble up the steep debris slope in front of him or to strike off to the right along a strip of grass, gay with gentians, that went winding between lichened rocks. He elected the second route and in due course reached the pass.

Great fallen crags diversified the wayside. The *nippern* (domed hills or "reeks") to the south were broken by a rock and grass slope into light and shadow. Northward melted the green, gray, bluish mountains—Falkberg with its hood of snow, Mutraberg with the fan of its avalanche, Paberg (Mt. Peacock), and others,—separated by narrow dim valleys with intercalated cotton-wool bits of cloud that seemed placed between the receding sets of ridges to prevent their flanks from scraping against one another. Beyond them, in the final blue, loomed Mt. Glitterntin, a serrated edge of bright foil; and southward, a tender haze enveloped more distant ridges which led to one another in an endless array, through every grade of soft evanescence.

The pass had been reached, granite and gravity had been overcome; but the most dangerous stretch lay ahead. Westward a succession of heathered slopes led down to the shining sea. Up to this moment the mountain had stood between him and the gulf; now he was exposed to that arching blaze. He began the descent.

Three hours later he trod level ground. Two old women working in an orchard unbent in slow motion and stared after him. He had passed the pine groves of Boscobel and was approaching the quay of Blawick, when a black police car turned out of a transverse road and pulled up next to him: "The joke has gone too far," said the driver. "One hundred clowns are packed in Onhava jail, and the ex-King should be among them. Our local prison is much too small for more kings. The next masquerader will be shot at sight. What's your real name, Charlie?" "I'm British. I'm a tourist," said the King. "Well, anyway, take off that red *fufa*. And the cap. Give them here." He tossed the things in the back of the car and drove off.

The King walked on; the top of his blue pajamas tucked into his skiing pants might easily pass for a fancy shirt. There was a pebble in his left shoe but he was too fagged out to do anything about it.

He recognized the seashore restaurant where many years earlier he had lunched incognito with two amusing, very amusing, sailors. Several heavily armed Extremists were drinking beer on the geranium-lined veranda, among the routine vacationists, some of whom were busy writing to distant friends. Through the geraniums, a gloved hand gave the King a picture postcard on which he found scribbled: *Proceed to R.C. Bon voyage!* Feigning a casual stroll, he reached the end of the embankment.

It was a lovely breezy afternoon with a western horizon like a luminous vacuum that sucked in one's eager heart. The King, now at the most critical point of his journey, looked about him, scrutinizing the few promenaders and trying to decide which of them might be police agents in disguise, ready to pounce upon him as soon as he vaulted the parapet and made for the Rippleson Caves. Only a single sail dyed a royal red marred with some human interest the marine expanse. Nitra and Indra (meaning "inner" and "outer"), two black islets that seemed to address each other in cloaked parley, were being photographed from the parapet by a Russian tourist, thickset, many-chinned, with a general's fleshy nape. His faded wife, wrapped up floatingly in a flowery *écharpe*, remarked in singsong Moscovan "Every time I see that kind of frightful disfigurement I can't help thinking of Nina's boy. War is an awful thing." "War?" queried her consort. "That must have been the explosion at the Glass Works in 1951—not war." They slowly walked past the King in the direction he had come from. On a sidewalk bench, facing the sea, a man with his crutches beside him was reading the Onhava *Post*

which featured on the first page Odon in an Extremist uniform and Odon in the part of the Merman. Incredible as it
may seem the palace guard had never realized that identity
before. Now a goodly sum was offered for his capture. Rhythmically the waves lapped the shingle. The newspaper reader's
face had been atrociously injured in the recently mentioned
explosion, and all the art of plastic surgery had only resulted
in a hideous tessellated texture with parts of pattern and parts
of outline seeming to change, to fuse or to separate, like fluctuating cheeks and chins in a distortive mirror.

The short stretch of beach between the restaurant at the
beginning of the promenade and the granite rocks at its end
was almost empty: far to the left three fishermen were loading
a rowboat with kelp-brown nets, and directly under the sidewalk, an elderly woman wearing a polka-dotted dress and having for headgear a cocked newspaper (Ex-King Seen—) sat
knitting on the shingle with her back to the street. Her bandaged legs were stretched out on the sand; on one side of her
lay a pair of carpet slippers and on the other a ball of red
wool, the leading filament of which she would tug at every
now and then with the immemorial elbow jerk of a Zemblan
knitter to give a turn to her yarn clew and slacken the thread.
Finally, on the sidewalk a little girl in a ballooning skirt was
clumsily but energetically clattering about on roller skates.
Could a dwarf in the police force pose as a pigtailed child?

Waiting for the Russian couple to recede, the King stopped
beside the bench. The mosaic-faced man folded his newspaper, and one second before he spoke (in the neutral interval
between smoke puff and detonation), the King knew it was
Odon. "All one could do at short notice," said Odon, plucking at his cheek to display how the varicolored semitransparent
film adhered to his face, altering its contours according to
stress. "A polite person," he added, "does not, normally, examine too closely a poor fellow's disfigurement." "I was looking for *shpiks* [plainclothesmen]," said the King. "All day,"
said Odon, "they have been patrolling the quay. They are
dining at present." "I'm thirsty and hungry," said the King.
"There's some stuff in the boat. Let those Russians vanish.
The child we can ignore." "What about that woman on the
beach?" "That's young Baron Mandevil—chap who had that

duel last year. Let's go now." "Couldn't we take him too?" "Wouldn't come—got a wife and a baby. Come on, Charlie, come on, Your Majesty." "He was my throne page on Coronation Day." Thus chatting, they reached the Rippleson Caves. I trust the reader has enjoyed this note.

Line 162: With his pure tongue, etc.

This is a singularly roundabout way of describing a country girl's shy kiss; but the whole passage is very baroque. My own boyhood was too happy and healthy to contain anything remotely like the fainting fits experienced by Shade. It must have been with him a mild form of epilepsy, a derailment of the nerves at the same spot, on the same curve of the tracks, every day, for several weeks, until nature repaired the damage. Who can forget the good-natured faces, glossy with sweat, of copper-chested railway workers leaning upon their spades and following with their eyes the windows of the great express cautiously gliding by?

Line 167: There was a time, etc.

The poet began Canto Two (on his fourteenth card) on July 5, his sixtieth birthday (see note to line 181, "today"). My slip—change to sixty-first.

Line 169: survival after death

See note to line 549.

Line 171: A great conspiracy

For almost a whole year after the King's escape the Extremists remained convinced that he and Odon had not left Zembla. The mistake can be only ascribed to the streak of stupidity that fatally runs through the most competent tyranny. Airborne machines and everything connected with them cast a veritable spell over the minds of our new rulers whom kind history had suddenly given a boxful of these zipping and zooming gadgets to play with. That an important fugitive would not perform by air the act of fleeing seemed to them inconceivable. Within minutes after the King and the actor had clattered down the backstairs of the Royal Theater, every wing in the sky and on the ground had been accounted for—such was the efficiency of the government. During the next weeks not one private or commercial plane was allowed to take off, and the inspection of transients became so rigorous and lengthy that international lines decided to cancel stopovers at Onhava. There were some casualties. A crimson balloon was enthusiastically shot down and the aeronaut (a well-known meteorologist) drowned in the Gulf of Surprise. A pilot from a Lapland base flying on a mission of mercy got lost in the fog and was so badly harassed by Zemblan fighters that he settled atop a mountain peak. Some excuse for all this could be found. The illusion of the King's presence in the wilds of Zembla was kept up by royalist plotters who decoyed entire regiments into searching the mountains and woods of our rugged peninsula. The government spent a ludicrous amount of energy on solemnly screening the hundreds of impostors packed in the country's jails. Most of them clowned their way back to freedom; a few, alas, fell. Then, in the spring of the following year, a stunning piece of news came from abroad. The Zemblan actor Odon was directing the making of a cinema picture in Paris!

It was now correctly conjectured that if Odon had fled, the King had fled too. At an extraordinary session of the Extremist government there was passed from hand to hand, in grim silence, a copy of a French newspaper with the headline: L'EX-ROI DE ZEMBLA EST-IL À PARIS? Vindictive exasperation rather than state strategy moved the secret organization of which Gradus was an obscure member to plot the destruction of the royal fugitive. Spiteful thugs! They may be compared to hoodlums who itch to torture the invulnerable gentleman whose testimony clapped them in prison for life. Such convicts have been known to go berserk at the thought that their elusive victim whose very testicles they crave to twist and tear with their talons, is sitting at a pergola feast on a sunny island or fondling some pretty young creature between his knees in serene security—and laughing at them! One supposes that no hell can be worse than the helpless rage they experience as the awareness of that implacable sweet mirth reaches them and suffuses them, slowly destroying their brutish brains. A group of especially devout Extremists calling themselves the Shadows had got together and swore to hunt down the King and kill him wherever he might be. They were, in a sense, the shadow twins of the Karlists and indeed several had cousins or even brothers among the followers of the King. No doubt, the origin of either group could be traced to various reckless rituals in student fraternities and military clubs, and their development examined in terms of fads and anti-fads; but whereas an objective historian associates a romantic and noble glamor with Karlism, its shadow group must strike one as something definitely Gothic and nasty. The grotesque figure of Gradus, a cross between bat and crab, was not much odder than many other Shadows, such as, for example, Nodo, Odon's epileptic half brother who cheated at cards, or a mad Mandevil who had lost a leg in trying to make anti-matter. Gradus had long been a member of all sorts of jejune leftist organizations. He had never killed, though coming rather close to it several times in his gray life. He insisted later that when he found himself designated to track down and murder the King, the choice was decided by a show of cards—but let us not forget that it was Nodo who shuffled and dealt them out. Perhaps our man's foreign origin secretly prompted a nomination that would not cause any son of Zembla to incur the dishonor of actual regicide. We can well imagine the scene: the ghastly neon lights of the laboratory, in an annex of the Glass Works, where the Shadows happened to hold their meeting that night; the ace of spades lying on the tiled floor; the vodka gulped down out of test tubes; the many hands clapping Gradus on his round back, and the dark exultation of the man as he received those rather treacherous congratulations. We place this fatidic moment at 0:05, July 2, 1959—which happens to be also the date upon which an innocent poet penned the first lines of his last poem.

Was Gradus really a suitable person for the job? Yes and no.

One day in his early youth, when he worked as messenger boy for a large and depressing firm of cardboard box manufacturers, he quietly helped three companions to ambush a local lad whom they wished to beat up for winning a motorcycle at a fair. Young Gradus obtained an axe and directed the felling of a tree: it crashed improperly, though, not quite blocking the country lane down which their carefree prey used to ride in the growing dusk. The poor lad whizzing along toward the spot where those roughs crouched was a slim delicate-looking Lorrainer, and one must have been vile indeed to begrudge him his harmless enjoyment. Curiously enough, while they were lying in wait, our future regicide fell asleep in a ditch and thus missed the brief affray during which two of the attackers were knuckledusted and knocked out by the brave Lorrainer, and the third run over and crippled for life.

Gradus never became a real success in the glass business to which he turned again and again between his wine-selling and pamphlet-printing jobs. He started as a maker of Cartesian devils—imps of bottle glass bobbing up and down in methylate-filled tubes hawked during Catkin Week on the boulevards. He also worked as teazer, and later as flasher, at governmental factories—and was, I believe, more or less responsible for the remarkably ugly red-and-amber windows in the great public lavatory at rowdy but colorful Kalixhaven where the sailors are. He claimed to have improved the glitter and rattle of the so-called *feuilles-d'alarme* used by grape growers and orchardmen to scare the birds. I have staggered the notes referring to him in such a fashion that the first (see note to line 17 where some of his other activities are adumbrated) is the vaguest while those that follow become gradually clearer as gradual Gradus approaches in space and time.

Mere springs and coils produced the inward movements of our clockwork man. He might be termed a Puritan. One essential dislike, formidable in its simplicity, pervaded his dull soul: he disliked injustice and deception. He disliked their union—they were always together—with a wooden passion that neither had, nor needed, words to express itself. Such a dislike should have deserved praise had it not been a by-product of the man's hopeless stupidity. He called unjust and deceitful everything that surpassed his understanding. He worshiped general ideas and did so with pedantic aplomb. The generality was godly, the specific diabolical. If one person was poor and the other wealthy it did not matter what precisely had ruined one or made the other rich; the difference itself was unfair, and the poor man who did not denounce it was as wicked as the rich one who ignored it. People who knew too much, scientists, writers, mathematicians, crystalographers and so forth, were no better than kings or priests: they all held an unfair share of power of which others were cheated. A plain decent fellow should constantly be on the watch for some piece of clever knavery on the part of nature and neighbor.

The Zemblan Revolution provided Gradus with satisfactions but also produced frustrations. One highly irritating episode seems retrospectively most significant as belonging to an order of things that Gradus should have learned to expect but never did. An especially brilliant impersonator of the King, the tennis ace Julius Steinmann (son of the well-known philanthropist), had eluded for several months the police who had been driven to the limits of exasperation by his mimicking to perfection the voice of Charles the Beloved in a series of underground radio speeches deriding the government. When finally captured he was tried by a special commission, of which Gradus was member, and condemned to death. The firing squad bungled their job, and a little later the gallant young man was found recuperating from his wounds at a provincial hospital. When Gradus learned of this, he flew into one of his rare rages—not because the fact presupposed royalist machinations, but because the clean, honest, orderly course of death had been interfered with in an unclean, dishonest, disorderly manner. Without consulting anybody he rushed to the hospital, stormed in, located Julius in a crowded ward and managed to fire twice, both times missing, before the gun was wrested from him by a hefty male nurse. He rushed back to headquarters and returned with a dozen soldiers but his patient had disappeared.

Such things rankle—but what can Gradus do? The huddled fates engage in a great conspiracy against Gradus. One notes with pardonable glee that his likes are never granted the ultimate thrill of dispatching their victim themselves. Oh, surely, Gradus is active, capable, helpful, often indispensable. At the foot of the scaffold, on a raw and gray morning, it is Gradus who sweeps the night's powder snow off the narrow steps; but his long leathery face will not be the last one that the man who must mount those steps is to see in this world. It is Gradus who buys the cheap fiber valise that a luckier guy will plant, with a time bomb inside, under the bed of a former henchman. Nobody knows better than Gradus how to set a trap by means of a fake advertisement, but the rich old widow whom it hooks is courted and slain by another. When the fallen tyrant is tied, naked and howling, to a plank in the public square and killed piecemeal by the people who cut slices out, and eat them, and distribute his living body among themselves (as I read when young in a story about an Italian despot, which made of me a vegetarian for life), Gradus does not take part in the infernal sacrament: he points out the right instrument and directs the carving.

All this is as it should be; the world needs Gradus. But Gradus should not kill kings. Vinogradus should never, never provoke God. Leningradus should not aim his peashooter at people even in dreams, because if he does, a pair of colossally thick, abnormally hairy arms will hug him from behind and squeeze, squeeze, squeeze.

Line 172: books and people

In a black pocketbook that I fortunately have with me I find, jotted down, here and there, among various extracts that had happened to please me (a footnote from Boswell's *Life of Dr. Johnson*, the inscriptions on the trees in Wordsmith's famous avenue, a quotation from St. Augustine, and so on), a few samples of John Shade's conversation which I had collected in order to refer to them in the presence of people whom my friendship with the poet might interest or annoy. His and my reader will, I trust, excuse me for breaking the orderly course of these comments and letting my illustrious friend speak for himself.

Book reviewers being mentioned, he said: "I have never acknowledged printed praise though sometimes I longed to embrace the glowing image of this or that paragon of discernment; and I have never bothered to lean out of my window and empty my skoramis on some poor hack's pate. I regard both the demolishment and the rave with like detachment." Kinbote: "I suppose you dismiss the first as the blabber of a blockhead and the second as a kind soul's friendly act?" Shade: "Exactly."

Speaking of the Head of the bloated Russian Department, Prof. Pnin, a regular martinet in regard to his underlings (happily, Prof. Botkin, who taught in another department, was not subordinated to that grotesque "perfectionist"): "How odd that Russian intellectuals should lack all sense of humor when they have such marvelous humorists as Gogol, Dostoevski, Chekhov, Zoshchenko, and those joint authors of genius Ilf and Petrov."

Talking of the vulgarity of a certain burly acquaintance of ours: "The man is as corny as a cook-out chef apron." Kinbote (laughing): "Wonderful!"

The subject of teaching Shakespeare at college level having been introduced: "First of all, dismiss ideas, and social background, and train the freshman to shiver, to get drunk on the poetry of *Hamlet* or *Lear*, to read with his spine and not with his skull." Kinbote: "You appreciate particularly the purple passages?" Shade: "Yes, my dear Charles, I roll upon them as a grateful mongrel on a spot of turf fouled by a Great Dane."

The respective impacts and penetrations of Marxism and Freudism being talked of, I said: "The worst of two false doctrines is always that which is harder to eradicate." Shade: "No, Charlie, there are simpler criteria: Marxism needs a dictator, and a dictator needs a secret police, and that is the end of the world; but the Freudian, no matter how stupid, can still cast his vote at the poll, even if he is pleased to call it [smiling] *political pollination*."

Of students' papers: "I am generally very benevolent [said Shade]. But there are certain trifles I do not forgive." Kinbote: "For instance?" "Not having read the required book. Having read it like an idiot. Looking in it for symbols; example: 'The author uses the striking image *green leaves* because green is the symbol of happiness and frustration.' I am also in the habit of lowering a student's mark catastrophically if he uses 'simple' and 'sincere' in a commendatory sense; examples: 'Shelley's style is always very simple and good'; or 'Yeats is always sincere.' This is widespread, and when I hear a critic speaking of an author's sincerity I know that either the critic or the author is a fool." Kinbote: "But I am told this manner of thinking is taught in high school?" "That's where the broom should begin to sweep. A child should have thirty specialists to teach him thirty subjects, and not one harassed schoolmarm to show him a picture of a rice field and tell him this is China because she knows nothing about China, or anything else, and cannot tell the difference between longitude and latitude." Kinbote: "Yes. I agree."

Line 181:   Today

Namely, July 5, 1959, 6th Sunday after Trinity. Shade began writing Canto Two "early in the morning" (thus noted at the top of Card 14). He continued (down to line 208) on and off throughout the day. Most of the evening and a part of the night were devoted to what his favorite eighteenth-century writers have termed "the Bustle and Vanity of the World." After the last guest had gone (on a bicycle), and the ashtrays had been emptied, all the windows were dark for a couple of hours; but then, at about 3 A.M., I saw from my upstairs bathroom that the poet had gone back to his desk in the lilac light of his den, and this nocturnal session brought the canto to line 230 (card 18). On another trip to the bathroom an hour and a half later, at sunrise, I found the light transferred to the bedroom, and smiled indulgently, for, according to my deductions, only two nights had passed since the three-thousand-nine-hundred-ninety-ninth time—but no matter. A few minutes later all was solid darkness again, and I went back to bed.

On July 5th, at noontime, in the other hemisphere, on the rain-swept tarmac of the Onhava airfield, Gradus, holding a French passport, walked towards a Russian commercial plane bound for Copenhagen, and this event synchronized with Shade's starting in the early morning (Atlantic seaboard time) to compose, or to set down after composing in bed, the opening lines of Canto Two. When almost twenty-four hours later he got to line 230, Gradus, after a refreshing night at the summer house of our consul in Copenhagen, an important Shadow, had entered, with the Shadow, a clothes store in order to conform to his description in later notes (to lines 286 and 408). Migraine again worse today.

As to my own activities, they were I am afraid most unsatisfactory from all points of view—emotional, creative, and social. That jinxy streak had started on the eve when I had been kind enough to offer a young friend—a candidate for my third ping-pong table who after a sensational series of traffic violations had been deprived of his driving license—to take him, in my powerful Kramler, all the way to his parents' estate, a little matter of two hundred miles. In the course of an all-night party, among crowds of strangers—young people, old people, cloyingly perfumed girls—in an atmosphere of fireworks, barbecue smoke, horseplay, jazz music, and auroral swimming, I lost all contact with the silly boy, was made to dance, was made to sing, got involved in the most boring bibble-babble imaginable with various relatives of the child, and finally, in some inconceivable manner, found myself transported to a different party on a different estate, where, after some indescribable parlor games, in which my beard was nearly snipped off, I had a fruit-and-rice breakfast and was taken by my anonymous host, a drunken old fool in tuxedo and riding breeches, on a stumbling round of his stables. Upon locating my car (off the road, in a pine grove), I tossed out of the driver's seat a pair of soggy swimming trunks and a girl's silver slipper. The brakes had aged overnight, and I soon ran out of gas on a desolate stretch of road. Six o'clock was being chimed by the clocks of Wordsmith College, when I reached Arcady, swearing to myself never to be caught like that again and innocently looking forward to the solace of a quiet evening with my poet. Only when I saw the beribboned flat carton I had placed on a chair in my hallway did I realize that I had almost missed his birthday.

Some time ago I had noticed that date on the jacket of one of his books; had pondered the awful decrepitude of his breakfast attire; had playfully measured my arm against his; and had bought for him in Washington an utterly gorgeous silk dressing gown, a veritable dragon skin of oriental chromas, fit for a samurai; and this was what the carton contained.

Hurriedly I shed my clothes and, roaring my favorite hymn, took a shower. My versatile gardener, while administering to me a much-needed rubdown, informed me that the Shades were giving that night a big "buffet" dinner, and that Senator Blank (an outspoken statesman very much in the news and a cousin of John's) was expected.

Now there is nothing a lonesome man relishes more than an impromptu birthday party, and thinking—nay, feeling certain—that my unattended telephone had been ringing all day, I blithely dialed the Shades' number, and of course it was Sybil who answered.

"*Bon soir*, Sybil."

"Oh, hullo, Charles. Had a nice trip?"

"Well, to tell the truth—"

"Look, I know you want John but he is resting right now, and I'm frightfully busy. He'll call you back later, okay?"

"Later when—tonight?"

"No, tomorrow, I guess. There goes that doorbell. Bye-bye."

Strange. Why should Sybil have to listen to doorbells when, besides the maid and the cook, two white-coated hired boys were around? False pride prevented me from doing what I should have done—taken my royal gift under my arm and serenely marched over to that inhospitable house. Who knows—I might have been rewarded at the back door with a drop of kitchen sherry. I still hoped there had been a mistake, and Shade would telephone. It was a bitter wait, and the only effect that the bottle of champagne I drank all alone now at this window, now at that, had on me was a bad *crapula* (hangover).

From behind a drapery, from behind a box tree, through the golden veil of evening and through the black lacery of night, I kept watching that lawn, that drive, that fanlight, those jewel-bright windows. The sun had not yet set when, at a quarter past seven, I heard the first guest's car. Oh, I saw them all. I saw ancient Dr. Sutton, a snowy-headed, perfectly oval little gentleman arrive in a tottering Ford with his tall

daughter, Mrs. Starr, a war widow. I saw a couple, later identified for me as Mr. Colt, a local lawyer, and his wife, whose
blundering Cadillac half entered my driveway before retreating in a flurry of luminous nictitation. I saw a world-famous
old writer, bent under the incubus of literary honors and his
own prolific mediocrity, arrive in a taxi out of the dim times
of yore when Shade and he had been joint editors of a little
review. I saw Frank, the Shades' handyman, depart in the station wagon. I saw a retired professor of ornithology walk up
from the highway where he had illegally parked his car. I saw,
ensconced in their tiny Pulex, manned by her boy-handsome
tousle-haired girl friend, the patroness of the arts who had
sponsored Aunt Maud's last exhibition. I saw Frank return
with the New Wye antiquarian, purblind Mr. Kaplun, and his
wife, a dilapidated eagle. I saw a Korean graduate student in
dinner jacket come on a bicycle, and the college president in
baggy suit come on foot. I saw, in the performance of their
ceremonial duties, in light and shadow, and from window to
window, where like Martians the martinis and highballs
cruised, the two white-coated youths from the hotel school,
and realized that I knew well, quite well, the slighter of the
two. And finally, at half past eight (when, I imagine, the lady
of the house had begun to crack her finger joints as was her
impatient wont) a long black limousine, officially glossy and
rather funereal, glided into the aura of the drive, and while
the fat Negro chauffeur hastened to open the car door, I saw,
with pity, my poet emerge from his house, a white flower in
his buttonhole and a grin of welcome on his liquor-flushed
face.

Next morning, as soon as I saw Sybil drive away to fetch
Ruby the maid who did not sleep in the house, I crossed over
with the prettily and reproachfully wrapped up carton. In
front of their garage, on the ground, I noticed a *buchmann*,
a little pillar of library books which Sybil had obviously forgotten there. I bent towards them under the incubus of curiosity: they were mostly by Mr. Faulkner; and the next
moment Sybil was back, her tires scrunching on the gravel
right behind me. I added the books to my gift and placed the
whole pile in her lap. That was nice of me—but what was that
carton? Just a present for John. A present? Well, was it not

his birthday yesterday? Yes, it was, but after all are not birthdays mere conventions? Conventions or not, but it was my birthday too—small difference of sixteen years, that's all. Oh my! Congratulations. And how did the party go? Well, you know what such parties are (here I reached in my pocket for another book—a book she did not expect). Yes, what are they? Oh, people whom you've known all your life and simply *must* invite once a year, men like Ben Kaplun and Dick Colt with whom we went to school, and that Washington cousin, and the fellow whose novels you and John think so phony. We did not ask you because we knew how tedious you find such affairs. This was my cue.

"Speaking of novels," I said, "you remember we decided once, you, your husband and I, that Proust's rough masterpiece was a huge, ghoulish fairy tale, an asparagus dream, totally unconnected with any possible people in any historical France, a sexual *travestissement* and a colossal farce, the vocabulary of genius and its poetry, but no more, impossibly rude hostesses, please let me speak, and even ruder guests, mechanical Dostoevskian rows and Tolstoian nuances of snobbishness repeated and expanded to an unsufferable length, adorable seascapes, melting avenues, no, do not interrupt me, light and shade effects rivaling those of the greatest English poets, a flora of metaphors, described—by Cocteau, I think—as 'a mirage of suspended gardens,' and, I have not yet finished, an absurd, rubber-and-wire romance between a blond young blackguard (the fictitious Marcel), and an improbable *jeune fille* who has a pasted-on bosom, Vronski's (and Lyovin's) thick neck, and a cupid's buttocks for cheeks; but—and now let me finish sweetly—we were wrong, Sybil, we were wrong in denying our little *beau ténébreux* the capacity of evoking 'human interest': it is there, it is there—maybe a rather eighteenth-centuryish, or even seventeenth-centuryish, brand, but it is there. Please, dip or redip, spider, into this book [offering it], you will find a pretty marker in it bought in France, I want John to keep it. *Au revoir*, Sybil, I must go now. *I think my telephone is ringing.*"

I am a very sly Zemblan. *Just in case*, I had brought with me in my pocket the third and last volume of the *Bibliothèque de la Pléiade* edition, Paris, 1954, of Proust's work, wherein I had marked certain passages on pages 269–271. Mme. de Mortemart, having decided that Mme. de Valcourt would *not* be among the "elected" at her soirée, intended to send her a note on the next day saying "Dear Edith, I miss you, last night I did not expect you too much (Edith would wonder: how could she at all, since she did not invite me?) because I know you are not overfond of this sort of parties which, if anything, bore you."

So much for John Shade's last birthday.

Lines 181–182:   waxwings . . . cicadas

The bird of lines 1–4 and 131 is again with us. It will reappear in the ultimate line of the poem; and another cicada, leaving its envelope behind, will sing triumphantly at lines 236–244.

Line 189:   Starover Blue

See note to line 627. This reminds one of the Royal Game of the Goose, but played here with little airplanes of painted tin: a wild-goose game, rather (go to square 209).

Line 209:   gradual decay

Spacetime itself is decay; Gradus is flying west; he has reached gray-blue Copenhagen (see note to 181). After to-morrow (July 7) he will proceed to Paris. He has sped through this verse and is gone—presently to darken our pages again.

Lines 213–214:   A syllogism

This may please a boy. Later in life we learn that we *are* those "others."

Line 230:   a domestic ghost

Shade's former secretary, Jane Provost, whom I recently looked up in Chicago, told me about Hazel considerably more than her father did; he affected not to speak of his dead daughter, and since I did not foresee this work of inquiry and comment, I did not urge him to talk on the subject and un-burden himself to me. True, in this canto he has unburdened himself pretty thoroughly, and his picture of Hazel is quite clear and complete; maybe a little too complete, architecton-ically, since the reader cannot help feeling that it has been expanded and elaborated to the detriment of certain other richer and rarer matters ousted by it. But a commentator's obligations cannot be shirked, however dull the information he must collect and convey. Hence this note.

It appears that in the beginning of 1950, long before the barn incident (see note to line 347), sixteen-year-old Hazel was involved in some appalling "psychokinetic" manifesta-tions that lasted for nearly a month. Initially, one gathers, the poltergeist meant to impregnate the disturbance with the identity of Aunt Maud who had just died; the first object to perform was the basket in which she had once kept her half-paralyzed Skye terrier (the breed called in our country "weep-ing-willow dog"). Sybil had had the animal destroyed soon after its mistress's hospitalization, incurring the wrath of Hazel who was beside herself with distress. One morning this basket shot out of the "intact" sanctuary (see lines 90–98) and traveled along the corridor past the open door of the study, where Shade was at work; he saw it whizz by and spill its humble contents: a ragged coverlet, a rubber bone, and a partly discolored cushion. Next day the scene of action switched to the dining room where one of Aunt Maud's oils (*Cypress and Bat*) was found to be turned toward the wall. Other incidents followed, such as short flights accomplished by her scrapbook (see note to line 90) and, of course, all kinds of knockings, especially in the sanctuary, which would rouse Hazel from her, no doubt, peaceful sleep in the adjacent bed-room. But soon the poltergeist ran out of ideas in connection with Aunt Maud and became, as it were, more eclectic. All the banal motions that objects are limited to in such cases, were gone through in this one. Saucepans crashed in the kitchen; a snowball was found (perhaps, prematurely) in the icebox; once or twice Sybil saw a plate sail by like a discus and land safely on the sofa; lamps kept lighting up in various parts of the house; chairs waddled away to assemble in the impassable pantry; mysterious bits of string were found on the floor; invisible revelers staggered down the staircase in the middle of the night; and one winter morning Shade, upon rising and taking a look at the weather, saw that the little table from his study upon which he kept a Bible-like Webster open at M was standing in a state of shock outdoors, on the snow (subliminally this may have participated in the making of lines 5–12).

I imagine, that during that period the Shades, or at least John Shade, experienced a sensation of odd instability as if parts of the everyday, smoothly running world had got unscrewed, and you became aware that one of your tires was rolling beside you, or that your steering wheel had come off. My poor friend could not help recalling the dramatic fits of his early boyhood and wondering if this was not a new genetic variant of the same theme, preserved through procreation. Trying to hide from neighbors these horrible and humiliating phenomena was not the least of Shade's worries. He was terrified, and he was lacerated with pity. Although never able to corner her, that flabby, feeble, clumsy and solemn girl, who seemed more interested than frightened, he and Sybil never doubted that in some extraordinary way she was the agent of the disturbance which they saw as representing (I now quote Jane P.) "an outward extension or expulsion of insanity." They could not do much about it, partly because they disliked modern voodoo-psychiatry, but mainly because they were afraid of Hazel, and afraid to hurt her. They had however a secret interview with old-fashioned and learned Dr. Sutton, and this put them in better spirits. They were contemplating moving into another house or, more exactly, loudly saying to each other, so as to be overheard by anyone who might be listening, that they were contemplating moving, when all at once the fiend was gone, as happens with the *moskovett*, that bitter blast, that colossus of cold air that blows on our eastern shores throughout March, and then one morning you hear

the birds, and the flags hang flaccid, and the outlines of the
world are again in place. The phenomena ceased completely
and were, if not forgotten, at least never referred to; but how
curious it is that we do not perceive a mysterious sign of equa-
tion between the Hercules springing forth from a neurotic
child's weak frame and the boisterous ghost of Aunt Maud;
how curious that our rationality feels satisfied when we plump
for the first explanation, though, actually, the scientific and
the supernatural, the miracle of the muscle and the miracle
of the mind, are *both* inexplicable as are all the ways of Our
Lord.

Line 231: How ludicrous, etc.

A beautiful variant, with one curious gap, branches off at
this point in the draft (dated July 6):

Strange Other World where all our still-born dwell,
And pets, revived, and invalids, grown well,
And minds that died before arriving there:
Poor old man Swift, poor—, poor Baudelaire

What might that dash stand for? Unless Shade gave prosodic value to the mute *e* in "Baudelaire," which I am quite
certain he would never have done in English verse (cp.
"Rabelais," line 501), the name required here must scan as a
trochee. Among the names of celebrated poets, painters,
philosophers, etc., known to have become insane or to have
sunk into senile imbecility, we find many suitable ones. Was
Shade confronted by too much variety with nothing to help
logic choose and so left a blank, relying upon the mysterious
organic force that rescues poets to fill it in at its own convenience? Or was there something else—some obscure intuition,
some prophetic scruple that prevented him from spelling out
the name of an eminent man who happened to be an intimate
friend of his? Was he perhaps playing safe because a reader in
his household might have objected to that particular name
being mentioned? And if it comes to that, *why* mention it at
all in this tragical context? Dark, disturbing thoughts.

Line 238:   empty emerald case

This, I understand, is the semitransparent envelope left on
a tree trunk by an adult cicada that has crawled up the trunk
and emerged. Shade said that he had once questioned a class
of three hundred students and only *three* knew what a cicada
looked like. Ignorant settlers had dubbed it "locust," which
is, of course, a grasshopper, and the same absurd mistake has
been made by generations of translators of Lafontaine's *La
Cigale et la Fourmi* (see lines 243–244). The *cigale*'s companion piece, the ant, is about to be embalmed in amber.

During our sunset rambles, of which there were so many,
at least nine (according to my notes) in June, but dwindling
to two in the first three weeks of July (they shall be resumed
Elsewhere!), my friend had a rather coquettish way of pointing
out with the tip of his cane various curious natural objects.
He never tired of illustrating by means of these examples the
extraordinary blend of Canadian Zone and Austral Zone that
"obtained," as he put it, in that particular spot of Appalachia
where at our altitude of about 1,500 feet northern species of
birds, insects and plants commingled with southern representatives. As most literary celebrities, Shade did not seem to
realize that a humble admirer who has cornered at last and
has at last to himself the inaccessible man of genius, is considerably more interested in discussing with him literature and
life than in being told that the "diana" (presumably a flower)
occurs in New Wye together with the "atlantis" (presumably
another flower), and things of that sort. I particularly remember one exasperating evening stroll (July 6) which my poet
granted me, with majestic generosity, in compensation for a
bad hurt (see, frequently see, note to line 181), in recompense
for my small gift (which I do not think he ever used), and
with the sanction of his wife who made it a point to accompany us part of the way to Dulwich Forest. By means of astute
excursions into natural history Shade kept evading me, me,
who was hysterically, intensely, uncontrollably curious to
know what portion exactly of the Zemblan king's adventures
he had completed in the course of the last four or five days.
My usual shortcoming, pride, prevented me from pressing him
with direct questions but I kept reverting to my own earlier

themes—the escape from the palace, the adventures in the mountains—in order to force some confession from him. One would imagine that a poet, in the course of composing a long and difficult piece, would simply jump at the opportunity of talking about his triumphs and tribulations. But nothing of the sort! All I got in reply to my infinitely gentle and cautious interrogations were such phrases as: "Yep. It's coming along nicely," or "Nope, I'm not talkin'," and finally he brushed me off with a rather offensive anecdote about King Alfred who, it was said, liked the stories of a Norwegian attendant he had but drove him away when engaged in other business: "Oh, there you are," rude Alfred would say to the gentle Norwegian who had come to weave a subtly different variant of some old Norse myth he had already related before: "*Oh there* you are again!" And thus it came to pass, my dears, that a fabulous exile, a God-inspired northern bard, is known today to English schoolboys by the trivial nickname: Ohthere.

However! On a later occasion my capricious and henpecked friend was much kinder (see note to line 802).

Line 240: That Englishman in Nice

The sea gulls of 1933 are all dead, of course. But by inserting a notice in *The London Times* one might procure the name of their benefactor—unless Shade invented him. When I visited Nice a quarter of a century later, there was, in lieu of that Englishman, a local character, an old bearded bum, tolerated or abetted as a tourist attraction, who stood like a statue of Verlaine with an unfastidious sea gull perched in profile on his matted hair, or took naps in the public sun, comfortably curled up with his back to the lulling roll of the sea, on a promenade bench, under which he had neatly arranged to dry, or ferment, multicolored gobbets of undeterminable victuals on a newspaper. Not many Englishmen walked there, anyway, though I noticed quite a few just east of Mentone, on the quay where in honor of Queen Victoria a bulky monument, with difficulty embraced by the breeze, had been erected, but not yet unshrouded, to replace the one the Germans had

taken away. Rather pathetically, the eager horn of her pet
monoceros protruded through the shroud.

Line 246: . . . my dear

The poet addresses his wife. The passage devoted to her
(lines 246–292) has its structural use as a transition to the
theme of his daughter. I can, however, state that when dear
Sybil's steps were heard upstairs, fierce and sharp, above our
heads, everything was not always "all right"!

Line 247: Sybil

John Shade's wife, née Irondell (which comes not from a
little valley yielding iron ore but from the French for "swallow"). She was a few months his senior. I understand she
came of Canadian stock, as did Shade's maternal grandmother
(a first cousin of Sybil's grandfather, if I am not greatly mistaken).
From the very first I tried to behave with the utmost courtesy toward my friend's wife, and from the very first she disliked and distrusted me. I was to learn later that when alluding
to me in public she used to call me "an elephantine tick; a
king-sized botfly; a macaco worm; the monstrous parasite of
a genius." I pardon her—her and everybody.

Line 270: My dark Vanessa

It is *so* like the heart of a scholar in search of a fond name
to pile a butterfly genus upon an Orphic divinity on top of
the inevitable allusion to *Van*homrigh, *Es*ther! In this connection a couple of lines from one of Swift's poems (which in
these backwoods I cannot locate) have stuck in my memory:

> When, lo! *Vanessa* in her bloom
> Advanced like *Atalanta*'s star

As to the Vanessa butterfly, it will reappear in lines 993–995 (to which see note). Shade used to say that its Old English name was The Red Admirable, later degraded to The Red Admiral. It is one of the few butterflies I happen to be familiar with. Zemblans call it *harvalda* (the heraldic one) possibly because a recognizable figure of it is borne in the escutcheon of the Dukes of Payn. In the autumn of certain years it used to occur rather commonly in the Palace Gardens and visit the Michaelmas daisies in company with a day-flying moth. I have seen The Red Admirable feasting on oozy plums and, once, on a dead rabbit. It is a most frolicsome fly. An almost tame specimen of it was the last natural object John Shade pointed out to me as he walked to his doom (see, see now, my note to lines 993–995).

I notice a whiff of Swift in some of my notes. I too am a desponder in my nature, an uneasy, peevish, and suspicious man, although I have my moments of volatility and *fou rire*.

Line 275: We have been married forty years

John Shade and Sybil Swallow (see note to line 247) were married in 1919, exactly three decades before King Charles wed Disa, Duchess of Payn. Since the very beginning of his reign (1936–1958) representatives of the nation, salmon fishermen, non-union glaziers, military groups, worried relatives, and especially the Bishop of Yeslove, a sanguineous and saintly old man, had been doing their utmost to persuade him to give up his copious but sterile pleasures and take a wife. It was a matter not of morality but of succession. As in the case of some of his predecessors, rough alderkings who burned for boys, the clergy blandly ignored our young bachelor's pagan habits, but wanted him to do what an earlier and even more reluctant Charles had done: take a night off and lawfully engender an heir.

He saw nineteen-year-old Disa for the first time on the festive night of July the 5th, 1947, at a masked ball in his uncle's palace. She had come in male dress, as a Tirolese boy, a little knock-kneed but brave and lovely, and afterwards he drove her and her cousins (two guardsmen disguised as flowergirls) in his divine new convertible through the streets to see the tremendous birthday illumination, and the fackeltanz in the park, and the fireworks, and the pale upturned faces. He procrastinated for almost two years but was set upon by inhumanly eloquent advisers, and finally gave in. On the eve of his wedding he prayed most of the night locked up all alone in the cold vastness of the Onhava cathedral. Smug alderkings looked at him from the ruby-and-amethyst windows. Never had he so fervently asked God for guidance and strength (see further my note to lines 433–434).

After line 274 there is a false start in the draft:

> I like my name: Shade, *Ombre*, almost "man"
> In Spanish . . .

One regrets that the poet did not pursue this theme—and spare his reader the embarrassing intimacies that follow.

Line 286:   A jet's pink trail above the sunset fire

I, too, was wont to draw my poet's attention to the idyllic beauty of airplanes in the evening sky. Who could have guessed that on the very day (July 7) Shade penned this lambent line (the last one on his twenty-third card) Gradus, alias Degré, had flown from Copenhagen to Paris, thus completing the second lap of his sinister journey! Even in Arcady am I, says Death in the tombal scripture.

The activities of Gradus in Paris had been rather neatly planned by the Shadows. They were perfectly right in assuming that not only Odon but our former consul in Paris, the late Oswin Bretwit, would know where to find the King. They decided to have Gradus try Bretwit first. That gentleman had a flat in Meudon where he dwelt alone, seldom going anywhere except the National Library (where he read theosophic works and solved chess problems in old newspapers), and did not receive visitors. The Shadows' neat plan sprung from a piece of luck. Suspecting that Gradus lacked the mental equipment and mimic gifts necessary for the impersonation of an enthusiastic Royalist, they suggested he had better pose as a completely apolitical commissioner, a neutral little man interested only in getting a good price for various papers that pri-

vate parties had asked him to take out of Zembla and deliver
to their rightful owners. Chance, in one of its anti-Karlist
moods, helped. One of the lesser Shadows whom we shall call
Baron A. had a father-in-law called Baron B., a harmless old
codger long retired from the civil service and quite incapable
of understanding certain Renaissance aspects of the new regime. He had been, or thought he had been (retrospective
distance magnifies things), a close friend of the late Minister
of Foreign Affairs, Oswin Bretwit's father, and therefore was
looking forward to the day when he would be able to transmit
to "young" Oswin (who, he understood, was not exactly *per-
sona grata* with the new regime) a bundle of precious family
papers that the dusty baron had come across by chance in the
files of a governmental office. All at once he was informed
that now the day had come: the documents would be immediately forwarded to Paris. He was also allowed to prefix a
brief note to them which read:

> Here are some precious papers belonging to your fam-
> ily. I cannot do better than place them in the hands of
> the son of the great man who was my fellow student in
> Heidelberg and my teacher in the diplomatic service.
> *Verba volant, scripta manent.*

The *scripta* in question were two hundred and thirteen long
letters which had passed some seventy years ago between Zule
Bretwit, Oswin's grand-uncle, Mayor of Odevalla, and a
cousin of his, Ferz Bretwit, Mayor of Aros. This correspondence, a dismal exchange of bureaucratic platitudes and fus-
tian jokes, was devoid of even such parochial interest as letters
of this sort may possess in the eyes of a local historian—but
of course there is no way of telling what will repel or attract
a sentimental ancestralist—and this was what Oswin Bretwit
had always been known to be by his former staff. I would like
to take time out here to interrupt this dry commentary and
pay a brief tribute to Oswin Bretwit.

Physically, he was a sickly bald-headed man resembling a
pallid gland. His face was singularly featureless. He had café-
au-lait eyes. One remembers him always as wearing a mourning band. But this insipid exterior belied the quality of the
man. From beyond the shining corrugations of the ocean I

salute here brave Bretwit! Let there appear for a moment his hand and mine firmly clasping each other across the water over the golden wake of an emblematic sun. Let no insurance firm or airline use this insigne on the glossy page of a magazine as an ad badge under the picture of a retired businessman stupefied and honored by the sight of the technicolored snack that the air hostess offers him with everything else she can give; rather, let this lofty handshake be regarded in our cynical age of frenzied heterosexualism as a last, but lasting, symbol of valor and self-abnegation. How fervently one had dreamed that a similar symbol but in verbal form might have imbued the poem of another dead friend; but this was not to be . . . Vainly does one look in *Pale Fire* (oh, pale, indeed!) for the warmth of my hand gripping yours, poor Shade!

But to return to the roofs of Paris. Courage was allied in Oswin Bretwit with integrity, kindness, dignity, and what can be euphemistically called endearing naïveté. When Gradus telephoned from the airport, and to whet his appetite read to him Baron B.'s message (minus the Latin tag), Bretwit's only thought was for the treat in store for him. Gradus had declined to say over the telephone what exactly the "precious papers" were, but it so happened that the ex-consul had been hoping lately to retrieve a valuable stamp collection that his father had bequeathed years ago to a now defunct cousin. The cousin had dwelt in the same house as Baron B., and with all these complicated and entrancing matters uppermost in his mind, the ex-consul, while awaiting his visitor, kept wondering not if the person from Zembla was a dangerous fraud, but whether he would bring all the albums at once or would do it gradually so as to see what he might get for his pains. Bretwit hoped the business would be completed that very night since on the following morning he was to be hospitalized and possibly operated upon (he was, and died under the knife).

If two secret agents belonging to rival factions meet in a battle of wits, and if one has none, the effect may be droll; it is dull if both are dolts. I defy anybody to find in the annals of plot and counterplot anything more inept and boring than the scene that occupies the rest of this conscientious note.

Gradus sat down, uncomfortably, on the edge of a sofa (upon which a tired king had reclined less than a year ago), dipped into his briefcase, handed to his host a bulky brown paper parcel and transferred his haunches to a chair near Bretwit's seat in order to watch in comfort his tussle with the string. In stunned silence Bretwit stared at what he finally unwrapped, and then said:

"Well, that's the end of a dream. This correspondence has been published in 1906 or 1907—no, 1906, after all—by Ferz Bretwit's widow—I may even have a copy of it somewhere among my books. Moreover, this is not a holograph but an apograph, made by a scribe for the printers—you will note that both mayors write the same hand."

"How interesting," said Gradus noting it.

"Naturally I appreciate the kind thought behind it," said Bretwit.

"We were sure you would," said pleased Gradus.

"Baron B. must be a little gaga," continued Bretwit, "but I repeat, his kind intention is touching. I suppose you want some money for bringing this treasure?"

"The pleasure it gives you should be our reward," answered Gradus. "But let me tell you frankly: we took a lot of pains in trying to do this properly, and I have come a long way. However, I want to offer you a little arrangement. You be nice to us and we'll be nice to you. I know your funds are somewhat—" (Small-fish gesture and wink).

"True enough," sighed Bretwit.

"If you go along with us it won't cost you a centime."

"Oh, I could pay *something*" (Pout and shrug).

"We don't need your money" (Traffic-stopper's palm). "But here's our plan. I have messages from other barons for other fugitives. In fact, I have letters for the most mysterious fugitive of all."

"What!" cried Bretwit in candid surprise. "They know at home that His Majesty has left Zembla?" (I could have spanked the dear man.)

"Indeed, yes," said Gradus kneading his hands, and fairly panting with animal pleasure—a matter of instinct no doubt since the man certainly could not realize intelligently that the ex-consul's faux pas was nothing less than the first confirmation of the King's presence abroad: "Indeed," he repeated with a meaningful leer, "and I would be deeply obliged to you if you would recommend me to Mr. X."

At these words a false truth dawned upon Oswin Bretwit and he moaned to himself: Of course! How obtuse of me! He is one of us! The fingers of his left hand involuntarily started to twitch as if he were pulling a kikapoo puppet over it, while his eyes followed intently his interlocutor's low-class gesture of satisfaction. A Karlist agent, revealing himself to a superior, was expected to make a sign corresponding to the X (for Xavier) in the one-hand alphabet of deaf mutes: the hand held in horizontal position with the index curved rather flaccidly and the rest of the fingers bunched (many have criticized it for looking too droopy; it has now been replaced by a more virile combination). On the several occasions Bretwit had been given it, the manifestation had been preceded for him, during a moment of suspense—rather a gap in the texture of time than an actual delay—by something similar to what physicians call the aura, a strange sensation both tense and vaporous, a hot-cold ineffable exasperation pervading the entire nervous system before a seizure. And on this occasion too Bretwit felt the magic wine rise to his head.

"All right, I am ready. Give me the sign," he avidly said.

Gradus, deciding to risk it, glanced at the hand in Bretwit's lap: unperceived by its owner, it seemed to be prompting Gradus in a manual whisper. He tried to copy what it was doing its best to convey—mere rudiments of the required sign.

"No, no," said Bretwit with an indulgent smile for the awkward novice. "The other hand, my friend. His Majesty is left-handed, you know."

Gradus tried again—but, like an expelled puppet, the wild little prompter had disappeared. Sheepishly contemplating his five stubby strangers, Gradus went through the motions of an incompetent and half-paralyzed shadowgrapher and finally made an uncertain V-for-Victory sign. Bretwit's smile began to fade.

His smile gone, Bretwit (the name means Chess Intelligence) got up from his chair. In a larger room he would have paced up and down—not in this cluttered study. Gradus the

Bungler buttoned all three buttons of his tight brown coat and shook his head several times.

"I think," he said crossly, "one must be fair. If I bring you these valuable papers, you must in return arrange an interview, or at least give me his address."

"I know who you are," cried Bretwit pointing. "You're a reporter! You are from that cheap Danish paper sticking out of your pocket" (Gradus mechanically fumbled at it and frowned). "I had hoped they had given up pestering me! The vulgar nuisance of it! Nothing is sacred to you, neither cancer, nor exile, nor the pride of a king" (alas, this is true not only of Gradus—he has colleagues in Arcady too).

Gradus sat staring at his new shoes—mahogany red with sieve-pitted caps. An ambulance screamed its impatient way through dark streets three stories below. Bretwit vented his irritation on the ancestral letters lying on the table. He snatched up the neat pile with its detached wrapping and flung it all in the wastepaper basket. The string dropped outside, at the feet of Gradus who picked it up and added it to the *scripta*.

"Please, go," said poor Bretwit. "I have a pain in my groin that is driving me mad. I have not slept for three nights. You journalists are an obstinate bunch but I am obstinate too. You will never learn from me anything about my king. Good-bye."

He waited on the landing for his visitor's steps to go down and reach the front door. It was opened and closed, and presently the automatic light on the stairs went out with the sound of a kick.

Line 287:   humming as you pack

The card (his twenty-fourth) with this passage (lines 287–299) is marked July 7th, and under that date in my little agenda I find this scribble: DR. AHLERT, 3.30 P.M. Feeling a bit nervous, as most people do at the prospect of seeing a doctor, I thought I would buy on my way to him something soothing to prevent an accelerated pulse from misleading credulous science. I found the drops I wanted, took the aromatic draught in the pharmacy, and was coming out when I noticed the Shades leaving a shop next door. She was carrying a new traveling grip. The dreadful thought that they might be going away on a summer vacation neutralized the medicine I had just swallowed. One gets so accustomed to another life's running alongside one's own that a sudden turn-off on the part of the parallel satellite causes in one a feeling of stupe-faction, emptiness, and injustice. And what is more he had not yet finished "my" poem!

"Planning to travel?" I asked, smiling and pointing at the bag.

Sybil raised it by the ears like a rabbit and considered it with my eyes.

"Yes, at the end of the month," she said. "After John is through with his work."

(The poem!)

"And where, pray?" (turning to John).

Mr. Shade glanced at Mrs. Shade, and she replied for him in her usual brisk offhand fashion that they did not know for sure yet—it might be Wyoming or Utah or Montana, and perhaps they would rent somewhere a cabin at 6,000 or 7,000 feet.

"Among the lupines and the aspens," said the poet gravely. (Conjuring up the scene.)

I started to calculate aloud in meters the altitude that I thought much too high for John's heart but Sybil pulled him by the sleeve reminding him they had more shopping to do, and I was left with about 2,000 meters and a valerian-flavored burp.

But occasionally black-winged fate can display exquisite thoughtfulness! Ten minutes later Dr. A.—who treated Shade, too—was telling me in stolid detail that the Shades had rented a little ranch some friends of theirs, who were going else-where, had at Cedarn in Utana on the Idoming border. From the doctor's I flitted over to a travel agency, obtained maps and booklets, studied them, learned that on the mountainside above Cedarn there were two or three clusters of cabins, rushed my order to the Cedarn Post Office, and a few days later had rented for the month of August what looked in the snapshots they sent me like a cross between a mujik's izba and Refuge Z, but it had a tiled bathroom and cost dearer than my Appalachian castle. Neither the Shades nor I breathed a word about our summer address but I knew, and they did not, that it was the same. The more I fumed at Sybil's evident intention to keep it concealed from me, the sweeter was the forevision of my sudden emergence in Tirolese garb from behind a boulder and of John's sheepish but pleased grin. During the fortnight that I had my demons fill my goetic mirror to overflow with those pink and mauve cliffs and black junipers and winding roads and sage brush changing to grass and lush blue flowers, and death-pale aspens, and an endless sequence of green-shorted Kinbotes meeting an anthology of poets and a brocken of their wives, I must have made some awful mistake in my incantations, for the mountain slope is dry and drear, and the Hurleys' tumble-down ranch, lifeless.

Line 293: She

Hazel Shade, the poet's daughter, born in 1934, died 1957 (see notes to lines 230 and 347).

Line 316: The Toothwort White haunted our woods in May

Frankly, I am not certain what this means. My dictionary defines "toothwort" as "a kind of cress" and the noun "white" as "any pure white breed of farm animal or a certain genus of lepidoptera." Little help is provided by the variant written in the margin:

In woods Virginia Whites occurred in May

Folklore characters, perhaps? Fairies? Or cabbage butterflies?

Line 319: wood duck

A pretty conceit. The wood duck, a richly colored bird, emerald, amethyst, carnelian, with black and white markings, is incomparably more beautiful than the much-overrated swan, a serpentine goose with a dirty neck of yellowish plush and a frogman's black rubber flaps.

Incidentally, the popular nomenclature of American animals reflects the simple utilitarian minds of ignorant pioneers and has not yet acquired the patina of European faunal names.

Line 334: Would never come for her

"Would he ever come for me?" I used to wonder waiting and waiting, in certain amber-and-rose crepuscules, for a ping-pong friend, or for old John Shade.

Line 347: old barn

This barn, or rather shed, where "certain phenomena" occurred in October 1956 (a few months prior to Hazel Shade's death) had belonged to one Paul Hentzner, an eccentric farmer of German extraction, with old-fashioned hobbies such as taxidermy and herborizing. Through an odd trick of atavism, he was (according to Shade who liked to talk about him—the only time, incidentally, when my sweet old friend became a tiny bit of a bore!) a throwback to the "curious Germans" who three centuries ago had been the fathers of the first great naturalists. Although by academic standards an uneducated man, with no real knowledge of far things in space or time, he had about him a colorful and earthy something that pleased John Shade much better than the suburban refinements of the English Department. He who displayed such fastidious care in his choice of fellow ramblers liked to trudge with the gaunt solemn German, every other evening, up the wood path to Dulwich, and all around his acquaintance's fields. Delighting as he did in the right word, he esteemed Hentzner for knowing "the names of things"—though some of those names were no doubt local monstrosities, or Germanisms, or pure inventions on the old rascal's part.

Now he was walking with another companion. Limpidly do I remember one perfect evening when my friend sparkled with quips, and marrowskies, and anecdotes which I gallantly countered with tales of Zembla and harebreath escapes! As we were skirting Dulwich Forest, he interrupted me to indicate a natural grotto in the mossy rocks by the side of the path under the flowering dogwoods. This was the spot where the good farmer invariably stopped, and once, when they happened to be accompanied by his little boy, the latter, as he trotted beside them, pointed and remarked informatively: "Here Papa pisses." Another, less pointless, story awaited me at the top of the hill, where a square plot invaded with willow herb, milkweed and ironweed, and teeming with butterflies, contrasted sharply with the goldenrod all around it. After Hentzner's wife had left him (around 1950) taking with her their child, he sold his farmhouse (now replaced by a drive-in cinema) and went to live in town; but on summer nights he used to take a sleeping bag to the barn that stood at the far end of the land he still owned, and there one night he passed away.

That barn had stood on the weedy spot Shade was poking at with Aunt Maud's favorite cane. One Saturday evening a young student employee from the campus hotel and a local hoyden went into it for some purpose or other and were chatting or dozing there when they were frightened out of their wits by rattling sounds and flying lights causing them to flee in disorder. Nobody really cared what had routed them—whether it was an outraged ghost or a rejected swain. But the *Wordsmith Gazette* ("The oldest student newspaper in the USA") picked up the incident and started to worry the stuffing out of it like a mischievous pup. Several self-styled psychic researchers visited the place and the whole business was so blatantly turning into a rag, with the participation of the most notorious college pranksters, that Shade complained to the authorities with the result that the useless barn was demolished as constituting a fire hazard.

From Jane P. I obtained however a good deal of quite different, and much more pathetic information—which explained to me why my friend had thought fit to regale me with commonplace student mischief, but also made me regret that I prevented him from getting to the point he was confusedly and self-consciously making (for as I have said in an earlier note, he never cared to refer to his dead child) by filling in a welcome pause with an extraordinary episode from the history of Onhava University. That episode took place in the year of grace 1876. But to return to Hazel Shade. She decided she wanted to investigate the "phenomena" herself for a paper ("on any subject") required in her psychology course by a cunning professor who was collecting data on "Autoneurynological Patterns among American university students." Her parents permitted her to make a nocturnal visit to the barn only under the condition that Jane P.—deemed a pillar of reliability—accompany her. Hardly had the girls settled down when an electric storm that was to last all night enveloped their refuge with such theatrical ululations and flashes as to make it impossible to attend to any indoor sounds or lights. Hazel did not give up, and a few days later asked Jane to come with her again, but Jane could not. She tells me she suggested that the White twins (nice fraternity boys accepted by the Shades) would come instead. But Hazel flatly refused this new arrangement, and after a row with her parents took her bull's-eye and notebook and set off alone. One can well imagine how the Shades dreaded a recrudescence of the poltergeist nuisance but the ever-sagacious Dr. Sutton affirmed—on what authority I cannot tell—that cases in which the same person was again involved in the same type of outbreaks after a lapse of six years were practically unknown.

Jane allowed me to copy out some of Hazel's notes from a typescript based on jottings made on the spot:

> 10:14 P.M. Investigation commenced.
>
> 10:23. Scrappy and scrabbly sounds.
>
> 10:25. A roundlet of pale light, the size of a small doily; flitted across the dark walls, the boarded windows, and the floor; changed its place; lingered here and there, dancing up and down; seemed to wait in teasing play for evadable pounce. Gone.
>
> 10:37. Back again.

The notes continue for several pages but for obvious reasons I must renounce to give them verbatim in this commentary. There were long pauses and "scratches and scrapings" again, and returns of the luminous circlet. She spoke to it. If asked something that it found deliciously silly ("Are you a will-o-the-wisp?") it would dash to and fro in ecstatic negation, and when it wanted to give a grave answer to a grave question ("Are you dead?") would slowly ascend with an air of gathering altitude for a weighty affirmative drop. For brief periods of time it responded to the alphabet she recited by staying put until the right letter was called whereupon it gave a small jump of approval. But these jumps would get more and more listless, and after a couple of words had been slowly spelled out, the roundlet went limp like a tired child and finally crawled into a chink; out of which it suddenly flew with extravagant brio and started to spin around the walls in its eagerness to resume the game. The jumble of broken words and meaningless syllables which she managed at last to collect came out in her dutiful notes as a short line of simple letter-groups. I transcribe:

> pada ata lane pad not ogo old wart alan ther tale feur
> far rant lant tal told

In her *Remarks*, the recorder states she had to recite the alphabet, or at least begin to recite it (there is a merciful preponderance of a's) eighty times, but of these, seventeen yielded no results. Divisions based on such variable intervals cannot be but rather arbitrary; some of the balderdash may be recombined into other lexical units making no better sense (e.g., "war," "talant," "her," "arrant," etc.). The barn ghost seems to have expressed himself with the empasted difficulty of apoplexy or of a half-awakening from a half-dream slashed by a sword of light on the ceiling, a military disaster with cosmic consequences that cannot be phrased distinctly by the thick unwilling tongue. And in this case we too might wish to cut short a reader's or bedfellow's questions by sinking back into oblivion's bliss—had not a diabolical force urged us to seek a secret design in the abracadabra,

812   Some kind of link-and-bobolink, some kind
813   Of correlated pattern in the game.

I abhor such games; they make my temples throb with abominable pain—but I have braved it and pored endlessly, with a commentator's infinite patience and disgust, over the crippled syllables in Hazel's report to find the least allusion to the poor girl's fate. Not one hint did I find. Neither old Hentzner's specter, nor an ambushed scamp's toy flashlight, nor her own imaginative hysteria, express anything here that might be construed, however remotely, as containing a warning, or having some bearing on the circumstances of her soon-coming death.

Hazel's report might have been longer if—as she told Jane—a renewal of the "scrabbling" had not suddenly jarred upon her tired nerves. The roundlet of light that until now had been keeping its distance made a pugnacious dash at her feet so that she nearly fell off the wooden block serving her as a seat. She became overwhelmingly conscious that she was alone in the company of an inexplicable and perhaps very evil being, and with a shudder that all but dislocated her shoulder blades she hastened to regain the heavenly shelter of the starry night. A familiar footpath with soothing gestures and other small tokens of consolation (lone cricket, lone streetlight) led her home. She stopped and let forth a howl of terror: a system of dark and pale patches coagulating into a phantastic figure had risen from the garden bench which the porch light just reached. I have no idea what the average temperature of an October night in New Wye may be but one is surprised that a father's anxiety should be great enough in the present case to warrant conducting a vigil in the open air in pajamas and the nondescript "bathrobe" which my birthday present was to replace (see note to line 181).

There are always "three nights" in fairy tales, and in this sad fairy tale there was a third one too. This time she wanted her parents to witness the "talking light" with her. The minutes of that third session in the barn have not been preserved but I offer the reader the following scene which I feel cannot be too far removed from the truth:

THE HAUNTED BARN

Pitch-darkness. Father, Mother *and* Daughter *are heard breathing gently in different corners. Three minutes pass.*

FATHER (*to Mother*)
Are you comfortable there?

MOTHER
Uh-huh. These potato sacks make a perfect—

DAUGHTER (*with steam-engine force*)
Sh-sh-sh!

Fifteen minutes pass in silence. The eye begins to make out here and there in the darkness bluish slits of night and one star.

MOTHER

That was Dad's tummy, I think—not a spook.

DAUGHTER (*mouthing it*)

Very funny!

Another fifteen minutes elapse. Father, deep in workshop thoughts, heaves a neutral sigh.

DAUGHTER

Must we sigh all the time?

Fifteen minutes elapse.

MOTHER

If I start snoring let Spook pinch me.

DAUGHTER (*overemphasizing self-control*)

Mother! Please! Please, Mother!

Father clears his throat but decides not to say anything. Twelve more minutes elapse.

MOTHER

Does anyone realize that there are still quite a few of those creampuffs in the refrigerator?

That does it.

DAUGHTER (*exploding*)

Why must you *spoil* everything? Why must you *always* spoil everything? Why can't you leave people *alone*? Don't touch me!

FATHER

Now look, Hazel, Mother won't say another word, and we'll go on with this—but we've been sitting an hour here and it's getting late.

Two minutes pass. Life is hopeless, afterlife heartless. Hazel is heard quietly weeping in the dark. John Shade lights a lantern. Sybil lights a cigarette. Meeting adjourned.

The light never came back but it gleams again in a short poem "The Nature of Electricity," which John Shade had sent to the New York magazine *The Beau and the Butterfly*, some time in 1958, but which appeared only after his death:

The dead, the gentle dead—who knows?—
In tungsten filaments abide,
And on my bedside table glows
Another man's departed bride.

And maybe Shakespeare floods a whole
Town with innumerable lights,
And Shelley's incandescent soul
Lures the pale moths of starless nights.

Streetlamps are numbered, and maybe
Number nine-hundred-ninety-nine
(So brightly beaming through a tree
So green) is an old friend of mine.

And when above the livid plain
Forked lightning plays, therein may dwell
The torments of a Tamerlane,
The roar of tyrants torn in hell.

Science tells us, by the way, that the Earth would not merely fall apart, but vanish like a ghost, if Electricity were suddenly removed from the world.

Lines 347–348: She twisted words

One of the examples her father gives is odd. I am quite sure it was I who one day, when we were discussing "mirror words," observed (and I recall the poet's expression of stupefaction) that "spider" in reverse is "redips," and "T. S. Eliot," "toilest." But then it is also true that Hazel Shade resembled me in certain respects.

Lines 367–370: then—pen, again—explain

In speech John Shade, as a good American, rhymed "again" with "pen" and not with "explain." The adjacent position of these rhymes is curious.

Line 376:   poem

I believe I can guess (in my bookless mountain cave) what poem is meant; but without looking it up I would not wish to name its author. Anyway, I deplore my friend's vicious thrusts at the most distinguished poets of his day.

Lines 376–377:   was said in English Litt to be

This is replaced in the draft by the more significant—and more tuneful—variant:

the Head of our Department deemed

Although it may be taken to refer to the man (whoever he was) who occupied this post at the time Hazel Shade was a student, the reader cannot be blamed for applying it to Paul H., Jr., the fine administrator and inept scholar who since 1957 headed the English Department of Wordsmith College. We met now and then (see Foreward and note to line 894) but not often. The Head of the Department to which I belonged was Prof. Nattochdag—"Netochka" as we called the dear man. Certainly the migraines that have lately tormented me to such a degree that I once had to leave in the midst of a concert at which I happened to be sitting beside Paul H., Jr., should not have been a stranger's business. They apparently were, very much so. He kept his eye on me, and immediately upon John Shade's demise circulated a mimeographed letter that began:

> Several members of the Department of English are painfully concerned over the fate of a manuscript poem, or parts of a manuscript poem, left by the late John Shade. The manuscript fell into the hands of a person who not only is unqualified for the job of editing it, belonging as he does to another department, but is known to have a deranged mind. One wonders whether some legal action, etc.

"Legal action," of course, might be taken by somebody else too. But no matter; one's just anger is mitigated by the satisfaction of foreknowing that the *engagé* gentleman will be less worried about the fate of my friend's poem after reading the passage commented here. Southey liked a roasted rat for supper—which is especially comic in view of the rats that devoured his Bishop.

Line 384: book on Pope

The title of this work which can be found in any college library is *Supremely Blest*, a phrase borrowed from a Popian line, which I remember but cannot quote exactly. The book is concerned mainly with Pope's technique but also contains pithy observations on "the stylized morals of his age."

Lines 385–386: Jane Dean, Pete Dean

The transparent pseudonyms of two innocent people. I visited Jane Provost when passing through Chicago in August. I found her still unmarried. She showed me some amusing photos of her cousin Peter and his friends. She told me—and I have no reason to disbelieve her words—that Peter Provost (whom I desired very very much to meet, but he was, alas, selling automobiles in Detroit) might have exaggerated a wee bit, but certainly did not fib, when explaining that he had to keep a promise made to one of his dearest fraternity friends, a glorious young athlete whose "garland" will not, one hopes, be "briefer than a girl's." Such obligations are not to be treated lightly or disdainfully. Jane said she had tried to talk to the Shades after the tragedy, and later had written Sybil a long letter that was never acknowledged. I said, displaying a bit of the slang I had recently started to master: "You are telling me!"

Lines 403–404: it's eight fifteen (And here time forked)

From here to line 474 two themes alternate in a synchronous arrangement: television in the Shades' parlor and the replay, as it were, of Hazel's (already adumbrated) actions from the moment Peter met his blind date (406–407) and apologized for having to leave in a hurry (426–428) to Hazel's ride in the bus (445–447 and 457–459), ending with the watchman's finding her body (475–477). I have italicized the Hazel theme.

The whole thing strikes me as too labored and long, especially since the synchronization device has been already worked to death by Flaubert and Joyce. Otherwise the pattern is exquisite.

Line 408: A male hand

On July 10, the day John Shade wrote this, and perhaps at the very minute he started to use his thirty-third index card for lines 406–416, Gradus was driving in a hired car from Geneva to Lex, where Odon was known to be resting, after completing his motion picture, at the villa of an old American friend, Joseph S. Lavender (the name hails from the laundry, not from the laund). Our brilliant schemer had been told that Joe Lavender collected photographs of the artistic type called in French *ombrioles.* He had *not* been told what exactly these were and dismissed them mentally as "lampshades with landscapes." His cretinous plan was to present himself as the agent of a Strasbourg art dealer and then, over drinks with Lavender and his house guest, endeavor to pick up clues to the King's whereabouts. He did not reckon with the fact that Donald Odon with his absolute sense of such things would have immediately deduced from the way Gradus displayed his empty palm before shaking hands or made a slight bow after every sip, and other tricks of demeanor (which Gradus himself did not notice in people but had acquired from them) that wherever he had been born he had certainly lived for a considerable time in a low-class Zemblan environment and was therefore a spy or worse. Gradus was also unaware that the *ombrioles* Lavender collected (and I am sure Joe will not resent this indiscretion) combined exquisite beauty with highly indecent subject matter—nudities blending with fig trees, oversize ardors, softly shaded hindercheeks, and also a dapple of female charms.

From his Geneva hotel Gradus had tried to get Lavender on the telephone but was told he could not be reached before noon. By noon Gradus was already under way and telephoned again, this time from Montreux. Lavender had been given the message and would Mr. Degré drop in around tea time. He luncheoned in a lakeside café, went for a stroll, asked the price of a small crystal giraffe in a souvenir shop, bought a newspaper, read it on a bench, and presently drove on. In the vicinity of Lex he lost his way among steep tortuous lanes. Upon stopping above a vineyard, at the rough entrance of an unfinished house, he was shown by the three index fingers of three masons the red roof of Lavender's villa high up in the ascending greenery on the opposite side of the road. He decided to leave the car and climb the stone steps of what looked like an easy short cut. While he was trudging up the walled walk with his eye on the rabbit foot of a poplar which now hid the red roof at the top of the climb, now disclosed it, the sun found a weak spot among the rain clouds and next moment a ragged blue hole in them grew a radiant rim. He felt the burden and the odor of his new brown suit bought in a Copenhagen store and already wrinkled. Puffing, consulting his wrist watch, and fanning himself with his trilby, also new, he reached at last the transverse continuation of the looping road he had left below. He crossed it, walked through a wicket and up a curving gravel path, and found himself in front of Lavender's villa. Its name, Libitina, was displayed in cursive script above one of the barred north windows, with its letters made of black wire and the dot over each of the three i's cleverly mimicked by the tarred head of a chalk-coated nail driven into the white façade. This device, and the north-facing window grates, Gradus had observed in Swiss villas before, but immunity to classical allusion deprived him of the pleasure he might have derived from the tribute that Lavender's macabre joviality had paid the Roman goddess of corpses and tombs. Another matter engaged his attention: from a corner casement came the sounds of a piano, a tumult of vigorous music which for some odd reason, as he was to tell me later, suggested to him a possibility he had not considered and caused his hand to fly to his hip pocket as he prepared to meet not Lavender and not Odon but that gifted hymnist, Charles the Beloved.

The music stopped as Gradus, confused by the whimsical shape of the house, hesitated before a glassed-in porch. An elderly footman in green appeared from a green side door and led him to another entrance. With a show of carelessness not improved by laborious repetition, Gradus asked him, first in mediocre French, then in worse English, and finally in fair German, if there were many guests staying in the house; but the man only smiled and bowed him into the music room. The musician had vanished. A harplike din still came from the grand piano upon which a pair of beach sandals stood as on the brink of a lily pond. From a window seat a gaunt jet-glittering lady stiffly arose and introduced herself as the governess of Mr. Lavender's nephew. Gradus mentioned his eagerness to see Lavender's sensational collection: this aptly defined its pictures of love-making in orchards, but the governess (whom the King had always called to her pleased face Mademoiselle Belle instead of Mademoiselle Baud) hastened to confess her total ignorance of her employer's hobbies and treasures and suggested the visitor's taking a look at the garden: "Gordon will show you his favorite flowers" she said, and called into the next room "Gordon!" Rather reluctantly there came out a slender but strong-looking lad of fourteen or fifteen dyed a nectarine hue by the sun. He had nothing on save a leopard-spotted loincloth. His closely cropped hair was a tint lighter than his skin. His lovely bestial face wore an expression both sullen and sly. Our preoccupied plotter did not register any of these details and merely experienced a general impression of indecency. "Gordon is a musical prodigy," said Miss Baud, and the boy winced. "Gordon, will you show the garden to this gentleman?" The boy acquiesced, adding he would take a dip if nobody minded. He put on his sandals and led the way out. Through light and shade walked the strange pair: the graceful boy wreathed about the loins with ivy and the seedy killer in his cheap brown suit with a folded newspaper sticking out of his left-hand coat pocket.

"That's the Grotto," said Gordon. "I once spent the night here with a friend." Gradus let his indifferent glance enter the mossy recess where one could glimpse a collapsible mattress with a dark stain on its orange nylon. The boy applied avid lips to a pipe of spring water and wiped his wet hands on his black bathing trunks. Gradus consulted his watch. They strolled on. "You have not seen anything yet," said Gordon.

Although the house possessed at least half-a-dozen water closets, Mr. Lavender in fond memory of his grandfather's Delaware farm, had installed a rustic privy under the tallest poplar of his splendid garden, and for chosen guests, whose sense of humor could stand it, he would unhook from the comfortable neighborhood of the billiard room fireplace a heart-shaped, prettily embroidered bolster to take with them to the throne.

The door was open and across its inner side a boy's hand had scrawled in charcoal: *The King was here.*

"That's a fine visiting card," remarked Gradus with a forced laugh. "By the way, where is he now, that king?"

"Who knows," said the boy striking his flanks clothed in white tennis shorts, "that was last year. I guess he was heading for the Côte d'Azur, but I am not sure."

Dear Gordon lied, which was nice of him. He knew perfectly well that his big friend was no longer in Europe; but dear Gordon should not have brought up the Riviera matter which happened to be true and the mention of which caused Gradus, who knew that Queen Disa had a palazzo there, to mentally slap his brow.

They had now reached the swimming pool. Gradus, in deep thought, sank down on a canvas stool. He should wire headquarters at once. No need to prolong this visit. On the other hand, a sudden departure might look suspicious. The stool creaked under him and he looked around for another seat. The young woodwose had now closed his eyes and was stretched out supine on the pool's marble margin; his Tarzan brief had been cast aside on the turf. Gradus spat in disgust and walked back towards the house. Simultaneously the elderly footman came running down the steps of the terrace to tell him in three languages that he was wanted on the telephone. Mr. Lavender could not make it after all but would like to talk to Mr. Degré. After an exchange of civilities there was a pause and Lavender asked: "Sure you aren't a mucking snooper from that French rag?" "A what?" said Gradus, pronouncing the last word as "vot." "A mucking snooping son of a bitch?" Gradus hung up.

He retrieved his car and drove up to a higher level on the hillside. From the same road bay, on a misty and luminous September day, with the diagonal of the first silver filament crossing the space between two balusters, the King had surveyed the twinkling ripples of Lake Geneva and had noted their antiphonal response, the flashing of tinfoil scares in the hillside vineyards. Gradus as he stood there, and moodily looked down at the red tiles of Lavender's villa snuggling among its protective trees, could make out, with some help from his betters, a part of the lawn and a segment of the pool, and even distinguish a pair of sandals on its marble rim—all that remained of Narcissus. One assumes he wondered if he should not hang around for a bit to make sure he had not been bamboozled. From far below mounted the clink and tinkle of distant masonry work, and a sudden train passed between gardens, and a heraldic butterfly *volant en arrière*, sable, a bend gules, traversed the stone parapet, and John Shade took a fresh card.

Line 413:   a nymph came pirouetting

In the draft there is the lighter and more musical:

413   A nymphet pirouetted

Lines 417–421:   I went upstairs, etc.

The draft yields an interesting variant:

417   I fled upstairs at the first quawk of jazz
      And read a galley proof: "Such verses as
      'See the blind beggar dance, the cripple sing,
      The sot a hero, lunatic a king'
      Smack of their heartless age." Then came your call

This is, of course, from Pope's *Essay on Man*. One knows not what to wonder at more: Pope's not finding a monosyllable to replace "hero" (for example, "man") so as to accommodate the definite article before the next word, or Shade's replacing an admirable passage by the much flabbier final text. Or was he afraid of offending an authentic king? In pondering the near past I have never been able to ascertain retrospectively if he really had "guessed my secret," as he once observed (see note to line 991).

Line 426: Just behind (one oozy footstep) Frost

The reference is, of course, to Robert Frost (b. 1874). The line displays one of those combinations of pun and metaphor at which our poet excels. In the temperature charts of poetry high is low, and low high, so that the degree at which perfect crystallization occurs is above that of tepid facility. This is what our modest poet says, in effect, respecting the atmosphere of his own fame.

Frost is the author of one of the greatest short poems in the English language, a poem that every American boy knows by heart, about the wintry woods, and the dreary dusk, and the little horsebells of gentle remonstration in the dull darkening air, and that prodigious and poignant end—two closing lines identical in every syllable, but one personal and physical, and the other metaphysical and universal. I dare not quote from memory lest I displace one small precious word.

With all his excellent gifts, John Shade could never make *his* snowflakes settle that way.

Line 431: March night . . . headlights from afar approached

Note how delicately at this point the television theme happens to merge with the girl's theme (see line 440, *more* headlights in the fog . . .).

Lines 433–434: To the . . . sea Which we had visited in thirty-three

In 1933, Prince Charles was eighteen and Disa, Duchess of Payn, five. The allusion is to Nice (see also line 240) where

the Shades spent the first part of that year; but here again, as
in regard to so many fascinating facets of my friend's past life,
I am not in the possession of particulars (who is to blame,
dear S.S?) and not in the position to say whether or not, in
the course of possible excursions along the coast, they ever
reached Cap Turc and glimpsed from an oleander-lined lane,
usually open to tourists, the Italianate villa built by Queen
Disa's grandfather in 1908, and called then *Villa Paradiso*, or
in Zemblan *Villa Paradisa*, later to forego the first half of its
name in honor of his favorite granddaughter. There she spent
the first fifteen summers of her life; thither did she return in
1953, "for reasons of health" (as impressed on the nation) but
really, a banished queen; and there she still dwells.

When the Zemblan Revolution broke out (May 1, 1958), she
wrote the King a wild letter in governess English, urging him
to come and stay with her until the situation cleared up. The
letter was intercepted by the Onhava police, translated into
crude Zemblan by a Hindu member of the Extremist party,
and then read aloud to the royal captive in a would-be ironic
voice by the preposterous commandant of the palace. There
happened to be in that letter one—only one, thank God—
sentimental sentence: "I want you to know that no matter
how much you hurt me, you cannot hurt my love," and this
sentence (if we re-English it from the Zemblan) came out as:
"I desire you and love when you flog me." He interrupted
the commandant, calling him a buffoon and a rogue, and insulting everybody around so dreadfully that the Extremists
had to decide fast whether to shoot him at once or let him
have the original of the letter.

Eventually he managed to inform her that he was confined
to the palace. Valiant Disa hurriedly left the Riviera and made
a romantic but fortunately ineffectual attempt to return to
Zembla. Had she been permitted to land, she would have
been forthwith incarcerated, which would have reacted on the
King's flight, doubling the difficulties of escape. A message
from the Karlists containing these simple considerations
checked her progress in Stockholm, and she flew back to her
perch in a mood of frustration and fury (mainly, I think, because the message had been conveyed to her by a cousin of
hers, good old Curdy Buff, whom she loathed). Several weeks

passed and she was soon in a state of even worse agitation owing to rumors that her husband might be condemned to death. She left Cap Turc again. She had traveled to Brussels and chartered a plane to fly north, when another message, this time from Odon, came, saying that the King and he were out of Zembla, and that she should quietly regain Villa Disa and await there further news. In the autumn of the same year she was informed by Lavender that a man representing her husband would be coming to discuss with her certain business matters concerning property she and her husband jointly owned abroad. She was in the act of writing on the terrace under the jacaranda a disconsolate letter to Lavender when the tall, sheared and bearded visitor with the bouquet of flowers-of-the-gods who had been watching her from afar advanced through the garlands of shade. She looked up—and of course no dark spectacles and no make-up could for a moment fool her.

Since her final departure from Zembla he had visited her twice, the last time two years before, and during that lapse of time her pale-skin, dark-hair beauty had acquired a new, mature and melancholy glow. In Zembla, where most females are freckled blondes, we have the saying: *belwif ivurkumpf wid snew ebanumf*, "A beautiful woman should be like a compass rose of ivory with four parts of ebony." And this was the trim scheme nature had followed in Disa's case. There was something else, something I was to realize only when I read *Pale Fire*, or rather reread it after the first bitter hot mist of disappointment had cleared before my eyes. I am thinking of lines 261–267 in which Shade describes his wife. At the moment of his painting that poetical portrait, the sitter was twice the age of Queen Disa. I do not wish to be vulgar in dealing with these delicate matters but the fact remains that sixty-year-old Shade is lending here a well-conserved coeval the ethereal and eternal aspect she retains, or should retain, in his kind noble heart. Now the curious thing about it is that Disa at thirty, when last seen in September 1958, bore a singular resemblance not, of course, to Mrs. Shade as she was when I met her, but to the idealized and stylized picture painted by the poet in those lines of *Pale Fire*. Actually it was idealized and stylized only in regard to the older woman; in regard to

Queen Disa, as she was that afternoon on that blue terrace, it represented a plain unretouched likeness. I trust the reader appreciates the strangeness of this, because if he does not, there is no sense in writing poems, or notes to poems, or anything at all.

She seemed also calmer than before; her self-control had improved. During the previous meetings, and throughout their marital life in Zembla, there had been, on her part, dreadful outbursts of temper. When in the first years of marriage he had wished to cope with those blazes and blasts, trying to make her take a rational view of her misfortune, he had found them very annoying; but gradually he learned to take advantage of them and welcomed them as giving him the opportunity of getting rid of her presence for lengthening periods of time by not calling her back after a sequence of doors had slammed ever more distantly, or by leaving the palace himself for some rural hideout.

In the beginning of their calamitous marriage he had strenuously tried to possess her but to no avail. He informed her he had never made love before (which was perfectly true insofar as the implied object could only mean one thing to her), upon which he was forced to endure the ridicule of having her dutiful purity involuntarily enact the ways of a courtesan with a client too young or too old; he said something to that effect (mainly to relieve the ordeal), and she made an atrocious scene. He farced himself with aphrodisiacs, but the anterior characters of her unfortunate sex kept fatally putting him off. One night when he tried tiger tea, and hopes rose high, he made the mistake of begging her to comply with an expedient which she made the mistake of denouncing as unnatural and disgusting. Finally he told her that an old riding accident was incapacitating him but that a cruise with his pals and a lot of sea bathing would be sure to restore his strength.

She had recently lost both parents and had no real friend to turn to for explanation and advice when the inevitable rumors reached her; these she was too proud to discuss with her ladies in waiting but she read books, found out all about our manly Zemblan customs, and concealed her naïve distress under a great show of sarcastic sophistication. He congratulated her on her attitude, solemnly swearing that he had given up, or at least would give up, the practices of his youth; but everywhere along the road powerful temptations stood at attention. He succumbed to them from time to time, then every other day, then several times daily—especially during the robust regime of Harfar Baron of Shalksbore, a phenomenally endowed young brute (whose family name, "knave's farm," is the most probable derivation of "Shakespeare"). Curdy Buff—as Harfar was nicknamed by his admirers—had a huge escort of acrobats and bareback riders, and the whole affair rather got out of hand so that Disa, upon unexpectedly returning from a trip to Sweden, found the Palace transformed into a circus. He again promised, again fell, and despite the utmost discretion was again caught. At last she removed to the Riviera leaving him to amuse himself with a band of Eton-collared, sweet-voiced minions imported from England.

What had the sentiments he entertained in regard to Disa ever amounted to? Friendly indifference and bleak respect. Not even in the first bloom of their marriage had he felt any tenderness or any excitement. Of pity, of heartache, there could be no question. He was, had always been, casual and heartless. But the heart of his dreaming self, both before and after the rupture, made extraordinary amends.

He dreamed of her more often, and with incomparably more poignancy, than his surface-life feelings for her warranted; these dreams occurred when he least thought of her, and worries in no way connected with her assumed her image in the subliminal world as a battle or a reform becomes a bird of wonder in a tale for children. These heart-rending dreams transformed the drab prose of his feelings for her into strong and strange poetry, subsiding undulations of which would flash and disturb him throughout the day, bringing back the pang and the richness—and then only the pang, and then only its glancing reflection—but not affecting at all his attitude towards the real Disa.

Her image, as she entered and re-entered his sleep, rising apprehensively from a distant sofa or going in search of the messenger who, they said, had just passed through the draperies, took into account changes of fashion; but the Disa wearing the dress he had seen on her the summer of the Glass Works explosion, or last Sunday, or in any other antechamber of time, forever remained exactly as she looked on the day he had first told her he did not love her. That happened during a hopeless trip to Italy, in a lakeside hotel garden—roses, black araucarias, rusty, greenish hydrangeas—one cloudless evening with the mountains of the far shore swimming in a sunset haze and the lake all peach syrup regularly rippled with pale blue, and the captions of a newspaper spread flat on the foul bottom near the stone bank perfectly readable through the shallow diaphanous filth, and because, upon hearing him out, she sank down on the lawn in an impossible posture, examining a grass culm and frowning, he had taken his words back at once; but the shock had fatally starred the mirror, and thenceforth in his dreams her image was infected with the memory of that confession as with some disease or the secret aftereffects of a surgical operation too intimate to be mentioned.

The gist, rather than the actual plot of the dream, was a constant refutation of his not loving her. His dream-love for her exceeded in emotional tone, in spiritual passion and depth, anything he had experienced in his surface existence. This love was like an endless wringing of hands, like a blundering of the soul through an infinite maze of hopelessness and remorse. They were, in a sense, amorous dreams, for they were permeated with tenderness, with a longing to sink his head onto her lap and sob away the monstrous past. They brimmed with the awful awareness of her being so young and so helpless. They were purer than his life. What carnal aura there was in them came not from her but from those with whom he betrayed her—prickly-chinned Phrynia, pretty Timandra with that boom under her apron—and even so the sexual scum remained somewhere far above the sunken treasure and was quite unimportant. He would see her being accosted by a misty relative so distant as to be practically featureless. She would quickly hide what she held and extend her arched hand to be kissed. He knew she had just come across a telltale object—a riding boot in his bed—establishing beyond any doubt his unfaithfulness. Sweat beaded her pale, naked forehead—but she had to listen to the prattle of a chance visitor or direct the movements of a workman with a ladder who was nodding his head and looking up as he carried it in his arms to the broken window. One might bear—a strong merciless dreamer might bear—the knowledge of her grief and pride but none could bear the sight of her automatic smile as she turned from the agony of the disclosure to the polite trivialities required of her. She would be canceling an illumination, or discussing hospital cots with the head nurse, or merely ordering breakfast for two in the sea cave—and through the everyday plainness of the talk, through the play of the charming gestures with which she always accompanied certain readymade phrases, he, the groaning dreamer, perceived the disarray of her soul and was aware that an odious, undeserved, humiliating disaster had befallen her, and that only obligations of etiquette and her staunch kindness to a guiltless third party gave her the force to smile. As one watched the light on her face, one foresaw it would fade in a moment, to be replaced—as soon as the visitor left—by that impossible little frown the dreamer could never forget. He would help her again to her feet on the same lakeside lawn, with parts of the lake fitting them-selves into the spaces between the rising balusters, and pres-ently he and she would be walking side by side along an anonymous alley, and he would feel she was looking at him out of the corner of a faint smile but when he forced himself to confront that questioning glimmer, she was no longer there. Everything had changed, everybody was happy. And he absolutely had to find her at once to tell her that he adored her, but the large audience before him separated him from the door, and the notes reaching him through a succession of hands said that she was not available; that she was inaugurat-ing a fire; that she had married an American businessman; that she had become a character in a novel; that she was dead.

No such qualms disturbed him as he sat now on the terrace of her villa and recounted his lucky escape from the Palace. She enjoyed his description of the underground link with the theater and tried to visualize the jolly scramble across the mountains; but the part concerning Garh displeased her as if, paradoxically, she would have preferred him to have gone through a bit of wholesome houghmagandy with the wench. She told him sharply to skip such interludes, and he made her a droll little bow. But when he began to discuss the political situation (two Soviet generals had just been attached to the Extremist government as Foreign Advisers), a familiar vacant expression appeared in her eyes. Now that he was safely out of the country, the entire blue bulk of Zembla, from Embla Point to Emblem Bay, could sink in the sea for all she cared. That he had lost weight was of more concern to her than that he had lost a kingdom. Perfunctorily she inquired about the crown jewels; he revealed to her their unusual hiding place, and she melted in girlish mirth as she had not done for years and years. "I do have some business matters to discuss," he said. "And there are papers you have to sign." Up in the trellis a telephone climbed with the roses. One of her former ladies in waiting, the languid and elegant Fleur de Fyler (now fortyish and faded), still wearing pearls in her raven hair and the traditional white mantilla, brought certain documents from Disa's boudoir. Upon hearing the King's mellow voice behind the laurels, Fleur recognized it before she could be misled by his excellent disguise. Two footmen, handsome young strangers of a marked Latin type, appeared with the tea and caught Fleur in mid-curtsey. A sudden breeze groped among the glycines. Defiler of flowers. He asked Fleur as she turned to go with the *Disa* orchids if she still played the viola. She shook her head several times not wishing to speak without addressing him and not daring to do so while the servants might be within earshot.

They were alone again. Disa quickly found the papers he needed. Having finished with that, they talked for a while about nice trivial things, such as the motion picture, based on a Zemblan legend, that Odon hoped to make in Paris or Rome. How would he represent, they wondered, the *narstran*, a hellish hall where the souls of murderers were tortured under a constant drizzle of drake venom coming down from the foggy vault? By and large the interview was proceeding in a most satisfactory manner—though her fingers trembled a little when her hand touched the elbow rest of his chair. Careful now.

"What are your plans?" she inquired. "Why can't you stay here as long as you want? Please do. I'll be going to Rome soon, you'll have the whole house to yourself. Imagine, you can bed here as many as forty guests, forty Arabian thieves." (Influence of the huge terracotta vases in the garden.)

He answered he would be going to America some time next month and had business in Paris tomorrow.

Why America? What would he do there?

Teach. Examine literary masterpieces with brilliant and charming young people. A hobby he could now freely indulge.

"And, of course, I don't know," she mumbled looking away, "I don't know but perhaps if you'd have nothing against it, I might visit New York—I mean, just for a week or two, and not this year but the next."

He complimented her on her silver-spangled jacket. She persevered: "Well?" "And your hairdo is most becoming." "Oh, what does it matter," she wailed, "what on earth does anything matter!" "I must be on my way," he whispered with a smile and got up. "Kiss me," she said, and was like a limp, shivering ragdoll in his arms for a moment.

He walked to the gate. At the turn of the path he glanced back and saw in the distance her white figure with the listless grace of ineffable grief bending over the garden table, and suddenly a fragile bridge was suspended between waking indifference and dream-love. But she moved, and he saw it was not she at all but only poor Fleur de Fyler collecting the documents left among the tea things. (See note to line 80.)

When in the course of an evening stroll in May or June, 1959, I offered Shade all this marvelous material, he looked at me quizzically and said: "That's all very well, Charles. But there are just two questions. How can you know that all this intimate stuff about your rather appalling king is true? And if true, how can one hope to print such personal things about people who, presumably, are still alive?"

"My dear John," I replied gently and urgently, "do not worry about trifles. Once transmuted by you into poetry, the stuff *will* be true, and the people *will* come alive. A poet's purified truth can cause no pain, no offense. True art is above false honor."

"Sure, sure," said Shade. "One can harness words like performing fleas and make them drive other fleas. Oh, sure."

"And moreover," I continued as we walked down the road right into a vast sunset, "as soon as your poem is ready, as soon as the glory of Zembla merges with the glory of your verse, I intend to divulge to you an ultimate truth, an extraordinary secret, that will put your mind completely at rest."

Line 469: his gun

Gradus, as he drove back to Geneva, wondered when he would be able to use it, that gun. The afternoon was unbearably hot. The lake had developed a scaling of silver and a touch of reflected thunderhead. As many old glaziers, he could deduce rather accurately water temperature from certain indices of brilliancy and motion, and now judged it to be at least 23°. As soon as he got back to his hotel he made a long-distance call to headquarters. It proved a terrible experience. Under the assumption that it would attract less attention than a BIC language, the conspirators conducted telephone conversations in English—broken English, to be exact, with one tense, no articles, and two pronunciations, both wrong. Furthermore, by their following the crafty system (invented in the chief BIC country) of using two different sets of code words— headquarters, for instance, saying "bureau" for "king," and Gradus saying "letter," they enormously increased the difficulty of communication. Each side, finally, had forgotten the meaning of certain phrases pertaining to the other's vocabulary so that in result, their tangled and expensive talk combined charades with an obstacle race in the dark. Headquarters thought it understood that letters from the King divulging his whereabouts could be obtained by breaking into Villa Disa and rifling the Queen's bureau; Gradus, who had said nothing of the sort, but had merely tried to convey the results of his Lex visit, was chagrined to learn that instead of looking for the King in Nice he was expected to wait for a consignment of canned salmon in Geneva. One thing, though, came out clearly: next time he should not telephone, but wire or write.

Line 470: Negro

We were talking one day about Prejudice. Earlier, at lunch in the Faculty Club, Prof. H.'s guest, a decrepit emeritus from

Boston—whom his host described with deep respect as "a true Patrician, a real blue-blooded Brahmin" (the Brahmin's grandsire sold braces in Belfast)—had happened to say quite naturally and debonairly, in allusion to the origins of a not very engaging new man in the College Library, "one of the Chosen People, I understand" (enunciated with a small snort of comfortable relish); upon which Assistant Professor Misha Gordon, a red-haired musician, had roundly remarked that "of course, God might choose His people but man should choose his expressions."

As we strolled back, my friend and I, to our adjacent castles, under the sort of light April rain that in one of his lyrical poems he calls:

A rapid pencil sketch of Spring

Shade said that more than anything on earth he loathed Vulgarity and Brutality, and that one found these two ideally united in racial prejudice. He said that, as a man of letters, he could not help preferring "is a Jew" to "is Jewish" and "is a Negro" to "is colored"; but immediately added that this way of alluding to two kinds of bias in one breath was a good example of careless, or demagogic, lumping (much exploited by Left-Wingers) since it erased the distinction between two historical hells: diabolical persecution and the barbarous traditions of slavery. On the other hand (he admitted) the tears of all ill-treated human beings, throughout the hopelessness of all time, mathematically equaled each other; and perhaps (he thought) one did not err too much in tracing a family likeness (tensing of simian nostrils, sickening dulling of eyes) between the jasmine-belt lyncher and the mystical anti-Semite when under the influence of their pet obsessions. I said that a young Negro gardener (see note to line 998) whom I had recently hired—soon after the dismissal of an unforgettable roomer (see Foreword)—invariably used the word "colored." As a dealer in old and new words (observed Shade) he strongly objected to that epithet not only because it was artistically misleading, but also because its sense depended too much upon application and applier. Many competent Negroes (he agreed) considered it to be the only dignified word, emotionally neutral and ethically inoffensive; their endorsement obliged decent non-Negroes to follow their lead, and poets do not like to be led; but the genteel adore endorsements and now use "colored man" for "Negro" as they do "nude" for "naked" or "perspiration" for "sweat"; although of course (he conceded) there might be times when the poet welcomed the dimple of a marble haunch in "nude" or an appropriate beadiness in "perspiration." One also heard it used (he continued) by the prejudiced as a jocular euphemism in a darky anecdote when something funny is said or done by "the colored gentleman" (a sudden brother here of "the Hebrew gentleman" in Victorian novelettes).

I had not quite understood his *artistic* objection to "colored." He explained it thus: Figures in the first scientific works on flowers, birds, butterflies and so forth were hand-painted by diligent aquarellists. In defective or premature publications the figures on some plates remained blank. The juxtaposition of the phrases "a white" and "a colored man" always reminded my poet, so imperiously as to dispel their accepted sense, of those outlines one longed to fill with their lawful colors—the green and purple of an exotic plant, the solid blue of a plumage, the geranium bar of a scalloped wing. "And moreover [he said] we, whites, are not white at all, we are mauve at birth, then tea-rose, and later all kinds of repulsive colors."

Line 475:   A watchman, Father Time

The reader should notice the nice response to line 312.

Line 490:   Exe

Exe obviously stands for Exton, a factory town on the south shore of Omega Lake. It has a rather famous natural history museum with many showcases containing birds collected and mounted by Samuel Shade.

Line 493:   She took her poor young life

The following note is not an apology of suicide—it is the simple and sober description of a spiritual situation.

The more lucid and overwhelming one's belief in Providence, the greater the temptation to get it over with, this business of life, but the greater too one's fear of the terrible sin implicit in self-destruction. Let us first consider the temptation. As more thoroughly discussed elsewhere in this commentary (see note to line 550), a serious conception of any form of afterlife inevitably and necessarily presupposes some degree of belief in Providence; and, conversely, deep Christian faith presupposes some belief in some sort of spiritual survival. The vision of that survival need not be a rational one, i.e., need not present the precise features of personal fancies or the general atmosphere of a subtropical Oriental park. In fact, a good Zemblan Christian is taught that true faith is not there to supply pictures or maps, but that it should quietly content itself with a warm haze of pleasurable anticipation. To take a homely example: little Christopher's family is about to migrate to a distant colony where his father has been assigned to a lifetime post. Little Christopher, a frail lad of nine or ten, relies completely (so completely, in fact, as to blot out the very awareness of this reliance) on his elders' arranging all the details of departure, passage and arrival. He cannot imagine, nor does he try to imagine, the particular aspects of the new place awaiting him but he is dimly and comfortably convinced that it will be even better than his homestead, with the big oak, and the mountain, and his pony, and the park, and the stable, and Grimm, the old groom, who has a way of fondling him whenever nobody is around.

Something of this simple trust we too should have. With this divine mist of utter dependence permeating one's being, no wonder one is tempted, no wonder one weighs on one's palm with a dreamy smile the compact firearm in its case of suede leather hardly bigger than a castlegate key or a boy's seamed purse, no wonder one peers over the parapet into an inviting abyss.

I am choosing these images rather casually. There are purists who maintain that a gentleman should use a brace of pistols, one for each temple, or a bare botkin (note the correct spelling), and that ladies should either swallow a lethal dose

or drown with clumsy Ophelia. Humbler humans have preferred sundry forms of suffocation, and minor poets have even
tried such fancy releases as vein tapping in the quadruped tub
of a drafty boardinghouse bathroom. All this is uncertain and
messy. Of the not very many ways known of shedding one's
body, falling, falling, falling is the supreme method, but you
have to select your sill or ledge very carefully so as not to hurt
yourself or others. Jumping from a high bridge is not recommended even if you cannot swim, for wind and water
abound in weird contingencies, and tragedy ought not to cul-
minate in a record dive or a policeman's promotion. If you
rent a cell in the luminous waffle, room 1915 or 1959, in a tall
business center hotel browing the star dust, and pull up the
window, and gently—not fall, not jump—but roll out as you
should for air comfort, there is always the chance of knocking
clean through into your own hell a pacific noctambulator
walking his dog; in this respect a back room might be safer,
especially if giving on the roof of an old tenacious normal
house far below where a cat may be trusted to flash out of
the way. Another popular take-off is a mountaintop with a
sheer drop of say 500 meters but you must find it, because
you will be surprised how easy it is to miscalculate your de-
flection offset, and have some hidden projection, some fool
of a crag, rush forth to catch you, causing you to bounce off
it into the brush, thwarted, mangled and unnecessarily alive.
The ideal drop is from an aircraft, your muscles relaxed, your
pilot puzzled, your packed parachute shuffled off, cast off,
shrugged off—farewell, *shootka* (little chute)! Down you go,
but all the while you feel suspended and buoyed as you somersault in slow motion like a somnolent tumbler pigeon, and
sprawl supine on the eiderdown of the air, or lazily turn to
embrace your pillow, enjoying every last instant of soft, deep,
death-padded life, with the earth's green seesaw now above,
now below, and the voluptuous crucifixion, as you stretch
yourself in the growing rush, in the nearing swish, and then
your loved body's obliteration in the Lap of the Lord. If I
were a poet I would certainly make an ode to the sweet urge
to close one's eyes and surrender utterly unto the perfect
safety of wooed death. Ecstatically one forefeels the vastness
of the Divine Embrace enfolding one's liberated spirit, the

warm bath of physical dissolution, the universal unknown engulfing the minuscule unknown that had been the only real part of one's temporary personality.

When the soul adores Him Who guides it through mortal life, when it distinguishes His sign at every turn of the trail, painted on the boulder and notched in the fir trunk, when every page in the book of one's personal fate bears His watermark, how can one doubt that He will also preserve us through all eternity?

So what can stop one from effecting the transition? What can help us to resist the intolerable temptation? What can prevent us from yielding to the burning desire for merging in God?

We who burrow in filth every day may be forgiven perhaps the one sin that ends all sins.

Line 501:   L'if

The yew in French. It is curious that the Zemblan word for the weeping willow is also "*if*" (the yew is *tas*).

Line 502:   The grand potato

An execrable pun, deliberately placed in this epigraphic position to stress lack of respect for Death. I remember from my schoolroom days Rabelais' *soi-disant* "last words" among other bright bits in some French manual: *Je m'en vais chercher le grand peut-être.*

Line 502:   IPH

Good taste and the law of libel prevent me from disclosing the real name of the respectable institute of higher philosophy at which our poet pokes a good deal of fanciful fun in this canto. Its terminal initials, HP, provide its students with the abbreviation Hi-Phi, and Shade neatly parodies this in his IPH, or If, combinations. It is situated, most picturesquely, in a southwestern state that must remain anonymous here.

I am also obliged to observe that I strongly disapprove of the flippancy with which our poet treats, in this canto, certain aspects of spiritual hope which religion alone can fulfill (see also note to 549).

Line 549:   While snubbing gods including the big G

Here indeed is the Gist of the matter. And this, I think, not only the institute (see line 517) but our poet himself missed. For a Christian, no Beyond is acceptable or imaginable without the participation of God in our eternal destiny, and this in turn implies a condign punishment for every sin, great and small. My little diary happens to contain a few jottings referring to a conversation the poet and I had on June 23 "on my terrace after a game of chess, a draw." I transcribe them here only because they cast a fascinating light on his attitude toward the subject.

I had mentioned—I do not recall in what connection—certain differences between my Church and his. It should be noted that our Zemblan brand of Protestantism is rather closely related to the "higher" churches of the Anglican Communion, but has some magnificent peculiarities of its own. The Reformation with us had been headed by a composer of genius; our liturgy is penetrated with rich music; our boy choirs are the sweetest in the world. Sybil Shade came from a Catholic family but since early girlhood developed, as she told me herself, "a religion of her own"—which is generally synonymous, at the best, with a half-hearted attachment to some half-heathen sect or, at the worst, with tepid atheism. She had weaned her husband not only from the Episcopal Church of his fathers, but from all forms of sacramental worship.

We happened to start speaking of the general present-day nebulation of the notion of "sin," of its confusion with the much more carnally colored idea of "crime," and I alluded briefly to my childhood contacts with certain rituals of our church. Confession with us is auricular and is conducted in a richly ornamented recess, the confessionist holding a lighted taper and standing with it beside the priest's high-backed seat which is shaped almost exactly as the coronation chair of a

Scottish king. Little polite boy that I was, I always feared to stain his purple-black sleeve with the scalding tears of wax that kept dripping onto my knuckles, forming there tight little crusts, and I was fascinated by the illumed concavity of his ear resembling a seashell or a glossy orchid, a convoluted receptacle that seemed much too large for the disposal of my peccadilloes.

SHADE: All the seven deadly sins are peccadilloes but without three of them, Pride, Lust and Sloth, poetry might never have been born.

KINBOTE: Is it fair to base objections upon obsolete terminology?

SHADE: All religions are based upon obsolete terminology.

KINBOTE: What we term Original Sin can never grow obsolete.

SHADE: I know nothing about that. In fact when I was small I thought it meant Cain killing Abel. Personally, I am with the old snuff-takers: *L'homme est né bon*.

KINBOTE: Yet disobeying the Divine Will is a fundamental definition of Sin.

SHADE: I cannot disobey something which I do not know and the reality of which I have the right to deny.

KINBOTE: Tut-tut. Do you also deny that there are sins?

SHADE: I can name only two: murder, and the deliberate infliction of pain.

KINBOTE: Then a man spending his life in absolute solitude could not be a sinner?

SHADE: He could torture animals. He could poison the springs on his island. He could denounce an innocent man in a posthumous manifesto.

KINBOTE: And so the password is—?

SHADE: Pity.

KINBOTE: But who instilled it in us, John? Who is the Judge of life, and the Designer of death?

SHADE: Life is a great surprise. I do not see why death should not be an even greater one.

KINBOTE: Now I have caught you, John: once we deny a Higher Intelligence that plans and administrates our individual hereafters we are bound to accept the unspeakably dreadful notion of Chance reaching into eternity. Consider the situation. Throughout eternity our poor ghosts are exposed to nameless vicissitudes. There is no appeal, no advice, no support, no protection, nothing. Poor Kinbote's ghost, poor Shade's shade, may have blundered, may have taken the wrong turn somewhere—oh, from sheer absent-mindedness, or simply through ignorance of a trivial rule in the preposterous game of nature—if there be any rules.

SHADE: There are rules in chess problems: interdiction of dual solutions, for instance.

KINBOTE: I had in mind diabolical rules likely to be broken by the other party as soon as we come to understand them. That is why goetic magic does not always work. The demons in their prismatic malice betray the agreement between us and them, and we are again in the chaos of chance. Even if we temper Chance with Necessity and allow godless determinism, the mechanism of cause and effect, to provide our souls after death with the dubious solace of metastatistics, we still have to reckon with the individual mishap, the thousand and second highway accident of those scheduled for Independence Day in Hades. No-no, if we want to be serious about the hereafter let us not begin by degrading it to the level of a science-fiction yarn or a spiritualistic case history. The idea of one's soul plunging into limitless and chaotic afterlife with no Providence to direct her—

SHADE: There is always a psychopompos around the corner, isn't there?

KINBOTE: Not around *that* corner, John. With no Providence the soul must rely on the dust of its husk, on the experience gathered in the course of corporeal confinement, and cling childishly to small-town principles, local by-laws and a personality consisting mainly of the shadows of its own prison bars. Such an idea is not to be entertained one instant by the religious mind. How much more intelligent it is—even from a proud infidel's point of view!—to accept God's Presence— a faint phosphorescence at first, a pale light in the dimness of bodily life, and a dazzling radiance after it? I too, I too, my dear John, have been assailed in my time by religious doubts. The church helped me to fight them off. It also helped me not to ask too much, not to demand too clear an image of what is unimaginable. St. Augustine said—

SHADE: Why must one *always* quote St. Augustine to me?

KINBOTE: As St. Augustine said, "One can know what God is not; one cannot know what He is." I think I know what He is not: He is not despair, He is not terror, He is not the earth in one's rattling throat, not the black hum in one's ears fading to nothing in nothing. I know also that the world could not have occurred fortuitously and that somehow Mind is involved as a main factor in the making of the universe. In trying to find the right name for that Universal Mind, or First Cause, or the Absolute, or Nature, I submit that the Name of God has priority.

Line 550: debris

I wish to say something about an earlier note (to line 12). Conscience and scholarship have debated the question, and I now think that the two lines given in that note are distorted and tainted by wistful thinking. It is the *only* time in the course of the writing of these difficult comments, that I have tarried, in my distress and disappointment, on the brink of falsification. I must ask the reader to ignore those two lines (which, I am afraid, do not even scan properly). I could strike them out before publication but that would mean reworking the entire note, or at least a considerable part of it, and I have no time for such stupidities.

Lines 557–558: How to locate in blackness, with a gasp, Terra the Fair, an orbicle of jasp

The loveliest couplet in this canto.

Line 579: the other

Far from me be it to hint at the existence of some other woman in my friend's life. Serenely he played the part of exemplary husband assigned to him by his small-town admirers and was, besides, mortally afraid of his wife. More than once did I stop the gossipmongers who linked his name with that of one of his students (see Foreword). Of late, American novelists, most of whom are members of a United English Department that, with one thing and another, must be more soaked in literary talent, Freudian fancies, and ignoble heterosexual lust than all the rest of the world, have driven the topic to extinction; therefore I could not face the tedium of introducing that young lady here. Anyway, I hardly knew her. One evening I invited her to a little party with the Shades for the express purpose of refuting those rumors; and that reminds me I should say something about the curious rituals of invitation and counterinvitation in bleak New Wye.

Upon referring to my little diary, I see that during the five-month period of my intercourse with the Shades I was invited to their table exactly three times. Initiation took place on Saturday, March the 14th, when I dined at their house with the following people: Nattochdag (whom I saw every day in his office); Professor Gordon of the Music Department (who completely dominated the conversation); the Head of the Russian Department (a farcical pedant of whom the less said the better); and three or four interchangeable women (of whom one—Mrs. Gordon, I think) was enceinte, and another, a perfect stranger, steadily talked to me, or rather *into* me, from eight to eleven owing to an unfortunate afterdinner distribution of available seats. My next treat, a smaller but by no means cozier *souper* on Saturday, May 23, was attended by Milton Stone (a new librarian, with whom Shade discussed till midnight the classification of certain Wordsmithiana); good old Nattochdag (whom I continued to see every day); and an undeodorized Frenchwoman (who gave me a complete picture of language-teaching conditions at the University of California). The date of my third and last meal at the Shades is not entered in my little book but I know it was one morning in June when I brought over a beautiful plan I had drawn of the King's Palace in Onhava with all sorts of heraldic niceties, and a touch of gold paint that I had some trouble in obtaining, and was graciously urged to stay for an impromptu lunch. I should add that, despite my protests, at all three meals my vegetarian limitations of fare were not taken into account, and I was exposed to animal matter in, or around, some of the contaminated greens I might have deigned to taste. I revanched myself rather neatly. Of a dozen or so invitations that I extended, the Shades accepted just three. Every one of these meals was built around some vegetable that I subjected to as many exquisite metamorphoses as Parmentier had his pet tuber undergo. Every time I had but one additional guest to entertain Mrs. Shade (who, if you please—thinning my voice to a feminine pitch—was allergic to artichokes, avocado pears, African acorns—in fact to everything beginning with an "a"). I find nothing more conducive to the blunting of one's appetite than to have none but elderly persons sitting around one at table, fouling their napkins with the disintegration of their make-up, and surreptitiously trying, behind noncommittal smiles, to dislodge the red-hot torture point of a raspberry seed from between false gum and dead gum. So I had young people, students: the first time, the son of a padishah; the second time, my gardener; and the third time, that girl in the black leotard, with that long white face and eyelids painted a ghoulish green; but she came very late, and the Shades left very early—in fact, I doubt if the confrontation lasted more than ten minutes, whereupon I had the task of entertaining the young lady with phonograph records far into the night when at last she rang up somebody to accompany her to a "diner" in Dulwich.

Line 584: The mother and the child

Es ist die Mutter mit ihrem Kind (see note to line 664).

Line 596: Points at the puddles in his basement room

We all know those dreams in which something Stygian soaks through and Lethe leaks in the dreary terms of defective plumbing. Following this line, there is a false start preserved in the draft—and I hope the reader will feel something of the chill that ran down my long and supple spine when I discovered this variant:

> Should the dead murderer try to embrace
> His outraged victim whom he now must face?
> Do objects have a soul? Or perish must
> Alike great temples and Tanagra dust?

The last syllable of "Tanagra" and the first three letters of "dust" form the name of the murderer whose *shargar* (puny ghost) the radiant spirit of our poet was soon to face. "Simple chance!" the pedestrian reader may cry. But let him try to see, as I have tried to see, how many such combinations are possible and plausible. "Lenin*grad us*ed to be Petrograd?" "A pri*g rad* (obs. past tense of read) *us*?"

This variant is so prodigious that only scholarly discipline and a scrupulous regard for the truth prevented me from inserting it here, and deleting four lines elsewhere (for example, the weak lines 627–630) so as to preserve the length of the poem.

Shade composed these lines on Tuesday, July 14th. What was Gradus doing that day? Nothing. Combinational fate rests on its laurels. We saw him last on the late afternoon of July 10th when he returned from Lex to his hotel in Geneva, and there we left him.

For the next four days Gradus remained fretting in Geneva. The amusing paradox with these men of action is that they constantly have to endure long stretches of otiosity that they are unable to fill with anything, lacking as they do the resources of an adventurous mind. As many people of little culture, Gradus was a voracious reader of newspapers, pamphlets, chance leaflets and the multilingual literature that comes with nose drops and digestive tablets; but this summed up his concessions to intellectual curiosity, and since his eyesight was not too good, and the consumability of local news not unlimited, he had to rely a great deal on the torpor of sidewalk cafés and on the makeshift of sleep.

How much happier the wide-awake indolents, the monarchs among men, the rich monstrous brains deriving intense enjoyment and rapturous pangs from the balustrade of a terrace at nightfall, from the lights and the lake below, from the distant mountain shapes melting into the dark apricot of the afterglow, from the black conifers outlined against the pale ink of the zenith, and from the garnet and green flounces of the water along the silent, sad, forbidden shoreline. Oh my sweet Boscobel! And the tender and terrible memories, and the shame, and the glory, and the maddening intimations, and the star that no party member can ever reach.

On Wednesday morning, still without news, Gradus telegraphed headquarters saying that he thought it unwise to wait any longer and that he would be staying at Hotel Lazuli, Nice.

Lines 597–608:   the thoughts we should roll-call, etc.

This passage should be associated in the reader's mind with the extraordinary variant given in the preceding note, for only a week later Tana*gra du*st and "our royal hands" were to come together, in real life, in real death.

Had he not fled, our Charles II might have been executed; this would have certainly happened had he been apprehended between the palace and the Rippleson Caves; but he sensed those thick fingers of fate only seldom during his flight; he sensed them feeling for him (as those of a grim old shepherd checking a daughter's virginity) when he was slipping, that night, on the damp ferny flank of Mt. Mandevil (see note to line 149), and next day, at a more eerie altitude, in the heady blue, where the mountaineer becomes aware of a phantom companion. Many times that night our King cast himself upon the ground with the desperate resolution of resting there till dawn that he might shift with less torment what hazard soever he ran. (I am thinking of yet another Charles, another long dark man above two yards high.) But it was all rather physical, or neurotic, and I know perfectly well that my King, if caught and condemned and led away to be shot, would have behaved as he does in lines 606–608: thus he would look about him with insolent composure, and thus he would

> Taunt our inferiors, cheerfully deride
> The dedicated imbeciles and spit
> Into their eyes just for the fun of it

Let me close this important note with a rather anti-Darwinian aphorism: The one who kills is *always* his victim's inferior.

Line 603:   Listen to distant cocks crow

One will recall the admirable image in a recent poem by Edsel Ford:

> And often when the cock crew, shaking fire
> Out of the morning and the misty mow

A mow (in Zemblan *muwan*) is the field next to a barn.

Lines 609–614:   Nor can one help, etc.

This passage is different in the draft:

> 609   Nor can one help the exile caught by death
> In a chance inn exposed to the hot breath
> Of this America, this humid night:
> Through slatted blinds the stripes of colored light
> Grope for his bed—magicians from the past
> With philtered gems—and life is ebbing fast.

This describes rather well the "chance inn," a log cabin, with a tiled bathroom, where I am trying to coordinate these notes. At first I was greatly bothered by the blare of diabolical radio music from what I thought was some kind of amusement park across the road—it turned out to be camping tourists—and I was thinking of moving to another place, when they forestalled me. Now it is quieter, except for an irritating wind rattling through the withered aspens, and Cedarn is again a ghost town, and there are no summer fools or spies to stare at me, and my little blue-jeaned fisherman no longer stands on his stone in the stream, and perhaps it is better so.

Line 615:   two tongues

English and Zemblan, English and Russian, English and Lettish, English and Estonian, English and Lithuanian, English and Russian, English and Ukrainian, English and Polish, English and Czech, English and Russian, English and Hungarian, English and Rumanian, English and Albanian, English and Bulgarian, English and Serbo-Croatian, English and Russian, American and European.

Line 619: tuber's eye

The pun sprouts (see line 502).

Line 627: The great Starover Blue

Presumably, permission from Prof. Blue was obtained but even so the plunging of a real person, no matter how sportive and willing, into an invented milieu where he is made to perform in accordance with the invention, strikes one as a singularly tasteless device, especially since other real-life characters, except members of the family, of course, are pseudonymized in the poem.

This name, no doubt, is most tempting. The star over the blue eminently suits an astronomer though actually neither his first nor second name bears any relation to the celestial vault: the first was given him in memory of his grandfather, a Russian *starover* (accented, incidentally, on the ultima), that is, Old Believer (member of a schismatic sect), named Sinyavin, from *siniy*, Russ. "blue." This Sinyavin migrated from Saratov to Seattle and begot a son who eventually changed his name to Blue and married Stella Lazurchik, an Americanized Kashube. So it goes. Honest Starover Blue will probably be surprised by the epithet bestowed upon him by a jesting Shade. The writer feels moved to pay here a small tribute to the amiable old freak, adored by everybody on the campus and nicknamed by the students Colonel Starbottle, evidently because of his exceptionally convivial habits. After all, there were other great men in our poet's entourage—for example, that distinguished Zemblan scholar Oscar Nattochdag.

Line 629: The fate of beasts

Above this the poet wrote and struck out:

The madman's fate

The ultimate destiny of madmen's souls has been probed by many Zemblan theologians who generally hold the view that even the most demented mind still contains within its diseased mass a sane basic particle that survives death and suddenly expands, bursts out as it were, in peals of healthy and triumphant laughter when the world of timorous fools and trim blockheads has fallen away far behind. Personally, I have not known any lunatics; but have heard of several amusing cases in New Wye ("Even in Arcady am I," says Dementia, chained to her gray column). There was for instance a student who went berserk. There was an old tremendously trustworthy college porter who one day, in the Projection Room, showed a squeamish coed something of which she had no doubt seen better samples; but my favorite case is that of an Exton railway employee whose delusion was described to me by Mrs. H., of all people. There was a big Summer School party at the Hurleys', to which one of my second ping-pong table partners, a pal of the Hurley boys had taken me because I knew my poet was to recite there something and I was beside myself with apprehension believing it might be my Zembla (it proved to be an obscure poem by one of his obscure friends—my Shade was very kind to the unsuccessful). The reader will understand if I say that, at my altitude, I can never feel "lost" in a crowd, but it is also true that I did not know many people at the H.'s. As I circulated, with a smile on my face and a cocktail in my hand, through the crush, I espied at last the top of my poet's head and the bright brown chignon of Mrs. H. above the backs of two adjacent chairs. At the moment I advanced behind them I heard him object to some remark she had just made:

"That is the wrong word," he said. "One should not apply it to a person who deliberately peels off a drab and unhappy past and replaces it with a brilliant invention. That's merely turning a new leaf with the left hand."

I patted my friend on the head and bowed slightly to Eberthella H. The poet looked at me with glazed eyes. She said:

"You must help us, Mr. Kinbote: I maintain that what's his name, old—the old man, you know, at the Exton railway station, who thought he was God and began redirecting the trains, was technically a loony, but John calls him a fellow poet."

"We all are, in a sense, poets, Madam," I replied, and offered a lighted match to my friend who had his pipe in his teeth and was beating himself with both hands on various parts of his torso.

I am not sure this trivial variant has been worth commenting; indeed, the whole passage about the activities of the IPH would be quite Hudibrastic had its pedestrian verse been one foot shorter.

Line 662: Who rides so late in the night and the wind

This line, and indeed the whole passage (lines 653–664), allude to the well-known poem by Goethe about the erlking, hoary enchanter of the elf-haunted alderwood, who falls in love with the delicate little boy of a belated traveler. One cannot sufficiently admire the ingenious way in which Shade manages to transfer something of the broken rhythm of the ballad (a trisyllabic meter at heart) into his iambic verse:

662 Who rides so late in the night and the wind

663 . . . .

664 . . . . It is the father with his child

Goethe's two lines opening the poem come out most exactly and beautifully, with the bonus of an unexpected rhyme (also in French: *vent-enfant*), in my own language:

> *Ret woren ok spoz on natt ut vett?*
>
> *Eto est votchez ut mid ik dett.*

Another fabulous ruler, the last king of Zembla, kept repeating these haunting lines to himself both in Zemblan and German, as a chance accompaniment of drumming fatigue and anxiety, while he climbed through the bracken belt of the dark mountains he had to traverse in his bid for freedom.

Lines 671–672: The Untamed Seahorse

See Browning's *My Last Duchess.*

See it and condemn the fashionable device of entitling a collection of essays or a volume of poetry—or a long poem, alas—with a phrase lifted from a more or less celebrated poetical work of the past. Such titles possess a specious glamor acceptable maybe in the names of vintage wines and plump courtesans but only degrading in regard to the talent that substitutes the easy allusiveness of literacy for original fancy and shifts onto a bust's shoulders the responsibility for ornateness since anybody can flip through a *Midsummer-Night's Dream* or *Romeo and Juliet*, or, perhaps, the *Sonnets* and take his pick.

Line 678:   into French

Two of these translations appeared in the August number of the *Nouvelle Revue Canadienne* which reached College Town bookshops in the last week of July, that is at a time of sadness and mental confusion when good taste forbade me to show Sybil Shade some of the critical notes I made in my pocket diary.

In her version of Donne's famous Holy Sonnet X composed in his widowery:

> Death be not proud, though some have callèd thee
> Mighty and dreadful, for, thou art not so

one deplores the superfluous ejaculation in the second line introduced there only to coagulate the caesura:

> *Ne soit pas fière, Mort! Quoique certains te disent*
> *Et puissante et terrible, ah, Mort, tu ne l'es pas*

and while the enclosed rhyme "so-overthrow" (lines 2–3) is fortunate in finding an easy counterpart in *pas-bas*, one objects to the enclosing *disent-prise* rhyme (1–4) which in a *French* sonnet of *circa* 1617 would be an impossible infringement of the visual rule.

I have no space here to list a number of other blurrings and blunders in this Canadian version of the Dean of St. Paul's denouncement of Death, that slave—not only to "fate" and "chance"—but also to *us* ("kings and desperate men").

The other poem, Andrew Marvell's "The Nymph on the Death of her Fawn," seems to be, technically, even tougher to stuff into French verse. If in the Donne translation, Miss Irondell was perfectly justified in matching English pentameters with French Alexandrines, I doubt that here she should have preferred *l'impair* and accommodated with nine syllables what Marvell fits into eight. In the lines:

> And, quite regardless of my smart,
> Left me his fawn but took his heart

which come out as:

> *Et se moquant bien de ma douleur*
> *Me laissa son faon, mais pris son coeur*

one regrets that the translator, even with the help of an ampler prosodic womb, did not manage to fold in the long legs of her French fawn, and render "quite regardless of" by *"sans le moindre égard pour"* or something of the sort.

Further on, the couplet

> Thy love was far more better than
> The love of false and cruel man

though translated literally:

> *Que ton amour était fort meilleur*
> *Qu'amour d'homme cruel et trompeur*

is not as pure idiomatically as might seem at first glance. And finally, the lovely closule:

> Had it lived long it would have been
> Lilies without, roses within

contains in our lady's French not only a solecism but also that kind of illegal run-on which a translator is guilty of, when passing a stop sign:

> *Il aurait été, s'il eut longtemps*
> *Vécu, lys dehors, roses dedans.*

How magnificently those two lines can be mimed and rhymed in our magic Zemblan ("the tongue of the mirror," as the great Conmal has termed it)!

Id wodo bin, war id lev lan,
Indran iz lil ut roz nitran.

Line 680:   Lolita

Major hurricanes are given feminine names in America. The feminine gender is suggested not so much by the sex of furies and harridans as by a general professional application. Thus any machine is a she to its fond user, and any fire (even a "pale" one!) is she to the fireman, as water is she to the passionate plumber. Why our poet chose to give his 1958 hurricane a little-used Spanish name (sometimes given to parrots) instead of Linda or Lois, is not clear.

Line 681:   gloomy Russians spied

There is really nothing metaphysical, or racial, about this gloom. It is merely the outward sign of congested nationalism and a provincial's sense of inferiority—that dreadful blend so typical of Zemblans under the Extremist rule and of Russians under the Soviet regime. Ideas in modern Russia are machine-cut blocks coming in solid colors; the nuance is outlawed, the interval walled up, the curve grossly stepped.

However, not all Russians are gloomy, and the two young experts from Moscow whom our new government engaged to locate the Zemblan crown jewels turned out to be positively rollicking. The Extremists were right in believing that Baron Bland, the Keeper of the Treasure, had succeeded in hiding those jewels before he jumped or fell from the North Tower; but they did not know he had had a helper and were wrong in thinking the jewels must be looked for in the palace which the gentle white-haired Bland had never left except to die. I may add, with pardonable satisfaction, that they were, and still are, cached in a totally different—and quite unexpected—corner of Zembla.

In an earlier note (to line 130) the reader has already glimpsed those two treasure hunters at work. After the King's escape and the belated discovery of the secret passage, they

continued their elaborate excavations until the palace was all
honeycombed and partly demolished, an entire wall of one
room collapsing one night, to yield, in a niche whose presence
nobody had suspected, an ancient salt cellar of bronze and
King Wigbert's drinking horn; but you will never find our
crown, necklace and scepter.

All this is the rule of a supernal game, all this is the im-
mutable fable of fate, and should not be construed as reflecting on the efficiency of the two Soviet experts—who, anyway,
were to be marvelously successful on a later occasion with
another job (see note to line 747). Their names (probably
fictitious) were Andronnikov and Niagarin. One has seldom
seen, at least among waxworks, a pair of more pleasant, pre-
sentable chaps. Everybody admired their clean-shaven jaws,
elementary facial expressions, wavy hair, and perfect teeth. Tall
handsome Andronnikov seldom smiled but the crinkly little
rays of his orbital flesh bespoke infinite humor while the twin
furrows descending from the sides of his shapely nostrils
evoked glamorous associations with flying aces and sagebrush
heroes. Niagarin, on the other hand, was of comparatively
short stature, had somewhat more rounded, albeit quite manly
features, and every now and then would flash a big boyish
smile remindful of scoutmasters with something to hide, or
those gentlemen who cheat in television quizzes. It was delightful to watch the two splendid Sovietchiks running about
in the yard and kicking a chalk-dusty, thumping-tight soccer
ball (looking so large and bald in such surroundings). Andronnikov could tap-play it on his toe up and down a dozen
times before punting it rocket straight into the melancholy,
surprised, bleached, harmless heavens; and Niagarin could imitate to perfection the mannerisms of a certain stupendous
Dynamo goalkeeper. They used to hand out to the kitchen
boys Russian caramels with plums or cherries depicted on the
rich luscious six-cornered wrappers that enclosed a jacket of
thinner paper with the mauve mummy inside; and lustful
country girls were known to creep up along the *drungen*
(bramble-choked footpaths) to the very foot of the bulwark
when the two silhouetted against the now flushed sky sang
beautiful sentimental military duets at eventide on the rampart. Niagarin had a soulful tenor voice, and Andronnikov a

hearty baritone, and both wore elegant jackboots of soft black leather, and the sky turned away showing its ethereal vertebrae.

Niagarin who had lived in Canada spoke English and French; Andronnikov had some German. The little Zemblan they knew was pronounced with that comical Russian accent that gives vowels a kind of didactic plenitude of sound. They were considered models of dash by the Extremist guards, and my dear Odonello once earned a harsh reprimand from the commandant by not having withstood the temptation to imitate their walk: both moved with an identical little swagger, and both were conspicuously bandy-legged.

When I was a child, Russia enjoyed quite a vogue at the court of Zembla but that was a different Russia—a Russia that hated tyrants and Philistines, injustice and cruelty, the Russia of ladies and gentlemen and liberal aspirations. We may add that Charles the Beloved could boast of some Russian blood. In medieval times two of his ancestors had married Novgorod princesses. Queen Yaruga (reigned 1799–1800) his great-great-granddam, was half Russian; and most historians believe that Yaruga's only child Igor was not the son of Uran the Last (reigned 1798–1799) but the fruit of her amours with the Russian adventurer Hodinski, her *goliart* (court jester) and a poet of genius, said to have forged in his spare time a famous old Russian *chanson de geste*, generally attributed to an anonymous bard of the twelfth century.

Line 682:   Lang

A modern Fra Pandolf no doubt. I do not remember seeing any such painting around the house. Or did Shade have in mind a photographic portrait? There was one such portrait on the piano, and another in Shade's study. How much fairer it would have been to Shade's and his friend's reader if the lady had deigned answer some of my urgent queries.

Line 691:   the attack

John Shade's heart attack (Oct. 17, 1958) practically coincided with the disguised king's arrival in America where he descended by parachute from a chartered plane piloted by Colonel Montacute, in a field of hay-feverish, rank-flowering weeds, near Baltimore whose oriole is not an oriole. It had all been perfectly timed, and he was still wrestling with the unfamiliar French contraption when the Rolls-Royce from Sylvia O'Donnell's manor turned toward his green silks from a road and approached along the *mown-trop*, its fat wheels bouncing disapprovingly and its black shining body slowly gliding along. Fain would I elucidate this business of parachuting but (it being a matter of mere sentimental tradition rather than a useful manner of transportation) this is not strictly necessary in these notes to *Pale Fire*. While Kingsley, the British chauffeur, an old and absolutely faithful retainer, was doing his best to cram the bulky and ill-folded parachute into the boot, I relaxed on a shooting stick he had supplied me with, sipping a delightful Scotch and water from the car bar and glancing (amid an ovation of crickets and that vortex of yellow and maroon butterflies that so pleased Chateaubriand on *his* arrival in America) at an article in *The New York Times* in which Sylvia had vigorously and messily marked out in red pencil a communication from New Wye which told of the "distinguished poet's" hospitalization. I had been looking forward to meeting my favorite American poet who, as I felt sure at the moment, would die long before the Spring Term, but the disappointment was little more than a mental shrug of accepted regret, and discarding the newspaper, I looked around me with enchantment and physical wellbeing despite the congestion in my nose. Beyond the field the great green steps of turf ascended to the multicolored coppices; one could see above them the white brow of the manor; clouds melted into the blue. Suddenly I sneezed, and sneezed again. Kingsley offered me another drink but I declined it, and democratically joined him in the front seat. My hostess was in bed, suffering from the aftereffects of a special injection that she had been given in anticipation of a journey to a special place in Africa. In answer to my "Well, how are you?" she murmured that the Andes had been simply marvelous, and then in a slightly less indolent tone of voice inquired about a notorious actress with whom her son was said to be living in sin. Odon, I said,

had promised me he would not marry her. She inquired if I
had had a good hop and dingled a bronze bell. Good old
Sylvia! She had in common with Fleur de Fyler a vagueness
of manner, a languor of demeanor which was partly natural
and partly cultivated as a convenient alibi for when she was
drunk, and in some wonderful way she managed to combine
that indolence with volubility reminding one of a slow-speak-
ing ventriloquist who is interrupted by his garrulous doll.
Changeless Sylvia! During three decades I had seen from time
to time, from palace to palace, that same flat nut-colored
bobbed hair, those childish pale-blue eyes, the vacant smile,
the stylish long legs, the willowy hesitating movements.

A tray with fruit and drinks was brought in by a *jeune
beauté*, as dear Marcel would have put it, nor could one help
recalling another author, Gide the Lucid, who praises in his
African notes so warmly the satiny skin of black imps.

"You nearly lost the opportunity to meet our brightest
star," said Sylvia who was Wordsmith University's main trus-
tee (and, in point of fact, had been solely responsible for arranging my amusing lectureship there). "I have just called up
the college—yes, take that footstool—and he is much better.
Try this mascana fruit, I got it especially for you, but the boy
is strictly hetero, and, generally speaking, Your Majesty will
have to be quite careful from now on. I'm sure you'll like it
up there though I wish I could figure out why anybody should
be so keen on teaching Zemblan. I think Disa ought to come
too. I have rented for you what they say is their best house,
and it is near the Shades."

She knew them very slightly but had heard many endearing
stories about the poet from Billy Reading, "one of the very
few American college presidents who know Latin." And let
me add here how much I was honored a fortnight later to
meet in Washington that limp-looking, absent-minded, shab-
bily dressed splendid American gentleman whose mind was a
library and not a debating hall. Next Monday Sylvia flew away
but I stayed on for a while, resting from my adventures, musing, reading, taking notes, and riding a lot in the lovely countryside with two charming ladies and their shy little groom. I
have often felt when leaving a place that I had enjoyed, somewhat like a tight cork that is drawn out for the sweet dark

wine to be drained, and then you are off to new vineyards and conquests. I spent a couple of pleasant months visiting the libraries of New York and Washington, flew to Florida for Christmas, and when ready to start for my new Arcady deemed it nice and dutiful to send the poet a polite note congratulating him on his restored health and jokingly "warning" him that beginning with February he would have a very ardent admirer of his for neighbor. I never received any answer, and my civility was never recalled later so I suppose it got lost among the many "fan" letters that literary celebrities receive, although one might have expected Sylvia or somebody to have told the Shades of my arrival.

The poet's recovery turned out indeed to be very speedy and would have to be called miraculous had there been anything organically wrong with his heart. There was not; a poet's nerves can play the queerest tricks but they also can quickly recapture the rhythm of health, and soon John Shade, in his chair at the head of an oval table, was again speaking of his favorite Pope to eight pious young men, a crippled extramural woman and three coeds, one of them a tutorial dream. He had been told not to curtail his customary exercise, such as walks, but I must admit I experienced myself palpitations and cold sweats at the sight of that precious old man wielding rude garden tools or squirming up the college hall stairs as a Japanese fish up a cataract. Incidentally: the reader should not take too seriously or too literally the passage about the alert doctor (an alert doctor, who as I well know once confused neuralgia with cerebral sclerosis). As I gathered from Shade himself, no emergency incision was performed; the heart was not compressed by hand; and if it stopped pumping at all, the pause must have been very brief and so to speak superficial. All this of course cannot detract from the great epic beauty of the passage. (Lines 691–697)

Line 697: Conclusive destination

Gradus landed at the Côte d'Azur airport in the early afternoon of July 15, 1959. Despite his worries he could not help being impressed by the torrent of magnificent trucks, agile

motor bicycles and cosmopolitan private cars on the Promenade. He remembered and disliked the torrid heat and the
blinding blue of the sea. Hotel Lazuli, where before World
War Two he had spent a week with a consumptive Bosnian
terrorist, when it was a squalid, running-water place frequented by young Germans, was now a squalid, running-
water place frequented by old Frenchmen. It was situated in
a transverse street, between two thoroughfares parallel to the
quay, and the ceaseless roar of crisscross traffic mingling with
the grinding and banging of construction work proceeding
under the auspices of a crane opposite the hotel (which had
been surrounded by a stagnant calm two decades earlier) was
a delightful surprise for Gradus, who always liked a little noise
to keep his mind off things. (*"Ça distrait,"* as he said to the
apologetic hostlerwife and her sister.)

After scrupulously washing his hands, he went out again, a
tremor of excitement running like fever down his crooked
spine. At one of the tables of a sidewalk café on the corner of
his street and the Promenade, a man in a bottle-green jacket,
sitting in the company of an obvious whore, clapped both
palms to his face, emitted the sound of a muffled sneeze, and
kept masking himself with his hands as he pretended to wait
for the second installment. Gradus walked along the north
side of the embankment. After stopping for a minute before
the display of a souvenir shop, he went inside, asked the price
of a little hippopotamus made of violet glass, and purchased
a map of Nice and its environs. As he walked on to the taxi
stand in rue Gambetta, he happened to notice two young
tourists in loud shirts stained with sweat, their faces and necks
a bright pink from the heat and imprudent solarization; they
carried carefully folded over their arms the silk-lined double-
breasted coats of their wide-trousered dark suits and did not
look at our sleuth who despite his being exceptionally unob-
servant felt the undulation of something faintly familiar as they
brushed past. They knew nothing of his presence abroad or
of his interesting job; in point of fact, only a few minutes ago
had their, and his, superior discovered that Gradus was in Nice
and not in Geneva. Neither had Gradus been informed that
he would be assisted in his quest by the Soviet sportsmen,

Andronnikov and Niagarin, whom he had casually met once or twice on the Onhava Palace grounds when re-paning a broken window and checking for the new government the rare Rippleson panes in one of the ex-royal hothouses; and next moment he had lost the thread end of recognition as he settled down with the prudent wriggle of a short-legged person in the back seat of an old Cadillac and asked to be taken to a restaurant between Pellos and Cap Turc. It is hard to say what our man's hopes and intentions were. Did he want just to peep through the myrtles and oleanders at an imagined swimming pool? Did he expect to hear the continuation of Gordon's bravura piece played now in another rendition, by two larger and stronger hands? Would he have crept, pistol in hand, to where a sun-bathing giant lay spread-eagled, a spread eagle of hair on his chest? We do not know, nor did Gradus perhaps know himself; anyway, he was spared an unnecessary journey. Modern taximen are as talkative as were the barbers of old, and even before the old Cadillac had rolled out of town, our unfortunate killer knew that his driver's brother had worked in the gardens of Villa Disa but that at present nobody lived there, the Queen having gone to Italy for the rest of July.

At his hotel the beaming proprietress handed him a telegram. It chided him in Danish for leaving Geneva and told him to undertake nothing until further notice. It also advised him to forget his work and amuse himself. But what (save dreams of blood) could be his amusements? He was not interested in sightseeing or seasiding. He had long stopped drinking. He did not go to concerts. He did not gamble. Sexual impulses had greatly bothered him at one time but that was over. After his wife, a beader in Radugovitra, had left him (with a gypsy lover), he had lived in sin with his mother-in-law until she was removed, blind and dropsical, to an asylum for decayed widows. Since then he had tried several times to castrate himself, had been laid up at the Glassman Hospital with a severe infection, and now, at forty-four, was quite cured of the lust that Nature, the grand cheat, puts into us to inveigle us into propagation. No wonder the advice to amuse himself infuriated him. I think I shall break this note here.

Lines 704–707:   A system, etc.

The fitting-in of the threefold "cells interlinked" is most skillfully managed, and one derives logical satisfaction from the "system" and "stem" interplay.

Lines 727–728:   No, Mr. Shade . . . just half a shade

Another fine example of our poet's special brand of combinational magic. The subtle pun here turns on two additional meanings of "shade" besides the obvious synonym of "nuance." The doctor is made to suggest that not only did Shade retain in his trance half of his identity but that he was also half a ghost. Knowing the particular medical man who treated my friend at the time, I venture to add that he is far too stodgy to have displayed any such wit.

Lines 734–735:   probably . . . wobble . . . limp blimp . . . unstable

A third burst of contrapuntal pyrotechnics. The poet's plan is to display in the very texture of his text the intricacies of the "game" in which he seeks the key to life and death (see lines 808–829).

Line 741:   the outer glare

On the morning of July 16 (while Shade was working on the 698–746 section of his poem) dull Gradus, dreading another day of enforced inactivity in sardonically sparkling, stimulatingly noisy Nice, decided that until hunger drove him out he would not budge from a leathern armchair in the simulacrum of a lobby among the brown smells of his dingy hotel. Unhurriedly he went through a heap of old magazines on a nearby table. There he sat, a little monument of taciturnity, sighing, puffing out his cheeks, licking his thumb before turning a page, gaping at the pictures, and moving his lips as he climbed down the columns of printed matter. Having replaced everything in a neat pile, he sank back in his chair closing and opening his gabled hands in various constructions of tedium—when a man who had occupied a seat next to him got up and walked into the outer glare leaving his paper behind. Gradus pulled it into his lap, spread it out—and froze over a strange piece of local news that caught his eye: burglars had broken into Villa Disa and ransacked a bureau, taking from a jewel box a number of valuable old medals.

Here was something to brood upon. Had this vaguely unpleasant incident some bearing on his quest? Should he do something about it? Cable headquarters? Hard to word succinctly a simple fact without having it look like a cryptogram. Airmail a clipping? He was in his room working on the newspaper with a safety razor blade when there was a bright rap-rap at the door. Gradus admitted an unexpected visitor—one of the greater Shadows, whom he had thought to be *onhava-onhava* ("far, far away"), in wild, misty, almost legendary Zembla! What stunning conjuring tricks our magical mechanical age plays with old mother space and old father time!

He was a merry, perhaps overmerry, fellow, in a green velvet jacket. Nobody liked him, but he certainly had a keen mind. His name, Izumrudov, sounded rather Russian but actually meant "of the Umruds," an Eskimo tribe sometimes seen paddling their umyaks (hide-lined boats) on the emerald waters of our northern shores. Grinning, he said friend Gradus must get together his travel documents, including a health certificate, and take the earliest available jet to New York. Bowing, he congratulated him on having indicated with such phenomenal acumen the right place and the right way. Yes, after a thorough perlustration of the loot that Andron and Niagarushka had obtained from the Queen's rosewood writing desk (mostly bills, and treasured snapshots, and those silly medals) a letter from the King did turn up giving his address which was of all places— Our man, who interrupted the herald of success to say he had *never*—was bidden not to display so much modesty. A slip of paper was now produced on which Izumrudov, shaking with laughter (death is hilarious), wrote out for Gradus their client's alias, the name of the university where he taught, and that of the town where it was situated.

No, the slip was not for keeps. He could keep it only while memorizing it. This brand of paper (used by macaroon makers) was not only digestible but delicious. The gay green vision withdrew—to resume his whoring no doubt. How one hates such men!

Lines 747–748: a story in the magazine about a Mrs. Z.

Anybody having access to a good library could, no doubt, easily trace that story to its source and find the name of the lady; but such humdrum potterings are beneath true scholarship.

Line 768: address

At this point my reader may be amused by my allusion to John Shade in a letter (of which I fortunately preserved a carbon copy) that I wrote to a correspondent living in southern France on April 2, 1959:

> My dear, you are absurd. I do not give you, and will not give you or anybody, my home address not because I fear you might look me up, as you are pleased to conjecture: *all* my mail goes to my office address. The suburban houses here have open letter boxes out in the street, and anybody can cram them with advertisements or purloin letters addressed to me (not out of mere curiosity, mind you, but from other, more sinister, motives). I send this by air and urgently repeat the address Sylvia gave you: Dr. C. Kinbote, KINBOTE (*not* "Charles X. Kingbot, Esq.," as you, or Sylvia, wrote; *please,* be more careful—and more intelligent), Wordsmith University, New Wye, Appalachia, USA.
>
> I am not cross with you but I have all sorts of worries, and my nerves are on edge. I believed—believed deeply and candidly—in the affection of a person who lived here, under my roof, but have been hurt and betrayed, as never happened in the days of my forefathers, who

could have the offender tortured, though of course I do not wish to have anybody tortured.

It has been dreadfully cold here, but thank God now a regular northern winter has turned into a southern spring.

Do not try to explain to me what your lawyer tells you but have him explain it to my lawyer, and *he* will explain it to me.

My work at the university is pleasant, and I have a most charming neighbor—now do not sigh and raise your eyebrows, my dear—he is a very old gentleman— the old gentleman in fact who was responsible for that bit about the ginkgo tree in your green album (see again—I mean the reader should see again—the note to line 49).

It might be safer if you did not write me *too* often, my dear.

Line 782: your poem

An image of Mont Blanc's "blue-shaded buttresses and sun-creamed domes" is fleetingly glimpsed through the cloud of that particular poem which I wish I could quote but do not have at hand. The "white mountain" of the lady's dream, caused by a misprint to tally with Shade's "white fountain," makes a thematic appearance here, blurred as it were by the lady's grotesque pronunciation.

Line 802: mountain

The passage 797 (second part of line)–809, on the poet's sixty-fifth card, was composed between the sunset of July 18 and the dawn of July 19. That morning I had prayed in two different churches (on either side, as it were, of my Zemblan denomination, not represented in New Wye) and had strolled home in an elevated state of mind. There was no cloud in the wistful sky, and the very earth seemed to be sighing after our Lord Jesus Christ. On such sunny, sad mornings I always feel

in my bones that there is a chance yet of my not being excluded from Heaven, and that salvation may be granted to me
despite the frozen mud and horror in my heart. As I was ascending with bowed head the gravel path to my poor rented
house, I heard with absolute distinction, as if he were standing
at my shoulder and speaking loudly, as to a slightly deaf man,
Shade's voice say: "Come tonight, Charlie." I looked around
me in awe and wonder: I was quite alone. I at once telephoned. The Shades were out, said the cheeky ancillula, an
obnoxious little fan who came to cook for them on Sundays
and no doubt dreamt of getting the old poet to cuddle her
some wifeless day. I retelephoned two hours later; got, as
usual, Sybil; insisted on talking to my friend (my "messages"
were never transmitted), obtained him, and asked him as
calmly as possible what he had been doing around noon when
I had heard him like a big bird in my garden. He could not
quite remember, said wait a minute, he had been playing golf
with Paul (whoever that was), or at least watching Paul play
with another colleague. I cried that I must see him in the
evening and all at once, with no reason at all, burst into tears,
flooding the telephone and gasping for breath, a paroxysm
which had not happened to me since Bob left me on March
30. There was a flurry of confabulation between the Shades,
and then John said: "Charles, listen. Let's go for a good ramble tonight, I'll meet you at eight." It was my second good
ramble since July 6 (that unsatisfactory nature talk); the third
one, on July 21, was to be exceedingly brief.

Where was I? Yes, trudging along again as in the old days
with John, in the woods of Arcady, under a salmon sky.

"Well," I said gaily, "what were you writing about last
night, John? Your study window was simply blazing."

"Mountains," he answered.

The Bera Range, an erection of veined stone and shaggy
firs, rose before me in all its power and pride. The splendid
news made my heart pound, and I felt that I could now, in
my turn, afford to be generous. I begged my friend not to
impart to me anything more if he did not wish it. He said yes,
he did not, and began bewailing the difficulties of his self-
imposed task. He calculated that during the last twenty-four
hours his brain had put in, roughly, a thousand minutes of

work, and had produced fifty lines (say, 797–847) or one syllable every two minutes. He had finished his Third, penultimate, Canto, and had started on Canto Four, his last (see Foreword, see Foreword, at once), and would I mind very much if we started to go home—though it was only around nine—so that he could plunge back into his chaos and drag out of it, with all its wet stars, his cosmos?

How could I say no? That mountain air had gone to my head: he was reassembling my Zembla!

Line 803: a misprint

Translators of Shade's poem are bound to have trouble with the transformation, at one stroke, of "mountain" into "fountain": it cannot be rendered in French or German, or Russian, or Zemblan; so the translator will have to put it into one of those footnotes that are the rogue's galleries of words. However! There exists to my knowledge one absolutely extraordinary, unbelievably elegant case, where not only two, but *three* words are involved. The story itself is trivial enough (and probably apocryphal). A newspaper account of a Russian tsar's coronation had, instead of *korona* (crown), the misprint *vorona* (crow), and when next day this was apologetically "corrected," it got misprinted a second time as *korova* (cow). The artistic correlation between the crown-crow-cow series and the Russian *korona-vorona-korova* series is something that would have, I am sure, enraptured my poet. I have seen nothing like it on lexical playfields and the odds against the double coincidence defy computation.

Line 810: a web of sense

One of the five cabins of which this motor court consists is occupied by the owner, a blear-eyed, seventy-year-old man whose twisted limp reminds me of Shade. He runs a small gas station nearby, sells worms to fishermen, and usually does not bother me, but the other day he suggested I "grab any old book" from a shelf in his room. Not wishing to offend him,

I cocked my head at them, to one side, and then to the other, but they were all dog-eared paperback mystery stories and did not rate more than a sigh and a smile. He said wait a minute—and took from a bedside recess a battered clothbound treasure. "A great book by a great guy," the Letters of Franklin Lane. "Used to see a lot of him in Rainier Park when I was a young ranger up there. You take it for a couple of days. You won't regret it!"

I did not. Here is a passage that curiously echoes Shade's tone at the end of Canto Three. It comes from a manuscript fragment written by Lane on May 17, 1921, on the eve of his death, after a major operation: "And if I had passed into that other land, whom would I have sought? . . . Aristotle!—Ah, there would be a man to talk with! What satisfaction to see him take, like reins from between his fingers, the long ribbon of man's life and trace it through the mystifying maze of all the wonderful adventure. . . . The crooked made straight. The Daedalian plan simplified by a look from above—smeared out as it were by the splotch of some master thumb that made the whole involuted, boggling thing one beautiful straight line."

Line 819:   Playing a game of worlds

My illustrious friend showed a childish predilection for all sorts of word games and especially for so-called word golf. He would interrupt the flow of a prismatic conversation to indulge in this particular pastime, and naturally it would have been boorish of me to refuse playing with him. Some of my records are: hate-love in three, lass-male in four, and live-dead in five (with "lend" in the middle).

Line 822:   killing a Balkan king

Fervently would I wish to report that the reading in the draft was:

killing a Zemblan king

—but alas, it is not so: the card with the draft has not been preserved by Shade.

Line 830:   Sybil, it is

This elaborate rhyme comes as an apotheosis crowning the entire canto and synthesizing the contrapuntal aspects of its "accidents and possibilities."

Lines 835–838:   Now I shall spy, etc.

The canto, begun on July 19th, on card sixty-eight, opens with a typical Shadism: the cunning working-in of several inter-echoing phrases into a jumble of enjambments. Actually, the promise made in these four lines will not be really kept except for the repetition of their incantatory rhythm in lines 915 and 923–924 (leading to the savage attack in 925–930). The poet like a fiery rooster seems to flap his wings in a preparatory burst of would-be inspiration, but the sun does not rise. Instead of the wild poetry promised here, we get a jest or two, a bit of satire, and at the end of the canto, a wonderful radiance of tenderness and repose.

Lines 841–872:   two methods of composing

Really three if we count the all-important method of relying on the flash and flute of the subliminal world and its "mute command" (line 871).

Line 873:   My best time

As my dear friend was beginning with this line his July 20 batch of cards (card seventy-one to card seventy-six, ending with line 948), Gradus, at the Orly airport, was walking aboard a jetliner, fastening his seat belt, reading a newspaper, rising, soaring, desecrating the sky.

Lines 887–888:   Since my biographer may be too staid or know too little

Too staid? Know too little? Had my poor friend precognized *who* that would be, he would have been spared those conjectures. As a matter of fact I had the pleasure and the honor of witnessing (one March morning) the performance he describes in the next lines. I was going to Washington and just before starting remembered he had said he wanted me to look up something in the Library of Congress. I hear so clearly in my mind's ear Sybil's cool voice saying: "But John cannot see you, he is in his bath"; and John's raucous roar coming from the bathroom: "Let him in, Sybil, he won't rape me!" But neither he nor I could recall what that something was.

Line 894:   a king

Pictures of the King had not infrequently appeared in America during the first months of the Zemblan Revolution. Every now and then some busybody on the campus with a retentive memory, or one of the clubwomen who were always after Shade and his eccentric friend, used to ask me with the inane meaningfulness adopted in such cases if anybody had told me how much I resembled that unfortunate monarch. I would counter with something on the lines of "all Chinese look alike" and change the subject. One day, however, in the lounge of the Faculty Club where I lolled surrounded by a number of my colleagues, I had to put up with a particularly embarrassing onset. A visiting German lecturer from Oxford kept exclaiming, aloud and under his breath, that the resemblance was "absolutely unheard of," and when I negligently observed that all bearded Zemblans resembled one another—and that, in fact, the name Zembla is a corruption not of the Russian *zemlya*, but of Semblerland, a land of reflections, of "resemblers"—my tormentor said: "Ah, yes, but King Charles wore no beard, and yet it is his very face! I had [he added] the honor of being seated within a few yards of the royal box at a Sport Festival in Onhava which I visited with my wife, who is Swedish, in 1956. We have a photograph of him at home, and her sister knew very well the mother of one of his pages, an interesting woman. Don't you see [almost tugging at Shade's lapel] the astounding similarity of features—of the upper part of the face, and the eyes, yes, the eyes, and the nose bridge?"

"Nay, sir" [said Shade, refolding a leg and slightly rolling in his armchair as wont to do when about to deliver a pronouncement] "there is no resemblance at all. I have seen the King in newsreels, and there is no resemblance. Resemblances are the shadows of differences. Different people see different similarities and similar differences."

Good Netochka, who had been looking singularly uncomfortable during this exchange, remarked in his gentle voice how sad it was to think that such a "sympathetic ruler" had probably perished in prison.

A professor of physics now joined in. He was a so-called Pink, who believed in what so-called Pinks believe in (Progressive Education, the Integrity of anyone spying for Russia, Fall-outs occasioned solely by US-made bombs, the existence in the near past of a McCarthy Era, Soviet achievements including *Dr. Zhivago*, and so forth): "Your regrets are groundless" [said he]. "That sorry ruler is known to have escaped disguised as a nun; but whatever happens, or has happened to him, cannot interest the Zemblan people. History has denounced him, and that is his epitaph."

Shade: "True, sir. In due time history will have denounced everybody. The King may be dead, or he may be as much alive as you and Kinbote, but let us respect facts. I have it from him [pointing to me] that the widely circulated stuff about the nun is a vulgar pro-Extremist fabrication. The Extremists and their friends invented a lot of nonsense to conceal their discomfiture; but the truth is that the King walked out of the palace, and crossed the mountains, and left the country, not in the black garb of a pale spinster but dressed as an athlete in scarlet wool."

"Strange, strange," said the German visitor, who by some quirk of alderwood ancestry had been alone to catch the eerie note that had throbbed by and was gone.

Shade [smiling and massaging my knee]: "Kings do not die—they only disappear, eh, Charles?"

"Who said that?" asked sharply, as if coming out of a trance, the ignorant, and always suspicious, Head of the English Department.

"Take my own case," continued my dear friend ignoring Mr. H. "I have been said to resemble at least four people: Samuel Johnson; the lovingly reconstructed ancestor of man in the Exton Museum; and two local characters, one being the slapdash disheveled hag who ladles out the mash in the Levin Hall cafeteria."

"The third in the witch row," I precised quaintly, and everybody laughed.

"I would rather say," remarked Mr. Pardon—American History—"that she looks like Judge Goldsworth" ("One of us," interposed Shade inclining his head), "especially when he is real mad at the whole world after a good dinner."

"I hear," hastily began Netochka, "that the Goldsworths are having a wonderful time—"

"What a pity I cannot prove my point," muttered the tenacious German visitor. "If only there was a picture here. Couldn't there be somewhere—"

"Sure," said young Emerald and left his seat.

Professor Pardon now spoke to me: "I was under the impression that you were born in Russia, and that your name was a kind of anagram of Botkin or Botkine?"

Kinbote: "You are confusing me with some refugee from Nova Zembla" [sarcastically stressing the "Nova"].

"Didn't you tell me, Charles, that *kinbote* means regicide in your language?" asked my dear Shade.

"Yes, a king's destroyer," I said (longing to explain that a king who sinks his identity in the mirror of exile is in a sense just that).

Shade [addressing the German visitor]: "Professor Kinbote is the author of a remarkable book on surnames. I believe [to me] there exists an English translation?"

"Oxford, 1956," I replied.

"You do know Russian, though?" said Pardon. "I think I heard you, the other day, talking to—what's his name—oh, my goodness" [laboriously composing his lips].

Shade: "Sir, we all find it difficult to *attack* that name" [laughing].

Professor Hurley: "Think of the French word for 'tire': *punoo*."

Shade: "Why, sir, I am afraid you have only punctured the difficulty" [laughing uproariously].

"Flatman," quipped I. "Yes," I went on, turning to Pardon, "I certainly do speak Russian. You see, it was the fashionable language *par excellence*, much more so than French, among the nobles of Zembla at least, and at its court. Today, of course, all this has changed. It is now the lower classes who are forcibly taught to speak Russian."

"Aren't we, too, trying to teach Russian in our schools?" said Pink.

In the meantime, at the other end of the room, young Emerald had been communing with the bookshelves. At this point he returned with the T–Z volume of an illustrated encyclopedia.

"Well," said he, "here he is, that king. But look, he is young and handsome" ("Oh, that won't do," wailed the German visitor). "Young, handsome, and wearing a fancy uniform," continued Emerald. "Quite the fancy pansy, in fact."

"And you," I said quietly, "are a foul-minded pup in a cheap green jacket."

"But what have I said?" the young instructor inquired of the company, spreading out his palms like a disciple in Leonardo's *Last Supper*.

"Now, now," said Shade. "I'm sure, Charles, our young friend never intended to insult your sovereign and namesake."

"He could not, even if he had wished," I observed placidly, turning it all into a joke.

Gerald Emerald extended his hand—which at the moment of writing still remains in that position.

Lines 895–899: The more I weigh . . . or this dewlap

Instead of these facile and revolting lines, the draft gives:

895   I have a certain liking, I admit,
       For Parody, that last resort of wit:
       "In nature's strife when fortitude prevails
       The victim falters and the victor fails."
899   Yes, reader, Pope

Line 920: little hairs stand on end

Alfred Housman (1859–1936), whose collection *The Shropshire Lad* vies with the *In Memoriam* of Alfred Tennyson (1809–1892) in representing, perhaps (no, delete this craven "perhaps"), the highest achievement of English poetry in a hundred years, says somewhere (in a foreword?) exactly the opposite: The bristling of thrilled little hairs obstructed *his* barbering; but since both Alfreds certainly used an Ordinary Razor, and John Shade an ancient Gillette, the discrepancy may have been due to the use of different instruments.

Line 922: held up by Our Cream

This is not quite exact. In the advertisement to which it refers, the whiskers are held up by a bubbly foam, not by a creamy substance.

After this line, instead of lines 923–930, we find the following, lightly deleted, variant:

> All artists have been born in what they call
> A sorry age; mine is the worst of all:
> An age that thinks spacebombs and spaceships take
> A genius with a foreign name to make,
> When any jackass can rig up the stuff;
> An age in which a pack of rogues can bluff
> The selenographer; a comic age
> That sees in Dr. Schweitzer a great sage.

Having struck this out, the poet tried another theme, but these lines he also canceled:

> England where poets flew the highest, now
> Wants them to plod and Pegasus to plough;
> Now the prosemongers of the Grubby Group,
> The Message Man, the owlish Nincompoop
> And all the Social Novels of our age
> Leave but a pinch of coal dust on the page.

Line 929: Freud

In my mind's eye I see again the poet literally collapsing on his lawn, beating the grass with his fist, and shaking and howling with laughter, and myself, Dr. Kinbote, a torrent of tears streaming down my beard, as I try to read coherently certain tidbits from a book I had filched from a classroom: a learned work on psychoanalysis, used in American colleges, repeat, used in American colleges. Alas, I find only two items preserved in my notebook:

By picking the nose in spite of all commands to the contrary, or when a youth is all the time sticking his finger through his buttonhole . . . the analytic teacher knows that the appetite of the lustful one knows no limit in his phantasies.
(Quoted by Prof. C. from Dr. Oskar Pfister, *The Psychoanalytical Method*, 1917, N.Y., p. 79)

The little cap of red velvet in the German version of Little Red Riding Hood is a symbol of menstruation.
(Quoted by Prof. C. from Erich Fromm, *The Forgotten Language*, 1951, N.Y., p. 240.)

Do those clowns really *believe* what they teach?

Line 934: big trucks

I must say I do not remember hearing very often "big trucks" passing in our vicinity. Loud cars, yes—but not trucks.

Line 937: Old Zembla

I am a weary and sad commentator today.
Parallel to the left-hand side of this card (his seventy-sixth)

the poet has written, on the eve of his death, a line (from Pope's Second Epistle of the *Essay on Man*) that he may have intended to cite in a footnote:

> *At Greenland, Zembla, or the Lord knows where*

So this is all treacherous old Shade could say about Zembla—*my* Zembla? While shaving his stubble off? Strange, strange . . .

Lines 939–940: Man's life, etc.

If I correctly understand the sense of this succinct observation, our poet suggests here that human life is but a series of footnotes to a vast obscure unfinished masterpiece.

Line 949: And all the time

Thus, some time in the morning of July 21, the last day of his life, John Shade began his last batch of cards (seventy-seven to eighty). Two silent time zones had now merged to form the standard time of one man's fate; and it is not impossible that the poet in New Wye and the thug in New York awoke that morning at the same crushed beat of their Time-keeper's stopwatch.

Line 949: and all the time

And all the time he was coming nearer.

A formidable thunderstorm had greeted Gradus in New York on the night of his arrival from Paris (Monday, July 20). The tropical rainfall flooded basements and subway tracks. Kaleidoscopic reflections played in the riverlike streets. Vinogradus had never seen such a display of lightning, neither had Jacques d'Argus—or Jack Grey, for that matter (let us not forget Jack Grey!). He put up in a third-class Broadway hotel and slept soundly, lying belly up *on* the bedclothes, in striped pajamas—the kind that Zemblans call *rusker sirsusker* ("Russian seersucker suit'')—and retaining as usual his socks: not since July 11, when he had visited a Finnish bathhouse in Switzerland, had he seen his bare feet.

It was now July 21. At eight in the morning New York roused Gradus with a bang and a roar. As usual he started his blurry daily existence by blowing his nose. Then he took out of its nightbox of cardboard and inserted into his Comusmask mouth an exceptionally large and fierce-looking set of teeth: the only bad flaw really in his otherwise harmless appearance. This done, he fished out of his briefcase two petit-beurres he had saved and an even older but still quite palatable small, softish, near-ham sandwich, vaguely associated with the train journey from Nice to Paris last Saturday night: not so much thriftiness on his part (the Shadows had advanced him a handsome sum, anyway), but an animal attachment to the habits of his frugal youth. After breakfasting in bed on these delicacies, he began preparations for the most important day in his life. He had shaved yesterday—that was out of the way. His trusty pajamas he stuffed not into his traveling bag but into the briefcase, dressed, unclipped from the inside of his coat a cameo-pink, interdentally clogged pocket comb, drew it through his bristly hair, carefully donned his trilby, washed both hands with the nice, modern liquid soap in the nice, modern, almost odorless lavatory across the corridor, micturated, rinsed one hand, and feeling clean and neat, went out for a stroll.

He had never visited New York before; but as many near-cretins, he was above novelty. On the previous night he had counted the mounting rows of lighted windows in several skyscrapers, and now, after checking the height of a few more buildings, he felt that he knew all there was to know. He had a brimming cup and half a saucerful of coffee at a crowded and wet counter and spent the rest of the smoke-blue morning moving from bench to bench and from paper to paper in the westside alleys of Central Park.

He began with the day's copy of *The New York Times*. His lips moving like wrestling worms, he read about all kinds of things. Hrushchov (whom they spelled ''Khrushchev'') had abruptly put off a visit to Scandinavia and was to visit Zembla instead (here I tune in: ''*Vi nazïvaete sebya zemblerami*, you

call yourselves Zemblans, *a ya vas nazïvayu zemlyakami*, and
I call you fellow countrymen!" Laughter and applause). The
United States was about to launch its first atom-driven merchant ship (just to annoy the Ruskers, of course. J.G.). Last
night, in Newark, an apartment house at 555 South Street was
hit by a thunderbolt that smashed a TV set and injured two
people watching an actress lost in a violent studio storm (those
tormented spirits are terrible! C.X.K. *teste* J.S.). The Rachel
Jewelry Company in Brooklyn advertised in agate type for a
jewelry polisher who "must have experience on costume jewelry" (oh, Degré had!). The Helman brothers said they had
assisted in the negotiations for the placement of a sizable note:
$11,000,000, Decker Glass Manufacturing Company, Inc.,
note due July 1, 1979," and Gradus, grown young again, reread this twice, with the background gray thought, perhaps,
that he would be sixty-four four days after that (no comment).
On another bench he found a Monday issue of the same newspaper. During a visit to a museum in Whitehorse (Gradus
kicked at a pigeon that came too near), the Queen of England
walked to a corner of the White Animals Room, removed her
right glove and, with her back turned to several evidently observant people, rubbed her forehead and one of her eyes. A
pro-Red revolt had erupted in Iraq. Asked about the Soviet
exhibition at the New York Coliseum, Carl Sandburg, a poet,
replied, and I quote: "They make their appeal on the highest
of intellectual levels." A hack reviewer of new books for tourists, reviewing his own tour through Norway, said that the
fjords were too famous to need (his) description, and that all
Scandinavians loved flowers. And at a picnic for international
children a Zemblan moppet cried to her Japanese friend:
Ufgut, ufgut, velkam ut Semblerland! (Adieu, adieu, till we
meet in Zembla!) I confess it has been a wonderful game—
this looking up in the WUL of various ephemerides over the
shadow of a padded shoulder.

Jacques d'Argus looked for a twentieth time at his watch.
He strolled like a pigeon with his hands behind him. He had
his mahogany shoes shined—and appreciated the way the dirty
but pretty boy clacked taut his rag. In a restaurant on Broadway he consumed a large portion of pinkish pork with sauer-
kraut, a double helping of elastic French fries, and the half

of an overripe melon. From my rented cloudlet I contemplate him with quiet surprise: here he is, this creature ready to commit a monstrous act—and coarsely enjoying a coarse meal! We must assume, I think, that the forward projection of what imagination he had, stopped at the act, on the brink of all its possible consequences; ghost consequences, comparable to the ghost toes of an amputee or to the fanning out of additional squares which a chess knight (that skip-space piece), standing on a marginal file, "feels" in phantom extensions beyond the board, but which have no effect whatever on his real moves, on the real play.

He strolled back and paid the equivalent of three thousand Zemblan crowns for his short but nice stay at Beverland Hotel. With the illusion of practical foresight he transferred his fiber suitcase and—after a moment of hesitation—his raincoat to the anonymous security of a station locker—where, I suppose, they are still lying as snug as my gemmed scepter, ruby necklace, and diamond-studded crown in—no matter, where. On his fateful journey he took only the battered black briefcase we know: it contained a clean nylon shirt, a dirty pajama, a safety razor, a third petit-beurre, an empty cardboard box, a thick illustrated paper he had not quite finished with in the park, a glass eye he once made for his old mistress, and a dozen syndicalist brochures, each in several copies, printed with his own hands many years ago.

He had to check in at the airport at 2 P.M. The night before, when making his reservation, he had not been able to get a seat on the earlier flight to New Wye because of some convention there. He had fiddled with railway schedules, but these had evidently been arranged by a practical joker since the only available direct train (dubbed the Square Wheel by our jolted and jerked students) left at 5:13 A.M., dawdled at flag stations, and took eleven hours to cover the four hundred miles to Exton; you could try to cheat it by going via Washington but then you had to wait there at least three hours for a sleepy local. Buses were out so far as Gradus was concerned since he always got roadsick in them unless he drugged himself with Fahrmamine pills, and that might affect his aim. Come to think of it, he was not feeling too steady anyway.

Gradus is now much nearer to us in space and time than

he was in the preceding cantos. He has short upright black hair. We can fill in the bleak oblong of his face with most of its elements such as thick eyebrows and a wart on the chin. He has a ruddy but unhealthy complexion. We see, fairly in focus, the structure of his somewhat mesmeric organs of vision. We see his melancholy nose with its crooked ridge and grooved tip. We see the mineral blue of his jaw and the gravelly pointillé of his suppressed mustache.

We know already some of his gestures, we know the chimpanzee slouch of his broad body and short hindlegs. We have heard enough about his creased suit. We can at last describe his tie, an Easter gift from a dressy butcher, his brother-in-law in Onhava: imitation silk, color chocolate brown, barred with red, the end tucked into the shirt between the second and third buttons, a Zemblan fashion of the nineteen thirties—and a father-waistcoat substitute according to the learned. Repulsive black hairs coat the back of his honest rude hands, the scrupulously clean hands of an ultra-unionized artisan, with a perceptible deformation of both thumbs, typical of bobêche-makers. We see, rather suddenly, his humid flesh. We can even make out (as, head-on but quite safely, phantom-like, we pass through him, through the shimmering propeller of his flying machine, through the delegates waving and grinning at us) his magenta and mulberry insides, and the strange, not so good sea swell undulating in his entrails.

We can now go further and describe, to a doctor or to anybody else willing to listen to us, the condition of this primate's soul. He could read, write and reckon, he was endowed with a modicum of self-awareness (with which he did not know what to do), some duration consciousness, and a good memory for faces, names, dates and the like. Spiritually he did not exist. Morally he was a dummy pursuing another dummy. The fact that his weapon was a real one, and his quarry a highly developed human being, this fact belonged to *our* world of events; in his, it had no meaning. I grant you that the idea of destroying "the king" did hold for him *some* degree of pleasure, and therefore we should add to the list of his personal parts the capacity of forming notions, mainly general notions, as I have mentioned in another note which I will not bother to look up. There might be (I am allowing a lot) a slight, very slight, sensual satisfaction, not more I would say than what a petty hedonist enjoys at the moment when, retaining his breath, before a magnifying mirror, his thumbnails pressing with deadly accuracy on both sides of a full stop, he expulses totally the eely, semitransparent plug of a comedo—and exhales an Ah of relief. Gradus would not have killed anybody had he not derived pleasure not only from the imagined act (insofar as he was capable of imagining a palpable future) but also from having been given an important, responsible assignment (which happened to require he should kill) by a group of people sharing his notion of justice, but he would not have taken that job if in killing he had not found something like that rather disgusting anticomedoist's little thrill.

I have considered in my earlier note (I now see it is the note to line 171) the particular dislikes, and hence the motives, of our "automatic man," as I phrased it at a time when he did not have as much body, did not offend the senses as violently as now; was, in a word, further removed from our sunny, green, grass-fragrant Arcady. But Our Lord has fashioned man so marvelously that no amount of motive hunting and rational inquiry can ever *really* explain how and why anybody is capable of destroying a fellow creature (this argument necessitates, I know, a temporary granting to Gradus of the status of man), unless he is defending the life of his son, or his own, or the achievement of a lifetime; so that in final judgment of the Gradus versus the Crown case I would submit that if his human incompleteness be deemed insufficient to explain his idiotic journey across the Atlantic just to empty the magazine of his gun, we may concede, doctor, that our halfman was also half mad.

Aboard the small and uncomfortable plane flying into the sun he found himself wedged among several belated delegates to the New Wye Linguistic Conference, all of them lapel-labeled, and representing the same foreign language, but none being able to speak it, so that conversation was conducted (across our hunched-up killer and on all sides of his immobile face) in rather ordinary Anglo-American. During this ordeal, poor Gradus kept wondering what caused another discomfort which kept troubling him on and off throughout the flight, and which was worse than the babble of the monolinguists. He could not settle what to attribute it to—pork, cabbage, fried potatoes or melon—for upon retasting them one by one in spasmodic retrospect he found little to choose between their different but equally sickening flavors. My own opinion, which I would like the doctor to confirm, is that the French sandwich was engaged in an intestinal internecine war with the "French" fries.

Upon arriving after five at the New Wye airport he drank two papercupfuls of nice cold milk from a dispenser and acquired a map at the desk. With broad blunt finger tapping the configuration of the campus that resembled a writhing stomach, he asked the clerk what hotel was nearest to the university. A car, he was told, would take him to the Campus Hotel which was a few minutes' walk from the Main Hall (now Shade Hall). During the ride he suddenly became aware of such urgent qualms that he was forced to visit the washroom as soon as he got to the solidly booked hotel. There his misery resolved itself in a scalding torrent of indigestion. Hardly had he refastened his trousers and checked the bulge of his hip pocket than a renewal of stabs and queaks caused him to strip his thighs again which he did with such awkward precipitation that his small Browning was all but sent flying into the depths of the toilet.

He was still groaning and grinding his dentures when he and his briefcase re-offended the sun. It shone with all sorts of speckled effects through the trees, and College Town was gay with summer students and visiting linguists, among whom Gradus might have easily passed for a salesman hawking Basic-English primers for American schoolchildren or those wonderful new translating machines that can do it so much faster than a man or an animal.

A grave disappointment awaited him at Main Hall: it had closed for the day. Three students lying on the grass suggested he try the Library, and all three pointed to it across the lawn. Thither trudged our thug.

"I don't know where he lives," said the girl at the desk. "But I know he is here right now. You'll find him, I'm sure, in North West Three where we have the Icelandic Collection. You go south [waving her pencil] and turn west, and then west again where you see a sort of, a sort of [pencil making a circular wiggle—round table? round bookshelf?]— No, wait a minute, you better just keep going west till you hit the Florence Houghton Room, and there you cross over to the north side of the building. You cannot miss it" [returning pencil to ear].

Not being a mariner or a fugitive king, he promptly got lost and after vainly progressing through a labyrinth of stacks, asked about the Icelandic Collection of a stern-looking mother librarian who was checking cards in a steel cabinet on a landing. Her slow and detailed directions promptly led him back to the main desk.

"Please, I cannot find," he said, slowly shaking his head.

"Didn't you—" the girl began, and suddenly pointed up: "Oh, there he is!"

Along the open gallery that ran above the hall, parallel to its short side, a tall bearded man was crossing over at a military quick march from east to west. He vanished behind a bookcase but not before Gradus had recognized the great rugged frame, the erect carriage, the high-bridged nose, the straight brow, and the energetic arm swing, of Charles Xavier the Beloved.

Our pursuer made for the nearest stairs—and soon found himself among the bewitched hush of Rare Books. The room was beautiful and had no doors; in fact, some moments passed before he could discover the draped entrance he himself had just used. The awful perplexities of his quest blending with the renewal of impossible pangs in his belly, he dashed back—ran three steps down and nine steps up, and burst into a circular room where a bald-headed suntanned professor in a Hawaiian shirt sat at a round table reading with an ironic expression on his face a Russian book. He paid no attention to Gradus who traversed the room, stepped over a fat little white dog without awakening it, clattered down a helical staircase and found himself in Vault P. Here, a well-lit, pipe-lined, white-washed passage led him to the sudden paradise of a water closet for plumbers or lost scholars where, cursing, he hurriedly transferred his automatic from its precarious dangle-pouch to his coat and relieved himself of another portion of the liquid hell inside him. He started to climb up again, and

noticed in the temple light of the stacks an employee, a slim
Hindu boy, with a call card in his hand. I had never spoken
to that lad but had felt more than once his blue-brown gaze
upon me, and no doubt my academic pseudonym was familiar
to him but some sensitive cell in him, some chord of intuition,
reacted to the harshness of the killer's interrogation and, as if
protecting me from a cloudy danger, he smiled and said: "I
do not know him, sir."

Gradus returned to the Main Desk.

"Too bad," said the girl, "I just saw him leave."

"Bozhe moy, Bozhe moy," muttered Gradus, who sometimes
at moments of stress used Russian ejaculations.

"You'll find him in the directory," she said pushing it towards him, and dismissing the sick man's existence to attend
to the wants of Mr. Gerald Emerald who was taking out a fat
bestseller in a cellophane jacket.

Moaning and shifting from one foot to the other, Gradus
started leafing through the college directory but when he
found the address, he was faced with the problem of getting
there.

"Dulwich Road," he cried to the girl. "Near? Far? Very far,
probably?"

"Are you by any chance Professor Pnin's new assistant?"
asked Emerald.

"No," said the girl. "This man is looking for Dr. Kinbote,
I think. You are looking for Dr. Kinbote, aren't you?"

"Yes, and I can't any more," said Gradus.

"I thought so," said the girl. "Doesn't he live somewhere
near Mr. Shade, Gerry?"

"Oh, definitely," said Gerry, and turned to the killer: "I
can drive you there if you like. It is on my way."

Did they talk in the car, these two characters, the man in
green and the man in brown? Who can say? They did not.
After all, the drive took only a few minutes (it took me, at
the wheel of my powerful Kramler, four and a half).

"I think I'll drop you here," said Mr. Emerald. "It's that
house up there."

One finds it hard to decide what Gradus alias Grey wanted
more at that minute: discharge his gun or rid himself of the
inexhaustible lava in his bowels. As he began hurriedly fum-

bling at the car door, unfastidious Emerald leaned, close to him, across him, almost merging with him, to help him open it—and then, slamming it shut again, whizzed on to some tryst in the valley. My reader will, I hope, appreciate all the minute particulars I have taken such trouble to present to him after a long talk I had with the killer; he will appreciate them even more if I tell him that, according to the legend spread later by the police, Jack Grey had been given a lift, all the way from Roanoke, or somewhere, by a lonesome trucker! One can only hope that an impartial search will turn up the trilby forgotten in the Library—or in Mr. Emerald's car.

Line 957:   Night Rote

I remember one little poem from *Night Rote* (meaning "the nocturnal sound of the sea") that happened to be my first contact with the American poet Shade. A young lecturer on American Literature, a brilliant and charming boy from Boston, showed me that slim and lovely volume in Onhava, in my student days. The following lines opening this poem, which is entitled "Art," pleased me by their catchy lilt and jarred upon the religious sentiments instilled in me by our very "high" Zemblan church.

> From mammoth hunts and Odysseys
> And Oriental charms
> To the Italian goddesses
> With Flemish babes in arms.

Line 962: Help me, Will. Pale Fire.

Paraphrased, this evidently means: Let me look in Shakespeare for something I might use for a title. And the find is "pale fire." But in which of the Bard's works did our poet cull it? My readers must make their own research. All I have with me is a tiny vest pocket edition of *Timon of Athens*—in Zemblan! It certainly contains nothing that could be regarded as an equivalent of "pale fire" (if it had, my luck would have been a statistical monster).

English was not taught in Zembla before Mr. Campbell's time. Conmal mastered it all by himself (mainly by learning a lexicon by heart) as a young man, around 1880, when not the verbal inferno but a quiet military career seemed to open before him, and his first work (the translation of Shakespeare's *Sonnets*) was the outcome of a bet with a fellow officer. He exchanged his frogged uniform for a scholar's dressing gown and tackled *The Tempest*. A slow worker, he needed half a century to translate the works of him whom he called "dze Bart," in their entirety. After this, in 1930, he went on to Milton and other poets, steadily drilling through the ages, and had just completed Kipling's "The Rhyme of the Three Sealers" ("Now this is the Law of the Muscovite that he proves with shot and steel") when he fell ill and soon expired under his splendid painted bed ceil with its reproductions of Altamira animals, his last words in his last delirium being *"Comment dit-on 'mourir' en anglais?"*—a beautiful and touching end.

It is easy to sneer at Conmal's faults. They are the naïve failings of a great pioneer. He lived too much in his library, too little among boys and youths. Writers should see the world, pluck its figs and peaches, and not keep constantly meditating in a tower of yellow ivory—which was also John Shade's mistake, in a way.

We should not forget that when Conmal began his stupendous task no English author was available in Zemblan except Jane de Faun, a lady novelist in ten volumes whose works, strangely enough, are unknown in England, and some fragments of Byron translated from French versions.

A large, sluggish man with no passions save poetry, he seldom moved from his warm castle and its fifty thousand crested books, and had been known to spend two years in bed reading and writing after which, much refreshed, he went for the first and only time to London, but the weather was foggy, and he could not understand the language, and so went back to bed for another year.

English being Conmal's prerogative, his *Shakspere* remained invulnerable throughout the greater part of his long life. The venerable Duke was famed for the nobility of his work; few dared question its fidelity. Personally, I had never the heart to check it. One callous Academician who did, lost his seat in result and was severely reprimanded by Conmal in an extraordinary sonnet composed directly in colorful, if not quite correct, English, beginning:

> I am not slave! Let be my critic slave.
> I cannot be. And Shakespeare would not want thus.
> Let drawing students copy the acanthus,
> I work with Master on the architrave!

Line 991: horseshoes

Neither Shade nor I had ever been able to ascertain whence precisely those ringing sounds came—which of the five families dwelling across the road on the lower slopes of our woody hill played horseshoe quoits every other evening; but the tantalizing tingles and jingles contributed a pleasant melancholy note to the rest of Dulwich Hill's evening sonorities—children calling to each other, children being called home, and the ecstatic barking of the boxer dog whom most of the neighbors disliked (he overturned garbage cans) greeting his master home.

It was this medley of metallic melodies which surrounded me on that fateful, much too luminous evening of July 21 when upon roaring home from the library in my powerful car I at once went to see what my dear neighbor was doing. I had just met Sybil speeding townward and therefore nursed some hopes for the evening. I grant you I very much resembled a lean wary lover taking advantage of a young husband's being alone in the house!

Through the trees I distinguished John's white shirt and gray hair: he sat in his Nest (as he called it), the arborlike porch or veranda I have mentioned in my note to lines 47–48. I could not keep from advancing a little nearer—oh, discreetly, almost on tiptoe; but then I noticed he was resting rather than writing, and I openly walked up to his porch or perch. His elbow was on the table, his fist supported his temple, his wrinkles were all awry, his eyes moist and misty; he

looked like an old tipsy witch. He lifted his free hand in greeting without changing his attitude, which although not unfamiliar to me struck me this time as more forlorn than pensive.

"Well," I said, "has the muse been kind to you?"

"Very kind," he replied, slightly bowing his hand-propped
head: "Exceptionally kind and gentle. In fact, I have here [in-
dicating a huge pregnant envelope near him on the oilcloth]
practically the entire product. A few trifles to settle and [sud-
denly striking the table with his fist] I've swung it, by God."

The envelope, unfastened at one end, bulged with stacked
cards.

"Where is the missus?" I asked (mouth dry).

"Help me, Charlie, to get out of here," he pleaded. "Foot
gone to sleep. Sybil is at a dinner meeting of her club."

"A suggestion," I said, quivering. "I have at my place half
a gallon of Tokay. I'm ready to share my favorite wine with
my favorite poet. We shall have for dinner a knackle of wal-
nuts, a couple of large tomatoes, and a bunch of bananas. And
if you agree to show me your 'finished product,' there will be
another treat: I promise to divulge to you *why* I gave you, or
rather *who* gave you, your theme."

"What theme?" said Shade absently, as he leaned on my
arm and gradually recovered the use of his numb limb.

"Our blue inenubilable Zembla, and the red-capped Steinmann, and the motorboat in the sea cave, and—"

"Ah," said Shade, "I think I guessed your secret quite some
time ago. But all the same I shall sample your wine with pleasure. Okay, I can manage by myself now."

Well did I know he could never resist a golden drop of this
or that, especially since he was severely rationed at home. With
an inward leap of exultation I relieved him of the large envelope that hampered his movements as he descended the
steps of the porch, sideways, like a hesitating infant. We
crossed the lawn, we crossed the road. Clink-clank, came the
horseshoe music from Mystery Lodge. In the large envelope
I carried I could feel the hard-cornered, rubberbanded batches
of index cards. We are absurdly accustomed to the miracle of
a few written signs being able to contain immortal imagery,
involutions of thought, new worlds with live people, speaking,
weeping, laughing. We take it for granted so simply that in a

sense, by the very act of brutish routine acceptance, we undo
the work of the ages, the history of the gradual elaboration
of poetical description and construction, from the treeman to
Browning, from the caveman to Keats. What if we awake one
day, all of us, and find ourselves utterly unable to read? I wish
you to gasp not only at what you read but at the miracle of
its being readable (so I used to tell my students). Although I
am capable, through long dabbling in blue magic, of imitating
any prose in the world (but singularly enough not verse—I
am a miserable rhymester), I do not consider myself a true
artist, save in one matter: I can do what only a true artist can
do—pounce upon the forgotten butterfly of revelation, wean
myself abruptly from the habit of things, see the web of the
world, and the warp and the weft of that web. Solemnly I
weighed in my hand what I was carrying under my left armpit,
and for a moment I found myself enriched with an indescribable amazement as if informed that fireflies were making de-
codable signals on behalf of stranded spirits, or that a bat was
writing a legible tale of torture in the bruised and branded
sky.

I was holding all Zembla pressed to my heart.

Lines 993–995:   A dark Vanessa, etc.

One minute before his death, as we were crossing from his
demesne to mine and had begun working up between the
junipers and ornamental shrubs, a Red Admirable (see note
to line 270) came dizzily whirling around us like a colored
flame. Once or twice before we had already noticed the same
individual, at that same time, on that same spot, where the
low sun finding an aperture in the foliage splashed the brown
sand with a last radiance while the evening's shade covered
the rest of the path. One's eyes could not follow the rapid
butterfly in the sunbeams as it flashed and vanished, and
flashed again, with an almost frightening imitation of conscious play which now culminated in its settling upon my delighted friend's sleeve. It took off, and we saw it next moment
sporting in an ecstasy of frivolous haste around a laurel shrub,
every now and then perching on a lacquered leaf and sliding

down its grooved middle like a boy down the banisters on his birthday. Then the tide of the shade reached the laurels, and the magnificent, velvet-and-flame creature dissolved in it.

Line 998: Some neighbor's gardener

Some neighbor's! The poet had seen my gardener many times, and this vagueness I can only assign to his desire (noticeable elsewhere in his handling of names, etc.) to give a certain poetical patina, the bloom of remoteness, to familiar figures and things—although it is just possible he might have mistaken him in the broken light for a stranger working for a stranger. This gifted gardener I discovered by chance one idle spring day when I was slowly wending my way home after a maddening and embarrassing experience at the college indoor swimming pool. He stood at the top of a green ladder attending to the sick branch of a grateful tree in one of the most famous avenues in Appalachia. His red flannel shirt lay on the grass. We conversed, a little shyly, he above, I below. I was pleasantly surprised at his being able to refer all his patients to their proper habitats. It was spring, and we were alone in that admirable colonnade of trees which visitors from England have photographed from end to end. I can enumerate here only a few kinds of those trees: Jove's stout oak and two others: the thunder-cloven from Britain, the knotty-entrailed from a Mediterranean island; a weather-fending line (now lime), a phoenix (now date palm), a pine and a cedar (*Cedrus*), all insular; a Venetian sycamore tree (*Acer*); two willows, the green, likewise from Venice, the hoar-leaved from Denmark; a midsummer elm, its barky fingers enringed with ivy; a midsummer mulberry, its shade inviting to tarry; and a clown's sad cypress from Illyria.

He had worked for two years as a male nurse in a hospital for Negroes in Maryland. He was hard up. He wanted to study landscaping, botany and French ("to read in the original Baudelaire and Dumas"). I promised him some financial assistance. He started to work at my place the very next day. He was awfully nice and pathetic, and all that, but a little too talkative and completely impotent which I found discouraging.

Otherwise he was a strong strapping fellow, and I hugely enjoyed the aesthetic pleasure of watching him buoyantly struggle with earth and turf or delicately manipulate bulbs, or lay out the flagged path which may or may not be a nice surprise for my landlord, when he safely returns from England (where I hope no bloodthirsty maniacs are stalking him!). How I longed to have him (my gardener, not my landlord) wear a great big turban, and shalwars, and an ankle bracelet. I would certainly have him attired according to the old romanticist notion of a Moorish prince, had I been a northern king—or rather had I still been a king (exile becomes a bad habit). You will chide me, my modest man, for writing so much about you in this note, but I feel I must pay you this tribute. After all, you saved my life. You and I were the last people who saw John Shade alive, and you admitted afterwards to a strange premonition which made you interrupt your work as you noticed us from the shrubbery walking toward the porch where stood—(Superstitiously I cannot write out the odd dark word you employed.)

Line 1000:   [= *Line 1*: I was the shadow of the waxwing slain]

Through the back of John's thin cotton shirt one could distinguish patches of pink where it stuck to the skin above and around the outline of the funny little garment he wore under the shirt as all good Americans do. I see with such awful clarity one fat shoulder rolling, the other rising; his gray mop of hair, his creased nape; the red bandanna handkerchief limply hanging out of one hip pocket, the wallet bulge of the other; the broad deformed pelvis; the grass stains on the seat of his old khaki pants, the scuffed back seams of his loafers; and I hear his delightful growl as he looks back at me, without stopping, to say something like: "Be sure not to spill anything—this is not a paper chase," or [wincing] "I'll have to write again to Bob Wells [the town mayor] about those damned Tuesday night trucks."

We had reached the Goldsworth side of the lane, and the flagged walk that scrambled along a side lawn to connect with the gravel path leading up from Dulwich road to the

Goldsworth front door, when Shade remarked: "You have a caller."

In profile to us on the porch a short thickset, dark-haired man in a brown suit stood holding by its ridiculous strap a shabby and shapeless briefcase, his curved forefinger still directed toward the bell button he had just pressed.

"I will kill him," I muttered. Recently a bonneted girl had made me accept a bunch of religious tracts and had told me that her brother, whom for some reason I had pictured to myself as a fragile neurotic youth, would drop in to discuss with me God's Purpose, and explain anything I had not understood in the tracts. Youth, indeed!

"Oh, I will kill him," I repeated under my breath—so intolerable was it to think that the rapture of the poem might be delayed. In my fury and hurry to dismiss the intruder, I outstripped John who until then had been in front of me, heading at a good shamble for the double treat of revel and revelation.

Had I ever seen Gradus before? Let me think. Had I? Memory shakes her head. Nevertheless the killer affirmed to me later that once from my tower, overlooking the Palace orchard, I had waved to him as he and one of my former pages, a boy with hair like excelsior, were carrying cradled glass from the hothouse to a horse-drawn van; but, as the caller now veered toward us and transfixed us with his snake-sad, close-set eyes, I felt such a tremor of recognition that had I been in bed dreaming I would have awoken with a groan.

His first bullet ripped a sleeve button off my black blazer, another sang past my ear. It is evil piffle to assert that he aimed not at me (whom he had just seen in the library—let us be consistent, gentlemen, ours is a rational world after all), but at the gray-locked gentleman behind me. Oh, he was aiming at me all right but missing me every time, the incorrigible bungler, as I instinctively backed, bellowing and spreading my great strong arms (with my left hand still holding the poem, "still clutching the inviolable shade," to quote Matthew Arnold, 1822–1888), in an effort to halt the advancing madman and shield John, whom I feared he might, quite accidentally, hit, while he, my sweet awkward old John, kept clawing at me and pulling me after him, back to the protection of his laurels, with the solemn fussiness of a poor lame boy trying to get his spastic brother out of the range of the stones hurled at them by schoolchildren, once a familiar sight in all countries. I felt—I still feel—John's hand fumbling at mine, seeking my fingertips, finding them, only to abandon them at once as if passing to me, in a sublime relay race, the baton of life.

One of the bullets that spared me struck him in the side and went through his heart. His presence behind me abruptly failing me caused me to lose my balance, and, simultaneously, to complete the farce of fate, my gardener's spade dealt gunman Jack from behind the hedge a tremendous blow on the pate, felling him and sending his weapon flying from his grasp. Our savior retrieved it and helped me to my feet. My coccyx and right wrist hurt badly but the poem was safe. John, though, lay prone on the ground, with a red spot on his white shirt. I still hoped he had not been killed. The madman sat on the porch step, dazedly nursing with bloody hands a bleeding head. Leaving the gardener to watch over him I hurried into the house and concealed the invaluable envelope under a heap of girls' galoshes, furred snowboots and white wellingtons heaped at the bottom of a closet, from which I exited as if it had been the end of the secret passage that had taken me all the way out of my enchanted castle and right from Zembla to *this* Arcady. I then dialed 11111 and returned with a glass of water to the scene of the carnage. The poor poet had now been turned over and lay with open dead eyes directed up at the sunny evening azure. The armed gardener and the battered killer were smoking side by side on the steps. The latter, either because he was in pain, or because he had decided to play a new role, ignored me as completely as if I were a stone king on a stone charger in the Tessera Square of Onhava; but the poem was safe.

The gardener took the glass of water I had placed near a flowerpot beside the porch steps and shared it with the killer, and then accompanied him to the basement toilet, and presently the police and the ambulance arrived, and the gunman gave his name as Jack Grey, no fixed abode, except the Institute for the Criminal Insane, *ici*, good dog, which of course should have been his permanent address all along, and which the police thought he had just escaped from.

"Come along, Jack, we'll put something on that head of yours," said a calm but purposeful cop stepping over the body, and then there was the awful moment when Dr. Sutton's daughter drove up with Sybil Shade.

In the course of that chaotic night I found a moment to transfer the poem from under the booties of Goldsworth's four nymphets to the austere security of my black valise, but only at daybreak did I find it safe enough to examine my treasure.

We know how firmly, how stupidly I believed that Shade was composing a poem, a kind of *romaunt*, about the King of Zembla. We have been prepared for the horrible disappointment in store for me. Oh, I did not expect him to devote himself *completely* to that theme! It might have been blended of course with some of his own life stuff and sundry Americana—but I was sure his poem would contain the wonderful incidents I had described to him, the characters I had made alive for him and all the unique *atmosphere* of my kingdom. I even suggested to him a good title—the title of the book in me whose pages he was to cut: *Solus Rex*; instead of which I saw *Pale Fire*, which meant to me nothing. I started to read the poem. I read faster and faster. I sped through it, snarling, as a furious young heir through an old deceiver's testament. Where were the battlements of my sunset castle? Where was Zembla the Fair? Where her spine of mountains? Where her long thrill through the mist? And my lovely flower boys, and the spectrum of the stained windows, and the Black Rose Paladins, and the whole marvelous tale? Nothing of it was there! The complex contribution I had been pressing upon him with a hypnotist's patience and a lover's urge was simply not there. Oh, but I cannot express the agony! Instead of the wild glorious romance—what did I have? An autobiographical, eminently Appalachian, rather old-fashioned narrative in a neo-Popian prosodic style—beautifully written of course— Shade could not write otherwise than beautifully—but void of my magic, of that special rich streak of magical madness which I was sure would run through it and make it transcend its time.

Gradually I regained my usual composure. I reread *Pale Fire* more carefully. I liked it better when expecting less. And what was that? What was that dim distant music, those vestiges of color in the air? Here and there I discovered in it and especially, especially in the invaluable variants, echoes and spangles of my mind, a long ripplewake of my glory. I now felt a new, pitiful tenderness toward the poem as one has for a fickle young creature who has been stolen and brutally enjoyed by a black giant but now again is safe in our hall and park, whistling with the stableboys, swimming with the tame seal. The spot still hurts, it must hurt, but with strange gratitude we kiss those heavy wet eyelids and caress that polluted flesh.

My commentary to this poem, now in the hands of my readers, represents an attempt to sort out those echoes and wavelets of fire, and pale phosphorescent hints, and all the many subliminal debts to me. Some of my notes may sound bitter—but I have done my best not to air any grievances. And in this final scholium my intention is not to complain of the vulgar and cruel nonsense that professional reporters and Shade's "friends" in the obituaries they concocted allowed themselves to spout when misdescribing the circumstances of Shade's death. I regard their references to me as a mixture of journalistic callousness and the venom of vipers. I do not doubt that many of the statements made in this work will be brushed aside by the guilty parties when it is out. Mrs. Shade will not remember having been shown by her husband who "showed her everything" one or two of the precious variants. The three students lying on the grass will turn out to be totally amnesic. The desk girl at the Library will not recall (will have been told not to recall) anybody asking for Dr. Kinbote on the day of the murder. And I am sure that Mr. Emerald will interrupt briefly his investigation of some mammate student's resilient charms to deny with the vigor of roused virility that he ever gave anybody a lift to my house that evening. In other words, everything will be done to cut off my person completely from my dear friend's fate.

Nevertheless, I have had my little revenge: public misapprehension indirectly helped me to obtain the right of publishing *Pale Fire*. My good gardener, when enthusiastically relating to everybody what he had seen, certainly erred in several respects—not so much perhaps in his exaggerated account of my "heroism" as in the assumption that Shade had been

deliberately aimed at by the so-called Jack Grey; but Shade's
widow found herself so deeply affected by the idea of my having "thrown myself" between the gunman and his target that
during a scene I shall never forget, she cried out, stroking my
hands: "There are things for which no recompense in this
world or another is great enough." That "other world"
comes in handy when misfortune befalls the infidel but I let
it pass of course, and, indeed, resolved not to refute anything,
saying instead: "Oh, but there *is* a recompense, my dear Sybil.
It may seem to you a very modest request but—give me the
permission, Sybil, to edit and publish John's last poem." The
permission was given at once, with new cries and new hugs,
and already next day her signature was under the agreement
I had a quick little lawyer draw up. That moment of grateful
grief you soon forgot, dear girl. But I assure you that I do
not mean any harm, and that John Shade, perhaps, will not
be too much annoyed by my notes, despite the intrigues and
the dirt.

Because of these machinations I was confronted with nightmare problems in my endeavors to make people calmly see—
without having them immediately scream and hustle me—the
truth of the tragedy—a tragedy in which I had been not a
"chance witness" but the protagonist, and the main, if only
potential, victim. The hullabaloo ended by affecting the
course of my new life, and necessitated my removal to this
modest mountain cabin; but I did manage to obtain, soon
after his detention, an interview, perhaps even two interviews,
with the prisoner. He was now much more lucid than when
he cowered bleeding on my porch step, and he told me all I
wanted to know. By making him believe I could help him at
his trial I forced him to confess his heinous crime—his de-
ceiving the police and the nation by posing as Jack Grey, es-
capee from an asylum, who mistook Shade for the man who
sent him there. A few days later, alas, he thwarted justice by
slitting his throat with a safety razor blade salvaged from an
unwatched garbage container. He died, not so much because
having played his part in the story he saw no point in existing
any longer, but because he could not live down this last
crowning botch—killing the wrong person when the right one
stood before him. In other words, his life ended not in a feeble

splutter of the clockwork but in a gesture of humanoid despair. Enough of this. Exit Jack Grey.

I cannot recall without a shudder the lugubrious week that I spent in New Wye before leaving it, I hope, forever. I lived in constant fear that robbers would deprive me of my tender treasure. Some of my readers may laugh when they learn that I fussily removed it from my black valise to an empty steel box in my landlord's study, and a few hours later took the manuscript out again, and for several days *wore* it, as it were, having distributed the ninety-two index cards about my person, twenty in the right-hand pocket of my coat, as many in the left-hand one, a batch of forty against my right nipple and the twelve precious ones with variants in my innermost left-breast pocket. I blessed my royal stars for having taught myself wife work, for I now sewed up all four pockets. Thus with cautious steps, among deceived enemies, I circulated, plated with poetry, armored with rhymes, stout with another man's song, stiff with cardboard, bullet-proof at long last.

Many years ago—how many I would not care to say—I remember my Zemblan nurse telling me, a little man of six in the throes of adult insomnia: *"Minnamin, Gut mag alkan, Pern dirstan"* (my darling, God makes hungry, the Devil thirsty). Well, folks, I guess many in this fine hall are as hungry and thirsty as me, and I'd better stop, folks, right here.

Yes, better stop. My notes and self are petering out. Gentlemen, I have suffered very much, and more than any of you can imagine. I pray for the Lord's benediction to rest on my wretched countrymen. My work is finished. My poet is dead.

"And you, what will *you* be doing with yourself, poor King, poor Kinbote?" a gentle young voice may inquire.

God will help me, I trust, to rid myself of any desire to follow the example of two other characters in this work. I shall continue to exist. I may assume other disguises, other forms, but I shall try to exist. I may turn up yet, on another campus, as an old, happy, healthy, heterosexual Russian, a writer in exile, sans fame, sans future, sans audience, sans anything but his art. I may join forces with Odon in a new motion picture: *Escape from Zembla* (ball in the palace, bomb in the palace square). I may pander to the simple tastes of theatrical critics and cook up a stage play, an old-fashioned melodrama with three principles: a lunatic who intends to kill an imaginary king, another lunatic who imagines himself to be that king, and a distinguished old poet who stumbles by chance into the line of fire, and perishes in the clash between the two figments. Oh, I may do many things! History permitting, I may sail back to my recovered kingdom, and with a great sob greet the gray coastline and the gleam of a roof in the rain. I may huddle and groan in a madhouse. But whatever happens, wherever the scene is laid, somebody, somewhere, will quietly set out—somebody has already set out, somebody still rather far away is buying a ticket, is boarding a bus, a ship, a plane, has landed, is walking toward a million photographers, and presently he will ring at my door—a bigger, more respectable, more competent Gradus.

Index

The italicized numerals refer to the lines in the poem and the comments thereon. The capital letters G, K, S (which see) stand for the three main characters in this work.

A., Baron, Oswin Affenpin, last Baron of Aff, a puny traitor, *286.*

Acht, Iris, celebrated actress, d. 1888, a passionate and powerful woman, favorite of Thurgus the Third (*q.v.*), *130.* She died officially by her own hand; unofficially, strangled in her dressing room by a fellow actor, a jealous young Gothlander, now, at ninety, the oldest, and least important, member of the Shadows (*q.v.*) group.

Alfin, King, surnamed The Vague, 1873–1918, reigned from 1900; K.'s father; a kind, gentle, absent-minded monarch, mainly interested in automobiles, flying machines, motorboats and, at one time, sea shells; killed in an airplane accident, *71.*

Andronnikov and Niagarin, two Soviet experts in quest of a buried treasure, *130, 681, 741;* see Crown Jewels.

Arnor, Romulus, poet about town and Zemblan patriot, 1914–1958, his poem quoted, *80;* executed by the Extremists.

Aros, a fine town in E. Zembla, capital of Conmal's dukedom; once the mayorship of the worthy Ferz ("chessqueen") Bretwit, a cousin of the granduncle of Oswin Bretwit (*q.v.*), *149, 286.*

B., Baron, involuntary father-in-law of Baron A. and imaginary old friend of the Bretwit (*q.v.*) family, *286.*

Bera, a mountain range dividing the peninsula lengthwise; described with some of its glittering peaks, mysterious passes and picturesque slopes, *149.*

Blawick, Blue Cove, a pleasant seaside resort on the Western Coast of Zembla, casino, golf course, sea food, boats for hire, *149.*

Blenda, Queen, the King's mother, 1878–1936, reigned from 1918, *71.*

Boscobel, site of the Royal Summerhouse, a beautiful, piny and duny spot in W. Zembla, soft hollows imbued with the writer's most amorous recollections; now (1959) a "nudist colony"—whatever that is, *149, 596.*

Botkin, V., American scholar of Russian descent, *894;* king-bot, maggot of extinct fly that once bred in mammoths and is thought to have hastened their phylogenetic end, *247;* bottekin-maker, *71; bot,* plop, and *boteliÿ,* big-bellied (Russ.); botkin or bodkin, a Danish stiletto.

Bregberg. See Bera.

Bretwit, Oswin, 1914–1959, diplomat and Zemblan patriot, *286.* See also under Odevalla and Aros.

Campbell, Walter, b. 1890, in Glasgow; K.'s tutor, 1922–1931, an amiable gentleman with a mellow and rich mind; dead shot and champion skater; now in Iran; *130.*

Charles II, Charles Xavier Vseslav, last King of Zembla, surnamed The Beloved, b. 1915, reigned 1936–1958; his crest, *1;* his studies and his reign, *12;* fearful fate of predecessors, *62;* his supporters, *70;* parents, *71;* bedroom, *80;* escape from palace, *130;* and across the mountains, *149;* engagement to Disa recalled, *275;* parenthetical passage through Paris, *286;* and through Switzerland, *408;* visit to Villa Disa, *433;* night in mountains recalled, *597, 662;* his Russian blood, and Crown Jewels (*q.v.* by all means), *681;* his arrival in the U.S.A., *691;* letter to Disa stolen, *741;* and quoted, *768;* his portrait discussed, *894;* his presence in library, *949;* identity almost revealed, *991;* Solus Rex, *1000.* See also Kinbote.

Conmal, Duke of Aros, 1855–1955, K.'s uncle, the eldest half-brother of Queen Blenda (*q.v.*); noble paraphrast, *12;* his version of *Timon of Athens, 39, 130;* his life and work, *962.*

Crown Jewels, 130, 681; see Hiding Place.

Disa, Duchess of Payn, of Great Payn and Mone; my lovely, pale, melancholy Queen, haunting my dreams, and haunted by dreams of me, b. 1928; her album and favorite trees, *49;* married 1949, *80;* her letters on ethereal paper with a watermark I cannot make out, her image torturing me in my sleep, *433.*

Embla, a small old town with a wooden church surrounded by sphagnum bogs at the saddest, loneliest, northmost point of the misty peninsula, *149, 433.*

Emblem, meaning "blooming" in Zemblan; a beautiful bay with bluish and black, curiously striped rocks and a luxurious growth of heather on its gentle slopes, in the southmost part of W. Zembla, *433.*

Falkberg, a pink cone, *71;* snowhooded, *149.*

Flatman, Thomas, 1637–88, English poet, scholar and miniaturist, not known to old fraud, *894.*

Fleur, Countess de Fyler, an elegant lady-in-waiting, *71, 80, 433.*

G, see Gradus.

Garh, a farmer's daughter, *149, 433.* Also a rosy-cheeked gooseboy found in a country lane, north of Troth, in 1936, only now distinctly recalled by the writer.

Glitterntin, Mt., a splendid mountain in the Bera Range (*q.v.*); pity I may never climb it again, *149.*

Gordon, see Krummholz.

Gradus, Jakob, 1915–1959; alias Jack Degree, de Grey, d' Argus, Vin-ogradus, Leningradus, etc.; a Jack of small trades and a killer, *12, 17*; lynching the wrong people, *80*; his approach synchronized with S's work on the poem, *120, 131*; his election and past tribulations, *171*; the first lap of his journey, Onhava to Copenhagen, *181, 209*; to Paris, and meeting with Oswin Bretwit, *286*; to Geneva, and talk with little Gordon at Joe Lavender's place near Lex, *408*; calling headquarters from Geneva, *469*; his name in a variant, and his wait in Geneva, *596*; to Nice, and his wait there, *697*; his meeting with Izumrudov in Nice and discovery of the King's address, *741*; from Paris to New York, *873*; in New York, *949*[1]; his morning in New York, his journey to New Wye, to the campus, to Dulwich Rd., *949*[2]; the crowning blunder, *1000*.

Griff, old mountain farmer and Zemblan patriot, *149*.

Grindelwod, a fine town in E. Zembla, *71, 149*.

Hiding place, *potaynik* (*q.v.*).

Hodinski, Russian adventurer, d. 1800, also known as Hodyna, *681*; resided in Zembla 1778–1800; author of a celebrated pastiche and lover of Princess (later Queen) Yaruga (*q.v.*), mother of Igor II, grandmother of Thurgus (*q.v.*).

Igor II, reigned 1800–1845, a wise and benevolent king, son of Queen Yaruga (*q.v.*) and father of Thurgus III (*q.v.*); a very private section of the picture gallery in the Palace, accessible only to the reigning monarch, but easily broken into through Bower P by an inquisitive pubescent, contained the statues of Igor's four hundred favorite catamites, in pink marble, with inset glass eyes and various touched up details, an outstanding exhibition of verisimilitude and bad art, later presented by K. to an Asiatic potentate.

K, see Charles II and Kinbote.

Kalixhaven, a colorful seaport on the western coast, a few miles north of Blawick (*q.v.*), *171*; many pleasant memories.

Kinbote, Charles, Dr., an intimate friend of S, his literary adviser, ed-itor and commentator; first meeting and friendship with S, *Fore-word*; his interest in Appalachian birds, *1*; his good-natured request to have S use his stories, *12*; his modesty, *34*; his having no library in his Timonian cave, *39*; his belief in his having inspired S, *42*; his house in Dulwich Road, and the windows of S's house, *47*; Prof. H. contradicted and corrected, *61, 71*; his anxieties and insomnias, *62*; the map he made for S, *71*; his sense of humor, *79, 91*; his belief that the term "iridule" is S's invention, *109*; his weariness, *120*; his sports activities, *130*; his visit to S's basement, *143*; his trusting the reader enjoyed the note *149*; boyhood and the Orient Express re-called, *162*; his request that the reader consult a later note, *169*; his quiet warning to G, *171*; his remarks on critics and other sallies endorsed by S, *172*; his participation in certain festivities elsewhere, his being debarred from S's birthday party upon coming home, and his sly trick next morning, *181*; his hearing about Hazel's "poltergeist" phase, *230*; poor who? *231*; his futile attempts to have S get off the subject of natural history and report on the work in progress, *238*; his recollection of the quays in Nice and Mentone, *240*; his utmost courtesy towards his friend's wife, *247*; his limited knowledge of lepidoptera and the sable gloom of his nature marked like a dark Vanessa with gay flashes, *270*; his discovery of Mrs. S's plan to whisk S to Cedarn and his decision to go there too, *287*; his attitude towards swans, *319*; his affinity with Hazel, *334, 348*; his walk with S to the weedy spot where the haunted barn once stood, *347*; his objection to S's flippant attitude towards celebrated contemporaries, *376*; his contempt for Prof. H. (not in Index), *377*; his overworked memory, *384*; his meeting with Jane Provost and examination of lovely lakeside snapshots, *385*; his criticism of the 403–474 lines section, *403*; his secret guessed, or not guessed, by S, his telling S about Disa, and S's reaction, *433–434*; his debate on Prejudice with S, *470*; his discussion of Suicide with himself, *493*; his surprise at realizing that the French name of one melancholy tree is the same as the Zemblan one of another, *501*; his disapproval of certain flippant passages in Canto Three, *502*[2]; his views on sin and faith, *549*; his editorial integrity and spiritual misery, *550*; his remarks on a certain female student and on the number and nature of meals shared with the Shades, *579*; his delight and amazement at a portentous meeting of syllables in two adjacent words, *596*; his aphorism on the slayer and the slain, *597*; his logcabin in Cedarn and the little angler, a honey-skinned lad, naked except for a pair of torn dungarees, one trouser leg rolled up, frequently fed with nougat and nuts, but then school started or the weather changed, *609*; his appearance at the H——s, *629*; his severe criticism of quotational titles, from *The Tempest* etc., such as "pale fire," etc., *671*; his sense of humor, *680*; his arrival at Mrs. O'Donnell's country house recalled, *691*; his appreciation of a quodlibet and his doubts anent its purported authorship, *727*; his loathing for a person who makes advances, and then betrays a noble and naïve heart, telling foul stories about his victim and pursuing him with brutal practical jokes, *741*; his not being able, owing to some psychological block or the fear of a second G, of traveling to a city only sixty or seventy miles distant, where he would certainly have found a good library, *747*; his letter of April 2, 1959, to a lady who left it locked up among her treasures in her villa near Nice when she went that summer to Rome, *768*; divine service in the morning and ramble in the evening with the poet finally speaking of his work, *802*; his remarks on a lexical and linguistic miracle, *803*; his borrowing a collection of F. K. Lane's letters from the motor court owner, *810*; his penetrating into the bathroom where his friend sat and shaved in the tub, *887*; his participation in a Common Room discussion of his resemblance to the King, and his final rupture with E. (not in the Index), *894*; he and *S* shaking with mirth over tidbits in a college textbook by Prof. C. (not in the Index), *929*; his sad gesture of weariness and gentle reproach, *937*; a young lecturer in Onhava University vividly recollected, *957*; his last meeting with *S* in the poet's arbor, etc., *991*; his discovery of the scholarly gardener recalled, *998*; his unsuccessful attempt to save *S*'s life, and his success in salvaging the MS, *1000*; his arranging to have it published without the help of two "experts," *Foreword.*

Kobaltana, a once fashionable mountain resort near the ruins of some old barracks now a cold and desolate spot of difficult access and no importance but still remembered in military families and forest castles, not in the text.

Kronberg, a snow-capped rocky mountain with a comfortable hotel, in the Bera Range, *70, 130, 149.*

Krummholz, Gordon, b. 1944, a musical prodigy and an amusing pet; son of Joseph Lavender's famous sister, Elvina Krummholz, *408.*

Lane, Franklin Knight, American lawyer and statesman, 1864–1921, author of a remarkable fragment, *810.*

Lass, see Mass.

Lavender, Joseph S., see O'Donnell, Sylvia.

Male, see Word Golf.

Mandevil, Baron Mirador, cousin of Radomir Mandevil (*q.v.*), experimentalist, madman and traitor, *171.*

Mandevil, Baron Radomir, b. 1925, man of fashion and Zemblan patriot; in 1936, K's throne page, *130*; in 1958, disguised, *149.*

Marcel, the fussy, unpleasant, and not always plausible central character, pampered by everybody in Proust's *A la Recherche du Temps Perdu, 181, 691.*

Marrowsky, a, a rudimentary spoonerism, from the name of a Russian diplomat of the early 19th century, Count Komarovski, famous at foreign courts for mispronouncing his own name—Makarovski, Macaronski, Skomorovski, etc., *347.*

Mass, Mars, Mare, see Male.

Multraberg, see Bera.

Niagarin and Andronnikov, two Soviet "experts" still in quest of a buried treasure, *130, 681, 741*; see Crown Jewels.

Nitra and Indra, twin islands off Blawick, *149.*

Nodo, Odon's half-brother, b. 1916, son of Leopold O'Donnell and of a Zemblan boy impersonator; a cardsharp and despicable traitor, *171*.

Odevalla, a fine town north of Onhava in E. Zembla, once the mayorship of the worthy Zule ("chessrook") Bretwit, grand-uncle of Oswin Bretwit (*q.v., q.v.,* as the crows say), *149, 286.*

Odon, pseudonym of Donald O'Donnell, b. 1915, world-famous actor and Zemblan patriot; learns from K. about secret passage but has to leave for theater, *130*; drives K. from theater to foot of Mt. Mandevil, *149*; meets K. near sea cave and escapes with him in motorboat, *ibid.*; directs cinema picture in Paris, *171*; stays with Lavender in Lex, *408*; ought not to marry that blubber-lipped cinemactress, with untidy hair, *691*; see also O'Donnell, Sylvia.

O'Donnell, Sylvia, nee O'Connell, born 1895? 1890?, the much-traveled, much-married mother of Odon (*q.v.*), *149, 691*; after marrying and divorcing college president Leopold O'Donnell in 1915, father of Odon, she married Peter Gusev, first Duke of Rahl, and graced Zembla till about 1925 when she married an Oriental prince met in Chamonix; after a number of other more or less glamorous marriages, she was in the act of divorcing Lionel Lavender, cousin of Joseph, when last seen in this Index.

Oleg, Duke of Rahl, 1916–1931, son of Colonel Gusev, Duke of Rahl (b. 1885, still spry); K.'s beloved playmate, killed in a toboggan accident, *130.*

Onhava, the beautiful capital of Zembla, *12, 71, 130, 149, 171, 181, 275, 579, 894, 1000.*

Otar, Count, heterosexual man of fashion and Zemblan patriot, b. 1915, his bald spot, his two teenage mistresses, Fleur and Fifalda (later Countess Otar), blue-veined daughters of Countess de Fyler, interesting light effects, *71.*

Paberg, see Bera Range.

Payn, Dukes of, escutcheon of, *270*; see Disa, my Queen.

Poems, Shade's short: The Sacred Tree, 49; The Swing, 61; Mountain View, 92; The Nature of Electricity, 347; one line from *April Rain, 470*; one line from *Mont Blanc, 782*; opening quatrain of *Art, 957.*

Potaynik, taynik (*q.v.*).

Religion: contact with God, *47*; the Pope, *85*; freedom of mind, *101*; problem of sin and faith, *549*; see Suicide.

Rippleson Caves, sea caves in Blawick, named after a famous glass maker who embodied the dapple-and-ringle play and other circular reflections on blue-green sea water in his extraordinary stained glass windows for the Palace, *130, 149.*

Shade, Hazel, S's daughter, 1934–1957; deserves great respect, having preferred the beauty of death to the ugliness of life; the domestic ghost, *230*; the Haunted Barn, *347.*

Shade, John Francis, poet and scholar, 1898–1959; his work on *Pale Fire* and friendship with *K, Foreword*; his physical appearance, mannerisms, habits, etc., *ibid.*; his first brush with death as visualized by *K*, and his beginning the poem while *K* plays chess at the Students' Club, *1*; his sunset rambles with *K, 12*; his dim precognition of *G, 17*; his house seen by *K* in terms of lighted windows, *47*; his starting on the poem, his completing Canto Two, and about half of Three, and *K*'s three visits at those points of time, *ibid.*; his parents, Samuel Shade and Caroline Lukin, *71*; *K*'s influence seen in a variant, *79*; Maud Shade, *S*'s father's sister, *86*; *K* shown *S*'s clockwork *memento mori, 143*; *K* on *S*'s fainting fits, *162*; *S* beginning Canto Two, *167*; *S* on critics, Shakespeare, education, etc., *172*; *K*'s watching *S*'s guests arriving on his and *S*'s birthday, and *S* writing Canto Two, *181*; his worries over his daughter recalled, *230*; his delicacy, or prudence, *231*; his exaggerated interest in the local fauna and flora, *238, 270*; the complications of *K*'s marriage compared to the plainness of *S*'s, *275*; *K*'s drawing *S*'s attention to a pastel smear crossing the sunset sky, *286*; his fear that *S* might leave before finishing their joint composition, *287*; his waiting vainly for *S* on July 15th, *334*; his walk with *S* through old Hentzner's fields and his reconstitution of *S*'s daughter's expeditions to the Haunted Barn, *347*; *S*'s pronunciation, *367*; *S*'s book on Pope, *384*; his grudge against Peter Provost, *385*; his work on lines 406–416 synchronized with *G*'s activities in Switzerland, *408*; again his prudence, or considerateness, *417*; his having possibly glimpsed twenty-six years ago Villa Disa and the little Duchess of Payn with her English governess, *433*; his apparent assimilation of the Disa material and *K*'s promise to divulge an ultimate truth, *ibid.*; *S*'s views on Prejudice, *470*; *K*'s views on Suicide, *493*; *S*'s and *K*'s views on sin and faith, *549*; *S*'s crabbed hospitality and delight in meatless cuisine at my house, *579*; rumors about his interest in a female student, *ibid.*; his denial of a stationmaster's insanity, *629*; his heart attack synchronized with *K*'s spectacular arrival in the USA, *691*; *K*'s allusion to *S* in a letter to Disa, *768*; his last ramble with *S* and his joy at learning *S* is working hard on the "mountain" theme—a tragic misunderstanding, *802*; his games of golf with *S, 819*; his readiness to look up references for *S, 887*; *S*'s defense of the King of Zembla, *894*; his and *K*'s hilarity over the rot in a textbook compiled by Prof. C., psychiatrist and literary expert (!), *929*; his beginning his last batch of cards, *949*; his revealing to *K* the completion of his task, *991*; his death from a bullet meant for another, *1000*.

Shade, Sybil, S's wife, *passim.*

Shadows, the, a regicidal organization which commissioned Gradus (*q.v.*) to assassinate the self-banished king; its leader's terrible name cannot be mentioned, even in the Index to the obscure work of a scholar; his maternal grandfather, a well-known and very courageous master builder, was hired by Thurgus the Turgid, around 1885, to make certain repairs in his quarters, and soon after that perished, poisoned in the royal kitchens, under mysterious circumstances, together with his three young apprentices whose pretty first names Yan, Yonny, and Angeling, are preserved in a ballad still to be heard in some of our wilder valleys.

Shalksbore, Baron Harfar, known as Curdy Buff, b. 1921, man of fashion and Zemblan patriot, *433.*

Steinmann, Julius, b. 1928, tennis champion and Zemblan patriot, *171.*

Sudarg of Bokay, a mirror maker of genius, the patron saint of Bokay in the mountains of Zembla, *80;* life span not known.

Suicide, K's views on, *493.*

Taynik, Russ., secret place; see Crown Jewels.

Thurgus the Third, surnamed The Turgid, K's grandfather, d. 1900 at seventy-five, after a long dull reign; sponge-bag-capped, and with only one medal on his Jaeger jacket, he liked to bicycle in the park; stout and bald, his nose like a congested plum, his martial mustache bristling with obsolete passion, garbed in a dressing gown of green silk, and carrying a flambeau in his raised hand, he used to meet, every night, during a short period in the middle-Eighties, his hooded mistress, Iris Acht (*q.v.*) midway between palace and theater in the secret passage later to be rediscovered by his grandson, *130.*

Tintarron, a precious glass stained a deep blue, made in Bokay, a medieval place in the mountains of Zembla, *149;* see also Sudarg.

Translations, poetical; English into Zemblan, Conmal's versions of Shakespeare, Milton, Kipling, etc., noticed, *962;* English into French, from Donne and Marvell, *678;* German into English and Zemblan, *Der Erlkönig, 662;* Zemblan into English, *Timon Afinsken,* of Athens, *39;* Elder Edda, *79;* Arnor's *Miragarl, 80.*

Uran the Last, Emperor of Zembla, reigned 1798–1799; an incredibly brilliant, luxurious, and cruel monarch whose whistling whip made Zembla spin like a rainbow top; dispatched one night by a group of his sister's united favorites, *681.*

Vanessa, the Red Admirable (*sumpsimus*), evoked, *270;* flying over a parapet on a Swiss hillside, *408;* figured, *470;* caricatured, *949;* accompanying S's last steps in the evening sunshine, *993.*

Variants: the thieving sun and moon, *39–40;* planning the Primal Scene, *57;* the Zemblan King's escape (K's contribution, 8 lines), *70;* the Edda (K's contribution, 1 line), *79;* Luna's dead cocoon, *90–93;* children finding a secret passage (K's contribution, 4 lines),

130; poor old man Swift, poor—(possible allusion to *K*), *231*; Shade, *Ombre*, *275*; Virginia Whites, *316*; The Head of Our Department, *377*; a nymphet, *413*; additional line from Pope (possible allusion to *K*), *417*; Tanagra dust (a remarkable case of foreknowledge), *596*; of this America, *609–614*; first two feet changed, *629*; parody of Pope, *895–899*; a sorry age, and Social Novels, *922*.

Waxwings, birds of the genus *Bombycilla*, *1–4, 131, 1000*; *Bombycilla shadei*, *71*; interesting association belatedly realized.

Windows, Foreword; 47, 62, 181.

Word golf, S's predilection for it, *819*; see Lass.

Yaruga, Queen, reigned 1799–1800, sister of Uran (*q.v.*); drowned in an ice-hole with her Russian lover during traditional New Year's festivities, *681*.

Yeslove, a fine town, district and bishopric, north of Onhava, *149, 275*.

Zembla, a distant northern land.

APPENDIX

LOLITA

A SCREENPLAY

Foreword

Sometime at the end of July 1959 (my pocket diary does not give the exact date), in Arizona, where my wife and I were hunting butterflies, with headquarters at Forest Houses (between Flagstaff and Sedona), I received through Irving Lazar who was representing me a message from Messrs. Harris & Kubrick. They had acquired the film rights of *Lolita* in 1958, and were now asking me to come over to Hollywood and write the script. The honorarium they offered was considerable, but the idea of tampering with my own novel caused me only revulsion. A certain lull in the activity of the local lepidoptera suggested, however, that we might just as well drive on to the West Coast. After a meeting in Beverly Hills (at which I was told that in order to appease the censor a later scene should contain some pudic hint to the effect that Humbert had been secretly married to Lolita all along), followed by a week of sterile meditation on the shores of Lake Tahoe (where a calamitous growth of manzanita precluded the presence of good butterflies), I decided not to undertake the job and left for Europe.

We sojourned in Paris, London, Rome, Taormina, Genoa, and Lugano, where we arrived for a week's stay on December 9 (Grand Hotel, rooms 317–318, says my 1959 agenda, which now grows more talkative). I had long ceased to bother about the film, when suddenly I experienced a small nocturnal illumination, of diabolical origin, perhaps, but unusually compelling in sheer bright force, and clearly perceived an attractive line of approach to a screen version of *Lolita*. I regretted having had to decline the offer and was aimlessly revolving bits of dream dialogue in my mind when magically a telegram came from Hollywood urging me to revise my earlier decision and promising me a freer hand.

We spent the rest of the winter in Milan, San-Remo, and Mentone and on Thursday, February 18, 1960, left for Paris (2 singles Mentone-Paris, beds 6 and 8, car 9, leaving 7:15 P.M., arriving 8:55 A.M., these and other informative items from my diary are mentioned not only for mnemonic comfort but because I have not the heart to leave them ignored and unused). The first lap of the long journey to Los Angeles began with a rather ominous gag: the damned sleeping car stopped before reaching the platform, amid the mimosas and cypresses in the aquarelle elegance of a Riviera evening, and my wife and I, and the almost demented porter, had to swarm up from ground level to board the train.

By next evening we were at Le Havre, on the *United States*. We had booked an upper-deck cabin (61) but were transferred at no extra cost, with a bonus of fruit and whiskey, to a charming suite (65) by courtesy of the charming management—one of the many treats an American writer is granted. On Saturday, February 27, after four busy days in New York, we left for Chicago (10 P.M., car 551, bedrooms en suite E–F, enjoyable jottings, naive trivia of yore!) and next evening boarded the Super Chief on which the next installment of our bedrooms welcomed us with a twin burst of music, whereupon we scrambled frantically to stop, kill, stamp out, annihilate the heinous gadget and, not finding the switch, had to call for help (of course, the situation is incomparably worse on Soviet trains where you are strictly forbidden to turn off the muzakovitch).

On March 1, Kubrick and I, at his Universal City studio, debated in an amiable battle of suggestion and countersuggestion how to cinemize the novel. He accepted all my vital points, I accepted some of his less significant ones. Next morning, sitting on a bench under a lovely bright yellow-green *Pyrospodia* tree in a public park not far from the Beverly Hills Hotel (one of whose cottages Mr. Lazar had taken for us) I was already attending with all my wits to the speech and pantomime in my head. On March 9, Kubrick had us meet Tuesday Weld (a graceful ingénue but not my idea of Lolita). On March 10 we rented, from the late John Francis Fay, a pleasant villa (2088 Mandeville Canyon Road). On March 11, Kubrick sent me by messenger a rough outline of the scenes he and I had agreed upon: they covered Part One of the novel. By then his attitude had convinced me that he was willing to heed my whims more closely than those of the censor.

During the next months we met rather seldom—every fortnight or so, at his place or mine; outlines ceased altogether, criticism and advice got briefer and briefer, and by midsummer I did not feel quite sure whether Kubrick was serenely accepting whatever I did or silently rejecting everything.

I worked with zest, composing mentally every morning from eight to noon while butterfly hunting in the hot hills, which, except for some remarkably skittish individuals of a little-known Wood Nymph, produced nothing noteworthy, but *per contra* teemed with rattlers whose hysterical performance in the undergrowth or in the middle of the trail was more comical than alarming. After a leisurely lunch, prepared by the German cook who came with the house, I would spend another four-hour span in a lawn chair, among the roses and mockingbirds, using lined index cards and a Blackwing pencil, for copying and recopying, rubbing out and writing anew, the scenes I had imagined in the morning.

By nature I am no dramatist; I am not even a hack scenarist; but if I had given as much of myself to the stage or the screen as I have to the kind of writing which serves a triumphant life sentence between the covers of a book, I would have advocated and applied a system of total tyranny, directing the play or the picture myself, choosing settings and costumes, terrorizing the actors, mingling with them in the bit part of guest, or ghost, prompting them, and, in a word, pervading the entire show with the will and art of one individual—for there is nothing in the world that I loathe more than group activity, that communal bath where the hairy and slippery mix in a multiplication of mediocrity. All I could do in the present case was to grant words primacy over action, thus limiting as much as possible the intrusion of management and cast. I persevered in the task until I could tolerate the rhythm of the dialogue and properly control the flow of the film from motel to motel, mirage to mirage, nightmare to nightmare. Long before, in Lugano, I had adumbrated the sequence at the Enchanted Hunters Hotel, but its exact mechanism now proved tremendously difficult to adjust so as to render by the transparent interplay of sound effects and trick shots both a humdrum morning and a crucial moment in the lives of a desperate pervert and a wretched child. A small number of scenes (for example, McCoo's phantom house, the three poolside nymphs, or Diana Fowler starting to repeat the fatal cycle through which Charlotte Haze had passed) are based on unused material that I had kept after destroying the MS. of my novel, an act which I regret less than my having discarded those passages.

By the end of June, after having used up over a thousand cards, I had the thing typed, sent to Kubrick the four hundred pages it made, and, needing a rest, was driven by my wife in a rented Impala to Inyo County for a short stay at Glacier Lodge on Big Pine Creek, where we collected the Inyo Blue and other nice bugs in the surrounding mountains. Upon our returning to Mandeville Canyon, Kubrick visited us to say that my screenplay was much too unwieldly, contained too many unnecessary episodes, and would take about seven hours to run. He wanted several deletions and other changes, and some of these I did make, besides devising new sequences and situations, when preparing a shorter script which he got in September and said was fine. That last stretch was the toughest, but also the most exhilarating part of the six-month task. Ten years later, though, I reread my play and restored a few scenes.

My final meeting with Kubrick must have taken place on September 25, 1960, at his house in Beverly Hills: he showed me that day photographs of Sue Lyon, a demure nymphet of fourteen or so, who, said Kubrick, could be easily made to look younger and grubbier for the part of Lolita for which he already had signed her up. On the whole I felt rather pleased with the way things had worked out, when on October 12, at P.M., my wife and I took the Super Chief (bdr. E + F, car 181) for Chicago, changing there to the Twentieth-Century (bdr J–K, car 261) and reaching New York, at 8:30 A.M. on October 15. In the course of that splendid journey—and the following note can stir only the dedicated extrasensorialist—I had a dream (October 13) in which I saw written: "They say on the radio that she is as natural as Sarah Footer." I have never known anybody of that name.

Complacency is a state of mind that exists only in retrospective: it has to be shattered before being ascertained. Mine was to endure for a year and a half. As early as October 28 (New York, Hampshire House, room 503) I find the following plan penciled in my little book: "a novel, a life, a love—which is only the elaborate commentary to a gradually evolved short poem." The "short poem" started to become a rather long one soon after the *Queen Elizabeth* ("Buy dental floss, new pince-nez, Bonamine, check with baggage-master big black trunk on pier before embarcation, Deck A, Cabin 71") deposited us at Cherbourg on November 7. Four days later, at the Principe e Savoia in Milan and then throughout the winter in Nice, in a rented flat (57 Promenade des Anglais) and after that in Tessin, Valais, and Vaud ("Oct. 1, 1961, moved to Montreux-Palace") I was absorbed in *Pale Fire*, which I finished on December 4, 1961. Lepidopterology, work on the galleys of my *Eugene Onegin* mammoth, and the revising of a difficult translation (*The Gift*) took care of the spring of 1962, spent mostly in Montreux, so that (apart from the fact that nobody insisted on my coming to Elstree) the shooting of the *Lolita* film in England was begun and concluded far beyond the veil of my vanities.

On May 31, 1962 (almost exactly twenty-two years after we emigrated from St.-Nazaire aboard the *Champlain*), the *Queen Elizabeth* took us to New York for the opening of *Lolita*. Our cabin (main deck, cabin 95) was quite as comfortable as the one we had on the *Champlain* in 1940 and, moreover, at a cocktail party given by the purser (or surgeon, my scribble is illegible), he turned to me and said: Now you, as an American businessman, will enjoy the following story (story not recorded). On June 6 I revisited my old haunts, the entomological department at the American Museum of Natural History, where I deposited the specimens of Chapman's Hairstreak I had taken the previous April between Nice and Grasse, under strawberry trees. The première took place on June 13 (Loew's State, BW at 45, E2 + 4 orchestra, "horrible seats" says my outspoken agenda). Crowds were awaiting the limousines that drew up one by one, and there I, too, rode, as eager and innocent as the fans who peered into my car hoping to glimpse James Mason but finding only the placid profile of a stand-in for Hitchcock. A few days before, at a private screening, I had discovered that Kubrick was a great director, that his *Lolita* was a first-rate film with magnificent actors, and that only ragged odds and ends of my script had been used. The modifications, the garbling of my best little finds, the omission of entire scenes, the addition of new ones, and all sorts of other changes may not have been sufficient to erase my name from the credit titles but they certainly made the picture as unfaithful to the original script as an American poet's translation from Rimbaud or Pasternak.

I hasten to add that my present comments should definitely not be construed as reflecting any belated grudge, any high-pitched deprecation of Kubrick's creative approach. When adapting *Lolita* to the speaking screen he saw my novel in one way, I saw it in another—that's all, nor can one deny that infinite fidelity may be an author's ideal but can prove a producer's ruin.

My first reaction to the picture was a mixture of aggravation, regret, and reluctant pleasure. Quite a few of the extraneous inventions (such as the macabre ping-pong scene or that rapturous swig of Scotch in the bathtub) struck me as appropriate and delightful. Others (such as the collapsing cot or the frills of Miss Lyon's elaborate nightgown) were painful. Most of the sequences were not really better than those I had so carefully composed for Kubrick, and I keenly regretted the waste of my time while admiring Kubrick's fortitude in enduring for six months the evolution and infliction of a useless product.

But I was wrong. Aggravation and regret soon subsided as I recollected the inspiration in the hills, the lawn chair under the jacaranda, the inner drive, the glow, without which my task could not have been accomplished. I told myself that nothing had been wasted after all, that my scenario remained intact in its folder, and that one day I might publish it—not in pettish refutation of a munificent film but purely as a vivacious variant of an old novel.

Vladimir Nabokov
Montreux
December, 1973

Prologue

A feminine voice (Lolita's, or rather Dolly Schiller's) repeats exactly a fragment of speech from her last conversation with Humbert at the end of Act Three:

. . . Oh, what does it matter. Up in Parkington, I guess. He's got a house there, a regular old castle (*rustle of rummaging*). There was a picture of it somewhere. (*flip-flip*) Yes, here it is.

Pavor Manor, an Elaborate, Antiquated Wooden Mansion at the Top of a Winding Forest Road
This is Clare Quilty's lair, not far from Parkington, Ramsdale County. The sun is rising above the gnarled old trees. After a brief still, the CAMERA glides around an ornate turret and dips into an upper-story casement. A prone sleeper (Quilty) is glimpsed in dorsal view. The CAMERA also locates the drug addict's implementa on a bedside chair, and with a shudder withdraws. It slides down the gutter pipe, returns to the porch and meets a car which stops in the driveway. Humbert Humbert, hatless, raincoated, emerges. Lurching a little (he is drunk), he makes for the front door. He rings the doorbell. He uses the knocker. There is no response. He rings and knocks again. Still no response. With a petulant snarl, he pushes the door—and it swings open as in a medieval fairy tale.

CUT TO:

A Spacious and Ugly Hall with a Long Mirror and a Huge Boar's Head on the Wall
Humbert enters. With a drunkard's fussy care he closes the door behind him. He looks around. He produces a pistol.

CUT TO:

The Central Staircase
down which slowly comes a large man (Clare Quilty) in a silk dressing gown, the sash of which he is tying as he goes. The

host sees the visitor. They face each other. Now begins a silent shadowy sequence which should not last more than one minute. As Humbert levels his weapon, Quilty retreats and majestically walks upstairs. Humbert fires. Once more. We see him missing: the impact of a bullet sets a rocking chair performing on the landing. Then he hits a picture (photograph of Duk-Duk ranch which Lolita had visited). Next a large ugly vase is starred and smashed. Finally, on his fourth fire, he stops a grandfather clock in its clacking stride. The fifth bullet wounds Quilty, and the last one fells him on the upper landing.

CUT TO:

Dr. John Ray
a psychiatrist, perusing a manuscript on his desk. He swings around toward us in his swivel chair.

DR. RAY   I'm Dr. John Ray. Pleased to meet you. This here is a bundle of notes, a rough autobiography, poorly typed, which Mr. Humbert Humbert wrote after his arrest, in prison, where he was held without bail on a charge of murder, and in the psychopathic ward where he was committed for observation. Without this document his crime would have remained unexplained. Naturally, in my capacity of psychotherapist, I would have preferred obtaining the information revealed here not from the typewriter but from the couch.

The murder Humbert perpetrated is only a side product of his case. His memoir is mainly an account of his fatal infatuation with a certain type of very young girl and of the torments he underwent in his vortex of libido and guilt. I have no intention to glorify Humbert. He is horrible, he is abject. He is a shining example of moral leprosy. But there are in his story depths of passion and suffering, patterns of tenderness and distress, that cannot be dismissed by his judges. As a case history, his autobiography will no doubt become a classic in psychiatric circles. But more important to us is the ethical impact it should have on a serious audience. For here lurks a general lesson: the wayward child, the egotistic mother, the panting maniac—these are not only vivid characters in a unique story. They warn us of dangerous trends. They point out potent evils. They should make all of us— parents, social workers, educators—apply ourselves with still greater vigilance and vision to the task of bringing up a better generation in a safer world. Thank you.

CUT TO:

Humbert's Cell in The Tombs
He is writing at a table. Conspicuous among the reference books at his elbow are some tattered travel guides and maps. Presently his voice surfaces as he rereads the first sentences of his story.

HUMBERT'S VOICE   I was born in Paris forty dark years ago. My father was a gentle easy-going person, a Swiss citizen of mixed French and Austrian descent with a dash of the blue Danube in his veins. He owned a luxurious hotel on the Riviera. In a minute I am going to pass around some lovely picture postcards. My mother was an Englishwoman. Her death preceded that of my father by two decades: she was killed by a bolt of lightning during a picnic on my fourth birthday, high in the Maritime Alps.

CUT TO:

A Mountain Meadow—A thunderhead advancing above sharp cliffs
Several people scramble for shelter, and the first big drops of rain strike the zinc of a lunchbox. As the poor lady in white runs toward the pavilion of a lookout, a blast of livid light fells her. Her graceful specter floats up above the black cliffs holding a parasol and blowing kisses to her husband and child who stand below, looking up, hand in hand.

CUT TO:

HUMBERT'S VOICE   Aunt Sybil, my mother's eldest sister, a severe spinster, helped my father to bring me up. My childhood was spent in the bright world of the Hotel Mirana, at St.-Topaz.

CUT TO:

A Picture Postcard of the Mirana Palace flying its flag in a cloudless sky
There are palm trees in front of it, and a system of stone steps winding down from terrace to terrace, among rhododendrons and roses. Back to the memoirist's murmur:

HUMBERT'S VOICE   I remember a certain summer. My father was away in Naples attending to the affairs of an Italian lady he was courting at the time. In the east wing of our hotel an English family occupied a first-floor suite.

CUT TO:

Picture Postcard of Hotel
A clumsy cross is scrawled over one window.

HUMBERT'S VOICE   This was Annabel's room. How strange to recollect today, in the light of another love, those past pangs! I was fourteen and she was twelve, in that kingdom by the sea. Young as we were, we fell in love. My Aunt Sybil and Annabel's parents apparently realized that if she and I filched somehow five mad minutes of privacy, God knows what would come of it. Therefore, they saw to our not obtaining that privacy. In fact, *any* meeting between us was allowed only on condition we kept in the public domain. Good Lord, how I envy today's youngsters and their progressive Freudian freedom. Poor Humbert, poor Annabel. I would now like a shot of two hands.

CUT TO:

Two Young Hands—right boy's, left girl's—both slender, long-fingered, tanned, hers with the modest star of a topaz ring, his with fine glistening hair on the back of the wrist, and a wrist watch (11:55), creeping toward each other—belonging to Humbert and Annabel (who are prone on the beach, sunning their backs in symmetrical similar adjacent positions), now through shifting sifted sand, now under sand, now in the shimmer of midday—and now they meet like two wary sensitive insects—and suddenly separate, a pretty scene for the subtle camera as the shore-fortress gun booms noon.

CUT TO:

HUMBERT'S VOICE   I loved her more tenderly than Tristan adored Isolde, more hotly than Petrarca desired his Laura, more romantically than Poe loved little Virginia. Once, on a rosy rock in the purple sea, I made her promise me an old-fashioned assignation at night in the palmy hotel garden.

CUT TO:

Rocky Promontory
Annabel supine, Humbert murmuring passionate plaints. Two Englishmen, robust freckled swimmers, interrupt these throbbings.

CUT TO:

The Garden of the Mirana Palace at Night
On a lower lighted balcony Annabel's parents, Humbert's Aunt Sybil, and a Mr. Cooper are playing cards (poker, European fashion). Aunt Sybil narrowly fondles three kings. Annabel in pale pajamas slithers through the honeysuckle from a first-floor window into the dark garden where she is joined by young Humbert near the balustrade under the oleanders. She sits on a stone shelf, he worships her from below, his arms embracing her haunches, and the light of an ornamental lamp imprints on a stone wall the emblematic silhouettes of long leaves. He is groping his way to a secret fount when her mother claps down her cards and loudly calls her daughter's name.

HUMBERT'S VOICE   And then summer was over. Aunt Sybil, after a torrential rain, broke her leg on a slippery terrace, and I was supposed that evening to sit at her bedside and read to her *South Wind*, her favorite novel; instead of which I escaped to the little railway station where the great European expresses so grandly stopped. I just made it—and saw Annabel off.

CUT TO:

A Côte d'Azur Station—luminous evening—black cypresses and a young moon

The *train bleu* is pulling out. We follow a youth trotting alongside the sleeping car *Nice-Paris* from the window of which the young girl he is seeing off leans out in an ecstasy of blown kisses and streaming tears.

HUMBERT'S VOICE   We parted. Never again did I see her alive. A few months after she left the Riviera I was sent to school in England. That same year she died of pneumonia in a seaside town. I learned of her illness at the last moment and barely managed to arrive in time for the funeral. This is her tomb at the end of that vista.

CUT TO:

That Vista

We see her highborn kinsmen, in a romantic Poe-esque arrangement, bearing her away down an alley of tall cypresses. Our young mourner watches, cloaked in his grief. A related nymphet places a wreath on the tomb.

HUMBERT'S VOICE   I am writing this in prison, and the physical seclusion I am condemned to here strangely helps to encompass and concentrate the remote, diffuse, personal past I'm evoking. If I am given enough time before my trial I hope to proceed onward from that first young love and relate in all possible detail of circumstance and emotion the story of my later life in Europe and America. And if I manage to finish my difficult task, I shall place these pages in the capable hands of my adviser and physician, Dr. John Ray.

CUT TO:

Dr. Ray in His Study as Before, holding the typescript

DR. RAY   And here they are, those precious pages. From them we learn that Humbert could never forget graceful Annabel, and her shape and shadow haunted him in every alley of his love life. He finished college in England and continued his graduate studies—in the field of comparative literature—in Switzerland, where his nationality and temperament kept him away from the tumult of World War Two. He then moved to Paris, where he engaged in various literary pursuits and taught English at a boys' school. But we are not concerned with his intellectual life. We are interested in his emotional tribulations. Everywhere: In public parks——

CUT TO:

A Nymphet Readjusts the Straps of Her Roller Skate
She has placed her armored foot on the edge of Humbert's bench, and her shining curls tumble over her sun-dappled bare leg.

DR. RAY'S VOICE   —at bus stops——

CUT TO:

Chattering, Jostling Schoolgirls crowd into a bus and push against Humbert
One nymphet glances at him, nudges another lass, and both giggle.

DR. RAY'S VOICE   —on street corners——

CUT TO:

Two Nymphets play at marbles under a sidewalk maple

DR. RAY'S VOICE   —in the garden of an orphanage——

CUT TO:

Pale, Black-stockinged Girls performing tame calisthenics directed by a nun

DR. RAY'S VOICE   —and in many other haunts, Humbert wrestled with strange wretched urges and kept searching for the child of his shameful obsession, for some incarnation of his boyhood sweetheart. At thirty, he decided to marry. His choice fell on the daughter of a Polish-born doctor in Paris who was treating him for a heart condition.

CUT TO:

Humbert and the Doctor—playing chess

The doctor's daughter Valeria flirts with Humbert. She is in her late twenties and rather shopworn and pudgy, but imitates in attitudes and attire a little girl. "She looked fluffy and frolicsome, dressed *à la gamine* . . . and pouted, and dimpled, and romped, and dirndled, in the cutest and tritest fashion imaginable."*

DR. RAY'S VOICE   He married Valeria, but reality soon asserted itself, and presently unsatisfied Humbert had on his hands not a nymphet but a large, puffy, dull, adult woman.

CUT TO:

A Bourgeois Evening in a Tiny Parisian Flat
Humbert reads the evening paper. Plump-shouldered, in a rumpled slip, scratching her rump, Valeria looks after the *pot-au-feu.*

DR. RAY'S VOICE   The marriage dragged on for several years. In the meantime, Humbert went on with his literary and educational studies. A handbook of French translations from English poetry enjoyed some success, and an Institute of Comparative Literature in an American city invited him to come over for a series of lectures.

CUT TO:

The Prefecture in Paris. Humbert and Valeria come out.
He is checking a batch of documents, she looks perturbed.

HUMBERT   We have all our papers now.

DR. RAY'S VOICE   They have all their papers now. They are all set to go. Good-bye, gray Paree!

HUMBERT   Good-bye, gray Paree. Now, my dear, don't lose your passport. (*Gives it to her.*)

They follow the sidewalk. A taxi starts creeping along the curb as if inviting them to take it. Valeria is silent, and keeps shaking her poodle head.

DR. RAY'S VOICE   Watch that cab.

*Passages in quotation marks denote excerpts from the novel *Lolita*.

HUMBERT   Why are you shaking your head? Something in it? A pebble?

She shakes it.

HUMBERT   I can assure you it is quite empty.

VALERIA   No-no-no-no-no——

HUMBERT   That will do.

VALERIA   —I cannot go on with it. You will sail alone.

HUMBERT   What? What's that, you fool?

VALERIA   We must separate.

HUMBERT   I refuse to discuss this in the street. Taxi!

The cab that had been quietly escorting them glides up.

HUMBERT   *Quarante-deux, rue Baudelaire.*

DR. RAY'S VOICE   Forty-two Baudelaire Street.

They get into the taxi.

HUMBERT   May I inquire *why* you want us to separate?

VALERIA   Because life with you is sad and horrible. Because you've got impossible eyes. Because I cannot imagine your thoughts. Because I'm afraid of you and hate you.

DR. RAY'S VOICE   She had never been so voluble.

HUMBERT   You've never been so voluble before. All right. Let's get this straight——

DR. RAY'S VOICE   My patient is flabbergasted. As Professor Gast used to say: "Woe to him who gets stuck in his own guilt complex like an angry fly." Mr. Humbert cannot react rationally, he splutters. That's the famous *Place de l'Etoile*, Place of the Star. Need good brakes. Oops. See what I mean?

The taxi driver is strangely erratic.

VALERIA   It's all finished now. I'm going to be free. There's another man in my life and I'm leaving you.

HUMBERT   What man? What are you talking about? How
dare you?

DR. RAY'S VOICE   Dare indeed. A very curious situation.
Humbert is accustomed to making the decisions. Now
the fate of his marriage is no longer in his hands. I think
the cab driver ought to have turned left here. Oh, well,
he can take the next cross street.

VALERIA   He's a human being, not a monster. He's a
White Russian. He was a colonel in the Russian army.
His father was a Councilor of the Tsar.

HUMBERT   I don't know whom you are speaking of. I'll—
I don't know what I'll do to you if you go on like that.

DR. RAY'S VOICE   Look out! Close shave. When you analyze those jaywalkers you find they hesitate between the
womb and the tomb.

VALERIA   Oh, you can't do anything to me now—because
I love him.

HUMBERT   But damn you—who the devil is he?

VALERIA   Him, of course (*points at the thick backhead of
the driver who turns briefly revealing a Russian profile,
potato nose, and bristly moustache*).

The taxi pulls up at the curb.

CUT TO:

Sidewalk in Front of 42, rue Baudelaire.
The driver and both passengers get out of the cab.

DRIVER   I am Colonel Maximovich, allow me to present
myself. I have seen you often in the cinema of the corner, and she was sitting between us. (*Smiles fondly at
Valeria.*) Let us discuss.

HUMBERT   We have nothing to discuss.

MAXIMOVICH   Perhaps we can move her and her things
immediately in my auto. (*turning to Valeria*) You want?
You are prepared?

HUMBERT   I will not have anything to do with either of you. This is ridiculous.

MAXIMOVICH   She is quite pale today, the poor. You must permit me to help with her baggage.

VALERIA   The percolator!

MAXIMOVICH   Yes, all the presents of marriage. Also, the white dress, the black dress, library books which she must return, her furry coat, and her diet.

HUMBERT   I beg your pardon? What was that last fascinating item?

VALERIA   My diet. He means the printed list father gave me.

HUMBERT   Oh yes. Oh, of course. Anything else?

MAXIMOVICH   One will see. Let us mount upstairs.

DR. RAY'S VOICE   Divorce was inevitable. Valeria had found herself another, more suitable mate, and lone Humbert set out for America.

CUT TO:

Humbert Dramatically Standing on a Liner's Deck
The towers of New York loom in the autumnal mist.

DR. RAY'S VOICE   For the following year Humbert had been promised a lectureship at Beardsley College in Idaho. Meanwhile in New York he spent all his time in libraries preparing his course, a series of lectures under the general title of "Romanticists and Rebels."

CUT TO:

Library
In the vicinity of Humbert's carrel a brood of bored school-girls are shown by their teacher The Place Where Books Live.

DR. RAY'S VOICE   He also accepted lecture engagements out of town. A nervous breakdown in result of his solitary exertions and repressed dreams interrupted one such engagement at a Women's Club.

CUT TO:

A Women's Club
A full-blown matron, Mrs. Nancy Whitman (her name pinned
to her breast), rises above a carafe to introduce the speaker.

MRS. WHITMAN   Before introducing the distinguished vis-
    itor on tonight's program, you will be glad to learn that
    next Friday the well-known psychiatrist, Dr. John Ray,
    will talk to us on the sexual symbolism of golf.
        (*applause*)
    We have here tonight Dr. Humbert, who has spent
    many years in *very* continental surroundings, and who
    will talk to us right now on romantic poetry. Please, Dr.
    Humbert.

CUT TO:

Feminine Eyes Watching the Speaker—changing expressions
    come and go on various elastic faces—
some plump, but changing to eights and snapping in a distorted mirror; others, lean and long, developing abysmal dé-
colletés; others again blending with the flesh of rolling bare
arms, or turning into wax fruit in arty bowls.

HUMBERT'S FALTERING VOICE   Let me illustrate my point
    by reading to you Edgar's poem about . . . about . . .

CUT TO:

The Lecturer is now shown clearly except for a ripple or two
    of optical interference

HUMBERT   I put a marker in, but it dropped out, evidently.
    Somebody ought to collect all the markers we shed.
    I'm sure, though, it was in this volume. Oh God, oh
    God . . .

He fumbles feverishly through a volume to find a quotation
he needs.

HUMBERT   (*in a pearly sweat*) It is supposed to be a very
    complete anthology. There should be an index. Here it

is, here it is. Oh, I must find that poem. It is sure to be here. It began with an "N": n, y, m. N, y, m. . . . n. y. m . . . Oh, I'm sure it began with an "N" as in "Annabel."

HELPFUL VOICE   Title or first line?

HUMBERT   Don't ask me. This is atrocious. The term I wish to illustrate is "nymphet."

MURMURS IN AUDIENCE   What? What? What did he say?

HUMBERT   After all, I don't really need this stupid book. Stupid book, go!
                           (*Tosses it away.*)
So the term is nymphet. I intend to introduce the following idea: Between the age limits of nine and fourteen there are certain maidens: they bewitch the traveler who is twice their age and reveal to him their true nature, which is not human but nymphic—in other words, demoniac—and these chosen creatures I propose to designate as nymphets.

He is speaking very loud, almost screaming, and there is a rising rumble in the audience.

HUMBERT   Let me finish, ladies. Now the question is: between these age limits are *all* girl-children nymphets? 'Course, not. Otherwise the lone traveler would have long gone insane. Neither are good looks any criterion. I am speaking of a certain fey grace, of the elusive, shifty, soul-shattering, insidious charm that separates the preteen demon from the ordinary sweet round-faced child with a tummy and pigtails. You have to be an artist and a madman, a creature of infinite melancholy.——Silence!

His audience is coming out of its stunned stupefaction.

HUMBERT   Yes, only a madman can really distinguish at once—oh, at once—by ineffable signs—the feline outline of a cheekbone, the slenderness of a downy limb, and other indices which despair and shame and tears of tenderness forbid me to tab—tab—tabulate——

CUT TO:

Distorted Matronly Faces
and a good deal of rubbery, enveloping, adult flesh is now crowding Humbert out of the picture

HUMBERT   We cringe and hide, yes, but our dreams contain enchantments which normal men never know. What indeed could Edgar Poe see in Mother Clemm, the mother of his pubescent bride? Oh, how horrible full-grown women are to the nymphet-lover! Don't come near me! Hands off! I'm not well—I——

He faints.

CUT TO:

The Office of the Psychotherapeutic Home
Humbert, in a vicuña coat, applies for admission.

HUMBERT   I have come because I need help.

BUXOM RECEPTIONIST   And I'm sure you will get it. Have you filled that other form too? Okay.

HUMBERT   I want to say that I am perfectly aware of the real nature of my problems. All I need is some mental rest. Not a solution but solitude.

RECEPTIONIST   Dr. Ray will easily establish a working relationship with you.

HUMBERT   The point is I don't need a cure, because I'm incurable——

RECEPTIONIST   Oh, come. Everything and everybody can be cured. Sure.

HUMBERT   Well, anyway I'm not interested in being cured. What I need, what I badly need, is some kind of diversion, some peace of mind.

RECEPTIONIST   Our occupational therapy provides many fascinating contacts and outlets.

HUMBERT   I mean I have the feeling that something in my mind is poisoning everything else. I know this thing cannot be eliminated but perhaps it could be reduced to reasonable dimensions, watered down, so to speak.

RECEPTIONIST   Well, I'm sure Dr. Ray will fix all that. He'll assign you to a delightful group of patients we have here, mainly European immigrants. See these shoes?

(*Proffers her foot.*)

A wonderful Hungarian patient made them for me. Aren't they something!

HUMBERT   Please tell Dr. Ray that I want a private room. And then I must have silence and peace all the time.

RECEPTIONIST   Oh, I must disagree with you there. I think silence is terrible. Let me try again. Dr. Ray's office.

DR. RAY'S VOICE   So it happened that in the nursing home where Humbert spent three weeks I met him and talked with him. The patient refused to reveal the reasons for his breakdown, but it was plain he needed relaxation. Tranquilizers and a regular mental regime brought considerable improvement to his condition. An acquaintance of his, whose cousin had an attractive house in Ramsdale on the beautiful lake of that name, suggested that Humbert come to lodge there during the summer, before traveling west to the university where he had been invited to teach.

Act One

Ramsdale, a pretty, sedate town with opulent shade trees. The time is around noon in early summer.

The words LAST DAY OF SCHOOL are gradually scrawled across the blackboard.

CUT TO:

Three Girls Near Bay Window:
Virginia McCoo (polio cripple, sharp features, strident voice); Phyllis Chatfield (chubby, sturdy); and a third girl (head turned away, tying her shoe).

VIRGINIA   (*to Phyllis*) Well, Phyllis, what are your plans for the summer? Camp?

PHYLLIS   Yes, camp. My folks are going to Europe.

VIRGINIA   Getting rid of you, huh?

PHYLLIS   Oh well, I don't mind. I like camp.

VIRGINIA   Same place—Lake Climax?

PHYLLIS   Same old place. And what about you, Ginny?

VIRGINIA   I'm going to have a wonderful time. I'm going to have French lessons with our new paying guest.

PHYLLIS   Oh—has he come?

VIRGINIA   Coming tomorrow. My mother saw him in New York and she says he's a real man of the world and awfully handsome. I guess it will be fun.

PHYLLIS   (*to the third girl*) And you, Lolita?

Lolita turns toward them. A smile, a shrug.

CUT TO:

A Car Drives up to the School. Charlotte Haze Emerges.

LOLITA   There's my dear mother.

CUT TO:

A Teacher Coming out meets Charlotte Coming in.

TEACHER   How are you, Mrs. Haze?

CHARLOTTE   Fine. And you, Miss Horton—glad to be rid of them until the fall?

TEACHER   I should say so. Now it's Mama's turn to take over. Is Lolita going to the Lake Climax camp?

CHARLOTTE   I don't know. I sort of never got around to planning our summer yet.

CUT TO:

Charlotte Drives Lolita Homeward.
Heavy traffic. Red light.

LOLITA   Our luck as per usual. (*Pause.*)

Light changes

With our luck it is sure to be some ugly old hag.

CHARLOTTE   What are you talking about?

LOLITA   About the lodger you are trying to find.

CHARLOTTE   Oh, *that*. Well, I'm sure she will be a lovely person. When the time comes. The agency tells me it is going to be quite a season here this summer. What with the new casino.

LOLITA   Ginny McCoo was telling me about the roomer *they* are getting. He's a professor of French poetry. And her uncle's firm is going to publish a book he has written.

CHARLOTTE   We don't want any French poets. *Please*, stop rummaging in that glove compartment.

LOLITA   I had some candy there.

CHARLOTTE   You are wrecking your teeth on those mints. By the way, you have not forgotten you have Dr. Quilty at three and—oh, darn that dog!

CUT TO:

Mr. Jung's Dog, a Large Collie,
waits at the corner of Lawn Street, then races the car barking
lustily and nearly gets run over.

CHARLOTTE   Really, I am fed up with that beast.

CUT TO:

She Draws up at the Curb
where old Mr. Jung is inspecting the contents of his mailbox.
Over his spectacles he peers at Mrs. Haze.

CHARLOTTE   (*leaning out*) Mr. Jung, something *must* be
          done about that dog of yours.

Mr. Jung, beaming and a little gaga, walks around the car to
her window.

CUT TO:

Lolita, leaning out of her side of the car,
fondly stroking the pleased hound and speaking confidentially—

LOLITA   And I think he is a good, good dog—yes, a *good*
          dog.

CUT TO:

Mr. Jung, who is a little deaf
and seems to listen with his mouth, comes closer to the
driver's window.

CHARLOTTE   I am talking about your dog. Something
          must be done about him.

MR. JUNG   Why? What's he been up to?

CHARLOTTE   He's a nuisance. He chases every car. He has
          taught two other dogs to do it.

MR. JUNG   He's a gentle intelligent beast. Never hurt any-
          body. Most alert and intelligent.

CHARLOTTE   I'm not interested in his I.Q. All I know he's
          a nuisance. And it will be your fault if he gets hurt.

MR. JUNG   He won't hurt nobody. Come here, boy! You just don't mind him, Mrs. Haze. Come, boy!

LOLITA   Mother, I'm hungry. Let's be moving.

WIPE TO:

Dinner Time.
Quick view of Ramsdale. White church with clock against an inky sky. Lolita dines from a plate watching TV.

DISSOLVE TO:

A Ragged Sunset.
The plashing lake. A thunderhead looming.
   Details of approaching electric storm: an empty milk bottle overturned by a gust.
   The wind brutally turns the pages of the mangled magazine forgotten on the folding chair. It is suddenly whisked away in rotating mad flight.
   Nightfall. Lolita barefooted hastens to close a bedroom window. Lightning. Charlotte folds and drags in the garden chair. The thunder claps and rolls. Another flash.

CUT TO:

LOLITA   (*undressed, on landing, to her mother downstairs*) I'm going to bed. I'm scared!

Big Thunderclap

CUT TO:

Charlotte in the Living Room.
The storm never stops. Far away the fire engine is heard. Nearer. Far again. Charlotte looks out of the window. Details of nocturnal storm: gesticulating black trees, rain drumming on roof, thunder, lightning printing reflections on wall, Lolita sits up in bed. More sounds of firefighting.

CUT TO:

A Car,
shedding its moving beam on 342 Lawn Street, and then on 345 Lawn Street, turns in to the driveway next door. The Farlows, John and Jean. The storm is abating.

JEAN   John, while you are parking the car I'll dash over to Charlotte and tell her——

JOHN   Oh, but she must be fast asleep.

JEAN   No, she's in the living room. The lights are on.

CUT TO:

Charlotte, Who has noticed their return, opens the front door. A cat's eyes in the dripping-dark. Sheet lightning.

JEAN   Oh, what's that cat doing there? Have you heard about the fire, Charlotte?

CHARLOTTE   I heard the engines.

JEAN   Well, it was at the McCoos'.

CHARLOTTE   No!

JEAN   Yes. Their house got struck by lightning. We were at John's club and could see the blaze five blocks away.

CHARLOTTE   My goodness! Are they safe?

JEAN   Oh yes, they're okay. They even saved the TV. But the house is practically a burnt-out shell.

CHARLOTTE   But how *dreadful!*

JEAN   Naturally they were insured and all that—and they have that apartment in Parkington. Well, see you to-morrow. Bye-bye.

CUT TO:

Early Morning Next Day.
Robin pulling out worm on damp lawn. One new dandelion. Milkman collects empty bottles. Tinkle. Telephone takes over, rings.

Lolita in pajamas, barefoot, leaning over banisters, half a story above Charlotte, who attends to the telephone in the hallway. The conversation is nearing its end. We hear only her side.

CHARLOTTE   I certainly could, Mr. McCoo. Oh, I just keep thinking and thinking of you and that dreadful fire——

(*Listens.*)

No trouble at all. In fact it's just the kind of lodger—

(*Listens.*)

Yes, I see. Yes, of course.

(*Listens.*)

Well, I'm glad he's old-fashioned enough to prefer lakes to oceans. That means a quiet lodger.

(*Laughs demurely.*)

(*Listens.*)

Oh, I could fetch him if you'd like.

(*Listens.*)

I see.

(*Listens.*)

Look, why don't you meet him at the station, explain things to him, put him into Joe's taxi, and send him over here.

(*Listens.*)

Aha. Naturally. I understand that.

(*Listens.*)

Okay then. I'll be expecting him around noon.

(*Listens.*)

Not at all, not at all (*melodious laugh*). Everything in the world happens at short notice.

(*Listens.*)

Yes, do that. You know, I could not sleep all night thinking of that dreadful fire and your poor wife. You're so right to have sent her and Ginny to Parkington. Well, please do tell your wife that if there's anything I can do——

(*Hangs up.*)

LOLITA   Mother, is that man going to stay with us?

CHARLOTTE   He is. Oh dear, Louise is not coming until after tomorrow. You had better get dressed and pick up all those books and things you brought back from school. The hall is a mess.

CUT TO:

Humbert's Arrival

FADE IN

Ramsdale (a thriving resort, somewhere between Minnesota and Maine)
as seen by a traveler arriving by plane. We are served the dish of the large, pine-fringed, scintillating Ramsdale Lake, with, at one end, a recreation park and a stucco pleasure dome. A small cloud of dark smoke is hanging over part of the suburban development. Beyond this is the cheerful, neat-looking town in the sunshine of a serene May morning. The airport spreads out beneath us, flying its flags and gently gyrating as the plane's shadow sweeps over it.

CUT TO:

Alfalfa Fields, Asphalted Spaces, Parked Cars: Ramsdale Airport
Humbert carrying briefcase lands and enters the office. His bags follow. He looks around.

HUMBERT   Somebody was supposed to meet me. . . .

He consults a little black diary.

DESK CLERK   Can I help you, sir?

HUMBERT   May I use this phone?

He attempts to dial McCoo's number. Consults his diary again. Redials. There is no answer.

HUMBERT   Funny. (*to the clerk*) Where can I find a taxi?

CLERK   (*pointing with pencil*) Down there. He'll take your bags.

CUT TO:

Humbert in Taxi
They cross the town and turn in to Lake Avenue. Sounds of fire engines. Firefighters going back to their station.

TAXI DRIVER   We sure had a big storm last night. Lightning struck a house in Lake Avenue, and oh boy, did it burn!

(*does a double take*)
Say, mister, what number you said you were going?

HUMBERT   Nine hundred. Nine oh oh.

TAXI DRIVER   (*chuckling*) Well, "oh-oh" is about all that's
left of it.

CUT TO:

*The Black, Hosewater-drenched, Still Smoking Remains of a
Burned-Down House*
Policemen are still keeping away a thinning crowd of specta-
tors, most of whom have come by car or bicycle. The charred
ruins are those of the McCoo villa in a pine-treed, sparsely
populated part of Lake Avenue. Humbert's taxi stops at a
roped-off puddle.

TAXI DRIVER   (*continuously indulging in raw, ready humor*) Here you are, sir.

HUMBERT   My goodness! You mean this is the McCoo
residence?

TAXI DRIVER   Residence? Oh, brother!

Humbert, automatically carrying raincoat and briefcase,
climbs out of the car. Faint cheers from the crowd.

PATROLMAN   You can't come any closer.

HUMBERT   I'm supposed to live here.

PATROLMAN   Why don't you speak to the owner? That's
Mr. McCoo down there.

(In the following scene the grotesque humor turns upon
McCoo's conducting a kind of guided tour through a nonexistent house. He makes the belated honors of the home
Humbert would have shared.) McCoo, a small fat man,
emerges from the ruins of the patio. He staggers along with
a big barbecue roaster in his arms. He is dirty and wet, and
utterly bewildered. He stops and stares at Humbert.

HUMBERT   How do you do. I am your lodger. Or rather
I was to be your lodger.

McCOO   (*setting down his burden*) What do you know! Mr. Humbert, I must apologize. I thought my wife would leave you a message at the airport. I know she found other lodgings for you. Look at this dreadful disaster.

He gestures toward architectural ghosts in the aura of the vanished villa.

McCOO   Follow me. Look, sir, look. Your room was right here. A beautiful, sunny, quiet studio. That was your bed—with a brand-new mattress. Here you had a writing desk—you see, that's where the wall ran—where that hose lies now.

Humbert blankly considers a heap of water-soaked volumes.

McCOO   Ginny's encyclopedia. (*Glances up at a nonexistent upper story.*) Must have dropped through the floor of my daughter's room. Good illustrations. Cathedrals. Cocoa Industry. It's a wonder that bolt did not kill Mrs. McCoo and me in the master bedroom. Our little daughter was quite hysterical. Oh, it was such a lovely home. A regular showpiece. People came all the way from Parkington to see it.

Humbert stumbles over a board.

McCOO   Careful. I know there is not much left but I'd like you to see the patio. Here was the barbecue table. Well, that's all out now. I had planned to have you give lessons in French to my little Ginny, the poor pet. I've bundled them off to Parkington. And of course I'm fully insured. But still it's a terrible shock. Now, about that other place for you——

McCoo, wiping a dirty face with a dirty hand, walks back to the street with carefully high-stepping Humbert. The camera escorts them.

McCOO   We thought that other place would be the best arrangement, under these sad circumstances. We all have to rough it now. She's a widow, a delightful personality with a lot of culture. But it's not as grand as here,

though much nearer to town. The address is 342 Lawn
Street. Let me direct your taxi. Hullo, Joe.

CUT TO:

Hysterical Bark of a car-chasing *Collie* on Lawn Street, down
which Humbert's taxi arrives to stop at No. 342, an unattractive white clapboard suburban house, with a smooth philistine
lawn where only one dandelion has survived the leveling
power mower. Humbert emerges, watched by Charlotte from
an upper window. The driver is about to help with the suitcases.

HUMBERT   No, leave those bags. I want you to wait a few
    minutes.

DRIVER   Sure.

HUMBERT   I doubt very much that I'll stay here. (*in vocal
    brackets*) What a horrible house.

The door is ajar. Humbert enters. The hallway is graced with
Mexican knickknacks and the banal favorites of arty middle-
class (such as a Van Gogh reproduction). An old tennis racket
with a broken string lies on an oak chest. There is a telephone
on a small table near the living-room door, which is ajar.
    From the upper landing comes the voice of Mrs. Haze, who
leans over the banisters inquiring melodiously: "Is that Monsieur Humbert?"
    A bit of cigarette ash drops from above as Humbert looks
up. Presently the lady herself—sandals, slacks, silk blouse,
Marlenesque face (in that order)—comes down the steps, her
index finger still tapping upon the cigarette.
    Shake hands.

HUMBERT   How do you do. Allow me to explain the sit-
    uation.

CHARLOTTE   Yes—I know everything. Come on in.

CUT TO:

Humbert and Charlotte enter the parlor
She makes Javanese-like gestures: inviting him to choose a

seat. (N.B.: these gestures will be repeated by Dolly Schiller in last scene of play.) They sit down.

CHARLOTTE   Let's get acquainted and then I'll show you your room. I have only Dromes.

HUMBERT   Thanks, I don't smoke.

CHARLOTTE   Oh well, one vice the less. I'm a tissue of little vices. *C'est la vie.* (*Lights up.*) You're sure you're comfortable in that old chair?

He removes from under his thigh an old tennis ball.

HUMBERT   Oh, perfectly.

CHARLOTTE   (*relieving him of the ball*) I think, Mr. Humbert, I have exactly what you are looking for. I understand you wanted to stay at Ramsdale all summer?

HUMBERT   I'm not sure. No, I really could not say. The point is I have been very ill, and a friend suggested Ramsdale. I imagined a spacious house on the shore of a lake.

The CAMERA meanwhile examines ironically various crannies of the room.

CHARLOTTE   Well, the lake is only two miles from *my* spacious house.

HUMBERT   Oh, I know. But I envisaged a villa, white dunes, the accessible ripples, a system of morning dips.

CHARLOTTE   Frankly, between you and I, the McCoo residence, though perhaps a bit more modern than mine, is not at all on the lake front, not at all. You have to walk two blocks to see it.

HUMBERT   Oh, I'm sure there would have been some flaw, some disappointment. What I mean is that I was pursuing a particular dream, not *any* house but *that* house.

CHARLOTTE   I'm sorry for the McCoos—but they should not have promised too much. Well, I can offer you congenial surroundings in a very select neighborhood. If you like golf, as I am sure you do, we are practically at walking distance from the country club. And we are very intellectual, yes sir. You are a professor of poetry, aren't you?

HUMBERT   Alas. I shall be teaching at Beardsley College next year.

CHARLOTTE   Then you will certainly want to address our club, of which I am a proud member. Last time we had Professor Amy King, a very stimulating teacher type, talk to us on Dr. Schweitzer and Dr. Zhivago. Now let us take a peek at that room. I'm positive you're going to love it.

CUT TO:

Charlotte and Humbert reach the upper landing

CHARLOTTE   It's what you might call a semi-studio—or *almost* a semi-studio.

She closes quickly the door to Lolita's room, which is ajar, and opens a door opposite.

CHARLOTTE   Well here we are. Isn't that a cute bookshelf? Look at those colonial book ends. Now, in that corner (*meditative pause, with elbow in palm*) I shall put our spare radio set.

HUMBERT   No, no. Please, no radio.

He winces as he glances at a picture: a reproduction of René Prinet's "Kreutzer Sonata"—the unappetizing one in which a disheveled violinist passionately embraces his fair accompanist as she rises from her piano stool with clammy young hands still touching the keys.

CHARLOTTE   Now, that's a rug Mr. Haze and I bought in Mexico. We went there on our honeymoon, which was—let me see—thirteen years ago.

HUMBERT   Which was about the time I got married.

CHARLOTTE   Oh, you are married?

HUMBERT   Divorced, madam, happily divorced.

CHARLOTTE   Where was that? In Europe?

HUMBERT   In Paris.

CHARLOTTE   Paris must be wonderful at this time of the
year. As a matter of fact, we were planning a trip to
Europe just before Mr. Haze died, after three years of
great happiness. He was a lovely person, a man of complete integrity. I know you would have enjoyed talking
to him and he to you. Now, here we have——

Humbert opens a closet. A painted screen of the folding type
topples into his arms. Pictured on it is a nymphet in three
repeated designs: (1) gazing over a black gauze fan, (2) in a
black half-mask, (3) in bikini and harlequin glasses. There is
a rent in the fabric.

CHARLOTTE   Oops! I *am* sorry. We bought it at the store
here to match our Mexican stuff but it did not wear well.
I'll have Lolita remove it to her room. She loves it.

HUMBERT   You have a maid living in the house?

CHARLOTTE   Oh no, what do you think? Ramsdale is not
Paris. There's a colored girl who comes three times a
week and we think we're lucky to have her. I see this
bed-lamp does not work. I'll have it fixed.

HUMBERT   But I thought you said——

Carefully and rather wistfully, Charlotte closes the door of the
unsuccessful room. She opens another door next to it.

CHARLOTTE   This is the bathroom. I'm sure that as a European intellectual you hate our luxurious modern monstrosities—tiled tubs and golden faucets. This here is a
good old-fashioned type with the kind of quaint plumbing that should appeal to an Englishman. I must apologize for this dirty sock. Now, if we walk down again
I'll show you the dining room—and, of course, my
beautiful garden.

HUMBERT   I understood there would be a private bath.

CHARLOTTE   Sorry.

HUMBERT   I don't want to take so much of your time. It
     must be a frightful bother——

CHARLOTTE   No bother at all.

Humbert and Charlotte walk via the parlor into the dining
room, the camera trucking with them.

CHARLOTTE   Here we have our meals. Down there is the
     sun porch. Well, that's about all, *cher Monsieur.*
                    (*sigh*)
     I'm afraid you are not too favorably impressed.

HUMBERT   I must think it over. I have a taxi waiting out
     there. Let me take down your telephone number.

CHARLOTTE   Ramsdale 1776. So easy to remember. I won't
     charge you much, you know. Two hundred per month,
     all meals included.

HUMBERT   I see. Didn't I have a raincoat?

CHARLOTTE   I saw you leave it in the car.

HUMBERT   So I did. Well——

He bows.

CHARLOTTE   Oh, but you *must* visit my garden!

Humbert follows her.

CHARLOTTE   That's the kitchen there. You might like to
     know I'm a very good cook. My pastries win prizes
     round here.

Humbert follows Charlotte to the veranda. Now comes the
shock of dazzling enchantment and recognition. "From a mat
in a pool of sun, half-naked, kneeling turning about on her
knees, my Riviera love was peering at me over dark glasses."

It might be a good idea at this point to film the extended
metaphor of the next paragraph: "As if I were the fairy-tale
nurse of some little princess—lost, kidnapped, discovered in
Gypsy rags through which her nakedness smiled at the king
and his hounds, I recognized the tiny dark-brown mole on

her side." Humbert, much disturbed, follows Charlotte down into the garden.

CHARLOTTE   That was my daughter, and these are my lilies.

HUMBERT   (*mumbling*) Beautiful, beautiful. . . .

CHARLOTTE   (*with winsome abandon*) Well, this is all I can offer you—a comfortable home, a sunny garden, my lilies, my Lolita, my cherry pies.

HUMBERT   Yes, yes. I'm very grateful. You said fifty per week, including meals?

CHARLOTTE   So you *are* going to stay with us?

HUMBERT   Why—yes. I'd like to move in right now.

CHARLOTTE   You dear man. That's wonderful. Was my garden the decisive factor?

CUT TO:

Veranda where Lolita, in briefs and bra, is sunning herself on the mat
Charlotte and Humbert returning to the house mount the steps from the garden.

CHARLOTTE   I'll pay your taxi and have the luggage put in your room. Do you have many things?

HUMBERT   There's a briefcase and a typewriter, and a tape recorder, and a raincoat. And two suitcases. May I——

CHARLOTTE   No, it's okay. I know from Mrs. McCoo that you are not supposed to carry things.

HUMBERT   Oh yes, and there's also a box of chocolates I intended to bring the McCoos.

Charlotte smiles and exits.

LOLITA   Yum-yum.

HUMBERT   So you are Lolita.

LOLITA   Yes, that's me.

Turns from sea-star supine to seal prone. There is a pause.

HUMBERT   It's a beautiful day.

LOLITA   Very.

HUMBERT   (*sitting down on the steps*) Nice here. Oh, the floor is hot.

LOLITA   (*Pushes a cushion toward him.*) Make yourself comfortable.

She is now in a half-sitting position.

LOLITA   Did you see the fire?

HUMBERT   No, it was all over when I came. Poor Mr. McCoo looked badly shaken.

LOLITA   You look badly shaken yourself.

HUMBERT   Why, no. I'm all right. I suppose I should change into lighter clothes. There's a ladybird on your leg.

LOLITA   It's a ladybug, not a ladybird.

She transfers it to her finger and attempts to coax it into flight.

HUMBERT   You should blow. Like this. There she goes.

LOLITA   Ginny McCoo—she's in my class, you know. And she said you were going to be her tutor.

HUMBERT   Oh, that's greatly exaggerated. The idea was I might help her with her French.

LOLITA   She's grim, Ginny.

HUMBERT   Is she—well, attractive?

LOLITA   She's a fright. And mean. And lame.

HUMBERT   Really? That's curious. Lame?

LOLITA   Yah. She had polio or something. Are you going to help me with my homework?

HUMBERT   *Mais oui*, Lolita. *Aujourd'hui?*

Charlotte comes in.

CHARLOTTE   That's where you are.

LOLITA   He's going to help me with my homework.

CHARLOTTE   Fine. Mr. Humbert, I paid your taxi and had the man take your things upstairs. You owe me four dollars thirty-five. Later, later. Dolores, I think Mr. Humbert would like to rest.

HUMBERT   Oh no, I'll help her with pleasure.

Charlotte leaves.

LOLITA   Well, there's not much today. Gee, school will be over in three weeks.

A pause.

HUMBERT   May I—I want to pluck some tissue paper out of that box. No, you're lying on it. There—let me— thanks.

LOLITA   Hold on. This bit has my lipstick on it.

HUMBERT   Does your mother allow lipstick?

LOLITA   She does not. I hide it here.

She indraws her pretty abdomen and produces the lipstick from under the band of her shorts.

HUMBERT   You're a very amusing little girl. Do you often go to the lake shore? I shaw—I mean, I saw that beautiful lake from the plane.

LOLITA   (*lying back with a sigh*) Almost never. It's quite a way. And my mummy's too lazy to go there with me. Besides, we kids prefer the town pool.

HUMBERT   Who is your favorite recording star?

LOLITA   Oh, I dunno.

HUMBERT   What grade are you in?

LOLITA   This a quiz?

HUMBERT   I only want to know more about you. I know

that you like to solarize your solar plexus. But what else do you like?

LOLITA   You shouldn't use such words, you know.

HUMBERT   Should I say "what you *dig*"?

LOLITA   That's old hat.

Pause. Lolita turns over on her tummy. Humbert, awkwardly squatting, tense, twitching, mutely moaning, devours her with sad eyes; Lolita, a restless sunbather, sits up again.

HUMBERT   Is there anything special you'd like to be when you grow up?

LOLITA   What?

HUMBERT   I said——

Lolita, eyes shuttling, listens to the telephone ringing in the remote hallway and to her mother attending to it.

LOLITA   (*yelling*) Mother, is it for me?

HUMBERT   I said what would you like to be?

Charlotte enters from dining room. Humbert, interrupted in his furtive lust, scrambles up guiltily.

CHARLOTTE   It's Kenny. I suspect he wants to escort you to the big dance next month.

Lolita, groping, skipping on one foot, half-shod, shedding beach slipper, whirling, taking off, bumping into humid Humbert, laughing, exits barefoot.

CHARLOTTE   I'll be driving downtown in a few minutes. Like me to take you somewhere? Like to see Ramsdale?

HUMBERT   First I'd like to change. I never thought it would be so warm in Ramsdale.

CUT TO:

Humbert's Room. A few days have elapsed.
Humbert jots down last night's dream: A somewhat ripply shot reveals: a knight in full armor riding a black horse along

a forest road. Three nymphets, one lame, are playing in a sun-shot glade. Nymphet Lolita runs toward Humbert, the Dark Knight, and promptly seats herself behind. His visor closes again. At a walking pace they ride deeper into the Enchanted Forest.

DISSOLVE TO NEXT ENTRY:

We are on the piazza. Humbert takes up a strategic position in rocker, with voluminous Sunday paper, in the vicinity of two parallel mats. He rocks and feigns to read. Exaggerate the volume of the paper.

Mother and daughter, both in two-piece bathing suits, come to sun themselves.

CUT TO:

Charlotte transposes jar of skin cream from farther mat (mat 2) to nearer mat (mat 1) and sits down on mat 1. Lolita yanks the comics section, and the family section, and the magazine section out of Humbert's paper and makes herself comfortable on mat 2.

There is an area of shade beyond her. Into this area Humbert, the furtive writer, gently rocking arrives in his ambling chair. He is now near Lolita.

Mother, far, supine, on mat 1 (now the farthest) lavishly anointed, exhibits herself to the sun; daughter, near, prone, on mat 2, showing Humbert her narrow nates and the sea-side of her thighs, is immersed in the funnies.

Tenderly, the rocker rocks.

A mourning dove coos.

Charlotte gropes for her cigarettes but they are on mat 2, nearer to Humbert. She half rises and transfers herself to a new position, between him and her daughter, whom she shoves onto mat 1.

Charlotte, now on mat 2, near Humbert, fusses with lighter and casts a look at what he is grimly perusing: book review, a full-page ad:

WHEN THE LILACS LAST
most controversial novel of the year, 300,000 copies in print.

CHARLOTTE   Have you read that? *When the Lilacs Last.*

HUMBERT   (*Clears his throat negatively.*)

CHARLOTTE   Oh, you should. It was given a rave review
    by Adam Scott. It's about a man from the North and a
    girl from the South who build up a beautiful relation-
    ship—he is her father image and she is his mother image,
    but later she discovers that as a child she had rejected
    her father, and of course then he begins to identify her
    with his possessive mother. You see, it works out this
    way: he symbolizes the industrial North, and she sym-
    bolizes the old-fashioned South, and——

LOLITA   (*casually*) and it's all silly nonsense.

CHARLOTTE   Dolores Haze, will you go up to your room
    at once.

THREE WEEKS LATER,
THE DAY OF THE SCHOOL DANCE.

FADE IN:

Kitchen—the Cat and the Morning Milk are let in
Charlotte, dainty-aproned, prepares breakfast for Humbert.
He enters, wearing a silk jacket with frogs.

HUMBERT   Good morning.

He sits down at the breakfast-niche table. Puts his elbows on
it and meditates.

CHARLOTTE   Your bacon is ready.

Humbert considers the calendar on the wall and reaches into
his back pocket for his wallet.

HUMBERT   My fourth week starts today.

CHARLOTTE   The time certainly flies. Monsieur is served.

HUMBERT   Fifty, and the eight twenty I owe you for the
    wine.

CHARLOTTE   No, it's sixty-two thirty-five: I paid for the
    Glance subscription, remember?

HUMBERT   Oh, I thought I had settled that.

He settles.

CHARLOTTE   Well, today is the big party. I bet she'll be
   pestering me all morning with her dance dress.

HUMBERT   Isn't that rather normal?

CHARLOTTE   Oh, yes. Definitely. I am all for these formal
   affairs. It may suggest to the hoyden she is some elements of gracious living.
                    (*Sits down at the table.*)
   On the other hand—this is the end of that blessed era,
   school year. After which we'll be in for a period of
   slouching, disorganized boredom, vehement griping,
   feigned gagging, and all the rest of it.

HUMBERT   Hm. Aren't you exaggerating a bit?

CHARLOTTE   Oh, I leave *that* to her. Exaggerating is all
   hers. How I hate that diffused clowning—what they call
   "goofing off." In *my* day, which after all was only a
   couple of short decades ago, I never indulged in that
   sprawling, droopy, dopy-eyed style.

Lolita's voice is heard calling from the stairs.

CHARLOTTE   (*making a grimace of resignation*) See what I
   mean?
                    (*to Lolita*)
   Yes? What is it?

LOLITA   (*carrying a slip*) You promised to fix this.

CHARLOTTE   Okay. Later.

LOLITA   (*to Humbert*) Well: coming to our hop?

CHARLOTTE   My daughter means: Do you intend to attend
   her school dance.

HUMBERT   I understood. Yes, thank you.

CHARLOTTE   We parents are not supposed to dance, of
   course.

LOLITA   What do you mean "we"?

CHARLOTTE   (*flustered*) Oh, I mean adults. Parents and their friends.

Lolita exits singing.

HUMBERT   When does it start?

CHARLOTTE   Around four. I have some nice cold chicken for you afterwards.
(*seeing him rise*)
Back to Baudelaire?

HUMBERT   Yes. I wanted to write in the garden but our neighbor's gardener has again set loose his motor mower or whatever you call it. It's deafening and sickening.

CHARLOTTE   I always think of it as an exhilarating, cheerful kind of sound. It brings back heaps of green summers and that kind of thing.

HUMBERT   You Americans are immune to noise.

CHARLOTTE   Anyway, Lesley stops work at noon, and you'll have lots of time before the party.

CUT TO:

The Garden
Humbert in the leafy shade, writes in his little black book. Mourning doves moan, cicadas whirr, a jet beyond sight and sound leaves its twin wakelines of silvery chalk in the cloudless sky. A mother's voice is heard calling somewhere up the street: "Rosy! Ro-sy!" It is a very pleasant afternoon. Humbert consults his watch and glances up at the house. He gets up and strolls around, quietly trying to locate Lolita, whose voice is heard now in one room, now in another, while radio music comes from a third. Presently the bath water is heard performing, filling the tub, and then emptying into the drain. Humbert assembles his papers and walks to the house.

CUT TO:

The Living Room
Humbert feigning to read a magazine. Lolita swishes into the

room wearing a pale billowy-skirted dance dress and pale satin pumps. She gracefully gyrates in front of Humbert.

LOLITA   Well? Do you like me?

HUMBERT   (*a phony judge*) Very much.

LOLITA   Adoration? Beauty in the mist? Too dreamy for words?

HUMBERT   I am often amazed at your verbal felicity, Lolita.

LOLITA   Check my back zipper, will you?

HUMBERT   There's some talc on your shoulder blades. May I remove it?

LOLITA   It depends.

HUMBERT   There.

LOLITA   Silly boy.

HUMBERT   I am three times your age.

LOLITA   Tell it to Mom.

HUMBERT   Why?

LOLITA   Oh, I guess you tell her everything.

HUMBERT   Wait a minute, Lolita. Don't waltz. A great poet said: Stop, moment——. You are beautiful.

LOLITA   (*feigning to call*) Mother!

HUMBERT   Even when you play the fool.

LOLITA   That's not English.

HUMBERT   It's English enough for me.

LOLITA   D'you think this dress will make Kenny gulp?

HUMBERT   Who's Kenny?

LOLITA   He's my date for tonight. Jealous?

HUMBERT   In fact, yes.

LOLITA   Delirious? Dolly-mad?

HUMBERT   Yes, yes. Oh, wait!

LOLITA   And she flew away.

She flies away.

CUT TO:

The Landing
Humbert in a flannel suit and Charlotte in a glamorous gown
(from Rosenthal, The Rose of Ramsdale, 50 South Main
Street).

HUMBERT   Are we supposed to pick up her young man?

CHARLOTTE   No. He said he'd call for her. He lives two
    blocks from here. I'll bet she'll be prettying herself up
    to the last moment.

CUT TO:

The Driveway, Facing the Garage
Kenny helps Lolita to get into the back of the Haze two-door
sedan. On the other side Humbert opens the driver's door for
Charlotte. Daughter and Mother settle down with the same
preenings, the same rhythm of rustle and rerustle. Humbert
starts walking around the car. Charlotte turns to Kenny, who
is about to join Lolita.

CHARLOTTE   It's the new building, isn't it?

KENNY   Yes, ma'am.

CHARLOTTE   And Chestnut Street is closed for repairs?

KENNY   Yes. You have to turn after the church.

CHARLOTTE   Church? I thought it was the other way. Let
    me see—

LOLITA   Look, Kenny, why don't you get in beside Mother
    and direct her?

CHARLOTTE   Don't bother. I'll find it.

LOLITA   No, you won't. Please, Ken. And you come here.

Pats the seat next to her for Hum. Humbert, not without hitting his head against the lintel, climbs in and arranges his long limbs beside Lolita's bouffant skirt. The backrest of the passenger seat is pushed into place by Kenny who briskly seats himself next to Charlotte. She gives vent to her irritation by getting into reverse gear so abruptly that Lolita's purse leaps off her lap. Lolita and Humbert fumble for it.

LOLITA   (*laughing*) Easy, Mother.

CHARLOTTE   (*controlling herself*) No backseat driving, children.

And that is how Humbert obtains a few minutes of secret alliance with the nymphet. Deliberately, Lolita lets her hand rest on his, lets it slip into his, be enveloped by his.

CUT TO:

The New Hall
School punch and cookies are served in the gallery where teachers, parents, and their friends stand around in more or less garrulous groups. *Music* comes from the adjacent room, where the children are dancing. Charlotte introduces Humbert to the Chatfields.

CHARLOTTE   Ann, I want you to meet Professor Humbert, who is staying with us. Mrs. Chatfield, Mr. Chatfield.

How do you do's are exchanged.

MRS. CHATFIELD   (*to Charlotte*) Your Lolita looks perfectly enchanting in that cloud of pink. And the way she moves. . . . Oh, my!

CHARLOTTE   Thank you. And I was about to compliment you on your Phyllis. She's a darling. I understand you are sending her to the Climax Lake camp next week?

MRS. CHATFIELD   Yes. It's the healthiest place in the world. Run by a remarkable woman who believes in natural education. Which, of course, is progressive education combined with nature.

CHARLOTTE   Say, who is that gentleman in the fancy waistcoat whom those women are mobbing? He looks familiar to me.

MRS. CHATFIELD   Oh, Charlotte! That's Clare Quilty, the playwright.

CHARLOTTE   Of course. I quite forgot that our good old dentist had such a distinguished nephew. Didn't you adore his play which they had on the TV, *The Nymphet*?

CUT TO:

Another Part of the Gallery
In the meantime, after some dreary small talk with Mr. Chatfield (Chatfield: I hear, Professor, you're going to teach at Beardsley College. I believe the wife of our president—I work for the Lakewood corporation—majored there in Home Economics.), Humbert drifts away. He wanders toward the dance floor and watches Lolita. The second or third slow dance has terminated and now a more boisterous strain hits the eardrum. Kenny and Lolita go through an energetic rock 'n' roll. Humbert leans his shoulder against a pillar. The camera picks out his Adam's apple.

CUT TO:

The Refreshments Table Near Which Charlotte Stands
She casts a questing look around. She has lost Humbert. Two gigglers in full skirts rustle past rapidly, heading for the ballroom.

FIRST GIRL   (*to second*) D'you know who that was? Clare Quilty! Oh, gosh, I got a real bang out of seeing him.

Charlotte's roving eye meets the gaze of the English teacher, Miss Adams, in the Quilty group. Miss Adams beckons to her. Charlotte floats thither. Introductions. Quilty is a tremendously successful phony, fortyish, roguish, baldish, with an obscene little mustache and a breezy manner which some find insulting and others just love.

CHARLOTTE   Oh, but I have met Mr. Quilty before.
     (*Elegantly appropriates him.*)
     Mr. Quilty, I'm a great fan of yours.

QUILTY   Ah yes—ah yes——

CHARLOTTE   We met two years ago——

QUILTY   (*ironically purring*) An eternity——

CHARLOTTE   We had that luncheon in your honor at the club——

QUILTY   I can imagine it better than I recall it——

CHARLOTTE   And afterwards I showed you my garden and drove you to the airport——

QUILTY   Ah yes—magnificent airport.

He attempts to leave her orbit.

CHARLOTTE   Are you here for some time?

QUILTY   Oh, very briefly. Came to borrow a little cash from Uncle Ivor. Excuse me, I think I must go now. They are putting on a play of mine in Parkington.

CHARLOTTE   Recently we had the pleasure of enjoying your *Nymphet* on Channel 5.

QUILTY   Great fun those channels. Well, it was a joy chatting about the past.

He moves away sidling into the crowd but stops suddenly and turns.

QUILTY   Say, didn't you have a little girl? Let me see. With a lovely name. A lovely lilting lyrical name——

CHARLOTTE   Lolita. Diminutive of Dolores.

QUILTY   Ah, of course: Dolores. The tears and the roses.

CHARLOTTE   She's dancing down there. And tomorrow she'll be having a cavity filled by your uncle.

QUILTY   I know; he's a wicked old man.

MISS ADAMS   Mr. Quilty, I'm afraid I must tear you away. There's somebody come from Parkington to fetch you.

QUILTY   They can wait. I want to watch Dolores dance.

CUT TO:

Gallery Near Refreshments
Humbert appears.

CHARLOTTE   Where have you been all this time?

HUMBERT   Just strolling around.

CHARLOTTE   You look bored stiff, you poor man. Oh, hullo, Emily.

MRS. GRAY   Good evening, Charlotte.

CHARLOTTE   Emily, this is Professor Humbert, who is staying with us. Mrs. Gray.

Handshakes

MRS. GRAY   Isn't it a lovely party?

CHARLOTTE   Is your darling Rose having a good time?

MRS. GRAY   Oh, yes. You know, that child is insatiable. She got some new records for her birthday, so she plans to dance to them with Jack Beale and a couple of other kids after the party. She'd like to ask Lolita and Kenny. Could Lolita go with us from here? I'll give her supper.

CHARLOTTE   By all means. That's a delightful arrangement.

MRS. GRAY   Wonderful. I'll bring her back. Around ten?

CHARLOTTE   Make it eleven. Thank you very much, Emily.

Mrs. Gray joins another group.

CHARLOTTE   (*taking Humbert's arm*) And *we* can go home and have a nice cozy supper. Is that all right with you, *cher monsieur?*

CUT TO:

The Haze Living Room
Charlotte and Humbert have finished their cold chicken and salad and are now sipping liqueurs in the parlor.

CHARLOTTE   I consider crème de menthe to be the supremely divine nectar. This was given me by the Farlows. Cost them a small fortune, I suspect.

Humbert eyes casually a diminutive circular sticker with the price "$2.50." They clink and drink.

CHARLOTTE   Well—*votre santé*. Now let's have some good music.

Humbert looks at his wristwatch, and then at the clock.

CHARLOTTE   Bartók or Bardinski?

HUMBERT   Doesn't matter—Bardinski, rather. I am not at all sure that those parties are properly chaperoned.

CHARLOTTE   What parties? What are you talking about?

HUMBERT   Parties at the homes of mothers. Record-playing sessions in the basement with the lights out.

CHARLOTTE   Oh, that! Really, Mr. Humbert, I have more exciting things to think about than the manners of modern children. Look, let's change the subject. I mean, after all . . . can't we forget my tedious daughter? Here's a proposal: why don't I teach you some of the new dance steps? What say you?

HUMBERT   I don't even know the old ones. I'm an awkward tripper and have no sense of rhythm.

CHARLOTTE   Oh, come on. Come on, Humbert. May I call you Humbert? Especially as nobody can tell which it is of your two names? Or do you think the surname is pronounced a little different? In a deeper voice? No? Humbert. . . . Which is it now, first or second?

HUMBERT   (*getting more and more uneasy*) I wouldn't know.

CHARLOTTE   (*going to the phonograph*) I'll teach you the cha-cha-cha.
(*returning to her armrest perch and coyly questioning*) Cha-cha-cha?

He rises from his low armchair, not because he wants to be

taught but because the ripe lady might roll into his lap if he remains seated. The record clacks and croons. Charlotte demonstrates her ankles. Bored, helpless, Humbert, hands clasped on his fly, stands looking at her moving feet.

CHARLOTTE   It's as simple as that.
            (*Darts to the phonograph to restart*)
    Now come here, Humbert.
                    (*smiling*)
    That was *not* the surname.

Humbert surrenders. She leads him this way and that in a tactile drill. Releases him for a moment.

CHARLOTTE   Now do like this with your hands. More life. Fine. Now clasp me.

                          CUT TO:

Lawn Street in Front of No. 342
A station wagon with Mrs. Gray at the wheel, two or three boys and Lolita, stops at the lawn curb. Rigmarole of resonant good-byes. Car drives off. Lolita runs up the porch steps.

                          CUT TO:

Living Room
Charlotte pulsates and palpates Humbert's (stuffed) shoulder.

CHARLOTTE   In certain lights, when you frown like that, you remind me of somebody. A college boy I once danced with, a young blue-blooded Bostonian, my first glamour date.

The Door Chimes go into action.

CHARLOTTE   (*shutting off the record player*) Oh, darn it!

Humbert lets in Lolita.

LOLITA   (*casually*) Hullo, sweetheart.

She saunters into the living room.

CHARLOTTE   Well, you came earlier than I hoped— I mean, I did not hope you would be back so early.

LOLITA   You two seem to have been living it up here?

CHARLOTTE   How was your party?

LOLITA   Lousy.

CHARLOTTE   I thought Kenny looked cute.

LOLITA   I'm calling him Shorty from now on. I never realized he was so short. And dumb.

CHARLOTTE   Well, you've had your fling—and now to bed,
my dear.

During this exchange, Humbert in abject adoration, gloats
over the limp nymphet who has now filled a low chair with
her foamy skirt and thin arms.

HUMBERT   You remind me of a sleepy flamingo.

LOLITA   Cut it out, Hum.

CHARLOTTE   Do you permit, Mr. Humbert, this rude
child——

LOLITA   Oh, Mother, give us a break. May I take these
cookies upstairs?

CHARLOTTE   Well, if you want to pamper your pimples—

LOLITA   I don't have pimples!

CHARLOTTE   Take anything you want but go.

LOLITA   All in good time.
                    (*Stretches.*)
Did you talk to the famous author?

CHARLOTTE   Yes. Please go.

LOLITA   Rose is crazy about him. Okay, I go. Bye-bye.

Indolently she moves out of the room. At the bottom of the
stairs—as seen from the parlor—she stops, lingers, with her
fair arm stretched out on the rail and her cheek on her arm.
Meditates in this posture.

HUMBERT   What author did she mean?

CHARLOTTE   The author of *The Nymphet*. He's the nephew
  —will you *please* go upstairs, Lolita?

Lolita sighs, grimaces, and slowly comes into lazy motion.

HUMBERT   Thanks for this charming evening, Mrs. Haze.

CHARLOTTE   Thank *you*, Mr. Humbert. Oh, sit down.
  Let's have a nightcap.

HUMBERT   No, I think not. I think I'll go up to bed.

CHARLOTTE   It's quite early yet, you know.

HUMBERT   I know. But my neuralgia is about to strike.
  . . . With heartburn, an old ally.

CUT TO:

Stairs and Upper Landing
The nymphet is still there, now sliding up dreamily, half-
reclining on the banisters. Humbert and she reach the upper
landing together.

HUMBERT   Good night, Lolita.

LOLITA   Huh?

HUMBERT   I said "good night, Lolita."

LOLITA   Night.

She totters to her room.

CUT TO:

Humbert's Study, a Couple of Days Later
Humbert in his room is tape-recording his lecture, "Baudelaire and Poe." He plays back the last sentences:

HUMBERT'S VOICE   Before discussing Baudelaire's methods of translating Poe, let me turn for a moment to the
  romantic lines, let me turn to the romantic lines in which
  the great American neurotic commemorates his marriage
  to a thirteen-year-old girl, his beautiful Annabel Lee.

(*The machine clicks and stops.*)

Now Lolita is heard bouncing a tennis ball. Humbert softly

opens his door and listens. She is in the hallway. Humming to herself, Lolita walks upstairs plucking at the banisters and quietly clowning. Bluejeans, shirt. Humbert is back in his chair, Lolita is on the landing. With a good deal of shuffling and scraping she comes into Humbert's room. She potters around, fidgets, moves variously in the neighborhood of his desk.

LOLITA   (*bending close to him*) What are you drawing?

HUMBERT   (*considering his drawing*) Is it you?

LOLITA   (*peering still more closely—she is somewhat short-sighted*) Is it?

HUMBERT   Or perhaps it is more like a little girl I knew when I was your age.

One of the drawers of the desk comes out by itself in a kind of organic protractile movement, disclosing a photograph of Humbert's first love in a Riviera setting: a sidewalk café near a peopled *plage.*

LOLITA   Where's that?

HUMBERT   In a princedom by the sea. Monaco.

LOLITA   Oh, I know where that is.

HUMBERT   I'm sure you do. Many and many a year ago. Thirty, to be exact.

LOLITA   What was her name?

HUMBERT   Annabel—curiously enough.

LOLITA   Why curiously enough?

HUMBERT   Never mind. And this was me.

Same snapshot, same setting, but now in the photograph the chair next to Annabel is occupied by young Humbert, a moody lad. Morosely, he takes off his white cap as if acknowledging recognition, and dons it again.

   Actually it is the same actress as the one that plays Lolita but wearing her hair differently, etc.

LOLITA   She doesn't look like me at all. Were you in love
    with her?

HUMBERT   Yes. Three months later she died. Here, on that
    beach, you see the angels envying her and me.

He clears his throat.

LOLITA   (*now holding the photo*) That's not angels. That's
    Garbo and Abraham Lincoln in terrycloth robes.

She laughs. A pause. As she bends her brown curls over the
picture, Humbert puts his arm around her in a miserable imitation of blood relationship, and still studying the snapshot—
which now shows young Humbert alone—Lolita slowly sinks
to a half-sitting position upon his knee.
    The erotic suspense is interrupted.

CHARLOTTE   (*shouting up from hallway*) Lolita! Will you
    come down, please?

LOLITA   (*without changing her position*) I'm busy! What
    d'you want?

CHARLOTTE   Will you come down at once?

At the Foot of the Stairs
Charlotte and Lolita.

CHARLOTTE   Now, firstly I want you to change. Put on a
    dress: I'm going to the Chatfields, and I want you to
    come too. Secondly: I simply forbid you to disturb Mr.
    Humbert. He's a writer and should not be disturbed.
    And if you make that grimace again, I think I'll slap you.

CUT TO:

Humbert Transcribing from Pad to Diary
speaks as he deciphers his jottings.

HUMBERT   (*in a low faltering voice*) The hag said she
    would slap Lolita, my Lolita. For thirty years I mourned
    Annabel, and watched nymphets playing in parks, and
    never once dared—. And now Annabel is dead, and Lo-
    lita is alive—my darling—"my darling—my life and my
    bride."

CUT TO:

Dinner with Charlotte

HUMBERT   And where is your daughter tonight?

CHARLOTTE   Oh, I left her at the Chatfields'—she's going to a movie with Phyllis. By the way, I have a glorious surprise for you.

HUMBERT   What surprise? One of your dramatic sweets?

CHARLOTTE   Wrong, Monsieur. Try again.

HUMBERT   A new light bulb.

CHARLOTTE   Nope.

HUMBERT   I give up.

CHARLOTTE   After tomorrow, Lolita is leaving for summer camp.

HUMBERT   (*trying to conceal his consternation*) Really? This is only June, you know.

CHARLOTTE   Exactly. I think of myself as a good average mother, but I confess I'm looking forward to ten full weeks of tranquillity. Another slice of beef? No?

HUMBERT   Toothache.

CHARLOTTE   Oh, you poor man! Let me have Dr. Quilty take care of you.

HUMBERT   No, no, don't bother. It will pass. How far is that camp?

CHARLOTTE   About two hundred miles. It was a stroke of genius on Mama's part. I arranged everything without telling little Lolita, who dislikes Phyllis for no reason at all. Sprang it upon her at the Chatfields', so she could not talk back. Ain't I clever? Little Lolita I hope will be mollified by the movie. I just could not have faced her tonight.

HUMBERT   Are you sure she will be happy at that camp?

CHARLOTTE   She'd better. She'll go riding there, which is much healthier than banging a tennis ball against the garage door. And camp will be much healthier than moping here, and pursuing shy scholarly gentlemen. Camp will teach Dolores to grow in many ways—health, knowledge, temper. And particularly in the sense of responsibility toward other people. Shall we take these candles with us and sit for a while on the piazza? Or do you want to go to bed and nurse that tooth?

HUMBERT   Tooth.

He slowly ascends the stairs. Charlotte calls after him.

CHARLOTTE   By the way—I told Lolita *you* had advised it. I thought your authority
           (*crystalline little laugh*)
would have more weight than mine.

Night. Humbert in His Room at the Window
Car stops at 342 Lawn Street.

CHARLOTTE   Oh, do come in for a moment, Mary. I forgot to check a few items on that list for the girls. Do come in.

MRS. CHATFIELD   Well, just for a minute.

CHARLOTTE   We excuse you, Dolores. Straight to bed like a good girl.

Humbert meets Lolita on the landing.

HUMBERT   (*attempting small talk*) How was the picture?

Without answering, Lolita marches toward her room.

HUMBERT   What's the matter, Lolita?

LOLITA   Nothing. Except that you are revolting.

HUMBERT   I did not do anything. It's a mistake. I swear.

LOLITA   (*haughtily*) I'm through with you. *Envoyez votre jeune fille au camp, Madame.* Double-crosser!

HUMBERT   I never said that! It's not even French! I'd do
    anything to have you stay here. I really would.

She slams the door.

CUT TO:

Humbert Dictates His "Baudelaire and Poe" lecture into the recorder.

HUMBERT   Other commentators, commentators of the
    Freudian school of thought. No. Commentators of the
    Freudian prison of thought. Hm. Commentators of the
    Freudian nursery-school of thought, have maintained
    that Edgar Poe married the child Virginia Clemm merely
    to keep her mother near him. He—I quote—had found
    in his mother-in-law Mrs. Clemm the maternal image he
    had been seeking all his life. What piffle! Listen now to
    the passion and despair breathing in the letter he ad-
    dresses to Virginia's mother on August 29, 1835, when
    he feared that his thirteen-year-old little sweetheart
    would be taken away to be educated in another home.
    "I am blinded with tears while writing this letter. . . .
    My last, my last, my only hold on life is cruelly torn
    away. . . . My agony is more than I can bear. . . . for
    love like mine can never be gotten over. . . . It is use-
    less to disguise the truth . . . that I shall never behold
    her again. . . ."

CUT TO:

Humbert's Alarm Clock Rings
Seven-thirty. He hurries to the window.

SHOT FROM ABOVE

The maid helps to put a bag into the car. Lolita is leaving for
camp.

CHARLOTTE   Hurry up, Lolita.

Lolita is now half in and about to pull the car door to, but
suddenly she looks up—and scurries back into the house.

CHARLOTTE   (*furiously*) Dolores, get back into the car
    immediately!

She does not heed her mother's shout. She runs upstairs. She wears her Sunday frock—gay cotton, with ample skirt and fitting bodice. Humbert has come out on the landing. She stomps upstairs and next moment is in his arms. Hers is a perfectly innocent impulse, an affectionate bright farewell. As she rises on tiptoe to kiss him, he evades her approaching lips and imprints a poetical kiss on her brow.

CHARLOTTE   (*Blows the horn.*)

Lolita flies downstairs, gestures up to him in a ballerina-like movement of separation, and is gone.

The blond leg is drawn in, the car door slams, is reslammed as the car gathers momentum to the sound of the collie's *Bark.*

CUT TO:

Silence—except for the birds outside and the young Negro maid in the kitchen. The telephone *rings.*

MAID   No, there's no Miss Lee here. You must have got the wrong number. You're welcome.

Humbert has remained standing on the landing between his open door and the open door of Lolita's room opposite.

He surveys her deserted room. Abandoned clothes lie on the rumpled bed. A pair of white shoes with roller skates on the floor. He rolls one on his palm.

There is a full-page advertisement (back cover of magazine) tacked onto the wall: a distinguished playwright solemnly smoking ("I can write without a pen, but not without a Drome"). After a moment's brooding, Humbert goes to his room and incontinently starts to pack. Knock on his door.

The maid Louise knocks on Humbert's door. He opens. She hands him a letter.

LOUISE   Mrs. Haze asked me to give you this, Mr. Humbert.

Humbert inspects envelope.

LOUISE   I'll be doing the girl's room now. And when I've done I'd like to do yours. And then I'll go.

Humbert, puckering brow at envelope, walks slowly back to his desk.

The neat handwriting of the address turns momentarily into a schoolgirl's scribble, then reverts to the ladylike hand. He opens the letter.

Humbert, in a classical pattern of comments, ironical asides, and well-mouthed readings, scans the letter. In one SHOT, he is dressed as a gowned professor, in another as a routine Hamlet, in a third, as a dilapidated Poe. He also appears as himself.

HUMBERT   "This is a confession, this is an avowal of love."
          No signature—what, no signature? Ah, here it is. Good
          God! "I have loved you from the moment I saw you. I
          am a lonely woman and you are the love of my love."
          Of "my life," I suppose.

As in a pimp's sample album, Charlotte appears in various unattractive attitudes and positions.

HUMBERT   "Now, my dearest, *mon cher, cher Monsieur,*"
          that's a new one: she thinks it's a term of endearment.
          "Now, you have read this, now you know. So will you
          please, *at once*, pack and leave: this is a landlady's order.
          I shall be back by dinner time if I do eighty both ways
          and don't have an accident. But what would it matter?"
          I beg your pardon: it matters a lot *one* way. "You see,
          chéri," ah, French improving, "*if* you decided to stay, if
          I found you there when I got home, it would mean only
          one thing—that you want me as much as I do you—as
          a lifelong mate; and that you are ready to link up your
          life with mine forever and be a father to my little girl."
          My dear Mrs. Haze, or rather Mrs. Clemm, I am pas-
          sionately devoted to your daughter.

Pensively, with a dawning smile, Humbert starts to take out, one by one, slowly, then faster, the articles he had already packed. Then he goes into an awkward and grotesque jig (in striking contrast to his usual mournful and dignified de-meanor). Dancing, he descends the stairs.

CUT TO:

Humbert
making a long-distance call.

HUMBERT   Is this Camp Q on Lake Climax?
                         (*Listens.*)
        Is Mrs. Haze still there? She brought her daughter
        today.
                         (*Listens.*)
        Oh, I see. Could I speak to Dolores Haze, Lolita?

He listens, waits.

LOLITA   Hullo?

Now both parties are visible in a montage arrangement, with
the camp's various activities illustrated at the corners as in a
publicity folder.

HUMBERT   I have news for you.

LOLITA   Hullo?

HUMBERT   This is Humbert. I have news for you.

She is holding a big pup.

LOLITA   Oh, how are you? I have a friend here who wants
        to say hullo.

The pup licks the receiver.

HUMBERT   Listen, Lolita. I'm going to marry your
        mother. I'm going to propose to her as soon as she's
        back.

LOLITA   Gee, that's swell. Look, I've got to get rid of this
        beast, he's too heavy. One sec. There.

HUMBERT   Will you come to the wedding?

LOLITA   What? I can't hear too well.

HUMBERT   Will you come to the wedding?

LOLITA   I'm not sure. No, I guess, I have to stay here. It's
        a *fabulous* place! There's a water-sports competition
        scheduled. And I'm learning to ride. And my tentmate
        is the Ramsdale junior swimming champion. And——

DISSOLVE TO:

The Honeymooners
A month has elapsed. Kitchen at 342 Lawn Street.

Charlotte (radiant and demure, in tight velvet pants and bed slippers) prepares breakfast for two in the cute breakfast nook of the chrome-and-plastic kitchen. Shadows of sun and leaves play on the white refrigerator. Humbert, in the wake of his yawn, enters (dressing gown, rumpled hair).

Charlotte makes him a jocular Oriental bow. His face twitching with neuralgia, he glances at the scrambled eggs and starts clawing at a cupboard.

CHARLOTTE   What are you looking for?

HUMBERT   Pepper.

A tennis ball jumps out of the cupboard.

HUMBERT   I wonder if she can play tennis at that damned camp.

CHARLOTTE   I could not care less. Look what the *Ramsdale Journal* has to say about us. Here. Society Column.

Humbert glances at paper.

CHARLOTTE   Isn't that something? Look at your elegant bride. "Mr. Edgar H. Humbert, writer and explorer, weds the former——" I never knew you were Edgar.

HUMBERT   Oh, I called up a reporter and thought I'd inject a little glamour.

He yawns again.

CHARLOTTE   And what have you explored?

HUMBERT   Madame should not ask vulgar questions.

CHARLOTTE   (*very arch*) And Monsieur has certainly a grand sense of humor.

Charlotte Is Showing Bored Humbert
some of her treasures. A lamplit evening at the Humbert residence.

HUMBERT   (*suddenly interested*) Hey, a gun.

He examines a small automatic.

CHARLOTTE   It belonged to Mr. Haze.

HUMBERT   Hm. And then suddenly it went off.

CHARLOTTE   It's not loaded.

HUMBERT   That's what they all say: "I did not know it was
      loaded."

CHARLOTTE   Who—they?

HUMBERT   Boy shoots girl, banker shoots bitch, rapist
      shoots therapist.

CHARLOTTE   I told you many times that I appreciated your
      humor, but now and then it is misplaced. This is a sacred
      weapon, a tragic treasure. Mr. Haze acquired it when he
      thought he had cancer. He wanted to spare me the sight
      of his sufferings. Happily, or unhappily, he was hospi-
      talized before he could use it. And this is me just before
      I married him.

In the snapshot Charlotte at twenty-five resembles her daughter more than she does now. Humbert is moved.

HUMBERT   I like this one tremendously. May I have it?

CHARLOTTE   Oh, my dear, of course! Everything is yours.
      Wait, let me inscribe it.

Charlotte writes on the photo: For my *chéri* Humbert from
his Charlotte. April 1946 [if it is now 1960].

CUT TO:

Humbert and Wife in Car
He is driving her to the lake.

HUMBERT   What's that palazzo? A brothel?

CHARLOTTE   That's Jerome McFate's house. He's manager
      of our bank, if you please.

HUMBERT   What a name for a banker.

They leave the car at the edge of the pine forest and walk through it to the lake. They are sandaled and robed.

CHARLOTTE   Do you know, Hum, I have one most ambitious dream. I should love to get hold of a real French servant like that German girl the Talbots had, and have her live in the house.

HUMBERT   No room.

CHARLOTTE   Come.
(*with a quizzical smile*)
Surely, *chéri*, you underestimate the possibilities of the Humbert home. We would put her in Lo's room. I intended to make a guest room of that hole anyway. It's the coldest and meanest in the whole house.

HUMBERT   And where, pray, will you put your daughter when you get your guest or your maid?

CHARLOTTE   (*softly exhaling and raising one eyebrow*) Ah! Little Lo, I'm afraid, does not enter the picture at all, at all. Little Lo goes straight from camp to a good boarding school with strict discipline. I have it all mapped out, you need not worry.

The Brilliant Lake
There is a moored raft some forty yards off the lake shore. Humbert and Charlotte on the sandy strip. He, sitting, hands clasping knees, in a dreadful frame of mind; she, serenely and luxuriously reclining.

HUMBERT   The sand is filthy. Some oaf has been walking his filthy dog. And there's a chewing-gum wrapper.

CHARLOTTE   Oh, those are just leftovers from Sunday. There's not a soul anywhere. It's not at all like the east end of the lake where they built the casino.

HUMBERT   One would think there would be some decrepit cripple with a piked stick cleaning up on Mondays.

CHARLOTTE   No, I don't think so. In fact, even on weekends there is hardly anybody bathing at this end. This is the restricted part. We are alone, sweetheart, you and me. And we'll remain so forever. Just you and me. A red cent for your thoughts.

HUMBERT   I was wondering if you could make it to that raft, or whatever it is. I loathe this dirty gray sand. Out there we could sunbathe in the
(*wrinkling his nose*)
nude, as you genteel Americans say.

CHARLOTTE   I doubt it. This American's back is burnt as it is. Besides, I couldn't swim that far.

HUMBERT   Nonsense. Your merman will be at your side.

CHARLOTTE   How deep would you say it is?

HUMBERT   Twice your height. Two wives.

CHARLOTTE   I'm sure to panic and drown.

HUMBERT   All right, all right. If you don't want to swim, let's go home. This place bores me stiff.

CHARLOTTE   Well, I can always try.

DISSOLVE:

Humbert and Charlotte
reach the raft.

CHARLOTTE   Ah! I thought I would never make it.

HUMBERT   Yes, but there's still the return voyage.

An airplane passes overhead.

CHARLOTTE   That's a private plane, isn't it?

HUMBERT   I've no idea. That guardian angel has been circling above the lake during our entire swim. I think he's leaving now.

A butterfly passes in shorebound flight.

CHARLOTTE   Can butterflies swim?

HUMBERT   (*indistinct answer*)

CHARLOTTE   Shall I risk taking off my bra?

HUMBERT   I don't give a damn.

CHARLOTTE   Will you give a damn if I kiss you?

He grunts. Pause.

DISSOLVE TO:

Another Angle

CHARLOTTE   Not a cloud, not a soul, not a sound.

HUMBERT   Let's swim back.

CHARLOTTE   What—already? We haven't been here ten minutes.

HUMBERT   Come on, let's go in.

CHARLOTTE   Please, Humbert, stop pushing me.

HUMBERT   I'll roll you in the water.

CHARLOTTE   You'll do nothing of the sort. We are going to stay here till the Farlows come.

HUMBERT   They won't be here for another hour.

CHARLOTTE   Relax and enjoy yourself. Tell me about your first wife.

HUMBERT   To hell with her.

CHARLOTTE   You are very rude, sweetheart.

HUMBERT   I'm very bored. Look here. The Farlows will retrieve you. I'm going home. *Au revoir.*

He dives and swims away.

CHARLOTTE   Oh, please. Wait! I'm coming too. Oh, wait!

He swims on without turning his head. Awkwardly, she lowers herself into the water. He is now nearing the shore. She starts swimming and almost immediately is seized with a cramp.

A neat little diagram shows the relative positions of a drowning person (one arm sticking out of the water), a stationary raft, and the shoreline at equal distance from the sufferer.

For a few seconds, Humbert floats motionless in a vertical

position, his chin just above the surface, his eyes fixed on floundering Charlotte. There should be something reptilian and spine-chilling in his expectant stare. Then, as she gasps, and sinks, and splashes, and screams, he dashes toward her, reaching her in a few strokes.

He helps her out onto the beach.

CHARLOTTE   (*still panting*) You know—you know—for one moment—I thought you—would not come to save me—your eyes—you looked at me with dreadful, dreadful eyes——

He soothes her in a humid embrace.

CUT TO:

Car
They are driving home.

CHARLOTTE   You know, it's so funny. A drowning person is said to recollect his entire life but all I remembered was last night's dream. You were offering me some pill or potion, and a voice said: Careful, Isolda, that's poison.

HUMBERT   Rather pointless—what?

The car pulls up at 342 Lawn Street. They get out.

HUMBERT   Here, take this towel. Oh, blast it! I forgot my sunglasses on that bloody beach.

CHARLOTTE   Were they very expensive?

HUMBERT   (*still searching*) I loved them. They made a kind of taupe twilight. I bought them in St.-Topaz, never mislaid them before.

CHARLOTTE   Why don't you drive back to the lake and find them? Kiss?
                    (*Humbert obliges.*)
Meantime I'll tidy up——

CUT TO:

The "Semi-Studio"
Taking advantage of Humbert's absence, Charlotte lovingly

cleans his den. A small key drops out of a jacket. She considers it for a moment with amused perplexity; then tries it in the lock of a certain small drawer. The treasure turns out to be a little black book, Humbert's dark diary. She flips it open. Her daughter's name leers at her from every page. But the microscopic script is hard to decipher. She snatches up a magnifying glass. In its bland circle Humbert's jottings leap into formidable life:

". . . *but her grotesque mother butted in. . . . Friday: She is a bitch, that Haze woman. She is sending my darling away. Alas, Lolita! Farewell, my love! If the old cat expects me to stay on, she is——*"

CUT TO:

Humbert
opening the door of his living room. Charlotte, with her back to him, is writing at the desk in the far corner.

HUMBERT   I'm back. Couldn't find them.

Charlotte does not answer but her writing hand stops. She turns slowly toward him revealing a face disfigured by grief and wrath.

CHARLOTTE   "The Haze woman," "the old cat," "the obnoxious mama," "the—the old stupid Haze," is no longer your dupe.

HUMBERT   But what——

CHARLOTTE   You're a monster, you're a detestable, abominable, criminal fraud! If you come near me, I'll scream out the window.

HUMBERT   But really——

CHARLOTTE   I'm leaving today. This is all yours. Only you'll never, never see that miserable brat again.

HUMBERT   I can explain everything.

CHARLOTTE   Get out of here. Oh, I can see it all now. You tried to drown me, you would have shot me or poisoned me next. You disgusting satyr. I'm applying for a job in Parkington and you'll never see me again.

Furiously, she rummages for the stamps she needs. The convex block of them has fallen on the carpet. Tears off one, two. Fast and furious. Thumps on envelope.

CUT TO:

Humbert
goes swiftly upstairs to his study. There he contemplates the open and empty drawer. He crosses over to the bedroom and starts looking for his diary, which he suspects she has hidden. After some rapid ransacking, he finds it under her pillow. He walks downstairs again.

CUT TO:

Kitchen
He opens the refrigerator. Its roar, as well as the crepitation of the ice cubes in their cells under warm water, the noisy faucet, the fussing with the whiskey and soda, the banging of cupboard doors, and Humbert's own mutter, drown the *Sounds* from the street (such as the hideous screech of desperate brakes).

HUMBERT   (*muttering*) Tell her . . . Misunderstood . . .
        Civilized people . . . Brought you a drink . . . Don't
        be ridiculous . . . Fragments of novel . . . Provisional
        names . . . The notes you found were fragments of a
        novel. . . .

He has now prepared his defense. Carrying the two glasses he leaves the kitchen.

CUT TO:

Hallway-Door of Living Room Slightly Ajar
As Humbert approaches the *Telephone Rings* on table near door. He places the glasses on the table and lifts the receiver.

VOICE   This is Lesley Tompson, the gardener next door.
        Your wife, sir, has been run over and you'd better come
        quick.

HUMBERT   Nonsense. My wife is here—
                    (*Pushes the door open.*)
        man saying you've been killed, Charlotte. . . .

The room is empty. He turns back, the front door is not shut, the receiver is still throbbing on the table. He rushes out. "The far side of our steep little street presented a peculiar sight. A big black limousine had climbed Miss Opposite's sloping lawn at an angle from the sidewalk."

The picture now is a still. Humbert surveys the scene: The body on the sidewalk, the old gentleman resting on the grass near the car, various people attracted by the accident, the unfortunate driver, two policemen, and the cheerful collie walking from group to group.

A photographer from the Traffic Division is taking a picture.

In a projection room it is shown to a bunch of policemen by an instructor with a pointer:

THE INSTRUCTOR   Now, this is the picture of a real accident. To the ordinary spectator who has just arrived on the scene the situation may seem very, very unusual: it is not so, really. The lap robe there, on the sidewalk, covers a dead woman. The elderly person here on the grass is not dead but comfortably recovering from a mild heart attack. His nephew, the fat fellow talking to the police officers, was driving him to a birthday party when they ran over this woman. This is their car up on the slope of the lawn where it came to rest after leaving the road. It was moving down the street like so.

A diagram now appears with arrows and dotted lines.

INSTRUCTOR   The driver was trying to avoid the dog. The woman was crossing here. She was in a great hurry to mail a letter but never made it to the mailbox.
          (*still picture again*)
That man there who stands looking stunned is her husband.

The still comes to life. A little girl picks up the letter which Charlotte was about to post and hands it to Humbert. Old Mr. Jung is sobbing uncontrollably. The ambulance arrives. The Farlows lead Humbert away.

Act Two

The Office of Camp Q, a Stucco Cottage—early afternoon
The camp mistress hangs up and calls a camp counselor.

CAMP MISTRESS   (*to counselor*) Mr. Humbert has just
    telephoned. Lolita's mother has been killed in a street
    accident.

COUNSELLOR   Oh, my gosh.

CAMP MISTRESS   He's on the way here to fetch her. He
    asked me to tell her that her mother is sick. Find the
    girl, please, and have her get ready to leave. By the way,
    where's that lazy son of mine—make him move the gar-
    bage cans to the back of the shed.

CUT TO:

The Search for Lolita
Her name is cried out in different voices and keys at various
points. We pass in review the awfully quaint cabins and tents
in a pine grove. The camera looks behind trees and bushes.
Two shadows hastily unclip in the undergrowth. Distant cries
swell and recede.
   Lolita! Lolita!

CUT TO:

Dirt Road
leading to cabins and tents. Humbert drives up. Charlie, the
camp mistress's fourteen-year-old son, is rolling an empty garbage can across the road.

HUMBERT   (*out of car window, pointing questioningly*) Is
    that the office?

Charlie mutely directs him with a jerk of his thumb.

CUT TO:

Camp Office—Humbert and the Camp Mistress

CAMP MISTRESS   (*computing the bill and not raising her eyes from her writing*) What a terrible accident! When is the funeral?

HUMBERT   Oh, that was yesterday. It was decided not to have the child attend. Spare her the shock.

He settles the bill.

CAMP MISTRESS   Thank you. The poor kid. Here's your receipt.

Lolita arrives, dragging and bumping her valise.

LOLITA   Hi.

He lets his hand rest on her head and takes up her bag. She wears her brightest gingham and saddle oxfords.

As Humbert and she walk toward the car, Lolita waves to Charlie.

LOLITA   Good-bye, Charlie boy!

Moodily, not without some regret, he follows her with his pale, fair-lashed eyes.

CUT TO:

The Hot Car (*inside*)
She settles down beside Humbert, slaps a prompt fly on her lovely knee; then, her mouth working violently on chewing gum, she rapidly cranks down the window. The car speeds through the striped and speckled forest.

LOLITA   (*dutifully*) How's mother?

HUMBERT   It's something abdominal.

LOLITA   Abominable?

HUMBERT   No, abdominal. A stomach ailment. She's been moved to a hospital in the country. Not far from Lepingsville.

LOLITA   Are we going to, what you called it—Lepersville?

HUMBERT   Lepingsville. Yes, I expect we'll have to hang around a bit while she gets better or at least a little better. And then we'll go to the mountains. Is that a peachy idea?

LOLITA   Uh-huh. How far is it to her hospital?

HUMBERT   Oh, two hundred miles. Did you have a marvelous time at the camp?

LOLITA   Uh-huh.

HUMBERT   Sorry to leave?

LOLITA   Un-un.

HUMBERT   Talk, Lolita, don't grunt. Tell me something.

LOLITA   What thing, *Dad*?

HUMBERT   Any old thing.

LOLITA   Okay if I call you that?

HUMBERT   Quite.

LOLITA   It's a sketch, you know——

HUMBERT   A what?

LOLITA   A scream: you falling for my mummy.

HUMBERT   There are also such things as mutual respect and spiritual happiness.

LOLITA   Sure, sure.

(The lull in the dialogue is filled in with some landscapes.)

HUMBERT   Look at all those cows on the hillside.

LOLITA   I'll vomit if I see another cow.

HUMBERT   You know I missed you terribly, Lolita Lo. Really and truly.

LOLITA   I didn't. Fact I've been revoltingly unfaithful to you, but it doesn't matter a bit because you've stopped caring for me, anyway. You drive much faster than my mummy, mister.

He slows down from 70 to 50 as seen on speedometer.

HUMBERT   Why do you think I've stopped caring for you?

LOLITA   Well, you haven't kissed me yet, have you?

Humbert wobbles into the roadside weeds and stops. She cuddles up to him. A highway patrol car draws up alongside.

POLICEMAN   Having trouble?

HUMBERT   No, no. I just wanted to look at the map.

LOLITA   (*eagerly leaning across H.H. and speaking with unusual urbanity*) I'm afraid we have parked where we shouldn't but there was some question of taking a short cut, and we thought——

POLICEMAN   Well, if you want to stop there's a picnic area three hundred yards from here.

LOLITA   Oh, thank you.

The beetle-browed trooper gives the little colleen his toothiest smile and glides away. Lolita presses a fluttering hand to her breastbone.

LOLITA   The fruithead! He should have nabbed you.

HUMBERT   Why me, for heaven's sake?

LOLITA   Because the speed limit in this bum state is fifty. No, don't slow down. He's gone now.

HUMBERT   We have still quite a stretch, so be a good girl.

LOLITA   That light was red. I've never seen such driving.

They roll silently through a silent townlet.

HUMBERT   You said you'd been—I don't know—naughty? Don't you want to tell me about that?

LOLITA   Are you easily shocked?

HUMBERT   No. What did you do?

LOLITA   Well, I joined in all the activities that were offered.

HUMBERT   *Ensuite?*

LOLITA   Ansooit, I was taught to live happily and richly

with others and to develop a wholesome personality. Be a cake, actually.

HUMBERT   Yes, I saw that in the camp booklet.

LOLITA   We loved the sings around the fire.

HUMBERT   Anything else?

LOLITA   (*rhapsodically*) The Girl Scout's motto is also mine. My duty is to be useful to animals. I obey orders. I am cheerful. And I am absolutely filthy in thought, word, and deed.

HUMBERT   Is that all, young wit?

LOLITA   We baked in a reflector oven. Isn't that terrific? Oh, gee! We made shadowgraphs. We identified the three birds teacher knew. What fun!

HUMBERT   *C'est bien tout?*

LOLITA   *C'est.* Except one little thing that I may tell you later in the dark.

CUT TO:

The Road
A sign by the side of the road says 8 MILES TO ENCHANTED HUNTERS. Further, another sign BRICELAND, ELEV. 759 FEET. Finally a sign at a crossing 3 MILES TO ENCHANTED HUNT-ERS—YE UNFORGETTABLE INN.

LOLITA   Oh, let's stop at the unforgettable!

HUMBERT   I've reserved rooms in a tourist home at Lep-ingsville, but——

LOLITA   Oh, please. Let's go to the Enchanted. It's a famous romantic place. We'll make people think you've eloped with me. Please!

. . . And there it was, marvelously and inexorably there, at the top of a graded curve under spectral trees, at the top of a graveled drive—the pale palace of The Enchanted Hunters.

LOLITA   (*getting out of the car*) Wow! Looks swank.

Old Tom, a hunchbacked and hoary Negro, takes out the bags.

It is a large old heavily quaint family hotel with a pillared porch. Humbert and Lolita enter the ornate lounge. Two conventions, a medical one on the ebb and a floral one on the flow, throng the reception rooms.

Lolita sinks down on her haunches to caress a cocker spaniel sprawling and melting under her hand.

HUMBERT   (*at the reception desk* talks to Mr. Potts, the clerk, *indistinctly*) I want a room for the night.

POTTS   Excuse me, sir?

HUMBERT   I want two rooms or one room with two beds.

POTTS   I'm not sure we can accommodate you. We have the overflow of a convention of doctors from another hotel and we also have a reunion of rose growers just budding. Is it for you and your little girl?

He looks kindly at Lolita.

HUMBERT   Her mother is ill. We are very tired.

POTTS   Mr. Swoon!

Swoon, another clerk, appears.

POTTS   What about Dr. Love, has he called?

SWOON   He has canceled his reservation.

POTTS   And what about the Bliss family?

SWOON   They are supposed to check out tonight.

POTTS   (*to Humbert*) Well, I could give you 342. But it has one bed.

HUMBERT   Could you put in a cot perhaps?

POTTS   We have none available at the moment but the situation may improve later.

HUMBERT   Well, I'll register.

POTTS   It's really quite a large

(*opens the book*)
bed. The other night we had three doctors sleeping in
it, and the middle one was a pretty broad
(*offers the desk pen to Humbert whose own pen has stalled*)
gentleman.

Third-Floor Corridor
Uncle Tom, with bags and key, opens the door for Humbert
and Lolita. There is some fussing with the key.

LOLITA   Oh, look! It's the same number as our house. 342.

HUMBERT   Funny coincidence.

LOLITA   Yes. Very funny. You know
                              (*laughing*)
           last night I dreamt mother got drowned in Ramsdale
           Lake.

HUMBERT   Oh.

                              CUT TO:

Room
There's a double bed, a mirror, a double bed in the mirror, a
closet door with mirror, a bathroom door ditto, a blue-dark
window, a reflected bed there, the same in the closet mirror,
two chairs, a glass-topped table, two bed tables, a double bed:
a big panel bed, to be exact, with a Tuscan rose chenille
spread, and two frilled, pink-shaded nightlamps, left and
right.
   Humbert tips old Tom one dollar, calls him back, and adds
another. Exit Tom, gratefully grinning.

LOLITA   (*her features working*) You mean we are *both* going
           to sleep *here*?

HUMBERT   I've asked them to give me a separate room or
           at least to put in a cot—for you or me, as you wish.

LOLITA   You are crazy.

HUMBERT   Why, my darling?

LOLITA   Because, my dahrling, when dahrling Mother finds
           out, she'll divorce you and strangle me.

She stands slitting her eyes at herself contentedly in the closet door mirror. Humbert has sat down on the edge of a low chair, nervously rubbing his hands and leaning toward her pleased reflection.

HUMBERT   Now look here, Lo. Let's settle this once for all. I'm your stepfather. In your mother's absence I'm responsible for your welfare. We shall be a lot together. And since we are not rich, we won't be able
(*Gets up and hangs up his raincoat,
    which however slips off the hanger.*)
to have *always* two rooms.

LOLITA   Okay. I want my comb.

Humbert tries to embrace her—casually, a bit of controlled tenderness before dinner.

LOLITA   Look, let's cut out the kissing game and get something to eat.

He opens the suitcase with the articles he bought for her.

HUMBERT   By the way—here are some frocks and things I got for you at Parkington.

"Oh, what a dreamy pet! She walked up to the open suitcase as if stalking it from afar, at a kind of slow-motion walk, peering at that distant treasure box on the luggage support." She raises by the armlets a garment, pulls out the slow snake of a brilliant belt, tries it on. "Then she crept into my waiting arms, radiant, relaxed, caressing me with her tender, mysterious, impure, indifferent twilight eyes—for all the world like the cheapest of cheap cuties. For that is what nymphets imitate—while we moan and die." Their kiss is interrupted by a knock on the door. Old Tom enters with a vase of magnificent roses.

HUMBERT   Well! Where do these come from?

TOM   *I* don't know.

HUMBERT   What do you mean—you don't know? Is it the management?

TOM   I don't know. I was given them at the flower
       counter. For Mister—
                    (*Glances at the card.*)
       Mister Homberg and his little girl.

Exit Uncle Tom, with a quarter.

HUMBERT   (*shrugging it off*) Seems that flower show had
       a surplus of roses. I detest flowers. And I also detest
       when my name is misspelt.

LOLITA   Oh, but they are gorgeous!

(The point is, of course, that the bouquet is from an old admirer of little Dolores, Clare Quilty, whom we shall glimpse
presently.)

CUT TO:

Dining Room at the Enchanted Hunters
A pretentious mural depicts enchanted hunters in various postures and states of enchantment amid a medley of animals,
dryads, cypresses, and porticoes.

LOLITA   (*considering the mural*) What does it *mean*?

HUMBERT   Oh, mythological scenes, modernized. Bad art,
       anyway.

LOLITA   What's bad art?

HUMBERT   The work of a mediocre derivative artist. Look
       at that crummy unicorn. Or is it a centaur?

LOLITA   He's not crummy. He's wonderful.

Waitress brings food.

CUT TO:

End of Meal
Humbert produces a vial of sleeping pills, removes the stopper
and tips the container into his palm. He claps a hand to his
mouth and feigns swallowing.

LOLITA   Purple pills—what are they?

HUMBERT   Vitamin P. Purple seas and plums, and plumes

of paradise birds. And peat bog orchids. And Priap's orchard.

LOLITA   And double talk. Gimme one quick!

HUMBERT   Here.

Out of his fist the pill he had palmed is slipped into her gay cupped little hand.

LOLITA   (*swallowing*) I bet it's a love philter.

HUMBERT   Good gracious! What do you know about philters?

LOLITA   Just a movie I saw. *Stan and Izzie*. With Mark King. Oh, look who's here.

A man in a loud sports jacket comes into the dining room and walks to a distant table. It is Quilty. He recognizes Mrs. Haze's fascinating little girl but except for a glance of amused appraisal does not pay any attention to Humbert and her.

LOLITA   Doesn't he look exactly, but exactly, like Quilty?

HUMBERT   (*frightened*) What? Our fat dentist is here?

Lolita arrests the mouthful of water she has just taken and sets down her dancing glass.

LOLITA   (*with a splutter of mirth*) 'Course not. I meant the writer fellow in the *Drome* ad.

HUMBERT   O Fame, O Femina.

WAITRESS   What would you like for dessert? We have ice cream—raspberry, chocolate, vanilla and let me see——

LOLITA   Chocolate and raspberry for me.

HUMBERT   And for me just a cup of coffee. And the check, please.

Lolita shakes her curls trying to dismiss somnolence.

HUMBERT   When did they make you get up at camp?

LOLITA   Half past

(*She stifles a big yawn.*)

SIX.

(*yawn in full swell, shiver of all her frame*)
Half past six.

(*throat fills up again*)
I went canoeing this morning, and after that——

WAITRESS   We did not have the raspberry after all.

DISSOLVE TO:

The Elevator
Enter Humbert and Lolita; three rose-growing ladies each
looking like a rock garden; two old men; and the elevator girl.
Humbert and Lolita face each other closely, then still more
closely as others crowd in. The two men get out. Lolita somnolent and sly, pressed against Humbert, raises her eyes to
him and laughs softly.

HUMBERT   What's the matter?

LOLITA   Nothing.

The three smiling matrons get out. There is now sufficient
room for H. and L. to stand apart.

OPERATOR   Watch your step, please.

CUT TO:

Corridor to Room 342

LOLITA   You ought to carry me as they do in cartoons. Oh,
    I'm so sleepy. Guess I'll have to tell you how naughty
    Charlie and me have been.

CUT TO:

Room 342

LOLITA   This bed sleeps two.

HUMBERT   It's yours.

LOLITA   Where is *your* room?

Yawning, she sits on the edge of the bed, removes her shoes and peels off one sock.

HUMBERT   I don't know yet. Brush your teeth or whatever you're supposed to do and go to bed.
(*Opens her overnight case.*)
Here are your things. I want you to be asleep when I come back. I'm going downstairs. Please, Lolita. No, that's the closet. The bathroom is there.

LOLITA   Mirror, mirror——

She laughs drowsily and exits.

CUT TO:

Humbert Leaves the Room and Walks Downstairs
As he nears the lobby and turns a corner he is brushed by the shoulder of a lurching, elated man (Quilty).
Humbert asks a bellboy the way to the bar.

BELLBOY   There is no bar.

HUMBERT   I wonder where that lush got his liquor.

BELLBOY   Oh, that's Mr. Quilty, sir. And he would not want to be bothered. He comes here to write.

HUMBERT   I see. Can you direct me to the washroom.

BELLBOY   To your left and down.

CUT TO:

Humbert
emerging from the lavatory. A hearty old party, Dr. Braddock, on the way in, greets him.

DR. BRADDOCK   Well, how did you like Dr. Boyd's speech? Oh, I'm sorry. I mistook you for Jack Bliss.

Humbert passes a group of women who are bound for the Rose Room. He consults his watch. He lingers for a moment in the lobby. Mr. Potts, noticing him but by him unnoticed, lifts a finger, then calls old Tom and gives him an order. Humbert consults his watch again and continues his restless loitering. He strolls out onto the dimly lit pillared porch. To one

side in the darkness two or more people are sitting. We distinguish vaguely a very old man, and beyond him another
person's shoulder. It is from these shadows that a voice (Quilty's) comes. It is preceded by the rasp of a screwing off, then
a discrete gurgle, then the final note of a placid screwing on.

QUILTY'S VOICE   Where the devil did you get her?

HUMBERT   I beg your pardon?

QUILTY'S VOICE   I said: the weather is getting better.

HUMBERT   Seems so.

QUILTY'S VOICE   Who's the lassie?

HUMBERT   My daughter.

QUILTY'S VOICE   You lie—she's not.

HUMBERT   I beg your pardon?

QUILTY'S VOICE   I said: July was hot. Where's her mother?

HUMBERT   Dead.

QUILTY'S VOICE   I see. Sorry. By the way, why don't you
    two lunch with me tomorrow. That dreadful crowd will
    be gone by then.

HUMBERT   We'll be gone, too. Good night.

QUILTY'S VOICE   Sorry. I'm pretty drunk. Good night.
    That child of yours needs a lot of sleep. Sleep is a rose,
    as the Persians say. Smoke?

HUMBERT   Not now.

CUT TO:

Humbert Leaves the Porch
Sufficient time has elapsed. He tries not to display any hurry.
As he makes his way through a constellation of fixed people
in one corner of the lobby near the dining room, there comes
a blinding flash, as beaming Dr. Braddock and some matrons
are photographed.

DR. BRADDOCK   (*pointing to part of the mural which con-*

tinues around the corner) And here the theme changes.
The hunter thinks he has hypnotized the little nymph
but it is she who puts him into a trance.

Humbert Walks up the Stairs
and turns in to the corridor. The door key with its large unwieldly hangpiece of polished wood is dangling from his hand.
He takes off his coat. He stands for a moment immobile before door 342. It is a moment of wholesome hesitation. From
the service elevator old Tom, the gray-haired Negro, hobbles
out trundling a folded cot. Humbert turns guiltily.

TOM   342. I've brought you the cot, sir.

HUMBERT   Oh? Yes, yes, of course. But I'm afraid she is
    fast asleep. She has had a strenuous day.

TOM   That's quite all right. We'll put it in gently.

Humbert opens the door. Soft and slow, the rhythm of the
young sleeper's respiration is kept ajar for ten seconds.

HUMBERT   Please, very quietly. I don't want the child to
    be disturbed.

Crablike, crippled old Tom unfolds the cot alongside the bed
and shuffles out. Once out, he performs very slowly the act of
closing a creaky door but at the last moment (the poor devil
being somewhat spastic) he bangs it shut. Lolita does not
wake up. Humbert (now in pajamas) tests and retests the security of her drugged sleep. He turns on the radio. She does
not stir. A fist pounds on the wall. He shuts off the radio and
touches her shoulder. Still she sleeps. That drug certainly
works. He is about to take advantage of this safe sleep, but as
the moon reaches her face, its innocent helpless fragile infantine beauty arrests him. He slinks back to his cot.

CUT TO:

Humbert Lying on His Cot supine, traversed by pale strips of
moonlight coming through the slits in the blinds. Clouds en-
gulf the moon.

"There is nothing louder than an American hotel; and,
mind you, this was supposed to be a quiet, cozy, old-fash-

ioned, homey place—'gracious living' and all that stuff. The clatter of the elevator's gate—some twenty yards northeast of my head but as clearly perceived as if it were inside my left temple—alternated with the banging and booming of the machine's various evolutions and lasted well beyond midnight. Every now and then, immediately east of my left ear, the corridor would brim with cheerful, resonant, and inept exclamations ending in a volley of good nights. When *that* stopped, a toilet immediately north of my cerebellum took over. It was a manly, energetic, deep-throated toilet, and it was used many times. Its gurgle and gush and long afterflow shook the wall behind me. Then someone in a southern direction was extravagantly sick, almost coughing out his life with his liquor, and his toilet descended like a veritable Niagara, immediately beyond our bathroom. And when finally all the waterfalls had stopped, and the enchanted hunters were sound asleep, the avenue under the window of my insomnia, to the west of my wake—a staid, eminently residential, dignified alley of huge trees—degenerated into the despicable haunt of gigantic trucks roaring through the wet and windy night."

In the first antemeridian hours there is a lull. The sky pales. A breeze sighs. A bird discreetly twitters. Lolita wakes up and yawns (a childish, cozy, warm yawn). Humbert feigns sleep.

LOLITA   (*sitting up, looking at him*) What d'you know! I thought you got another room. Hey! Wake up!

Humbert gives a mediocre imitation of that process.

LOLITA   I never heard you come in. Oh, you're handsome in bed, Hum. Is that cot comfortable?

HUMBERT   Awful.

LOLITA   Come and sit here. Shall we eat that fruit in the brown bag? You need a shave, pricklepuss.

HUMBERT   Good morning, Lolita.

LOLITA   My tan is much darker than yours. Say, I have a suggestion. Are you listening?

HUMBERT   Yes?

LOLITA   It's something we did at the camp, Charlie and me. It's fun.

HUMBERT   Yes?

LOLITA   Gosh, how your heart is thumping! Shouldn't you see a doctor? You aren't dying?

HUMBERT   I am dying of curiosity. What was that suggestion?

LOLITA   It's playing a game. A game we played in the woods—when we should have been picking berries. I did it strictly for kicks, but oh well, it was sort of fun. It's a game lots of kids play nowadays. Kind of fad. Still don't get it? You're dense, aren't you?

HUMBERT   I'm dying.

LOLITA   It's—sure you can't guess?

HUMBERT   I can't.

LOLITA   It's not tiddledywinks, and it's not Russian roulette.

HUMBERT   I'm a poor guesser.

With a burst of rough glee she puts her mouth to his ear (could one reproduce this hot moist sound, the tickle and the buzz, the vibration, the thunder of her whisper?).

She draws back. Kneeling above recumbent Humbert (who is invisible except for a twitching toe), she contemplates him expectantly. Her humid lips and sly slit eyes seem to anticipate and prompt an assent.

HUMBERT'S VOICE   I don't know what game you children played.

In an eager gesture, she brushes the hair off her forehead and applies herself again to his tingling ear.

HUMBERT'S VOICE   (*faintly*) I never played that game.

LOLITA'S VOICE   Like me to show you?

HUMBERT   If it's not too dangerous. If it's not too difficult. If it's not too—*Ah, mon Dieu!*

CUT TO:

Various Rooms in the Enchanted Hunters
The CAMERA glides from room to room at dawn, with some
of the guests still fast asleep. The purpose of these shots is to
construct a series of situations contrasting with the atmosphere in Room 342. The movement of the CAMERA reveals
the following scenes, all of very brief duration:

Room 13: Mr. Potts, the hotel clerk, old, chubby, and bald,
is awakened by his alarm clock, which he knocks over in his
fussy attempt to stop its ringing.

Room 180: Dr. and Mrs. Braddock—he snoring lustily; she
is awakened by two pigeons on the window sill.

Room 423: The playwright Quilty, dead to the world,
sprawls prone among the emblems of drunkenness.

Room 342: (balcony) Pigeons. Early sunlight effects. A
truck rumbles by below. From the inside of the room comes
the laughter of a child (Lolita!).

Room 344: The laughter of a child in the neighboring room
rouses Dr. Boyd, who looks at his watch and smiles.

Room 442: A very large woman, Miss Beard, has risen and
indulges in some ponderous exercises causing the flowers to
shake in her small room.

Room 342: Lolita, sitting up in her tumbled bed, looks up
at the loud ceiling. She is messily consuming a peach. A banana skin hangs from the edge of the bed table. The cot is
empty. Humbert is in the bathroom, the door of which is ajar.
The faucet whines.

Room 242: Mr. Rose is shaving in the bathroom. The faucet
in the bathroom above whines. Mrs. Rose urges her daughter,
a dark-haired child Lolita's age, to get up.

Murals in the dining room: The hunters are still in a trance.

Corridor on third floor: Negro maids load a wagon with
linen.

The morning grows in brightness and blare. The elevator is
active. It is now around 9 A.M. One of the maids attempts to
open the door of 342. Humbert's nervous snarl from within.

CUT TO:

Room 342
Lolita combs her hair before the mirror.

HUMBERT'S VOICE   I love you. I adore you . . .

LOLITA   Oh, leave me alone now. We must get dressed.

HUMBERT'S VOICE   Lolita, Lolita, Lolita! Please, not yet.
Oh, my darling. This is——

CUT TO:

Hotel Dining Room

DR. BRADDOCK   (*pointing out details of mural to the Rose
family*) This is paradise, or at least a pagan shadow of
paradise. Note those ecstatic flowers and things sprout-
ing everywhere. In this corner we have one of the enchanted   hunters   courting   a   young   nymph.   The
coloration of the sky is dreamlike. I knew well Lewis
Ruskin who painted this remarkable mural. He was a
gentle soul, a melancholy drawing master who eventually became the head of a select girls' school in Briceland. He developed a romantic attachment for one of
his young charges and committed suicide when she left
his school. She is now married to a missionary.

MRS. ROSE   How very sad. Don't you just love those three
maidens dancing around the sleeping hunter? And that
shaggy animal with the mauve horn?

MRS. ROSE' LITTLE DAUGHTER   Why has one of the girls a
bandage on her leg?

CUT TO:

Lounge to Dining Room
Humbert, followed by Lolita, drifts in. She acquires a movie
magazine which she reads throughout breakfast, and continues to read as they trail out, and reads it in the lounge while
Humbert is paying the bill.

A VOICE   Hullo there, Lolita!

She looks around. There is no one. Humbert joins her. Old Tom carries out the bags.

CUT TO:

The Highway to Lepingsville
They drive in silence. A queer dullness has replaced Lolita's cheerfulness.

HUMBERT   (*attempting small talk*) My, my. I wonder what Mrs. Chatfield would say if she discovered the things her pretty Phyllis did with your filthy Charlie.

LOLITA   (*making a weeping grimace*) Look, let us get off the subject.

Silence. Some landscape.

HUMBERT   Why are you fidgeting like that? What is the matter?

LOLITA   Nothing, you brute.

HUMBERT   You what?

She turns away.
   They drive on in silence. "Cold spiders of panic crawled down my back. This was an orphan . . ."

CUT TO:

Receding Road

LOLITA   Oh, a squashed squirrel! What a shame.

HUMBERT   (*hopefully*) Yes, isn't it? The little animals are imprudent. You know, there should be——

LOLITA   Stop at the next gas station. I want to go to the washroom.

HUMBERT   Righto. Tummy-ache?

LOLITA   (*smiling sweetly at him*) You chump, you creep, you revolting character. I was a daisy-fresh girl and look what you've done to me. I ought to call the cops and tell them you raped me. Oh, you dirty, dirty old man!

Humbert frowns, sweats, glances at her askance.

LOLITA   (*wincing and making a sizzling sound as she in-
      takes through parted lips*) You hurt me. You've torn
      something inside.

CUT TO:

A Filling Station
She scrambles out and disappears. Slowly, lovingly, the old
mechanic soaps and wipes the windshield, etc. Lolita re-
appears.

LOLITA   Look, give me some dimes and nickles. I want to
      call Mother at that hospital. What's the number?

HUMBERT   Get in. You can't call.

LOLITA   Why?

HUMBERT   Get in and slam the door.

The old garage man beams. They swing onto the highway.

LOLITA   Why can't I call my mother if I want to?

HUMBERT   Because your mother is dead.

CUT TO:

Lepingsville—a Travel Agency on Main Street
A thick smear crayon traces across a map the itinerary which
Humbert and Lolita will follow through three or four mountain states, to Beardsley, Idaho. Besides the folding map, they
are given a strip map and a tour book.

CUT TO:

Humbert and Lolita Shopping in Lepingsville
The purchases are: a beribboned box of chocolates, comic
books, toilet articles, a manicure set, a travel clock, a ring with
a real topaz, field glasses, a portable radio, chewing gum, a
transparent raincoat, various playsuits and summer frocks. She
remains rather sullen throughout though some of the purchases do provoke a transient gleam in her gloom.

CUT TO:

A Forest Road at Nightfall
They have stopped by the side of the road.

HUMBERT We must have taken the wrong turning. This is awful.

He gets the map and a torch light.

LOLITA Give me that map.

HUMBERT We should have turned left half an hour ago and taken 42 south, not north.

LOLITA We? Leave me out of it.

HUMBERT (*over her shoulder*) I am sure we'll find some place to stop, if we just drive on.

He nuzzles her tentatively.

LOLITA (*flinching*) Leave me alone. I despise you. You deceived me about Mother. You took advantage of me.

CUT TO:

We see the Car moving on
This is the first, rather ominous, lap in their trip. Things will pick up, however—and then degenerate again.

It is assumed that Humbert and Lolita are traversing by car a distance of some three thousand miles, including side trips, from Lepingsville (which is anywhere between Massachusetts and Minnesota) westward through several mountain states to Beardsley, a college town in Idaho. Their journey is a leisurely, sightseeing tour, so that it takes them not less than two or three weeks to reach, in mid-September, their destination. All along their route there is an evolution of the motel theme, illustrated by six examples beginning with the modest log cabin (Acme Cabins), through cottages in a row (Baskerville Cottages), garage-connected units (Crest Court), fused units (Dymple Manor), and the patio-and-pool type (Eden Lodge), to the fancy two-story affair (Foxcreek Ranch), a gradation which, if pursued further, would lead us back to the country hotel. There is also a (shorter) series of eating places, from the breakfast counter of the Truckers Welcome, through the coffee-shop type, to the more or less smart restaurant.

While the accommodations improve, and their pretentions climb, Lolita's attitude takes an opposite, downward, course, starting with a forlorn semblance of affection and passing through a gamut of deterioration, to end in the wretchedness of their last night before reaching Beardsley.

We have now put up at The Humble Log Cabin, where Humbert and Lolita will conclude a pathetic pact—soon to be broken.

CUT TO:

Acme Cabins—a Modest Cabin, One of Five, Higgledy-piggledy in a Pine Forest

None has a bath. The separate privy is garlanded with wild roses. A brisk, buxom, unkempt woman shows our tired travelers the wood-burning stove and the two dissimilar beds, separable by a curtain on rings. There is a Bible on the chest of drawers. A fly buzzes drowsily. Above Humbert's bed there is the picture of a girl garlanded with wild roses.

Humbert, in his curtained-off section, sits on the bed with his face between his fists in mournful meditation. Presently, he puts out the light and lies down; silence. The moon rises, a disturbed fly buzzes and is still again. Humbert lies in the mottled dark with eyes open, his arms under his nape.

A child sob sounds and is followed by more. He sits up, listening. The curtain is drawn aside.

Lolita with tears streaming down her face, her nightgown white and infantine in the moonlight, comes to be comforted. He gently caresses her hair, as she weeps on his shoulder.

HUMBERT   I beseech you not to cry. I love you. I cannot exist without you. Everything will be all right.

LOLITA   (*with a snuffle and a wail*) Nothing will ever be all right.

HUMBERT   I'm sure we are going to be very happy, you and I.

LOLITA   But everything has *changed*, all of a sudden. Everything was so—oh, I don't know—normal: the camp, and the lake, and Charlie, and the girls, and the—

oh, everything. And now there is no camp, and no Ramsdale, nothing!

There is the patter of some little night beast on the roof.

HUMBERT   I don't want you to cry. We'll see things, we'll go places.

LOLITA   There's no place to go back to.

HUMBERT   We'll find a new home.

LOLITA   But there's no old one. And I've left all my things there.

HUMBERT   What, for instance?

LOLITA   My roller skates, my—oh, lots of things.

HUMBERT   You silly darling, why didn't you tell me in Lepingsville?

LOLITA   (*tearfully*) I forgot.

HUMBERT   We'll get every blessed thing you want. It's over two thousand miles to Beardsley but we've got a month before the fall term begins. We can dawdle as much as you want.

LOLITA   But what next? Oh, where is that handkerchief?

HUMBERT   Next you'll go to school in Beardsley, and have a wonderful time there. I love you. I'm also going to cry if you don't stop. Remember, I'll die if you ever leave me.

LOLITA   Leave you? You know perfectly well I have no-where to go.

CUT TO:

Baskerville Cottages
Ten white-washed cottages in a row, with a vast well-kept lawn in front, separating them from the highway.

Lolita and Humbert in a Leafy Spot not far from their cottage. Humbert with a book on the grass. Lolita in an old garden swing, swinging gently.

HUMBERT   You have been a very sweet child so far. It would be a pity to break the precious rhythm we have now established. I suggest we spend another night here, in this fairy-tale cabin. We shall ramble and read. Do you know, these notes on Edgar Poe that I have prepared for Beardsley College always remind me of Ramsdale and the first time I touched you. Come here, sit down beside me. I'll read you my favorite poem.

LOLITA   (*in the swing, just behind him*) I want to sit here.

HUMBERT   All right, but don't make it creak. I want you to follow very closely the intonation, the inner construction of these lines.
> *It was night in the lonesome October*
> *Of my most immemorial year*

Marvelous emphasis on "immemorial." Makes you step up from one dim rim to a dimmer one.
> *It was hard by the dim lake of Auber,*
> *In the misty mid region of Weir*

Notice how nicely the "dim" is read back and becomes "mid"—"misty mid region"?
                    (*The swing creaks.*)

HUMBERT   Darling, please don't do that. I skip a few stanzas. Now listen again:
> *Thus I pacified Psyche and kissed her*
> *And tempted her out of her gloom . . .*
> *And we passed to the end of the vista,*
> *But were stopped by the door of a tomb*
> *. . . And I said: "What is written, sweet sister? . . ."*
> *She replied: "Ulalume, Ulalume!"*

LOLITA   I think that's rather corny.

HUMBERT   Really? What exactly do you object to?

LOLITA   Vista-sister. That's like Lolita-sweeter.

HUMBERT   Oh, that's true. A very fine observation.

(A more or less tame rabbit stops, nibbles, lopes on.)

HUMBERT   In my class you'd get an A-plus and a kiss. But what I'm really driving at is that there is a certain intonation in this poem which is so much more original and mysterious than the rather trivial romanticism of Annabel Lee. (*He turns his head and notices the swing is empty.*)

HUMBERT   (*getting up to his feet*) Lolita!

(She has disappeared)

HUMBERT   Lolita, where are you hiding?

He looks for her among the trees and shrubs. He is in a state of distress and distraction hardly warranted by the circumstances. (She has wandered away in dim-smiling, stooping pursuit of the soft elusive rabbit)

HUMBERT   (*emerging from a thicket*) Lolita!

She is crouching behind the circumspect bunny. A very low-class young couple with an unattractive baby are on the back porch of a cabin. They talk to Lolita. The young man is not unlike (and should be played by the same actor as) Lolita's future husband.

THE YOUNG MAN   I guess he doesn't want to be caught.

Humbert, excited and angry, appears on the scene.

HUMBERT   Will you please come at once. I've been calling you for hours. This is preposterous.
            (*Does not quite know what he is saying.*)

Lolita turns and walks back to their cabin, followed by Humbert and the CAMERA. She stops near their parked car, and jiggles the door handle.

LOLITA   Unlock, please.

HUMBERT   Darling, you must forgive me.

LOLITA   You've insulted me in front of those people.

HUMBERT   I lost my head. I was reading a poem. I got the nightmare notion that you had disappeared for good— that perhaps you never existed. Don't be mad at me, my love. I'll unlock if you like, but don't be mad. Your mother once told me that when you were quite small and wanted to sulk, you'd get into the family car all alone.

LOLITA   I don't care. You can't do this to me.

HUMBERT   I know, I know. I'm asking your pardon. It won't happen again. I'm a fool. I thought you were gone.

LOLITA   I've nowhere to go.

CUT TO:

Breakfast Counter in a Diner Called TRUCKERS WELCOME
A very plain place with a deer head and adman's visions of celestial sundaes on the wall. At the counter, Lolita has Humbert on her right and a tremendous trucker with hairy forearms on her left. The trucker and Lolita wear identical clothes: dungarees and T-shirts. The man is messily finishing his meal. Humbert and Lolita are waiting for theirs.

CUT TO:

Lolita, Humbert, Driving on
The road is bordered by hilly farmlands and then winds through sparsely settled country interspersed with pine groves.

CUT TO:

Crest Court—a semicircle of stucco units connected by narrow garages
The lawn in front is shaded by ample maples. Inside, two identical pictures (stylized dahlias) hang over the twin beds. The hideous drone of an air-conditioning apparatus provides a constant sonic background.

CUT TO:

Long Shot—Humbert and Lolita Arriving
It is the ordinary procedure. They both get out of the car in front of the office. The woman who runs the motel cries out, "I'll be with you in a moment," as she hurriedly escorts some other people back to the office from the room they have seen.

It is now Humbert's and Lolita's turn. They follow the side-walk in the wake of the bustling woman. She shows them the room. Humbert nods his head. Listless, Lolita drops into a low chair. Humbert follows the woman back to the office and registers there.

HUMBERT   Where can I get some soft drinks round here?

THE WOMAN   It's just one block down the road.

Humbert walks out to follow her directions but then thinks better of it and returns to the room, where Lolita is sprawling in the chair with a magazine.

HUMBERT   We'll be going out in five minutes for a bite. Do lay aside that old magazine and come talk to me.

Lolita scans magazine without replying.

HUMBERT   Do you hear me, darling? I want a little chat with you, *mon petit chat*. Please.

LOLITA   If you give me a dime. From now on I am coin operated.

She continues to read.
    Humbert, who has taken off his shirt, notices the approach of the motel woman and steps into the bathroom. The woman enters bringing a jug of ice cubes.

THE WOMAN   There. You can have a nice cold drink, dearie. Long way from home?

LOLITA   Home? Yes, I guess so. Very long way.

WOMAN   Must be fun to travel all alone with your daddy?

LOLITA   Oh, I dunno——

WOMAN   Depends on what you call fun?

LOLITA   Uh-huh.

WOMAN   Left your mama up at the farm?

LOLITA   Uhn-uhn. We don't have a farm.

WOMAN   Get along with your daddy?

LOLITA   Yah.

WOMAN   You don't talk the way he does. I mean, he talks foreign, and you don't.

LOLITA   Oh, well—I went to school in this country.

WOMAN   And he didn't? Is he French Canadian?

LOLITA   Sort of.

WOMAN   Look, there's a Canadian couple living across the road. Maybe you'd like to talk to them?

LOLITA   Why?

HUMBERT   (*from the threshold of the bathroom*) Yes—why indeed?

WOMAN   Oh, I thought you had gone out for a drink.

HUMBERT   By the way, can you stop that ventilator, or whatever you call it? I can't stand that whirr.

CUT TO:

Another Stretch of Road
For the first time sagebrush and juniper appear. There is some uncertainty whether it is a bank of clouds or a range of mountains that have started looming just above the horizon. By the side of the road, a granite obelisk commemorates a bloody battle—the defeat of Blue Bull.

A Crowded Coffee Shop
A hard-working harried young waitress is doing her best to satisfy too many customers.

LOLITA   (*to Humbert*) Give me a coin for the juke box. Oh, they have my song.

She starts the juke box. The following song is produced:

> Lolita, Lolita, Lolita!
> For ever tonight we must part:
> Because separation is sweeter
> Than clasping a ghost to one's heart.

Because it's a maddening summer,
Because the whole night is in bloom,
Because you're in love with a strummer
Who brings his guitar to your room.

You know he's a clown and a cheater,
You know I am tender and true—
But *he* is now singing, Lolita,
The songs I've been making for you!

CUT TO:

The Route now offers spectacular scenery
as it snakes up a gigantic mountainside. At the top of the pass,
tourists take pictures and feed the marmots. In the next valley
we inspect the collection of frontier lore in a Ghost Town
museum. We have a little trouble when the car stalls on a steep
incline but some kind youths help. The radiator grill is plastered with dead butterflies.

CUT TO:

A Dirt Road in a Canyon
Humbert pulls up at the bloomy and lush wayside.

HUMBERT   I should not have attempted to take a short cut.
    We're lost.

LOLITA   Ask that nut with the net over there.

The Butterfly Hunter. His name is Vladimir Nabokov. A fritillary settles with outspread wings on a tall flower. Nabokov
snaps it up with a sweep of his net. Humbert walks toward
him. With a nip of finger and thumb through a fold of the
marquisette Nabokov dispatches his capture and works the
dead insect out of the netbag onto the palm of his hand.

HUMBERT   Is that a rare specimen?

NABOKOV   A specimen cannot be common or rare, it can
    only be poor or perfect.

HUMBERT   Could you direct me——

NABOKOV   You meant "rare species." This is a good spec-
    imen of a rather scarce subspecies.

HUMBERT   I see. Could you please tell me if this road leads
   to Dympleton?

NABOKOV   I haven't the vaguest idea. I saw some loggers
   (*pointing*) up there. They might know.

CUT TO:

Dymple Manor—twenty units firmly fused together in a Row
The screen doors never cease banging as people come in and
out, and the only way to confound one's neighbor's canned
music is to start one's own full blast. Sprinklers irrigate the
parched-looking lawn and its border of trembling petunias. In
the adjacent lot a bulldozer is at work, and another motel is
rising.

LOLITA   Give me a quarter for the TV.

HUMBERT   It's free, my pet, in this, as they say, joint.

A notice under glass says PETS ACCEPTED.

LOLITA   I need a quarter anyway.

HUMBERT   My pet must earn it.

CUT TO:

The Television Screen
A commercial is melting:

A FRUITY VOICE   . . . soft, soft as the bloom on a peach.

SUPREMELY HAPPY ANNOUNCER   And now we return to
   Act One of *The Nymphet.*

LOLITA'S VOICE   Oh, I saw it at home last winter. It's
   good.

On the TV screen, an art collector is seen examining a miniature statue: a tiny bronze nude.

HIS SUBDUED NARRATIONAL VOICE   I had bought it on a
   hunch; but now, as I stroked each curve, I knew it was
   a unique masterpiece.

CLOSE-UP of the statuette, which is called "Playing Hooky."

A teen-age girl is about to take a dip, her dress and school books are lying at the foot of a gnarled willow.

NARRATIVE UNDERVOICE CONTINUES   I knew that the artist who made it was traveling in a distant country with his young wife. A strange urge possessed me. Next day I was flying over the jungle.

HUMBERT'S VOICE   Must we look at this trash?

LOLITA'S VOICE   It's not trash. It will get quite exciting. He finds the girl and he shoots her.

CUT TO:

High Altitude
We stop at Sapphire Lake. Snow banks and wild flowers. Two boys from another car engage Lolita in a snowball fight. Humbert, who has incongruously put on rubbers, slips on an icy patch and ignominiously lands on his back. Lolita and the boys laugh at his discomfiture. A scenic drive takes our travelers to the Pueblo dwellings. A rodeo is advertised in the next town.

CUT TO:

Eden Lodge
We are now in the patio-and-pool belt. The arrangement of fused whitewashed units brackets a square of green grounds with a heated swimming pool in the middle. The rooms are smarter and more expensive than at Crest or Dymple; unfortunately, a tented roller-skate rink on the opposite side of the road impairs Eden's elegancy with a sustained blare of rowdy music.

In the Room

LOLITA   (*reading a notice*) Children free. Goody-goody.

HUMBERT   (*laughing tenderly*) No quarter tonight, free child.

LOLITA   That's what you think. From now on *this* child is paid half a dollar.

HUMBERT   My Persian peach.

LOLITA   And moreover—moreover you must promise
          you'll let me go roller-skating—no, wait a sec—it's not
          only that, but you must promise you'll not supervise
          me—I mean, you may wait outside, or at the chuck
          wagon, but the inside is reserved for teen-agers. See?

HUMBERT   My carissa, my liquidambar, my early delicious.

CUT TO:

Swimming Pool
At poolside Lolita (satin pants, shirred bra) and two other
nymphets (one dark, with a striped ball in her scanty lap, the
other fair, with a long scar on her leg) recline. A lad of their
age, in bathing trunks, sits on the cement brink, paying not
the slightest attention to the three maidens.

FAIR   (*in response to Lolita's index finger*) Rock climbing
        in Pink Pillar Park. Skinned my fanny too. That's a cute
        bracelet you've got.

LOLITA   Thank you.

DARK   You can't be Spanish, Lolita?

LOLITA   (*smile, shrug*)

FAIR   (to DARK) Are your folks like mine—playing cards
        all day?

DARK   My father is an admiral, and my mother's an actress.

FAIR   Good for you. (*pause*) That character there (*pointing
        with her bare toe at owlish Humbert, who at some distance
        beyond the pool is sitting in a shadow-dappled garden
        chair*), I know why *he* wears sunglasses.

(Dark girl and Lolita exchange a glance, and both laugh.)

DARK   It's her dad, bright kid.

FAIR   I'm sorry.

All three wince as the lad dives, splashing them.

FAIR   And who's the nitwit?

DARK   He belongs to this motor court.

Humbert, in the dappled distance, raises his hand beckoning Lolita. She makes a grimace of resignation, and leaves the poolside.

DARK   (*to Fair*) I bet her folks are divorced.

FAIR   (*to Dark*) Yah. She looks like one of those mixed-up kids you see on TV.

CUT TO:

Poolside

HUMBERT   (*closing his book*) I see from this point of vantage they have finished cleaning up our room. I therefore suggest we retire for a brief siesta, my love.

LOLITA   I want a hamburger first.

HUMBERT   And then a humburger.

LOLITA   Those two bitch girls are watching us.

HUMBERT   A propos: I don't mind your playing with girls of your age. In fact, I rather welcome it if I can be present. You may exchange wisecracks with them to your heart's content. But I must repeat: be careful.

LOLITA   Telling me what to say—huh?

HUMBERT   Telling you what not to say.

CUT TO:

The Motel Room

HUMBERT   Now let me rub this in. I may well be a middle-aged morals offender, *d'accord*, but *you* are a minor female who has impaired the morals of an adult in a respectable inn. I go to jail—*d'accord*. But what happens to you, neglected incorrigible orphan? Let me tell you: a nice grim matron takes away your fancy clothes, your lipsticks, your life. For me, it is jail. But for you, little waif, it is the correctional school, the bleak reformatory, the juvenile detention home where you knit things, and sing hymns, and have rancid pancakes on Sundays. Oh, horrible! My poor wayward girl (come, give me a kiss) should realize, I think, that under the circumstances she'd better be very careful, and not talk to strangers too freely. What were you giggling about with those two girls?

CUT TO:

A Roadside Sign: PINK PILLAR NATIONAL MONUMENT. Another sign further on: SADDLE HORSES. PERSONALIZED TOURS.

DISSOLVE TO:

A Slow Cavalcade of Tourists
weaving along a bridle trail, topped by digitate and phallic cliffs. Lolita is bobbing at a walking pace immediately behind the leader, a lanky ranger who keeps turning to her and kidding the cocky lass. A fat dude rancher in a flowery shirt rides behind her, then come two small boys, then a Mrs. Hopson, and then Humbert.

Edda Hopson (her name is on her back) takes advantage of a widening in the path to fall back and engage reluctant Humbert in polite conversation (oh, shade of Charlotte!).

MRS. HOPSON   What a lovely child you've got! I kept admiring her last night in the lounge. Those cheekbones! That virgin bloom on her arms and legs! I'm a bit of an artist, and in fact have exposed. Keep her pure! I do hope she has a good heart. I used to hurt my parents as a savage hurts dumb animals. Is she kind to you? Does she love you?

HUMBERT   No.

MRS. HOPSON   Ah, teen-agers are dreadfully cruel. And such a little beauty! A word of advice: don't let that redhaired brute of a ranger tease her the way he is doing. I rode with him alone once, and he exhibited his—well, emotion most shamelessly. I must say I thought it rather thick: knowing I was a divorcee and taking advantage.

CUT TO:

A Fairly Good Restaurant

Tablecloths and napkins. Waiters. A three-man orchestra. Lolita and Humbert sit at a table in shaded light.

LOLITA   (*to Humbert*) What's a roast caponette?

HUMBERT   Chicken.

LOLITA   No. I'll have the charcoal-broiled filet mignon.

The orchestra plays "Lolita, Lolita, Lolita." Humbert has ordered half a bottle of wine.

LOLITA   Give me some.

HUMBERT   If nobody's looking. Well, here's to your
health, my life and my bride.

LOLITA   Okay, okay.

HUMBERT   I'm so anxious to make you happy. Just don't
know what to suggest. I'm rather awkward and sometimes a brute. But I adore every inch of you. I'd like to
kiss your kidneys and fondle your liver. Tell me, what
shall we do tomorrow? Let's stay here a couple of days
longer and take in Phantom Lake and perhaps hire a
boat there. Would you like that?

LOLITA   A boat? What do you know about boats?

HUMBERT   Why are you laughing?

LOLITA   I just remembered. One day we went in the rowboat, Phyl, Agnes, and me, and we found a cove, and
went for a swim, and Charlie came out of the wood just
like that. And of course he was not supposed to go
swimming with us, and Phyllis said——

THE WAITER   Would the young lady like some more milk?

LOLITA   Yes, I guess so.

HUMBERT   So what did Phyllis say?

LOLITA   Nothing.

HUMBERT   I had hoped I was getting another racy account
of your camp activities.

LOLITA   No, that's all.

Three days are spent in this region, and some side trips are
made. Humbert photographs Lolita among the rocks of the
Devil's Paint Box—hot springs, baby geysers, bubbling mud,
pouting puddles. Another trip takes them to Christmas Tree
Cavern, a deep damp place where Humbert shivers and is rude
to the guide. A long drive toward a disappointing objective—
the display of a local lady's home-made sculptures—does not
improve Lolita's mood. She feigns gagging. They traverse an
incredibly barren and boring desert. Timbered hills rise again.

CUT TO:

Foxcreek Ranch
This is the last and most pretentious motel of the series, a
two-story affair, very fancy and ugly, in the heart of the train
and truck traffic. The office is brightly illumined. The time is
rather late at night.

THE MANAGER   Well, all I have left is this one room with
     a double bed.

Lolita is examining some Indian souvenirs on the counter.

LOLITA   (*to Humbert, who is about to register*) I want this
     money purse.

HUMBERT   Wait a moment, my dear.

LOLITA   I want this purse.

HUMBERT   *Mais c'est si laid.*

LOLITA   *Si laid* or not *si laid*—I want it.

HUMBERT   All right, all right.

MANAGER   (*giving Humbert his change*) Fifteen, and—let
     me see—three ninety-five for this. One silver dollar and
     one new nickel. Would the young lady like her mono-
     gram upon it?

LOLITA   Yes. It's D.H.

MANAGER   Aha. Very well. Where did my old dad put
     those initials? Dad! Oh, here they are.

LOLITA   D.H. Dolores Haze.

Humbert has started to write his name on a register slip. He has got as far as "Humbert Hu." With great presence of mind he changes "u" to "a," and adds "ze."

MANAGER   Ask your dad for that dollar, Dolores. That's a tongue twister—dollar doll—isn't it?

CUT TO:

Front of Hacienda
The manager shows Humbert where to park.

CUT TO:

Room
Wall-to-wall carpeting and floor-to-ceiling picture windows; dressing alcove; ceramic-tiled bath; trucks and trains accompany the dialogue.

HUMBERT   That "Haze" was a bad slip of your adorable little tongue. While we put up at hotels, you are—remember—Dolores Humbert. Let's keep "Haze" for the reformatory.

LOLITA   Meaning that school at Beardsley?

HUMBERT   You're going to an extremely good private school at Beardsley. But one hot whisper to a girl friend, one stupid boast, may send me to jail and you to a juvenile detention home.

LOLITA   By the way, you said "private." Is it a girls' school?

HUMBERT   Yes.

LOLITA   Then I'm not going there. I want to go to an ordinary public school.

HUMBERT   Let's not fight and argue tonight. I'm fagged out. We have to start quite early tomorrow. Please, Dolly Humbert.

LOLITA   I loathe your name. It's a clown's name: Humlet Hambert. Omelette Hamburg.

HUMBERT   Or plain "Hamlet." I daresay, you hate me
even more than my name. Oh, Lolita, if you knew what
you are doing to me. Some day you'll regret.

LOLITA   That's right. Just go clowning on and on.

HUMBERT   Well, let's struggle with these blinds. The war
with Venice. I can't do anything with these slats and
slits.

LOLITA   I'm not listening to you, you know.

HUMBERT   Pity. This is our last night on the road. I wonder what kind of house the Beardsley people have prepared for us. I hope it's brick and ivy.

LOLITA   I could not care less.

HUMBERT   But don't you think it has been an enchanting
journey? Tell me, what did you like best of all? I think,
yesterday's canyon, eh? I think I've never seen such iridescent rocks.

LOLITA   I think iridescent rocks stink.

HUMBERT   (*affecting a good-natured laugh*) Have it your
way.

She takes off her shoes. Her movements are slumber-slow.

LOLITA   I'm thirsty.

HUMBERT   There's ice in this jug.

Tinkle.

LOLITA   (*hazily*) I want a soda.

HUMBERT   Shall I bring you one from the Coke dispenser?

LOLITA   (*yawns and nods*)

HUMBERT   Grape? Cherry?

LOLITA   Cherry. No, make it grape.

She yawns.

CUT TO:

Spacious Patio, Neon-flooded Solitude
Humbert walks to the vending machine which is outside the
motel office. Dime. Bottle. Repeat performance. He opens
both bottles on the cap-bite.

AN OLD MAN'S VOICE   The missus thirsty?

It is the deaf old father of the hotel manager sitting and smoking in the shadows.

HUMBERT   I beg your pardon?

OLD MAN   Women sure get thirsty.

HUMBERT   It's my daughter. . . .

OLD MAN   What's that?

HUMBERT   . . . who wants a drink.

OLD MAN   No, thank you, very kind of you.

HUMBERT   (*after a moment's hesitation*) Well, good night.

OLD MAN   My wife was also like that—but *her* drink was
     beer.

Chuckles, mumbles, expectorates in the dark.

CUT TO:

Humbert
walking back to his door with the two bottles. He reaches the
door. He has not got the key. As he frees his hand to knock,
the telephone rings somewhere in an adjacent room and for
a moment the shadow of a past combination of memorable details is imposed upon the present (". . . better come
quick . . .") Humbert taps gently on the door. No answer.

HUMBERT   (*not too loud*) Lolita!

No answer. He taps again, then peers through the slits of the
Venetian blind. A blurry light is on in the room. Lolita, half
undressed, lies supine on the bed, fast asleep.
     It is hopeless. Humbert is disinclined to get the manager
to come and unlock: the nymphet's sleep is not that of an
acceptable child.

CUT TO:

Humbert

mouth open, asleep in the car. It is dawn. From one of the motel rooms there gradually emerges a big family—sleepy children, portable icebox, accepted pet, crib—and fills a big station wagon which has the stickers of various resorts and natural marvels affixed to it: a summary also of Humbert's honeymoon. One of the children turns on the radio.

Act Three

Beardsley School

A private school for girls at Beardsley, Idaho. It is a sunny spring day. There are catkins in all the vases. We are in the music room of the school. It is here that the drama classes are held. Several girls, including Lolita, mostly in gym suits, some barefoot, sit around, some on the floor. Miss Cormorant, a lean faded Lesbian, is discussing the play which they will stage at the Spring Festival of Arts.

MISS CORMORANT   For our Spring Festival next month, we are going to do a play by Clare Quilty. When I taught at Onyx, Mr. Cue, as we called him, would sometimes drive over from Briceland to direct a dance pantomime. The girls adored him. One day he told me that he and a famous painter, the late Lewis Ruskin, were engaged in writing a play for children. Eventually, Mr. Quilty published it under the intriguing title, *The Enchanted Hunters*. And this is the play we are going to do. Why are you laughing, Lolita? Did I say anything hilarious?

LOLITA   No, Miss Cormorant.

CORMORANT   The play is a charming fantasy. Several hunters are lost in a wood, and a strange girl they meet puts them into a kind of trance. They fraternize with mythical creatures. Of course, later the girl turns out to be a student at a nearby Institute for Extra-Sensorial Studies, and all ends quite plausibly. Mr. Quilty will be giving a lecture at Beardsley College at the end of this month, and I'm sure he'll help us to rehearse.

CUT TO:

Beardsley College (A coeducational institution where Humbert Humbert teaches)

The flowers that were budding in the first scene are now opening. A shrill whirring bell rings through the corridors. Students are leaving the classroom, where Humbert is collecting his notes. Miss Shatzki, an intense unkempt young woman in a formless sweater, speaks to him.

HUMBERT   Yes, I see what you mean, Miss Shatzki.

MISS SHATZKI   I would also like to ask you about Poe's other love affairs. Don't you think——

CUT TO:

College Corridor with moving sunlight at the far end
Humbert walks down this long passage toward the exit. At one point various publicity items are tacked onto a cork board hanging on the wall. Humbert's glance passes across:

MISS EMMA KING, PIANO LESSONS

SPRING IS HERE—SAY IT WITH ADELE'S DAFFODILS
AT THE CAMPUS FLOWER SHOP

FOUND: : A GIRL'S LEATHER BELT

FRIDAY, 8 P.M., MAIN AUDITORIUM
FAMOUS PLAYWRIGHT CLARE QUILTY
WILL LECTURE ON THE LOVE OF ART

CUT TO:

Campus—Humbert
walks across the turfy expanse toward the parking lot, a small group issues from the college library. An instructor of English and a couple of students have been conducting a distinguished visitor, Quilty, and his constant companion, Vivian Dark-bloom, on a tour through the stacks. Vivian is a stylish, bob-haired, lanky lady in a well-tailored suit, with striking exotic features marred by a certain coarseness of epiderm. The following scene is accompanied by a strong spring wind blowing across the campus.

INSTRUCTOR   (*to Quilty*) Next week the Department of Anthropology is arranging a special exhibition in the Rare Books department. It will feature some rugs, and, I think, sacred pictures, which Professor and Mrs. Brooks brought back from Moscow.

QUILTY   Fascinating.

INSTRUCTOR   (*noticing Humbert, who is passing by*) Oh, Professor Humbert!

Humbert stops.

INSTRUCTOR   Mr. Quilty, this is Professor Humbert, our visiting lecturer in Comparative Literature.

QUILTY   I don't think we have actually met—or have we? Seen you a couple of times in Ramsdale and elsewhere. Happy occasions.

He mumbles and smirks.

VIVIAN DARKBLOOM   (*very distinctly*) And I am Vivian Darkbloom.

QUILTY   (*his sparse hair and necktie stirring in the strong wind*) My collaborator, my evening shadow. Her name looks like an anagram. But she's a real woman—or anyway a real person. You're an inch taller than me, aren't you, m'dear?

VIVIAN   (*training her brilliant smile upon Humbert*) My niece Mona goes to Beardsley School with your daughter.

HUMBERT   Step.

QUILTY   (*addressing the instructor and the two students*) You know the first thing people usually say when I'm introduced to them is how much they like, or simply adore, my *Nymphet* on TV.

HUMBERT   I do have a vague recollection . . .

QUILTY   Good for you. I often wonder what is technically more vague—a vague recollection or a vague premonition.
(*to Vivian*)
This is a philosophic question, my dear, way above your pretty head. Ghouls of the past or phantoms of the future—which do we choose?

HUMBERT   Some of my best friends are phantoms.

QUILTY   Sense of humor, I see. What a wind! *Quel vent!* Lucky I'm not wearing my toupee. Have a cigarette.

Humbert declines.

QUILTY   It should have been a Drome, but it is not. It's a
very special Spanish brand made especially for me, for
my urgent needs.
   (*Dissolves in ghoulish giggles.*)
Does it always blow like this on your campus?

A photographer and a reporter, led by a lion-haired faculty
member, are seen approaching across the wind-rippled lawn.

FACULTY MEMBER   Mr. Quilty, the town paper would like
a picture of you.

REPORTER   How long will you be staying in Beardsley?

QUILTY   Oh, I don't know. A week. Perhaps longer.

REPORTER   You're on your way from the East to Arizona.
Correct?

QUILTY   Yes. I share a ranch there with a few merry
companions.

REPORTER   You are lecturing here on the Love of Art.
How do you define "Art"?

Front of Humbert's Rented House
in Thayer Street, Beardsley. It is a two-story brick-and-stucco
affair, with an unkempt dandelion-invaded lawn which is in
striking contrast to the adjacent neat garden of Miss Fenton
Lebone, whose name is on the mailbox. She is inspecting the
progress of certain bulbs when Humbert drives up. As he
walks past her along the gravel path to his porch, the sound
track registers his rapid mental supplication: Don't let Lebone
notice me, don't have Miss Fenton Lebone talk to me, please
don't let——. But the old lady's hawk eye has followed her
neighbor's passage, and now she greets him sternly from behind her frontier of lilacs and laurels.

MISS LEBONE   Good afternoon, Professor.

HUMBERT   Oh. Hallo. (*Attempts to reach the safety of his
door, but she will not be shaken off.*)

MISS LEBONE   I hate to intrude but don't you think you

should do something about that jungle (*denouncing the dandelions*).

HUMBERT   (*trying a feeble quip*) Kindness to flowers. They are immigrants. We all are in a sense.

LEBONE   I'm certainly not. Couldn't I lend you my mower?

HUMBERT   Yes. Thanks. Perhaps Sunday.

LEBONE   You look exhausted.

HUMBERT   Yes, lots of work.

LEBONE   Incidentally, are you sure your pretty little girl gets enough sleep? I notice the light in her bedroom off and on, off and on, at all hours of the night. That *is* her bedroom window, isn't it? There's a string dangling from your pocket.

HUMBERT   Oh, thank you. Every time I undo a parcel I put the string in my pocket. So stupid.

LEBONE   Now tell me—why doesn't your Dolly come over to my house, any time, and curl up in a comfortable chair, and look at the *loads* of beautiful books my dear mother gave me when *I* was a child. Wouldn't that be much more wholesome than having the radio at full blast for hours on end?

HUMBERT   Certainly. By all means. We'll do that. (*He reaches the porch.*)

HUMBERT   (*mental monologue*) Should have said, as we all are refugees in this world. Staircase wit. Abominable woman!

CUT TO:

The Humbert Home
There is a depressing atmosphere of disorder and neglect in every room of the house.

HUMBERT   (*calling*) Lo! Lolita! Not in.

Leaning against the hallway telephone there is an empty Cola bottle with its straw. In the living room, a stool is askew, pushed away from the easy chair with a medley of magazines spilled on the floor; a plate with crumbs stands on the TV; a heap of bluebooks (ruins of a college examination) have been left by Humbert on and around the divan. On a small table there are the implements from Lolita's manicure set: a bottle of nail polish has stuck to the varnished top of the table where it leaves a bald spot when removed; one ballet shoe sits on the piano, its mate lies sole up on the threshold to the next room. In the kitchen there is a mountain of dirty dishes in the sink; bottle caps strew the table where flies stroll around a chicken drumstick.

CUT TO:

Hallway—Lolita with her school chum, Mona Dahl
(a smartly dressed, experienced-looking, cool brunette), and two boys come in and troop into the living room, where with magic instantaneousness, as if awaiting them, music starts mewing and moaning. Humbert comes out on the upper landing from his study.

HUMBERT   (*calling down*) Lolita? Who's that?

LOLITA   (*climbing the stairs*) It's me, and Mona, and Roy, and Rex.

HUMBERT   Where have you been?

LOLITA   Oh, at the candy bar. And now I've come to fetch my sweater and swimsuit.

HUMBERT   What for?

LOLITA   (*pulling on the sweater, which she finds on the banister*) We are going to the BB River Club.

HUMBERT   The *what*?

LOLITA   (*laughing as she emerges Bardotesquely disheveled through the neckhole*) The Beach and Boat Club. Roy's father's a member.

HUMBERT   Now, first of all I don't want that racket in the living room. And in the second place, it's much too windy on the river today.

LOLITA   Oh, maybe we'll just hang around——

HUMBERT   Besides, my pet, the theme of boating has not been a particularly fortunate one in your young life.

LOLITA   Okay, okay, there are other things we can do there——

HUMBERT   You are not going.

LOLITA   They have a bowling alley and table tennis——

HUMBERT   You have your homework to do. And house-work!

LOLITA   Jees——

HUMBERT   You tell your friends you're not going.

LOLITA   I'll do nothing of the sort.

HUMBERT   Then I will.

He clears his throat and descends the stairs. From the landing Lolita sees him entering the living room. The music stops, stunned. Swearing under her breath, Lolita runs down the steps toward her friends, as they are herded into the hallway from the living room by Humbert, whose constrained nervous smile and jaunty manner cannot mask his awkward boorishness.

MONA   Really, sir, we would not stop long out there.

HUMBERT   No-no-no.

ROY   I'm sure, sir, you have nothing to worry about.

HUMBERT   I'm sorry, children, but it will be some other time.

He dismisses them and ascends the staircase repeating that rasping sound in his throat. In the hallway, Lolita talks to her friends as they file out into the sun.

LOLITA   Well, you see—this is the way it is.

MONA   I'll call you later, Dolly. I think your sweater's dreamy.

LOLITA   Thank you. It's virgin wool.

MONA   The only thing about you that is, kiddo.

Mona's husky laugh recedes as Lolita closes the door after her. Humbert from the stairs has heard that exchange. Lolita runs up past him to her room. She fumbles for the key to lock herself in. Humbert, rumbling, follows her.

CUT TO:

Lolita's Very Untidy Bedroom

HUMBERT   I've removed that key long ago, my dear. There is no place in the world where you could——

LOLITA   You get out!

HUMBERT   *You* have no reason to be mad at *me*. Yes, I shall leave you to your meditations, but first I want to say something about that girl, Mona.

LOLITA   You can't have her. She belongs to a marine.

HUMBERT   I shall ignore that idiotic remark. What I mean to say is—can it possibly be that you have betrayed me to her?

LOLITA   Very melodramatic.
                    (*Clowns.*)
          You make me sick.
                    (*in a quieter smaller voice*)
          Why can't I have fun with my friends?

HUMBERT   Because, Lolita, whenever you leave me, whenever you go somewhere without me, I start imagining all sorts of things.

LOLITA   So I never can have *any* fun?

HUMBERT   But you do have fun. You asked for a bicycle— I gave you one. You wanted music lessons—I got you Miss Emperor, I mean, Miss King, who is the best pianist in town.

LOLITA   I want to act in the school play.

HUMBERT   My darling, we went into that before. Can't
    you see, the more exposed you are to contacts, to peo-
    ple, the more dangerous it all becomes. You and I have
    to guard our secret constantly. You say you want to act
    in a play. You *are* in a play as it is. In a very difficult play
    where you have the part of an innocent schoolgirl. Stick
    to that role. It's quite big enough for one little
    performer.

LOLITA   Some day . . . Some day you'll be sorry.

HUMBERT   I know it's all very simple really. You don't love
    me. You never loved me. Isn't that the main problem?

LOLITA   Will you let me act in the play?

HUMBERT   Do you love me just a little, Lolita?

She looks at him, mysterious and meretricious, pondering
whether to get what she wants by granting or by refusing.

CUT TO:

Living Room
Lolita is rehearsing. Mimeos of her part litter the furniture.
From the kitchen threshold, Humbert tenderly observes her.
She, like a hypnotic subject or a performer in a mystic rite,
touches mirages of make-believe objects with her sly, slender,
girl-child hands.

LOLITA   (*in romantic monotone*) Sleep, hunter. Velvet pet-
    als flutter down upon you. In this bower you will recline.

She gestures toward an invisible partner—and then, with a
more normal movement, forehead puckered, searches for the
rest of her part on a mimeographed sheet.

HUMBERT   (*gently*) If you have finished, come and have
    something to eat.

LOLITA   (*continuing her incantations*) I'll recite to you,
    hunter, a lullaby song about the mourning dove you lost
    when you were young. Listen!

> *Gone is Livia, love is gone:*
> *Strong wing, soft breast, bluish plume;*
> *In the juniper tree moaning at dawn:*
> *doom, doom.*

HUMBERT   What an ominous last line. A perfect spondee but how depressing.

LOLITA   Lay off, will you? And now sleep, hunter, sleep. Under the raining rose petals, sleep, hunter.
(*to Humbert*)
What do you want?

HUMBERT   A five-minute pause. I want you to forget Mr. Hunter whoever he is.

She goes on with her tactile make-believe, stroking the air before her with kneading fingers.

HUMBERT   What are you doing? Plucking a fruit?

LOLITA   Look—what does it matter to you?

HUMBERT   One would like to know.

LOLITA   Suppose I'm stroking the horn of my pet unicorn—what the heck is it to you?

HUMBERT   Okay, Hecuba.

LOLITA   Will you go, please? I'll come in a minute.

He looks at her with dewy eyes, in an ecstasy of tenderness and adoration. She, exasperated, bangs her fist on the piano keys and falls into an easy chair, her legs sideways over the armrest.

LOLITA   You will never leave me alone, is that it?

He goes down on his knees literally crawling toward her, adumbrating an amphoric embrace, almost like a lover of yore.

LOLITA   Oh, no! Not again.

HUMBERT   My love, my mourning dove! I'm so miserable! There is something gathering around us which I cannot understand. You are not telling me all, you——

Doorbell

LOLITA   Get up! Get up from the floor! It's Mona. I quite
    forgot. Let her in. I'll be down in a sec.

She rushes through the kitchen, picking up the wedge of pizza
on the way, and runs upstairs to her room. From the upper
landing she cries down to Mona, whom Humbert has let in:

LOLITA   I'm changing and coming down!

CUT TO:

Living Room
Mona saunters in, followed by Humbert.

HUMBERT   Are you going to rehearse? She's been at it all
    day.

MONA   Well, no. I'm driving Dolly to her piano lesson.

HUMBERT   But today's Saturday? I thought Miss Emperor
    had changed the hour to Monday afternoon.

MONA   It's been changed back again.
                (*picking up a book*)
    Is this novel as good as some people say?

HUMBERT   Oh, I don't know. It's just an old love story
    with a new twist. Superb artist, of course, but who cares?
    We live in an age when the serious middlebrow idiot
    craves for a literature of ideas, for the novel of social
    comment.

MONA   I wish I could attend your lectures at Beardsley
    College, sir. We young people of today are so much in
    need of spiritual guidance.

HUMBERT   Tell me, young person of today, how was that
    party at your aunt's the other night?

MONA   Oh, it was sweet of you to allow Dolly to come.

HUMBERT   So the party was a success?

MONA   Oh, a riot, terrific.

HUMBERT   Did Dolly, as you call her, dance a lot?

MONA   Not a frightful lot. Why?

HUMBERT   I suppose all the boys are mad about her?

MONA   Well, sir, the fact is Dolly isn't much concerned with mere boys. They bore her.

HUMBERT   What about that Roy what's-his-name?

MONA   Oh, him.

A languorous shrug.

HUMBERT   What do you think of Dolly?

MONA   Oh, she's a swell kid.

HUMBERT   Is she very frank with you?

MONA   Oh, she's a doll.

HUMBERT   I mean, I suppose you and she——

Lolita runs into the room.

MONA   Dolly, your piano lesson is today. Remember? Not Monday. I came to fetch you as we agreed. Remember?

HUMBERT   Eight o'clock punctually, Lolita.

The two girls leave.

CUT TO:

The School Auditorium
A gauze curtain has just come down and the young performers are taking a last bow. Quilty's pudgy hands are briefly seen meatily clapping, as Lolita dreamily smiles across the footlights. Vivian Darkbloom, darkly blooming, blows her a kiss. The applause gradually subsides.

CUT TO:

Backstage
An atmosphere of exuberant success. Miss King, the piano teacher, greets tuxedo-clad Humbert.

HUMBERT   Glad to see you, Miss Emperor.

MISS KING   King.

HUMBERT   Yes, of course. Miss King. A thousand excuses. I keep thinking of the piano teacher in *Madame Bovary*. Well, I must thank you for giving Lolita so much time.

MISS KING   So much time? Why, on the contrary, she seems to have been much too busy with rehearsals. Let me see: she must have missed at least four lessons.

Lolita emerges from the greenroom. She is glamorous. She is excited. She has not yet shed her wings.

LOLITA   (*to Humbert*) You can go home now. Mona is taking me to her aunt's place for refreshments.

HUMBERT   You're coming with me. Home. At once.

LOLITA   I've promised Mona. Oh, please!

HUMBERT   No.

LOLITA   I'll do anything if you let me go.

HUMBERT   No.

LOLITA   I love you.

HUMBERT   Love me? With that lethal hate in those painted eyes? No, my girl, you'll come home and practice the piano.

He grasps her by the hand. A struggle would be indecorous. Exeunt.

CUT TO:

Car

It pulls up. Humbert and Lolita come out in front of their house. Lolita attempts to move away.

HUMBERT   Where are you going? Come here.

LOLITA   I want to ride my bike. I need some fresh air, you brute.

HUMBERT   You're coming in with me.

LOLITA   For Christ's sake——

CUT TO:

Hallway

HUMBERT   I know you are unfaithful to me. There's a tangled web around me. But I will not surrender. You cannot torment me like that. I have a right to know, I have a right to struggle.

LOLITA   Finished?

HUMBERT   And that's all you can answer?

LOLITA   If you've finished, I'll get something to eat. You cheated me out of a luscious supper.

CUT TO:

The Kitchen
Lolita has finished her sandwich and is messily fishing out slippery peach halves from a can. Humbert, throbbing with rage, makes himself a drink. She eats, reading a comic book and scratching her calf.

HUMBERT   What a fool—what a fool, this Humbert! Giving little Lolita numberless humbertless opportunities! Dreamy bicycle rides, sunsets, lovers' lanes, piano lessons, rehearsals, ditches, garages, coal sheds.

Lolita, having finished her meal, walks to the door.

CUT TO:

Living Room
Lolita sprawling in an overstuffed chair. She bites at a hangnail and mocks Humbert with her heartless eyes. She has placed one outstretched shoeless foot in coarse white sock on a stool which she rocks with heel and toe.

LOLITA   Well, speak, lover.

Humbert paces the room rubbing his cheek with his fist in a tremor of exasperation.

LOLITA   Because, if you don't want to speak to me, in a couple of minutes, I'll go riding my bicycle.

Humbert sinks down in a chair facing her. She continues to stare at him and to rock the stool.

HUMBERT   I doubt you'll be using your bicycle much longer now.

LOLITA   Oh, yah?

He controls himself and tries to speak calmly but in the course of his speech his voice gradually rises to a hysterical pitch. And the window is open with the lilacs listening.

HUMBERT   Dolores, this must stop right away. You are ruining our relationship and jeopardizing your own safety. I don't know, nor wish to know, what young hoodlum, Roy or Foy, you are dating in secret. But all this must stop or else anything may happen.

LOLITA   Anything may happen, huh?

He snatches away the stool she is toe-heel rocking, and her foot falls with a thud.

LOLITA   Hey, take it easy!

Humbert grabs her by her thin wrist as she attempts to run out of the room.

HUMBERT   No, you'll listen to me! I'll break your wrist, but you'll listen. Tomorrow—yes tomorrow—we'll leave, we'll go to Mexico, we'll start a completely new life.

She manages to twist out of his grip and runs out of the house.

Humbert rushes out into the street and sees her pedaling townward. With one hand pressed to his palpitating heart, he makes for the corner, and then continues to the familiar drugstore. In the lamplight her bicycle, self-conscious and demure, is leaning against a post. Humbert enters the drugstore. At its far end, Lolita is revealed through the glass of a telephone booth, a little mermaid in a tank. She is still speaking. To whom? Me? Cupping the tube, confidentially hunched over it, she slits her eyes at Humbert, hangs up, and walks out of the booth.

LOLITA   (*brightly*) Tried to reach you at home.

HUMBERT   You did? That's odd. I saw you speaking, I saw
    your lips move.

LOLITA   Yes, I got the wrong number. Look, I don't want
    you to be mad at me any more. Everything is going to
    be all right from now on. I've reached a great decision.

HUMBERT   Oh, Lolita. If only I could still believe you.

She smiles at him and straddles her bike.

Thayer Street, leading home
A glistening night. Along the damp pavement Lolita half-rides
her bike, pushing against the curb with one foot, waiting for
Humbert to catch up, and then propelling herself again. He
walks behind, agitated, moist-eyed, jerkily trying to keep up
with her. A dog strains on its leash, and its owner allows it to
sniff at a lamppost. The CAMERA follows Humbert and Lolita
as they approach the house. Lilacs in bloom. The neighbor's
lighted window goes out.

CUT TO:

Hallway. Lolita and Humbert enter

LOLITA   Carry me upstairs. I feel kind of romantic tonight.

He gathers her up. The telephone rings.

LOLITA   (*raising her index finger*) Telephone.

HUMBERT   Oh, let it ring!

LOLITA   Put me down, put me down. Never disappoint a
    telephone.

HUMBERT   My aphoristic darling! All right.

On the telephone Quilty speaks in a disguised muffled croak-
voice.

QUILTY   How are you, Prof?

HUMBERT   Fine. May I——

QUILTY   Sorry to disturb you at such a late hour. Are you
    enjoying your stay at Beardsley?

HUMBERT   Yes. May I inquire who's calling?

QUILTY   This is the best time of the year but we might do with some rain.

HUMBERT   Sorry—who's calling?

QUILTY   (*with a pleasant laugh*) We haven't actually met but I've been keeping a friendly eye on you. Could I talk to you on the phone for a minute?

HUMBERT   Are you connected with the college?

QUILTY   In a way. I am a kind of extramural student. You see, I am studying your case.

HUMBERT   What case? I don't understand.

QUILTY   Is Dolores in bed?

HUMBERT   Oh, that's what it is. Are you disguising your voice, Roy Walker?

QUILTY   No, no. You are mistaken.

HUMBERT   Well, all I can tell you is that neither she nor I welcomes calls from strangers.

QUILTY   (*very suavely*) This is a complete misunderstanding. The group I represent is merely anxious that children should not keep late hours. You see, Mr. Humbert, I am a private member of the Public Welfare Board.

HUMBERT   What's your name?

QUILTY   Oh, it's an obscure unremarkable name. My department, sir, wants to check some bizarre rumors concerning the relationship between you and that pretty child. We have certain plans for her. We know an elderly gentleman, a bachelor of independent means, who would be eager to adopt her.

In the course of this speech Humbert takes a pillbox out of his waistcoat and swallows a tablet.

HUMBERT   This is ridiculous.

QUILTY   Have you adopted her? Legally, I mean?

HUMBERT   Well, I——

QUILTY   Have you filed a petition? Your stutter proclaims you have not.

HUMBERT   I assume that a stepfather is a relative and that a relative is a natural guardian.

QUILTY   Are you aware that the word "natural" has rather sinister connotations?

HUMBERT   Not in my case, no.

QUILTY   But you agree that a minor female must have a guardian?

HUMBERT   I suppose so.

QUILTY   And that she is not merely a pet?

HUMBERT   I really——

QUILTY   You moved here from Ramsdale, Professor?

HUMBERT   That's right. But——

In the meantime Lolita has crept into the hallway and enlaced Humbert with her bare arm.

QUILTY   Are you aware that some states prohibit a guardian from changing the ward's residence without an order of the court?

HUMBERT   Which states?

QUILTY   For example, the state you are in: a state of morbid excitement. Have you seen your psychiatrist lately?

HUMBERT   I neither have nor need one.

QUILTY   You are classified in our files as a white widowed male. Are you prepared to give our investigator a report on your present sex life, if any?

HUMBERT   Investigator?

Humbert nervously strokes caressive Lolita's wrist.

QUILTY   Yes. We intend our Dr. Blanche Schwarzman, a
    very efficient lady, to visit you at your convenience.

HUMBERT   I'm afraid I have nothing to tell her.

QUILTY   "Afraid" is Freudian lingo.

HUMBERT   I do not follow you. Give me your address and
    I shall write you.

QUILTY   That's unnecessary. After tomorrow our doctor
    will examine you and your protégée. I now hang up.

DISSOLVE TO:

Living Room
Humbert walking about nervously.

HUMBERT   It's a hoax. It's a hoax. But that's immaterial.
    Rumors, he said. Oh, *mon Dieu!*

LOLITA   We must go away.

HUMBERT   We must flee as in an old melodrama. Our
    safest bet is to go abroad.

LOLITA   Okay—let's go to Mexico. I was conceived there.

HUMBERT   I'm sure I'll find a lecturing job there. Marvel-
    ous! I know a Spanish poet in Mexico City. He is full
    of black bulls and symbols, and as corny as a matador.
    But he is influential.

LOLITA   One condition. This time *I* am going to trace out
    our route. I want to take in Arizona. I want to see the
    Indian dances in Elphinstone.

HUMBERT   (*weeping*) I'm in your hands, your hot little
    hands, my love.

It is assumed that from Beardsley (which is situated in Idaho)
to the Mexican border (via Arizona) the distance is at least
1,000 miles. Our fugitives start Wednesday morning. Humbert, who is eager to reach with the least delay Borderton, S.
Arizona (and thence, Mexico's West Coast Highway) intends
to be there Friday morning. In a naive effort to be inconspicuous he plans to sleep two nights in the car (the first, within

the parking area of a trailer court and the second, somewhere in the Arizona desert). It is further assumed that Quilty, using three or four different rented cars, so as to avoid identification and confuse his victim, pursues Humbert from Idaho, through Nevada (or Utah), to Arizona. Quilty's plan is to have Humbert transport the minor female across two state lines down to Elphinstone, Arizona, where he will kidnap her and take her to his ranch in that vicinity. During the journey, there arises the problem how to get Lolita's luggage out of the car. This is attempted at the stop in Wace, Thursday morning (and successfully brought off on the following Monday, with the unplanned help of Lolita's hospitalization). The glimpses Humbert has had of Quilty before (e.g., in Briceland and Beardsley) had been too casual and brief to allow recognition. Quilty takes care to remain a fleet shadow, a ghostly predator, as he keeps up with Humbert on the road, now overtaking him, now awaiting his passage. Humbert's anxiety and rage are increased by his not quite knowing if it is a sleuth or a suitor.

CUT TO:

Humbert's Eyes in the Rearview Mirror
He and Lolita are driving along a canyon into the small burg of Cottonwood: three poplars and alfalfa fields.

LOLITA   We'll crash into something if you keep looking back.

HUMBERT   What a bizarre situation!

LOLITA   You're telling me. I've been riding with a nut all day.

HUMBERT   —bizarre because there's no general way of dealing with this kind of case. That car has been following us, on and off, for the last two hundred miles. I can't very well complain to the highway patrol.

LOLITA   (*laughing*) You certainly can't!

HUMBERT   But I can try to give him the slip.

LOLITA   Not with this jalopy.

HUMBERT   (*going through a changing light in Cottonwood*)
Ah, the red light will stop him.

LOLITA   You'll get arrested if you do that.

HUMBERT   And here we'll turn and hide for a minute. In
this nice little lane.

LOLITA   It's a one-way little lane.

HUMBERT   True.

He backs out.

LOLITA   Besides it's illegal to play games with other cars
on the road.

HUMBERT   Will you stop chattering. I almost hit that van.

LOLITA   Look. Let's get back to the highway and just ignore the whole business.

CUT TO:

*The Highway Again—evening of the same day—low blinding
sun*
Lolita is eating a banana in the moving car.

CUT TO:

Service Station
Needing a pair of new sunglasses, Humbert leaves Lolita in
the car and walks into the office of the station. His pursuer
quietly pulls up just across the street while Humbert is selecting the glasses. He glances through a side window.

CUT TO:

Humbert's Car
Quilty has walked up to it and Lolita is leaning out and talking
to him rapidly, her hand with outspread fingers going up and
down, as it does when she is very serious and emphatic. Humbert is struck by the voluble familiarity of her manner. The
conversation is not heard (except, perhaps, for the word
"Elphinstone"), and Quilty's face is not seen. He bolts back
to his convertible, which disappears as Humbert comes out
of the office.

CUT TO:

Humbert's Car moving up a steep grade

HUMBERT   What did that man ask you, Lo?

LOLITA   (*studying a road map*) Man? Oh, that man. Oh, yes. Oh, I don't know. He wondered if I had a map. Lost his way, I guess.

A pause.

HUMBERT   Now listen, Lo. I don't know if you are lying or not. I don't know if you are insane or not—but that person has been following us all day, and I think he is a cop.

LOLITA   (*laughing*) If he's really a cop the worst thing we could do would be to show that we are scared. Oh, look: all the nines are changing into the next thousand. When I was a little kid I used to think they'd stop and go back to nines if only my mother would agree to back the car.

CUT TO:

Market

HUMBERT   Let me see—we wanted——

He broods among the fruit, a rotting Priap, listening to a melon, questioning a peach, pushing his wire cart toward the lacquered strawberries. Lolita has been loitering near the window where the magazine rack is. She sees Quilty haunting the sidewalk. Satisfying herself that Humbert is engrossed in his shopping, she slips out. Presently, burdened with his cornucopian paper bag, Humbert comes out of the store looking around for Lolita. He leaves the bag in the parked car, locks it again, and then paces the sidewalk peering into various shops as he proceeds along a series of Drugs, Real Estate, Auto Parts, Café, Sporting Goods, Real Estate, Furniture, Drugs, Western Union, Cleaners, Appliances, Betty's Beauty Parlor. As he walks back, in pain and panic, he suddenly descries her trying to retrieve her new coat and traveling case out of the car; but the doors are locked, and she can't pull out her things through the three-quarters closed window

(Quilty the shadow is ambushed in a side street, the idea being that she join him with some of her treasured possessions). She notices Humbert approaching—and, slitting her eyes, walks toward him with feigned nonchalance.

LOLITA   Oh, there you are.

For a few seconds Humbert looks at her in grim silence.

LOLITA   What's the matter?

HUMBERT   You were gone twenty minutes. I cannot tolerate these vanishing acts. I want to know exactly where you've been—and with whom.

LOLITA   I ran into a girl friend.

HUMBERT   Really?

LOLITA   You calling me a liar?

HUMBERT   Her name, please.

LOLITA   Oh, just a kid I went to school with.

HUMBERT   Beardsley School?

LOLITA   Yes. Oh, yes. Beardsley.

HUMBERT   Her name?

LOLITA   Betty. Betty Parker.

HUMBERT   Perfect. Here, in this little black book, Volume 2, I have a list of your schoolmates. Let's see. Hm. There's a Mary Paddington, and a Julia Pierce. But no Parker. What say you?

LOLITA   She was not in my group.

HUMBERT   That's the entire school I have listed here.

LOLITA   She enrolled just before we left.

HUMBERT   Well, let's try another angle. Where exactly did you meet her?

LOLITA   Oh, I saw her from the grocery. She was just loafing around like me.

HUMBERT   And what did you do next?

LOLITA   We went to a drugstore.

HUMBERT   And you had there——?

LOLITA   Couple of Cokes.

HUMBERT   Careful, my girl. We can check that, you know.

LOLITA   At least, she had. I had a glass of water.

HUMBERT   The anonymous fluid. I see. Very good. Was it that place over there?

LOLITA   Sure.

HUMBERT   Good. Come on, we'll grill the soda jerk.

LOLITA   Wait a sec. Come to think, it might have been the other store, on the corner.

HUMBERT   Confrontation delayed. But it's all right. We'll try both.

LOLITA   Or perhaps in one of the side streets.

HUMBERT   We'll find it. Here, let's go into this telephone booth. You rather like telephone booths, don't you? Now, let's consult the directory. This dirty book. This chained and battered book. Dignified Funeral Service. No, we don't need that yet. Here we are. Druggists, Retail. Hill Drug Store. Corner Drug Store. Cypress Lane Drugs. And Larkin's Pharmacy. Well, that's all they have around here. And we'll check them one by one.

LOLITA   Go to hell.

HUMBERT   My dear, rudeness will get you nowhere.

LOLITA   You are not going to trap me. Okay. So we didn't have a pop. We just talked and walked, and looked at dresses in show windows.

HUMBERT   That window, for example?

LOLITA   Yes, that window for example.

HUMBERT   Oh, Lolita! Let us look closer at it.

CUT TO:

The Show Window of a dress store
A man, on his hands and knees, is rearranging the carpet on which a wedding group stands in a more or less dismantled state ("as if a blast had just worked havoc with them"): one wigless and armless figure is naked except for white spats. Another, a sexless little nude, stands in a smirking pose, with a posy, and would represent, when clothed, a flower girl of Lolita's size. The taller, lavishly veiled bride is complete but lacks one arm. On the floor, where the employee crawls, there lies a cluster of three bare arms and a blond wig. Two of the arms, not necessarily a pair, happen to be twisted and seem to suggest a clasping gesture of horror and supplication. Humbert, tense and bitter, his face twitching, points out these details to sullen Lolita.

HUMBERT   Look, Lolita. Look well. Isn't this a gruesome symbol of something or other? Doesn't it make your delicate flesh creep a little?

CUT TO:

A Highway, low sun, Shadow of Car running and fluctuating on a rock bank—a Sign:
ELPHINSTONE 20 M.
Lolita is ill. She covers her eyes with her hand, throws her head back, moans.

HUMBERT   Tired?

She does not respond.

HUMBERT   Would you like me to stop? You might nap for an hour or two.

She shrugs her shoulders.

HUMBERT   Don't you feel well?

LOLITA   I feel utterly rotten.

HUMBERT   Why, what's the matter, my darling? Tummy?

LOLITA   Everything. I want to stop at Elphinstone for the night.

HUMBERT   Oh, but we'll never make Borderton at this
rate.

LOLITA   I'm dying, you dope. We'll spend the night in
Elphinstone.

HUMBERT   I wanted to avoid motels.

LOLITA   Well, this time we'll go to the best one in Elphinstone. I underlined it in the AAA book. Dream Hacienda. Oh, I've never felt so awful in all my life! You're
sitting on my sweater.

HUMBERT   My poor darling! What a setback. Tsk-tsk. I
know what we'll do. At the next turnout I'll take your
temperature. I have a thermometer in my overnight bag.

CUT TO:

Turnout—a sheer cliff rising on the far side of the highway
and a misty abyss melting just beyond the rim of the turnout.
Lolita, her head on the nape rest, eyes closed, endures the
thermometer stuck in her mouth. The CAMERA gingerly inspects the litter receptacles with their cans and containers, and
a small child's sneaker forgotten on the stone parapet. Humbert consulting his wristwatch.

HUMBERT   Well, I think we can peep now.

Tenderly he removes the glass tube from her mouth. She licks
her parched lips and shivers. Humbert tries to make out the
level of the mercury.

HUMBERT   These tricky American thermometers are meant
to conceal their information from the layman. Ah, here
we are. Good God, one hundred and three. I must take
you straight to a hospital.

Quilty has pulled up at the next turnout.

CUT TO:

Dream Hacienda Motel at Elphinstone, Arizona—a fine
morning
Humbert is seen coming out of his unit with several books

under his arm and a bunch of rather straggly wild flowers. The landlady talks to him as he goes to his car.

LANDLADY   I hope she's much better today.

HUMBERT   Well, I'm driving over to see. The doctor said that in this kind of flu there's a distinct drop in temperature on the fourth day, and indeed she had hardly any fever yesterday.

LANDLADY   She'll love the flowers.

HUMBERT   I picked them in the ravine at the back of your place. Cold breeze today. Is it the elevation?

LANDLADY   Oh, it's hot enough for me.

HUMBERT   I'm not feeling well. Guess I'll lie down when I return.

LANDLADY   Wait a minute. I'll remove this basket of linen so you can turn more easily.

CUT TO:

A Sunny Private Room in the Elphinstone Hospital
Lolita, looking happy and innocent, lies in her neat bed with a magazine, her lips freshly painted, her hair brilliantly brushed. There is a white telephone, a topaz ring, and one rose in a glass with bubble-gemmed stem on the bedside table. Mary Lore, a plump, comely, arrogant young nurse who is in cahoots with the nymphet, is folding very rapidly a white flannel blanket as Humbert enters with his pathetic bouquet and books.

HUMBERT   *Bonjour, mon petit.*

LOLITA   What gruesome funeral flowers. Thanks all the same. But do you mind cutting out the French, it annoys everybody.

Her eyes go back to her magazine.

HUMBERT   Temperature normal? Well, that's splendid. Who gave you that rose?

LOLITA   Mary.

MARY LORE   (*glancing window-ward at the yard below*)
You can't park there, Mister. You have to go around to
the other end.

HUMBERT   Sorry. I was in a hurry—and I don't feel too
well.

MARY   There is a sign saying "staff only."

HUMBERT   All right, all right.

Exit Mary with blanket.

LOLITA   Mary was trying to be helpful.

HUMBERT   Mary is arrogant and nosy. I would not wonder, my dear, if you two had swapped every kind of
crummy confession. That rump of hers must make in-
terns pant.

LOLITA   Your English is showing vahst improvement, my
deah. You'll be using delinquent lingo next.

A pause.

HUMBERT   I brought you some rather fascinating books:
The History of Dancing. The Romantic Poets by my friend
Professor Behr. *Flowers of the Rockies*, with excellent illustrations. And *Carmen* by Mérimée—not a very good
translation, I'm afraid, but do read it, it's a marvelous
melancholy story.

Lolita emits a grunt of indifferent gratitude and continues to
consume her magazine. Mary Lore bustles in again.

HUMBERT   (*picking up a pair of sunglasses from the top of
a chest of drawers*) Oh—whose are these? Not mine, not
yours.

MARY   (*after exchanging a quick glance with Lolita*) Then
it's a visitor left them.

HUMBERT   Visitor? You had a visitor, Lolita?

MARY   (*pocketing the glasses*) Another patient had. I found
them in the corridor and thought they might be yours.

HUMBERT   *Est-ce que tu ne m'aimes plus, ma Carmen?* My
    Carmen does not love me any more?

LOLITA   There we go again.

She flips through her magazine, finds the continuation, and
reads on.

HUMBERT   The thermometer broke in the glove compart-
    ment but I took my pulse this morning and it was one
    hundred and ten. I shall soon leave you and go to bed.
    Don't you want to look at the nice books I brought you?

Lolita emits again her neutral grunt and picks her nose as she
plunges deeper into "They called me a Harlot." Humbert
lowers himself into a cretonne chair, opens the botanical work
he has brought her, and attempts to identify his flowers. This
proves impossible.

HUMBERT   (*with a sigh*) I'll be going away in a minute.
    I'm not feeling well at all. Don't you want to talk to
    me?

LOLITA   What?

HUMBERT   I said don't you want to talk to me? You'll read
    your magazine when I'm gone.

LOLITA   What do you want me to tell you?

Mary Lore reenters with a vase for the flowers.

HUMBERT   I'm wondering if you should not leave the hos-
    pital tomorrow. You look the image of radiant health.

MARY   She will stay till Tuesday. Doctor's orders. Horse
    mint, poison oak. And this goldenrod will give her hay
    fever.

HUMBERT   Oh, throw them out, throw them out.

MARY   Yes, I think I had better remove them.

She exits.

HUMBERT   Lolita! My love! Just think—Tuesday if we start
    early we'll be in Mexico by noon. No mysterious agents,

no ghosts, no ghouls will follow us any longer. We shall be free to live as we like, my Lolita. I'll make you a formal proposal. An old priest will bless us, and we shall live happily forever after, in lovely Rosamorada.

Both realize that Mary Lore is again in the room.

LOLITA   He's reciting poetry. Don't mind him, Mary.

HUMBERT   Yes, poetry. The only reality on this earth. Well, I'll be on my way.

LOLITA   I want all my things. The brown bag, mother's blue one, the car sack, everything.

HUMBERT   They are still in the car. I did not take them to the motel.

LOLITA   Well, I want them right now.

HUMBERT   Couldn't you wait till Tuesday? I mean, you don't want *all* your frocks immediately.

LOLITA   That's for me to decide. Where's that hand mirror, Mary?

HUMBERT   I don't feel strong enough to carry all that luggage.

MARY   Oh, we'll have Joe do it, don't you worry.

HUMBERT   All right. I think I'll go now. Well, good-bye, Lolita.

LOLITA   (*looking at herself in the hand mirror*) Bye-bye.

HUMBERT   Girl with a Hand Glass. Artist unknown.

He considers her, softly swinging the car keys he holds. Mary waits at the door.

CUT TO:

Motel Room
Humbert is asleep asprawl on one of the twin beds. He is in the throes of a virus infection and has been drinking freely from the bottle of gin beside him. The bedside telephone rings. It takes him some time to come out of his sick slumber.

VOICE   Hi there, Professor.

HUMBERT   Who's calling?

VOICE   Are you all right?

HUMBERT   Not exactly.

VOICE   Not feeling too good, eh?

HUMBERT   No. Who is it?

VOICE   Not enjoying your trip? That's too bad.

HUMBERT   What d'you want?

VOICE   I'm not sure what to call it. Cooperation? Surrender to fate?

HUMBERT   All right. If you are not a hallucination, not a mere tinnitus——

VOICE   A *what*?

HUMBERT   Tinnitus—a singing in the ears, because I have a high fever——

VOICE   Frankly, I'm also nursing some sort of bug. Guess, we both caught it from her.

HUMBERT   From her? What d'you mean?

VOICE   Oh, lots of things are feminine—cars, carpets, car pets, haha! I've even heard a fireman refer to a fire as she.

HUMBERT   If you're not my delirium——

VOICE   Skip it. Look, Bertie, I just wanted to make sure you're safe in bed. Good-nitus.

HUMBERT   If I'm not fancying things, then you must be the person who's been following me.

VOICE   Well, that's all finished now. You're not followed any more. I'll be leaving in a minute with my little niece. (Aside: You stay out of this.)

HUMBERT   Wait!

VOICE   Good-nitus, good-nitus. (*with a laugh*) I know ex-
     actly what you'll do as soon as I hang up.

He hangs up. Humbert frantically searches for the scrap of
paper on which he has jotted down the telephone number
connecting him with Lolita at the hospital. Finds it and dials.
A nurse's voice answers, but is engulfed in Quilty's rich
baritone.

VOICE   I'll take it. It's for me. Well, isn't that pat. I told
     you I knew you would do it. Sorry I can't talk now.
     She's in my lap and quite lively.

Hangs up guffawing.
     Humbert is about to dial again—but thinks better of it and
in a frenzy of horror and hurry pulls on some clothes and
stumbles out.

CUT TO:

The Vestibule of Elphinstone Hospital—a spacious lobby with a
     staircase on either side and offices at the farther end.
There are several people around. Joking Joe, a robust male
nurse, is in the act of wheeling a mummylike patient out of
the elevator. Nurse Mary Lore is preening herself on the first
landing. Doctor Blue is coming out of the x-ray department
perusing a cloudy picture, the galaxy of a lung. Two old men
in a corner are playing chess, and a third old-timer is inspecting the titles of several books (*Flowers of the Rockies*, etc.)
heaped on a chair. As Humbert rushes in and launches into
his dramatic, drunken, sick, hysterical expostulations, the various people around freeze in various positions.

HUMBERT   Lolita! Lolita! Lolita!

MARY LORE   (*tripping down the steps*) We don't want a
     scene——

HUMBERT   Where is she?

MARY   You know perfectly well that her uncle was to come
     for her today.

HUMBERT   I know nothing of the sort.

DR. BLUE   Take it easy. What's the matter, Mary?

MARY   He's sick and doesn't know what he's saying. The girl's uncle just took her away.

HUMBERT   It's a hellish conspiracy.

MARY   She warned me her stepfather had a feud with the rest of the family.

HUMBERT   A hellish lie! Where is she? I demand an answer.

DR. BLUE   Now, now, don't get excited.

Humbert tries to get hold of Mary Lore. He almost manages to clutch her. She gives a melodious yelp and twists free. The patient, who has been wheeled out by Joe, rises like Lazarus and joins Joe and Dr. Blue who are subduing Humbert.

CUT TO:

Psychiatrist
speaking (this is Dr. Ray who appears in the Prologue and will appear again at the very end of Act Three):

PSYCHIATRIST   As we now know from his notes, Humbert Humbert spent many a dismal month trying in vain to locate his lost Lolita and to establish the identity of her mysterious abductor. His quest merely resulted in impairing his health. At the sanatorium where he was treated for a heart condition, attention was also given to his mental state. The present speaker and two other psychiatrists endeavored to help Mr. Humbert but dissimulation had become second nature with him. My assistants and I tried to open channels of communication for the patient by providing a background of refinement and ease, soft music, amusing hobbies, and a permissive atmosphere in which he might dare express his most dangerous thoughts. However, the patient not only refused to indulge in voluptuous or vengeful fantasies, but insulted the therapist by calling him "the rapist of Psyche the Soul." He sneered at cooperation. He was abusive, he was taciturn. And Dr. Christina Fine, a lovely lady and a very strong analyst, complained that the patient kept trying to hypnotize her and make her divulge her innermost cravings. I am happy to say she is now my wife.

By the beginning of the following year, the patient's physical condition had improved so much that he was able to check out and join again the faculty of Beardsley College.

CUT TO:

A Neutral Place
The detective whom Humbert had hired to look for Lolita is reporting to him for the last time.

DETECTIVE   I'm afraid we'll have to give it up.

HUMBERT   Couldn't you go on? You said you would investigate the New Mexico clue.

DETECTIVE   Proved a dud. Dolores Hayes, H, A, Y, E, S, is a fat old dame selling homemade Tokay to the Indians.

HUMBERT   What about Canada?

DETECTIVE   What about the wide world? She might be a model in Brazil or a dancer in Paris.

HUMBERT   But isn't it merely a question of time? Can't *everybody* be tracked down finally?

DETECTIVE   Look, mister. We don't even have good pictures of her, she's just a kid in them. By now she may have three babies of her own.

HUMBERT   You are sure you could not keep trying?

DETECTIVE   It would just mean taking your money.

HUMBERT   I want the photos back.

DETECTIVE   We'll keep one or two in our files just in case. This one, in fancy dress, for instance.

He returns a number of photographs to Humbert. They should give a brief pictorial summary of Lolita's past life with him: Kneeling, half-naked, in a patch of sun on a mat; stand-

ing beside her mother on the dappled lawn; attending a school
ball in full-skirted flamingo dress; in blue jeans and T-shirt,
sprawling with a comic book; in dirty shorts, getting into a
canoe (Charlie handing her a paddle from the bushy bank);
in the passenger seat of Humbert's car; feeding a chipmunk;
riding a pony; wearing black tights; in fancy dress on the stage.

CUT TO:

Beardsley College
Men and women students are seen streaming out into a courtyard. Humbert, with books and papers under his arm, walks
to the parking lot. Mrs. Fowler, a lean, elegant, forty-year-old
flirt, the wife of the Head of the Department, calls out to
Humbert from inside her car.

MRS. FOWLER   Hullo, Humbert.

HUMBERT   Hullo, Diana.

MRS. FOWLER   Do you know if my husband is through
    with his seminar?

HUMBERT   Yes, I think I saw him going to his office.

MRS. FOWLER   He said he would finish a little earlier. We
    are to pick up a niece of mine at the airport. The poor
    kid lost her mother last year, and now her father has
    cancer.

HUMBERT   Oh.

MRS. FOWLER   I am so sorry for the child. We'll take her
    to the Riviera in spring. When is *your* sabbatical,
    Humbert?

HUMBERT   Alas, I've been here only two years.

He stands leaning with his elbows on the sill of her car. She
puts her hand on his.

MRS. FOWLER   You must come to see us more often. Frank
    will be away on a lecture tour next month, and I will be
    very lonesome. Would you teach me chess? I think it's
    such a glamorous medieval game.

Frank Fowler comes up.

MRS. FOWLER   (*to her husband*) I was telling Humbert we
     must get together soon.

FOWLER   Yah. What about Sunday? Come have dinner
     with us.

CUT TO:

The Fowlers' Living Room
Bourgeois abstract art on the walls. They are having preprandial drinks with their guests. Frank Fowler gulps down the
contents of a tall tumbler.

FOWLER   (*to Humbert*) Another Scotch? Well, I think I
     shall.

MRS. FOWLER   No, Frank, that's enough before dinner.

FOWLER   How does it feel to be a bachelor, Humbert?
     Must be a heavenly sensation.

HUMBERT   I was twice married.

MRS. FOWLER   Oh, were you?

HUMBERT   My second wife died four years ago. I inherited
     a stepdaughter.

MRS. FOWLER   But that's fascinating, Humbert. How old
     is she?

HUMBERT   Oh, she must be quite old by now. More than
     seventeen. She's living her own life somewhere. I've lost
     track of her.

A nymphet comes in.

MRS. FOWLER   This is Nina, my niece.

In the course of the following dialogue Humbert pays no attention to the child, and only at the last moment, as she turns
away, and he sinks back into his chair with a tidbit picked
from a remote plate, does he permit himself one brief, sad,
ember-hot, tiger-quick glance.

MRS. FOWLER   When is Rosemary coming to fetch you?

NINA   I dunno. Soon, I guess.

MRS. FOWLER   What picture are you going to see?

NINA   Oh, some western. I don't care.

MRS. FOWLER   (*smiling*) Okay. Run along.

Nina indolently leaves.

MRS. FOWLER   She is twelve and in her blasé period, if you please.

FOWLER   I think I'll spank her if she perseveres in that droopy style.

MRS. FOWLER   Oh, she'll be all right after we take her to Europe.

FOWLER   What's your vacation going to be, Humbert, m'boy?

HUMBERT   I have no definite plans.

FOWLER   Come with us to Cap Topaz. It's the best spot on the Riviera.

HUMBERT   I know it well. My father owned a big hotel not far from there. The Mirana. It has degenerated now into an apartment house.

MRS. FOWLER   Will you come, Humbert? We'll gamble at the casino.

HUMBERT   I dare not gamble any more.

MRS. FOWLER   Well, Frank and I will, and you can sprawl on the *plage*, and build sand castles with Nina. Is that a deal? Will you come?

HUMBERT   What again? The old pang? The perilous magic? No. I'm not coming with you. The excitement would be too much. I have a weak heart, you know.

MAID   Dinner is served.

CUT TO:

An Exchange of Good Nights

on the lighted steps of the Fowler home. Humbert walks off. His steps resound on the deserted sidewalk.

HUMBERT   I'm very lonely and I'm very drunk. The old magic. Kill Frank Fowler, marry Diana, drown Diana, inherit Nina, kill self. Oh, my Lolita, Lolita, Lolita. . . .

Next Day.

CUT TO:

Lecture Hall
Humbert has just finished his routine lecture and is collecting his notes. A male student comes up to the lectern.

STUDENT   I've been auditing your lectures, Professor. My name is Shatzki, Norbert Shatzki, you had my sister in your class three years ago, she sends you her kindest regards.

HUMBERT   Oh yes. Yes.

SHATZKI   She's married now. I was wondering, sir, if you would also cover Edgar Poe's other loves?

In the meantime, another student, a girl, has entered the classroom.

GIRL   May I audit your lectures, Professor Humbert?

HUMBERT   (*absentmindedly, paying little attention to either of them, still collecting his notes*) If you like. No, I'll ignore his other romances.

GIRL   I'm taking philosophy, but I hope to enroll in your courses next year.

HUMBERT   Yes. Yes.

He is now ready to leave.

GIRL   I see you don't recognize me at all, at all, monsieur.

HUMBERT   Good God—Mona!

MONA   It has been three years since we met. Time certainly flies.

HUMBERT   Let's walk across the campus and have some coffee at The Den.

MONA   I'm afraid I have a class in ten minutes.

HUMBERT   Well, let's go to my office. It's right opposite.

CUT TO:

Humbert's Office

HUMBERT   Three long years . . .

MONA   You don't live on Thayer Street any more?

HUMBERT   Oh no. I've a room in Clemm Hall. And you—how have you been?

MONA   Oh, fine. I left Beardsley School at the same time as—as—anyway, I mean, I never finished Beardsley School.

HUMBERT   I see.

MONA   Your temples are a little gray, which is most becoming.

HUMBERT   You don't ask me an obvious question, Mona.

MONA   Sorry. Have you remarried, sir?

HUMBERT   You haven't changed. Evasive Mona, strange girl.

MONA   I'm not strange. I merely know life rather well. Okay: how's Lolita?

HUMBERT   She's attending a school, a kind of junior college in Europe.

MONA   Oh, so it's true. That's what one of your colleagues told me. What college exactly?

HUMBERT   You would not know it. A small college in Paris.

MONA   Oh.

A pause.

HUMBERT   Old schoolmates seldom write to each other—isn't that so?

MONA   It depends.

HUMBERT   Naturally. Well, let's chat—let's reminisce, as Americans say. Why do you look at me like that?

MONA   Mr. Humbert . . . My parents sent me to Europe, too; I, too, went to school in Paris. It's odd that I never ran into Dolly.

HUMBERT   She never gave you her address, did she?

MONA   Oh, I knew you were still teaching in Beardsley. I could always reach her through you, couldn't I?

HUMBERT   But you didn't.

MONA   Well, no.

HUMBERT   And you completely lost track of her?

MONA   Why don't you give me her address?

HUMBERT   It's hardly worth while: she'll be leaving next week. As a matter of fact, she may be already in this country.

MONA   You are still very fond of your stepdaughter, sir?

HUMBERT   Still? What do you mean—"still"?

MONA   Everybody loves a child, but the child grows up, and something fades, something diminishes.

HUMBERT   Philosophy major.

MONA   But isn't it true? Or would you say that nothing changes?

HUMBERT   Nothing.

MONA   And you'd still be ready to forgive——?

HUMBERT   Forgive? Forgive what?

MONA   We are taking a purely abstract case. Assuming she had done something wrong——

HUMBERT   Mona, will you stop acting the impenetrable vamp?

MONA   Why, everything is crystal clear now. I'm very fond of Dolly, and it's such a comfort to know that you always intend to be kind to her.

HUMBERT   Did she write you? Please, tell me.

MONA   Doesn't she write to *you*?

HUMBERT   She's a poor correspondent—but that's not the point.

MONA   Oh, the point is clear, sir. I'm afraid I must be going now.

HUMBERT   She did write you? You *do* know where she is?

MONA   In those faraway schools we were talking about, in those schools one can be very unhappy, their lamps are dim, but one learns a good deal. I'm sure you needn't worry about our Dolly. I've got a class now.

The bell violently rings announcing the beginning of the next class period.

It should now have been established that Mona has had a letter from Lolita, apparently asking her to find out if it is safe for her, Lolita, to write to Humbert.

CUT TO:

University Post Office—The time is 8:55 a.m.
Professor Fowler takes out his letters. Humbert comes up and tweaks open *his* pigeonhole.

PROFESSOR FOWLER   If your mail is as dull as mine, I'm sorry for you, Humbert.

HUMBERT   I never expect anything—that's my advantage. This is a circular. This is from a Mrs. Richard Schiller— some graduate student, I presume. This is a fenestrated bill. This is a publisher's list. And this is not for me but for Professor Humphries.

FOWLER   Not gay, as the French say.

HUMBERT   Well, I must be rushing to my exam. Room
342,
                         (*repeats*)
342.

                              CUT TO:

The Door with That Number
He stares at it for a moment.

HUMBERT   How strange.

                              CUT TO:

A Large Classroom
The questions have been handed out by a monitor, and the
examination is under way. Humbert from his lectern morosely
observes the bent heads. A crew-cut footballer shoots up an
arm, and then buoyantly walks up to the lectern.

FOOTBALLER   It says here, "How did Poe define the Poetic
     Sentiment?" Do you want us to give a general answer,
     or actually quote the poem?

HUMBERT   I don't think there is any specific poem
     implied.

FOOTBALLER   (*utterly at his wit's end but with optimism
     unshattered*) I see. Thank you, sir.

He buoyantly walks back to his seat. Humbert, sitting at the
lectern, takes his mail out of his pocket and scans it. The monitor turns to the blackboard to write on it "9:10." The footballer, gratefully but mutely, receives from his neighbor a
secret note which reads "Poetry is the sentiment of intellectual
happiness." The letter that Humbert has opened begins talking to him in a small, matter-of-fact, agonizingly familiar,
voice:

LOLITA'S VOICE   Dear Daddy, how's everything? I'm mar-
     ried. I'm Mrs. Richard Schiller. I'm going to have a
     baby. I guess he's going to be a big one. I guess this is
     a hard letter to write. I'm going nuts because we don't
     have enough to pay our debts and get out of here. Dick
     is promised a big job in Alaska, in his specialized corner

of the mechanical field. That's all I'm told about it but it's really grand. Please, do send us a check, Dad. We could manage with three or four hundred, or even less. Anything is welcome. I have gone through much sadness and hardship. Your expecting Dolly (Mrs. Richard F. Schiller).

Most of the students having filled a bluebook page in the same number of minutes simultaneously turn it, which makes a brief whistling rustle.

Humbert has risen from his chair, dazed and unstable. He leaves the room followed by all eyes.

CUT TO:

Coalmont—a bleak foggy town

CUT TO:

Hunter Road—a dismal district
all dump and ditch, and wormy vegetable garden. Clapboard shacks line the wasteland. An old man is shoveling mud by the roadside. Humbert speaks to him from his car.

HUMBERT   Would you know if the Schillers live around here?

OLD MAN   (*pointing*) It's the fourth house after the junkyard.

CUT TO:

Humbert
driving up to the fourth house. Sounds of hammering and of two male voices exchanging loud but indistinct comments come from the back of the shack. Humbert turns off the motor and for a few seconds sits motionless. A shaggy dog with a muddy belly comes out and woofs. Humbert fingers his pistol, transfers it to a handier pocket, gets out of the car, slamming the door.

DOG   (*perfunctorily*) Woof.

Humbert presses the bell button, keeping one hand in his pocket.

DOG   Woof, woof.

A rush and a shuffle—the door explodes—and Lolita stands
on the threshold. She wears glasses. She has a new heaped-up
hairdo, new bare ears. She is frankly pregnant. Her pale arms
and neck are bare. But neither the maternity dress nor the
sloppy felt slippers can disguise her Botticellian grace.

LOLITA   (*after a pause, exhaling with all the emphasis of
    wonder and welcome*) We-e-ll!

HUMBERT   (*in a croaking voice*) Husband home?

LOLITA   Come on in.

She lets him pass, crucifying herself against the open door.

LOLITA   (*to the dog*) No, you stay here.

CUT TO:

*A Small, Shabby, Meagerly Furnished Parlor with the connubial
    bed disguised as a couch*
Lolita, emitting interrogatory "hm's," makes familiar Javanese
gestures with her wrists, offering her guest a choice between
the couch and the rocker. He chooses the latter.

LOLITA   Dick's mending the back porch with a pal. I'll call
    him.

She goes out. "Dick!" Dick and a friend come lumbering in.
Humbert's hand comes empty out of his trouser pocket. How
disappointing!

LOLITA   (*in a resounding violent voice*) Dick, this is my
    stepfather, Professor Humbert.

DICK   How do you do, Professor.

LOLITA   (*to Humbert*) Dick is very deaf. Speak loud, please.
    Oh, and this is our kind neighbor, Bill Crest.

BILL   Glad to meet you, Prof.

LOLITA   This calls for a celebration. I'll get some
    refreshments.

BILL   Let me help you, Dolly.

They go out. Humbert sits in a rocker, Dick on the edge of the couch. He wears overalls, has a shock of dark hair, a nice boyish face. He needs a shave and a hearing aid.

DICK   This is a grand surprise, Professor. Hope you're here to stay. You'll have this couch.

Humbert shakes his head.

DICK   No trouble. We can sleep on a spare mattress in the kitchen.

HUMBERT   I'm on a lecturing tour . . .

Lolita and Bill have reentered.

LOLITA   (*very loud*) He's on a lecturing tour. He chanced to visit this town. I wrote him to look us up.

DICK   (*nodding sagely*) I see, I see.

There is a pause. Beer is quaffed. Nobody knows what to say. Lolita greedily crunches potato chips. Bill signals to Dick.

DICK   Well
                    (*slapping his knees and rising*)
I guess you two have a lot to talk about. Come along, Bill. Back to work.
                    (*to Lolita*)
You just holler, sweetheart, when it's time for K.P.

HUMBERT   That's not the fellow I want.

LOLITA   Not *who*?

HUMBERT   You know very well. Where is the swine you eloped with?

LOLITA   (*inclining her head to one side and shaking it in that position*) Look, you are not going to bring that up.

HUMBERT   I certainly am. Three years—during three years I've been trying to find him. Who is he? Where is he?

LOLITA   I should never have written you. Oh, it was a great mistake. Now you are going to spoil everything.

HUMBERT   Could your husband give me that information?

LOLITA   (*blazing and bristling*) Leave out Dick! See? Leave
out my poor Dick. He does not know a thing about the
whole mess. He thinks I ran away from an upper-class
home just to wash dishes in a diner. Why should you
make things harder by raking up all that muck?

HUMBERT   Be a sensible girl—if you expect help from me.
Come, his name!

LOLITA   (*Half turns away, fumbling for something on a
crowded table.*) I thought you had guessed long ago.
     (*with a mischievous and melancholy smile*)
It's such a sensational name. You would never believe. . . . I can hardly believe it myself—and there's no
one I can brag to about it.

HUMBERT   His name, please.

LOLITA   Skip it. It does not matter now. Want a cigarette?

HUMBERT   No. His name.

LOLITA   (*Lights up, shakes her head firmly*) It's too late now
to raise hell.

HUMBERT   All right. I'm afraid I must be on my way. Regards to your husband. Nice to have seen you.

LOLITA   Oh, you are so silly to insist. I really should not
tell you. On the other hand—do you want to know it
that badly? Well, it was——

Softly, confidentially, arching her thin eyebrows and puckering
her parched lips, with a note of fastidious, not untender,
mockery, she emits in a kind of muted whistle, the name:

LOLITA   —Quilty.

Humbert regards her with stupefaction.

LOLITA   Yes, Clare Quilty, the playwright. Oh, you must
have seen his face lots of times in those cigarette ads!
And he was staying at that cute hotel at Briceland—
remember? And he wrote that play we chose for the
Beardsley School show. And he came to rehearsals. And
he followed our car in that absurd fashion for miles and

miles. Do you know the word "cynic"? Well, that sums him up—a bold laughing cynic. Yes, that's him all over. Clare Quilty. The only man I was ever crazy about.

HUMBERT   There is also Dick.

LOLITA   Oh, Dick is a lamb. We are very happy together. I meant something quite different.

HUMBERT   And *I*? I have never counted, of course?

Lolita considers him for a moment as if trying to grasp the tedious and confusing fact that Humbert had been her lover. That poor romance is dismissed by her like a dull party, a gray picnic, a raindrop of boredom.

He manages to jerk his knee out of the range of a sketchy tap—one of her acquired gestures.

LOLITA   Don't be dense. The past is the past. You've been a good stepdaddy, I guess. Watch your step, Daddy— remember that joke?

HUMBERT   No, that must have been after my time. Where can I find him?

LOLITA   Clare Quilty? Oh, what does it matter? Up in Parkington, I guess. He's got a house there, a regular old castle.
      (*Gropes and rummages in a pile of magazines
          on the lower shelf of a console.*)
There was a picture of it somewhere.
      (*Pulls out a bedraggled issue of* Glance.)
Yes, here it is.

The magazine opens in her slender hands revealing a photograph of Pavor Manor as shown in the first shot of the Prologue. She says with a deep sigh:

LOLITA   This world is just one wild gag after another. If somebody wrote up my life nobody would believe it.

She directs the dart of her cigarette toward the hearth, index rapidly tapping as her mother used to do. Lolita had never smoked under Humbert the Terrible.

HUMBERT   No. I suppose not. Well, let's recapitulate. So it was in Beardsley that you betrayed me.

LOLITA   Betrayed? No. In fact, Cue—everybody called him Cue, you know—Cue was very understanding and sympathetic toward you. You must not tell anybody but many years ago he actually was questioned once by the police about some kid who had complained. So you see you were among friends. Oh, he knew everything about you and me, and it tickled him no end.

She smiles, exhales smoke, shakes her head, darts her cigarette.

LOLITA   You know—that guy saw through everything and everybody. He was not like you or me—he was a genius. He had an Oriental philosophy of life. He believed in Life. Oh, he was—wonderful. Funny—I speak of him in the past as though we were all dead.

HUMBERT   Where exactly did he take you when you gave me the slip?

LOLITA   Yes, that was awfully mean, I must admit that. He took me to a dude ranch near Elphinstone. Duk-Duk Ranch. Silly name.

HUMBERT   Where exactly? What highway?

LOLITA   No highway—a dirt road up a small mountain. Anyway—that ranch does not exist any more. Pity, because it was really something. I mean you can't imagine how utterly lush it was, that ranch, I mean it had everything, but everything, even an indoor waterfall. You know when Cue and I first came the others had us actually go through a coronation ceremony.

HUMBERT   The others? Who were *they*?

LOLITA   Oh, just a bunch of wild kids, and a couple of fat old nudists. And at first everything was just perfect. I was there like a princess, and Cue was to take me to Hollywood, and make a big star of me, and all that. But somehow nothing came of it. And, instead, I was supposed to cooperate with the others in making filthy movies while Cue was gadding about the Lord knows where. Well, when he came back I told him I wanted *him* and not that crowd of perverts, and we had a fight, and he kicked me out, and that's all.

HUMBERT   You could have come back to me.

LOLITA   (*smile, shrug*) Oh, well. . . . I suppose I was afraid you'd kill me. And anyway I was a big girl now, on my own. So—I worked in motels, cleaning up and that sort of job, and in roadside cafés. And then after a year I could not stand it any longer, and thumbed my way back to the place where the ranch should have been. But it just was not there any more, it had burned down completely. So strange.
(*Smokes meditatively.*)
Well, I drifted back to cheap diners, and one day on the highway Dick picked me up, and we both were lonesome, and so it began.

She closes her eyes leaning back on the cushions of the couch, her belly up, one felted foot on the floor.
"I knew all I wanted to know. I had no intention of torturing my darling. Somewhere, beyond the shack, an afterwork radio had begun singing of folly and fate, and there she was with her ruined looks, and her adult rope-veined hands, there she was, my Lolita, hopelessly worn at seventeen—and I looked and looked, and knew that I loved her more than anything I had ever seen, or imagined, or hoped for. . . . She was only the dead-leaf echo of my nymphet—but thank God it was not that echo alone that I worshipped. I loved my Lolita, *this* Lolita, pale and polluted, and big with another's child, but still gray-eyed, still sooty-lashed, still auburn and almond, still Carmencita, still mine. 'Changeons de vie ma Carmen, allons vivre quelque part où nous ne serons jamais séparés' [this is a quotation from Mérimée's novel], no matter, even if those eyes of hers would fade to myopic fish, and her nipples swell and crack—even then I would go mad with tenderness at the mere sight of your dear worn face, at the mere sound of your raucous young voice, my Lolita."

HUMBERT   Lolita, this may be neither here nor there, but I have to say it. Life is very short. From here to that old car there are twenty-five paces. Make them. Now. Right now. Come just as you are. Take that plate of peanuts with you. And we shall live happily ever after.

LOLITA   You mean you'll give us some money only *if*? Only if I go to a motel with you? Is *that* what you mean?

HUMBERT   No, you got it all wrong. I want you to leave your incidental Dick, and this awful hole, and come to live with me, and die with me, and everything with me, eternally. . . .

LOLITA   (*her features working*) You're crazy.

HUMBERT   Think it over, Lolita. I'll wait for any length of time if you want to think. There are no strings attached—except that—well, that a life would be spared. But even if you refuse to come you shall still get your dowry.

LOLITA   No kidding?

HUMBERT   Here. Here's three, four hundred in cash—and here's a check for nine thousand six hundred.

Gingerly, uncertainly, Lolita takes the money, and speaks with agonized emphasis.

LOLITA   You mean you are giving us ten thousand bucks?

He covers his face and breaks into tears. They trickle through his fingers down his chin, his nose is clogged, he can't stop. He gropes for a handkerchief. She touches his wrist. He draws back abruptly.

HUMBERT   I'll die if you touch me. You are sure that you are not coming with me? Is there no hope of your ever coming?

LOLITA   No, honey, no.

His shoulders heave. She provides him with a paper napkin.

LOLITA   No, it's quite out of the question. I'd sooner go
back to Quilty. I mean——

HUMBERT   I know. *He* broke your heart. I merely broke
your life.

LOLITA   Oh, but everything is so wonderful now. I think
it's so utterly grand of you to give us all that dough. It
settles everything. We can pay all our debts. We can fly
to Alaska tomorrow. Stop crying, please. You should understand. Let me get you some more beer. Oh, don't
cry. I'm so sorry I cheated so much—but that's the way
things are.

He wipes his face. She smiles at the money.

LOLITA   (*exulting*) May I call Dick?

HUMBERT   No, no. Please don't. I don't want to see him
at all. I must leave in a moment.

LOLITA   Oh, don't go yet.

HUMBERT   I love you and this is sheer torture. By the
way—about these money matters. There'll be more
coming. I must go now.

LOLITA   It has been nice——

HUMBERT   All right, all right.
              (*evading her hand*)
Yes, good-bye, I have a piece of very important business
to take care of. A ragged, raw, horrible piece.

                    CUT TO:

The Front Porch
A remote sound of voices and hammering comes from the
back of the house. The song "Lolita, Lolita, Lolita" is repeated. Lolita and the shaggy dog see Humbert off.

LOLITA   What do you know—the same old car.

HUMBERT   One last word. Are you quite, quite sure that—
well, not tomorrow of course, and not after-tomorrow,

but some day, any day—you'd not come to live with me?
I'll create a brand-new God and thank him with piercing
cries, if you give me that small hope.

Lolita smiles, shakes her head in smiling negation.

HUMBERT   It would have made all the difference.

He hurries toward the car.

LOLITA   Good-bye. There's a bad storm coming.

HUMBERT   What?

LOLITA   A storm. Take care of yourself.

Her cry and the sound of the motor attract Bill followed by
Dick, as Humbert drives off, with the old shaggy dog loping
heavily alongside the car, and soon giving up. We dissolve
briefly to Lolita's delirious cry of joy and to Dick's incredulous
stare at the gift she brandishes.

CUT TO:

Desolate Road—Storm brewing
Humbert drives off, but a little way down the road, stops and
weeps uncontrollably, slumped over the wheel, with the windshield wipers vainly warring against a cloudburst.

A NARRATIONAL VOICE (DR. RAY'S)   Poor Lolita died in
childbed a few weeks later, giving birth to a stillborn
girl, in Gray Star, a settlement in the remote Northwest.
She never learned that Humbert finally tracked down
Clare Quilty and killed him. Nor did Humbert know of
Lolita's death when shortly before his own dissolution
he wrote in prison these last words of his tragic life's
story:

HUMBERT'S VOICE   (*clear and firm*) . . . While the blood
still throbs through my writing hand, you are still as
much part of blest matter as I am. I can still talk to you
and make you live in the minds of later generations. I'm
thinking of aurochs and angels, the secret of durable

pigments, prophetic sonnets, the refuge of art. And this
is the only immortality you and I may share, my Lolita.

THE END

VLADIMIR NABOKOV
Revised December 1973   *Summer 1960*
Montreux   *Los Angeles*

CHRONOLOGY

NOTE ON THE TEXTS

NOTES

Chronology

1899   Born Vladimir Vladimirovich Nabokov on April 23 (April 10 Old Style) at 47 Bolshaya Morskaya Street in St. Petersburg, first child of Vladimir Dmitrievich Nabokov, b. 1870, and Elena Ivanovna Nabokov, b. 1876. Christened in Orthodox ceremony in late spring. Father is a lecturer in criminal law at the Imperial School of Jurisprudence, and an editor of the liberal law journal *Pravo*. Family lives in plush Morskaya Street home with many servants and spends summer on the three neighboring estates of Rozhdestveno and Vyra (maternal grandfather's) and Batovo (paternal grandmother's), about 50 miles south of St. Petersburg. (Grandfather Dmitri Nikolaevich Nabokov, b. 1826, married Baroness Maria Ferdinandovna von Korff, b. 1842, in 1859. Grandfather became a member of the State Council and served as a liberal minister of justice from 1878 to 1885. Grandfather Ivan Vasilievich Rukavishnikov, b. 1841, a wealthy landowner and magistrate, married Olga Nikolaevna Kozlov, b. 1845, a daughter of the first president of the Royal Academy of Medicine. Mother was privately tutored in the natural sciences by a university professor. Parents were married in November 1897 and had a stillborn son in 1898.)

1900   Brother Sergey born in March. Nabokov speaks, and learns numbers, at an early age.

1901   Grandfather Rukavishnikov dies in March and grandmother Rukavishnikov dies in June, both of cancer. Mother inherits Vyra estate and uncle Vasiliy "Ruka" Rukavishnikov inherits Rozhdestveno. Doctors advise mother to go abroad for her health, and she takes Nabokov and Sergey to Pau and Biarritz in the south of France (father remains in St. Petersburg to teach).

1902   Nabokov and Sergey learn English from Rachel Home, first of a succession of British governesses. Spends summers at Vyra, enjoying the company of both sides of large extended family whose estates dot the area. Mother tells him to remember details they admire on walks in country, and reads him fairy tales and adventure stories in English at bedtime.

1903   Sister Olga born in January (brothers and sisters will be reared separately within household; Nabokov remains the favorite of parents). Father becomes a member of the St. Petersburg City Duma (council). After major pogrom at Kishinev in April, he writes article for *Pravo* charging government with tacitly encouraging pogroms. Family travels abroad in autumn and visits grandfather Nabokov, now senile, in Nice. In St. Petersburg Nabokov toboggans and takes long walks with new English governess; reads English juvenile magazines *Chatterbox* and *Little Folks* (has not yet learned to read Russian).

1904   Japan attacks Russia in February. Attends opera, which he does not enjoy, and theater with parents. Plays chess and cards with family. Grandfather Nabokov dies on March 28 in St. Petersburg. Father takes family to Rome and Naples for three weeks and then Beaulieu for the summer; there Nabokov falls in love with a Romanian girl. Family returns in fall to Russia, where setbacks in the Russo-Japanese War have increased pressure for political reform. Father plays active role in first national congress of zemstvos (local assemblies); congress, whose final session is held in the Nabokov home, calls for a written constitution, a national legislative assembly, and guaranteed civil rights, and effectively launches the 1905 (or First) Russian Revolution. Father, told his political activities are incompatible with his post at the Imperial School of Jurisprudence, resigns.

1905   Tsarist troops fire on a peaceful demonstration in St. Petersburg on January 22 ("Bloody Sunday"), killing more than a hundred people. Father denounces killings in the St. Petersburg Duma and is deprived of his court title. Advised to remove family from strife, father takes them in February to Abbazia (now Opatija, Croatia), where they stay with paternal aunt Natalia de Peterson and family. Nabokov misses Vyra and nostalgically traces details of the estate on his pillow with his finger. Father called back in October to Russia, where general strike spreads throughout country. Father goes to Moscow for founding sessions of Constitutional Democratic (CD) party; remainder of family moves to Wiesbaden, where Nabokov becomes friends with his cousin, Baron Yuri Rausch von Traubenburg, son of paternal aunt Nina.

1906   Family returns to Russia, but remains at Vyra through winter. Swiss governess Cécile Miauton arrives (she will be part of the household for seven years). Miauton tutors Nabokov and Sergey in mornings and in afternoons reads children her favorite French novels, poetry, and stories, beginning with Corneille and Hugo. Nabokov soon becomes fluent in French and memorizes passages from Racine. Sister Elena is born in March. Father, as leading speaker of the CDs, the largest party in the First State Duma, challenges Chief Minister Ivan Goremykin's rejection of the Duma's reform program in May: "Let the executive power submit to the legislative!" Nabokov is now taught to read and write in Russian over the summer by the village schoolmaster, Vasily Zhernosekov, a Socialist Revolutionary. Begins to catch butterflies (lepidopterology will become a lifelong passion). After Duma is unexpectedly dissolved by Tsar Nicholas II in July, father signs Vyborg manifesto (calling populace to civil disobedience) in protest and is stripped of his political rights; he becomes editor of *Rech'*, St. Petersburg's leading liberal daily and unofficial CD newspaper.

1907   Has severe bout of pneumonia, and loses his prodigious capacity for mathematical calculation. Studies books on Lepidoptera and specimens brought by mother while convalescing. Begins regular lessons with a succession of Russian-speaking tutors. Studies drawing and painting and learns tennis and boxing. Family travels to Biarritz in August, where Nabokov falls in love with Serbian girl, Zina.

1908   Father serves three-month prison sentence for signing Vyborg manifesto. Nabokov masters the known butterflies of Europe. Is permitted to stop going to church after telling father that he finds services boring.

1909   Sees father stop to chat with Leo Tolstoy during a walk. Becomes infatuated and spends much time with nine-year-old girl, Claude Deprès, during fall vacation at Biarritz. Though he still enjoys English juvenile magazines and *Punch*, Nabokov reads widely in his father's library, which contains 10,000 volumes. Early favorites include Jules Verne, Conan Doyle, Kipling, Conrad, Chesterton, Wilde, Pushkin, and Tolstoy.

1910   Continues friendship with cousin Yuri; they provoke each
            other to repeated tests of courage. Translates into French
            alexandrines Mayne Reid's *The Headless Horseman*, rears
            caterpillars, keeps notes in English on the butterflies he
            collects, reads entomological journals, and "dreams" his
            way through A. Seitz's *Macrolepidoptera of the World*. Af-
            ter fall family vacation in Germany, Nabokov and Sergey
            stay in Berlin with tutor for three months while under-
            going orthodontic work; reads Tolstoy's *Voyna i mir* (*War
            and Peace*).

1911   Begins classes at elite but liberal Tenishev School, helped
            in studies by tutors at home. Rankles at conformity of
            school life but copes easily with courses, which include
            history, geography, geometry, algebra, physics, chemistry,
            Russian, French, German, Scripture, and woodworking.
            Plays soccer, always as goalkeeper. Closest school friends
            are Samuil Rosov and Samuil Kyandzhuntsev. Brother
            Kirill is born in June. Father publicly challenges editor
            of conservative newspaper to duel for personal insult in
            October; Nabokov, in agony of apprehension, imagines
            father's death, but an apology averts the duel.

1912–13   Miauton returns to Switzerland. Nabokov begins two
            years of drawing lessons with leading St. Petersburg artist
            Mstislav Dobuzhinsky (who will later call him his most
            hopeless pupil). Begins reading new Symbolist, Acmeist,
            and Futurist poetry along with works of Pushkin, Poe,
            Browning, Keats, Verlaine, Rimbaud, Gogol, Chekhov,
            Dostoevsky, Shakespeare, Tolstoy, Flaubert, and William
            James.

1914   H. G. Wells, whose work Nabokov admires, dines at Na-
            bokovs' home during his tour of Russia. School report in
            spring describes Nabokov: "zealous football-player, excel-
            lent worker, respected as comrade of both flanks (Rosov-
            Popov), always modest, serious and restrained (though not
            adverse to a joke), Nabokov creates a most agreeable im-
            pression by his moral decency." Composes what he later
            calls his first poem in July and becomes prey to "the numb
            fury of versemaking." Germany declares war on Russia
            August 1; father, a reserve officer, is called up on August
            3 and leaves with his regiment for Vyborg while mother

volunteers as nurse in hospital for wounded soldiers. Nabokov continues to write poetry almost daily. Evgenia Hofeld, governess for Elena and Olga, arrives (will remain with family for many years and become closest companion of mother in her last years).

1915   Confined to bed with typhus in early summer. After recovering, begins love affair with Valentina "Lyussya" Shulgin, who is vacationing with her family near Vyra; writes many love poems to her. Father is transferred in September to the General Staff in Petrograd (as capital has been renamed). Nabokov is taught Russian literature by poet and critic Vladimir Gippius, whose verse he likes but whose pressure towards social concern he resists. Often skips classes throughout school year to meet with Lyussya. Smokes heavily. In November co-edits the school journal *Yunaya mysl'* (*Young Thought*), which contains his first publication, poem "Osen'" ("Autumn"). Translates Alfred de Musset's "La Nuit de décembre," dedicating it to Lyussya.

1916   Translation of "La Nuit de décembre" appears in *Yunaya mysl'*. Publishes at own expense *Stikhi* (*Poems*), collection of 68 love poems; another poem appears in leading literary journal *Vestnik Evropy* in July. Sees cousin Yuri, now in the army. Uncle "Ruka" Rukavishnikov dies in France in fall, leaving Nabokov 2,000-acre Rozhdestveno estate and manor. Is compelled to take extra lessons, having received "not satisfactory" grade in algebra at end of spring term. Affair with Lyussya ends and Nabokov begins what he later describes as "an extravagant phase of sentiment and sensuality." By end of year he is conducting affairs with three married women, including his cousin Tatiana Segerkranz, Yuri's 27-year-old sister.

1917   Sick with pneumonia, then measles. While recuperating at Imatra resort in Finland in January, begins romance with Eva Lubryjinksa. In Petrograd on March 12 soldiers refuse to fire on demonstrators and then mutiny, leading to the collapse of the Tsarist regime. Father becomes head of chancellery in the first Provisional Government. Nabokov has his appendix removed in May; writes "Dozhd' proletel" (later translated as "The Rain Has Flown"), the earliest poem he will include in his collected poems. Selects verses he will publish with schoolmate Andrey Balashov in *Dva puti* (*Two Paths*; printed 1918). Begins album of verses dedicated to Eva Lubryjinksa. Bolsheviks seize power in Petrograd in coup on November 7. Father sends family to Gaspra, estate outside Yalta in the Crimea, before being imprisoned by Bolsheviks for five days in December; after his release, he joins family in Crimea. Nabokov plays chess with him nightly and composes his first chess problems.

1918   After the Bolsheviks seize the Yalta area in late January, father adopts "disguise" of medical doctor. Nabokov writes first short verse play, "Vesnoy" ("In Spring"). German army occupies Crimea in April. Father begins to write his memoir *The Provisional Government*. Nabokov hunts butterflies, sees Yuri while he is on leave in Yalta. Family moves to Livadia, nearer Yalta, so that Sergey, Olga, and Elena can attend school. Nabokov studies Latin with tutor, continues writing poetry; publishes two poems in CD newspaper *Yaltinsky golos*. Meets poet Maximilian Voloshin, who suggests reading Andrey Bely on metrical patterns in Russian verse. Applies Bely's method to classics of Russian poetry and his own works; finds his poems metrically featureless and for about a year constructs his new verse to yield arresting Belian diagrams. Tutors favorite sister, Elena. After German troops withdraw in November, father becomes minister of justice in the Crimean Provisional Regional Government, civilian regime organized by CDs and Tatars.

1919   Writes "Dvoe" ("The Two"), 430-line riposte to Aleksandr Blok's "Dvenadstat" ("The Twelve"). Considers enlisting in White Army commanded by General Anton Denikin when cousin Yuri visits. Yuri is killed in battle soon after returning to the front; Nabokov serves as a pallbearer at his funeral in Yalta on March 14. Red Army begins advance into Crimea on April 3. Family sails from Sebastopol on April 15 aboard Greek freighter and arrives in Athens on April 23, then goes in late May to London, where they rent house in South Kensington with money from sale of mother's jewels. Nabokov spends time with other Russian emigrés including old schoolmate Samuil Rosov; renews romance with Eva Lubryjinksa. Enters Trinity College, Cambridge, on partial scholarship, in October. Studies Modern and Medieval Languages (French and Russian) and Natural Sciences (zoology). Shares room with Russian emigré Mikhail Kalashnikov. Writes poetry in Russian and plays goal for Trinity soccer team. Buys Dahl's four-volume Russian dictionary and reads in it every night, jotting down verbal finds. Writes first entomological paper, "A Few Notes on Crimean Lepidoptera" (published in *Entomologist*, Feb. 1920). Also reads Housman, Rupert Brooke, and Walter de la Mare and writes a few English poems.

1920   Spends time with brother Sergey, now at Christ's College, Cambridge, and becomes friends with Prince Nikita Romanov. Drops zoology to leave time for verse, women, soccer. Family moves to Berlin and father helps found liberal daily emigré newspaper *Rul'* (*The Rudder*). Nabokov receives advance from emigré publishing house Slovo for Russian translation of Romain Rolland's *Colas Breugnon*. Moves into lodgings next to Trinity with Kalashnikov in October. Argues with George Wells, son of H. G. Wells, about politics. Poem "Remembrance" published in *The English Review* (November).

1921   Three poems and story "Nezhit'" (later translated as "The Wood-Sprite") appear in *Rul'* on January 7 under name Vladimir Sirin, pseudonym adopted to distinguish himself from father (Nabokov will retain the Sirin pseudonym for his Russian writings into the 1960s). Begins regular contributions to *Rul'* of poems, plays, stories, chess problems, crossword puzzles, and reviews. Completes *Nikolka Persik*, translation of *Colas Breugnon* (published Nov. 1922). Spends summer in Berlin, where he falls in love with Svetlana Siewert, Kalashnikov's cousin. Visitors to family's house in Wilmersdorf include poet Sasha Chorny, Iosif Hessen, head of Slovo, cousin Nicolas Nabokov, Konstantin Stanislavsky, and actors from Stanislavsky's Moscow Art Theater. Returns to Cambridge and becomes friend of Count Robert de Calry, English student of Russian ancestry. During winter ski trip to Switzerland with de Calry visits Cécile Miauton in Lausanne.

1922   Father is shot and killed on March 28 while struggling with one of the monarchist gunmen attempting to assassinate fellow CD leader Pavel Milyukov. Nabokov attends funeral in Tegel, near Berlin, then returns to Cambridge to study for exams. Writes mother: "At times it's all so oppressive I could go out of my mind—but I have to hide. There are things and feelings no one will ever find out." Graduates with second-class honors B.A. degree in June. Returns to Berlin and becomes engaged to Svetlana Siewert. Takes job in bank but leaves after three hours. Receives advance of $5 from Gamayun publishers to translate *Alice's Adventures in Wonderland*. With several writers including friends Gleb Struve and Ivan Lukash, forms literary circle they name Bratstvo kruglogo stola (Brotherhood of the Round Table). *Grozd'* (*The Cluster*), collection of poems written 1921 to 1922, published by Gamayun in December.

1923   *Gorniy put'* (*Empyrean Path*), collection of poems written 1918 to 1921, published by Grani in January. Engagement to Svetlana is broken off by her parents, who object to Nabokov's not having steady job. *Anya v strane chudes* (translation of *Alice's Adventures in Wonderland*) published by Gamayun in March. At masquerade charity ball on May 8 Nabokov meets Véra Evseevna Slonim (b. 1902), formerly of St. Petersburg, daughter of a Russian Jewish emigré businessman. Works briefly as film extra, then for three months as agricultural laborer in south of France; writes verse plays. Returns in August to Berlin where he courts Véra Slonim; begins writing stories regularly. Hoping that theatrical work will earn more money, writes sketches with his good friend Ivan Lukash. Mother goes with Elena and Olga to find apartment in Prague, where she is eligible for a pension. Nabokov takes Kirill and Hofeld to join them in December; while in Prague, writes five-act verse play *Tragediya gospodina Morna* (*The Tragedy of Mr. Morn*; still unpublished). Evsey Slonim's businesses fail in hyperinflation.

1924   Meets Russian poet Marina Tsvetaeva. Returns to Berlin and takes room at 21 Lutherstrasse. Pantomime "Voda zhivaya" ("Living Water"), written with Lukash, is performed at emigré cabaret for more than a month. As center of Russian emigration shifts to Paris, Nabokov remains in Berlin (later attributes decision in part to his fear that his Russian would atrophy if he lived in a country whose language he knew well). Becomes engaged to Véra and begins to earn living tutoring in English, French, tennis, and boxing (tutoring will be his major source of income until 1929 and continue sporadically until 1941). Works on scenarios for cabarets and theater alone or with Lukash. Publishes nine stories in emigré journals and newspapers and begins contributing poems, chess problems, and crossword puzzles to new *Rul'* Sunday supplement, *Nash mir* (*Our World*).

1925   Marries Véra in civil ceremony on April 15. Nabokov acts as private tutor to two Russian Jewish schoolboys; he has them read and discuss Proust and Joyce's *Ulysses.* Increased income allows him to send more money to his mother. Often visits with Slonim family. Takes Véra to meet his family in Prague in August; they go to Konstanz, Germany, for a week before returning to Berlin, where they move into two rooms at 31 Motzstrasse. Writes novel *Mashen'ka* (later translated as *Mary*), September–November. Joins literary club organized by Raisa Tatarinov and critic Yuli Aykhenvald (will remain a member and contribute talks until 1933). Publishes six stories during year.

1926   Forms close friendships with George Hessen, son of *Rul'* editor Iosif Hessen, and Mikhail Kaminka, son of his father's CD and publishing colleague and best friend, Avgust Kaminka. Gives reading of *Mashen'ka* at local literary club where Aykhenvald proclaims: "A new Turgenev has appeared"; novel is published by Slovo in March to good reviews. Writes play *Chelovek iz SSSR* (later translated as *The Man from the USSR*) for new emigré Group Theater. Continues publishing stories. Composes 882-line Pushkinian poem, "Universitetskaya poema."

1927   *Chelovek iz SSSR*, performed in April, is well received. Poem "Bilet" (*Rul'*, June 26), about returning to a Russia freed from Communism, is printed in *Pravda* on July 17 along with a reply by Soviet poet Demyan Bedny ("Bilet" will be Nabokov's only work published in the Soviet Union in his lifetime). Has idea for *Korol', dama, valet* (later translated as *King, Queen, Knave*) while acting as chaperone with Véra for three boys at Baltic beach of Binz in summer. Goes with Véra to Misdroy, Germany, where he hunts moths; on return to Berlin they move into rented rooms at 12 Passauer Strasse. Nabokov becomes poetry reviewer for *Rul'*; continues publishing stories and poems, doing some translations with Véra, giving readings, and tutoring, though he has fewer pupils.

1928   Signs agreement in March with major newspaper *Vossische Zeitung* for serialization in German of *Mashen'ka*. With Véra begins attending Poets' Club, whose members include Raïsa Blokh and Vladimir Korvin-Piotrovsky. Véra's father dies in June and her mother dies in August; Véra takes job as secretary in French embassy to pay their medical bills. *Korol', dama, valet* (written January–June) published by Slovo in September to good reviews. Sells German rights to Ullstein publishing company for 7,500 marks. Aykhenvald, the first major critic to hail Nabokov, is killed by a streetcar as he returns from party at the Nabokovs' on December 16.

1929   Goes with Véra to the Pyrenees, February–June, where he hunts butterflies and begins novel *Zashchita Luzhina* (later translated as *The Defense*). Buys a small lakefront property in Kolberg with Anna Feigin, Véra's cousin; completes novel there in August and it is serialized in *Sovremennye zapiski* (*Contemporary Annals*), leading emigré literary review published in Paris, October 1929–April 1930. (All Nabokov's remaining Russian novels will be published serially in the journal, which pays better than emigré book publishers.) Moves with Véra into furnished rooms at 27 Luitpoldstrasse. *Vozvrashchenie Chorba* (*The Return of Chorb*), collection of stories and poems, published in December by Slovo.

1930   Completes novella *Soglyadatay* (later translated as *The Eye*) in February. Begins novel *Podvig* (later translated as *Glory*) in May; later that month goes to Prague, where he visits his family, counsels Kirill on his poetry, and gives public readings. Economic depression in Germany causes further decline in numbers of Berlin emigré community and viability of *Rul'*, but Nabokov's publication in *Sovremennye zapiski* provokes high praise from some writers like Vladislav Khodasevich and Nina Berberova, and attacks from others, like Georgy Adamovich and Georgy Ivanov, associated with new rival journal *Chisla* (*Numbers*). Véra takes job as secretary in a firm of German Jewish lawyers. *Zashchita Luzhina* is published as book in September and

Soglyadatay appears in *Sovremennye zapiski* in November. Completes *Podvig*.

1931   Writes novel *Kamera obskura* (later translated as *Camera Obscura* and as *Laughter in the Dark*) between January and May. *Podvig* is serialized in *Sovremennye zapiski* (Feb. 1931–Jan. 1932). Writes "Les Écrivains et l'époque" (*Le Mois*, June–July), his first French article. Continues publishing stories. *Rul'* fails in October. Joins soccer team of Russian sports club as goalkeeper.

1932   Writes appeal for assistance for the unemployed in emigré paper *Poslednie novosti* (*The Latest News*). In severe financial straits, Nabokov and Véra take a room in a crowded family apartment on 29 Westfälische Strasse. Meets Hollywood director Sergey Bertenson, a Russian emigré; offers him *Kamera obskura* but Bertenson pronounces it unsuitable for filming. Visits family in Prague; is delighted with nephew Rostislav Petkevitch, infant son of sister Olga. *Kamera obskura* appears in *Sovremennye zapiski* (May 1932–May 1933). Writes first draft of *Otchayanie* (later translated as *Despair*) between June and September. Moves with Véra into apartment of Anna Feigin on 22 Nestorstrasse in the Wilmersdorf district in July. Travels to Paris in fall where he gives highly successful public reading and explores opportunities for work. Sees brother Sergey and cousin Nicolas Nabokov, who live in France. Meets Vladislav Khodasevich, Nina Berberova, Mark Aldanov, Jean Paulhan, Gabriel Marcel, and Jules Supervielle. Visits with *Sovremennye zapiski* editors. Completes *Otchayanie*. Gives reading in Antwerp before returning to Berlin. *Podvig* is published in book form in November by Sovremennye zapiski.

1933   Adolf Hitler is appointed chancellor of Germany on January 30. Nabokov begins gathering materials on Nikolay Chernyshevsky and on Russian naturalist-explorers of Central Asia for projected novel *Dar* (later translated as *The Gift*). Is sick with neuralgia intercostalis for most of winter. Véra loses her secretarial job when law firm is forced to close in March and begins working as a free-lance stenographer, tourist guide, and interpreter. Nabokov writes Gleb Struve, now at the University of London, asking for help arranging English translations of his works. Applies for teaching position in Switzerland, but is rejected. Reads Virginia Woolf and Katherine Mansfield for story "Admiralteyskaya igla" ("The Admiralty Spire"). At invitation of emigré publisher, writes to James Joyce in November, offering to translate *Ulysses*: "the Russian language can be made to convey in a most subtle way the musical peculiarities and intricacies of the original." Sees Ivan Bunin, who has just been awarded the Nobel Prize, and speaks at meeting in his honor. *Kamera obskura* published as a book in December by Sovremennye zapiski.

1934   *Otchayanie* is serialized in *Sovremennye zapiski* (Jan.–Oct.). *La Course du fou*, translation of *Zashchita Luzhina*, is published in France. Continues working on Chernyshevsky chapter of *Dar*; writes Khodasevich that it is "monstrously difficult." Son, Dmitri Vladimirovich Nabokov, is born May 10. In June, begins anti-totalitarian novel *Priglashenie na kazn'* (later translated as *Invitation to a Beheading*), which he completes in December. Continues publishing stories in journals.

1935   Helps care for Dmitri; calls it "a mixture of hard labor and heaven." Continues publishing stories. In June, begins new chapter of *Dar*. *Priglashenie na kazn'* published serially in *Sovremennye zapiski* (June 1935–Feb. 1936). Writes in English autobiographical piece, "It Is Me" (later lost), about his English education. Contacts Gleb Struve about possibility of teaching Russian or French literature in England. Dissatisfied with Winifred Roy's translation, *Camera Obscura* (published in England by John Long in 1936), Nabokov translates *Otchayanie* into English as *Despair*, September–December.

1936   Makes successful reading tour of Brussels, Antwerp, and Paris in January and February; "Mademoiselle O," memoir in French of Cécile Miauton written for the tour, is especially well received. In Brussels, sees brother Kirill, who is studying at Louvain University. Shares a reading in Paris with Khodasevich, whom he considers the greatest contemporary Russian poet. *Otchayanie* published as book by Petropolis (Berlin) in February. Véra is fired in May from her job with an engineering firm because she is Jewish. Nabokov learns that one of his father's murderers,

Sergey Taboritsky, is deputy secretary in new Reich department of Russian emigré affairs and begins search for work in England or America. By August, begins final consecutive composition of *Dar*. Avoids government's registration of emigrés.

1937   Leaves Germany on January 18 for reading tour of Brussels, Paris, and London, planning to find employment in France or England, while Véra winds up their affairs in Berlin. Visits Kirill in Brussels. In Paris is pleased to see James Joyce in audience during a reading. Begins four-month affair with Russian emigré Irina Guadanini in February; plagued by guilt, develops severe psoriasis and comes near suicide. Goes to England late in February; gives readings in London, visits Cambridge, and unsuccessfully seeks work. Returns to France and obtains permits for him and Véra to stay there. In April *Despair* is published in London by John Long and first chapter of *Dar* appears in *Sovremennye zapiski*. Meets Sylvia Beach, Adrienne Monnier, and Henry Church. Receives free radiation treatments for psoriasis from emigré physician. Véra and Dmitri leave Germany for Prague in April to visit Nabokov's mother, who has not yet seen her grandson; Nabokov joins them in May (last time he sees mother) and on June 30 returns with them to Paris. Sells French rights to *Despair* to Gallimard, then settles with Véra and Dmitri in Cannes, where it is cheaper to live. Tells Véra of his affair with Guadanini. Cherynshevsky chapter of *Dar* is turned down by *Sovremennye zapiski* in August; Nabokov protests political censorship but, needing money, agrees to continue publishing novel in the journal (remaining chapters appear Sept. 1937–Oct. 1938). Signs contract with New York publisher Bobbs-Merrill for *Kamera obskura* and begins translating and rewriting it under title *Laughter in the Dark*. Moves with family to Menton in October; works on *Dar* and writes three-act play *Sobytie* (later translated as *The Event*) for new Russian theater in Paris.

1938   Completes *Dar* in January. *Sobytie* is successfully produced in March and appears in *Russkie zapiski* in April. *Laughter in the Dark*, published in New York by Bobbs-Merrill on April 22, receives some good reviews but does not sell well. Moves with family to Moulinet, above Menton, in July,

and captures what seems to be his first new species of butterfly (after Nabokov's death it proves to be a hybrid).
Redescends to Cap d'Antibes in late August where he
writes play *Izobretenie Val'sa* (published by *Russkie zapiski*
in November and later translated as *The Waltz Invention*).
Receiving only small remuneration for his works, requests
monthly support from Russian Literary Fund in the U.S.;
they send him $20. *Soglyadatay* (*The Eye*), collection of
1930 novella and other stories, published by Russkie zapiski. After receiving official identity card, moves with family to Paris in October and rents small apartment at 8 rue
de Saigon. Often sees friends, including Khodasevich,
George Hessen, Mark Aldanov, and *Sovremennye zapiski*
editors Ilya Fondaminsky and Vladimir Zenzinov. *Priglashenie na kazn'* published in book form by Dom Knigi,
emigré house in Paris. Continues publishing stories in emigré papers and journals. In December begins novel in
English, *The Real Life of Sebastian Knight*, completing it
the following month.

1939   Asks Lucie Léon Noel to check his English in *The Real
          Life of Sebastian Knight*. At Paul Léon's home, meets
          James Joyce. Moves with family to larger apartment at 59
          rue Boileau. Financially desperate without a work permit
          in France, travels to England in April in unsuccessful
          search for literary or academic work. Mother dies in
          Prague on May 2. Seeks work in England again in June.
          Khodasevich dies of cancer on June 14. Publishes "Poety"
          ("The Poets") over pseudonym "Vasily Shishkov" to
          catch out influential critic Georgy Adamovich, who has
          regularly condescended to Nabokov's and Khodasevich's
          work. Adamovich enthusiastically announces arrival of ma-
          jor new talent; Nabokov obliquely discloses hoax in story
          "Vasily Shishkov." Summers with family at Fréjus on the
          Riviera. Germany invades Poland on September 1 and
          France declares war on Germany September 3. Fearing
          Paris will be bombed, sends Dmitri to stay with Anna
          Feigin in Deauville. Fails to find publisher for *Sebastian
          Knight*; with no other work to sell, begins accepting 1,000
          francs monthly from Samuil Kyandzhuntsev, old Tenishev
          friend, which he supplements by tutoring. Aldanov, who
          has been offered a job teaching summer course in Russian
          literature at Stanford University in California, recommends
          Nabokov in his place. Nabokov receives and accepts

Stanford offer and applies for U.S. visa. Writes novella *Volshebnik* (posthumously published as *The Enchanter*), October–November, about a man who desires a 12-year-old girl. Dmitri returns to Paris in December.

1940   Writes lectures on Russian literature over spring and summer in preparation for teaching in the U.S. Begins Russian novel, *Solus Rex* (never completed). Germans begin offensive against France and the Low Countries on May 10. With help of the Hebrew Immigrant Aid Society, given in appreciation of Nabokov's father's championing of Jews in pre-revolutionary Russia, Nabokov, Véra, and Dmitri sail for New York aboard the *Champlain*, arriving on May 27 with $600. Meets Sergei Rachmaninoff, who had twice sent him money in Europe. Unsuccessfully seeks employment and receives small grant from Russian Literary Fund. With Véra and Dmitri vacations at Vermont summer home of Harvard professor Mikhail Karpovich, then rents New York apartment at 35 West 87th Street; begins tutoring in Russian and seeking ways to bring Anna Feigin and other emigré friends to the U.S. Abandons *Solus Rex* after realizing his English prose style can develop only if he renounces composing in Russian. Through cousin Nicolas Nabokov, meets Edmund Wilson, acting literary editor of *The New Republic*, and is soon writing literary reviews for the journal; also writes reviews for New York *Sun* and *The New York Times*. Sees old friends including Roman Grynberg, Mstislav Dobuzhinsky, Aldanov, and Zenzinov, meets Max Eastman, and becomes friends with Wilson and his wife, Mary McCarthy, and Harry and Elena Levin. Receives final terms of offer from Stanford to teach Modern Russian Literature and Art of Writing in summer of 1941. Begins preparing full set of lectures on Russian literature in fall. Researches Lepidoptera at American Museum of Natural History. Receives advance from Wilson to translate Pushkin's "Mozart and Salieri" for *The New Republic* (published April 21, 1941).

1941   Tutors privately in Russian, writes two papers on Lepidoptera, and establishes himself on lecture roster of Institute of International Education. Has eight teeth extracted and dentures fitted. Receives $750 and bonus for two weeks of extremely successful lectures at Wellesley College in March. His frank anti-Sovietism particularly appeals to

Wellesley president Mildred McAfee. Begins translating Pushkin and other Russian poets in April for Stanford course. Through Wilson, meets Edmund Weeks, editor of *Atlantic Monthly*; "Cloud, Castle, Lake," translation of 1937 story "Ozero, oblako, bashnya," appears in June (the first of many Nabokov stories and poems published in *Atlantic* over next two years). Is appointed to one-year position at Wellesley College as Resident Lecturer in Comparative Literature, with salary of $3,000. In late May Dorothy Leuthold, whom Nabokov has tutored in Russian, drives Nabokov, Véra, and Dmitri to California for Stanford course. During stops Nabokov hunts butterflies and moths and on June 9 discovers new species on rim of Grand Canyon; names it *Neonympha dorothea* in Leuthold's honor. Meets Yvor Winters and Henry Lanz over summer. In July, learns that *The Real Life of Sebastian Knight* has been accepted by James Laughlin for New Directions on recommendation of reader Delmore Schwartz. Returns east by train to begin position at Wellesley College, renting house at 19 Appleby Road in Wellesley, Massachusetts. Translates three poems of Khodasevich (published in *New Directions in Prose and Poetry*) and translates Gogol, Pushkin, Lermontov, and Tyutchev for teaching. Begins traveling regularly to Harvard's Museum of Comparative Zoology in Cambridge, where he volunteers to set the Lepidoptera collection in order. Writes poem in English, "Softest of Tongues" (*Atlantic Monthly*, Dec.). *The Real Life of Sebastian Knight*, published by New Directions December 18, receives mostly good reviews but sells poorly. Begins writing a new novel (later titled *Bend Sinister*).

1942   Commissioned by New Directions to write volume of verse translations of Pushkin and Tyutchev and critical book on Gogol. Despite faculty backing and student enthusiasm, is not reappointed at Wellesley through opposition of president Mildred McAfee, who now disapproves of Nabokov's hostility toward the Soviet government (U.S. is now allied with the Soviet Union in World War II and McAfee has entered government service as head of the Women's Naval Reserve, WAVES). Appointed in June to part-time position as Research Fellow in Entomology at the Museum of Comparative Zoology for 1942–43 academic year at salary of $1,000 (over next four years will

spend more time researching and writing on Lepidoptera than in writing fiction). "The Refrigerator Awakes," first of his poems published in *The New Yorker*, appears June 6. Long poem "Slava" (later translated as "Fame") published in New York emigré journal *Novy zhurnal*. Spends most of summer with Mikhail and Tatiana Karpovich in Vermont, where Nabokov works in attic for eight to ten hours a day on Gogol book. Rents apartment at 8 Craigie Circle, Cambridge, where he and his family remain until 1948; often sees Harry and Elena Levin, and Edmund Wilson and Mary McCarthy. Undertakes lecture and reading tour for Institute of International Education, traveling to colleges in South Carolina, Georgia, and Tennessee in October and in Illinois and Minnesota in November. Begins friendship with Florence Read, president of Spelman, college for black women in Atlanta. Gives Dmitri lessons in Russian grammar while Véra is hospitalized with pneumonia in December. Completes book on Gogol.

1943   Writes first story in English, "The Assistant Producer" (published *Atlantic Monthly*, May) and begins teaching noncredit course in elementary Russian at Wellesley College. Awarded Guggenheim Fellowship of $2,500 to complete new novel. Visits emigré friends in New York including George Hessen and Anna Feigin, whom he helped bring to America; on return to Cambridge writes story "That in Aleppo Once . . ." (*Atlantic Monthly*, Nov.). Continues writing poems in Russian for *Novy zhurnal*. Dictates book tentatively titled *Gogol Through the Looking-Glass* to Véra (she types all Nabokov's works for publication) and sends it to New Directions. Travels with Véra and Dmitri to Wasatch Mountains in Utah, where he hunts butterflies and moths and captures several species. In fall, resumes teaching noncredit course at Wellesley and receives $200 salary increase on new annual contract at Museum of Comparative Zoology (museum appointment will be renewed annually until 1948). Responding to Laughlin's complaint that the Gogol needs more factual information, Nabokov adds a chronology. Publishes "The Nearctic Forms of *Ly* Hüb." in *Psyche* (Sept.–Dec.). Has upper teeth removed and a dental plate fitted in November. Corresponds regularly with Wilson and often visits him.

1944 Persuaded by Véra to devote more time to new novel, soon completes four chapters under working title *The Person from Porlock* (later retitled *Bend Sinister*). Gives lecture on Russian literature at Yale in March and a reading at Cornell in May. Through Katharine White, an admirer of his *Atlantic* stories, signs first reading agreement with *The New Yorker* in June (agreement will be maintained over three decades); White also arranges a $500 advance, having been informed by Wilson that Nabokov is short of money. Devises system for studying butterfly markings and their evolution by counting rows of scales on wings, and writes major paper revising the neotropical Plebejinae. Vacations with Véra near Wilson and McCarthy in Wellfleet, Massachusetts, and, after Dmitri returns from summer camp, spends August with family in Wellesley, often playing tennis with poet Jorge Guillén. *Nikolai Gogol* published by New Directions August 15. Writes story "Time and Ebb" (*Atlantic Monthly*, Jan. 1945). Dmitri enters Dexter School in Brookline, Massachusetts, in fall and Nabokov begins appointment as lecturer in Russian at Wellesley College on year's contract for $800 salary, teaching elementary Russian.

1945 Lectures at St. Timothy's College in Maryland and Smith College in Massachusetts. *Three Russian Poets*, verse translations of Pushkin, Lermontov, and Tyutchev, published by New Directions in February. *The New Yorker* accepts first story from Nabokov, "Double Talk" (published July 23), paying $817.50, the most he has ever received for a story. After suffering heart palpitations, gives up smoking on doctor's advice in spring and begins "inhaling" molasses candies (gains 60 pounds over the summer). Nabokov and Véra become American citizens on July 12. Begins teaching a second course, intermediate Russian, at Wellesley, with salary increased to $2,000. In September learns in a letter from Kirill, who is working as an interpreter for American occupation forces in Germany and has traced him through *New Yorker* story, that Sergey died from malnutrition in a German concentration camp after being arrested as a "British spy" for criticizing Nazi Germany. Also hears from sister Elena Sikorski and Evgenia Hofeld, who is caring for nephew Rostislav Petkevich; sends them money and packages and seeks a way to bring them out of Czechoslovakia.

1946   Meets W. H. Auden; compliments him on work of Conrad
        Aiken, with whom he has confused him. Third course, on
        Russian literature in translation, is approved for the next
        academic year at Wellesley; anticipating its demands, Na-
        bokov hurries to complete novel and submits it under pro-
        visional title *Solus Rex* to Allen Tate at Henry Holt in
        June. Suffering from exhaustion, goes with family to New-
        found Lake in New Hampshire, then to town of Wellesley
        for August. Rereads Tolstoy and Dostoevsky in prepara-
        tion for new lectures. Begins research for monograph on
        nearctic *Lycaeides* (completes research in spring 1947, hav-
        ing examined 2,000 specimens). Continues seeking a per-
        manent job; is passed over for positions at the Voice of
        America, Harvard, and Vassar. Just before novel goes to
        printer in November, settles on title *Bend Sinister*. Earns
        extra money by speaking to women's clubs.

1947   Begins planning autobiography and a novel about "a man
        who likes little girls." Finishes first draft of *Lycaeides* mon-
        ograph in May. *Bend Sinister* published June 12 to mixed
        reviews; since Tate has left Henry Holt, it is poorly pro-
        moted and does not sell well. Loses 20 pounds hunting
        butterflies and climbing with Dmitri and Véra in and
        around Estes Park in Colorado during summer. Writes au-
        tobiographical essay "Portrait of My Uncle" (*The New
        Yorker*, Jan. 3, 1948). Dmitri begins at St. Mark's boarding
        school in Southborough, Massachusetts, in fall. Nabokov
        resumes work at Museum of Comparative Zoology and
        Wellesley on new annual contracts. Receives offer of a per-
        manent position teaching Russian literature at Cornell
        University at $5,000 salary, which he accepts after Welles-
        ley refuses him a permanent appointment. Helps obtain
        position for Elena Sikorski at United Nations library in
        Geneva; continues sending money to Hofeld and Rostislav
        and writes affidavit in unsuccessful attempt to bring Ros-
        tislav to America. *Nine Stories* published by New Direc-
        tions in December.

1948   Story "Signs and Symbols" published with minor editorial
        intervention by *The New Yorker* (May 15) after Nabokov
        tells Katharine White planned alterations are unnecessary
        and in some cases "murderous." Seriously ill throughout
        spring from broken blood vessel in lung. Véra reads his
        lectures at Wellesley and takes students through final

exams while Nabokov writes in bed three additional chapters
of autobiography (published in *The New Yorker* July 1948–
Jan. 1949). Completes "The Nearctic Members of the Genus *Lycaeides Hübner*" in June (published as whole issue
of *Bulletin of the Museum of Comparative Zoology*, Feb.
1949). Moves to Ithaca, New York, in July and settles with
Véra and Dmitri into furnished house at 802 East Seneca
Street. Still convalescing, prepares lectures and completes
"First Poem" chapter of autobiography (published in *Partisan Review*, Sept. 1949). Becomes close friend of Morris
Bishop, who initiated job offer from Cornell. Dmitri enters Holderness School in New Hampshire, with tuition
costing about a third of Nabokov's salary. Buys eight-year-
old Plymouth that Véra drives (Nabokov never learns to
drive) and takes in lodger to help pay rent. Teaches two
surveys of Russian literature (one in Russian). Translates
medieval heroic poem *Slovo o polku Igoreve* (*The Song of
Igor's Campaign*) for classes. Véra acts as his teaching
assistant, drives him to school, continues typing up his
writing, and begins conducting most of his business correspondence in her own name.

1949   Teaches seminar, Russian Poetry 1870–1925, in spring
            term, holding classes in his home, in addition to the two
            survey courses. Writes two more chapters of autobiogra-
            phy. Publishes negative review of Sartre's *La Nausée* and
            its English translation in *The New York Times Book Review*.
            Drives with Véra in May to New York City for reading
            from his Russian works and visits with emigré friends and
            relatives. Travels west in summer in newly purchased 1946
            Oldsmobile. Conducts classes at University of Utah
            Writers' Workshop in July, where he enjoys company of
            Wallace Stegner and son Page, Theodore Geisel ("Dr.
            Seuss"), Martha Foley, and John Crowe Ransom. Hunts
            butterflies in Utah and Wyoming with Véra. Returns to
            Cornell where he teaches Russian literature surveys and
            seminar on Pushkin. Katharine and E. B. White visit in
            October. Submits "Student Days" chapter of autobiog-
            raphy to *The New Yorker*; cannot agree to changes sug-
            gested by White and withdraws it (published as "Lodgings
            in Trinity Lane," *Harper's Magazine*, Jan. 1951).

1950   Needing money, lectures at University of Toronto for $150
            during semester break. Meets Harold Ross at *New Yorker*

party in March and sees Edmund Wilson for first time since Wilson went to Europe in 1948. Hospitalized in April for two weeks with severe pain, eventually determined to be from intercostal neuralgia; has relapse and is unwell until May. Véra conducts classes during his absences. Finishes autobiography, *Conclusive Evidence*, in May and in June has his remaining six teeth extracted in Boston; while returning to Ithaca with Véra, captures specimens of rare *Lycaeides melissa samuelis*, which he had been the first to classify. Under pressure to teach larger classes, spends summer writing lectures for new Masterpieces of European Fiction course on Austen, Dickens, Flaubert, Tolstoy, Stevenson, Proust, Kafka, and Joyce. Begins novel under title *The Kingdom by the Sea* (later, *Lolita*). Dissatisfied, decides to burn the manuscript but is dissuaded by Véra.

1951   *Conclusive Evidence*, published in February by Harper and Brothers, receives excellent reviews but sells poorly (book is published in England as *Speak, Memory*). Receives National Institute of Arts and Letters award of $1,000 at ceremony in New York City on May 25. Dmitri is accepted by Harvard without scholarship. Nabokov borrows $1,000 from emigré friend Roman Grynberg, explaining: "I can't write stories for money . . . and something else has me, a novel . . ." He and Véra sell their furniture and piano and move out of rented house before going west for summer. Works on *Lolita* in car and motels; catches first female of *Lycaeides argyrognomon sublivens* in Telluride, Colorado, where Dmitri joins them, then hunts butterflies in Wyoming and Montana. Moves with Véra into a professor's home for fall semester at Cornell (will live in homes of absent professors throughout remaining time there). Does research on schoolgirls for *Lolita*. Suffers from severe insomnia while writing story "The Lance" (*The New Yorker*, Feb. 2, 1952). Reads and lectures at Nabokov evening staged by Russian emigré community in New York City.

1952   As visiting lecturer for second semester at Harvard, teaches courses on Russian modernism, on Pushkin, and on the novel, including *Don Quixote*. With Véra, often sees Dmitri, Harry and Elena Levin, Alice and William James (son of the philosopher), and old Wellesley friends, as well as

Edmund Wilson and his fourth wife, Elena. Meets Richard Wilbur and May Sarton. Reads in Morris Gray Poetry Series; gives reading at Wellesley and lectures on Gogol at Dartmouth. In April, *Dar* (*The Gift*) is published for the first time complete by Chekhov, Russian publishing house in New York. Agrees to do a Russian version of *Conclusive Evidence* for Chekhov and receives $1,500 advance. Receives second Guggenheim award, which he plans to use to write an annotated literal translation of Pushkin's *Evgeniy Onegin*. Goes to Wyoming with Véra to hunt butterflies in summer. Resumes Cornell teaching in fall and works on *Lolita*.

1953   Takes unpaid semester's leave from Cornell to do research for his *Eugene Onegin* in Cambridge. Hunts butterflies with Véra in Arizona in spring and Oregon in summer; writes story about Professor Pnin as first installment of novel he can publish as sketches (four chapters are published in *The New Yorker* April 23, 1953–Nov. 12, 1955). Chiefly through efforts of Morris Bishop, Nabokov's Cornell salary is increased to $6,000 in fall. Completes *Lolita* on December 6 and while in New York to record talk for BBC on translation gives typescript to Pascal Covici of Viking. Plans to have the novel published anonymously to avoid scandal that would endanger his position at Cornell.

1954   Viking turns down *Lolita* for fear of prosecution. Second chapter of *Pnin* is rejected by *The New Yorker* as "unpleasant." In February and March, rushes to complete *Drugie berega* (*Other Shores*), expanded and revised Russian translation of autobiography (published by Chekhov). Records reading in New York for BBC program and lectures for three days at University of Kansas. During summer in New Mexico with Véra and Dmitri, works on notes (never completed) for projected Simon and Schuster edition of *Anna Karenina*. Simon and Schuster rejects *Lolita* in July as "pure pornography." Returns to Cornell and works intensely on *Eugene Onegin*. Gives paper, "Problems of Translation: *Onegin* in English" (published in *Partisan Review*, Autumn 1955), at English Institute conference at Columbia University. Sends *Lolita* manuscript to Edmund Wilson, who reads half of it and responds that he likes it less than anything of Nabokov's that he has read (Nabokov later urges Wilson to read the whole work carefully; tells Wilson that it is "a highly moral affair"). *Lolita* is turned down by New Directions, Farrar, Straus, and in December by Doubleday, despite editor Jason Epstein's support of it. Philip Rahv of *Partisan Review* counsels Nabokov that publishing the book anonymously will destroy its best defense.

1955   Convinced that he will not find an American publisher for *Lolita*, Nabokov sends typescript to literary agent Doussia Ergaz in Paris. Maurice Girodias, founder of new Olympia Press, agrees to publish it on condition that it carry Nabokov's name. Dmitri graduates cum laude from Harvard and enrolls in Longy School of Music in Cambridge, where he concentrates on singing. Epstein visits in June and arranges for Nabokov and Dmitri to translate Lermontov's *Geroy nashego vremeni* (*A Hero of Our Time*) and for Nabokov to translate *Anna Karenina* (his translation is never completed). Nabokov is hospitalized for eight days during summer with attack of lumbago. *Lolita* is published in Paris in September in Olympia's Traveler's Edition, a line consisting mostly of pornographic books aimed at English-speaking tourist market. Nabokov receives copies of the book in October and discovers that copyright has been assigned to Olympia Press as well as to him. Pnin novel, provisionally titled *My Poor Pnin*, is rejected as too short by Viking and then by Harper and Brothers. Nabokov is distressed when Katharine White moves from editorial to general policy department at *The New Yorker*. Graham Greene names *Lolita* one of the three best books of 1955 in London *Sunday Times* Christmas issue.

1956   On sabbatical for spring semester, conducts final research for *Eugene Onegin* in Cambridge. Meets John Dos Passos. Scandal begins to break around *Lolita* when John Gordon attacks Greene for praising it and denounces the novel as "Sheer unrestrained pornography" in the London *Sunday Express*. After *The New York Times Book Review* reports on the dispute and cites letters praising the quality of *Lolita*, Nabokov receives offers for rights from several American publishers. *Vesna v Fial'te i drugie rasskazy* (*Spring in Fialta and Other Stories*) published by Chekhov in March. Nabokov records reading from his *Eugene Onegin* for BBC. In June U.S. Customs seizes, and then releases, copies of *Lolita* (it will do so again in November). Travels with Véra to Utah, Wyoming, Montana, Minnesota, and Michigan, hunting butterflies and working on translation, *A Hero of Our Time*. In New York in October discusses with Epstein, Fred Dupee, and Melvin Lasky, editor of *Anchor Review*, plans to publish excerpts from *Lolita* in the magazine to test public reaction to it. Writes afterword, "On a Book Entitled *Lolita*." The French Ministry of Interior bans *Lolita* and 24 other Olympia titles in December and Girodias sues to have the ban lifted (he wins the case in January 1958).

1957   Harvard University, seeking a new Russian professor, almost appoints Nabokov; opposition to him is led by Roman Jakobson, who comments during faculty meeting: "Gentlemen, even if one allows that he is an important writer, are we next to invite an elephant to be professor of zoology?" *Pnin*, published March 7 by Doubleday to extremely favorable reviews, goes into second printing in two weeks. Begins work on novel (later *Pale Fire*) but puts it aside to complete *Eugene Onegin* and stays in Ithaca over summer. *Anchor Review* publishes nearly a third of *Lolita* in June, with Nabokov's afterword and critical commentary by Dupee. Nabokov contracts with publishers in Italy, France, Germany, and Sweden for translation rights to *Lolita*. Doubleday and then MacDowell, Obolensky, withdraw their offers for American rights when Girodias demands up to 62.5 percent of Nabokov's royalties. In December completes revisions of *Eugene Onegin*.

1958   *A Hero of Our Time* published by Doubleday in March. Hunts butterflies in Montana, Alberta, and Wyoming with Véra in summer. Hears from George Weidenfeld in England and Gallimard in France that they want to publish as many Nabokov works as possible. Putnam's works out contract for *Lolita* in March, assigning to Nabokov royalties of 7.5 percent and the same to Girodias. Published on August 18, *Lolita* sells 100,000 copies in three weeks, the fastest sales for an American novel since *Gone With the Wind*. *Nabokov's Dozen*, collection of 13 stories, published in September by Doubleday. Nabokov contracts with Harris-Kubrick Pictures in November for film rights to *Lolita* for $150,000 plus share of profits. Is awarded a year's leave of absence from Cornell, and searches for replacement so that leave can commence in February; finds novelist Herbert Gold to fill the position.

1959   Delivers last Cornell lectures on January 19. Makes first notes for "Texture of Time" (later a part of *Ada*) and stores belongings before leaving with Véra for New York City on February 24. Is interviewed by major American and English publications, meets George Weidenfeld, and sees Anna Feigin and Dmitri. Reworks translation, *Song of Igor's Campaign*, and begins preparing annotations. Hunts butterflies in Tennessee and Texas in April, then in Arizona, where he revises *Invitation to a Beheading*, Dmitri's translation of *Priglashenie na kazn'*. Asked to write *Lolita* screenplay, travels to Los Angeles with Véra in late July for discussions with director Stanley Kubrick and producer James Harris; cannot agree to changes they propose and soon rejects offer. Persuaded by Véra that the combination of teaching and writing is too burdensome for him, resigns from Cornell and sails to Europe on September 29 to visit sister Elena and brother Kirill, planning to return in a few months. Spends two weeks in Geneva with Elena, a UNESCO librarian, and Kirill, a Brussels travel agent, then goes with Véra to Paris for reception at Gallimard where Nabokov encounters Girodias, but fails to realize who he is. Gives numerous press interviews. Asks to meet Alain Robbe-Grillet, whose work he admires, and is interviewed by him. In London, meets Graham Greene and appears on *The Bookman* television show. Delivers lecture in Cambridge, then returns to London for November 6 Weidenfeld and Nicolson publication of *Lolita*, which immediately sells out. For next two months travels with Véra in Italy and Sicily; when he can elude the press, works on *Letters to Terra* project (later a part of *Ada*). Begins giving interviews in groups. Kubrick cables request that Nabokov write *Lolita* screenplay, with more artistic freedom. In Milan for reception by Mondadori, arranges audition for Dmitri with singing teacher Maestro Campogalliani. Spends Christmas holidays in San Remo, joined by Dmitri and Elena and nephew Vladimir Sikorski. Dmitri begins translating *Dar* as *The Gift*.

1960   During stay in Menton, Nabokov accepts offer of $40,000 for writing *Lolita* screenplay, plus an additional $35,000 if script is credited solely to him. Dmitri begins studying with Campogalliani. Nabokov turns down membership in the American National Institute of Arts and Letters, writing "all my thinking life I have declined to 'belong' " (will continue to reject all offers of honorary degrees and memberships). Arrives in Los Angeles with Véra in early March. Finishes screenplay July 9; told that it would take seven hours to run, produces a shorter version by September 8. Rostislav Petkevich dies in Prague of the effects of alcoholism. *Song of Igor's Campaign* published by Vintage. Nabokov hears that Dmitri has won first prize among basses in international opera competition in Italy. Returns to Europe in November to be near him, settling with Véra in Nice; works intensively on *Pale Fire* over winter.

1961   Completes *Pale Fire* poem February 11 and begins work on prose portion of novel. Attends Dmitri's operatic debut in *La Bohème* in Reggio, in which Luciano Pavarotti also debuts, then sees Dmitri in *Lucia da Lammermoor* (Nabokov and Véra try to see each of his new roles). In Stresa in May, revises Dmitri's translation of the first chapter of *Dar* (*The Gift*). Hunts butterflies in Valais, Switzerland, in August, then goes to Montreux, where he finds atmosphere conducive to writing. On advice of Peter Ustinov, who lives in the Montreux Palace Hotel, Nabokov and Véra take rooms there in October, planning to stay until spring. Completes *Pale Fire* on December 4.

1962   Corrects French translation of *Pnin* and Michael Scammell's English translation of the last four chapters of *Dar* (*The Gift*). Regularly reads New York *Herald Tribune* and American magazines and literary journals. Hears from agent Irving Lazar in February that Harris and Kubrick have extensively reworked *Lolita* screenplay. *Pale Fire* published by Putnam's in April. Sails aboard *Queen Elizabeth* with Véra for premiere of *Lolita* in New York. Sees film at screening a few days before attending opening on June 13 and praises the director and cast; conceals his disappointment that little remains of his original screenplay. Gives numerous interviews before returning to Montreux in late June. Featured in cover story in *Newsweek* (June 25) and in July hears that *Pale Fire* has made the bestseller list. Visited by former schoolmate Samuil Rosoff, whom he has not seen since 1919, and Elena. Moves with Véra into sixth-floor apartment of Montreux Palace, facing Lake

Geneva. Dmitri becomes ill with painful swelling of joints; in October, while in remission, he begins racing car in competitions. During visit by George Weidenfeld, Nabokov plans reissue of *Speak, Memory* and projected *Butterflies of Europe*, complete illustrated catalog of all species and main subspecies with notes by Nabokov on classification, habitat, and behavior. Compiles index for *Eugene Onegin.* Dmitri's illness recurs and is diagnosed as Reiter's syndrome.

1963   Dmitri is hospitalized in January and February, and again in summer. Nabokov revises *Eugene Onegin*, begins translating *Lolita* into Russian, and goes over *The Eye*, Dmitri's translation of *Soglyadatay.* Interviewed by Alvin Toffler in March for *Playboy* (published Jan. 1964). *The Gift*, translation with Michael Scammell and Dmitri of *Dar*, published in May by Putnam's; reviews stress the extent and achievement of Nabokov's work. Hunts butterflies with Véra in Valais and in Vaud, Switzerland, where they are joined by Dmitri; visitors include George Hessen, Raisa Tatarinov, Elena, Anna Feigin, and Véra's sister Sonia Slonim. Writes introduction for Time-Life reissue of *Bend Sinister* (published 1964).

1964   With Dmitri well enough to resume singing lessons in March, leaves with Véra for publication of *Eugene Onegin* in New York. Goes to Ithaca to retrieve some papers from storage and to visit with Morris Bishop. Gives reading at Harvard (his last public reading), where he meets graduate student Andrew Field. Kirill dies of a heart attack in Munich on April 16. After April 21 reception for *Eugene Onegin* (published by Bollingen in June), returns to Switzerland. Véra is hospitalized for several weeks of tests in May and has appendix removed. Makes revisions in *The Eye* for *Playboy* (published March 1965). Hunts butterflies at Valais in summer. *The Defense*, translation with Michael Scammell of *Zaschita Luzhina*, published by Putnam's in September. Works on *The Texture of Time* while awaiting British Museum's response to his queries for *Butterflies of Europe.* Resumes translating *Lolita* into Russian in December.

1965   Begins extensively revising *Despair* (1936 translation of *Otchayanie*). Composes first chess problem in years. Com-

pletes Russian translation of *Lolita*. During construction
work at Montreux Palace Hotel in spring, travels with
Véra to Gardone, then St. Moritz, for butterflies, taking
side trip to Milan to research paintings for projected work
Butterflies in Art (never completed). Is relieved to learn
that Dmitri will give up car racing to concentrate on singing. Reads Edmund Wilson's harshly critical review of *Eugene Onegin* for *New York Review of Books* (July 15) and
writes immediate response (letter appears Aug. 26); the
controversy draws in writers including Anthony Burgess,
Robert Lowell, and George Steiner. Unable to endure
publishing uncertainties about ever-expanding *Butterflies
of Europe* and finding his creative energies being drained,
cancels project despite Weidenfeld's offer of a $10,000 ad-
vance. *The Eye* published by Phaedra in early fall. Interviewed and filmed by Robert Hughes in and around
Montreux in September for New York Educational Television. Writes new afterword for Russian *Lolita* about difficulties of translating from English to Russian. Extensively
rewrites parts of *The Waltz Invention*, Dmitri's translation
of *Izobretenie Val'sa*. Over winter revises autobiography as
Speak, Memory: An Autobiography Revisited. Agrees to allow Radio Liberty to publish some of his works for free
clandestine distribution in Soviet Union, under imprint
Editions Victor (they will publish *Priglashenie na kazn'* in
1966 and *Zaschita Luzhina* in 1967). In December has first
detailed flash of a section of *Ada*.

1966   Completes work on *Speak, Memory*. "Nabokov's Reply,"
            article on *Eugene Onegin* controversy, appears in *Encoun-
            ter* (Feb.). Writes "*Lolita* and Mr. Girodias" (*Evergreen
            Review*, Feb. 1967), refutation of Girodias' "*Lolita*, Na-
            bokov, and I" (*Evergreen Review*, Sept. 1965). Begins
            composing *Ada* at a rapid rate. *The Waltz Invention* pub-
            lished by Phaedra in February. Visited by cartoonist Saul
            Steinberg. Revised *Despair* published by Putnam's in May.
            Explores Italian galleries for butterflies in art project in
            spring and summer; continues working on *Ada*. Véra flies
            to New York to discuss Nabokov's publishing future with
            Putnam. Dissatisfied with Putnam's response concerning
            advances and advertising, Nabokov seeks another pub-
            lisher. Stops work on *Ada* in November to revise *Eugene
            Onegin*, making translation still more literal. Extensively

revises *King, Queen, Knave*, Dmitri's translation of *Korol',
dama, valet* (completes revisions in March 1967).

1967   *Speak, Memory: An Autobiography Revisited* published by
Putnam's in January. French court rules agreement be-
tween Olympia Press and Nabokov canceled as of December 1964. Nabokov spends April to August with Véra in
northern Italy, working intensively on *Ada*; they are
joined in Camogli by Dmitri and Elena, and visited by
Peter Kemeny of McGraw-Hill. Russian translation of
Lolita published by Phaedra in August. Véra flies to New
York in November to settle with McGraw-Hill final details
of contract for 11 books at $250,000 advance. Andrew
Field, who is updating and expanding Dieter Zimmer's
Nabokov bibliography for McGraw-Hill, visits in December.

1968   Visited by Irving Lazar, who discusses film rights for *Ada*
and a *Lolita* musical proposed by Harold Prince, and by
Alfred Appel, who goes over notes for his *Annotated Lolita* with Nabokov. Véra brings Anna Feigin, now 80 years
old and ailing, from New York to live near her and Nabokov in Montreux. *King, Queen, Knave* published by
McGraw-Hill in April. Nabokov agrees to Andrew Field's
request to undertake his biography. Hunts butterflies in
Vaud and Valais, Switzerland, from May to July. Receives
from sister Olga in Prague about 150 letters he had written
to his mother. Completes *Ada* in October and begins
choosing and translating Russian poems for collection
(later titled *Poems and Problems*).

1969   Joseph Papp stages Russell McGrath's adaptation of *Invitation to a Beheading* at New York Shakespeare Festival
in March. Film rights for *Ada* are bought by Columbia
for $500,000 (film is not produced). *Ada* published by
McGraw-Hill on May 5 to initial critical acclaim and strong
sales. Summers with Véra in Ticino and Bernese Oberland,
Switzerland; enjoys visit from Carl and Ellendea Proffer,
who are setting up Ardis Press to publish Russian works.
Writes "Notes to Ada by Vivian Darkbloom" (published
in 1970 Penguin edition in England). Gives numerous interviews to Italian journalists in Montreux for Mondadori
translation of *Ada*. In October, begins writing *Transparent Things*, but makes slow progress.

1970　　Completes compilation of *Poems and Problems* in January. Drafts notes for inclusion in *Tri-Quarterly* issue devoted to his work (published Winter 1970). Visits Vatican Museum for *Butterflies in Art* project. Goes with Véra to Sicily in spring and Valais during summer for butterflies. *Transparent Things* "bursts into life" on June 30. Visited by Alan Jay Lerner to discuss musical of *Lolita*, and by Alfred and Nina Appel for five days in November. With Dmitri now singing in North and South America, Véra completes the translation of *Podvig* (*Glory*) while Nabokov revises the translations. *Mary*, translation by Nabokov with Michael Glenny of *Mashen'ka*, published in September by McGraw-Hill. Field arrives December 31 for month's stay in Montreux to discuss Nabokov biography.

1971　　Musical *Lolita, My Love* staged unsuccessfully in Philadelphia and Boston. Nabokov starts translating Russian stories with Dmitri in spring for McGraw-Hill collections. *Poems and Problems*, collection of 39 Russian poems with translations, 14 English poems, and 18 chess problems, published by McGraw-Hill in March. Flies to Portugal with Véra for spring, but finds few butterflies and soon returns. Cuts short butterfly hunting in France in summer when Véra is hospitalized for reaction to antibiotics; reads her Solzhenitsyn's *Avgust chetyrnadtsatogo* (*August 1914*) while she recovers. Vacations near Gstaad with Véra, Dmitri, Anna Feigin, Elena, and Sonia Slonim in August; hunts butterflies and hikes with Dmitri. Receives reply to a recent letter to Wilson, first friendly exchange since their *Eugene Onegin* quarrel. Soon after, Nabokov receives copy of passage about him in Wilson's *Upstate* and writes letter to *The New York Times Book Review* (Nov. 7) refuting statements "on the brink of libel." After five-month pause, begins intensive work on *Transparent Things*. *Glory* published by McGraw-Hill in December.

1972　　Completes *Transparent Things* on April 1; published by McGraw-Hill in November to mixed reviews, it sells poorly. In spring and summer hunts butterflies in France and Switzerland. Edmund Wilson dies on June 12. At request of Edmund White, Nabokov writes article, "On Inspiration," for *Saturday Review of the Arts* (Jan. 6, 1973) Nabokov issue. Revises Dmitri's translations of stories for collection *Tyrants Destroyed and Other Stories*.

1973　　Anna Feigin dies on January 6. Véra is hospitalized in mid-January with two slipped discs; Nabokov writes that the "feeling of distress, désarroi, utter panic and dreadful presentiment every time V. is away in hospital, is one of the greatest torments of my life." In January and February reads and corrects manuscript of Andrew Field's *Nabokov: His Life in Part*, distressed by its inaccuracies. Begins writing *Look at the Harlequins!* In April, starts translating stories with Dmitri for *Details of a Sunset and Other Stories*. *A Russian Beauty and Other Stories*, translations with Simon Karlinsky and Dmitri, published by McGraw-Hill in April. Gives Elena a list of details to check for his *Look at the Harlequins!* on her summer trip to Leningrad. Spends June and July with Véra in Italy hunting butterflies. During August and September reads and corrects revised manuscript of Field's biography, strongly disapproving of it; beyond a letter asking him to acknowledge corrections, will never communicate directly with Field again. Learns that he has won National Medal for Literature prize of $10,000. *Strong Opinions*, collection of interviews and other public prose, published by McGraw-Hill in November.

1974　　*Lolita: A Screenplay*, published by McGraw-Hill in February, sells very poorly. Writes letter welcoming Solzhenitsyn to West after his expulsion from the Soviet Union. Signs new agreement with McGraw-Hill for six books over next four years. Goes over Edmund Wilson's letters for his widow, Elena, who is preparing a book on Wilson's correspondence; writes her that it is "agony" to go over the exchanges from the "early radiant era of our correspondence." Spends eight days revising German translation of *Ada*. Composes chess problems in April. Begins writing letters on behalf of Soviet dissidents. Has new novel (eventually called *The Original of Laura*) "mapped out rather clearly for next year." Works on revisions to French edition of *Ada* during summer butterfly expedition to Zermatt, then travels on with Véra for a week with Dmitri in Sarnico. Visited by Viktor Nekrasov and Vladimir Maximov. Is distressed when Solzhenitsyn fails to arrive for visit due to a miscommunication. *Look at the Harlequins!* published by McGraw-Hill in August to mixed reviews. *Mashen'ka* and *Podvig* are reissued in November by Ardis

(Ardis will republish all of Nabokov's Russian fiction over next decade).

1975   *Tyrants Destroyed and Other Stories*, translated with Dmitri, published by McGraw-Hill in January. Names J. D. Salinger, John Updike, and Edmund White as his favorite American writers in interview for *Esquire*. After completing revisions to French *Ada ou l'ardeur* in February, exhausts himself checking proofs to meet May publication deadline. Goes to Davos in June for butterflies and in late July has severe fall on mountainside. Continues to feel unwell and has tests that disclose tumor on prostate, found to be benign after October operation. Returns to writing *The Original of Laura* in December. Revised translation of *Eugene Onegin* published by Princeton University Press.

1976   Suggests that McGraw-Hill bring out a volume of the Nabokov-Wilson correspondence with Simon Karlinsky as editor (*The Nabokov-Wilson Letters, 1940–1971*, is posthumously published in 1979). *Details of a Sunset and Other Stories* published by McGraw-Hill in March to good reviews. Suffers concussion from fall on May 1 and is hospitalized for ten days. Lumbago attack forces postponement of summer butterfly excursion and an infection causes fever. Readmitted to hospital, semi-conscious, in June and remains until September, delirious much of the time, then undergoes two weeks of convalescence and physiotherapy in Valmont Clinic with Véra, who had damaged her spine attempting to support him after fall. Selects poems for collection *Stikhi* (*Poems*) for Ardis in autumn; weak, with almost no sleep, can write out little of *The Original of Laura*.

1977   Has last interview with BBC Television in February. Develops high fever during bout of influenza and is hospitalized in Lausanne from March 17 to May 7. Reenters Nestlé Hospital in Lausanne when fever returns on June 5 and is placed in intensive care on June 30 with severe bronchial congestion. Dies at 6:50 P.M. on July 2, with Véra and Dmitri at bedside. After cremation at a non-religious funeral service in Vevey attended by a dozen family members and friends, ashes are interred in Clarens cemetery on July 8.

Note on the Texts

This volume presents three novels and a screenplay by Vladimir Nabokov, *Lolita* (1955), *Pnin* (1957), *Pale Fire* (1962), and, in the Appendix, *Lolita: A Screenplay* (1974). The texts presented here incorporate revisions and corrections Nabokov noted in his own copies. The text of *Lolita* printed here is that of the first American edition, published by Putnam in 1958. The texts of the other three works are those of the first editions.

Nabokov began writing *Lolita* in 1950, using the working title "The Kingdom by the Sea," and completed it in December 1953. After five American publishers (Viking; Simon and Schuster; New Directions; Farrar, Straus; and Doubleday) had rejected the novel for fear of prosecution for obscenity, Nabokov sent it to his European agent, Doussia Ergaz, in Paris. Maurice Girodias of the Olympia Press accepted the book for publication, and a contract was signed on June 6, 1955. *Lolita* was published in Paris in a two-volume paper-bound edition in the English-language Olympia Traveller's Companion series on September 15, 1955. From the beginning of their relationship, Nabokov had difficulty working with Girodias. He read galley proofs but did not receive page proofs, though he had requested them and considered reading page proofs to be an essential part of seeing a book to press. (In a January 22, 1968, letter to his McGraw-Hill editor, Frank E. Taylor, Nabokov wrote: "I absolutely must see the page proofs . . . no book of mine has ever appeared without my having checked those last proofs—except a few paperbacks, with dreadful consequences.") In addition, some corrections requested by Nabokov in letters to Girodias were not made in the later chapters because Girodias was eager to publish the book during the summer tourist season. When Nabokov received his copies from the Olympia Press, he found the volumes filled with typographical errors and discovered that Girodias (without permission) had assigned copyright to the Olympia Press as well as to Nabokov.

In the first two years after its publication *Lolita* gained international recognition and was translated into Danish and Swedish, with offers being made for Italian, German, Dutch, and French editions. Nabokov continued to seek an American publisher, but though several companies expressed interest they were discouraged by Girodias' royalty demands. To demonstrate the artistic merit of the novel, Nabokov published excerpts from *Lolita* in *The Anchor Review*, #2, 1957, published by Doubleday, for which he wrote the essay "On a Book Entitled Lolita." Eventually, G. P. Putnam's Sons negotiated an agreement with Girodias in which he agreed to split a 15 percent royalty with Nabokov, and a contract for American publication was signed on March 1, 1958. Putnam set the book from Nabokov's corrected copies of the Olympia edition. Nabokov made further corrections and revisions in the proofs, some of which were quite extensive. *Lolita* was published in New York on August 18, 1958, and immediately became a bestseller. (Nabokov's essay "On a Book Entitled Lolita" appeared as an afterword in the Putnam first edition.) The text printed here is that of the Putnam edition, incorporating corrections and revisions that Nabokov subsequently made in his own copies of the work as well as the addition of a dedication to his wife, Véra. It also includes the corrections requested by him in his earlier letters to Girodias that were never made in the Olympia and later editions.

Nabokov began writing *Pnin* in 1953 and finished the book late in September 1955. Four chapters from the novel were published in *The New Yorker*: Chapter One, titled "Pnin," on November 28, 1953; Chapter Three, "Pnin's Day," on April 23, 1955; Chapter Four, "Victor Meets Pnin," on October 15, 1955; and Chapter Six, "Pnin Gives a Party," on November 12, 1955. Two chapters were rejected by *The New Yorker*: Chapter Two, "Pnin Had Not Always Been Single," and Chapter Five, "Pnin Under the Pines." Nabokov did not submit the last chapter to the magazine, although he did give it the title "I Knew Pnin." Nabokov had expected Viking to publish the work, but it was rejected for being too short and seeming too much like a collection of sketches rather than a novel. After also being rejected by Harper and Brothers, it was accepted by Doubleday & Company in August 1956, under the working title of "My Poor Pnin." By October 1956 the title *Pnin* had been selected. The book was published by Doubleday in Garden City, New York, on March 7, 1957. It received good reviews and sold better than any of Nabokov's previous works, going into a second printing two weeks after publication. The text offered here is that of the first printing, incorporating the revisions and corrections marked by Nabokov in his own copies; it also includes the dedication to Véra not present in the first edition.

Although Nabokov began work in 1956 on the novel that eventually became *Pale Fire* and had chosen the title by March 1957, the finished novel was very different from the book he initially planned. He put the novel aside in 1958 to work on other projects and did not resume writing it until late November 1960, shortly after he had conceived a new structure (a poem with commentary) for the work. The completed typescript was sent from Montreux, Switzerland, to G. P. Putnam's Sons in early December 1961. *Pale Fire* was published in New York by Putnam in June 1962. The dedication to Véra was included in the first edition. Reviews were good, and the book appeared on

the bestseller list in *The New York Times* in July. The text printed here
is that of the first edition, incorporating the revisions and corrections
marked by Nabokov in his own copies.

Lolita: A Screenplay, included as an appendix here, was written by
Nabokov in Beverly Hills, California, between March and September
1960 for Harris-Kubrick Pictures. Although Nabokov received screen
credit for the screenplay, the finished film, released in June 1962, was
substantially different from the version he wrote. Nabokov wanted to
publish his screenplay soon after the film's release, but the rights were
withheld by Harris-Kubrick Pictures, and it was not until late in 1971
that he finally obtained permission. The screenplay was published by
McGraw-Hill in 1974. There were few reviews, and the book did not
sell well. The text printed here is that of the first edition.

This volume presents the texts of the original printings chosen for
inclusion here, but it does not attempt to reproduce features of their
typographic design, such as display capitalization of chapter openings.
The texts are printed without change, except for correction of typographical errors and the incorporation of revisions and corrections
made by Nabokov in letters and in his own copies of his books.

The following three lists record, by page and line number, Nabokov's revisions and corrections (other than corrections of typographical errors) incorporated into the texts of the novels presented in this
volume; in each case the reading of the present text comes first, followed by that of the first edition.

Lolita

3.31, *September–October*] September   5.28, August 5, 1955] [*no date in
first editions*]   16.30, perineum] peritonium   39.39, tip] top   47.32,
Fantasia] Fantazia   55.38, Krause] Krauze   73.36, hoped they]
hoped, and we all hoped, they   110.7, rubious] rubous   138.4, Patti]
Patty   151.26, Gobbert] Gobert   187.6, Marsh] March   203.19, con-
vertible] Convertible   213.22, convertible] Convertible   216.13–14,
flashlight] torchlight   248.36, late] early   288.38, ('Bye, Melmoth,]
(Hi, Melmoth,   289.37, voices—] voices,   296.2, America] American   297.20, spring of 1955] winter of 1954

Pnin

336.35, *shepchu*] shepchi   354.38, *Krieg*] Krief   386.30, half dozen]
half-a-dozen   396.28, Louise of] Louise—of   396.28, Department—] Department   396.33, Mandeville] Mandoville   411.26, *sizyy*] sizïy   415.9–10, caryatids] caryatides   424.40–425.1, as big]
bigger

Pale Fire

472.6, on] or   488.21, *Finnegans*] Finnigan's   488.38, *émaillée*]
émailée   523.28, closet door] closet   535.25, rusty] rustic   600.4,

549] 550   612.28, rhyme] lines   662.10, *287*] *288*   662.18, *433–434*]
417   663.38, etc., *347*] etc.   665.19, *287*] *288*   665.20, *334*] *338*

The following is a list of typographical errors corrected, cited by page and line number: 4.4, *sophomore,*; 5.2, *"unusual;"*; 20.35, *brune!"*); 28.5, *In Italy*; 28.19, *who*; 28.28, follows.]; 32.20, funeral; 37.8, Journal; 37.32, Ping.; 58.15, twelve-year old; 58.39, "brace"; 68.13, reak; 85.25, rightaway; 94.15, don'; 97.28, Farlow; 98.33, lamb; 98.36, Q.; 99.12, Q.; 113.32, notabene; 114.17, Droms; 127.37, course,; 130.19, Schwob's; 132.22, Oh you,; 132.32, nose,; 140.11, act; 140.11–12, nine-year old; 140.15, act; 145.23, street; 149.12, eight-year old; 150.24–25, girl children; 153.13, A; 167.19, girl children; 171.23, was; 172.1, twenty one; 173.12, Star; 181.9, Why, no; 182.17, teachers; 185.11, girls; 191.34, pommettes; 194.23, birchtree; 203.1, humming bird; 204.28, travellers'; 212.13, girl child; 218.32, fifty three; 224.35, seven-thousand foot high; 228.39, afterthought); 229.19, sometimes); 238.15, eighty-year old; 239.27, humming birds; 240.20, starling).; 240.32, snarlin').; 243.39, colombine; 246.18, Gazette's; 246.38, Dark Age; 258.26, pointilistic; 259.24, coincidence— . . . —; 260.16, start).; 261.9, baby,; 261.20, *péché*; 269.21, Avis; 269.22, dad; 272.4, nieces,; 279.28, said.; 281.19, readers,; 288.3, me,; 290.28, But; 333.22, night——"); 349.27, anyhere; 366.37, millenium; 371.32, diner,; 380.32, prosperious; 381.17, Emigré; 391.7, teemed; 405.28, action).; 503.21, he lane; 508.1, fateful; 529.36, erroneus; 546.20, Catskin; 578.15, Forword; 605.27, puddle; 607.12, *dust*; 608.29, Ukranian; 609.26, For; 620.15, sister).; 633.18, visitor.); 637.2, bathouse; 660.6, *130*; 660.17, 1000; 661.16, (q.v.); 661.17, 681; 661.35, 34; 663.24, 810; 666.37, 681; 684.3, girl; 686.21, *moustache.*); 688.16, faces; 688.25, interference / He fumbles . . . needs.; 701.17, knicknacks; 702.2, play).; 704.28, goldern; 728.27, sevent thirty; 733.24, 1960.]; 743.20, landscapes).; 755.33, that yours; 764.28, *sister?* . . . ; 764.29, *Ulalume, Ulalume!*; 765.21, scence; 770.23, *Nymphet*; 800.7, Elphinestone; 800.10, Waco; 805.2, *store.*; 806.15, turnout; 822.16, Sentiment"?; 825.18, guess,.

Notes

In the notes below, the reference numbers denote page and line of this volume (the line count includes titles and headings). No note is made for material included in standard desk-reference books such as Webster's *Collegiate, Biographical,* and *Geographical* dictionaries. Quotations from Shakespeare are keyed to *The Riverside Shakespeare,* ed. G. Blakemore Evans (Boston: Houghton Mifflin, 1974). For further background, more detailed notes, and references to other studies, see Brian Boyd, *Vladimir Nabokov, The Russian Years* and *Vladimir Nabokov, The American Years* (Princeton: Princeton University Press, 1990 and 1991); *The Nabokov-Wilson Letters, 1940–1971,* ed. Simon Karlinsky (New York: Harper & Row, Publishers, 1979); *Vladimir Nabokov: Selected Letters, 1940–1977,* ed. Dmitri Nabokov and Matthew J. Bruccoli (San Diego and New York: Harcourt, Brace, Jovanovich / Bruccoli Clark Layman, 1989); *The Annotated Lolita,* Revised and Updated Edition, ed. Alfred Appel Jr. (New York: Vintage Books, 1991), Vladimir Nabokov, *Strong Opinions* (New York: McGraw-Hill Book Company, 1973).

The publishers thank Dmitri Nabokov for his cooperation and assistance in the preparation of this volume and Glenn Horowitz for generous access to Vladimir Nabokov's personal copies of his books.

LOLITA

4.8   "*Vivian Darkbloom*"]   Anagram of "Vladimir Nabokov"; in part Nabokov's way of signing his novel at a time when he expected to publish *Lolita* anonymously. See also note 294.32.

4.24–25   *another . . . book*]   James Joyce's *Ulysses* (1922). In the 1934 Random House edition of *Ulysses,* the standard American edition at the time of *Lolita,* Woolsey's decision, which ruled the book publishable in the U.S., appeared as a preface.

4.34   *Blanche Schwarzmann*]   White (Fr.) Blackman (Ger.) See also note 284.14.

7.4–5   taking a trip . . . teeth.]   Since in an English "t" the tongue taps on the alveolar ridge, Humbert here indicates that he wants Lolita's name to be pronounced with a crisp Spanish "t," not a thick American one ("Low-leed-uh").

7.13–14   In a princedom . . . sea]   Cf. "Annabel Lee" (1849) by Edgar Allan Poe (1809–49), which opens: "It was many and many a year ago, / In a kingdom by the sea, / That a maiden there lived whom you may know /

By the name of Annabel Lee;—/ And this maiden she lived with no other thought / Than to love and be loved by me. // *She* was a child and *I* was a child, / In this kingdom by the sea." *The Kingdom by the Sea* was Nabokov's provisional title for *Lolita.*

7.18–19   what the seraphs . . . envied] Cf. "Annabel Lee," lines 9–12: "But we loved with a love that was more than love— / I and my Annabel Lee— / With a love that the winged seraphs of Heaven / Coveted her and me."

9.9   *Graphics*] London illustrated periodical.

10.15   *plage*] Beach.

10.34   *chocolat glacé*] At the time of *Lolita* this meant: "iced chocolate drink"; later, "chocolate ice cream."

13.19   uranists] Homosexuals.

13.19   Deux Magots] Café and famous haunt of intellectuals on Paris's Left Bank.

13.21–24   Fräulein . . . Gull.] Pastiche from lines 28–29, 67, and 69 of "Gerontion" (1920) by T. S. Eliot.

13.27–28   "*Histoire . . . anglaise*"] *Abridged History of English Poetry.*

13.35   Auteuil] Area of Paris on the Right Bank between the Seine and the Bois de Boulogne.

14.10   "nymphets."] At the time Nabokov wrote this, the word "nymphet" had not yet acquired the sense of "sexually loose girl or young woman" that evolved after the publication of *Lolita.*

16.23   Hugh Broughton] Puritan divine (1549–1612).

16.25   Rahab] Canaanite prostitute, Joshua 2:1–21.

16.29   Virgil . . . nymphet sing in single tone] Under "nymphet" the *Oxford English Dictionary* lists an example from Robert Singleton's translation of *The Works of Virgil* (1855): "who could the nymphets sing."

17.15–16   "*enfante . . . fourbe,*"] Charming and sly child.

18.23   voluptas] Latin, "pleasures, delights."

18.28   Madeleine] Church on Paris's Right Bank.

18.37   *frétillement*] Wiggle.

19.11   *petit cadeau*] Little present.

19.13   *dix huit*] Eighteen.

19.24–25   "*Oui, ce n'est pas bien,*"] Yes, that's no good.

19.31   *grues*] Prostitutes.

19.33–34   *"Il etait . . . true-là,"*]   It was a clever guy who thought up this trick.

19.38   *posé un lapin*]   Stood someone up.

20.1   *"Tu es . . . ça,"*]   You are very kind to say that.

20.6   *avant qu'on se couche*]   Before we go to bed.

20.15–16   *"Je vais . . . bas!"*]   I'm going to buy myself some stockings!

20.34–35   (*"Regardez-moi . . . brune!"*)]   Just look at this beautiful brunette!

20.39   *qui pourrait . . . chose*]   Who could arrange it.

21.21–22   Marie . . . stellar]   The Virgin Mary has traditionally been associated with *stella maris*, star of the sea.

22.10   *mes malheurs*]   My misfortunes.

22.19   *français moyen*]   Average Frenchman, man in the street.

22.28   merkin]   False hair for the female genitalia.

22.36   *à la gamine*]   Like a pert young girl.

23.4   *mairie*]   Town hall.

23.16   *baba*]   Nabokov told Alfred Appel Jr., who was preparing *The Annotated Lolita* (1970), that in Russian *baba* refers to "any female on the common side; a blousy, vulgar woman."

23.23   *Paris-Soir*]   Paris evening newspaper.

24.12   Nansen . . . passport]   A passport issued to stateless persons by the League of Nations.

25.2   *"Mais qui est-ce?"*]   But who is it?

25.31   *Jean Christophe*]   Ten-volume novel (1906–1912) by French novelist Romain Rolland (1868–1944).

26.23   *le gredin*]   The scoundrel.

34.16–17   René Prinet's "Kreutzer Sonata."]   For Nabokov's description of the 1898 painting, see *Lolita: A Screenplay*, page 703.24–28.

35.40–36.1   "Roches Roses."]   Red Rocks.

36.11   my dead bride]   Annabel Lee, after "my darling, my darling, my life and my bride" at the end of Poe's poem (see note 7.13–14).

36.12   *nouvelle*]   New girl.

36.21   *fruit vert . . . égal.*]   "Green fruit. Ultimately it's all the same to me." Nabokov noted to Appel that *fruit vert* is French slang for " 'unripe' females attractive to ripe gentlemen."

36.30   *en escalier*] In zigzag steps.

37.39   le Bel] The Fair.

39.10   *Delectatio morosa*] Morose delectation, the sin of letting the mind dwell at length on a pleasure, whether the pleasure be sinful or not.

39.18   Virginia . . . Harry Edgar] Virginia Clemm and Edgar Allan Poe married in 1836.

39.19   *Je m'imagine cela.*] I can just picture that.

40.16–17   *ne montrez . . . zhambes*] Don't show your legs.

40.19   *à mes heures*] In the right mood.

43.9–10   *"la vermeillette fente"*] "Little red slit"; from "Blason du sexe feminin" by Pierre de Ronsard (1524–85).

43.10–11   *"un petit . . . escarlatte"*] "A hillock felted in delicate moss, and marked along the middle with a scarlet thread"; from a poem by Remy Belleau (1528?–77).

43.14   my darling . . . bride] See note 36.11.

45.14   *"Ces matins . . . doux*] These gray mornings, so mild.

49.17   *"Mais allez-y, allez-y!"*] Go ahead, go ahead!

50.26   *manège*] Tactics.

61.11–12   Berthe *au Grand Pied*] Bigfoot Bertha, Charlemagne's mother and the wife of Pépin the Short.

64.8–9   Morell . . . hero."] "See the conquering hero comes" is from Handel's *Joshua* (1748), pt. 3, words by Thomas Morell (1703–84).

65.4   *pavor nocturnus*] Night tremor.

65.20–22   "To hold . . . kiss . . . "] Byron, *Childe Harold's Pilgrimage* (1812–18), Canto III, stanza 116.

65.29   (*quel mot!*)] What a word!

67.31   *Une petite attention*] A little act of thoughtfulness.

70.9   *rubrique*] Section (of newspaper).

73.17   *arrière-pensée*] Ulterior motive.

78.6   *c'est . . . décide*] It's I who decide.

83.34–35   *"Ce qui . . . comme ça."*] What drives me crazy is that I don't know what you're thinking about when you're like this.

88.13   olisbos-like] An olisbos was a leather phallus worn in Greek Dionysian celebrations.

90.33   pin] Cf. "gin and pineapple," p. 67.29.

98.24–25   *Eh bien, . . . tout!*] Well, not at all!

100.17–18   as Vee was Poe's] See note 39.18.

104.11   *aux yeux battus*] With rings around her eyes.

104.11   plumbaceous umbrae] Leaden shadows.

104.15   *mägdlein*] Little girl.

106.6   backfisch] German, adolescent or teenage girl.

107.12   *"Ensuite?"*] Then?

107.35–36   *C'est bien tout? / C'est.*] And that's all? It is.

111.38   *Enfins seuls*] Alone at last.

113.19–22   *Seva ascendes . . . quidquam*] Mixture of mock-Latin with English, French, German and Italian: "The sap rising, pulsing, burning, itching, most insane. Elevator clattering, pause, people in the corridor. Let no one but death take her from me now! Slender little girl, I thought most fondly, observing nothing at all."

116.5–6   *sicher ist sicher*] Sure is sure, steady does it.

118.2   *comme on dit*] As they say.

120.24   *entre nous soit dit*] Just between us.

121.31–32   *La Petite . . . Ridicule.*] Little Girl Sleeping or the Ridiculous Lover.

126.21   callypygean] With beautiful buttocks.

127.21   *die Kleine*] The little one.

129.29   clathrate] Latticed.

130.31   *le découvert*] The nude.

135.21–22   *nous connûmes . . .* Flaubertian intonation] Flaubert is famous for the special way he uses this verb tense, the *passé simple*.

135.22–23   Chateaubriandesque] After the description of America in *Atala* (1801) by François-René de Chateaubriand (1768–1848).

137.11   do you remember, Miranda] From Hillaire Belloc's poem "Tarantella" (1923): "Do you remember an Inn, / Miranda?"

138.3–4   Sammy . . . Patti] Band leader Sammy Kaye and popular singers Jo Stafford, Eddie Fisher, Tony Bennett, Peggy Lee, Guy Mitchell, and Patti Page.

138.19   Huncan Dines] Duncan Hines (1880–1959), author of *Adventures in Good Eating, Duncan Hines' Food Odyssey*, etc.

139.23   *comme . . . gentille*] As you know too well, my sweet one.

140.11   Mann Act] Passed in 1910, the act made it a federal felony to aid
or participate in the transportation of women or girls in interstate or foreign
commerce for immoral purposes.

141.3   *c'est tout*] That's all.

143.24   *ce qu'on appelle*] What one calls.

144.6   *partie de plaisir*] Outing.

144.11   Magnolia Garden] Near Charleston, South Carolina.

144.25   "Kurort"] Spa, health resort.

144.38   Battle of Blue Licks] Battle, August 19, 1782, in which Kentucky
settlers were defeated by a force of Indians and Canadians; the site is now
Blue Licks Battlefield State Park, northeast Kentucky.

145.2–3   plaque . . . author of "Trees"] The plaque is at Big Poplar Cave,
Joyce Kilmer Memorial Forest, in North Carolina's Smoky Mountains.

145.11   "millionaires' colony"] Jekyll Island, southeast Georgia, later a
state park.

145.34   Menninger Foundation] In Topeka, Kansas.

145.36–37   creeping white flies] Nabokov noted for Appel: "The insects
that poor Humbert mistakes for 'creeping white flies' are the biologically fascinating little moths of the genus *Pronuba* whose amiable and indispensable
females transport the pollen that fertilizes the yucca flowers (see, what Humbert failed to do, 'Yucca Moth' in any good encyclopedia)."

146.17   *comme on dit*] As one says.

146.26–27   hummingbirds in the dusk] Nabokov noted for Appel that
these were "hawkmoths which do move exactly like hummingbirds (which
are neither gray nor nocturnal)."

147.11   Scotty's Castle] In northern Death Valley, built as a home in the
1920s by Walter Scott of Buffalo Bill's Wild West Show.

147.13–14   Stevenson's footprint . . . . Mission Dolores] A Robert Louis
Stevenson Monument on Mount St. Helena in California commemorates the
writer's honeymoon stay there. Mission Dolores is in San Francsico.

147.16   Russian Gulch State Park] Near Mendocino, California.

147.21–22   chateau . . . French marquess] Chateau de Mores, Medora,
North Dakota.

147.23–25   The Bearded Woman . . . single.] Jingles were solicited by the
Burma Shave Company, 1925–63, for its roadside advertising signs; those selected were paid for. In 1953 Vladimir and Véra Nabokov offered one: "He
passed two cars; then five; then seven; and then he beat them all to heaven."

147.25   zoo in Indiana]   In Evansville, Indiana.

148.32–33   *face à claques*]   Face (that deserves) to be slapped.

149.2–3   *coulant un regard*]   Casting an eye.

151.3   *mais je divague.*]   But I digress.

151.9   *les yeux perdus*]   With a lost look in her eyes.

151.11–13   *brun adolescent . . . se tordre*—oh Baudelaire!]   "Dark-haired adolescent . . . to twist"; from Baudelaire's 1852 poem, "Le Crépuscule du matin" ("Morning Twilight"): "C'était l'heure où l'essaim des rêves malfaisants / Tord sur leurs oreillers les bruns adolescents" ("It was the hour when the swarm of hurtful dreams / Twists dark-haired adolescents on their pillows").

151.19–20   famous coach . . . boys]   Tennis star William "Big Bill" Tilden (1893–1953). When Alfred Appel asked if he should be identified by name, Nabokov imagined him now "consorting with ball boys . . . on Elysian turf. Shall we spare his shade?"

151.26   the great Gobbert]   André Gobbert. Nabokov noted for Appel: "I saw him beaten by Patterson in 1919 or 1920 at Wimbledon. He had a tremendous (old-fashioned) serve, but would double fault up to four times in a game. Big dark fellow, doubled with Decugis against Brookes and Patterson, I think."

151.36   *ange gauche*]   Awkward angel.

154.19   bobby-soxer]   In Harry Haenigsen's comic strip *Penny*, begun 1943.

155.25   *hors concours*]   Beyond competition.

155.33   leporine]   Resembling a hare.

157.17   *que dis-je*]   What am I saying.

158.32   *un monsieur très bien*]   A real gentleman.

162.22   *A Girl of the Limberlost*]   1914; by Gene Stratton Porter.

162.38   *dans la force de l'âge*]   In my prime.

162.40   *vieillard encore vert*]   An old man still green (unwithered, potent).

163.27   *casé*]   Settled.

165.29   *recueillement*]   Abstraction, gathering oneself.

169.18   *mes goûts*]   My tastes.

170.14   *"Oui, ils sont gentils."*]   Yes, they are nice.

170.16   *toiles*]   Canvases.

170.20–22   *"Prenez . . . j'exècre."*]   "Please take one of these pears. The good lady opposite offers me more than I can relish." Or: "Mrs. Taylor has just given me these dahlias, pretty flowers that I abhor."

170.29–30   *Au roi!*]   Check!

171.13   *"Et toutes . . . bien?"*]   And are all your little girls doing well?

171.20   *sale histoire*]   Sordid business.

185.14   Reynolds' "Age of Innocence"]   Joshua Reynolds' painting (1788) shows a girl of six or seven seated barefoot on the ground.

187.3   Doris Lee]   (1905–83); the painting described is her "Noon."

189.28   Miss Emperor . . . French scholars]   In Gustave Flaubert's *Madame Bovary* (1857), Emma Bovary uses lessons with her piano teacher Mlle Lempereur as an alibi for her adulterous trysts with Léon.

190.11–15   (*mon pauvre . . . saluent*)]   My poor friend, I have never seen you again and although there is very little chance you will read my book, allow me to say I give you a very cordial handshake and all my daughters send their greetings.

190.19   *d'un petit . . . contrit*]   With a little look of false contrition.

191.34   *pommettes . . . maman*]   Cheekbones . . . mother.

194.2   passes by . . . Pippa]   Cf. A. A. Milne's *Mr. Pim Passes By* (1919) and Robert Browning's *Pippa Passes* (1842).

194.4   *J'ai . . . Dublinois.*]   "I have always admired the ormonde work of the sublime Dubliner." A chapter of James Joyce's *Ulysses* is set in the Ormond Hotel in Dublin; *hors de ce monde* is French for "out of this world."

194.14   *C'est entendu?*]   It's agreed?

194.22   *qui prenait son temps.*]   Who was taking its time.

196.32   *le montagnard émigré*]   The emigré mountaineer; title of a Chateaubriand song (1806).

196.32–33   *Felis tigri goldsmithi*]   Goldsmith's tiger; cf. line 356 of Oliver Goldsmith's "The Deserted Village" (1770): "where crouching tigers wait their hapless prey."

197.34   French detective tale]   By Maurice Leblanc (1864–1941).

200.13–14   "Bertoldo" . . . comedy]   In the *commedia dell'arte.*

201.5–6   *adolori d'amoureuse langueur*]   "Saddened by the languor of love."

202.6   *Gros*]   Fat.

202.13   luizettas]   Humbert's invention, from "louis d'or," a French gold coin.

203.27   *donc*]   Therefore.

203.38   Jutting Chin]   Dick Tracy, in the comic strip created by Chester Gould in 1931.

206.6   *O lente . . . equi!*]   "Oh run slowly, horses of night!"; cf. Ovid's *Amores*, I.xiii.39, (where the line begins *lente*) and Christopher Marlowe's *The Tragical History of Dr. Faustus* (1605), xvi (where it begins *O lente, lente*).

207.10   kurortish]   See note 144.25.

207.15–23   garland of seven . . . Joyce]   Cf. the seven rainbow girls of *Finnegans Wake*.

209.26–28   *Ne manque . . . Qu'il t'y—*]   "Do not fail to tell your suitor, Chimène, how beautiful the lake is, for he must take you there." (*Qu'il'ty* literally means "that he you there.") Chimène is the heroine of Corneille's *Le Cid* (1636), the style of which is parodied here.

209.36   *à titre documentaire*]   For the record.

212.35   *la pomme de sa canne*]   The knob of his cane.

215.33–35   'Hedda . . . Orchard"]   Henrik Ibsen's *Hedda Gabler* (1890) and Anton Chekhov's *The Cherry Orchard* (1904). "Love Under the Lindens" is a play on Eugene O'Neill's *Desire Under the Elms* (1924) and Berlin's boulevard Unter den Linden.

216.26   *petit rat*]   Young ballet trainee at the Paris Opera.

219.33   Decugis or Borman]   Paul de Borman, Belgian tennis champion, of whom Nabokov recalled for Appel: "He was left-handed, and one of the first Europeans to use a sliced (or twist) service." For Max Decugis, see note 151.26.

224.14   *Soyons logiques*]   Let's be logical.

224.38–225.1   José . . . Carmen]   José is the Basque who tells the tale-within-the-tale—of his fatal love for Carmen—in Prosper Mérimée's novella *Carmen* (1845).

225.24   40.4]   104 degrees F.

225.40   heterosexual Erlkönig]   In Goethe's ballad "Erlkönig," the elf king accosts a little boy riding through the night with his father, who flies at a gallop to "safety" only to find his son dead in his arms. See also page 562.27–28 and note.

226.29   *haute montagne*]   Upper mountain area.

226.31   *que sais-je!*]   Who knows!

228.10   *chassé-croisé*]   Repeated sidestepping to pass someone else.

228.17   *"Je croyais . . . billet doux."*]   I thought it was a bill—not a love letter.

228.38–40   sister Ann . . . . brothers]   In Perrault's fairy tale, Ann is the sister of the heroine; their brothers slay Bluebeard.

228.40–229.1   *Est-ce . . . Carmen?*]   "Do you not love me anymore, my Carmen?" (from Chapter 3 of Mérimée's novella).

229.3   Zemfirian]   From "Zemfira," the heroine of Alexander Pushkin's long poem *Tsigany* (*The Gypsies*, 1824).

229.12   Professor Humbertoldi]   In the *commedia dell'arte*.

229.22   gitanilla]   Little gypsy.

229.38–39   *une belle . . . bleu*]   A beautiful lady all in blue.

230.20–23   *Saint . . . magazine*]   Parody of the opening of Browning's "Soliloquy of the Spanish Cloister" (1842).

231.34   telestically]   With an end or purpose in view.

233.16–17   ("N. Petit, Larousse, Ill.")]   Cf. the French dictionary *Nouveau petit Larousse illustré* (*New Illustrated Little Larousse*).

233.38–39   Dr. Gratiano . . . Comedy]   Gratiano, Forbeson, and Mirandola are figures from the *commedia dell'arte*.

234.40   logodaedaly and logomancy]   Word-coinage and word-divination.

235.3   Quelquepart Island]   Somewhere Island.

237.19   *garçon*]   Boy, young man.

238.20   *"Dolorès Disparue,"*]   "Dolores Disappeared," a play on *Albertine disparue*, the title of the penultimate volume of *A la recherche du temps perdu* (*In Search of Lost Time*, 1913–27) until the 1954 Pléiade edition restored Proust's own title, *La Fugitive.*

238.36–37   *chambres garnies*]   Furnished rooms.

239.10   *que . . . cela!*]   How distant it was, all of that!

239.21–22   *Et . . . génie*]   And I who was offering you my genius.

240.20   I cannot . . . starling]   From Sterne's *A Sentimental Journey Through France and Italy* (1768), II: "The Passport: Hotel de Paris."

241.3   *Soleil Vert*]   Green Sun

241.5–8   *L'autre . . . vie?*]   "The other night a cold opera air landed me in bed: / Broken note—whoever trusts that is quite mad! / It is snowing, the decor is crumbling, Lolita! / Lolita, what have I made of your life?" Parody of a passage from IV.ii of Victor Hugo's 1832 play *Le Roi s'amuse.*

242.23–24   *ensellure*]   The inward curve of the lower back.

243.1   *cavalier servant*]   In the courtly love tradition of medieval literature, a knight who serves the lady he loves as a vassal.

244.35   "Mimir]   In Norse myth, a giant god who dwelled in Mimir's
Well (the ocean) by a root of the world-tree Yggdrasil and could see the past
and future by drinking its water.

245.4   *travaux*]   Works.

245.13–14   *très digne*]   Very dignified.

245.26–27   *souvenir . . . veux-tu?*]   "Memory, memory, what do you want
of me?" The opening line of "Nevermore" (1866) by Paul Verlaine (1844–
96).

245.33   NEAR CHURCHES]   In the 1940s and 1950s, hotels frequently so-
advertised to indicate that Jews were not welcome.

245.39   *petite nymphe accroupie*]   Crouching nymphet.

246.10   *Bruder!*]   Brother!

246.30–31   *Brute Force* and *Possessed*]   1947 films, the former directed by
Jules Dassin and starring Burt Lancaster, the latter directed by Curtis Bern-
hardt and starring Joan Crawford.

246.33   Omen Faustum]   Lucky Omen (cf. Lucky Strike cigarettes).

247.7   *vin triste*]   Glum from drink.

248.15   *Mes fenêtres!*]   "My windows!" Parody of Verlaine's autobiographical prose pieces, with titles like *Mes hôpitaux* (1891), *Mes prisons* (1893), *Ma
candidature* (1893).

248.26–27   *"Savez-vous . . . vous?"*]   Do you know that at ten my little
girl was mad about you?

249.15–16   Emma . . . Flaubert's father's]   Emma Bovary takes arsenic at
the end of *Madame Bovary* and her father does not arrive until after her death;
Flaubert is reported to have said of her: "*Emma Bovary? c'est moi.*"

251.5   *Pas tout à fait.*]   Not completely.

253.13–14   *Personne . . . Repersonne.*]   No one. I ring. Re-no one.

253.37–38   *pommettes*]   Cheekbones.

257.11   *frileux*]   Susceptible to cold.

258.2   Florentine]   Alluding to Botticelli's "Birth of Venus" (c. 1484–86,
Uffizi, Florence).

259.5   *Streng verboten*]   Strictly forbidden.

259.25–26   Duk Duk]   A native secret society of the island of New Britain
whose members pose as sorcerers; also, an obscene word for copulation in

The Perfumed Garden (16th-century Arabic erotology, English version 1886 by Richard Burton).

260.28   *souffler*]   Blow.

261.20–21   *mon grand péché radieux*]   "My great radiant sin"; from Verlaine's poem "Lunes."

261.27–29   *Changeons . . . séparés*]   "Let's change our lives, my Carmen, let's go somewhere where we shall never be separated"; this and the quotations translated in notes 262.1 and 263.31 are from Mérimée's *Carmen*.

262.1   *Carmen . . . moi?*]   "Carmen, do you want to come with me?"

262.18   *mon petit cadeau*]   My little present.

263.27   to Jupiter]   To Juneau, Alaska, a homophone of Juno, the wife of Jupiter and the goddess of marriage.

263.31   *Carmencita, lui demandais-je*]   "Carmencita, I asked her."

267.34   stippled Hopkins]   Gerard Manley Hopkins' "Pied Beauty" (1877) celebrates his love of "dappled things . . . rose-moles all in stipple upon trout that swim."

268.4–5   *mais je t'aimais*]   But I loved you.

270.10   Moulinet]   Village in the Alpes-Maritimes, in the hills north of Menton.

270.29   *Bonzhur*]   *Bonjour* (Good day).

271.26   Turgenev story]   "Prizraki" ("Ghosts," written 1861–63).

272.26   *mille grâces*]   A thousand thanks.

273.23–24   *"Réveillez-vous . . . mourir!"*]   Wake up, Laqueue (or: Cue), it is time to die!

278.28–29   *vaterre*]   Toilet (French-accented "water," here short for "water-closet").

278.39   *Fierté de la Chair*]   *Pride of the Flesh.*

279.26   *une femme . . . cigarette*]   "A woman is a woman, but a Caporal is a cigarette" (Caporal: a cigarette brand name); cf. Kipling's "The Betrothed," stanza 25: "And a woman is only a woman, but a good cigar is a smoke."

280.33–34   *"Vous voilà . . . vieux."*]   You're in a fine mess, old chap.

280.38   *"Alors, que fait-on?"*]   So, what next?

282.2–283.5   Because you . . . die]   Parody of T. S. Eliot's "Ash Wednesday" (1930).

283.18–19   *rencontre*]   Duel.

283.33   *soyons raisonnables.*]   Let's be reasonable.

283.38–39   Bard . . . to borrow.]   Cf. *Macbeth* V.vii.19.

284.6   Maeterlinck-Schmetterling]   *Schmetterling* is German for "butter-fly." The repetition of a word, prefaced by "sch", is a Yiddish idiom of disgust.

284.8   herculanita]   A kind of heroin.

284.14   Melanie Weiss]   Black (from the Greek) White (German).

284.17   Barda Sea]   *Barda* is Russian for dregs from alcohol production, fed as slops to livestock.

284.21   *Feu*]   Fire.

284.40–285.1   old . . . Nijinski]   Nabokov wrote to Carl Proffer (May 1, 1968): "A reference to a famous photograph that . . . showed poor mad Nijinsky, then almost fifty, executing a pathetic entrechat for the reporters."

285.1   Old Faithful]   Geyser in Yellowstone National Park.

285.40   trudging from room to room]   Nabokov wrote to Alfred Appel (April 2, 1967): "I have corrected in my Russian [*Lolita*] a curious dream-distortion . . . Q could not be trudging from room to room since H. H. had locked their rooms, but this is okay on second thought and need not be corrected in your edition."

288.8   Thomas had something.]   Cf. the "Doubting" Thomas of John 20:24.

290.16   the nastiness]   Nabokov told Robert Hughes in September 1965: "The sound of Humbert is both pompous and somehow dingy."

293.35   two social revolutionaries . . . doctor]   Ilya Fondaminsky, Vladimir Zenzinov, and Dr. Elizaveta Kogan-Bernstein.

294.32   anonymously]   Translating the afterword to the Russian *Lolita*, Nabokov added: "The anagram of my name in one of my characters [Vivian Darkbloom] is a memorial of this covert authorship."

295.44   reader]   Professor Harry Levin of Harvard.

298.7–8   an American critic]   John Hollander, in *Partisan Review*, Fall 1956.

PNIN

301.27   *faux col*]   The old-fashioned removable collar attached to a shirt by a stud.

302.34   Dub]   In Russian literally "oak," but colloquially "thick, stupid."

303.29   University of Prague]   The major academic center for Russian emigrés in the 1920s.

304.21–22   Leskovian . . . verbal contortions.]   Nicolai Leskov (1831–95); cf. his story "Levsha" ("Lefty"; 1881).

304.24–25   Moscow Artists]   The Moscow Art Theatre, founded in 1898 by Konstantin Stanislavsky and Vladimir Nemirovich-Danchenko, set new standards of artistic integrity.

305.16–17   *der zestreute Professor*]   The absent-minded professor.

306.6–7   "the rest is silence"]   *Hamlet* V.ii.356.

306.7   "nevermore"]   The refrain in Poe's poem "The Raven" (1845).

307.30   the Yalta conference]   Meeting at Yalta in the Crimea, February 4–11, 1945, attended by Winston Churchill, Franklin D. Roosevelt, and Joseph Stalin, and held to plan for the end of World War II and for the post-war world.

312.22   pyrographic]   Produced by scorching.

315.36–37   Khodotov]   Nikolai Khodotov (1878–1932), a star of the Aleksandrinskiy Theater in St. Petersburg, invented his own declamatory mode.

319.14–15   'I know . . . brooch—']   *Hamlet* IV.vii.93.

320.14   scientific]   From Russian *nauchnye*, "scientific," which also has the meanings "research" and "academic."

320.33   Hoecker's]   German salon painter Paul Hoecker (1854–1910).

320.34   Hunt's]   American artist William Morris Hunt (1824–79).

321.13   The Egg and We]   Cf. *The Egg and I*, film (1949, from Betty McDonald's novel) directed by Chester Erskine; between 1949 and 1957 it was followed by nine popular films featuring its characters Ma and Pa Kettle.

322.18   *"Zdravstvuyte . . . spasibo,"*]   Hello how are you fine thanks.

322.21–22   *Ougolok*]   Nook, cozy little corner.

323.12–13   Chateaubriand . . . *chef*]   François-René de Chateaubriand (1768–1848) was a leading French writer; chateaubriand is also the name of a steak dish.

324.8   *petite histoire*]   History on the small scale, of everyday life and customs.

325.36–37   *espace meublé*]   Furnished space; the term derives from philosopher Henri Bergson.

326.8   *mahnut', vsplesnut', razvesti*]   To wave, to "splash," and to spread one's hands.

326.35–36   Turgenev's poem . . . roses."]   1879; in *Senilia* (1879–83).

326.39   Pauline Viardot]   Celebrated French opera singer and teacher Pauline Viardot-Garcia (1821–1910). Turgenev (1818–83) became her admirer in 1843 and later left Russia to be near her. In his Cornell lectures, Nabokov called her the "great, the only true love" of Turgenev's life.

326.40–327.1   Madam Pushkin . . . verses, Pushkin'] Recorded by Olga Smirnov in a footnote in *Zapiski A. O. Smirnovoi* (St. Petersburg, 1895), the unreliable memoirs of her mother, who was Pushkin's confidante.

327.2–3   wife . . . moozishan] From 1895 to the early 1900s Countess Sofia Tolstoy had a brief and one-sided infatuation with musician Sergei Taneyev (1856–1915) that caused her husband agonies of jealousy.

328.11–12   Aksakov . . . Gresset] Cf. Sergei Aksakov (1791–1859), author of the autobiographical novels *A Family Chronicle* (1856), which includes a portrayal of his grandfather as Stepan Bagrov, and *The Childhood Years of Bagrov's Grandson* (1858), and Jean Baptiste Louis de Gresset (1709–70), author of the humorous poem *Vert Vert* (1734) .

328.16   Meudon] Southwestern suburb of Paris.

329.2   Zhorzhik Uranski . . . dinner] "Zhorzhik" is a diminutive of Georgy, and "Uranski" implies "uranist" (homosexual). Russian emigré readers recognized the allusion to Georgy Adamovich (1894–1972), minor poet and critic who in his emigré years in Paris freely traded favorable reviews for dinners.

329.19   *taper dessus*] Beat up.

330.23   *dragées*] Sugar-coated almonds.

330.40–331.1   *("Wenn . . . fliegt")*] When you so, then I so, and horse [knight] flies.

331.2   *entschuldigen Sie*] Excuse me.

331.32   *"Lasse mich*] Leave me.

331.39   *koschmarische*] "Nightmare" is *koshmar* in Russian, *cauchemar* in French, but in German *Alpdrücken* or *böser Traum*.

334.21   *("Timofey, zdrastvuy!")*] Timothy, hello!

334.28–29   *"Nu . . . vot"*] Well, well, this is good, well now.

336.29–36   *Ya nadela . . . tvoyo!*] A parody of Akhmatova's early verse.

340.19–20   "Lermontov," . . . two poems.] "Rusalka" ("The Mermaid"; 1832) and "Morskaia tsarevna" ("The Sea Princess"; 1841).

341.35   *kabinet*] Study.

343.14–15   Duchess of Wonderland chin] As in John Tenniel's illustrations of Lewis Carroll's *Alice's Adventures in Wonderland* (1865), Chapters 6 and 9.

345.23   He died——"] Pushkin died on January 29, 1837, Old Style, February 10, New Style.

346.16   ticonderoga-ticonderoga] Cf. the Dixon Ticonderoga pencil manufacturing company at Ticonderoga, New York.

348.13   *antikvarnïy liberalizm*] Antiquated liberalism.

348.34   *"Huligani,"*] Hooligans.

349.1   *portfel'*] Briefcase.

351.15   *feuilleton*] Article.

351.20   *Petite Histoire*] See note 324.8.

352.1   Roaring Sixties] Like the geographical Roaring Forties (the stormy areas of ocean between the 40th and 50th parallels of latitude), the reformist 1860s could be seen as a windy or stormy time in Russia; it was a decade of political strife and strident political journalism, carried out especially in "thick magazines."

352.3–6   Russian classics . . . Pushkin's] The series *Biblioteka velikikh pisateley* (*Library of Great Writers*), published in St. Petersburg in the early 20th century; Pushkin was published in six volumes, 1907–15.

353.25   Vengerov's . . . edition.] Semion Vengerov's *Shekspir* (1903). Kroneberg's translation, an inexact paraphrase, long held sway in Russia.

354.29   Glupishkin . . . Linder] André Deed (1884–1931), Franco-Italian actor, stage names Cretinetti, Gribouille, Glupyshkin (all meaning "Simpleton"), and Gabrielle Leuvielle (1883–1925), French film comedian, film name Max Linder.

354.32   Soviet documentary film] *U.S.S.R. Today*, directed by G. Bobrov and S. Gurov, screened in New York in spring 1953. Nabokov saw the film.

354.36–38   *"Ruki . . . Krieg."*] "Hands off Korea" (in poor Russian and French) and "Peace will conquer war" (in Spanish and German).

355.15   Zim] From Zavod imeni Molotova (Molotov Factory).

357.18–19   Orient Express] Luxury train, running from Paris to Istanbul.

358.21   Bohemian Sea] Cf. the geographic absurdity in Shakespeare's *The Winter's Tale*, III.iii.1–2.

358.27   Italian film] Roberto Rossellini's *Germany Year Zero* (1949).

358.30   *The Scarlet Pimpernel*] Novel (1905) by Baroness Emmuska Orczy; its hero is Sir Percy Blakeney.

360.31   country pope] Russian parish priest.

361.30–31   Godunov . . . Test] Cf. the Drawing-a-Person test, introduced as a measure of children's intelligence in 1926 by W. H. Goodenough.

362.31–32   the wheel . . . Morphos] Cf. Alexander Pope's "Who breaks a butterfly upon a wheel?" ("Epistle to Dr. Arbuthnot," line 308), which became proverbial for using unnecessary force to destroy something fragile. Morphos are the generally large and showy blue South American butterflies of the genus *Morpho* Fabricius.

363.32–34   coffin . . . Lipari Island] St. Bartholomew (1st C.) is believed to have been martyred in Albanopolis and his relics translated to Lipari in 508, then to Benevenutum, and finally to Rome.

363.38   *"Sursum."*] Upwards.

365.10   Gertrude Käsebier] American photographer (1852–1934).

366.8–9   if Degas . . . *calèche*] Degas's "Carriage at the Races" (1872; also called "Aux Courses en province," "Country races").

367.1–2   Moinet] French, "monk" (pejorative).

372.29–31   *—vous comprenez . . . peu,"*] "—you understand French? Well? Fairly well? A little?" "Very a little."

372.33–34   box . . . Lermontov] In his 1838 poem "The Song of Tsar Ivan Vasilievich, of the Young *Oprichnik*, and of the Brave Merchant Kalashnikov," Lermontov describes a Russian fist fight quite unlike English boxing.

374.23–24   story of Tolstoy] *The Death of Ivan Ilich* (1886).

378.9   Glidden Tour] Automobile excursions organized 1905–13 by the American Automobile Association to promote motor vehicles.

380.19   Old-Believers] Those who by refusing to follow official reforms of ritual in the Russian Orthodox Church precipitated the Great Schism in the mid-17th century.

380.25–26   Harbin] In Manchuria, along the major eastward route for Russian emigrés in the 1920s.

381.21   Sirin] Pen-name in emigration of Nabokov.

382.27–28   local elective . . . seventeenth century] Exact translation of the title of M. Bogoslovski's *Zemskoe samoupravlenie na russkom severe v XVII v.* (Moscow, 1909).

382.29   history . . . medical schools in Russia] Exact translation of the title of Iakov Chistovich's *Istoriia pervykh meditsinskikh shkol v Rossii* (St. Petersburg, 1883).

384.28   *"Avtomobil', kostyum—*] Automobile, suit—.

386.5–7   "well adapted . . . towers."] The quotations are from *Sloan's Homestead Architecture* (Philadelphia, 1861).

389.23–30   small butterflies . . . . Vladimir Vladimirovich] The butterflies belong to the very local Eastern subspecies that Nabokov identified in 1943 as *Lycaeides melissa samuelis*, and that he first encountered in Karner, near Albany, New York, in 1950. The popular name is the Karner Blue.

395.18   Raskolnikov]   The central character, a murderer, in Dostoevsky's *Crime and Punishment.*

395.18–19   other great and good men]   In his notes to *Ada* Nabokov glosses "great good man" as "a phrase that Winston Churchill, the British politician, enthusiastically applied to Stalin."

401.28   fifty arshins]   Nearly forty yards (an arshin is about 28 inches).

401.40–402.3   a tall deciduous tree . . . leaves]   A paulownia (named for Russian princess Anna Pavlovna Romanov).

403.23   Turgenev's prose poem]   See page 326.35–36 and note.

404.16   teach Lethean and Fenugreek]   Lethean: from the river of forgetfulness in the Greek Hades; Fenugreek: the herb *Trigonella foenum-grae-cum;* Nabokov implies Latin, Lettish, Lithuanian, Finnish, and Greek, as well as the entire Finno-Ugric family of languages.

404.26–32   Thomas Wynn . . . "Twynn"]   Cf. John 11:16: "Thomas, who was called the Twin."

405.31   Skoff]   Pskov.

405.38–39   *zhavoronki . . . alouettes*]   Russian and French for "larks."

406.31   Gretchen-like]   After the maiden who becomes Faust's lover in Goethe's *Faust.*

408.27–28   somewhat *en jeune*]   In a somewhat younger version.

408.28–29   Jan van Eyck's . . . Paele]   Originally an altarpiece, often called "The Madonna with Canon van der Paele" (1436), now in the Musée communal des Beaux-Arts in Bruges.

410.40   *à la fourchette*]   To be eaten with forks; more than finger food.

411.14   Lake Dunmore]   In Vermont.

411.23   *verre*]   Glass.

418.13   *cruchon*]   Small jug.

419.16–17   Armenian massacres]   By the Turks, in 1894–95 and especially in 1915, when about 600,000 Armenians were killed in an attempt to deport the Armenian population of the Ottoman Empire to Syria and Mesopotamia.

421.5   *"Der arme Kerl,"*]   The poor fellow.

423.13–14   rosy-stone . . . Morskaya]   The Nabokovs' St. Petersburg house was a rosy-stone building at 47, Bolshaya Morskaya.

425.12   Paphia Fritillary]   A large nymphalid butterfly of the Palaearctic, *Argynnis paphia* Linnaeus.

427.23   *auf Bruderschaft*]   To brotherhood.

428.5   *cour d'amour*]   Court of love.

428.20   Poor Liza!]   Cf. the title of Nikolay Karamazin's novella *Bednaya Liza* (1792).

429.8–9   The letter . . . it is:]   A parody of Pushkin's *Eugene Onegin*, VI: xxi:1–2 (in Nabokov's translation: "The verses chanced to be preserved; / I have them; here they are: . . . ").

430.6–7   "To a Stranger . . . *neznakomki*)]   Allusion to Aleksandr Blok's poem "Neznakomka" ("The Stranger"; 1906).

430.19   Cheka]   The Soviet security police, 1917–22, from *Chrezvychaynaya Kommissiya po bor'be s kontrerevolyutsiey i sabotazhem* (Extraordinary Commmission for Combatting Counter-Revolution and Sabotage); its successors included the NKVD and the KGB. Members of the Soviet security police continued to be known as "chekists" until the collapse of the U.S.S.R. in 1991.

431.18–19   great writer's death]   Nikolay Gogol (1809–52).

431.22   *vos'midesyatniki . . .* Eighties)]   The term *shestidesyatniki* (men of the Sixties) refers to those active in the reformist fervor of Russia's 1860s.

433.26   Sobakevich]   *Sobaka* is Russian for "dog," and "Sobakevich" (son of a dog) the name of a land-owner in Gogol's *Dead Souls.*

435.4   fez wearers]   Shriners.

PALE FIRE

444.18–19   saw . . . darkly]   Cf. I Corinthians 13:12: "For now we see through a glass, darkly; but then, face to face."

446.12–13   only begetter]   From the dedication of Shakespeare's *Sonnets* (1609): "To the onlie begetter of these insuing sonnets Mr. W. H. all happinesse and that eternitie promised by our ever-living poet."

448.6   sleezy]   Nabokov explained to Riccardo Minaudi (March 3, 1964): "A door with slits in it, drafty."

450.9   Parthenocissus]   A genus of ivy.

452.30   Odin's Hall . . . Finnish epic]   The Valhalla of Norse mythology and the Finnish national epic, *Kalevala.*

457.30–31   *Sherlock . . .* shoes?]   In Arthur Conan Doyle's "The Empty House" (*The Return of Sherlock Holmes*, 1905), Holmes explains that he could have "reversed my boots, as I have done on similar occasions" during the encounter with Moriarty described in "The Final Problem" (*The Memoirs of Sherlock Holmes*, 1893).

459.12   preterist]   One whose chief interest or pleasure is in the past.

459.30–31   *Red Sox . . . Chapman's Homer*]   An actual newspaper head-line, referring to Ben Chapman, an outfielder who played for the Boston Red Sox, 1937–38.

463.18   Flemish hells]   Cf. the vivid depictions of hell in Flemish painting, especially in the work of Hieronymus Bosch.

463.35–36   *je nourris . . . cigales*]   "I feed the poor cicadas." *Cigales* (ci-cadas) sounds almost identical to "seagulls"; the Englishman mispronounces *nourris* as "noor-ees" if it were almost English (it should be pronounced somewhat like "noo-ree").

464.1   Lafontaine was wrong]   In his fable "La Cigale et la Fourmi" ("The Cicada and the Ant," often mistranslated "The Grasshopper and the Ant," cf. p. 559.4–9), the cicada sings all summer while the ant toils away storing food; when winter comes, the grasshopper begs the ants for food in vain.

464.28   Vanessa]   The nymphalid butterfly *Vanessa atalanta* Linnaeus, blackish-brown with red bars on its wingtips; popularly known as the Red Admirable or Red Admiral.

466.2   Toothwort White]   The pierid butterfly *Pieris virginiensis* W. H. Edwards.

466.16   Sorosa Hall]   "Sorosis" was the name of a women's club formed in the U.S. in 1869; by extension, any women's club.

467.15–20   *grimpen . . . sempiternal*]   Three words from T. S. Eliot's *Four Quartets* (1936–43): *grimpen* ("East Coker" II, line 93): the name of a bog in Conan Doyle's *The Hound of the Baskervilles*, *chthonic* ("Dry Salvages" V, line 225): infernal, of the underworld, ghostly; *sempiternal* ("Little Gid-ding" I, line 2): eternal.

468.32   *"See . . . cripple sing"*]   Pope, *An Essay on Man* (1732–34), II.267.

469.29   The famous face]   A description of Marilyn Monroe (1926–62).

469.30–31   grain . . . odd gallicism]   *Grain de beauté* is French for "mole."

469.36   *stang*]   Pole, upright bar.

472.33   orbicle of jasp.]   Little orb of jasper.

474.17   *le grand néant*]   The great nothing.

474.23   Grabermann's]   From German *Gräber*, "digger, gravedigger."

475.4–5   Fra Karámazov . . . *allowed*]   Cf. Dostoevsky's *The Brothers Karamazov* (1879–80), V.v. "Fra" indicates the monastic brother, the saintly Alyosha.

478.4   Old Faithful!]   Geyser in Yellowstone National Park, so called be-cause of its regular eruptions.

482.18   Newport Frill]   A Newgate Frill is a fringe of beard under the chin.

483.29   versipel]   A creature capable of changing from one form to another, like a werewolf.

484.4   *Dim Gulf*]   Cf. Poe's poem "To One in Paradise," line 12.

484.4   *Night Rote*]   A pun on "wrote" and *rote* as "routine": poems written in a nightly routine.

484.5   *Hebe's Cup*]   Hebe, daughter of Zeus and Hera, was cupbearer to the gods, until Zeus, desiring Ganymedes, the most beautiful youth alive, appointed him cupbearer before ravishing him.

484.9   moondrop title . . . *Pale Fire.*]   Cf. *Timon of Athens* IV.iii.436–40: "The sun's a thief, and with his great attraction / Robs the vast sea; the moon's an arrant thief, / And her pale fire she snatches from the sun; / The sea's a thief, whose liquid surge resolves / The moon into salt tears."

484.12   ament . . . noun I meant]   Some aments are also called catkins (in another sense, "ament" means "without mind," a mentally deficient person).

484.14–15   *consonne / D'appui*]   Supporting consonant. In English verse, rhyme is considered flat when the rhyming sounds begin with matching consonants, as in the "meant / cement" in these lines; in French verse, this supporting consonant is seen as an extra grace.

486.32–33   proper . . . crined or]   Naturally colored . . . hair golden.

486.34   Charles the Beloved]   Charles VI of France (1368–1422) was known as Le Bien-Aimé (the Well-Beloved) or Le Fol (the Mad).

487.18   bad gray poet]   Walt Whitman was known as "the good gray poet."

488.2   Muscovy glass]   Mica.

488.7–8   *Sosed* . . . neighbor)]   *Sosed* is Russian for "neighbor," but also suggests *Sovetsky Soyuz* (Soviet Union).

488.22–23   MacDiarmid's "incoherent transactions"]   From draft notes in Nabokov's archive: "The 'little language' used by Jonathan Swift in his letters to Stella and the 'incoherent transactions' of Angus M'Diarmid the author of 'A Description of the Beauties of Edinample and Lochearnhead' 1841 are heard through the worst parts of James Joyce like the 'incremental exorbitance' of a cataract 'which is antecedently token of the venitseason.' "

488.23–24   Southey's . . . Stumparumper,"]   Robert Southey's letters to his friend Grosvenor C. Bedford, Sept. 14, 1821 ("Dear Stumparumper . . . she . . . calls me detesty, a maffrum, a goffrum, a chatterpye, a sillycum, and a great mawkinfort. . . ."), and Dec. 24, 1822 ("the peculiar language . . .

which I have denominated the Lingo-Grande"), reflect a language actually invented in play by Samuel Taylor Coleridge's wife (and Southey's sister-in-law), Sara, whose name was indicated only by dashes in Victorian editions of Southey's writings.

488.25 *Kongs-skugg-sio*] Literally "King's Shadow-show" ("shadow-show" means "mirror"). Nabokov came across this work in *Notes and Queries*, 51 (Oct. 19, 1850), while doing research for *Eugene Onegin*. (In later reference works, the title has been spelled *Konungs-Skuggsja* and dated to the 13th century.)

490.20 Case . . . Footprints] See note 457.30–31.

490.21–33 stillicide . . . Hardy] "Friends Beyond" (1898), lines 6–8: "They've a way of whispering to me—fellow-wight who yet abide— / In the muted, measured note / Of a ripple under archways, or a lone cave's stillicide."

491.8–19 *Timon of Athens* . . . moon.] Cf. note 484.9.

492.39 star ghost] A faint image often seen accompanying the main image of brighter stars and planets, and due usually to reflection from the lenses of the eyepiece.

493.10–11 witty exchange . . . heroic couplet] Although Goldsmith wrote in heroic couplets, Wordsworth earnestly avoided them. (Pope and Dryden are usually considered the masters of the heroic couplet.)

493.37 Picasso . . . horse] "Boy Leading a Horse," 1905–6.

494.5 Amber] Cf. Kathleen Winsor's *Forever Amber* (1944), a popular novel depicting the life of a courtesan in Charles II's England.

495.24 *damnum infectum*] Damage threatened but not yet done.

497.5–6 *Hero* . . . *Time Lost*] Lermontov's *A Hero of Our Time* (1840–41) and Proust's *In Search of Lost Time*.

497.34 sectile mosaic] One cut into relatively large pieces shaped to fit one another.

499.31–32 St. Swithin's Day] July 15.

499.33 *"promnad vespert mid J.S.,"*] Evening walk with J.S. ("Zemblan").

500.33 Ozero] Russian, "lake."

501.17 chrysoprase] Apple-green marble.

502.4–5 an old-fashioned . . . In shape] Nabokov noted for his French translators: "Two hundred years ago collectors spread butterflies thus" and made a drawing of a butterfly with its forewing pulled back under the hindwing, making an outline very much like a ginkgo leaf.

504.26   Rodnaya]   Russian, "native, one's own."

505.35   Balthasar]   Traditionally, the black king among the three Magi.

505.37–39   *(Heliotropum turgenevi)* . . . . bench]   The scent of heliotrope repeatedly pervades the air (e.g., in *Smoke*, ch. 6), and dusk and garden benches abound, in the works of Turgenev.

506.23   *zhiletka* blades]   Russian, "vest"; Gilette razor blades originally came in vest-like paper covers.

507.15   *Bombycilla Shadei*]   The genus if not the species name is real.

508.20   Amphitheatricus]   The name of Vladimir Aleksandrovich Amfiteatrov (1862–1938) appeared frequently as a newspaper critic in the Russian emigré press of the 1920s and 1930s in which Nabokov published.

510.17–18   *Lord Ronald's Coronach*]   Walter Scott contributed his own "Glenfinlas; or, Lord Ronald's Coronach" to his edition of ballads, *Minstrelsy of the Scottish Border* (1802–3). *Coronach* means "dirge."

510.23   ingledom]   From *ingle*, "catamite."

511.7   adeling]   "Young nobleman" (Nabokov to Riccardo Mainardi, March 3, 1964).

511.26   luciola-like]   Variant spelling of the Italian *lucciola*, "firefly."

512.2   demilune]   Ditch before a fort; ravelin.

513.1   the Elder Edda]   A collection of poems compiled c. 1270, some from a much earlier age, and considered to include the masterpieces of Old Norse verse.

513.32   *maussade*]   Surly, gloomy.

514.18–19   Thormodus Torfaeus]   Icelandic scholar (1640–1719), court historian of Denmark and author of *History of Vinland*.

518.11–20   *Life* . . . Brief]   The advertisements are genuine.

519.27–28   peacock-herl]   "Herl," barb of feather used for artificial flies.

524.5   after Teniers]   The works of Flemish artist David Teniers the Yonger (1610–90) were so widely copied and imitated until the end of the 18th century that it is still impossible to establish a Teniers canon and chronology.

525.8   Varangian]   Norse rovers who invaded Russia and sailed down the Volga into the Caspian Sea.

526.40   *escalier dérobé*]   Secret staircase.

533.3   *lumbarkamer*]   Lumber room ("Zemblan").

534.20–22   with black traveling . . . the other]   Cf. Charlie Chaplin in his role as "the tramp."

539.13–14   elfinwood]   Stunted forest characteristic of alpine regions; "a flat matting of creeping branches hugging the ground" (Nabokov to Marie Schebeko, Sept. 30, 1965).

539.32   tintarron]   See Index, p. 666.

540.18   "reeks"]   British dialect, "heap, pile."

540.38   pine groves of Boscobel]   Farm near Shifnal in Shropshire, where in 1651 Charles II of England hid in the "royal oak" after the battle of Worcester.

541.33   écharpe]   Scarf.

544.32–33   L'EX-ROI . . . PARIS?]   Is the Ex-King of Zembla in Paris?

546.21   teazer . . . flasher]   A teazer is a fireman of a glass-melting furnace, a flasher is a worker who reheats glass articles at the furnace aperture to restore its plastic condition.

546.26   feuilles-d'alarme]   Literally, "alarm leaves."

549.2   skoramis]   From the ancient Greek word for "closet stool" found only in Aristophanes. Véra Nabokov wrote to Reuben Abel (Jan. 31, 1968): "says VN, was used for chamber pot by English dons in the past."

553.11   Pulex]   Latin, "flea."

554.15   asparagus dream]   Cf. Proust's lyrical description of the asparagus served at Combray in the first, "Combray," section of Swann's Way.

554.17   travestissement]   "Travesty": alluding to the widespread judgment that In Search of Lost Time is flawed by what some suppose is Proust's transposition of his own homosexual loves into heterosexual terms.

554.24–25   Cocteau . . . gardens,']   In his lecture on The Walk by Swann's Place (Nabokov's translation of the title Du Côté de chez Swann), published in Lectures on Literature, Nabokov wrote: "Jean Cocteau has called the work 'A giant miniature, full of mirages, of superimposed gardens, of games conducted between space and time.' "

554.28   jeune fille]   Girl.

554.28–29   Vronski's (and Lyovin's)]   The two main male characters in Tolstoy's Anna Karenina.

554.31   beau ténébreux]   Byronically gloomy hero.

557.38   moskovett]   From Russian, moskovskiy, "of Moscow," and veter, "wind."

559.25   the "diana"]   The butterfly Speyeria diana Cramer.

559.26   "atlantis"]   The butterfly Speyeria atlantis Edwards.

560.9–18   King Alfred . . . Ohthere.]   Alfred the Great (849–99) adapted the *Universal History* of Orosius, especially by adding material from the Norwegian landowner and explorer Ohthere, who visited Alfred about A.D. 890.

561.2   monoceros]   The unicorn in the British coat of arms.

561.11–12   French for "swallow"]   *Hirondelle.*

561.20   macaco worm]   The larva of a botfly (*Dermatobia hominis*) parasitic on man and monkey in South America.

561.22–25   Vanessa . . . *Van*homrigh, E*st*her.]   For the butterfly, see note 464.28. Esther Vanhomrigh (1690–1723) met Jonathan Swift in 1708 and fell passionately in love with him; he wrote for her the poem "Cadenus and Vanessa" (1713).

561.28–29   When, lo! . . . star]   "Cadenus and Vanessa," lines 305–6.

562.16   *fou rire*]   Mad laughter.

562.27–28   rough alderkings . . . boys]   Véra Nabokov wrote to Reuben Abel (Jan. 31, 1968): "Goethe's *Erlkönig* was mistranslated into French as 'Roi des Aulnes'—'King of the Alders' (Alnus) ('Erl,' of course, means 'elf')." For the Goethe poem, see note 225.40.

562.29–30   what an earlier . . . Charles had done]   Charles I of England was alleged to have been infatuated with his favorite, the Duke of Buckingham (1592–1628). Charles married in 1625 but did not father an heir until after Buckingham's assassination.

563.1   fackeltanz]   Torchdance.

563.11–12   Ombre . . . Spanish]   *Ombre* is French for "shade," *hombre* is Spanish for "man."

563.21–22   Even in Arcady . . . scripture.]   *Et in Arcadia ego* is an inscription on a tomb in a painting by Guercino (1591–1666); it was also used by later artists.

564.22   *Verba . . . manent.*]   Words fly, writing remains.

570.7   goetic]   Black magic.

570.12   brocken]   Name of a German mountain where witches assembled on Walpurgis Night.

570.18   Toothwort White]   See note 466.2.

570.24   Virginia Whites]   Another name for the Toothwort White.

571.13   herborizing]   Botanical collecting.

571.16–18   "curious Germans" . . . naturalists]   Alexander Pope's *Imitations of English Poets: Earl of Dorset*: II: "Phryne" (1709) ends: "So have I known those Insects fair, / (Which curious *Germans* hold so rare,) / Still vary

Shapes and Dyes; / Still gain new Titles with new Forms; / First Grubs obscene, then wriggling Worms, / Then painted Butterflies."

571.32　　marrowskies] See Index, p. 663.

571.34–572.6　　Dulwich . . . "Here Papa pisses"] Robert Browning is said to have had the first flash of inspiration for his verse drama *Pippa Passes* (1842) in Dulwich Wood.

574.13–14　　pada . . . told] Nabokov wrote to Andrew Field (Sept. 26, 1966): "a garbled warning to her father and hint at the title of his poem to be written many years later. *Padre* should *not go* to the *lane* to be mistaken for *old Goldswart* (worth) after finishing his *tale* (pale) *feur* (fire) [which in Shakespeare is accompanied by] the word 'arrant' (farant) [and this] with 'lant' makes up the Atalanta butterfly in Shade's last scene. It is '*told*' by the spirit in the barn."

576.35　　*The Beau and the Butterfly*] After the dandy Eustace Tilley who appeared on the first cover of *The New Yorker* peering through his monocle at a butterfly (1925; drawn by Rea Irvin) and has reappeared frequently on *New Yorker* covers since then.

578.2–3　　what poem] See note 467.15–20.

579.2–4　　Southey . . . Bishop] Southey's 1799 poem "God's Judgement on a Wicked Bishop" tells of Archbishop Hatto of Mainz being eaten by rats for killing the paupers whose hunger he blamed for a famine.

579.7–8　　*Supremely* . . . Popian line] "The starving chemist in his golden views / Supremely blest, the poet in his muse" (*Essay on Man*, II, 269–70).

579.21–22　　young athlete . . . a girl's."] Cf. A. E. Housman, *A Shropshire Lad*, poem xix, "To An Athlete Dying Young," lines 25–28: "And round that early-laurelled head / Will flock to gaze the strengthless dead, / And find unwithered on its curls / The garland briefer than a girl's."

580.7–8　　synchronization . . . Flaubert and Joyce.] In the agricultural fair scene of *Madame Bovary* (II, viii), and in the synchronization of chapters 1 and 3 and within chapter 10 of *Ulysses*.

580.16–17　　Lavender (the name . . . laund)] The word lavender was once thought to derive from the Italian "lavanda" (washing). The old form *laund* means "glade, grassy patch."

583.29　　woodwose] Faun, young satyr.

584.16　　*volant en arrière*] Flying backwards.

584.17　　a bend gules] (Heraldic): "with a diagonal red bar."

584.26–27　　'See the blind . . . king'] Pope, *Essay on Man*, II.267–68.

585.15–19　　poem . . . closing lines] "Stopping by Woods on a Snowy Evening" (1923). Its repeated closing line: "And miles to go before I sleep."

587.14   flowers-of-the-gods] The orchid *Disa uniflora.*

587.23–24   compass rose] A circle graduated to degrees or quarter points and printed on a chart for reference, usually showing both magnetic and true directions.

590.28   Phrynia . . . Timandra] The two whores in *Timon of Athens* IV.iii.

591.36   houghmagandy] Scottish: "fornication."

592.18–19   glycines] Apios: a genus of trailing or climbing herbs with small racemose flowers.

592.28–29   *narstran,*] The *Nastrond* (from Old Norse *nar*, "corpse" and *strönd*, "strand, shore") of Norse myth.

594.14   BIC] Behind the Iron Curtain.

597.34–35   boy's seamed purse] Nabokov wrote to his French translators in 1964: "le petit sac conturé d'un bambin *or better* le scrotum d'un garçonnet. (Dr. Kinbote is not a nice person.)"

598.28   *shootka* (little chute)] *Shootka* means "joke" in Russian; the joke here is the allusion to Chekhov's story "Shutochka," "A Little Joke" (1886), which involves a "chute" (sleigh run) and the fear of falling.

599.23–24   *Je m'en . . . peut-être.*] I'm off to search the great perhaps.

601.8–603.11   SHADE: All . . . priority.] A parody of James Boswell's interviews with Samuel Johnson on subjects sure to provoke the latter to memorable replies. The capitalizations follow 18th-century practice.

601.18   *L'homme est né bon*] Man is born good.

602.12   goetic] See note 570.7.

605.5–6   Parmentier . . . pet tuber] Antoine-Augustin Permentier (1737–1813) devoted himself to turning the French into potato-eaters (they had previously considered the potato fit only as animal fodder and a possible cause of leprosy) and wrote treatises on the tuber.

605.16   padishah] Chief ruler, great king; the title especially of the Shah of Persia.

606.4   Tanagra dust] A figurine of terra-cotta like those found in the ancient Boeothian town of Tanagra.

606.6   *shargar*] Scottish: lean, faded, or stunted person or animal.

607.3   Boscobel] See note 540.38.

607.23–26   Many times . . . he ran.] Adapted from the account of Charles II's flight after the battle of Worcester, 1651, in Edward Hyde the Earl of Clarendon's *History of the Rebellion* (1702–4): "he many times cast himself upon the ground, with a desperate and obstinate resolution to rest there till the morning, that he might shift with less torment, what hazard soever he run."

607.26–27   another Charles, . . . two yards high.]   Charles II of England (1630–85) was tall and dark.

609.19–20   Kashube]   A Pomeranian people distinct from the Poles.

610.32–33   Eberthella]   A genus of bacteria, usually associated with inflammation; the type species causes typhoid fever.

611.9–10   erlking . . . alderwood]   See notes 225.40 and 562.27–28.

611.28–29   Untamed Seahorse . . . *My Last Duchess*]   Browning's poem (1842) ends: "Notice Neptune, though, / Taming a sea horse, thought a rarity, / Which Claus of Innsbruck cast in bronze for me!"

612.13   *Nouvelle Revue Canadienne*]   *New Canadian Review*, invented in imitation of the prestigious *Nouvelle Revue Française*.

612.22–30   one deplores . . . visual rule.]   Sybil's translation is actually highly accurate.

612.33–34   "fate" . . . men").]   Line 9: "Thou art slave to fate, chance, kings, and desperate men."

613.1–2   "The Nymph . . . Fawn,"]   The full title is "The Nymph Complaining for the Death of Her Fawn" (1681).

613.6   *l'impair*]   Odd, uneven (number); blunder.

613.7–31   In the lines . . . *roses dedans*]   Again, Kinbote quibbles at translations of exemplary accuracy.

615.12–616.3   One has seldom seen . . . ethereal vertebrae]   Parody of the idealized wholesomeness of the heroes in the Socialist Realism decreed as the Soviet Union's official literary mode in 1934.

616.25–26   Russian *chanson de geste* . . . twelfth century.]   The medieval heroic poem *Slovo o polku Igoreve* (translated with notes by Nabokov as *The Song of Igor's Campaign*). The *Slovo* was first published in 1800, from a manuscript (a 16th-century transcript) supposedly acquired in 1790; this transcript perished in the Moscow fire of 1812. Although it has been alleged that the *Slovo* is a late 18th-century fabrication, the evidence to prove forgery is lacking and Nabokov accepted the poem as authentic in his edition, though he would also teasingly invite Slavists to find the forger.

616.28   Fra Pandolf]   The name of the painter in Robert Browning's "My Last Duchess."

617.18–20   (amid . . . America)]   In *Mémoires d'Outre-Tombe*, Chateaubriand wrote of seeing butterflies in America about six weeks after his landing in Chesapeake Bay on July 2, 1791, and again, perhaps another six weeks later, of seeing "mayflies and butterflies which, in their brilliant array, vied with the speckled flora" (this passage is in fact mostly taken from William Bartram's *Travels*, 1791).

618.15–16 Gide the Lucid . . . black imps.] A play on *Jude the Obscure* (1895) by Thomas Hardy; André Gide wrote of Africa and Africans especially in *Amyntas* (1906), *Voyage au Congo* (1927), *Retour du Tchad* (1928), as well as in parts of his *Journal* (1889–1949), and in the Biskra sections of *L'Immoraliste* (*The Immoralist*, 1902), in which the boys Bachir, Lassif, and Moktir appear.

619.24–25 Japanese fish . . . cataract] In honor of Hokusai's *ukiyo-e* print of "Carp in a Waterfall," c. 1832–33.

621.31 Radugovitra] "Rainbowglass," from Russian *raduga*, "rainbow," and Latin *vitrum*, "glass."

623.23 Izumrudov] Russian, "of emeralds."

626.9 ancillula] Latin, "little handmaid."

628.5–6 Letters of Franklin Lane] *The Letters of Franklin K. Lane, Personal and Political*, ed. Anne Wintermute Lane and Louise Herrick Wall (Boston, 1922), p. 464.

629.26 Orly airport] In Paris.

630.31 Russian *zemlya*] Land, country.

630.31–32 Semblerland . . . "resemblers"] French *sembler*, "seem."

631.21 *Dr. Zhivago*] By Boris Pasternak (1957).

632.24 Botkin or Botkine] Botkin is a distinguished Russian surname; *botkin* is a variant spelling of *bodkin*, which can, as in Shakespeare, mean "a dagger, poniard, stiletto, etc." or "a person closely wedged between two other persons."

632.27 *kinbote*] In English a *kinbote* is "a bote given by a homicide to the kin of his victim"; a *bote* is "a compensation paid by way of composition for a wrong or injury; amends; satisfaction."

633.1 French word for 'tire'] *Pneu.*

633.34–37 Parody . . . Pope.] Pastiche especially of lines 56–57 of Pope's *Essay on Criticism* (1709): "Nature to all things fix'd the Limits fit, / And wisely curb'd proud Man's pretending Wit: / As on the Land while here the Ocean gains, / In other Parts it leaves wide sandy Plains; / Thus in the Soul while Memory prevails, / The solid Pow'r of Understanding fails; / Where Beams of warm Imagination play, / The Memory's soft Figures melt away" (lines 52–59).

634.2–3 Housman . . . Tennyson] Housman laments the loss of young men in *A Shropshire Lad* and Tennyson expresses grief for his closest friend, Arthur Hallam, in *In Memoriam*.

634.6–8   says . . . barbering]   In "The Name and Nature of Poetry"
(1933), Housman wrote: "Poetry indeed seems to me more physical than intellectual . . . . Experience has taught me, when I am shaving of a morning,
to keep watch over my thoughts, because, if a line of poetry strays into my
memory, my skin bristles so that the razor ceases to act."

636.2–4   Pope's Second . . . *knows where*]   Line 224.

637.7–9   Comus-mask . . . set of teeth]   Play on the title of Milton's *Comus, A Maske presented at Ludlow Castle*, 1634. In it Comus offers "to every
weary traveller, / His orient liquor in a crystal glass / . . . which as they taste
/ . . . their human countenance, / The express resemblance of the gods, is
changed / Into some brutish form of wolf, or bear, / Or ounce, or tiger,
hog, or bearded goat, / All other parts remaining as they were, / And they,
so perfect is their misery, / Not once perceive their foul disfigurement, / But
boast themselves more comely than before . . . " (lines 63–75).

637.36   day's copy . . . *New York Times*]   Real items are drawn from the
July 21, 1959, issue, although with a few transpositions ("Charel Jewelry Company" to "Rachel Jewelry Company," "Lehman" to "Helman," etc.) and
substitutions: "Adieu . . . Norway!" becomes "Adieu . . . Zembla!" The
"reviewer" is Orville Prescott—"who gave *Lolita* its most idiotic review"
(Véra Nabokov to Alfred Appel Jr., Dec. 17, 1971).

644.11   *Bozhe moy*]   Good God!

645.26–31   Help me, Will . . . . *Athens*]   See note 484.9.

646.18–19   *"Comment . . . anglais?"*]   How do you say "die" in English?

648.17   knackle]   As a verb, "to cause to crack or break sharply, as a nut."

648.24   inenubilable]   That cannot be cleared of clouds.

650.22–30   those trees: . . . Illyria]   Trees named by Shakespeare. Jove's
stout oak (*The Tempest* V.i.45); the thunder-cloven (*King Lear* III.ii.5); the
knotty-entrailed, weather-fending line (now lime), a phoenix (now date palm),
a pine and a cedar (*The Tempest*, I.ii.295, V.i.10, III.iii.23, V.i.48); a Venetian
sycamore tree (*Othello* IV.iii.40); two willows, the green from Venice, the
hoar-leaved from Denmark (*Othello* IV.iii.41, *Hamlet* IV.vii.166–67); a midsummer elm, midsummer mulberry (*A Midsummer Night's Dream* IV.i.44;
V.i.148); clown's sad cypress from Illyria (*Twelfth Night* II.iv.52).

651.8   shalwars]   Oriental trousers.

652.36–37   "still clutching . . . Arnold]   "The Scholar Gypsy" (1853), line
212.

653.38   *ici*]   French, "here."

663.20   *Krummholz*]   Elfinwood (see note 539.13–14).

666.38   (*sumpsimus*)]   A strictly correct expression substituted for an old
popular error.

667.15   distant northern land] Pope, *Rape of the Lock*, IV.154–7: "Oh had I rather unadmir'd remained / In some lone Isle, or distant Northern Land; / Where the gilt Chariot never marks the Way, / Where none learn Ombre, none ever taste Bohea!'"

LOLITA: A SCREENPLAY

675.15   Elstree] Film studio in London.

678.7   Duk-Duk] See note 259.25–26.

680.18   kingdom by the sea] See note 7.13–14.

681.32   *South Wind*] By Norman Douglas (1917).

682.12–15   tomb . . . Poe-esque] Reference to Poe's "Ulalume—A Ballad"; see also page 764.13–29 and note.

684.4   *à la gamine*] See note 22.36.

701.26   Marlenesque] Like Marlene Dietrich's.

707.28   *Mais . . . Aujourd'hui?*] Certainly, Lolita. Today?

708.9–10   school . . . three weeks.] Cf. page 692.4; Nabokov prepared two alternative versions of Act I. In assembling the screenplay for publication, he used parts of both versions but did not reconcile the different time schemes.

720.5   *votre santé*] Your health.

724.17   *plage*] Beach.

725.33–34   "my darling . . . bride."] See note 36.11.

727.30–31   *Envoyez . . . camp*] Send your girl to camp.

730.18   *mon cher, cher Monsieur*] My dear, dear Sir.

744.29   *Ensuit?*] And then?

745.14–15   *C'est bien . . . C'est.*] And that's all? It is.

750.10–11   *Stan and Izzie . . . . Mark King.*] Cf. Tristran, his lover Isolda, and her husband King Mark, of medieval legend.

764.13–29   *It was night . . . Ulalume!"*] From stanzas 1 and 8 of "Ulalume" (1847).

767.15   *mon petit chat*] My little cat.

772.6   carissa] A plum-like fruit of the genus *Carissa* of spiny shrubs.

776.24   *Mais c'est si laid*] But it's so ugly.

782.21–22   Vivian Darkbloom] See note 4.8.

788.32   Miss Emperor]   See note 189.28.

790.1–4   *Gone is Livia . . . doom, doom.*]   Combines Joyce's Anna Livia Plurabelle in *Finnegans Wake* (1939) with a Poesque poetics.

792.29–793.2   Miss Emperor . . . *Madame Bovary*]   See note 189.28.

799.1   Blanche Schwarzman]   See note 4.34.

829.32–34   'Changeons . . . séparés']   See note 261.27–29.

Cataloging Information

Nabokov, Vladimir Vladimirovich, 1899–1977.
   [Selections. 1996]
   Novels 1955–1962 / Vladimir Nabokov.
      p. cm. — (The Library of America ; 88)
   Contents: Lolita — Pnin — Pale fire —Lolita: A screen
play.

   1. Nabokov, Vladimir Vladimirovich, 1899–1977.
I. Title.   II. Series.
PS3527.A15A6   1996a
813'.54—dc20   96-15256
ISBN 1–883011–19–1 (alk. paper)   CIP

THE LIBRARY OF AMERICA SERIES

1. Herman Melville, *Typee, Omoo, Mardi* (1982)
2. Nathaniel Hawthorne, *Tales and Sketches* (1982)
3. Walt Whitman, *Poetry and Prose* (1982)
4. Harriet Beecher Stowe, *Three Novels* (1982)
5. Mark Twain, *Mississippi Writings* (1982)
6. Jack London, *Novels and Stories* (1982)
7. Jack London, *Novels and Social Writings* (1982)
8. William Dean Howells, *Novels 1875–1886* (1982)
9. Herman Melville, *Redburn, White-Jacket, Moby-Dick* (1983)
10. Nathaniel Hawthorne, *Collected Novels* (1983)
11. Francis Parkman, *France and England in North America* vol. I, (1983)
12. Francis Parkman, *France and England in North America* vol. II, (1983)
13. Henry James, *Novels 1871–1880* (1983)
14. Henry Adams, *Novels, Mont Saint Michel, The Education* (1983)
15. Ralph Waldo Emerson, *Essays and Lectures* (1983)
16. Washington Irving, *History, Tales and Sketches* (1983)
17. Thomas Jefferson, *Writings* (1984)
18. Stephen Crane, *Prose and Poetry* (1984)
19. Edgar Allan Poe, *Poetry and Tales* (1984)
20. Edgar Allan Poe, *Essays and Reviews* (1984)
21. Mark Twain, *The Innocents Abroad, Roughing It* (1984)
22. Henry James, *Essays, American & English Writers* (1984)
23. Henry James, *European Writers & The Prefaces* (1984)
24. Herman Melville, *Pierre, Israel Potter, The Confidence-Man, Tales & Billy Budd* (1985)
25. William Faulkner, *Novels 1930–1935* (1985)
26. James Fenimore Cooper, *The Leatherstocking Tales* vol. I, (1985)
27. James Fenimore Cooper, *The Leatherstocking Tales* vol. II, (1985)
28. Henry David Thoreau, *A Week, Walden, The Maine Woods, Cape Cod* (1985)
29. Henry James, *Novels 1881–1886* (1985)
30. Edith Wharton, *Novels* (1986)
31. Henry Adams, *History of the United States during the Administrations of Jefferson* (1986)
32. Henry Adams, *History of the United States during the Administrations of Madison* (1986)
33. Frank Norris, *Novels and Essays* (1986)
34. W. E. B. Du Bois, *Writings* (1986)
35. Willa Cather, *Early Novels and Stories* (1987)
36. Theodore Dreiser, *Sister Carrie, Jennie Gerhardt, Twelve Men* (1987)
37. Benjamin Franklin, *Writings* (1987)
38. William James, *Writings 1902–1910* (1987)
39. Flannery O'Connor, *Collected Works* (1988)
40. Eugene O'Neill, *Complete Plays 1913–1920* (1988)
41. Eugene O'Neill, *Complete Plays 1920–1931* (1988)
42. Eugene O'Neill, *Complete Plays 1932–1943* (1988)
43. Henry James, *Novels 1886–1890* (1989)
44. William Dean Howells, *Novels 1886–1888* (1989)
45. Abraham Lincoln, *Speeches and Writings 1832–1858* (1989)
46. Abraham Lincoln, *Speeches and Writings 1859–1865* (1989)
47. Edith Wharton, *Novellas and Other Writings* (1990)
48. William Faulkner, *Novels 1936–1940* (1990)
49. Willa Cather, *Later Novels* (1990)
50. Ulysses S. Grant, *Personal Memoirs and Selected Letters* (1990)
51. William Tecumseh Sherman, *Memoirs* (1990)
52. Washington Irving, *Bracebridge Hall, Tales of a Traveller, The Alhambra* (1991)
53. Francis Parkman, *The Oregon Trail, The Conspiracy of Pontiac* (1991)
54. James Fenimore Cooper, *Sea Tales: The Pilot, The Red Rover* (1991)

55. Richard Wright, *Early Works* (1991)
56. Richard Wright, *Later Works* (1991)
57. Willa Cather, *Stories, Poems, and Other Writings* (1992)
58. William James, *Writings 1878–1899* (1992)
59. Sinclair Lewis, *Main Street & Babbitt* (1992)
60. Mark Twain, *Collected Tales, Sketches, Speeches, & Essays 1852–1890* (1992)
61. Mark Twain, *Collected Tales, Sketches, Speeches, & Essays 1891–1910* (1992)
62. *The Debate on the Constitution: Part One* (1993)
63. *The Debate on the Constitution: Part Two* (1993)
64. Henry James, *Collected Travel Writings: Great Britain & America* (1993)
65. Henry James, *Collected Travel Writings: The Continent* (1993)
66. *American Poetry: The Nineteenth Century,* Vol. 1 (1993)
67. *American Poetry: The Nineteenth Century,* Vol. 2 (1993)
68. Frederick Douglass, *Autobiographies,* (1994)
69. Sarah Orne Jewett, *Novels and Stories* (1994)
70. Ralph Waldo Emerson, *Collected Poems and Translations* (1994)
71. Mark Twain, *Historical Romances* (1994)
72. John Steinbeck, *Novels and Stories 1932–1937* (1994)
73. William Faulkner, *Novels 1942–1954* (1994)
74. Zora Neale Hurston, *Novels and Stories* (1995)
75. Zora Neale Hurston, *Folklore, Memoirs, and Other Writings* (1995)
76. Thomas Paine, *Collected Writings* (1995)
77. *Reporting World War II: American Journalism 1938–1944* (1995)
78. *Reporting World War II: American Journalism 1944–1946* (1995)
79. Raymond Chandler, *Stories and Early Novels* (1995)
80. Raymond Chandler, *Later Novels and Other Writings* (1995)
81. Robert Frost, *Collected Poems, Prose, & Plays* (1995)
82. Henry James, *Complete Stories 1892–1898* (1996)
83. Henry James, *Complete Stories 1898–1910* (1996)
84. William Bartram, *Travels and Other Writings* (1996)
85. John Dos Passos, *U.S.A.* (1996)
86. John Steinbeck, *The Grapes of Wrath and Other Writings 1936–1941* (1996)
87. Vladimir Nabokov, *Novels and Memoirs 1941–1951* (1996)
88. Vladimir Nabokov, *Novels 1955–1962* (1996)
89. Vladimir Nabokov, *Novels 1969–1974* (1996)
90. James Thurber, *Writings and Drawings* (1996)

This book is set in 10 point Linotron Galliard,
a face designed for photocomposition by Matthew Carter
and based on the sixteenth-century face Granjon. The paper is
acid-free Ecusta Nyalite and meets the requirements for permanence
of the American National Standards Institute. The binding
material is Brillianta, a woven rayon cloth made by
Van Heek-Scholco Textielfabrieken, Holland.
The composition is by The Clarinda
Company. Printing and binding by
R.R.Donnelley & Sons Company.
Designed by Bruce Campbell.

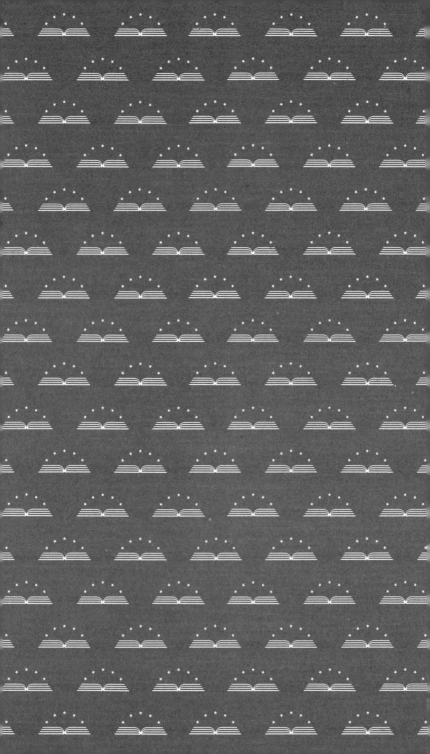